One explosive event creating four love stories.

Cover Photographer: Tonya Clark Photography- All About the Covers

Cover Designer: Tonya Clark Photography - All About the Covers

Editor: Ink It Out Editing

Page Edges: Painted Wings Publishing

An author is only as good as the support group they have behind them and mine is incredible. Family, friends and readers have kept me writing story after story. There are no words to describe how lucky I am to have the support that cheers me on, book after book. I thank everyone from the bottom of my heart for supporting and encouraging me to follow my dreams.

Silent Burn

BOOK 1

CHAPTER
One

CHARLIEE

THE DAY IS FINALLY OVER, and I just want to pick up dinner from my favorite Italian restaurant and go home. I swear, every teenager in my class today was trying to see how far they could push me. I need to remind myself to look and see if we have a full moon tonight, give their attitudes at least some excuse.

I step out of my jeep and instantly I smell the amazing aroma of spicy sauces, meatballs, and all around mouthwatering food. The chicken fettuccini alfredo that I ordered online is calling my name, along with a hot bath after I eat. Wait, maybe I'll eat while I'm in the bath. Warm bath, bubbles, glass of wine, and alfredo. I do believe I just planned my perfect evening. Now, in more of a hurry to get home and on with my perfect night, I start walking a little faster around the corner, only to be plowed down. A little winded from the fall, I feel my arm being tugged by Levi's leash. I look over at my dog to see him lunging at the man who just ran into me. I look up at the guy, he looks to be around my age I would say and he has his hands up in a surrender fashion. With everything today, this just added to the perfect ending of a bad day.

I'm really looking forward to my bubble bath now. Almost comically, this man is just standing there. He doesn't even offer to help me. He is just staring at my 95 pound German Shepherd, with his hands in the air, looking very nervous. I tug on Levi's leash once more, but he isn't responding. I stand back up and brush off my pants. "Levi," is all I have to say and my dog is instantly by my side. The man takes the opportunity of not having my dog's attention and runs off. This is all a sign, I just need to be home. I'm definitely starting to believe we may be having a full moon. They say all the crazy comes out with a full moon, and today can definitely be listed as crazy. "Come on, boy, let's get my food and go home."

Walking into the door, I'm instantly greeted by Trina, the hostess. "Hi, Charliee! Your dinner should be ready, let me just go check."

I nod my head, smile and watch as she heads to the back. It's almost sad that they all know me by name in here. What do I expect, though, I eat here at least four times a week. Maybe I should start cooking a little more. Wait, why would I do that? This place has amazing food and the best part is I have no kitchen to clean after the meal is over.

Trina comes back out, "It will be about five minutes."

"Thank you." I move myself to the side as a couple comes in the door. I recognize them as one of our student's parents.

"Miss Brooksman, how nice to see you." I watch her lips and hands move together as she greets me.

I smile, "Hello, Mr. and Mrs. Tovaren! Good to see both of you."

Trina has two menus in hand and points in a direction for the couple to follow her to a table. Mrs. Tovaren turns back to me, "Have a good evening, hon."

"Thank you! You two enjoy your dinner."

I feel a tug on my arm. Looking down at Levi, I notice he is pacing and looking toward the door. He has been acting strange ever since that guy knocked into me. "Levi, come sit," I command.

He looks back at me, over toward the door, and then once again back at me. I point down at the floor to my left, "Sit."

He walks over and slowly starts to sit on his haunches, his behind never sitting completely down. He looks as though he is ready to bolt. He never acts this way, I start to become a little more aware of my surroundings.

A touch on my right shoulder startles me, I jump a little and turn my head seeing Trina standing there with my dinner in hand.

"Charliee, I'm sorry, I didn't mean to scare you."

I laughed, "Sorry, I was in my own little world."

She hands me my check. I reach into my wallet, take out a twenty and hand it to her. "Just keep the change."

She smiles at me, "Thank you, Charliee. Have a good evening." I watch as her lips move.

I smile back, "Thank you, you, too." I grab my bag and turn to Levi, "Come on, boy, let's go home."

Levi lunges for the door, pulling my arm so hard it almost causes me to drop my dinner. "All right, all right, slow down. What is wrong with you tonight?"

I push open the door and take a step outside. That's when all at once I feel the ground shake and scorching heat slams into my back, throwing me forward, then darkness!

CHAPTER
Two

TRAVIS

"COME ON, man, we would like to eat some time tonight."

I walk in carrying a pan of chicken that I just pulled off the barbecue, "You know, any one of you lazy asses can help instead of sitting there pounding your fist on the table demanding food." I walk into the kitchen and place the pan on the counter.

Bryan, the new kid here at the station, walks in and stands next to me, "What can I help with, Trav?"

"Grab the salad and the ranch out of the fridge. Thanks, man." I place the chicken on a plate and head out behind the new kid, placing the plate in the middle of the table.

"Damn, it's about time! I'm starving."

"One of you guys can cook anytime you would like to volunteer. I have no problem handing the grill off to one of you." I take my seat and the food begins being passed around.

"You can't blame anyone but yourself Trav. If you sucked at cooking then just maybe one of us would step up, but we have no reason to with you here," Jim, our captain at the station, states plainly.

I didn't mind doing the cooking at the station. It's kind of relaxing. Plus, this way I know we are eating something good. We are a group of brothers here and each and every one of us knows that we would do anything for each other or to protect each other, but damn, they are a bunch of lazy assholes sometimes.

First bite off the fork and the tones go off. Each of us groans as we drop whatever is in hand and jump up from the table and out to the bay, to our engine. Stepping into my boots and pulling my turn-outs up, the voice over the station speaker announces our call. Explosion, the word sounds through the bay in an echo. Next, the address is given to us, we all know the place. It's our favorite Italian restaurant about five blocks away.

Captain and Trey, our engineer, jump up front taking their spots. Bryan and I jump in behind Trey. Randy and Pete jump in behind the captain. Lights on and sirens blaring, we pull out of the bay and are on our way within minutes.

"This sucks," Pete's voice comes through our headsets, "I wonder how long the place is going to be closed for. They have the best lasagna around."

Laughing, I shake my head, Pete is always thinking of food. "Don't worry, man, I'm sure it's just a small kitchen thing."

"Shit," I hear the captain's voice.

"What's up, Cap?" Bryan turns his head around to look over his shoulder to the front cab.

"Mass casualties. They are calling in more stations. Get ready, boys, this doesn't sound like a small kitchen problem."

The engine stops and we all jump out. I'm not sure if any of us were really prepared for the scene that we just rolled up to. Bodies and debris are thrown everywhere on the sidewalk. People are frantic all around. Some are walking around dazed, some are running away and others are running to the scene trying to help out. What the hell happened here?

Red lights are everywhere from all of the emergency crews on site. Police, ambulances, fire engines and trucks are parked in every direction you look. Orders are being barked out, putting everyone in motion.

"Bryan, Travis, start getting in for recovery. Pete and Randy, grab the hose, Trey is on controls." Our Cap orders all of us into motion.

Bryan and I walk over the debris heading in the direction of where the front door used to be. "Where do we start?" Bryan asks as he looks around.

The kid has only been with us for five months, straight out of the academy. I feel a little sorry for him, his face is a little ashen at the moment. I have been doing this job for about seven years now and if I am being honest with myself, I feel a little sick to my stomach. I look down by my foot and see a person's detached leg just lying there.

"Let's start moving things around out here. I don't have much hope of finding someone alive under this mess, but you never know. You start over there," I point to my left. "I will start on this side," I point to my right.

I am pulling boards back when I think I hear a noise. I stop and listen for a moment. Nothing, it must have been something else. I take a couple more steps and stop again. I hear it again, it is almost like a whining sound. I wait a couple of seconds again and nothing. It must be my imagination playing tricks. You want to think of a miracle happening and find someone who might have survived this mess. I pull a couple more boards away and again, I hear it. Now, damn it, I know that isn't my imagination. I take a couple more steps, my eyes scanning the area around me for any signs. I look to my right just as a board bounces up a little. "Bryan, over here!" I yell and start quickly pulling boards back.

Bryan runs over and starts pulling boards and bricks away with me. "What did you see? I'm not finding anything."

"Keep pulling the boards off, I'm not sure. I heard a noise, and then saw a board move."

Just as the words finish, I pull a board back and find a dog's head. I hear him whine again. "Hold on, buddy, we will get you out."

I pulled back a couple more and that's when I noticed his red collar and a leash attached. One more board and my heart stops, there is a hand. "Bryan, we have a body! Help me!"

Bryan joins me on one side, but I haven't really paid too much attention to the person on my other side until I hear, "Oh my god, Levi."

I look to my right, a cop is helping us, one I have seen on a couple of calls but I can't tell you his name. "You know the dog?"

My question goes unanswered. "Derrick!" the guy yells, "Get over here, it's Levi!"

Before I know it, an identical look-alike to the man beside me joins us. "Are you sure?"

"That's him. Charliee eats here all of the time," the other one yells as we all continue to move the debris. "Hurry up, get this stuff off of her. Come on, Charliee, be alive. Please, be alive."

Together, the four of us quickly pull the broken building away, slowly uncovering a young lady and the rest of the dog. He whines and tries to move. "No, boy, stay still, we'll get you guys out." I pat the dog on the head and try to get him to stay still. If by some miracle this lady is alive then we don't want the dog pulling away since the leash is still wrapped around her arm.

"Levi, stay," the one named Derrick commands.

The dog looks over at the man then lays his head back down, whining.

What feels like an hour, but is probably only minutes, passes and we finally uncover the young lady. She is laying on her stomach, her blonde hair is blown all around her face. The back of her shirt is burnt and torn. Her right arm lays in a very awkward position.

"Bryce, I don't think she's breathing." The one brother places his hand on the girl's shoulders as though he is going to try and flip her over.

"Don't move her!" I yell. I push past both men and kneel down next to the girl. I put my two fingers onto her neck, feeling for a pulse.

"Do you feel a pulse?" Bryan asks as he kneels down next to me.

I shake my head and look up at the brothers.

"No, she isn't dead," I hear one of them say.

I move my hand slightly and there it is, the slightest vibration in the neck. "Hurry, get a medic over here," I yell over my shoulder.

"Hurry!" one of the brothers yells after me.

With all the commotion, the dog starts getting antsy again. I look up at the brothers. "The dog seems to listen to you guys. Can one of you please try and calm him down?"

"Levi." The guy bends down at the dog's head and starts petting him. "Stay, boy. Charliee is going to be fine."

The medics make their way over to us with a back board. "What do we have?"

"Her name is Charliee Brooksman, 25-year-old..."

"Brooksman?" The male medic stops and looks up at the brother. "Derrick, is this your sister?"

"Yes, Tom, please hurry and get her out of here."

I move to the side and allow the medics full access. Noticing the leash can be freed from the girl's hand, I begin to work it off. The dog starts to get restless again and I believe he growls at me. "It's all right, boy, we are going to get you guys some help."

"What do we do with the dog?" Bryan asks.

I shrug my shoulders. I have no idea.

"He isn't going to leave Charliee without a fight." The brother, Derrick, starts petting the dog's head. "He's injured, too. We need to get him to a vet to get checked out."

"Bring us another back board!" I yell.

I watch the exchange between the brothers. How do you choose who goes with whom? I can tell that both are very close to their sister. "Guys, we can get someone to take good care of the dog."

"Like Derrick says, the moment we take them in two different directions, Levi is going to do anything to get back to Charliee. He is her service dog. Charliee is deaf."

"Here is the back board for the dog, Travis," Bryan comes up next to me and sets it down, "Do you want me to help?"

"I'll help with Levi." The brother I've now figured out is Derrick squats down next to the dog.

"All right, buddy, let's get you out of here." With Derrick's help, we both lift the large German Shepherd onto the back board.

We have just gotten the dog secured to the back board when a piercing scream sounds around us. We all look over at the medics who are working on the young lady, both brothers are there in a flash.

"Ma'am, it's okay, it's okay," the female medic keeps repeating.

Now Levi is thrashing around and whining, it is a good thing we already had the straps on. I place my hand on the dog's head. "Hey, boy, calm down, she's okay."

"Move, she can't hear you." Bryce is pushing the female medic away.

The medic starts pushing back, "Sir, stay back. We can handle this."

"Tom, tell your partner here to move before I move her myself," Bryce yells at the medic who seems to know the brothers.

"It's okay, Darryn, let him in," Tom informs his partner.

The female medic moves to the side and Bryce gets right in view of his sister. "Charliee, calm down. You are going to be all right but you need to stay still."

I watch as Bryce tries to calm his sister down. The whole time he is talking to her his hands are moving in front of her face.

"Levi? Where is Levi?" she yells.

For a moment I am a little confused on her talking, I thought her brother said she was deaf? Her yelling her dog's name, though, stirs up Levi again, so the thought quickly leaves my mind. Every time she yells for the dog, he barks and thrashes around, then whines. He is hurting himself trying to get to her. I look over at the woman who is now strapped down to a board, and she is trying to move her head around, looking for her dog. If we don't do something soon, they are both going to be in worse shape than they are already in. I have an idea. "Bryan, help me bring the dog over to the girl. Maybe if they see each other, they will both calm down." We both grab an end and drag him next to her.

"Charliee, look, here is Levi. You both need to calm down, please." Bryce tries again.

I look over, her eyes are wide as she watches her brother, but she stops moving. Her head is strapped down to the board, but I see her eyes try and look over. Her hand on the side moves as far as the strap will allow as she tries to reach for the dog. I push the board with Levi on it a little closer to her, until her hand can touch the dog's fur. Levi instantly begins to calm down. I watch as the lady's fingers lightly brush against her dog.

"We need to go, Bryce," Tom, the medic, informs him.

He nods and tenderly touches his sister's forehead. Her eyes go to him, "We have to get you both some help. Derrick is going to take Levi and get him to a vet." He speaks to her so tenderly, while the whole time his hands are moving in front of her so that she can see them.

I watch this whole exchange between brother and sister. He is signing to her and it's amazing to watch. Derrick brings my attention back to him and then Levi. "Can you please help me carry Levi over to my squad car?"

I nod and move to grab the bottom end of the board. Levi begins to thrash and bark again, making it hard to keep a hold of him.

"Bryce, tell Charliee to tell Levi that it's okay," Derrick yells at his brother.

Bryce only signs to his sister this time, then we hear her voice, "Levi, it's all right, boy. Derrick will take care of you and I'm all right. Let them help you, boy."

Her voice instantly calms the dog. I look over and Derrick nods to me and together we start walking out of the debris and down to the car. After getting the dog settled, Derrick walks over to the ambulance that his sister is being loaded into. Derrick and his brother exchange a few words about contacting their parents and which hospital they will be taking their sister to. I try not to listen but for reasons that I can't explain, I want to know. I'm staring up into the ambulance where the medics are busy with Charliee and a strange feeling washes over me. I want to crawl back in there and go with her, protect her. I'm not sure what is causing me to feel this way but something is tugging at me.

Derrick turns to me, "Hey, man, thank you for everything."

I smile, "All in the job, right?"

He nods and gives a small smile, "Yeah, man. All the same, though, thank you."

We shake hands, Derrick heads to his patrol car and a waiting Levi. I watch as the ambulance doors shut and they begin to drive away, sirens blaring. Following shortly behind is Derrick with his lights and sirens on.

I watch as both drive away, almost a little angry that I'm not going with them. A hand on my shoulder brings my attention around, "Good job, Trav, but we have a lot more to do," Cap informs me.

I do a quick look again at the red lights fading away and then turn to look at the tragedy we still have to help out with.

14

CHAPTER
Three

CHARLIEE

THE PAIN IS UNBEARABLE. I want to scream, but I can't. I can't open my eyes, I can't tell them to stop, my hands won't move. Why are they torturing me like this? Why won't they just leave me alone? The pain is getting worse. I can't handle this, please someone make them stop. Where are my parents or my brothers? Why are they allowing whoever this is to do this to me? I can't take it anymore.

"Doctor, are you sure she isn't feeling any of the cleanings? How do we know she isn't in pain if she can't tell us?"

"Mrs. and Mr. Brooksman, I honestly can't tell you what she is feeling and not feeling while she is unconscious. We're watching her blood pressure and heart rate while we work on her back and I'm not going to tell you we don't see an increase, but that's to be expected."

"How long will she stay unconscious?"

"That's something I can't give you a time frame on, I'm sorry. Luckily she didn't have any major injury to the head, a slight concussion is all.

While we are having to scrub her back, I believe her being in this state is better for her than being awake. The process is very painful, and it's a good portion of her lower back that has been burnt. The good news is she won't need any skin grafts. We will keep an eye on the area for infection, and we will continue to clean the area to keep the dead skin away. Her right arm is broken, two ribs are cracked and we had to place fifteen stitches across her right shoulder blade." The doctor looked down at their daughter, then back up at the couple. "She is a very lucky girl, it could have been a lot worse."

"Steven, we almost lost our baby today." Karen buries her face into her husband's chest as he wraps his arms around her, holding her close.

"Thank you, Doctor." Steven rubs his wife's back, "She's going to be all right, honey, and we need to concentrate on the fact that we didn't lose her!"

The pain has become bearable again, I need to open my eyes and I need to flip over onto my back. Laying like this is very uncomfortable. I try to lift my right arm, not working. Neither is the left. Why is nothing working right now? I start to feel nervous, panicked, what the hell is wrong with me? Wait, where is Levi? If I can't move, what's wrong with him? I need to open my eyes now. I need to know where Levi is. Okay, concentrate, Charliee, move your right arm. I try and I feel my fingers move; my arm, though, feels heavy. I try my left fingers, they move, now my arm.

"Steven, she just moved her arm!" Karen shouts as she spots her daughter's arm move slightly. She pulls away from her husband and moves to her daughter's side. She wraps her fingers with her daughter's, encouraging her to keep moving, "Come on, honey, wake up! I know you are trying," she chants softly.

"Are you sure, honey? I don't see any movement." Steven wants his daughter to wake up, too, but he isn't seeing anything.

I feel someone take my hand, my nerves relax a little. It is comforting knowing someone is here with me. I squeeze the hand that holds mine.

"She just squeezed my hand!" Karen shouts. "Come on, sweetie, open your eyes. I can't talk to you until you open your eyes." Karen knows her daughter can't hear her plea, so she squeezes her hand harder.

It's getting lighter, my eyes can move under my eyelids. I'm almost there. Although, the closer I get to opening my eyes, it seems like the more pain I begin to feel. My back is the worst! It feels like it's on fire. I can now feel the extra weight on my right arm and my shoulder has a slight throb. What the heck happened to me? If I'm hurting like this, what is wrong with Levi? I need to know where he is. If for no other reason, that is why I need to open my eyes. Maybe I can call him, "Levi."

"Doctor, she is trying to say something." Steven barely hears his daughter's words. "I think she is trying to wake up."

"Charliee, come on, sweetheart." Karen once again repeats and squeezes her hand, she would feel so much better if she would wake up.

"Mom, what's going on?" Bryce walks in carrying two cups of coffee for his parents.

"Charliee is trying to wake up. She is squeezing my hand, and your dad just heard her try to say something."

Something is wrong, Levi always comes to me when I call his name. Panic sets in and my eyes fly open. I look around and instantly my mom is eye level with me. She is crying but smiling. She is trying to say something but between her crying and not signing, I don't understand her. My mouth is dry and my head is pounding. What in the heck happened to me? My mom's lips are going a mile a minute and I'm not understanding a thing she is trying to tell me. Looking around, I notice I'm in a hospital room. I try to think back, I remember going and getting dinner. I remember seeing one of our student's parents. Levi was acting very strange, that I do remember very clearly. I'm drawing a blank on anything after that though. I look around, I see my father and Bryce. The guy in the white must be the doctor. "Where is Levi?"

My mom's lips stop moving and she looks over at my dad and brother. "Mom, where is Levi?" I ask again.

Bryce's hands begin to move, along with his lips, "Charliee, don't worry. Derrick is with him, but we haven't heard anything from him yet. If I don't hear from him soon then I will call him and see what I can find out. I'm sure he is fine. He was alert when they left."

"What do you mean when they left? Where did they go?" I couldn't move my hands to sign and it was only adding to my frustration.

My dad sat down next to my mom, more in front of me, "Charliee, do you remember anything?"

I looked between the three of them and shake my head slightly. "No, I remember grabbing dinner and walking out the front door, but nothing after that."

My mom looks up at Bryce, but no one answers me. "Would someone please tell me what the hell happened? Why am I laying like this and where is Levi?" I hope I am shouting because I am meaning to.

Dad's hands go up in a surrender sign, "Okay, honey, calm down." He signs, "There was an explosion at the restaurant. You and Levi were found buried under some debris. You have burns along your lower back, which is why you are laying on your stomach. A couple of broken ribs, your right arm is broken and you have stitches along your right shoulder blade. Honey, you are very lucky to be alive." He places his hands over my mom's, who is now crying again.

Bryce begins to sign and I watch, "Derrick took Levi over to an animal hospital, and I came with you here in the ambulance. A couple of firemen found you and Levi. Derrick and I were on scene, the four of us dug you guys out. Levi was alert when we all left. You woke up once when we were trying to get you guys on backboards, you don't remember?" I shake my head, I don't remember any of it. "Derrick took him in the patrol car. We knew you wouldn't want him to be alone. I'm sure we will hear something from him soon."

My mind feels like it is spinning trying to take in all he is telling me. An explosion, what the heck? That must have been why Levi was acting so weird while we were there waiting on my food. He must have sensed something wasn't right. Wait, my dad said I was lucky to be alive. "How many people died?"

I watch my brother take a deep breath, his hands are on his hips and he looks down at the floor. "Bryce, how many people died?" I ask once more.

I can see the sadness in his eyes when he looks back up at me. "I'm not real sure to be honest. We found you pretty quickly after arriving on the scene, and I left with you once we got you out. The whole front dining room area was down, though. I will be honest, it didn't look good for survivors in that area inside."

Oh no, Mr. and Mrs. Tovaren were in there. "Bryce, one of our student's parents had just walked in, please try and find out what you can. I need to know how they are."

He nods his head, "I'll see what I can find out."

"Thank you."

"All right, everyone," the doctor cuts in, my mom signs for me as the doctor speaks. "I need to check Charliee out now that she is awake. I'm going to have Mrs. Brooksman stay and help me translate, but ask you two gentlemen to wait in the waiting room for a little bit."

I look up at my dad and then over at my brother. "Can you please call Garrett while you are waiting? I would like to know how Levi is doing."

"Sure." Bryce comes over and kisses me on the head. "You scared the hell out of me, sis. We'll take care of Levi, you take care of getting yourself better. I love you."

"I love you, too." I watch as he turns to follow my dad out of the room. "Bryce," I call him.

He turns around right before leaving the room, "Thank you."

A small smile appears on his lips. "You have nothing to thank me for. You have no idea how bad I want to hug you right now."

I smile back, "You have no idea how much I would love a hug right now."

CHAPTER

Four

THROWING my keys down on the dining table, I walk over to my couch and plop myself down. I'm exhausted. With my elbows on my knees, I bury my face into my hands. What a night! Never have I questioned if I had chosen the right career with becoming a firefighter. I've wanted to be one since I was little kid and I watched firefighters put our neighbor's house fire out. After last night, though, I've done nothing but wonder if I made the right choice. We deal with death, but it's usually in small numbers at a time and usually caused by accidents. This, I believe, was no accident and the number of deaths were not just a couple or a few. Other than the girl we pulled out last night, only four other people were found alive inside. When we were getting ready to leave the scene and go back to the station, the Cap had told us the death number was at eighteen. Today all the investigating would be under way and hopefully they will find out what caused the explosion. It wasn't from the kitchen, most of that was still intact. All the damage happened in the dining area. Finding the five alive does make you realize why you do this kind of work though.

All night, though, my mind kept going back to the girl, Charliee. I keep finding myself wondering how she is doing, even how the dog is doing. Crazy thing is, on this job you train yourself to do your job, rescue the person, help and care for them as best as you can and hope that after they leave the scene you have done enough. You really can't sit there and think about it for too long or you will drive yourself crazy with the whole "What if" scenario. With her, though, it was different. It took everything I had not to jump in the back of that ambulance with her. I knew she was in good care, her brother was with her, but I wanted to be there. I wanted to make sure nothing else happened to her. Even now I was feeling myself becoming restless just thinking about her and not knowing how she is doing. I have no way of contacting her brothers. I'm sure I could go through the police station and see if they would give me a way to contact one of them, but right now everyone is busy with what's going on. I know the hospital that they took her to, I heard one brother tell the other one before they left, but I'm pretty sure that if I call they won't give me any information. I lay my head back against the couch. My body is exhausted and begging me to go take a shower and then sleep. My mind, however, is on a completely different track. I'm not going to be able to sleep anyway, so with my mind made up, I get up and head for a quick shower and then to the hospital.

Walking into the hospital, I approach the front desk, "Yes, sir how may I help you?" A little lady probably in her seventies wearing a pair of pink scrubs greets me.

"Yes, ma'am. I'm looking for a girl who was brought in here last night by the name of Charliee."

"Do you know her last name?"

Damn, no, I don't know her last name. "No, I don't."

"Sorry, hon, but without a last name I can't find her in the computers."

"She was brought in last night. She was one who was rescued from the restaurant explosion." I'm hoping that small bit of information will help out a little, but with the small smile the receptionist is giving me, I am getting the idea it isn't helping.

"I'm sorry but without a last name, I have no way of finding her. I heard about that explosion, though, what a shame."

I am tired and I know this lady isn't trying to be annoying but I am finding it hard to not reach across and shake her. I take a deep breath. "So there is no way to look up females with the name Charliee?" I am getting desperate and I know it. I am sounding crazy to myself.

She shakes her head, "Sorry."

I turn away from the counter and just as I am thinking about heading out, I spot one of the brother's along with two other people coming out of the elevator. I walk up to them, "Hey."

The brother stops and stares at me for a moment. I can tell he doesn't know who I am, "I'm sorry. I'm Travis Kendricks." I put my hand out to shake his. "I'm one of the firefighters that found your sister last night."

I watch the brother relax and then he shakes my hand. "Yeah, sorry, I didn't recognize you without all the gear. I'm Bryce Brooksman, and this is my mom, Karen, and my dad, Steven."

"Mr. and Mrs. Brooksman, it's nice to meet you." I shake Mr. Brooksman's hand and when I go to shake Mrs. Brooksman's hand, she pulls me into a hug.

"Oh thank you, Travis, for saving our girl."

"Ma'am, I didn't do it alone. I'm just glad we found her."

"So, what are you doing here?" Bryce asks.

I'm feeling a little foolish now, but I can't leave until I find out how she is. "I just got off my shift and figured I would stop by and see how she was doing."

"Thanks to you guys, she is alive," Mr. Brooksman answers.

"We were just on our way to go and get something to eat, you can go up if you want. She is in room 407." Mrs. Brooksman surprises me by offering the information so quickly.

"Mom…" Bryce begins to object.

"I appreciate it but…" I begin at the same time.

Mrs. Brooksman puts her hand up, "It's all right, Bryce, he saved her life. I don't think any harm will come of him going up."

Bryce is very protective of his sister, that I can sense already. I don't blame him, I am pretty protective of my sister, too. I would react the same way.

"You're right, Mom. Sorry, man."

"No hard feelings. I have a sister, I would react the same way."

"Well, let's go you two." Mr. Brooksman cuts in, "I want to go and get back."

Mrs. Brooksman smiles at me and then gives me another hug. "Thank you again, Travis."

I watch as the three of them leaves the hospital. I turn to the elevator and I stand staring at it for a moment. Do I need to go up there? What is my problem? I came to see how she is, I'll just go up pop in and say hello and then leave. I push the up button on the panel and wait.

I stand at the door to room 407 for a moment. What am I supposed to say once I get in there? She has no clue who I am. Just as I decide to leave, a nurse walks out of the room. "Hello, are you here to see Charliee? You can go in now."

Well, no way out now, I think to myself. "Thank you."

The nurse keeps the door open for me and walks away toward the nurse's station.

I walk in, past the small bathroom, and the hospital bed with Charliee laying on her stomach, face toward me came into view. She is awake and instantly sees me. I stop and we just stare at each other. Her eyes scrunch together as she tries to figure out who I am. Her left hand is tucked up under the pillow that her head is on and her right arm is casted and resting on the other side of the bed. A blanket is up over her legs and stops right above her backside. The back of her hospital gown is tied at the top and covering most of the top of her back, but the gown is open and a cloth is covering her lower back. I can see a bandage along her right shoulder blade peeking out from the gown where it begins to open up.

"Hi." I decide to break the silence.

She just continues to stare at me. "I'm Travis Kendricks."

Again, nothing. Maybe I shouldn't have come in here alone.

"Your mom said it would be all right to come up. Hope you don't mind."

Still nothing. She adjusts her pillow under her head with her left hand and as she bends up a little, I see her eyes close and pain etches across her features. I want to go and help but my feet aren't moving. This was a stupid idea, I'm just going to leave.

"Well, I just wanted to see how you were." I turn my body toward the door and point with my hand. "I'm just going to leave now."

I began to finish turning around and her voice stops me, "You have to look at me when you talk."

Surprised, I turn back around and look down at her. "What?"

"If you don't look at me when you are talking, I have no idea what you are saying."

That's when it hits me. Last night her brother had said she was deaf. Now I know I shouldn't have come up here alone. I have no idea how to tell her who I am or what I am doing in her room. Wait, if I can find paper and a pen, I can talk to her that way and at least let her know who I am. I look around, no paper in sight, damn. The nurse's station might have something, I put a hand up. "I will be right back," I start to say, then stop myself. What the hell am I doing? She can't hear me. I want to slap myself in the head. I put my hand up to signal what I hope comes across as "I will be right back" and turn and leave the room.

I walk down the hallway a little and up to the station. "Excuse me, do you by chance have a piece of paper and pen I can borrow?" I ask the nurse who just left Charliee's room.

"Sure." She hands me over a small notepad and a pen.

"Thank you," I head back to the room.

I wave as I enter the room again, something jumps in my chest when she gives me a small smile back. I walk over to the chair that is beside her bed and point at it. She nods slightly and I sit down. I began to write down my name and who I am, half way through her hand comes out and grabs the paper. "Are you drawing me a picture?"

I look over at her and she is smiling, "My name is Travis Kendricks, I'm the…." She reads off the paper, it's as far as I got before she pulled it out of my hands.

I watch as she put the notebook on the bedside table. "Well, Travis Kendricks, my name is Charliee Brooksman and I'm, as you must know, deaf. I'm going to save you a little time here, though. As long as you talk to me where I can see your mouth move, I can read your lips and you won't have to write everything down." She is laughing at me now.

I hang my head down for a moment, when I look back up my breath catches. Her smile and those green eyes shoot electricity right through me. "I'm sorry."

"For what?"

"Acting so stupid. Let's start over. I'm Travis Kendricks. I'm one of the firefighters that found you last night."

Her smile fades with the mention of last night for a moment, but quickly comes back. "Well then I guess I should be thanking you."

I shake my head. "I didn't come by for a thank you."

"Why did you come by then?"

Well hell, how am I supposed to answer that question? I can't tell her that I couldn't stop thinking about her all night and today. I look anywhere but at her. "How is Levi doing?" I hope that is more subtle than it seemed. Judging by the look she is giving me, it wasn't.

"He is doing all right. We spoke to my brother early this morning and they said his rib cage is bruised, but by some miracle nothing was broken. Some cuts needed a couple stitches."

"That's great."

Silence stretches between us. "Well, I guess I should go and let you get some rest."

I stand up and start to turn to leave but she grabs my hand. I look down at her.

"I know you said you didn't come by for a thank you, Travis, but I want to say thank you very much. If you hadn't found us, we wouldn't be alive." I watch as a single tear rolls down her cheek.

I squat down so that I am eye level with her, keeping her hand in mine. I wipe the tear from her cheek. "If it hadn't been for Levi, I'm not sure if I would have found you. That is one amazing animal you have there."

She smiles again, "He's my best friend."

It takes everything in me not to lean forward and kiss those lips. This is crazy, how can she be affecting me like this? We didn't even know each other before I walked into this room. Now I am finding it hard to leave.

"Are we interrupting?" I hear the voice from behind me. I jump up and let go of her hand. Behind me are her parents and brother.

"Bryce, be nice." His mother smacks him on the arm.

She walks toward us with a bag of food in hand. I step out of the way and watch as she sets the bag down on the small table and turns to her daughter, her hands in motion. Charliee laughs and Bryce frowns. "Really, Mom!"

I look down at Charliee who is laughing. "What did she say?"

She looks at her mom and then back at me. "She said you're hot."

"Oh," is all I can think to say. Charliee, her mom and dad are laughing. Bryce, on the other hand, is glaring.

"Well thank you, Mrs. Brooksman."

"Please, call me Karen."

I smile and nod, "I should be going, thank you for letting me visit."

Charliee reaches up and grabs my hand again. "Are you going to come by again?"

Surprised, I look around the room. The only one who seems to be showing any sign that might not be okay with me coming back is Bryce. "I have tomorrow off, I'll try and stop in and say hi."

The smile I get is worth any reaction I would receive from her brother, "It was nice meeting everyone." I turn and leave.

While waiting on the elevator, I hear my name being called. I turn to find Bryce walking down the hallway toward me, "Hey."

"I don't want to be one of those overbearing brothers or anything. If anything. Charliee can take care of herself. but…"

"Bryce, listen," I stop him before he can finish. "I'm not here to make a move on your sister. I sincerely wanted to stop by today and see how she was doing. It had been a long night. We saw a lot through the night that wasn't good. I needed to see something that came out of last night that was good. Come on, man, you have to understand where I'm coming from with that."

Bryce stares at me for a moment, "I understand, Travis, I'm sorry for jumping all over you. We almost lost her last night, I think it just made me a little protective of her."

"I understand that, take care of her." The elevator doors open and I shake his hand. "See you around."

I do stop by the next day, but when I walk in she is asleep. The nurse tells me they have just cleaned her burns on her back and with the pain, it has exhausted her. I sit there next to her for almost an hour just staring at her. Her long blonde hair is in a French braid, her hand lays resting next to her cheek on the pillow. Every once in a while, her eyes scrunch together and she groans a little, I assume it is from the pain in her back. Every time it happens, I feel like someone is taking their fist and punching me in the chest knowing she is in pain and I can't do anything to relieve it. It is crazy. How do you not really know someone and have these kinds of feelings for them? The colorful cast on her arm tells me a couple of people have been by and before I leave, I walk over, pick up the red permanent marker that is sitting there and draw some flames. Next with the black marker, I write "TK" over the flames.

CHAPTER
Five

TODAY HAS BEEN a day from hell. First thing this morning, Derrick stopped by letting me know that Levi was resting at his house and that he would bring him by in a couple of days. I know I don't really need him here in the hospital but I miss him and want him here regardless. Levi isn't just my hearing dog, he is my best friend. Plus I know they said he was fine, but I still want to see for myself.

Bryce came by with the worst news. Both Mr. and Mrs. Tovaren had died in the explosion along with sixteen other people. He told me they found what looked to be a bomb under one of the tables. Who would want to bomb a restaurant? Who would want to kill a bunch of inno- cent people? My mind is spinning as I think back to the people I saw while I was in there. I hadn't known many of them but my heart broke for their families.

There have been times when they were cleaning my back and the pain was so fierce, I wished I had died. Now I feel guilty for even thinking that. I know it is all the pain talking at those moments, but now I feel ashamed for even thinking it. I am alive, so is Levi by some miracle. I am able to feel pain, to see my family, and what makes me feel even worse—I know my pain will heal. Those families who lost a loved one will carry that pain around for the rest of their lives. I feel the tears roll down my cheek.

I fell asleep after they scrubbed my back, I was exhausted between the pain and the news. When I wake up, no one was around. I find myself thinking about Travis. He had told me yesterday he would try and stop by today. I look up at the clock, it is already a little after five. The disappointment I feel surprises me. I don't even know this man and here I am upset because he didn't stop by and see me. I turn my head to look out the window of the hospital room, and the large red flames on my cast catch my eye. The initials TK are written in the middle of the flames, he had stopped by. He must have been here while I was asleep. Excitement and disappointment are two feelings that are strange to have at the same time. Why didn't he wake me when he was here? How long did he stay? Is he going to come back again? All these questions and no one to answer them for me. A tap on my shoulder startles me, I jump and quickly bring my head back to look at the other side.

"I'm sorry, I didn't mean to startle you." The nurses were all told to make sure I was looking at them when talking to me and they are all doing great. The one here now is named Teresa, and I have to say she is my favorite. She looks to be in her mid-fifties, she wears her hair in a tight bun, and her scrubs always have some kind of Disney character on them.

"It's okay, I was thinking."

She checks my blood pressure, "Is there anything you need, hon?"

"To turn over onto my back would be great."

"I can't imagine you're very comfortable. Hopefully you have only a day or so before we can get you up and moving around a little."

That gives me a little to be happy about I guess. "Can I ask you a question?"

"Of course."

She sits down in the chair next to me, which I am grateful for, it puts her more at eye level. "Do you remember that guy that stopped by yesterday?"

"The cute one who asked for paper and pen?"

I nod, "Yes, did he come by today?"

"Yes, he was here for about an hour. You had just fallen asleep."

Again, excitement races through me. He had stayed for an hour. "Did he by chance mention if he was going to come by again later?"

She places her hand on mine. "I'm sorry, hon, I didn't talk to him before he left."

"Never fear, the best friend is here." Jayden, my best friend and coworker, comes sweeping into the room at that moment, hands moving as she enters, something that looks to be a bag of food clutched between her teeth.

I laugh, the nurse stands up. "I'll be back later to check on you. I'm assuming she brought you dinner so I won't bring you any of our delicious food." She winks at me before she turns to leave.

"Thank you, Teresa." She turns and smiles at me, and then leaves.

Jayden places the bag on the tray next to my bed and plops herself down in the chair. "It's about time you're awake. I need to know everything about the hotness of a guy I saw leaving out of here as I came in earlier." Her hands sign, "We're best friends and I'm not going to get all hurt thinking that you haven't told me you were seeing someone. So start spilling all the info."

I love this woman, she is always running a mile a minute, her hands and mouth included. She talks so fast most of the time that she had learned early on in our friendship she had to sign. Those lips run way too fast for me to read.

"I'm not holding any information from you. His name is Travis and he is one of the firefighters that found me and helped pull me out. He is only being nice and stopping by to see how I'm doing, nothing more, I promise."

Jayden sits back in the chair and folds her arms across her chest as though she doesn't believe me. "What?"

"Come on, Charliee, that nurse told me today he stayed here an hour while you slept. No man does that unless there is more."

I laugh, "I swear, yesterday was the first time we met."

"Is he coming back?"

"I don't know." Again, disappointment over the fact that I didn't see him today settles in my chest.

Jayden stretches her neck up and looks over my back. "Firefighter, you say. Well then I'm going to take a huge guess in that large area of your cast covered in flames, and TK written in it is from him."

I turn my head to my other side and stare at the flames across my cast. "I'm going to say yes, but I wasn't awake when he did it."

Jayden now stands in front of me on my other side pointing at the flames. "I'm going to take another small guess and say I'll bet that man comes back again."

IT HAS BEEN a month now since the bombing. Levi and I have been home for about two weeks and both of us are healing well. The stitches on my shoulder were taken out two weeks ago, although I will admit it still burns like crazy if I stretch it too much. Same goes for the ribs, as long as I don't make quick movements, they are fine. I still have two weeks in the cast which feels like forever. Signing with one hand in a cast isn't as easy as some may think. I haven't been so thankful to my parents for the years and years of speech therapy as I am now for communication. My back is healing, but the scars will forever be a reminder of that day; they cover my entire lower back. Levi is pretty much all healed up and is back at my side no matter where I am. It seems like more now than before. If I get up and leave the room, he is right behind me. If I send him to go lay down, he hesitates. We are both still shaken from the whole event.

The investigation on what happened is still going. They have no suspects as of yet. I wanted to be at the funereal for Mr. and Mrs. Tovaren, but unfortunately I was still in the hospital when they held the services. Jacob, their son, is one of our students at the deaf school that Jayden and I teach at. I think about him every day. I am off work until the cast comes off but I think about stopping by to check up on him.

My phone screen shines next to me, catching my attention from the magazine I am staring at. I pick it up and open my message box. It is from my brother, Derrick.

** I did some checking and found which station Travis is at.

I smile, oh how I love my brother. Although, when I asked him to find out where Travis worked, he wasn't very happy about doing it. He kept going on about how I had to be careful and brotherly stuff like that. Both of my brothers have been more protective lately. One of them has stopped by every day since I have been home to check on me. My mom texts every couple of hours daily to try and get me to come home and stay a couple of weeks with them. I love my family dearly, but I need to get back to my life as it was before the bombing. My phone screen lights up again. This time when I check it is the address to the station.

I text back a quick thank you and sit there staring at the address he sent. Travis hasn't stopped by again after that one day he signed my cast. I should take the hint that he was giving and just forget about him, but I can't. I think about him multiple times a day. I told Derrick that I wanted the station address so that I could stop by and thank all of the guys that helped out that night. I think about the chocolate chip and peanut butter cookies I made earlier today and before I can change my mind or chicken out, I decide I am going to do exactly what I told

Derrick I was going to do. I am going to take the guys at the station some thank you cookies.

I run to my bedroom, Levi following right behind me, and quickly change out of my sweatpants and t-shirt. It is the middle of April and still a little cool outside so I grab my favorite jeans and a shirt I can tuck in to keep my pants from rubbing too much on my back and a sweater. I grab my black combat boots, slide them on real fast, and run to the bathroom. Quick makeup fix, hair out of the bun. I stare at myself in the mirror, I want to look good but not like I am trying to catch someone's attention.

I quickly run into the kitchen and pull out two plates and fill them with all of the cookies I have made. I grab Levi's leash and harness, "Come on, boy."

I grab my phone and shove it into my back pocket, then snatch my wallet and keys off the kitchen table. Thankfully I got my Jeep back a couple of days ago. There had been minor damage from the explosion but everything was fixable. I love my Jeep. I quickly walk out the front door, open the passenger door of the car for Levi to jump in, place the plates on the floor and get in the driver's side. Wait, what if he isn't at the station today? If I take the cookies today and he isn't there, what other reason would I have to go back another day? I sit there and argue with myself for probably five minutes. I take a deep breath, if it's meant to be then he will be there. If not then I'll know and I'll have to forget about him. I take a deep breath, my mind is made up. Here goes nothing.

CHAPTER
Six

TRAVIS

I CAN'T GET her off my mind. What is wrong with me? A woman has never had this kind of effect on me. It has been a month and there isn't a day that goes by that I don't think about her at least once. How a woman who I have only seen three times, once covered in building and the next two times laying in a hospital bed, could stir me the way Charliee did has completely puzzled me. I went back to the hospital but she had been released. There was no way the hospital would give me information about where she lived, and I didn't know her brothers, plus Bryce already warned me to keep my distance.

"Trav, are you trying to wipe the paint off, man?" Trey comes up behind me.

Damn, I need to get her out of my mind. I throw the towel that I was using to dry the engine off with at Trey. "Here, why don't you finish drying? You haven't done much anyway."

Trey laughs as I walk away. "Come on, man, don't go getting all mad at me because you got caught daydreaming."

I flip him off as I walk into the bay and back into the station. I am walking past the front window when I notice someone standing outside the front door. Everyone is out back, how long has this person been standing here? I walk over and pull the door open, not expecting the person on the other side. Charliee is standing in front of me with a plate of cookies in each hand and Levi at her side.

"I wasn't sure if I was supposed to knock, or just come in." Her voice brings me back.

"How long have you been standing there?"

"Not long." She stretches her hands out in front of her with the plates of cookies in them. "I wanted to stop by and say thank you to you guys for saving my life. I know cookies aren't much compared to what you guys had to deal with that night, but I made them myself."

Her unsure smile about knocks me down. I feel a moment of jealousy that she didn't come to just see me. I look down at the two plates, one arm is still in a cast. My signature is the largest one on it, only now it has the whole area marked off around it so that no one can sign near it, which makes me smile. I grab the one plate she holds with that hand and step aside for her. "You didn't have to bring us anything, but I'm sure the guys won't complain."

As she walks past me, my eyes travel her length. Seeing Charliee up and well isn't going to help me with forgetting her. Her blonde hair lays down to the middle of her back and my hands itch to grab it. Her backside is nicely shaped in her jeans, and her legs…damn, I have to stop. I turn to shut the door, "So how have you been doing?"

No answer. I turn back around, her back is to me and she seems to be looking around the room. Damn, that's right, I hurry around her so that she can see me and then repeat myself. "How are you feeling?"

She shrugs her shoulders. "Good, except this thing," she holds her casted arm up. "I can't wait for it to come off."

"How much longer?"

"Two weeks."

I grab the second plate from her and place them onto the table, then turn and bend down to Levi. "How you doing, boy?"

I look back up at her, "He looks to be doing well, too."

The noise coming in from behind has me standing back up. Bryan, Trey and Randy are all coming in. "Guys, we have a guest and she came offering cookies."

"Cookies?" Trey goes straight to the table. The guy is well-built and never stops eating, his wife must go crazy trying to keep him fed.

Bryan just stares at her, and I have a sudden urge to punch the kid. I move to her side.

"Guys, this is Charliee, she was one of the survivors we pulled from the explosion, and that's Levi, her hearing dog." I introduce her to them.

Suddenly, I feel very protective. My arm aches to move around her waist and hold her in tight against me. Just the mention of that night sends flashes of her under all the building. I shove my hands into my pockets to keep from reaching out and grabbing her. I can feel her watching me as I speak. She then looks over at the guys and waves with her casted hand, "Hi, guys."

She looks back at me, I point at Bryan. "That's Bryan, he was the one who was with me when we found you and helped with Levi." I wait for her to look over at him, and then back at me. "Next to him is Randy, and the one taking care of all the cookies is Trey."

She laughs as she looks over the guys, "It's nice to meet all of you guys." She walks over to Bryan and gives him a hug. "Thank you so much for everything." The kid is going to get punched if he doesn't move away from her soon.

How in the hell does the kid get a hug within minutes of meeting her and I haven't? He has felt her body pressed against his and I haven't. I want to go and pull her away. My eyes meet Bryan's and he must read me well because he pulls away from her. "Please don't say thank you.

We were just doing our job, but it's great to see both of you doing so well."

I grab her hand and she turns to me. "Let's go out back and I'll introduce you to the rest of the guys."

She nods and smiles then follows me out to the bay. The engine has already been pulled back in but I don't see Cap or Pete anywhere which doesn't break my heart. It just means I am alone again with her. "Well, I have no clue where they are."

"That's all right, I should probably be going anyway. I just wanted to stop by and say thank you real quick. Bryce was able to find out which station you guys were at for me."

So that's how she found which station to come to, her brother looked it up for her, which kind of surprises me a little. "I'll walk you out to your car, we can go around this way." I lead her through the bay, out back and then around the side. I don't want to go back through the front where all the guys are.

I follow her over to her Jeep where she opens her passenger side and Levi jumps right in. I scratch him behind his ears. "You take care of her, boy." I follow her over to the driver side. She gets up into the seat but turns her body toward me. I stand with one hand on the open door and the other on the top of the door frame.

"I'm sorry I slept through the last visit at the hospital, you should have woken me up."

Her hands are playing with her keys in her lap, almost like she is nervous. "The nurse told me they had just cleaned your burns and that you were exhausted from that, I didn't want to wake you up. You needed your rest."

"Oh," is all she says!

I stare at her for a moment, I've done nothing but think about her for the past month. I have no way of contacting her, but she went and figured out how to contact me. I look down at her cast again, she has made sure no one signed near where I had. I may be reading a little too much into that action, but it is a chance I have to take, "Can I call you tomorrow when I get off work?"

She shakes her head no, it feels like she has just punched me in the stomach. "I won't be able to hear you if you call me." Laughter is in her voice.

Damn it, I really need to think before I speak around her. I drop my head, shaking it. "I'm sorry."

I watch her hand come up from her lap to my chin and she pushes my face back up so that I am looking into the most amazing green eyes. "You can text me tomorrow after you get off work if you would like, though."

Her hand goes from my chin to my chest and warmth spreads through and straight to my stomach. What is this woman doing to me? I grab my phone out of my pocket and hand it to her, "Here, put your number in and I'll text you tomorrow. Do you work?"

"I can't go back until the cast comes off. I'm a teacher at the deaf school and signing right now isn't the easiest." She finishes putting her number in and hands me back my phone.

A teacher. Why didn't that surprise me? "What do you teach?"

"High school English."

Just then the tones go off. "I have to go, we have a call. I'll text you tomorrow." Damn the timing, but at least I got her number.

CHAPTER
Seven

CHARLIEE

I FEEL like a high school girl waiting around for the boy to call, or should I say text. Here I am, sitting on my couch, my phone on my lap so that I can feel it vibrate when it goes off. I don't want to miss his text. What's wrong with me? I've never been one of those girls who waited around for the guy. Wait, what am I talking about? There really haven't been many guys for me to wait around on.

Yesterday when Travis answered the door at the station, it took everything in me not to sag with relief that he was working. I've no idea how many times on the way over I almost turned around and went home. I laugh when I think back to when he grabbed my hand and dragged me away from the other guy who helped pull me out that night. Or when we started talking about the night of the bombing and he moved a little closer to me, almost in a protective manner. It's true when they say when one of your senses stops working all of the others pick up because I picked up on all of his actions. All my life I've learned to pay a little closer attention to a person's body language, facial expressions and my all around surroundings. When I placed my hand on his chest, I felt his heart rate pick up. I'm pretty sure that was a good sign.

The vibration from my phone on my leg causes me to jump, which in turn causes Levi to jump up. "Sorry, boy, just my phone."

I swipe the screen over and hit my message box. Dang, it is from Jayden.

**What are you doing today?

All right, how am I going to answer this one? If I tell her I am waiting to hear from Travis, she will start shooting off a hundred questions. I haven't even told her I went to the station. If I tell her that I am just staying home and being lazy, she'll want to come over. If I ignore the text all together then she'll panic, probably call my brothers or my parents and I'll have everyone here. Wait, I got it.

**I thought about going to the gym.

Jayden hates the gym. How she keeps the amazing body she has without working out is beyond me, but right now it is my saving grace.

**Well you have fun with that. Let me know if you want to do anything afterwards.

I laugh, do I know my best friend or what?

**Sounds good.

This is crazy! What am I going to do, wait all day on the couch for him to get a hold of me? I look up at the clock, it's already almost twelve. Maybe I should go to the gym, I haven't been back since getting out of the hospital. Actually a run would be good, Levi could get some exercise that way. "Boy, you want to go for a run?"

Levi jumps up from his spot on the floor. Laughing, I get up and head for my room to change. While walking down the hall, I feel my phone vibrate again. This time I am expecting Jayden, but I'm surprised to see Travis's name appear on the screen. I'm sure the smile on my face is as goofy looking as it feels. I push the screen on his message.

**I was wondering if you had any plans for tonight.

I lean up against the wall in the hallway and stare down at the screen for a moment. Travis is asking me out. This guy doesn't beat around the bush, does he? No hi, how has your morning been?

**No plans that I'm aware of.

I push send and start back down the hall toward my room. His reply comes back instantly.

**There's a great restaurant and bar down by the beach if you are interested.

I sit down on the edge of my bed and Levi sits down next to my legs, one paw up on my knee. "I know, boy, we are going to go for a run, give me just a minute."

**What time would you be picking me up?

His response is quick.

**How does around 6 sound?

**Sounds good!

I text him my address and quickly switch over to Jayden's name.

**Travis just asked me out for tonight.

I laugh at how fast she responds.

**As in the firefighter who saved you Travis?

I smile. *Yes, the firefighter who looks great in his uniform,* I think to myself.

**That's the one.

I send back quickly. A few minutes go by and then she responds.

**Wait! I thought you said you hadn't seen him since that day at the hospital?

Crap, that's right, I haven't told Jayden about going to the station and seeing him yesterday. I know where this lecture is heading later.

Right into the whole "I'm your best friend and you didn't tell me" speech.

**Kind of a funny story, I'll tell you about it later.

**You're damn lucky you're deaf and I can't call you right now. It would take too long to yell at you in text!!

This is why she is my best friend. From the moment we met, she would make jokes about me being deaf. Where most people would tip toe around the subject, Jayden would shoot it straight at me.

**What time is this date tonight?

**He said he's picking me up at 6.

**I'll be there around 2. You can grovel for me to forgive you, and then we can find the perfect outfit.

I love this girl.

**Sounds good, I'm on my way out for a run with Levi, so talk to you later.

JAYDEN'S CAR is at the curb when I get home from my run. I should have known she couldn't wait until two. Walking through the front door, I'm greeted with my best friend sitting on the couch. "It's about time you got home," she signs.

I take Levi's leash off and he heads directly to his water bowl. I follow behind him to grab a bottle of water. "I thought you said you would be here at two."

When I turn back around, she is sitting on my kitchen counter. "Charliee, it's twenty after two now."

I look up at the clock over my sink. Holy crap, I've been gone for almost two hours. I wasn't paying attention to the time while I was out, I was too busy thinking about tonight. "Sorry, I lost track of time."

"All right, stop procrastinating, I want the whole story."

"Can I take a shower first?"

She shakes her head, "No, you may not. I need information now and I can't talk to you while you are in the shower."

"Fine, the story is short, I believe you're going to be a little disappointed."

"Stop stalling and get on with it then."

I almost choke myself downing a half bottle of water trying not to laugh while she glares at me. "Last week I asked my brother to see if he could find out which station Travis worked at so that I could go and thank the guys for everything."

"Which one of them were gullible enough to believe that story?"

"I went through Derrick for this one. He wasn't at the hospital when Travis visited, so I hoped he would be more willing to help. Bryce threw a few brotherly looks Travis's direction while he was there. So anyway, I took a couple of plates of cookies with me and went and visited the station yesterday."

"So you didn't even know if he would be there, you just chanced it."

Nodding, I take another drink of water. "Charliee, that is so unlike you. I'm very proud of you."

Out of the two of us, Jayden was the outgoing one. She has no problem walking up to a guy and talking to him, or maybe I should say flirting with him. Where I, on the other hand, stand back and wait for them to approach me.

I push myself away from the counter and start down the hallway to my bedroom. I grab a pair of my favorite sweats and a t-shirt and turn to find Jayden standing in the doorway of my bathroom shaking her head, "Out with the rest of the story."

I push past her, place my clothes on the counter and start the shower. "There isn't much more to tell really. I was only there for about twenty minutes. I met the guys that he works with. We exchanged numbers and they got a call. He texted me earlier today and asked me to dinner."

Jayden stands there staring at me, "That's it?"

"I told you it wasn't that exciting of a story. Can I take a shower now?"

She watches me for a moment, like she is trying to read my mind or something. "Fine, take a shower, but you better not be leaving any information out of that story."

I wait for her to leave the bathroom, then I quickly undress and jump into the shower. "Just the part about the amazing sex we had on top of the fire engine."

The shower door flies open, Jayden's eyes are huge and her mouth is open in shock. I laugh as I push her back out and shut the door, "I'm kidding. He's hot and in the uniform even hotter, but I wouldn't have sex with him at least until after the first date."

The door opens again. "You are driving me crazy, my friend. This kind of behavior is so unlike you, but I have to say I like it."

"I have to admit, I'm kind of liking it myself. Now leave me alone and let me take a shower."

CHAPTER
Eight

TRAVIS

PULLING up to the address that Charliee texted me, I see her Jeep in the driveway. I park behind it and sit there for a moment. Should I text her and let her know I'm here? I know I can't walk up and knock on the door, or can I? I notice the other car sitting along the curb. Maybe she has a roommate. That would make more sense. Well, that is as long as the roommate can hear. Why am I making this so damn difficult? I need to just walk up to the front door. I jump out of my truck and go up to the door. Right there on the door is a sign, "Please ring the doorbell". All I can do is laugh at myself and ring the doorbell.

After a few moments, the front door opens but it's not Charliee. "Hi, you must be Travis."

Well, I'm at the right house I guess. "Yes, I am."

She stands there for a moment and looks me over, I believe she is checking me out actually. "I'm Jayden, Charliee's best friend."

"It's nice to meet you." We stand there in silence for a moment more, then Levi comes to the door. I bend down to pet him, "Hey, boy."

Charliee shows up behind her friend, "Jayden, what are you doing? Let him in."

With her back still to Charliee, she warns me, "You better be good to her." She then turns to Charliee, signs something to her, and gives her a hug. "I'm out of here, have fun." She pushes past me and walks to her car.

Hearing Charliee apologize, "Sorry about her," has my attention brought back around to her.

"What did she say to you?" I'm going to have to check out a book of sign language or something on the internet because this is now the second time someone has signed something to her and it's been about me. It's almost like being talked about behind your back but worse because they are doing it in front of you.

Charliee steps aside and motions for me to come in, "It's between girls, sorry."

She shuts the door and I wait for her to turn back to me.

"Seems a little unfair. You have this whole other language you can use and I wouldn't have the slightest idea what you were saying."

She laughs at me, "To make it fair, all you have to do is turn your back to me and talk to someone and I wouldn't know what you were saying either."

She has a point. I guess she is more at the disadvantage. I can learn sign language, she can't see through my head.

"But I'll be nice and warn you on one thing."

"Really, what's that?"

"I can read lips from a pretty good distance away, people have a tendency to forget that."

Her sense of humor is amazing. She doesn't allow her disability to slow her down in the least. "I'll try and keep that in mind."

"Give me just another minute, I have to put Levi's vest on him. He hates it so it may take a minute."

"Take your time, I'm in no hurry." I watch as she and Levi walk down the hallway, then take a quick look around. Her living room is simple and clean. A picture of her and her brothers is sitting on the end table by the couch. I sit down and grab it. It wasn't taken that long ago. They are all down at the beach. One of the boys has her thrown over their shoulder, the other one looks to be tickling her. It makes me think of my sister, Samantha. We are close like these three.

Someone rings the doorbell and all the lights in the house begin to flash. So that's how she knows someone is here, that's pretty neat. I place the picture back down on the table and wait for Charliee to walk out. Again, the doorbell rings, lights flash and still I don't hear Charliee. Maybe she doesn't have the lights in the back that flash, which would be strange, I would think they would be hooked up to go off through the entire house. Again it rings, should I answer it? No, I'll walk down the hall and see if I can find her. Just as I begin down the hall, the door crashes open. I turn and find myself in direct line of her brother and his gun, pointed right at me. I throw my hands up, "Hey, easy." I have no idea which brother it is but it doesn't really matter.

Levi comes running out of what I figure is Charliee's bedroom barking, and before I know it, Charliee is standing in front of me, shielding me from the pointed gun. "Derrick, what the hell are you doing?"

I am pretty sure her brother isn't going to shoot, but we have a loaded gun pointed at both of us and if for some reason it goes off, she isn't going to be the first hit. I push her back behind me.

Derrick looks between the two of us for a moment and then puts his gun away. "I saw the truck outside and didn't recognize it."

Charliee comes from behind me once again and walks up to her brother, who towers over her. "Maybe you should try ringing the door-bell, not just running in here with your gun drawn." Her hands are going just as angry as her tempered words. It is amazing how even through her hands you can tell she is pissed.

"I did ring the doorbell, three or more times. When you didn't answer I got worried."

Charliee turns to me with a questioning look on her face. I nod, "He did."

Now she turns her wrath onto me, "Why didn't you answer it then?"

"This isn't my house. I haven't been here more than maybe five minutes. I usually don't just answer someone's door. I saw the lights flash and figured that was how you were signaled that someone was at the door. I was actually on my way to look for you when he busted in." I defend myself to the little firecracker in front of me.

She stares at me for a moment, and then turns back to her brother. "So what, you just bust in here with your gun drawn? Why are you here anyway?"

Derrick rolls his eyes and takes a deep breath. "Look, I was just getting off work and I wanted to check on you. I saw the truck, didn't recognize it, so after I rang the doorbell a few times and you didn't answer, I got a little worried and reacted. Why didn't you answer it? He said the lights flashed." Derrick points over at me. "Better yet, why didn't Levi let you know?"

I notice Charliee backing down a little, her back relaxes and her shoulders slump a little. "I was putting his vest on. He did try and let me know, I just figured he was being stubborn, you know he hates having that thing on. I guess I didn't see the lights. I was trying to hurry, Travis was out here waiting. That doesn't excuse you barging in, gun drawn."

"Charliee, I said I was sorry."

I place my hand on her shoulder to get her attention, "It's all right, he was just worried. I can't say I blame him."

Reaching around Charliee, I extend my hand out to Derrick. "Hi, I'm Travis." This isn't the one I had talked to at the hospital, but I remember him from the night we pulled Charliee out.

"The firefighter from that night, right?"

I nod my head and wait for him to shake my hand. After a moment he extends his hand and shakes mine. "I'm Derrick. Sorry about all of that."

Shrugging it off, I assure him, "It's no problem. I have a sister, and like I said, I understand."

Derrick stands there for a moment staring at his sister, he was worried. The fear is still in his eyes. He takes a deep breath, walks over to her and gives her a kiss on her forehead. "Be careful and have fun." Then he signs something else at her and turns to me. "You better take care of her." I nod my understanding and watch as the second person tonight walks out of the house after warning me to take care of her.

I understand where everyone is coming from when it comes to this woman. I have felt the same need to protect her since we pulled her out. Watching Charliee roll her eyes at her brother as he walks away, I am getting the feeling she is feeling smothered. She needs to under-stand what her brothers went through that night, they have the right to be this protective of her.

"I'm real sorry about all of that. If you want to cancel tonight, I understand."

"Charliee, don't worry about it. I have a younger sister, I understand his feelings. I just don't carry a gun that I can pull out on the guys she dates."

She stares up at me for a moment. She is thinking, about what I have no clue, but it is taking everything in me to not bend down and kiss her. We need to get going before I rush everything a little too fast. I hold my hand out to her, "Are you ready to go?"

• • •

"SO TELL me how you and Jayden met." We moved from the dining area after eating and over to the bar of the restaurant for a beer.

"We met in college actually, she was one of the few people who never treated me different because I was deaf. We were both studying to be teachers and after she met me, she decided to learn sign language and we both got jobs at the deaf school."

"Do you only sign when you're mad?" I noticed she talked more than signed, with the exception of tonight with her brother.

"Actually no, but with this thing on my arm." She holds up the arm that is still in a cast, "It makes signing a little difficult at times."

"Really, because today when you were yelling at your brother your hands were a flying."

She laughs, looking down at her hands, "Yeah, that's a natural reaction. Signing is so natural that when I get mad, they start moving." She holds up her hands.

I take the arm with a cast on it and look at all the names signed onto it. Where I signed is the largest one on there.

"Why didn't you come back after the day you signed this?" she asks me.

How much should I tell her? I couldn't sit here and tell her that the feelings I was having for her were confusing the hell out of me, so I decided not to come back thinking they would go away. Or that all I have wanted to do since we uncovered her that night was take her in my arms and keep her safe. Seeing her in the hospital was hell. That hour I sat there, I knew she was in pain, and I couldn't do anything to take it away. All I could do was sit there and watch. That's not what I do, I don't just stand back and watch someone go through pain. I go and help them. Plus she needed the time to heal, not worry about me being there all of the time. Staying away was hard though. Every day I was off from the station it took everything not to go to the hospital, but I would talk myself out of it. Finally when I decided I couldn't stay away, I go and find out she was already home.

"Actually I did go back again, but you had already been released to go home."

"But that was a couple of weeks after, why didn't you come back before then?"

Her green eyes don't leave mine. She is trying to read me. I look away and take a drink of my beer. She isn't going to let this go. "Work was crazy. So when do you get the cast off?"

She knows I am lying. I won't look at her, but I can feel her eyes on me. I take one more drink of my beer, finishing it, and look at her. Nope, she isn't buying my crap one bit. She keeps silent for a moment longer, I can tell she is at war with herself on whether she should keep this conversation going, or just answer my question. She looks disappointed, which drives to me almost tell her everything, but I want to see her again, not scare her away.

"Next Tuesday, I hope." My relief is hard to hide, she lets the conversation go, for now. I am pretty sure it isn't the last time it will come up.

"Are you back to work already?'

She shakes her head, "No, I'm waiting until the cast comes off. It's not real easy to sign with this thing on. Plus everyone thought it would be best if I wait a little longer. Hopefully if I get it off next week, I can start back the following Monday. I miss being there. I'm also going a little crazy with being home all the time. I think once I get back to work, it will hopefully feel like my life is back to normal again. Between my brothers, my parents and Jayden, I think I may go crazy with how much they check up and worry about me."

I know she thinks they are crowding her for no reason, but they have every right, they almost lost her. I didn't even know her before that night and I went crazy fighting with myself to not go to the hospital every day.

"Charliee, I know you may think they are smothering you a little, I saw it in your eyes when the whole thing with your brother happened tonight. But you need to think about what they went through. Especially your brothers. I was there when they realized it was you buried under there. We uncovered Levi first and the moment they recognized him, both of them went into action."

I don't know how much she really wants to hear about that night, or how much her brothers have told her, but I think she needs to know what they went through. "Have your brothers talked about that night at all with you?"

She is playing with the napkin on the bar shaking her head. "Charliee, at one point when we finally uncovered you, we weren't sure you were alive. It took me a second to find your pulse and it was weak. I'm sure your brothers didn't take a solid breath until you opened your eyes. I know I didn't."

She looks up at me, tears are in her eyes. I want to pull her into my arms and hold her, comfort her and myself knowing she is all right, but instead I grab her hand, threading my fingers with hers. "I know this can't be easy to hear, all the stuff from that night. I can only imagine how you feel about it and your life now. I can't blame you for wanting to get back to a normal life, but you need to cut them all a little slack."

She doesn't say anything, she just stares down at our hands. I watch as a single tear falls down her cheek. I tap my finger against her hand to get her attention back up to me. "Hey, why don't we head out of here?"

She wipes the tear away, and I watch as Levi sits up from where he is lying down and nestles against her leg, sensing her mood change. "No, I'm sorry. I don't want to ruin our evening. I'm having a good time."

"So am I," I assure her, "But with you crying and all, people are looking at us like we are breaking up or something."

She laughs at my joke, her smile causing a need in me for her. "We don't have to end the night. We can go and take a walk, or whatever you want."

She takes the last drink of her beer and stands up from the stool. That is my cue that she is all right with leaving. We start out toward the exit and she freezes. I stop and look over at her. She is staring at the door, fear in her eyes. No one is standing there so that can't be causing her to stop. I look around, what the heck is wrong? A couple behind us walks around and leaves. I look back at Charliee and she is shaking, Levi is starting to whine a little.

I step out in front of her, "Hey, what's wrong?"

Her breathing is rapid, I look down at her hands. The one holding Levi's leash has the knuckles turning white from grasping it so hard. She is shaking all over. "Charliee, talk to me, what's wrong?" I try again.

"The explosion, it happened when we were leaving the restaurant. I had just walked out the door. I felt the heat hit my back and all I remember from there is darkness. You say I woke up after you guys uncovered us, but I have no memory of it. I only remember waking up in the hospital."

I take her face in between my hands. "You need to calm your breathing down before you start hyperventilating. Come on, breathe in slow and let it out slow. "I talk her into calming down. Once her breathing evens out, I work on reassuring her, "I promise you while you are with me, nothing is going to happen to you."

A little laugh escapes past her lips, which makes me smile. It has to be a good sign if she can smile a little, "You can't keep that promise, Travis. You can't protect me from everything."

"Actually, I'll do everything I can to make sure I do keep that promise. I have already pulled you out from under a building and seen you in a hospital bed. I don't ever want to feel like that again, Charliee. I'll do whatever I can to make sure of it."

Her surprise shines through her eyes and the force between us can't be held at bay any longer, I need to kiss this woman. My hands are still cupping her cheeks, I tip her head up and lean down. Ever so gently, my lips brush hers. I want her to know she can stop me if she wants to.

I hear her intake of breath, I smile against her lips. She wraps her arms around my waist and pulls me closer, that's my clue she wants this as much as I do.

I don't care that we are standing in the middle of the waiting area of the restaurant, or that people are going around us entering and exiting the place. We are probably getting the evil eyes by everyone, but right now the most important person to me is this woman in my arms. I feel her hands grip the back of my shirt. She is going to be my undoing, I'm sure of that now. All those days I fought going to see her, now I wonder, what the hell was I thinking? I could have already had this woman in my arms. One thing is for sure, I'm not letting her go now. One taste of these lips and I'm hooked.

I pull back and look down at her, an idea comes to me. "Do you trust me?"

She nods her head without hesitation. "I want you to close your eyes and keep them closed."

Again, no hesitation, she closes her eyes and I turn her around twice. She never even attempts to open her eyes, she just follows my lead. For her to have that much trust in me without even really knowing me surprises me.

I look up at the hostess, who is giving me a strange look. "Can you please open the door and hold it open for me?"

She looks at us strangely for a moment, then walks over to the door and opens it. 'Lady, don't even worry about it, just do what I ask' I want to tell her. I start walking backwards toward the door leading Charliee forward with me. As we pass the hostess, I smile a thank you. I move us out a couple of feet and out of the way of the door.

CHAPTER
Nine

CHARLIEE

WHEN TRAVIS ASKED me if I trusted him, I knew the answer right away. I didn't even have to think about it, something about this man drew me to him. When he kissed me, I thought I was going to melt to the floor. The light brush of his lips against mine, I knew he was telling me I could stop him, which made me want to kiss him all the more.

When he starts turning me around, I wonder what is happening and then I figure it out, he is leading me out of the restaurant. My nerves almost have me opening my eyes, but something about having him leading me and touching me calms me. We start walking, I can feel Levi walking along side of me and Travis in front of me. Levi isn't nervous like he was last time, he isn't trying to pull me back or rush me out like last time. We walk a ways, I start to wonder when we were going to be out. We weren't that far from the front door to begin with. He hasn't released either one of my hands to open the door, but then before the thought is done, we stop. The feel of his lips once again against mine relaxes me. I would walk through fire to have these lips against mine. He tastes of beer and it is intoxicating. I wrap my arms around his neck pulling him closer to me, deepening the kiss. I find his tongue with mine. I feel his arms tighten around my waist, pulling me into him. We can't get any closer. Travis pulls away from me and taps a finger on my right temple. He is telling me to open my eyes. When I open them, I am staring right into ice blue eyes. I'm hooked!

"Hey, if we don't stop we are going to give every customer of this place a little show before they enter for their dinner."

Laughing and a little embarrassed, I tilt my head down and put my forehead against his chest. How is this man, with one kiss, able to make me forget everything around me? His chest rumbles a little, he is laughing as well. He places a hand under my chin and makes me look back up at him.

"Don't hide, trust me, I felt the same way. I knew if I didn't end that kiss there was no telling where we would have ended up. I'm just as affected as you are, Charliee."

This is crazy. I have dated, had boyfriends. Not a lot, men usually weird out once they find out I'm deaf. No one has affected me this fast or this much though. I haven't stopped thinking of Travis since I met him when he visited me at the hospital. He has made adjustments to me being deaf without making it obvious. The man tapped my temple to make me open my eyes. He thinks before he acts with me, that just makes me fall a little more for him. Then there are the kisses, and I have never felt like I do when he kisses me. I'm lost, completely unaware of my surroundings and honestly, I'm okay with it.

"So, do you want to go somewhere else, take a walk on the beach, or call it a night?"

I'm not ready to say goodnight to him, but after the whole leaving the restaurant thing, him kissing me and the emotional rollercoaster of the evening, I'm exhausted. Plus, we need to slow things down a little. "I think maybe we should call it a night."

I see the disappointment in his eyes, it almost has me changing my mind. "I would like to go out again though. That is if you want to."

He smiles at me, leans forward and for the third time tonight, kisses me. "Is that a yes?" I ask after.

"I believe I can handle one more date," he teases me. He takes my hand and we head to his truck.

WE ARE STANDING at my front door and Levi pulling on my arm breaks our kiss. I open the door and Levi runs in.

"How long have you had Levi?"

I look over at my best friend who is now lying in his favorite spot next to the couch. "Since I was sixteen. My parents wanted to make sure when I went to college and moved out on my own I had the extra ears, I guess you can say."

"Is he your first hearing dog?"

"Yes, I thought my parents were being ridiculous when they mentioned getting him for me, but now I couldn't imagine not having him."

I look back up at Travis, he is staring down at me. I want to invite him in, I think he is waiting for me to ask. "I would invite you in but I think we better at least get through the second date before we reach second base."

Travis laughs. This is the first time that I can remember wishing that for once I could hear. I would love to hear his laugh and his voice. "What makes you think I wanted to go to second base?"

I'm pretty sure he's joking with me, but I can't tell. I'm usually pretty good at reading people and their reactions, but with Travis it's not as easy. I feel my cheeks heat up from embarrassment. I look back into the house where Levi is laying, trying to avoid eye contact with Travis.

His hand on my cheek pulls my attention back to him and his lips. He kisses me again, my embarrassment is gone. He was joking! "I'm sorry for teasing you. I'm not sure if standing out here would keep me from trying to get to second base, so with that said I'm going to say good night."

"I had fun tonight."

"Me, too! I'll text you tomorrow. I have to work the next two days, but I'd like to get together this weekend if you're interested."

I shrug my shoulders, "I'll think about it."

Travis stares at me for a moment, now he's trying to figure out if I'm joking or not. Good, I can make him think a little as well. He searches my eyes for a moment, I can't stop from laughing. I push up onto my toes and claim his lips. "You better go, or this is going to go on all evening."

He smiles down at me, nods and then turns and walks back to his truck. I wait as he pulls out of my driveway, waving one last time before he drives away. What an evening. I walk into the house, closing the door behind me, then turn and stare at it. Tonight was the first time I feared anything since the night of the bombing. I've gone in and out of doors, lots of them, but tonight at the restaurant I froze. I remember looking up at the door as we began to leave but my legs froze. I just kept flashing back to the night of the bombing, I could even feel the heat at my back. I feel the burn now and find myself unknowingly rubbing my back. If Travis hadn't lead me out the way he did, I've no idea how I would have left the building. Is this something I am going to go through now every time I leave a restaurant? I don't have nightmares. I assumed that was because I didn't remember anything after opening the door to leave. My brothers and Travis have both mentioned me waking up after they uncovered us, but I have absolutely no memory of it at all. The earliest memory I have is waking up in the hospital room. I close my eyes and think back to that night. Nothing new. I think of before the explosion. Now all I'm seeing is Mr. and Mrs. Tovaren and my heart breaks. I feel the tears roll down my face. I have wondered why I was the one to survive when so many lives were lost that night. I remember the families I had seen in there, the hostess. Why would someone want to do what they did and take so many lives? The pressure against my legs has me opening my eyes. Levi is standing next to me, he moves his head under my hand. "I'm all right, boy." I kneel down and pet him for a moment. I don't want to be selfish and not appreciate that we lived. I know we were lucky, but there hasn't been a day that goes by that I don't think of all those families who lost loved ones that night. I need to ask Jayden how Jacob, the Tovarens' son, is doing.

I feel my phone go off, pulling it out of my back pocket I see that it's Jayden.

**Soooo, how did tonight go?

I laugh a little, wiping the tears from my face. Maybe I shouldn't answer her and let her wonder for a little while. My phone goes off again, man she is being really impatient, but looking down I see it's not from Jayden, it's from Travis.

**I wanted to make sure you were doing all right?

I look around, here I am sitting on the floor in front of my door, crying.

**I'm good thank you.

It only takes a matter of seconds for him to respond.

**Good, if you ever need to talk or just need a kissing partner please let me know.

I laugh, he has been good at making a serious moment seem a little flirty.

**I appreciate both offers. I'm sorry about my little hitch in the evening, but kissing you did make it kind of worth it.

I can flirt back. It's strange how easy it is with him. I haven't dated a lot, but I have never felt this comfortable with a guy and this quickly. Even the first time he came to the hospital, I remember feeling very comfortable around him. I was laying on my stomach, my back burnt, bruised and cut up, and an arm in a cast and never once do I remember wondering what he thought about how I looked. Of course that could be because he had been the one to pull me out from under a building and I'm pretty sure I didn't look too great then either. Another text vibrates through.

**My job is to serve and protect. I had a damsel in distress, I rescued and then was rewarded!

I quickly text back.

**You're very good at your job sir.

Just thinking about kissing him stirs up my insides.

**Which job would you be referring to? The rescuing or the kissing?

**So kissing me is considered a job now?

I wait for a response, my cheeks hurt from the huge smile. Again he has come to my rescue, only this time he has no clue. Just minutes ago I was balling my eyes out, now I sit here smiling like a fool, still on my floor.

**A job that I look forward to doing again and again.

Damn, he's quick! I hate that it's going to be another two or three days before I see him again.

**Smooth! Thank you again for tonight I had a great time.

**So does this mean you have thought it over and have decided to go out with me again?

It takes me a moment to figure out what he is talking about, but then I remember before he left I told him I would think about going out with him again.

**Will there be kissing involved?

**I have been taught that I need to work hard at everything I do to make myself better, so I look forward to that work load.

Yep, I'm in trouble with this one. He has a response for everything.

**I will see you in a few days, good night.

**Look forward to it, good night.

Staring at the last text, I realize I may be falling too fast for this one. I can still feel his arms around me. I felt safe. He's strong, that's obvious for anyone who was to look at him. His full sleeve tattoos on both arms give him that bad boy look, but his personality shows you his tenderness. We didn't talk endlessly about me being deaf, like most first dates I have gone on. Or the guy is so worried about offending me or doing something wrong that it's uncomfortable for the both of us. Travis adjusted to everything without making a big deal out of it. He thinks before he acts and if he forgets for a moment, he can laugh at himself. To top everything off, the man can kiss. I can still feel his lips, his tongue. I don't think I have ever wanted to crawl up a man's body and wrap my legs around him like I did when he kissed me tonight.

Looking over at Levi, he is still next to me, both of us still on the floor in front of my door. He hasn't left my side since I laid here and cried. I love this dog. He is the only one who knows how that night of the bombing has affected me. Around my family and friends I act as though everything is fine. Like it's all in the past and will stay there. Between my parents, brothers and Jayden, there is enough worrying going around. If I was to tell them what's rolling around in my head, they would never leave me alone. I can sit here and cry or talk to Levi and he will just listen and cuddle. I realize I haven't taken his vest off, which surprises me he hasn't bugged me to take it off. "Come on, boy, let's go get this stupid thing off you."

He shoots up off the floor and toward the hall. He turns and looks at me. If he could talk I'm sure he would be asking what I was waiting for. I laugh as I get up from the floor. "All right, I'm coming." Damn, what a night.

CHAPTER

Ten

TRAVIS

I DIDN'T WANT to leave Charliee tonight. I wanted to stay and hold her. That night of the bombing affects her more than she lets on. She's strong, that I'll give her and if you weren't paying attention you would think she has moved on from it all. When her brother busted in with his gun drawn, she was pissed, but her eyes spoke nothing but love for her brother for caring. I still believe she needs to give them all a little break about being so protective, but I fully believe she loves each one of them for caring as much as they do. She likes them checking on her, they're like her security she doesn't want to let on she needs. If they just keep showing up, she can keep acting like they are overreacting and she doesn't have to admit she is still scared.

Tonight I saw some of her fear. The look in her eyes when she stared at the door of the restaurant tore me apart. I wanted to grab her and carry her out through the back if need be. I knew she would have hated me for that, though. She was already embarrassed for showing a weakness, but we needed to get out of there. The way she trusted me without question hit me straight in the chest. When we kissed, her arms were tightly wrapped around me, like she didn't want to let go. She may fool everyone else but I see through all of it. Driving away tonight was hard. Her words were telling me she was fine but her eyes still had that look of fear and pain in them. She says she doesn't remember much from that night, but she remembers enough. Our playful texting was what helped me keep myself from jumping back in my truck and driving back over.

I have never wanted to call in sick to work like I want to right now. Working the next two days means not seeing Charliee for the next two days. It can't be normal to want to be with someone this much after just one date. Damn, what's wrong with me? A woman has never gotten to me like Charliee has. Then again she isn't like most women either. She's grounded, easy to talk to and doesn't use her disability to get attention. She is very independent, which is why she isn't allowing her family to see her fears. I'm falling for this woman and I'm falling hard. I'm all right with that, I think.

CHAPTER
Eleven

CHARLIEE

"SO SPILL IT. You never texted me back last night, so I'm going to assume you got home late. Now I need all the details, please."

Jayden texted me again this morning telling me that I needed to come to the school on her lunch and fill her in on what happened. I haven't been back since everything happened and I am happy she suggested me coming by. Even if it was just to get information out of me about last night. It's strange how many days I've sat here and wished I was anywhere but here. I don't think I've ever been this excited to be sitting in the teacher's lounge. I want this damn cast off more than ever, I need to be back at work. There isn't much time left before school gets out for the summer, I miss the kids.

"We went to dinner and had a couple of beers."

"Oh, come on, you have to give me more detail than that."

Laughing at her I realize my friend needs a boyfriend. Maybe then she wouldn't be so interested in my love life. "What kind of details would you like? I had a bacon burger and fries for dinner. Two beers at the restaurant bar after that. Wait…" I held my hand up for her, "We also had mozzarella sticks for an appetizer."

Jayden smacks my hand away and sits back in her chair, arms crossed. "You're not funny."

I personally thought it was funny. Teasing her about all of this I think is pretty damn funny. She wants to be nosy? Then she will have to take the joking. "It was the first date, Jay, what did you think was going to happen?"

Shrugging her shoulders, she almost looks as though she is pouting. "I don't know. I thought he might at least try and get a kiss or something."

I instantly feel the heat rise in my body when she mentions him kissing me. I try looking around so that she won't notice but no such luck.

"He did kiss you." She flings herself forward in the chair, I know she must have yelled that.

I'm thankful when I look around and notice there is only one other teacher in the lounge right now and she is also deaf. From the look on her face, she is very interested in the book she is reading and not the conversation that we are having.

Jayden grabs my arm, basically pulling me across the table. "Spill it, my friend."

Rolling my eyes, I pull away from her. "Yes, we kissed. Are you happy now?"

She sits back in her chair again, shaking her head at me. A smile is on her face from ear to ear. "Was it just a sweet little kiss to say good night, or one that said please invite me in?"

Oh my gosh, she isn't going to let this go without the full details. I can feel my cheeks heat up a little more. "You, my friend, need a boyfriend."

I notice Jayden's smile falls for a moment at the mention of her needing a boyfriend, but she quickly recovers it. "Then allow me to live my life through you, please, until that happens."

She's keeping something from me. The smile and teasing may have returned quickly but something is going on. Maybe I should hound her and see how she likes it, because she isn't giving me full details. Something in her eyes is pleading with me to let it go, though, so for now I will. Plus, I guess I'm keeping some stuff to myself as well. I'll tell her about the amazing kisser he is, really none of that really bothers me. That's what best friends do, share the steamy stuff. The incident at the restaurant, however, isn't being brought up. She would mention it to my brothers or parents and everyone would swarm more than they already do.

"Yes, we kissed. More than once and more than just a little good night peck, and no, he wasn't invited in no matter how much I wanted to offer."

She starts to say something and I hold up my hand, "Yes, it was not only nice, it was amazing. The curl your toes, I want to crawl up your body hot kind of kissing. Happy now?"

She just sits there nodding her head. I believe that answer may have satisfied her. "Then I will say it's safe to assume you want to see him again?"

"He is working today and tomorrow, but we did make plans to go out again."

Shoving a chip in her mouth, Jayden just stares at me.

"What?"

"You like this guy, don't you?"

Didn't I just say that? I'm a little confused. "Didn't I just say we made plans to see each other again?"

Shaking her head, she shoves another couple chips in her mouth. "No, I mean you like, like him. He is hot, I wouldn't blame you at all."

"All right, first stop talking to me with food in your mouth, it's gross. Either sign it or swallow, I don't want to see it as I'm trying to figure out what you are saying to me."

She throws a couple chips at me and opens her mouth wide, showing her chewed up food. I throw a chip back at her. "You're gross."

I wait as she swallows, and then gestures with her hand for me to continue. "I'm done, please continue to answer my question. You like, like this guy?"

"Yes, I like him," I confess.

"From the short time I met him, I can't say I blame you."

"I'm surprised we made it out onto the date. Right after you left, Derrick stopped by. He rang the doorbell a couple of times but I was putting on Levi's vest and didn't pay attention to the lights going off. Anyway, long story short. He didn't know whose truck was in my driveway, panicked when I didn't answer the door so he busted in, gun drawn."

Maybe I should have waited until she finished drinking before I told the story, she just sprayed water all over the table and me. "Are you serious?"

Taking a napkin, I wipe the water from my face. "Thanks for that. Yes, I'm serious. I walked out and found him standing in front of Travis, his gun pointed right at him."

"What did Travis do?"

"Surprisingly, he stayed calm. He even said he understood because he has a sister as well."

Elbows on the table and her chin in her hand, Jayden just shakes her head. "You need to keep that man. Anyone who isn't going to run when your brother barges in with a gun drawn is a keeper."

The lights flashing in the room signal for us that our time is up. Jayden needs to get back to work. "Damn, I have to go. I can't wait for you to get back. I've missed having you here."

I understand her feelings. I don't want to leave. All I've been doing lately is sitting around the house. "Hopefully only one more week. I go next week to see about getting this thing off." I hold up my cast. "I'm bored out of my mind all day long, everyone is working but me."

I follow Jayden as she gets up and throws away her trash, then turns back to me. "Since he's working for the next two days, why don't you stop by the station and say hi?"

"I've thought about that, trust me. I just keep talking myself out of it. It's his work place, how professional is it to have a girl stop by? I'm not even a girlfriend."

As we enter into the hallway, I feel a little more need to be back watching all the kids hurry to their next class. Jayden turns to me and signs, "I don't see anything wrong with you stopping by. Maybe wait until tomorrow though. That way you don't seem real pushy. You did just go out last night, we don't want to scare him away."

"I'll think about it." I give her a hug and promise to text her later.

I HAVE no idea where I'm at, it's too dark to see anything, but the heat is unbearable. My back feels as though it's on fire. The pain just keeps getting worse, I try to scream, but of course I can't tell if I am or not. Why isn't anyone helping me? Where is everyone? I'm on fire.

My eyes fly open. I look around, my hands go directly to my lower back. Levi has his front two paws up on my bed. I have never had nightmares about that night, why the hell am I having them now?

"I'm all right, boy, just a bad dream." I run my hand over his head a couple times reassuring him I'm all right. I must have woken him up. He sits there for a moment, you can tell he is trying to figure out if I'm really all right or not. After a moment he must be satisfied because he pushes himself off my bed and goes to lay back down in his.

I look over at my clock on my nightstand, it's almost six in the morning. I'm pretty sure I'm not going back to sleep, and I have a nervous, need air kind of feeling. Going for a run seems like a pretty good idea.

It's early and probably chilly outside, but right now chilly sounds very nice. I quickly jump out of bed and change, then grab Levi's leash. "Come on, boy, let's go for a run."

I'VE RAN, showered and now I'm just sitting here. Now what? Everyone is at work and I'm getting restless. That saying 'you never appreciate something until it's gone' is my motto right now. I'll promise never to complain about having to get up to go to work, deal with teenagers or anything work related if I can just go back. I do believe I may be going crazy. I could go see Travis but I'm still not sure if it's a good idea. Not only for the reason that I'm not sure if it's allowed for him to have people stop by, but I don't want to seem too eager either. Last time I stopped by I had a good reason, to thank everyone. This time I wouldn't have a reason. I probably should just wait until tomorrow. Plus, I haven't heard from him since that night, so maybe he doesn't want to see me.

My phone vibrates in my pants pocket. I pull it out and look at the screen. My stomach gets a fluttering feeling just seeing his name

**How are you doing?

**Good how are you doing?

**I'm bored

Well, I'm happy to see that I'm not the only one.

**That makes two of us. A couple days off from work is one thing. All this time off is driving me crazy.

His response it instant.

**Come visit me then.

There isn't even enough time for him to really think about that, he must really want me to stop by. I guess my questions about him having people at work are answered now, but just to make sure…

**It's all right to stop by? You're supposed to be working.

**We are all just hanging out. So are you coming to visit me?

Well, if I wanted a reason to go visit, I guess him wanting me there is a pretty good one. My phone vibrates with another text.

**You don't have to if you don't want to.

Crap, he thinks I don't want to see him.

**I'm leaving now.

**Hurry up, I need to practice that kissing job again. Drive careful please.

After telling me he's waiting to kiss me, he says drive careful. Really?!

CHAPTER
Twelve

Travis

WHEN I ASK to her to come by the station and don't get an instant response, I become a little nervous. Maybe she didn't enjoy the other night as much as I did. Just the idea of kissing her lips again is stirring a need in me. Then I think maybe it was a bad idea not to text her yesterday. It's not that I didn't want to, I had pulled my phone out a few times, but she hadn't text me either and I thought maybe I should slow down a little. The fire I felt when her hands grabbed the back of my shirt like it was what was keeping her standing while we kissed the other night almost sent me to my knees and begging her for more. At least with having her come by the station I can see her, but with the guys around it should help me to control my need to have her.

Sitting here on the front of the engine, bay door open, I see her when she pulls up. I watch as she jumps out of her seat, Levi following right behind. She waves and smiles and my body instantly reacts. Damn, just the woman smiling at me is causing a need inside. All I can do is watch as she walks over to me, her jeans fitting each of her curves perfectly. She stops just out of my reach. "Hi."

"Hi," is all she says back!

I watch her for a moment as she looks around. It's cute to see her cheeks a little red and a look in her in eyes like she is about to get caught for doing something she shouldn't. "I'm glad you decided to come by."

I look down at her hands that are nervously twisting around the leash that she is holding. Levi, on the other hand, must feel comfortable because he is sitting right next to my leg, looking up at me, waiting for me to acknowledge him. "Hey, boy, you keeping her out of trouble?" I scratch him behind this ears and down his muzzle. At least he likes me. That has to be a plus to getting Charliee's attention.

I look back up and Charliee is smiling now. "We wouldn't want you being bored."

That smile sparks something in me. I keep petting Levi to stop myself from grabbing her by the waist and pulling her to me. "It's been pretty quiet today."

She points at the engine behind me. "I would think in this line of work that's a good thing."

I nod, agreeing with her. "Yes, it's a very good thing. On the other side of it, though, I have to spend the day with the guys. I needed a little distraction."

"So I'm being used, is that what you're telling me?" Her stance becomes a little more relaxed, she has even taken another step closer to me.

"Absolutely, any complaints?" I can't keep my hands to myself any longer. I reach out and grab her by the waist, pulling her between my legs.

"I think I can say this is the first time I don't mind being used."

Her responses keep right up with mine. "Good, so can I kiss you now?"

She shakes her head no. I'm sure it's either the shock or the plea in my eyes that has her laughing at me. I'm not against begging her if it gives me her lips.

Her hands go to the back of my neck, her cast digs into my skin a little. I tilt my head back to look up at her. She brings her forehead down against mine. "Just a little bit of information for later. You look hotter than hell in this uniform. Even if I didn't know you, I would have a hard time not wanting to kiss you."

I have no time to register what she said, her lips claim mine. Who the hell cares what she said?!

The moment our lips touch, my body reacts to her. My hands are still on her waist, so I pull her in closer to me, my tongue seeking hers. The moment her tongue meets mine, every nerve in my body wakes up and wants more. Then, like cold water being thrown on me, I remember that we are sitting on the front of my engine. Even worse we are in the front of the station, doors open. I'm sure the hardest thing I will have to do today is pull away from this woman's lips.

It takes only a moment for Charliee to realize the same thing I gather because she quickly pulls out of my arms and a good distance away from me. Her reaction is so quick that her fast movement even causes Levi to jump up and look around wondering what just happened. "I'm so sorry."

It's hard to keep myself from laughing as I watch her look around frantically for anyone who may have seen us.

I walk over to her and grab her hand. She looks anywhere but at me. I wrap my arm around her waist and pull her up against me, still she doesn't look at me. With my two fingers under her chin, I push her face up so that she has to look at me. "I can't talk to you if you aren't looking at me."

A small smile joins those embarrassed cheeks, it's hard to keep myself from kissing her again. "Travis, I'm so sorry."

Her forehead falls to my chest. I can't keep from laughing this time. She slaps me. "Don't think that just because I can't see your face, it doesn't mean I don't know that you're laughing at me."

She tries to pull away from me, only I tighten my arms around her to keep her close. "I'm not laughing at you, Charliee, I promise. Although I will admit you are very cute when you're embarrassed. Stop apologizing. Trust me, I was into that as much as you were. I'm glad you are feeling the same for me as I am for you."

"Travis, we have had one date. I don't want you thinking I'm one of those girls who easily throws myself at a guy."

"Charliee, take a deep breath."

I wait a moment as she takes a couple breaths and I can feel her body relaxing against mine again. "First off, I don't think you easily throw yourself at guys. I know we have only had one date. I left my phone on my bunk all day yesterday just so that I wouldn't text you, but I haven't stopped thinking about you. You're right, we have only had one date, but I have felt a pull toward you since that night."

"Since you are confessing, so will I. I haven't stopped thinking about you since you first visited me in the hospital."

She holds her casted arm up so that I can see it. "I wouldn't even let people sign my cast close to where you signed it."

I am happy to hear I was right about the border being drawn around my name. "I found you, Charliee, literally if you want to put it that way. I've thought about you a lot in the last month, I even tried fighting the attraction I have for you and it hasn't worked. I'm done with all of that. I'm not planning on letting you go."

I watch as she stares at her fingers that are rubbing back and forth over my chest right above my heart. Her eyes smile when she looks back up at me. "So does this mean I'm your girlfriend now?"

I can't keep from kissing her again, but we keep it sweet this time, not steamy. "I'm not sharing you with anyone else, Charliee. So if you would like to call that being my girlfriend, that's fine with me. Are you good with that?"

Shrugging her shoulders, she looks around like she is thinking about it for a moment. "All right, boyfriend, let's make this a thing between us."

This is one of the reasons I am falling so fast, she always has a response that matches my sense of humor. "Maybe we should make it official with a kiss."

"Kissing you seems to get me in a little trouble and then embarrassed, especially here at your station."

"I'll behave, I promise." Just as our lips touch, the tones go off. Seriously, now we get a call?

The lights flashing catch Charliee's attention. "What's going on?"

"We have a call, I have to go."

The dispatchers voice over the speakers cause us guys to all freeze with one word—explosion. Everyone is looking at us, or probably more at Charliee.

"Travis, what's wrong?"

The guys get back to getting ready. There's movement around the whole area, the dispatcher is giving us our direction, the tones are still going off and Levi is pacing. I'm sure all the sounds aren't easy on his ears. I don't want to freak Charliee out. "Don't worry, all right? I will text you later."

I know my words will mean more to her when she finds out what is going on and she will find out, I just don't want her worrying about it as she drives home.

"Kendricks, let's go," the Cap yells at me.

"I've got to go." I kiss her quickly and run to my gear.

As the engine rolls out, I see her standing at her Jeep watching as we leave. This is the first time I have ever not wanted to be on a call. I want to be with Charliee!

CHAPTER
Thirteen

CHARLIEE

THE WHOLE DRIVE home I wonder what the call is that Travis is going to. Something changed in all the guys for a second. I saw it in all their faces. For that quick second, they all stopped what they were doing and I would swear they all looked at us, but then quickly went back to getting ready.

As I pull into my driveway, my phone in my pocket starts vibrating like crazy telling me that I have multiple text messages that are coming through. I unbuckle my seat belt and pull my phone out. I have seven text messages. The first one I open is from Jayden.

**Where are you?

Then my dad.

**Sweetie where are you?

Next is Derrick.

**Why aren't you answering your text messages?

All right, what in the blue blazes is going on? The messages are coming one right after the other, I don't even have time to answer any of them. Next two are my mom.

**Charliee we are worried please text us back.

**Text us now Charliee.

Next is Bryce, we can't leave him out of all this frenzy. There are two from him as well.

**Charliee text me back please.

**Damn it Charliee where are you? We are all worried!

That is the last one. I'm becoming a little pissed off now. I make a group text to everyone.

**Give a person a chance to text back. What is wrong with all of you?

All of these messages came in within a minute of each other. Not a one of them gave me even a second to respond. I'm still trying to figure out how they all contacted each other and then me that quick. I'm a little surprised they aren't all here at my house when I get home.

I jump out of my Jeep, of course none of them have texted me back yet. Maybe I should start shooting all of them text messages wondering where they are all at and why aren't they answering me back. My mom's car flies into my driveway right behind my Jeep. So much for them not being here.

Mom flies out of her car, I'm not even sure if it was completely parked, her hands flying at me. "Why aren't you texting anyone back?"

I put my hands up to stop her. "What's wrong with you guys? I did text you back, just as soon as I received several messages from all of you at one time and read them all. You guys didn't give me a chance to answer anyone back. I just got home."

Her phone must have rang because she doesn't answer me, she answers it instead. I watch as she paces back and forth as she talks to whoever called. I'm thinking it's my dad.

First Travis and the guys at the station and now my family. Something is definitely going on, I just wish someone would tell me what.

I wait until my mom ends her call. "Would you care to tell me what's going on?"

"Where were you?"

Wait, what? Since when do I check in with my parents on where I'm going on a daily basis? I'm about to ask just that but something is really wrong, I can tell by the look on my mom's face. So instead of getting a little mouthy with her, I just answer her question. "I was at the station visiting Travis. They had a call so I came home."

"Did he tell you what that call was?"

I'm a little taken back that she doesn't start asking a ton of questions about Travis. I really haven't talked to my parents or brothers about us yet. "No, he just said he would text me later."

She takes a deep breath, I can tell she is calming down a little. She walks over to me and gives me a hug. When she pulls back, tears are in her eyes. "Charliee, there was another bombing."

I'm sure I am giving my mom a look like she just grew another head. My chest feels heavy. "Where?"

"At one of the movie theaters."

That place would have been packed with people. A chill runs up my back. I don't even want to imagine how many lives were taken this time!

I HAVEN'T HEARD from Travis since yesterday at the station. From the news we learned that no one died during this bombing. There had been a handful of injuries but luckily a movie had just let out and the cleaning crew had just cleared out when the bomb went off. Jayden and my parents finally stopped checking in on me around ten last night.

I find myself running through so many emotions since I heard about everything. Anger, fear, sadness. The night of the bombing I was involved with runs over and over in my mind. The faces of the people who lost their lives keep bouncing around in my head. It doesn't surprise me at all this morning around two when I wake up from another nightmare. I haven't been back to sleep since. Maybe I should have taken Jayden up on her offer to stay with me last night, but I knew she had to work today so I told her I was fine.

It is around three in the afternoon now and both of my brothers have stopped by to check for themselves how I am doing. Both were on duty yesterday, they were able to answer a few of my questions, but neither one of them had seen Travis.

The lights starting flashing. Levi gets up and heads for the door with me following him. Jayden told me she might stop by after work, but I had texted her earlier and let her know she didn't need to. I kind of want to be alone today, but she must have decided to stop by anyway.

My breath catches when I open the door. Travis stands there, dark jeans and grey t-shirt that hugs all his muscle, tattoos on display. He has two bags in his hands.

"I know it's a little early for dinner, but I haven't eaten since lunch yesterday and I'm starving. Care to join me?"

I haven't eaten much since yesterday either. I realize now that I am starving, but I don't think it's the food that is making my mouth water, but the man holding it. "Depends, what did you bring?"

He holds up one of the bags. "How do carne asada burritos sound?"

All I can do is stare at him. My hands tighten around the door handle to keep from grabbing the front of his shirt and pulling him in. This is crazy. I'm starting to act like Jayden.

He holds up his other hand. "I brought beer as well."

"Burritos and beer, sounds perfect. Come on in."

I move aside so he can come in. I shut the door and watch as he sits the two bags down on the coffee table. "What time did you guys get back?"

He turns to me. "Couple of hours ago. I think the guys knew I needed to see you so they told me to go. I wasn't going to argue with them. I ran home, took a shower, went and grabbed the food and came here."

He grabs my hand and pulls me up against his chest. "How are you doing?"

I give him the same answer I have given everyone, "Fine!"

CHAPTER
Fourteen

TRAVIS

SHE ISN'T FINE, I can see it in her eyes, but she is trying to play it off as if it isn't affecting her. I, on the other hand, am shaken and exhausted. We have been up all night. Most of the employees had been accounted for last night except one. We spent most of the night pulling debris back looking for them. With every piece of building we lifted away, I saw Charliee's twisted body. Finally around eleven last night, we got confirmation that the employee had been so frightened that she ran all the way home.

Today, when we got back to the station, I think the guys knew I was going crazy with a need to see her. They told me to go and I didn't even question it, I left. I didn't even text to see if it was all right if I came over. When she opened the door, it took everything to not drop the bags I was holding and take her into my arms.

Having her now up against my chest and my arms tightly wrapped around her, I think I just took my first real breath since leaving her at the station yesterday. Her head is laying on my chest, her casted hand laid over my heart. I notice she does this a lot when I'm holding her. It feels right.

She pulls away a little and looks up at me. "Are you all right?"

"Fine," is all I say to answer her and I smile. Charliee realizes what I just did. She knows I just threw her response right back at her and with the same meaning behind it.

She stretches up onto the tips of her toes and softly kisses my lips, and then pulls away from me altogether. I hate the empty feeling I get when she leaves my arms.

"Let's eat, we can watch a movie as long as you don't mind subtitles.

"Subtitles are fine with me, what kind of movie do you have in mind?"

SOMETHING WAKES ME UP, I'm just not sure what. Charliee is asleep in my arms, head laying on my chest. It feels good to be holding her like this. It's dark outside, but I have no idea what time it is. My phone is in my pocket and I don't want to move and risk waking her up. I want to keep her right where she is.

The movie play screen is playing over and over on the television begging for someone to press play. I didn't make it long into the movie. Once we finished eating and Charliee settled against me, my whole body relaxed. It didn't take long for me to pass out.

Charliee's head starts moving back and forth, soft sounds are coming from her lips. She moves a little more now and when I look, I see her eyes scrunched together. It reminds me of the day in the hospital when I sat and watched her sleep. She was in pain that day. It killed me not to be able to wrap her in my arms and take the pain away. Tonight she is in my arms and I'm not sure how but I'm going to take the pain away, physically or mentally, whichever she needs me for. I rub her arm slightly and wrap her a little tighter with my other arm. She calms down a little and the lines between her eyes soften.

Right when I think she has settled down and relaxed again, she shoots up and out of my arms. She's not looking at me but I do notice both hands are on her lower back rubbing frantically. If I remember right, that's where she was burnt.

I watch as she looks around as if she is trying to figure out where she is. Levi is now sitting in front of her, his head on her leg. I place my hands over hers, she shoots around to face me.

I cradle her face in my hands, her eyes are huge and shining from the tears that want to escape. "Hey, you're all right. I'm here, Charliee, nothing is going to happen to you again."

The fear is still in her eyes, but she's coming around. Her breathing is starting to even out. "I don't know why I'm having these nightmares now. I haven't had any up until the other night."

"What are they about, exactly?"

Wait, that's a stupid question, I'm pretty sure I know what they are about. "What I mean is, I know you are having them of the night of the bombing, but what part?"

She lays back against me, her side to my chest, and her right hand over my heart. She doesn't answer right away, I'm starting to think she won't. "I don't see anything, it's just black. The heat is unbearable. I try to scream, but of course I hear nothing. It's strange when I wake up I remember the heat, but that's not what really scares me the most about it. It's not being able to see anything. I depend so much on my other senses because I have no hearing, sight being the most important. It's like the dream is mixing my two worst fears. The night of the bombing and the one thing I hope to never lose."

She bends her head back to look up at me. A single tear is escaping down her cheek. I wipe it away. "Hey, you've said you don't remember anything from feeling the heat at your back that night. I'm sure that's why everything is black in your dreams, it's the heat and darkness, the last two things you remember at all."

"But why now, why a month later?"

"Charliee, you hadn't been in any situations like that night up until now. Even though you weren't involved with yesterday's bombing, it's still bringing up everything that happened. You keep trying to be strong around your family about that night. Maybe you need to start talking to someone about it. Showing emotion over it doesn't mean you are weak."

"I haven't said anything to anyone about the other night, you are the only one who knows what happened. I don't want everyone worrying any more than they already do."

"I still think you need to talk to them, but I'm not going to push you. I am going to ask that you keep talking to me, though. Let me be here for you, Charliee."

Something changes in her eyes. A moment ago they looked scared and lost. They are lighter now, almost awakened. Her hand that was resting on my chest moves up and around my neck to the back of my head. She brings my head down to hers and our lips touch softly. We stare at each other for a moment. I know she has just woken up scared and I shouldn't be taking advantage of her emotions right now but her eyes are telling me a whole new thing. She needs me, she needs to know we are real and not her dreams. She wants to make sure she's awake.

Again she pulls me into her lips, this time the kiss has a little more energy to it. She has her arm gripped around my neck like I'm her life line. Her cast is digging into my skin but I couldn't care less. Her movement against me is causing parts of my body to awaken. Her tongue finds mine. I hear myself moan. I've wanted my hands on her since the moment she opened the door. Yesterday at the station when she kissed me like this, it took everything in me to pull away. Tonight, I don't have a good reason to pull away from her. We are alone, in her house. I have to remind myself she just went through an emotional rollercoaster the last two days, and ended it with a night-mare tonight. It's just that she feels amazing against me right now. Screw it, I'm done fighting this pull to her. When she stops me I will stop, until then I'm going to enjoy everything she is willing to give me.

She pulls away, for a moment my stomach sinks. I want to pull her back, but if that was what she was willing to give then I will take it. So it surprises me when she twists around and climbs up onto my lap, now straddling me. If she didn't know how she was affecting me before, she sure the hell does now. I lean my head back against the couch and look into the eyes of the goddess sitting in front of me.

"I'm glad you decided to stop by tonight." There's that smile she gives me that threatens to drop me to my knees.

Sinking my fingers into her hair around her face and pushing it back, I pull her head down to mine. "That makes two of us."

She has complete control right now and I'm more than happy to follow her lead. Each time her tongue dives into my mouth, her hips thrust slightly against mine. I can feel the heat from her core and if I thought my pants couldn't get any tighter, I was so very wrong. Her breasts are rubbing against my chest. My hands are tangled into her long hair. Her lips are intoxicating. I suck her bottom lip in between my teeth and run my tongue over the softness. She moans and her fingers dig into my scalp.

Charliee pulls back and I release her lips. As she sits up, her hands come down each side of my face, her fingers trace a path down both sides of my neck and they come to rest on my chest. My muscles flex under her touch from the electricity that shoots into me from her touch.

She doesn't need to say a word, her face is so expressive. Her hands begin to move down a trail again over my stomach, her eyes never leaving mine, like she is asking permission. As her hands reach the edge of my shirt, I dare her with my eyes. A small smile stretches across her lips. Soft fingers reach under my shirt and at the first touch on my skin, my breath stops. Her smile gets a little bigger. As her hands glide their way up my chest, my shirt rising with them, I find myself holding my breath.

Her hands stop for a moment. "Can you lift your arms, please?"

I'm not about to say no to that request, so I do as I'm asked.

My shirt continues up my arms and over my head. All I'm aware of is Charliee's eyes blazing green and her licking her lips as she runs her hands and eyes over my chest and arms. Her fingers begin to trace my tattoos that run across my chest and down my left arm. "How do you decide what you want for the rest of your life drawn on your body?"

"I go with what inspires me at the time."

"One day you are going to have to explain what they all mean."

"Anytime."

Nothing else is said as I watch her run her fingers over the designs, finishing as she traces the word "Faith" that I have drawn on my forearm. Her eyes are back to mine and then finally I have her lips once again.

Running my hands down her back and over her perfectly rounded backside, I stop with both hands around her thighs. I squeeze both legs and she tightens them around me, her knees squeezing my hips tighter between them. My hands begin the journey back only to stop at the bottom edge of her shirt. I grip her shirt tightly, waging a war with myself on if I should slow us both down or not.

Her lips pull away from mine. I don't want to open my eyes for fear that she is now putting a halt to this moment. I finally open them to find her sitting up, arms up over her head and an "I'm waiting" smile.

That's all of the permission I need. I quickly pull her shirt up and over her head and let it drop where it may. My hands travel back down her arms and around her back. Her skin is as soft as I imagined it to be. I lean forward and run a trail of kisses starting at her neck and down her chest, lightly kissing the top mound of each breast above her bra.

Her hands on my shoulders push me away. I sit back and watch as she reaches behind her back and as her arms come back around, her bra drops away from her perfectly rounded breasts. Her nipples already begging for my touch.

CHAPTER
Fifteen

THIS ISN'T ME. I don't usually move this fast with a guy, but there is something about Travis that I can't seem to stop myself with. If feels right, he feels right. When his arms are around me it feels like that's where I belong.

I like being independent, taking care of myself, not having to depend on anyone. I'm used to adjusting around people to try and make them not uncomfortable around me. I throw most people off when they first meet me. I talk but I'm deaf. I'm sure they all notice a difference in my speech, but most peoples' reactions when they find out I'm deaf is comical. They look almost panicked because they can't figure out how to communicate with me, although three seconds before we were communicating just fine.

Travis never acted that way, he just kept rolling with it. I remember back to the first time I saw him in the hospital. He walked in all shy and chatting away, but he would be looking everywhere but at me. It was hard making out what he was saying. After a moment he left. I remember even then I felt disappointed he didn't stay even though I had no idea who he was. He did, however, return and when he sat down with the paper and pen, I almost laughed. Relief washed over his face when I explained all he had to do was look at me when he talked, and from then on he has never treated or acted as though I'm missing something.

When I'm in his arms, I don't always have to be on alert, it's relaxing. I'm drawn to him in every sense and sexually is one of the highest right now. I'm willing to take this step if it means I can have his body against mine. The heat between us is sizzling but when I first felt his skin against mine, my body temperature topped off at smoldering. I can feel his hardness even through both our jeans. My fingers itch to reach between our bodies.

One of his hands cups my breast, his thumb running back and forth other my nipple. My hips push down more on him. Just the feel of his hands on me is going to drive me crazy with want.

I tilt his head back and claim his lips. He still tastes of beer, and it's intoxicating. He lightly pinches my nipple. I suck his tongue into my mouth and he rolls my nipple between his fingers causing my hips to push into his.

Travis trails his tongue down my chin, down my neck and over the top of my breast. I tilt my head back, which pushes my breasts out more to him, begging him for more. His lips against my skin feels electrifying. His teeth nip at my nipple and a bolt of fire goes straight to my core. My head flies up, eyes wide and my hands press his head closer to me, begging him for more.

I watch as his tongue lightly makes circles around my nipple. Another bolt shoots through me. Watching him and feeling his hardness pressed against my heat, I'm pretty sure I am going to fall apart right here.

When he pulls away from me, I feel a cold emptiness. "Charliee, I didn't come over here expecting anything."

I know he didn't, the thought never crossed my mind that he did. This heat between us has been there since the beginning and it feels right. "Travis, you brought food and beer, you can't fool me," I tease him.

His eyes go from lust to panic in a second. Maybe this isn't the best time to tease with him. He tries to lift me off his lap but I'm not allowing it. "Travis, I was joking. I'm sorry."

He stares at me for a moment, searching my eyes. I feel bad now, if anything I think I'm the one who started all of this between us. I'm the one who should probably be pleading my case that I didn't invite him in expecting this. "If I didn't want this, I wouldn't have started it, Travis. This isn't like me, I don't just sleep around, but there is something that flares up inside me every time you touch me. I want this. I want you."

Still he says nothing. He just stares up at me. Now I'm starting to think I'm pushing him and I become nervous.

"If you don't want this…" My words are cut short by his lips.

He pulls back slightly. "I want you, Charliee, but not here on the couch."

He easily stands up, still holding me. I wrap my legs around his waist. "Where is your room?"

"Down the hall, door to the right."

He walks as though he isn't carrying me wrapped around his body. Feeling all his muscles flex against me as he walks is more than I can almost handle. All I want is him naked and inside me. We walk into my room and he sets me down, my bed at the back of my legs. With his finger under my chin, he brings my eyes up to meet his. He lightly kisses my forehead, nose and then my lips.

"You can still tell me no."

I almost giggle. That's not an option my body is giving me at the moment. It kind of fuels the fire I already have running through me knowing he is still worried about me not being ready. Oh how wrong he is though. I race my hands over the muscles of his chest, down his stomach and stop when I hit the top of his jeans. I give him what I hope is a seductive smile and unbutton his jeans. Together I push his jeans and boxer briefs down his legs as far as my arms can reach.

"I don't want to say no."

He gives me that tilted smile of his that makes my heart skip every time and finishes removing his clothes. I begin to remove my jeans but he pushes my hands out of the way.

"This is a job I would like to do, if you don't mind."

I throw my hands up in surrender. "Work away."

His fingers touch my skin and all joking vanishes. Just one touch and my body starts turning up. My eyes never leave his. I watch as he unbuttons my pants and then begins pulling them down my legs. He crouches down in front of me, his eyes still connected to mine. One at a time he lifts one foot, pulling that leg free and then the other. We watch each other as he leans forward and lightly trails kisses down one thigh to my knee and then repeats with the other. It's taking everything in me not to fall back onto the bed. I feel my legs begin to shake and he smiles. He knows what effect he is having on me.

His hands run up from my ankles over my thighs and into the last little piece of clothing I have on, squeezing both butt cheeks. He leans forward and kisses right below my belly button. As he slides them down my legs, his tongue follows.

Now that I'm standing completely naked, he looks me over. I work hard to keep my body in shape so I'm not in the least bit embarrassed to be standing here with his eyes taking me in from head to toe. The small smile on his face and the blue in his eyes becoming molten have me believing the hard work has paid off.

"You are beautiful, Charliee."

Before I can say anything, he leans forward and kisses right above the juncture of my legs. I gasp at the feel of his breath against my already throbbing center. My knees threaten to buckle. I'm pretty sure if it wasn't for his hands holding onto my hips, I wouldn't be standing.

Slowly he stands up, our bodies blend together. The feel of his skin against mine is almost my undoing.

He leans his forehead against mine. "I want to taste every inch of you, you smell amazing."

My cheeks heat up. I'm not sure if it's from the meaning behind his words that make me blush a little, or from the fact that those words just turned me on that much more. Maybe a mixture of both.

"Right now, though, all I can think about is being inside of you."

"Please," is the only word I am able to push past my lips. It is a plea, or begging, whichever you would like to call it; however, I don't care. His teasing is going to send me over the edge before we even get started. Sitting down on the bed, I slowly lay myself out in front of him. From here I have to ability to see more of him. He is gorgeous. My hand itches to reach out and stroke him, but the rest of my body wants me to pull him down to me and not drag this out any longer.

He looks down at the floor and I watch as a concerned look crosses his face. "I have no protection with me."

I have to hold the laugh in that threatens to bubble up. He looks like a little boy who was just told he couldn't have an ice cream.

"Travis, I'm on the pill. I've only slept with one other guy and that was some time ago. My last physical was a clean bill of health."

"I can't say I have only been with one woman, Charliee, but we are required through work to have yearly physicals and I had a green light. I haven't been with anyone since and I have never not used protection."

A moment of jealousy hits me in the heart when he mentions the other women, but I have to push that aside. I lift my arms up over my head and smile. All that matters at the moment is his hands on me and him inside of me.

He kneels above me on the bed, one knee between my thighs, and then brings his weight down onto me. It feels good. I wrap my arms around his neck, one hand to the back of his head, bringing his lips down to mine. His tongue instantly finds mine, no more talking needed.

His lips leave mine and he begins to work his way down my neck across my chest until he finds one of my nipples. He slightly nibbles on it with his teeth. My legs clutch around his strong thighs. Trailing my hand down his side, I slide it between our bodies until I find his hardness, wrapping my hand around him. I stroke up the length once, he is heavy in my hand. I feel his chest vibrate against mine. I believe I just caused him to groan.

Once again, I stroke down and then back up his full length, running my finger over the tip, feeling the little moisture beaded there. With every stroke of my hand, the harder he sucks on my breast. The combination of the two and the friction against his leg, I'm about to lose myself.

"Travis, please." I'm not against begging.

My plea has him leaving my breast. I spread my legs further apart, inviting him between them. I feel the tip of him, but he doesn't enter fully.

"Charliee, are you sure?"

Is it possible that I'm falling in love with this man already? He is always worried about me and my feelings. I know he would be miserable if I said no to him right now, but I know he wouldn't force me. There is no doubt in me at all. I want this. I want him.

"Yes." I answer his question as I wrap my legs around his waist and thrust my hips toward him, hoping this makes him understand my need for him.

The blue in his eyes blaze. All at once he claims my lips and enters my body completely.

My head is spinning, my heart is racing and I feel him so deep inside, I feel complete. My tongue meets his in a duel. My hands are on his very nicely rounded backside. He hasn't moved, I know he is making sure I'm good. I thrust my hips up and with my hands push his hips into me. The feeling is amazing. I pull his bottom lip between my teeth and bite slightly. That is the signal for him and he realizes it because he takes over the pace.

I'm close, I tighten my legs around him. I feel the energy all collecting in my center, but he stops. *Wait, don't stop, I'm so close,* I want to scream. I open my eyes and see him staring down at me.

"I want you to keep your eyes open, Charliee. You can't hear what you are making me feel. I want you to see what you do to me. I want to watch your eyes as you explode around me."

If I had any questions before about my feelings for this man, I am no longer questioning them. I nod that I understand because I don't trust my words at the moment. I may be having these feelings but I'm not ready to voice them and I'm pretty sure he isn't ready to hear them.

Slowly, I feel his hips as he pulls out almost all the way. I swear his eyes change to a white blue as he slowly thrusts back into me. It takes everything in me not to close my eyes and savor every sensation I'm having as he is filling me with his length. On the other hand, watching the emotions change across his face, I don't want to miss that either. That alone is making it a lot easier to keep them open.

I want to speed the movements up, my body is screaming for one of us to. I feel my muscles starting to clutch around him, my body begging him for more. His fingers are threaded through my hair and as his movements quicken, he pulls my hair just a little. It doesn't hurt, it only pushes me a little closer to losing myself to him.

My hands are on his chest, my nails digging into his skin. Once more he pulls almost all the way out and then with one thrust, he's deep back in and I explode. My muscles tighten completely around him, but he doesn't stop. He pumps faster and harder into me. The building begins to happen again. A feeling I have never felt before or even knew was possible. My nails dig into his chest, I know he will have marks after this. My body quakes around his, begging. I know I have screamed his name. Thinking I couldn't handle more, he has one last thrust, he has completely filled my body and there isn't an inch of me not feeling his full length. His body begins to shake. He is pulling on my hair so hard, I may have bald spots but who cares. Our eyes never leave each other's, which just intensifies the whole sensation. I feel his warmth as he releases inside me. I have to bite my lip to keep from yelling out my feelings for him. I see my name leave his lips. His grip on my hair loosens and his forehead comes down to mine. As I run my hands over his chest, I feel the indentations from my nails. Never could I have ever imagined feeling this amazing with someone.

CHAPTER
Sixteen

TRAVIS

FOR THE SECOND TIME TONIGHT, I find myself holding Charliee as she sleeps. Only this time her naked body is pressed fully against mine and we are laying in her bed, after the mind blowing sex we just shared.

She said tonight she had only been with one other guy. I have very mixed feelings hearing her mention past guys. I want to find and beat the man who touched her because she is mine, even if at that time I had no part in her life. On the other hand, I am happy to hear I wasn't following a line of guys. One thing I do know, I am going to do whatever I can to make sure I am the last guy though.

I've had a couple of what people would call serious girlfriends. They weren't bad break ups. No horror stories of crazy exes. Charliee is different. I'm not anywhere near wanting to let her go, it's the complete opposite actually. I just want to hold on tighter.

Watching through her eyes as she came apart around me tonight was unexplainable. I knew she was expressive with her face and eyes. I've learned a lot about her without her saying a word to me. However, nothing could have prepared me for what I experienced with her tonight.

When I asked her to keep her eyes open, I knew we would have a connection far more expressive than not looking at each other. I wanted to make sure that even though she couldn't hear me, she knew everything I was feeling with her. She had mentioned how fast everything has been between us. I look at what we have in a different way. I've done nothing but think about her since that night. Being with her this past week has only made feelings I had that much stronger. I've never been one of those guys that hide from feelings. Swear to never fall in love or hide from a relationship. I'm not going to start now either. She has feelings for me. I saw that tonight. We didn't just have sex, we both felt more.

I rub my hand down her back and feel the roughness along her lower back. It's from the burns. I lightly brush my hand from one side of her waist to the other. You can still feel some of the scabbing. Now I'm a little worried that I may have hurt her. I didn't realize she wasn't completely healed yet.

"Don't worry, it doesn't hurt much anymore."

She's awake. When I look down at her, my heart skips. "Why didn't you tell me you weren't completely healed yet?"

She shrugs her shoulders. "We haven't really talked about it I guess. Besides my arm being in this cast, my back is the only part of me still healing some."

Her fingers are once again rubbing back and forth on my chest just above my heart. "I'm not complaining but I've noticed you're always placing a hand over my chest about there. Why?"

She smiles a little, but her cheeks redden like she is embarrassed that she got caught. "I like the feel of your heart. It tells me what you're feeling. When you first touched my lower back it started to speed up, that's how I knew you were worried."

"It may have something to do with whenever I think about that night or the asshole who caused it, I feel ready to pounce."

She smiles up at me. She looks small curled up against my side, her head bent back laying on my shoulder and her eyes still dreamy. Her light laugh causes her breast to rub against my side. My body reacts instantly. Hopefully she hasn't noticed certain members of my body starting to beg for a little attention. I need to distract myself.

"So what other injuries did you have?"

Her smile fades and her hand stills. "You really want to talk about this now?"

Brushing a piece of hair away from her face, I nod. "Like you said, we have never talked about it."

She looks away from me and I start to think she isn't going to tell me. Finally, she holds her cast up. "Well, you know about this. I had two cracked ribs. Fifteen stitches a cross my right shoulder and then the burns along my lower back. The burns for me were the worst. All in all, though, I guess it could have been a lot worse."

She's right, it could have been worse. She could have died. On the other side of it, it should never have happened to begin with. I lift her face back up to look at me. "Can I see your back?"

She only nods. She moves just enough away from me to flip herself over onto her stomach. She pulls her long hair over her shoulder, exposing her whole back.

I reach over and click the lamp on next to the bed. I make sure to keep myself in her line of vision. The first thing I see is the long scar across her shoulder. I trace it with my hand.

"Maybe I should get a tattoo to cover that one."

She's smiling again. Damn, she's a strong person. I run my hand down her back to the lower section. It's hard not to react the first time you see it. There isn't one section that isn't covered with a scar.

I've been lucky in my profession, I've never been burned. A couple of men I've worked with have had burns. I remember them describing the pain during the cleanings and recovery. Charliee's whole lower back and a couple small spots upward are raised from the burns. Trying to imagine the pain she went through with all of this makes me sick. Now I'm pissed at myself. I should have gone back to the hospital, been there with her when she was going through all of this. No, instead I stayed away from this amazing woman.

"Hey, why the face? Does it look that bad?"

Damn, I need to watch my facial expressions, she picks up on everything. I lay back down next to her. "No, nothing on you could look bad. I was just scolding myself."

Confusion etches across her forehead. "May I ask why?"

I wonder how much I should say. I don't want to scare her away. The road of honesty is the one I decide to go with. If she is going to run, might as well be now and not later.

"Charliee, I've had this connection to you since we uncovered you that night. I wanted to wrap you up in my arms and take care of you even from that moment. Watching that ambulance pull away and not be able to be in there with you was torturing me that night. I had no idea how you were doing or what was happening to you. Then the next day, I came to the hospital. There you were laying there on your stomach, I knew you had to be in pain, but you still found your smile. Your strength that day was just another thing that pulled me toward you. When Bryce stopped me out by the elevator asking me why I came by and what I was looking for, I told him that I just wanted to check on you. You were the one positive thing that happened that night around all the disaster. When he asked me if I was coming back, I had told him no. The next day I sat at home and tried to talk myself out of going back, but you had asked me. You were in no condition to keep having visitors you didn't know, but I convinced myself that since you did ask me, it would be all right."

I try to read her reaction to all of this but she is giving away nothing.

"When I got to the hospital, I was kind of relieved you were asleep. The nurse told me you had just fallen asleep so I just sat there and watched you. I could tell you were in pain, all I wanted to do was pull you into my arms and absorb your pain into my body. I realized that day sitting there watching you that I had feelings for you. You didn't need that then, you needed to worry about healing and that's when I decided I wouldn't come back again. I wasn't worried about having the feelings, I was wanting you to heal. I had told you I would come back so I decided if I signed your cast you would know I stopped by, but I wanted to leave before you woke up. As long as your eyes weren't looking at me in that way you do, I knew I could leave. There wasn't a day that went by that I didn't think about you. One day I told myself I just needed to know that you were all right, so I went back to the hospital, but you had already been released. I knew the hospital wouldn't give me any information about where you lived or anything so I figured I was too late and that was that. I did think about going to the station and asking one of your brothers, but then I remembered the protective look Derrick gave me at the hospital and figured that would be a dead end."

She laughs a little and shakes her head at the mention of how protective her brothers are and she is still next to me naked, so I am taking all of that as a sign that she isn't running yet.

"The day you showed up at the station, I couldn't believe it. When I opened the door and saw you standing there, I decided at that moment that I wasn't letting you get away again.

Silence stretches between the two of us. It is making me a little nervous that she isn't saying anything. At the moment she isn't even looking at me. Maybe it is a little too much too soon, but I feel like she needs to know what I am feeling. I am still holding some of it back, but I'm sure she knows enough. I will wait all night for her to talk to me if that's how long it takes her to figure out how she feels about all I've said.

She adjusts herself so that she is laying across my chest, her lips inches from mine. "I believe everything happens for a reason. If the reason I was involved that night was for us to be brought into each other's lives, then the pain I went through was completely worth it."

If I hadn't already been in love with her, I would have been after she said that. There are no words to say to her that would tell her what those words mean to me. When she leans forward and kisses me, I decide not to worry about words but to show her.

I devour her lips with mine, my tongue darting in to find hers. I roll us over so that she is under me and her hands go to my back, her nails scraping up and down. My hand finds her breast, they are perfect. She moans when my thumb skims over her nipple, instantly puckering up under my touch. I can already feel her heat against my leg. Earlier I only had a lick of her sweetness, now I want to taste all of her.

I run small kisses down over her chin, down her neck. I pay attention to each of her breasts, licking and nibbling on the nipples. Every time I suck hard on her breast, her hips thrust up toward me begging for some attention. I trail my tongue down over her belly to the junction between her legs. I thought she would get all shy, but once again she surprises me. The moment my tongue touches her heated core, her legs fall open for me. That action alone almost causes me to lose all control.

Her hands are in my hair, pushing me into her. The light is still on and when I look up, emerald green eyes are looking back. She is watching me. Her bottom lip is sucked in between her teeth, her face flush. My tongue darts out and I watch her as I lick her, tasting all her sweetness. Her grip on my hair tightens. I could taste and watch her all night. I dip my tongue deep into her, feeling her muscles tighten, she is close. Once more I run my tongue over her heat and then dip deep inside and she explodes, screaming my name as her back arches up off the bed.

I need to be inside her, I want to feel her pull me in deep with each contraction of her muscles. I quickly make my way up her body, capturing her breast with my mouth, causing her to yell out my name again. I quickly thrust into her, her tightness causing me to moan. The pulse of her orgasm pull me in deeper and deeper. I pull out and enter her once more, her hips thrusting up to meet me and that is all I can handle. Together, we spiral up and then back down again.

CHAPTER
Seventeen

SOMETHING COLD IS TOUCHING my arm. I turn my head and slowly open my eyes. Levi stands there, his eyes pleading with me to wake up and let him out. What time is it? I look up at the clock by my bed. Crap, no wonder he looks like he is begging, it is after ten.

Looking over, Travis is still sound asleep, laying on his stomach, arms stretched up under the pillow. It's tempting to run my fingers over his tattoos but I don't want to wake him. He looked exhausted when I opened my door yesterday. Our active evening probably didn't help with that either.

Trying not to move the bed too much so that I don't wake him, I scoot out of the sheets. Levi bolts out of the room, looking back to make sure I am following. I don't even bother with clothes, I'm just letting him out the back door, no one will see me.

As I'm trying to pull the door open, Levi is trying to push his way through. "Hold on, boy. If you back up, I'll be able to open it."

He takes a step back, but as soon as the door is half open he shoots through. I feel bad he had to wait.

He'll want back in shortly so I should probably just wait for him. I look around the living room and spot Travis's shirt still laying on the floor. I pick it up and bury my face into it, it smells like him. I pull it on. It's almost like being wrapped in his arms, which is where I would like to be right now. He needs his sleep, so the shirt will have to do for now.

The bag that had our dinner in it is still sitting on the table so I grab that and any other trash and walk back into the kitchen to throw it all away. I look out the window and see that Levi is still walking around the yard.

Last night was great. It felt so natural to sit on the couch, enjoying dinner and a movie with Travis there, even if he didn't make it far into the movie before falling asleep. He had eaten quickly and then once he pulled me between his legs and I laid back against his chest, I believe it took only minutes before he was asleep. Having him all wrapped around me relaxed me so much that I fell asleep not long after him.

My nightmare waking us both up, I could have done without. I have to admit, it felt good to talk to him last night about everything. I keep from saying too much around Jayden and my family. I need them to think I'm healing and moving on. Which I am, with the exception of the nightmares. Everyone has finally started backing away a little, not checking on me as much, or calling every hour. Well, they had until the other day when the second explosion happened, family worried mode went back in full swing.

It felt good to be able to lay there in Travis's arms, knowing I was safe and telling him what the nightmares were about. My fear of the darkness. I have never told anyone that fear. He just listened and then brought an idea of what is probably causing that part of the dreams.

Waking up this morning and having Travis next to me was natural. Last night was amazing. Just thinking about him touching me and inside me is causing me to heat up again. I can feel my core starting to pulse just thinking about all of it. I squeeze my thighs together hoping to extinguish some of the feelings starting. I need to get a grip, this can't be healthy to get this excited over just thinking about him.

I go let Levi in since he is now sitting at the back door waiting for me. That's when I see Travis standing there leaning up against the corner of the wall.

"Good morning." His eyes look me up and down.

He has no idea how good of a morning it just became. There he is standing there with no shirt on, his jeans hanging low because he doesn't have them buttoned. I have to hold onto the counter behind me to keep my legs from giving out on me. I am already getting turned on just thinking about last night and then I turn to find this amazing sight staring at me like he's ready to pounce on his prey.

I watch as he pushes away from the wall and walks over to me. "My shirt looks good on you."

"It feels good on me." I'm finally able to push words past my lips.

His arm hooks around my waist and he pulls me away from the counter and against his chest. My arms go up around his shoulders, causing the shirt to ride up my backside. The cool air against my skin feels good.

He squeezes my exposed cheeks. I watch as his eyes change to that blazing blue tone like last night, and a seductive smile spreads across his mouth. "I was going to ask what's for breakfast but I'm completely content with what I have in my arms."

"You sound pretty delicious to me as well."

His mouth crashes against mine, his other arm circles my waist and he lifts me up. I wrap my legs around his waist. Quickly he turns and heads back to my room. I pull his shirt up over my head and let it fall to the floor. We fall together onto the bed and I realize he is no longer wearing his jeans. How he managed to get out of those is beyond me, but I have little time to actually think about it. He claims my lips and body all at once.

. . .

TRAVIS'S HAND appears in front of my face and he wiggles his fingers. Laughing, I look up at him. "What are you doing?"

He smiles down at me. "Checking to see if you're awake."

"I'm awake. How many times did you say my name before you realized I wasn't answering?"

His smile becomes a shy one. That's right, buddy, you don't fool me.

"See now, I could lie to you and say I have no idea what you are talking about but I'll give this one to you and admit, I said your name twice before I felt a little foolish and remembered."

He is so cute when he is a little embarrassed. "Well, I think you're adorable when you are caught being foolish."

"Thanks, I think. Anyway, as much as I would like to keep you here in bed all day and take care of an appetite I have for you, both of our stomachs are yelling at us for some real food."

I'm hungry, but I could survive it if it meant I could lay here next to him, or should I say on him, a little longer. "I don't hear anything." I smile up at him.

"Being deaf has its advantages. I can't ignore them, yours is rumbling enough to shake the windows."

Smacking his chest, I roll away from him. "Fine, I'll get up."

Travis sits up and leans over, claiming my pouting lips. How am I supposed to talk myself into getting out of bed when he's doing this?

"Keep this up and I won't care how hungry either of us are," I tell him as he pulls slightly away from me.

"I probably wouldn't object, but it's raining outside and I think I swept you away and back to bed before you let Levi back in. He probably isn't very happy with us at the moment."

"Oh damn, I forgot about him being outside." I fly out of the bed, throwing on Travis's shirt once again.

Running to the bathroom first, I grab a towel to dry him off with. Then I rush to the kitchen, throwing open the back door. There Levi sits, soaking wet staring up at me and giving me the "How dare you forget about me" look.

I hold the towel out in front of me. "Come on in, boy. I'm so sorry, let's get you dried off."

I GRAB my phone that I left by the couch last night before I head back to the bedroom. I am kind of surprised no one has come by to check on me since I haven't spoken to anyone yet today. Looking down at it, I do have two text messages. One from my mom and one from Jayden.

As I walk back into the bedroom, Travis is just coming out of the bath-room. "Hope you don't mind I helped myself to a shower."

"No, not at all. If you would have waited then I would have joined you."

"Very tempting to use that as a reason to take another one, but I'll have to take a raincheck on that."

"Your loss!" I walk past him and head for the bathroom myself, only to be stopped when he grabs my arm.

"As much as I like seeing you in my shirt, I'm going to have to ask for it back. It's the only one I have with me."

"All right, so take it back," I dare him.

"As tempting as that sounds, I'm going to have to not touch you until you are fully dressed. I haven't eaten much in the last two days and I don't want to pass out. So I'll have to ask that you return it when you are finished with your shower."

I smile up at him as I pull it up and over my head. He wants his shirt, I will give it to him. Now standing naked in front of him, I hand it over to him. His eyes are changing colors again. I look down at his hand, it has a very tight grip on his shirt.

I smile and look back up at his face. "If you will excuse me, I'm going to go and take that shower now."

As I take a step away, his arm quickly circles around my waist and he pulls me into his chest, his lips quickly devouring mine. One hand goes around and grabs my backside, thrusting my hips into his. I can feel his hardness through his pants. Wrapping my arms around his neck, I rub my body against his.

Just when I think I'm going to get what I want, he quickly releases me. "Now, go and take a shower, I'm hungry."

After that, he wants me to just walk away? The smile on his face is telling me he is pretty proud of himself for getting me all worked up and being able to walk away. He is getting back at me for teasing him first, damn him.

This proves that I'm not great at the teasing game, I really haven't had much practice with it. Being with Travis has woken something up inside me, though, and I'm not ready to give up. He thinks he has won but I'm not giving up. I take a few steps backwards toward the bathroom.

"Fine, I'll just go and finish what you started by myself." I'm hoping that didn't sound too corny. By the fire that just erupted in his eyes, I would say final score goes to me. I almost want to skip into the bathroom.

I turn the water on and am getting ready to step inside when I am suddenly turned around and brought body to body against a now naked Travis. He walks us both into the shower and under the hot water.

"I think I would like finish what I started, if you don't mind."

"Please do." I want to scream yes. Or pump my fist in the air because I won. I like this game!

CHAPTER
Eighteen

TRAVIS

I HAVE NOTICED as we sat here in the driveway that Charliee seems a little nervous. I have tried to convince her that we could just order something in, or grab something and bring it back, but she says she needs to get over her fear. She is a fighter, and I am proud of her for that.

"So what are you hungry for?"

"Well, my parents have invited us over to dinner tonight, so how about something light to just hold us over for right now?"

Ahh, so that's why she is so nervous. Here I thought it was the whole going to get lunch somewhere but it is because her parents want us over tonight. She is nervous about asking me about going.

"Us?"

She gives me a nervous smile. "You picked up on that?"

"Charliee, I have no problem having dinner with your family. You should never be nervous to ask me that kind of stuff. I would like to get to know your family better. How bad could it be? I've already had a gun pointed at me," I tease with her.

Her shoulders slump a little as she relaxes. "So you don't mind coming with me tonight?"

She hasn't realized yet that there isn't much I wouldn't do for her. "Of course I don't mind. I've met them all already at the hospital anyway, so this isn't the first meeting."

She pulls out her phone and swipes her fingers across the screen. "All right, there is no backing out now, I sent my mom a message saying we were coming."

"Great, now I ask again, where do you want to go and eat, woman? I'm starving!"

"You are the one starving, what do you want?"

"I know this great place that has an amazing chef salad."

"Perfect." She leans across, giving me a quick kiss.

AFTER WE EAT, I take her to my place. I am still wearing the same clothes as yesterday and want to change before we head to her parents' house.

When I join her in the living room after changing, I find her looking at the picture of my family that I have hanging on the wall.

I take a deep breath and walk over to her. This is a perfect time. "My mom, dad and sister," I sign to her.

Charliee's eyes go wide, but she doesn't say anything. Maybe I didn't sign it all right. "Did I do that right?"

She only nods as tears collect in her eyes. "Was I that bad at it?"

She shakes her head, wiping the tears away from her eyes. "You're learning sign language?"

"There is a great app that I found. I figured you have adjusted to the hearing world your whole life. I want to learn to adjust to your world."

Tears now run down her cheeks. I wipe them away with my thumb. "Plus, I hate not knowing what everyone is signing about me."

She laughs." You did great. I'd be more than happy to help you learn to sign."

"I know my ABCs as well. It felt like being in Kindergarten all over again."

The sound of her laugh shoots straight to my chest. I love it when she laughs. She wipes the tears away. "I'm sorry, I hate crying in front of people. I'm an ugly crier."

"How do you sign the word beautiful?"

She brings her hand up to in front of her face, palm facing in, and makes a rainbow-like action across her face.

"I think you're beautiful," I sign the word she just showed me. "Even when you cry."

I lean down and kiss her, tasting the salty tears on her lips. She instantly deepens the kiss. I can't seem to get enough of her, but now isn't the time.

"We will have to put a hold on this. I'm not going to set a bad impression on your family by showing up late for dinner."

"So are you promising me later then?"

"Absolutely."

"Do you work tomorrow?"

I only nod.

"So then later isn't tonight?"

How tempting she is. She is making this pretty damn hard right now. "I'm afraid if I stay with you tonight then I'll be very tempted to call in sick tomorrow. Probably not a habit I should start getting into."

She pouts a little. "All right, but I'll be collecting on this promise on your next day off."

"I'll look forward to it." Leaning forward, I give her one last quick kiss and then lead her out of the apartment. If we don't leave now, we aren't going to make it to dinner.

DINNER WENT good with Charliee's family, I thought. I'm hoping that them getting to know me a little better, especially her brothers, will have them see what see means to me. I have a little sister, I know what it's like to be protective of her, wanting to know the guys she dates, make sure they are good enough for her, so I can't fault them at all for being protective of her, making sure I'm good enough. I can handle them and prove that she is in great care when she is with me.

I definitely won extra points tonight with her mom when I used the little sign language I had learned so far. Karen told me tonight that I am the first of Charliee's boyfriends who has actually gone and learned the language for her. How do you expect to be part of her life if you don't learn everything about her? Why would anyone think it's all right to have her change for them if they aren't willing to change for her?

I also notice tonight that Charliee is signing more. She told me she wasn't signing as much because of the cast, but I think now that she knows I'm trying to learn, she is going to sign more around me. The expression in her eyes tonight when I signed, only convinces me that I am doing the right thing by learning this for her. It actually makes me want to learn all that much faster.

Glancing over at the clock, I'm starting to realize I'm not going to get much sleep tonight. It is already two in the morning. I have to be up in four hours. Laying here is kind of useless, I'm not going to sleep. I have only had one night with Charliee but I am already missing her next to me, plus I worry that she is going to have another nightmare and I'm not there to talk through them with her. I've had my phone in my hands I don't know how many times almost texting her to see how she is doing. Then I think that's not the best idea at this time of night because she is probably sleeping. This is crazy, here I didn't stay with her because I thought I would be too tempted to not go to work, and now I'm not sleeping because I'm worried about her. Funny thing is, she has been handling all of this on her own up until last night. Difference is now she doesn't have to handle it alone, she has me.

This morning, I walked into her kitchen and found her standing there wearing nothing but my t-shirt and rubbing her thighs together and then to top it off, when she turned around her eyes were all glassed over and a slight pink covered her cheeks from being caught. I about lost myself. I had a good guess what she was thinking about and it took everything I had not to rush to her and take her right there against the counter. Thinking about this now, however, is not helping me to fall asleep. All it is doing is making me realize if I would have taken her up on her invitation to stay the night again tonight, I could be inside her right now instead of laying here, hard as a rock and miserable.

CHAPTER
Nineteen

"THIS WAS A GREAT IDEA, Jayden, my toes needed some attention." I wiggle my toes that are now soaking in a pedicure bath.

"I'm just surprised you were able to pull yourself away from your hunk of a boyfriend. I feel honored to have a little time with you."

She is teasing me, I know that, but I still feel a little guilty about not talking to her much lately. She is right, Travis has been taking up a lot of my time. With me not being back at work yet, we rarely see each other.

"I know and I'm sorry, but you can only blame yourself. You were the one always telling me I needed to find a guy."

"Well, I'm rethinking it all now. I didn't realize it would take you away from me like this."

She is smiling, so I'm not taking her too seriously. "Maybe it's time for you to find someone and we can double date."

There is that look again. It is the same one she gave me when I mentioned her getting a boyfriend when I went to the school the other day. This time I'm not going to let it go. She is hiding something from me and I want to know what it is.

"All right, Jayden, what's going on? Are you seeing someone and not telling me about it?"

She stares down at her soaking toes. I wait for a moment but I don't think she is going to tell me. "Come on, Jayden. You followed me into the shower, literally, to get the story about Travis. Who is this guy?"

Her shoulders shrug up and for a second, I don't think she is going to tell me anything, but then she looks over at me.

"There really isn't much to tell yet. I'm not sure if there is anything even starting. Honestly, he infuriates me more than anything."

I study her as she talks, she's facing my direction so that I can read her lips, but she isn't having any eye contact with me at all. This guy doesn't just make her mad, she has feelings for him. She forgets how well I know her. I'm a little hurt that she is keeping it from me, though. She demanded to know about Travis, and when she found out I had gone and saw him and kept it from her, she wasn't happy, but then she turns around and does the same thing. I guess I can say I know how she felt now, it kind of sucks.

"So I'm guessing you like this guy."

"I haven't really said anything because I'm not sure if there is anything to tell."

There is more to this than that excuse, but for some reason she doesn't want to say anything to me. It hurts, I won't lie. This isn't how our friendship works! She has a good reason for keeping all of this to herself. I just hope she will eventually tell me what's going on, but for now I let it go.

"So what do you have planned after our toes?"

Relief shows in her eyes and her smile returns. "Food because I'm starving and then some shopping."

She looks at me hopeful, she knows I hate shopping. I've never been one of those girls who love to shop and she has always loved it. That's where we are both very different. I am still feeling a little bad about not spending any time with her lately, so this once I'll give in.

"All right, we can go and do a little shopping." She bounces up and down in her chair like a little girl excited.

My phone vibrates in my pocket. I lean over and try not to move my feet too much and pull it out, glancing at the screen.

Jayden leans over, she taps me on the leg. I look up at her. "You, my friend, have got it bad."

"What are you talking about?"

She sits back against her chair, a knowing smile on her face. "From the look in your eyes, I'm going to assume that is from Travis."

"For your nosy information, yes, it is."

"You're in love with him, it's written all over your face."

I look back down at my phone, reading his text.

**I miss you! We are pretty slow today so Sign Language 101 has been in session all day. I do believe I'm catching on. Although the guys here may think I've lost my mind since I'm talking in weird sentences and waving my hands all around, and to top it off I'm sitting here alone.

Am I in love with Travis? I don't even have to wonder about it anymore. I am completely in love with him.

Looking over again, I find Jayden once again leaning over reading my text message. The poor lady working on her toes is having a heck of a time trying to follow her moving foot around.

I pull my phone back so that she can't see it. "Do you mind?"

"Is he really learning Sign Language for you?"

I know my smile is a goofy one. "Yes, he is. I found out last night. I asked him a question and he signed the answer back to me."

"Charliee, I really wish I could find something wrong with this guy, but I haven't yet. It's all a little irritating, he has to have a fault somewhere."

I have to agree with her. I know no one is perfect and I'm sure he has faults but I haven't found one yet.

"Maybe you should dump him. There is only one last place I can think he would have a fault and that's in bed." She signs this time.

I look down at the lady painting my toes. I know my cheeks have turned red. He definitely has no faults in bed. Jayden's hard smack across my arm tells me I'm not hiding anything from her. I glance to my side and her hands are flying.

"You've slept with him and you didn't mention this to me?"

"What are you expecting me to do? Walk up to you and tell you that I slept with him?"

Jayden rotates her whole body toward me, causing the lady who is polishing her toes to swipe nail polish across all of her toes. I give an apologetic smile to the lady even though it's not me causing the mess on my feet.

"Yes!" She signs big, but from what I can tell she also yells out loud.

I look around and just as I thought, Jayden has gotten the attention of all the other women in the shop. "Could you please not cause a scene? Turn back around, you screwed up your nails."

She glares at me for a moment and then she finally turns around. She says something to the woman who is now trying to clean all the nail polish off her toes. We both sit there, nothing else is said. Maybe she is going to drop the subject. I look over and she is still looking down at the lady working. Just when I think the subject is done, she turns to me.

Her hands are flying again. "Please tell me that's where his flaw is. Not that I want you to have bad sex, but Travis needs to be flawed somewhere. Is that why you didn't say anything?"

I almost laugh out loud, she only wishes.

"You're kidding me, right? Damn, the guy is perfect."

He's not perfect, but he is pretty damn close, I think to myself.

TUESDAY IS FINALLY HERE. Today I'm hoping the doctor takes this cast off my arm. Then maybe I can return back to work for the last couple weeks of school, before summer break.

"Travis, you didn't have to take today off from work. I could have seen the doctor by myself."

He takes my hand. "It was no big deal, I wanted to come with you."

I have already gone and had x-rays taken and now we are just sitting here in the waiting room waiting to be called back by the doctor. My phone vibrates, it's from my brother.

**Is there any way you can come by the station today?

The station? Why would he need me to stop by there?

Travis taps his fingers against mine. I look up at him.

"Everything all right?"

I show him the text from Bryce.

"Does he normally ask for you to stop by the station?"

I shake my head no. I send a text back to Bryce.

**Is everything all right?

His response doesn't take long to come back.

**We have a person of interest in the bombing. We are hoping you can help us with a video we have been given.

Travis is reading the text along with me. His hand tightens around mine, his leg starts a nervous bounce. Sometimes I think talking about the bombing bothers him more than it does me.

"Are you all right with us stopping by there, after we are done here?"

I'm not sure if he hears me. He just stares down at our hands. "Travis, if you don't want to go, you can just take me back to my house and I'll drive myself over there. It's no big deal."

He says something, but since he is looking down I can't make it all out.

"Travis, look at me."

He looks up at me, he looks mad. I've never seen him look pissed before. "Are you all right? Really, it's no big deal, you don't have to go."

His expression quickly changes. A softer look is in his eyes now. "Sorry. Of course I will go with you. You aren't going to do this alone."

I study him for a moment. I know that night bothers him, I'm just not used to him showing this much frustration in front of me. "Are you sure?"

He only nods. I quickly type out a text to Bryce letting him know that we are at the doctors and that we will stop by after we are done here.

Travis squeezes my leg, I look up at him. "They are calling your name."

Looking over, I see the nurse standing at the door. "Are you coming in with me?"

"If you want me to."

Standing up, I pull him with me. Of course I want him with me. I'm not sure if I like this mood he is in though.

I HAVE NEVER UNDERSTOOD why they call you back to see the doctor only to have you sit in the exam room for another twenty minutes waiting for the doctor to come in. Finally, the door opens and a doctor walks in. This isn't the same doctor.

"Hello, my name is Dr. Wallace. Dr. Samson had an emergency so I'm filling in for him today."

The doctor turns to Travis, I wait for him to turn back to me. He is still talking, I can tell by hand and body movement, and it's starting to irritate me that he is acting like I'm not here. I'm the patient, not Travis. I'm noticing I'm not the only one he is irritating, Travis looks like he did in the waiting room when I talked about going to the station. I am about to say something, but Travis beats me to it.

"No, I'm not her translator, I'm her boyfriend. We would both appreciate it if you would turn around and talk to Charliee. If that is a problem then we can reschedule this appointment for another day when Dr. Samson is available."

If it wasn't for wanting this cast off so badly, I probably would have gotten up and walked out. On the other hand, I can't figure out why I'm so irritated by the whole thing. This doctor doesn't know me. He probably only knows I'm deaf by reading my charts. I'm sure it doesn't say on there "she can read lips." So how is he supposed to know I can understand him without a translator? I take a deep breath, I need to calm us both down. Travis isn't usually this short either. We have both been a little edgy since my brother's text, especially Travis.

"Doctor, as long as you look at me when you talk then I will understand everything you are saying."

Dr. Wallace turns his attention back to me with an apologetic smile. "I'm sorry, I should have asked more questions when I came in and never assumed. Dr. Samson has spoken very highly of how well you communicate."

It not's fair for either of us to be taking our bad moods out on him either. "It's no problem."

I look over at Travis, his expression hasn't changed and he is still glaring at the doctor's back.

"So do you think I'm good to have the cast removed?" I ask, hopeful.

He places the x-ray up onto the screen and studies it for a moment. Travis comes over to stand next to me. I take his hand, he looks over at me. I smile, hoping it will help but it doesn't. He just looks back at the doctor.

Dr. Wallace turns back to us. "Everything looks great. I would say the cast can come off."

Jumping off the table, it's hard to hide my excitement. "Great! Thank you so much."

Holding up his hand, the doctor stops me, laughing. "Hold on, Charliee. Before you go, we need to check on everything else as well."

Laughing with him, I sit back up on the exam table. "Sorry, just ready for it to be removed."

"I understand, I'll be as quick as I can." He checks my shoulder, my ribs and lastly, my lower back.

"Well, I'll be happy to report back to Dr. Samson that you are healing great. There may be a couple tender spots on your lower back still, which is normal, but from what I can see I would say you can return back to work."

It takes a lot not to jump up and down like a little girl and hug the doctor, I am so excited.

Dr. Wallace finishes up with the paperwork, giving me a copy of everything and then sends us over to the casting room to have the cast removed. I thank him and drag a still not-so-happy-looking Travis out the door.

NOW ON OUR way to the station, my happy mood is starting to change again. My nerves are starting to reappear. Travis hasn't said a word since back at the doctor's office.

"Hey, are you all right?"

"It just irritated me when the doctor acted like you weren't there."

Okay, I don't doubt that irritated him a little. It did me and I'm used to that kind of reaction from people who don't know me, but I also know that isn't what caused this mood.

"Travis, there is more to it than just that, talk to me."

He looks out his window for a moment, then back to the road. When we pull up to a red light he looks back at me.

"I just don't see why you need to go to the station. Haven't you been through enough? Your brothers should know this."

Taking his hand, I kiss his knuckles. "Travis, I'm all right. If I can help in any way to catch the person who did this, then I want to help."

His hand tightens around mine. "Why you, though, Charliee?"

I lean over toward him and give him a light kiss. "I'm one of the only ones, besides the people in the kitchen, that survived that night Travis."

His expression softens a little. "I just don't want you to have to keep reliving it. You have been through so much already, when do you get to start putting it all behind you?"

It's at the tip of my tongue to tell him how much I love him. "Thanks to you, the guys at the station and my brothers, I did survive. I will get a chance to put it behind me. My family won't have to miss me, but there are so many other families who will now have to live with the loss and if I can help them move on then I want to help. One great thing happened that night, I found you."

He leans over to me, shaking his head. "No, don't forget I found you."

He kisses me and when he sits back, I'm happy to see him laughing.

"The people behind us are honking."

I lean over, wrapping a hand around the back of his neck, "I don't hear a thing." I kiss him back. The cars can wait or go around, I really don't care which.

. . .

DERRICK, Bryce and their Captain are in a small room with Travis and me. The moment we walk into the station my nerves almost get the best of me and cause me to turn around and leave. Knowing Travis is already having a problem with me coming, I try not to show him how much I worry about being here. Actually, walking into the building makes me realize it is going to be hard to keep acting this way. I don't know what kind of video they had found or what we will see on it. I do know that I don't want to see the actual explosion occur or what everything looked like after. I haven't been anywhere near that place since that night.

All of the guys are talking about something. What? I don't know. All I can do is stare at the large television in the room. I am pretty sure I'm not as ready as I tried to convince Travis I was.

Derrick appears in front of me, his hands signing, "Are you all right?"

I just stand there staring at him. I am scared, I hate feeling this way. Someone from behind me places their hands on my shoulders and turns me around. It's amazing how those eyes can calm me so easily.

"Charliee, you don't have to do this. We can leave."

I look between my brothers and the Captain. "I'm not sure if I'm ready to see what really happened that night." I finally find my voice.

Bryce shakes his head. "Charliee, you won't see anything like that actually. This video is of before you even entered the restaurant."

Now, I'm curious. How can I help with anything from before I went inside? "What are you talking about?"

"After that night, only one store had a video of the whole thing. Bad part was it was on the side of the restaurant, so we didn't have a good picture. For the last month, a number of officers have watched the video multiple times just looking for one thing that would start us on a lead. Bryce and I haven't even watched it because of your involvement. Trust me, we didn't want to see any of that any more than you want to."

I didn't even think about them having to see the video. I have a tendency to forget I wasn't the only one in my family affected by all of this.

Bryce continues, "Yesterday, when the video was being reviewed again, they caught something they hadn't seen before. They brought Derrick and me in to review it. I promise, you'll see nothing of the explosion or anything that follows. This part of the video is of you and a guy who ran into you before you went inside."

Bryce points with the controller and the screen lights up. After a moment of watching, I see myself park along the curb and Levi and I jump out. I remember all I wanted to do was grab a quick something to eat and go home to enjoy a hot bath after a trying day at work. We start to walk around the corner, then a guy runs into me, knocking me down. I remember all of this very clearly.

Bryce stops the video there. I take a deep breath, happy that is all I am going to have to watch.

"Yes, I remember all of that. He had come running around the corner and ran right into me. I had a rough day at school that day with the kids. Nothing major, just teenagers being teenagers. Anyway, all I wanted to do was grab my food and head home. When he slammed into me knocking me on my butt, I remember thinking it fit perfectly into the type of day I had experienced."

"Charliee, as you can see, the video isn't the best. We can't tell if he said anything to you or not. We can barely make out his features and the closer we zoom in, the worse it gets. Do you remember if he said anything to you?"

Disappointment is in all their eyes when I shake my head no. "He didn't say anything. Levi never really gave him a chance to. He began to lunge at him, I had to pull him back. He stood there for a moment, never offered to help me up, never said sorry or anything. He just ran off after a minute. Sorry I can't help more than that."

I look back at the screen. "Is that the man you guys think did it?"

Bryce nods, "When we push the video back a little more, we see him enter the restaurant with a back pack. About thirty minutes or so later, he comes out without the backpack and in a hurry. That's when he ran into you. We just don't have a clear picture of his face to use."

Thinking back to that night, I clearly see the man standing there, arms up in the air as Levi lunges at him. I remember almost laughing at the expression on his face.

"Maybe I can help with that. I do remember what the guy looked like."

They all look hopeful again. Bryce turns the screen off and turns to me. "Do you think you could describe him to our sketch artist?"

"Yes."

IT TAKES about another hour or so to finish up with the artist and get a picture drawn that they can use. When I walk out of the room, Travis is right there waiting. I go straight into his arms. He hasn't said much.

"Are you all right?"

He kisses my forehead. "I think I should be asking you that question."

"I'm exhausted. It's been a pretty eventful day. What sounds great to me is to go grab some quick food, go back to my place and relax with you in a bath."

"You want me to take a bath with you? I'm a guy, we don't take baths."

He has that look he gets when he is teasing me. "No, you don't have to. I could lie naked in that large bath tub and relax alone if you would like to drop me off and then go home."

He is shaking his head no before I even finish talking. "I'm not leaving you tonight. So I guess we are going to go get you some food and then head back to take a bath."

He leans down to kiss me but quickly pulls away. When he moves to my side, that's when I notice Derrick and Bryce standing there. According to the brotherly looks they were both giving Travis, I would say they heard our conversation.

"All right, boys, be nice."

Bryce is the first one to look away. It's kind of funny, out of the two he is the bad boy looking one, but in comparison he is the gentle one. "Charliee, thank you for coming in. This morning when they asked us to watch, we weren't jumping for joy, so I know you being asked to come in and watch wasn't easy. You giving the description was a huge help."

"I'll admit this wasn't the highlight of my day, but I'm glad I came and was able to help a little."

Derrick gives me a hug and then Bryce. "I love you both, but I'm going home now."

CHAPTER
Twenty

TRAVIS

WE GRABBED a quick bite to eat after leaving the station. I ran by my apartment and packed some clothes. By the time I get back to the truck, Charliee is asleep. Levi has moved from the back seat to the front and has his head in her lap. He is very protective of her and I don't blame him. Sure, she is independent and doesn't like to rely on people to help her, she has no problem taking care of herself. She also has this pull about her, a vulnerability that makes you want to wrap her up into your arms and never let go. She doesn't want other people fighting her battles for her. I know that, but today at the doctor's office I was ready to punch the doctor. When he turned his back to her and started telling me about her charts like she wasn't even in the room, I was ready to explode. It didn't help when I saw the irritation in her eyes about it. I'm sure this is something that happens to her a lot. I watched as she explained to the doctor how she could read his lips and the way her expression softened like she realized it was no big deal and easily looked pass it, she accepted the man's ignorance. I, on the other hand, didn't expect it. She is an adult, not a child. The doctor should have asked questions when he came in and not assumed he couldn't communicate with her. At least make the effort. I'm sure Charliee has dealt with people's different reactions all her life, so she would be more forgiving of it.

Of course it didn't help that I went into the room already in an irritated mood. When she told me about her brother's text and I saw a little fear enter her eyes, my mood changed. I couldn't believe her brothers were going to have her watch a video of the explosion or anything related to that night. Her strength today just made me fall deeper in love with her. She was scared, I knew it from the moment we walked into the station today. Her hand that I was holding gripped mine so tightly that she was shaking and her palms began to sweat.

When we entered the room with the large television screen, she froze. It took a lot not to pull her back out of the room and leave. What stopped me was her inner strength that I have come to learn about. I know she was terrified. I also know it bothers her more than she lets on, how she survived and so many others didn't. She wants to help in any way she can. Not for herself and what she went through but for those who lost their lives that night.

As I pull up behind her Jeep in the driveway, I look over at her. She is amazing and she is mine. I'm the lucky one. I hop out and wait for Levi to follow me out. Hurrying to the passenger side, I open the door, reach across and unbuckle the seat belt. When I get to the front door I realize I forgot her purse in the truck and her keys are probably in it. Starting to walk back to the truck, her voice stops me.

"Why don't you put me down?"

I look down at her half-open eyes, but she's smiling. "Next time I think I'm just going to sling you over my shoulder and carry you like we do when we pull people out of burning buildings."

Slapping me in the chest, she wiggles until I put her back on her feet. "I'll be right back, I'm going to get your purse out of the truck so we can get into the house. Don't fall asleep standing there."

I'm walking backwards as I'm talking to her and before I know it, my foot catches the edge of the walkway and I'm looking up at the night sky on my back in the grass.

Both Levi and Charliee appear above me, she is laughing. "Are you all right?"

"Yes, I can tell by your laugh that you are real concerned about my welfare."

She reaches down a hand. I take it and with her help pull myself back up onto my feet. As I stand, I wrap one arm around her waist and pull her tight against my chest, claiming her lips. Her tongue instantly darts out, finding mine. Now all I want to do is pull her back down to the grass.

She pulls away, her breathing is rapid. "I think we need that bath."

My hand on her backside, I thrust her hips into mine so that she knows exactly what I need. "I need you."

She pulls out of my arms and walks up to the front door. "Then hurry up and go get my keys so that we can get inside."

THE BATH WATER has started to cool but it could be ice cold and I wouldn't want to get out. It is nice sitting here holding Charliee's naked, wet body against mine. Earlier when she was filling up the bath tub, she explained how when she was house hunting there were only two things that were a must. A decent back yard for Levi and a huge bath tub for her. I've personally never sat in a bath, but after tonight I am thinking I need to take more, with her of course.

Charliee sits up and rotates her body around so that she is facing me. I push forward a little so that she can wrap her legs around my waist. This puts her breasts right at face level for me. I look up at her and smile like she just handed me the best dessert for me to feast on. "I'm thinking I'm going to like bath time from now on."

Before she can reply, I suck one of her breasts into my mouth, teasing the nipple with my tongue. She moans softly and her head falls back. Her long hair brushes against my legs in the water. I tangle my fingers into the wet strands, pulling slightly. She arches her back, thrusting her breast more into my mouth. Her nails dig into my shoulder and biceps. I can feel her heat against me, with her legs wrapped around me her core is open for me to take. The tip of me is just at the entrance to her body. She has all the control, all she has to do is take me. My attention moves to the other breast, the nipple already puckered up and begging for me to tease some more. I gently nibble and she tries to lift her head to look at me but I still have a hold on it. I pull gently and suck her breast into my mouth again.

After making sure she was fully worked up, I release her hair. When I look into her eyes, they are smoked over. "I want you now," she demands.

She lifts her hips slightly and rotates until she feels my tip at her very hot entrance. I'm letting her take charge this time, move at her pace. She pushes herself down just enough that my tip is just inside her. I hear myself moan. With my hands on her hips, all I want to do is pull her down the rest of the way, but I don't.

The water waves around us as she rotates her hips in tiny circles, her body massaging the tip of my hardness. I am going to lose it before we even get started with her doing this. Little by little she takes me further and further into her, the heat surrounding me along with her tight core. I dig my fingers into her hips to keep from thrusting into her completely. Finally, she lifts herself one last time and comes down on me completely, taking me deep inside. Her breasts are bouncing in front of my face, begging me. I take one breast, sucking it hard into my mouth and thrust my hips up, burying myself a little deeper inside her. Her arms wrap tightly around my shoulders, her nails now digging into my back and head. My face smothers into her chest. Her hips begin to thrust up and then quickly back down. Each time I nip at her nipple, she thrusts harder and faster.

Water is going everywhere, but who cares. The quicker my tongue circles her nipple, her hips follow. I switch to the other breast. The moment my teeth nip her, she explodes around me, her muscles pulling me in further and further. I shove my hips up once and that is all it takes for me to follow her.

MY PHONE RINGING is what wakes me up way too early this morning. Grabbing it, I see that it's my mom.

"Hey, Mom."

"Travis, I'm sorry, did I wake you?"

Rubbing my eyes, I pull my phone away to look at the time. It's eight-thirty. "It's all right, what's up?"

Looking over, Charliee is laying on her stomach, her face toward me.

"Sorry, honey, I thought you said you worked yesterday. I figured you would be driving home right now. If I had known you weren't work-ing, I wouldn't have called so early."

Levi appears next to me, he probably wants out. I climb out of bed, grabbing my pants and pulling them on. I don't want him to wake Charliee. "It's all right, Mom, really. I was supposed to work yesterday. I ended up taking the day off so I could go with Charliee to her doctor's appointment."

My parents haven't met Charliee yet but they know all about her. Actually, my dad and I have had many talks about her when she was in the hospital. He was kind of the one who convinced me to go back and see her.

"Your father took the week off from work and we were wondering if you and Charliee would like to meet us for lunch today. We would love to finally meet her."

When I open the back door, I realize it is raining again. I decide to wait for Levi to finish and then let him back in. I am surprised when he follows me into the living room afterwards. When I sit down on the couch, he lays down by my feet. I run my hand across his head a few times, petting him.

I would like for Charliee and my parents to meet. I am pretty sure she will be all right with it but I'm not sure if she has already made other plans for today.

"When she wakes up, I'll ask her and then call you back."

"You stayed the night with her?" The excitement in her voice is very noticeable. I wouldn't be surprised if she is already having us married off and giving her some grandchildren.

"Mom, let's not start this, but yes, I'm at her house. As soon as she wakes up, I'll ask her and let you know."

"All right, hon. Talk to you soon." She quickly hangs up.

I love my mom and her excitement.

"You know, he must really like you, he doesn't usually leave my side."

Charliee is standing against the wall watching us. She is wearing my shirt again, only this time she has on an old pair of sweats as well. Levi's head comes up but then relaxes down against my leg again. I scratch behind his ear.

"That's because when I let him out to go the bathroom and it's raining, I don't leave him out there like some people do," I tease her.

She comes over and sits on my lap. "I believe that was your fault. You distracted me, he just doesn't know that."

"I'm starting to think I'm going to have to start bringing extra shirts with me since you are always stealing the one I wore."

Her nails trace a light path across my chest. "Actually, I think you bring just enough. You see, if I'm wearing yours then you can't. I'm good with that."

"Before you go and distract me too much, my mom just called and asked if we would be interested in meeting them for lunch today."

"I would love to meet your parents."

We haven't been to a sit down restaurant since the night of our first date. I've kind of made sure we went to fast places, or brought food to her. "Charliee, are you going to be all right with going to another restaurant?"

"Travis, I'll be fine. I need to work past all of this. I can't spend the rest of my life not going into restaurants. That one time was probably because I hadn't been to one yet. I had to get past all the firsts, right? Anyway, I'm not going to have you tell your parents no because I may be afraid to exit the place. What kind of impression would that be?"

She gives me a small kiss.

"Charliee, my parents know what you've been through. They would understand."

Shaking her head, she moves off my lap. "Call your mom and find out when and where. I'm going to hop in the shower."

Yep, I am completely in love with that stubborn woman. I pick up my phone and call my mom.

"Hello," she answers.

"Mom..." Charliee appears around the corner, cutting me off.

"Hurry up and join me." Then she is gone down the hallway.

Wondering if my mother heard, I laugh. "Mom, Charliee is good for lunch, what time and where?"

CHAPTER

Twenty~One

I AM A LITTLE NERVOUS, I'm not going to lie. It's always important, I think, that the family approves. My parents like Travis, especially my mother. My brothers give him a hard time so that's a good sign. If they ignored him that would tell me they didn't like him. I'm pretty sure Jayden believes he can do no wrong and is a god. Now I just need to make a good impression with his family.

Travis squeezes my hand, which brings my attention to him and no longer out the window watching the view pass by. "Are you all right?"

I nod. "I'm just a little nervous. I want to make a good first impression. I don't want you to break up with me because your mom doesn't like me."

He smiles and brings my hand up to his mouth and kisses my knuckles. "First, I don't think you have ever met someone who didn't like you. Second, my parents are going to adore you. Just for the record, if for some strange reason they didn't, I would be convinced something was wrong with them and I would stay with you. I'm hooked and you aren't getting rid of me anytime soon."

He says that now. Smiling, I hope he thinks he has calmed my nerves when really they are still bouncing around like crazy inside. We pull up to the restaurant and Travis quickly jumps out of the truck and rounds to my side. He opens the door and holds his hand out to me.

"Come on, everything will be great."

Oh for heaven's sake, Charliee, snap out of it, I scold myself. If I just be myself everything will be fine.

When we walk into the building, there are only three people sitting in the waiting area. An older couple and a young girl. As we come inside, the younger lady, who is small and petite and has dark red colored hair, jumps up and throws herself into Travis's arms. After I look past the red hair, I recognize her from their family picture Travis has hanging on his wall. This is his sister, only she had blonde hair in the picture.

As I watch the exchange between brother and sister, I realize they have the same kind of relationship as I do with my brothers, and I love that. Family means everything to me and obviously the same is true with Travis. I watch as she pulls away and says something to Travis but with me to her side and her talking very quickly, I can't make out what she's saying, but Travis is nodding and smiling. Suddenly, they both turn and look at me and before I can react, she is hugging me.

When she pulls back, she is apologizing to me. "I'm so sorry, I forgot."

I glance at Travis, puzzled, and then back at his sister. "Why are you apologizing?"

Travis pulls me into his side, his arm around my waist. "Charliee, this is my sister Samantha. Sam, this is Charliee. She was apologizing because she was talking a mile a minute while she was hugging you, forgetting you weren't able to hear a word she was saying."

Samantha's cheeks are red, it is cute. "I'll let you in on a little secret. If you don't react to the times you forget, then most of the time I won't even know. Unless you are like your brother. I read it in his eyes every time, he just thinks I don't catch it."

Travis looks down at me with a shocked expression on his face. "I have no idea what you are talking about."

A couple who I am guessing are his parents walk up to join us. "It's nice to finally meet you, Charliee. My name is Anna and this is Kevin." She signs as she speaks.

I try to hide my surprise. Travis, on the other hand, has his mouth hanging open with surprise.

"Did I sign something wrong?" She looks nervously between Travis and me.

Shaking my head, I smile. "No, you did great! Travis never mentioned you signed. I'm sorry for my shock."

"That's because Travis didn't know his mother knew how to sign," he adds.

Relief washes over her face. "I don't sign. I tried learning a little before we met you. That's about all I have remembered so far."

It is hard to keep the tears at bay. I am pretty sure I have a goofy smile on my face. His mom is trying to make me comfortable. That small gesture speaks louder than any words, spoken or signed.

Anna steps forward and gives me a hug and then Kevin. "It's great to finally meet you, Charliee, we have heard a lot about you."

"It's great to meet all of you."

LUNCH with the Kendricks went great. Travis had no idea his sister was in town, she wanted to surprise him and meet me, I guess. She is going to college out of state for nursing. She is looking to graduate next year. His mom is a sweatheart. She kept asking me how to sign all these words. Then she would apologize to me for bugging me for a sign language class. It didn't bother me, I liked watching her get all excited when she would be talking and then she would throw a word she just learned in there. She is picking it all up pretty fast. Samantha and Kevin even joined in. Anna and Samantha even asked me for my number before we all left.

"I think you passed the test with my parents and sister."

"They are all great. Your sister is just one little ball of energy, isn't she? I had to really pay attention when she talked since she talks so fast."

"Ball of energy is a good way to describe her. Just ask her to slow down, she will."

"It's no big deal, it keeps me on my toes. "

Travis leans across and gives me a kiss. "I'm going to warn you. Now that they have your number, they will both be texting you all of the time."

I am all right with that.

FINALLY, back to work. I have never been so happy to see Monday morning as I was this morning. Travis spent the whole weekend with me at my place. He even stayed last night. Usually if he has to work the next morning he stays at his place, saying it's too tempting to call in sick and stay in bed with me. I think this morning was different because we were both getting up and going to work. That was something else that I had mixed feelings about. On one hand it felt very natural, like he belonged in my house, waking up with him in my bed. Putting on my makeup as he took a shower. Brushing our teeth side by side. Kissing each other good bye and then parting our separate ways to go to our jobs.

On the other hand, I kept thinking I should feel a little weird about it all. That we shouldn't already feel this comfortable with each other. I know I'll miss him tonight. I should be happy to have a little of my space back, but I don't feel that way at all. I feel like he belongs in my world, in my space. I've noticed a big difference with Levi as well. Before, he wouldn't leave my side. He would follow me room to room.

When Travis is at the house, he will stay in the living room when we go into another room. He trusts Travis to do his job at protecting and alerting me.

The lights in the class begin to flash, signaling the end of class and that it is time for lunch. I dismiss the kids and watch as they file out. Some let me know they were happy to have me back. A couple shyly tell me they are happy I am all right.

I grab my lunch and follow them out, locking the classroom door behind me. Coming around the corner, I stop when I see Jayden and some guy outside her classroom. I don't think they are yelling at each other or anything but from the facial expressions, they seem to be in a heated conversation. Their bodies, on the other hand, are speaking of something else completely, there is a lot of sexual tension there. I wonder if this is the guy she was talking about the day we were getting our toes done.

I know I should walk in a different direction and not stare or eaves drop, however, I am too curious, and Jayden has been very secretive lately. I have been standing here for a couple of minutes when Jayden looks over and sees me. She says a couple more things to the guy, I am too far away to really read her lips, and I'm going to assume he says a few things back. He never turns around, so I never get to see his face. He just walks away.

Jayden stands there for a moment watching him as he walks away from her. Her hands are on her hips, she is irritated with him for sure. Her eyes, on the other hand, look sad.

I walk over to her. "Are you ready for lunch?"

She looks at me in surprise. She was expecting me to drill her on the guy. She is right, I am going to, just not here in the hallway. I am hungry, I will drill her while we eat.

"Yeah, let me go and grab my lunch. I'll be right back."

• • •

THIS ISN'T JAYDEN. She is quiet and picking at her sandwich. She needs to start telling me what is going on. I'm not letting her keep it from me any longer.

"So when are you going to tell me who the guy was?"

I watch as she takes a couple of deep breaths. She sets her sandwich onto the paper towel on the table, then sits back in her chair.

"That was Cameron Tovaren."

The last name sends a stab through my heart. "So how is he related?"

"Cameron is their oldest son. He moved back to take care of Jacob after their parents died."

No longer hungry, I push the rest of my lunch away from me. "You guys seemed to be arguing."

Arms crossed at her chest, she is looking down, nodding her head.

"What were you two arguing about?"

She shrugs her shoulders. "It's not real important."

We have talked about how Jacob's grades have dropped. He is popular, on the football team and track team. He is a very talented kid.

"Were you guys arguing over Jacob?"

Sitting back up in her chair, she rests her elbows on the table, running her hands over her face. "In a nut shell, I'm trying to help Jacob get back on track and Cameron is telling me to mind my own business."

I don't have Jacob in any of my classes this year, although I did last year. He is a great kid, a teenager all parents wish they had. He always kept focus, never let his popularity get to his head. The girls all loved him. Losing both parents at one time I'm sure is going to make a person change.

There is more to this though. Knowing my friend as well as I do, there is more to this story and I have a feeling it is more about Cameron himself than Jacob.

"How close have you two become?"

No reaction. No surprised face that I figured it out. Not even an attempt to act like I just asked a crazy question. She just keeps staring down at the table.

"How long, Jayden?"

"We met about two weeks after the bombing. Jacob had taken a few weeks off from school. Cameron came in to get his school work so he wouldn't fall behind. I was asked by the office to be at a meeting they were having with Cameron to discuss how long Jacob would be out of school and implementing a teaching plan, no one wanted him falling behind. Jacob is a great student but he has always struggled a little in math so I told Cameron to let me know if Jacob wanted some tutoring while he was out. He called me a couple days later and we set up a time for me to go to their house and help Jacob with his math."

She stops for a moment, she is still holding something back.

"Anyway, after a couple days, Cameron asked me out for drinks. He said he needed someone to talk to, so I accepted. He's a great guy, we have a lot of chemistry. Things are great as long as I don't interfere or say anything about Jacob."

I can only imagine what those two guys are going through. "So you guys were arguing about Jacob."

She shakes her head no. "Today, surprisingly, wasn't about Jacob."

"Why was he here then?"

"He was here for a meeting with the track coach or something. I saw him walking down the hallway and he stopped to talk, that was right before you came around the corner."

Confused, I'm still not sure what they were arguing about.

She takes a deep breath again. "Charliee, the other day when we were getting our toes done, you mentioned double dating. I have asked Cameron a couple times if we could get together with you and Travis. This would be the other thing we always argue about. It's you."

"Wait, what?" How did I even get in between them? I haven't even met the guy.

Jayden holds her hand out to stop me from asking more. "Let me explain."

"Please do."

"Today I asked him again about us all getting together. Long story short, he isn't sure if he is ready to meet you. This is why I have been so secretive about the whole thing, I didn't want to hurt your feelings."

What the heck, is she serious right now? "I didn't blow up the place, what does he have against me?"

"Charliee, it's not like that."

The lights flicker, announcing the end of lunch. Well, my happy to be back to work mood just got trampled on. I grab my lunch, get up and throw it away. Jayden grabs my arm and turns me back to her.

"Charliee, please believe me, it's nothing like that. Cameron has a lot of mixed feelings right now. He needs to mourn his parents, but won't because he is staying strong for Jacob. I think he is afraid that if he meets someone who was involved, it will create or open up those emotions. He refuses to be weak, no matter how much I try to convince him that sadness isn't a weakness. It's not really you, it's what you may open up in him. Do you understand what I'm trying to say?"

She is begging me with her eyes to understand what she is trying to tell me. If I think for a moment on what she told me, I can admit to understanding. Not that it still doesn't sting a little, but like I said before, I can't imagine how the two of them are feeling. If I were to be honest with myself, I know I would have mixed feelings around him as well. Mostly guilt that I survived and both of their parents didn't.

"I understand, you just caught me off guard is all. If he changes his mind or you talk him into going out one night, just let me know."

Smiling, I give her a hug. I want her not to worry about it. Inside, though, I have to admit, I am still a little upset. I don't really think it is over the fact that Cameron doesn't want to meet me, but more over the fact that it woke me up to a little more reality of the whole situation.

When I get back to my classroom, I check my phone and find a text message from Samantha.

**Hey just wondering if you could meet up for dinner tonight? I know Travis is working and I would love to talk with you a little more before I head out of town.

Actually, dinner tonight sounds like a great idea. I don't really feel like being all alone, especially after all the stuff Jayden dropped on me at lunch.

**I would love to meet up with you, where did you have in mind?

I WALK into the little diner Samantha had suggested and spot her right away.

An older lady comes from around the counter as I approach. "How are you doing this evening?"

"Good, thank you." I point over in Samantha's direction. "I see who I'm meeting."

I start to walk by and I see the lady watching Levi. I'm waiting for her to ask me to either leave or take him outside. I put his service vest on but some places still question me about him. I am about to ask if everything is all right when she looks back at me and smiles. "Enjoy your meal."

I smile back. "Thank you."

Samantha greets me with a tight hug and then kneels down to Levi. "Hey, boy."

She sits back down in her seat and I sit across from her. "Charliee, thank you for having dinner with me tonight."

"Thank you for asking. Going home to an empty house wasn't sounding very appealing. Some girl time sounded a lot better."

I look around the little diner. "This place is cute."

Samantha glances around once herself. "It's little but it has great food. I used to come here all the time when I was in high school. I try to make sure I eat here at least once every time I come home."

Our waitress stops by to introduce herself. "Hi, ladies. My name is Wendy. Are you guys ready to order?"

I glance over the menu. "What do you recommend?" I ask Samantha.

"The chili cheese fries are amazing but they are huge. You up for sharing?"

"Sounds good to me. Can I get a coke as well, please?" I hand the menu back to Wendy.

"Make that two cokes, please," Samantha adds.

Wendy quickly writes down our order. "All right, I'll be back in just a few with your drinks."

Samantha leans forward, hands folded in front of her on the table. "All right, now that my brother and parents aren't here, I want to hear all about your first date with my brother."

Well, that's getting right to the point, I think to myself. I like that we can just sit down and act as though we have known each other for years instead of just days. "There is a pretty funny story to that night. Well, I didn't find it too funny that night, but I can laugh about it now."

"What did my brother do?" Samantha rolls her eyes and sits back in her seat.

"Actually, it wasn't your brother, it was mine."

"You have a brother, too?" she asks.

"I have two older brothers actually, Derrick and Bryce."

"So what happened?" she asks, all excited.

"Your brother had just gotten to my house. I went back to my room to put Levi's service vest on. My brother decided to stop by to check on me. Long story short, I wasn't paying attention to the lights flashing, alerting me that someone was at the front door. My brother panicked and barged in, gun drawn. When I came out into the hallway, I find my brother standing in the doorway, pointing his gun at Travis."

Samantha's eyes are wide. "What did Travis do?"

Our waitress comes back by with our drinks. We both thank her. After she walks away, I continue by answering Samantha's question.

"He didn't do anything. He stood there all calm, where I, on the other hand, was pissed and giving Derrick a piece of my mind. After Derrick had put his gun away and apologized, Travis told him it was no big deal. That he had a sister." I pointed over at her, "And that he would have probably done the same thing."

Samantha is sitting there nodding her head. "Yeah, he probably would have. So what happened after that?"

I am about to answer when someone taps me on my shoulder. I turn around, "Wow, were your ears ringing?"

He motions for me to move over so that he can sit down next to me. "Were you talking about me?"

"Your name was mentioned, yes. What are you doing here?"

"I just ended my shift. This place has a great burger. I stop here all the time and grab dinner before I head home," he explains.

"It seems that I'm the only one who hasn't been to this place before."

"You've been missing out, sis." He looks over at Samantha and holds his hand out. "Hi, I'm Derrick."

I want to elbow my brother. He is giving Samantha his flirting smile.

Samantha shakes his hand. "Oh, so you're the one who barged into the house, gun drawn and pointed at my brother. I'm Samantha, but everyone calls me Sam."

Derrick looks over at me. "You aren't going to let that one go, are you?"

I shrug my shoulder and point at Samantha. "She asked about Travis's and my first date. That was a pretty large part in it."

The waitress comes by and drops off our chili fries, setting them in the middle of the table. "Derrick, your order is ready and up at the front counter when you're ready for it."

"Thank you, Wendy." He leans over and gives Levi a little attention and then gives me a kiss on the cheek. "I'll let you two get back to your girl talk. Samantha, it was very nice to meet you, hopefully we will meet again. Charliee, I love you."

Samantha smiles. "It was nice to meet you, too, Derrick." You would have to be blind to miss the look exchanged between the two of them.

I look up at my brother. "I love you, too. See you later."

It is hard not to laugh as Samantha watches Derrick walk away. When she looks back at me, her smile says it all. The next time Samantha is in town, I need to introduce her to Jayden, the two of them are two of a kind. Neither one of them are shy when it comes to men. Going out with them would be very entertaining.

"Is he single?" she asks.

"Samantha, you don't even live here right now," I point out.

She shrugs her shoulders. "I visit a lot, though. Is your other brother as good looking as him?"

"They're identical twins."

Surprise shoots across her face. "You mean there are two guys walking around that look like him?"

I just nod my head and grab a fry, she would definitely get along great with Jayden!

CHAPTER

Twenty~Two

TRAVIS

THE KNOCK at my door I expected to be Charliee, but I'm surprised to see Sam.

"Hey, hope you don't mind me just stopping by. I wanted to see you before I left again tomorrow."

"Of course I don't mind, Charliee should be here shortly. I know she would love to see you."

She comes in and sits down on the couch. "Something smells great."

"I threw some steaks on the barbecue, you are welcome to stay and eat with us."

"Thank you, but I don't want to be in the way."

"Samantha, I don't think you could ever be in the way, plus I'm sure Charliee would love it. I hear you guys had dinner last night."

She nods. "I figured since you were at work it would be a great time to get her alone. She is a great person, Travis, I really like her."

"She is pretty amazing."

Sam stares at me for a moment, a smile across her lips. "You are in love with her, aren't you?"

Nodding, I'm not going to deny it with my sister. She would see right through me even if I tried. "Absolutely in love with her."

"Have you told her yet?"

I lay back in the couch shaking my head no. "I'm not sure if she is ready to hear it yet. I've told her I have feelings for her, but have I actually said I love you? No."

"I think she is ready to hear it, because I think she feels the same way about you."

I hope so. I know she has feelings for me, I'm just not sure if she is in love with me yet.

"Travis, stop questioning it. I know what is running through that head of yours. Anyone who watches the way she looks at you would tell you the same thing."

"I'll know when the time is right. So what did you guys talk about last night?"

I want to change the subject and from the way Sam is looking at me, she knows it.

"Well, she told me about her brother charging into the house on your first date with a gun."

"That was Derrick."

I notice the smile that appears when I mention Derrick's name.

"Yeah, I know, I met him last night as well. He showed up at the diner. He had ordered to go after he got off work. So do you and her brothers get along?" she asks, giving me that look I know a little too well. She likes him. She is leaving to go back to school tomorrow so I decide to leave the subject alone.

"About as well as I would get along with any guy who shows interest in you."

She laugh, she knows what I mean. I often got yelled at by her when she brought her boyfriends around, she would tell me I was being mean to them.

"Speaking of boyfriends, any right now?"

"No, just concentrating on graduating right now."

I am happy to hear that. I can't scare any boyfriends she has at school, she is too far away.

Another knock at the door gets me up from the couch, this would be Charliee. I walk over, opening it, and Levi comes right in like he owns the place.

"Hey, beautiful, come on in."

I give her a kiss as she walks by.

"Samantha, long time no see."

Sam gets up from the couch and comes and hugs Charliee. I'm happy these two get along.

"Hey, I just stopped by to spend a few minutes with my brother before I headed back tomorrow."

"Are you going to join us for dinner?" Charliee asks as she sets her bag down by the couch.

"I told her I had plenty, but she turned down my invitation."

"He did ask, and I did turn him down. Mom wants me to have dinner tonight with her and dad before I leave tomorrow. Sometimes I swear she acts like I live millions of miles away and I'm never coming home."

"Well, thank you for last night, it was great having some girl time." Charliee gives her another hug.

"Are you complaining that I'm taking you away from all your girl time?" I ask, acting offended.

Both girls ignore me of course. Samantha gives me a hug and then heads for the door.

"Anytime you need to chat, Charliee, just text me. All I'm really doing these days is studying. If my brother gets out of line, just let me know."

"Ha-ha, have a safe trip back. Call me tomorrow and let me know when you reach your dorms, please. Love you."

"Will do, love you, too." She waves and then closes the door behind her.

I turn back to Charliee who is now sitting on the couch. "So, whatever she told you last night about me was a complete lie."

Laughing, she takes off her shoes and curls her legs up under her. "Believe it or not, we didn't even talk about you that much."

"What did you guys talk about then? Or is this that whole girl code thing and you can't tell me."

She starts playing with a little string on her pants, something is wrong.

"Charliee, what's wrong?"

"I think I'm just overreacting."

"Overreacting about what?"

She rolls her eyes, "Yesterday at school Jayden informed me that she was seeing someone."

I'm a little confused on where this story is going. "This is a bad thing?"

"No, not at all, only it's Cameron Tovaren."

All right, still not seeing what she can be overreacting about. Then the last name clicks in my head.

"Any relation to…"

"Yes, their oldest son. After Mr. and Mrs. Tovaren died, he came back to stay with his brother Jacob who attends our school."

"So what are you overreacting about? I'm still a little confused on that. Do you have a problem with her seeing him?"

"No, not at all, but he does have a problem with me, I guess."

"Why would he have a problem with you?"

She throws her hands up in the air. "This is why I think I'm overreacting. He doesn't, per se, have the problem with me as a person. More for the fact that I remind him of what happened to his parents."

Got it. Well at least now I'm not going to have to beat the guy for hating my girl.

"Charliee, you have said it yourself, you couldn't imagine what all those families were going through who lost loved ones. This guy might not want to deal with the whole situation right now. I'm sure he has a lot on his plate just taking care of his brother."

"That's exactly what Jayden says, and I really don't blame the guy. Honestly, I'm not sure if I'm ready, but not being around Jayden is killing me right now."

"Come here." I put my arm out and she crawls over into my lap.

"Just give him some time, he is dealing with a lot. Don't take it all personally. Everyone who was involved has had their world turned upside down. That's not something that rights itself overnight as you know."

She is tracing the word Faith that I have tattooed on my forearm. "You're right and I have told myself all of this a thousand times since yesterday. I think I'm more upset that I don't have my best friend right now."

I kiss her forehead when she looks up at me. "She isn't far. You still have her, just give it a little more time. Everything will work back out. In the meantime, I know talking girl stuff with your boyfriend is kind of defeating the purpose but I'm always here to listen if you need me."

She hooks her arm around my neck and pulls my head down to meet hers, kissing me. "Thank you."

"Anytime, now let's get up and eat, I'm sure it's all cold by now." I push her up, smacking her backside as she stands.

I'm happy that she feels comfortable talking to me and opening up. She is usually trying to convince everyone she has everything under control and that nothing bothers her. Sam was right, I do need to tell her exactly how I feel about her and I almost do tonight. Just so that she knows she has someone here. I think better of it because I don't want her thinking I am just saying it to make her feel better. It's like I told her, lives were turned upside down that night, hers included. She is still getting her life back up to right. When I tell her I love her, I want to make sure she has no doubt about my feelings.

CHAPTER
Twenty~Three

CHARLIEE

THE LAST FEW weeks have flown by. I knew I would only be back to work for a short time before school let out for the summer, but I never expected it to go this quickly. Now the hallways are crazy with excited kids to be out of school for a little while.

Life is finally just feeling normal again. Travis has basically moved in. I feel bad he pays rent for a place he is never at. I've stayed a couple nights at his house but he feels more comfortable at my place. He says I have the yard for Levi and my house is already equipped for all of my needs. I've learned to stop asking.

I look around the classroom to make sure everything is good for the summer. I grab my purse and with Levi following me from behind, leave my room until September. Before I leave I want to go say bye to Jayden. When I enter her classroom, I find she isn't alone. Cameron and Jacob are both in there. Jayden still hasn't convinced Cameron to get together with us yet. She and I have had a couple girl days out and from the conversations we have had, I know she has very strong feelings for him. She hasn't admitted to the love word yet but I see it all over her face when she talks about him. I'm happy for her, she usually doesn't settle for one guy. The only thing I'm worried about is the timing for the two of them.

"I'm sorry, I didn't know you had people in here with you. I was finished in my room and just wanted to say bye before I headed home. I will text you later."

I am heading out the door when a hand on my arm stops me. When I look, it is Jacob.

"Miss. Brooksman, I would like you to meet my brother," he signs.

Jacob surprised me about a week ago when he came to my classroom asking to talk to me. I never thought he would ask me about that night, but I think he needed a little peace of mind. Jayden has told me he still struggles, he never went back to the track team this year and from what she was saying, he is giving his brother one hell of a hard time. However, when he approached me, I only saw a sad boy who wanted to talk, so we talked. It was hard answering some of his questions. Some I just didn't know or remember, others because it stirred a lot of emotions up in me.

I look over at Cameron, I see the anger in his eyes, but beyond that I see fear and sadness. That is the one thing that keeps me from leaving.

"Jacob, what are you doing?" Cameron signs to his brother.

Jacob walks over to his older brother. They look so much alike and stand about the same height.

"You need this, trust me. If you are that stubborn to admit it then do it for Jayden," Jacob signs back.

I don't think I've ever been more proud of a student than I am at this moment. I look at Jayden and see complete shock on her face as she stares at Jacob. She had told me she didn't think Jacob liked her much. I told her she was probably wrong and from what just happened, I do believe I was right.

Screw it, Cameron may not want to talk to me, but I'm not leaving without introducing myself. I walk over and hold out my hand.

"Hello, Cameron, it's nice to finally meet you. I'm Charliee."

I wait, but never pull back my hand. That night happened and there is nothing any of us can do about it. Do I wish I wasn't there? Every day! I have scars inside and out that will remind me of that night for the rest of my life. However, if he wants to be a part of my friend's life, we are a package deal. He needs to accept that.

Finally, he takes my hand. "Charliee, it's nice to meet you."

Relief washes over Jayden's face and Jacob smiles.

"I'll say this now and not bring it up again. If you ever want to ask questions or anything, I'm more than happy to answer what I can. I'm sorry for your loss, your parents were great people. You are becoming a very important person to my best friend over there," I point over at Jayden. "Which means you need to realize I'm going to be around."

Everyone laughs, including Cameron, who seems to relax a little.

"Well, Jacob just asked to stay the night at a buddy's house, so if you aren't already busy tonight, maybe we can all get together. Jayden has been bugging me for weeks."

Well, that isn't something I was expecting. I look over at Jayden and she is smiling from ear to ear. I'm relieved that Travis has today off. I would have hated to tell them thank you but maybe another day.

"Tonight would be great. I'm going to go let Travis know. Jayden, I'll text you in a while and we will plan something."

I don't wait for anyone to say anything back, I turn and walk out, leaving the three of them alone.

As I am walking to my Jeep, I text Travis about the extra company that is adding to our date night. I am pretty sure he won't mind that they are coming. It is dinner and a relaxing evening on the beach with a bonfire. I'm sure his idea was for some romantic time but we are changing it to some fun friend time.

My phone goes off as I get into the car.

**So you are telling me no cuddling on the beach and whispering sweet nothings in your ear, while I try to convince you to get naked with me?

A sad face follows that text.

**You can whisper all you want in my ear, it won't affect me at all.

I laugh, he is caught. I wish I could be there to see his face when he realizes what he just said.

**Damn!!!!

Is all the next text says with a little embarrassed face next to it. Another text from him follows quickly after.

**As long as I get you naked at some point tonight I'm good with everything else.

That's my man, only concerned about us being naked. I smile to myself. I knew he wouldn't mind, he knows how bummed I've been over this whole thing.

**Deal! I'll see you around five.

**Can't wait.

I quickly send a text to Jayden with the plans for tonight, then head home to get ready myself.

DINNER WENT GREAT. Cameron seemed relaxed. I haven't seen Jayden this giddy over a guy ever. It is kind of cute. If I wasn't sure before, I definitely know for sure tonight, she is falling hard and fast for this guy.

It is a perfect night to sit out on the beach. I even stopped by the store on the way home and grabbed stuff to make s'mores, which I think both men are more excited over than me.

We have been here an hour or so when I notice a change in Cameron, something seems to send his mood in a spiral downward. He doesn't seem mad, just very quiet while he just stares into the fire.

Travis is sitting in a chair as close as he can up against mine, my hand in his. Cameron looks up at me and signs. "Can you tell me anything about that night and my parents?"

Jayden's surprised eyes shoot from Cameron to me. Travis's hand tightens around mine. I actually look over at Travis in surprise, Cameron had signed the question, not spoken it at all.

"I picked up on enough to know what he asked. I've been studying," Travis answers my questioning look.

One of the things I love about Travis is he can make me smile. He always knows how to calm my nerves. Just a little comment about him studying is all that was needed.

"I'm sorry, that was rude of me. I wasn't sure if I could find actual words to ask so I signed them, forgetting that not everyone probably signs," Cameron explains.

Travis waves it off. "Don't worry about it. I started learning the language because all of her family and Jayden over there would only sign when they didn't want me to know something."

"Well, that's good to know now. Note to self, Travis knows signing," Jayden chimes in.

I don't know why she acts like she didn't already know this, but seeing Travis smile all proud of himself is worth her acting like she didn't already know.

"That's right, no more talking about me right in front of my face."

The easiness between all of us is nice. I look at Cameron and bring everything back to a serious note.

"I will tell you the same thing I told Jacob when he came to about a week ago and asked about it. There isn't much I can tell you that the police report doesn't already cover, but I will tell you what I can. I want to help you guys find some peace."

Cameron is shocked. "Jacob talked to you?"

I understand his surprise. "Trust me, I was just as surprised as you are now."

My heart breaks watching the play of emotions across Cameron's face. I won't cry, he doesn't need that right now. I squeeze Travis's hand a little tighter, he is my support, my rock.

"I don't even know what to ask really."

"Cameron, I was waiting for my dinner when I saw your parents. They passed me when they were following the hostess to be seated. I only got to say hello."

He looks down at his hands that are holding tightly onto one of Jayden's. When he looks back up, my chest feels like it is going to explode from the pain. Tears stream down both of his cheeks. "Did they go fast, or did they suffer?"

Gasping, I feel like I had all the air kicked out of my lungs. My back burns and my ribs throb, along with my shoulder and arm. It is like feeling everything all over. Tears can't be held back any longer. I take a couple deep breaths.

"I have no memory of that night past the part where I said hello to your parents. I was walking out the front door when the explosion happened. I remember lots of heat. If I had to say if they suffered or not, I would have to say I pray every day that they didn't."

I look over at Travis, pleading with him to say something. What I want him to say, I have no idea.

"Cameron, I was one of the firefighters who responded that night. I don't believe your parents suffered that night. In the area of the dining room, we found no survivors."

Cameron sits there staring at the fire for quite some time. No one says anything. Everyone seems to be in their own mind.

"I'm sorry for ruining the evening, we were having a great time." Cameron won't look at anyone, his eyes just stay focused on the fire as he speaks.

"I know I can't sit here and say I know what you are going through, Cameron. None of us can, but please don't ever apologize for wanting to talk about that night or your parents. I've learned that talking has helped me heal. It's hard sometimes. You wonder if you want to know the answer to certain questions but keeping it all bundled up will only hurt you and those around you."

I look at Travis, he has been my go to person. No one, not even Jayden, knows everything that I've gone through since that night. I needed to be strong for my family and her. To convince them I was all right. I wouldn't have been able to do that without having Travis to talk to.

"I know what it's like to have to put the smile on your face and be strong around the people you love to assure them everything is all right. You are the one who went through it all, yet you need to make sure the people around you are healing."

I squeeze Travis's hand to let him know this next part is because he is in my life.

"Find that one person, be it Jayden, an old friend, whoever and talk to them. Believe me when I tell you it will help you heal and accept and it will help those around you heal."

Cameron surprises me when he looks over at me with a small smile. "You are one tough woman, Charliee. Jayden has told me about how they found you and your injuries."

What do you say to that? All the quick witted responses don't sound right when you are speaking to someone who lost a lot that night. I choose to just smile.

Jayden stands up and reaches down for Cameron's hand. "I'm ready to go if you are?"

Cameron's expression relaxes a little. I'm pretty sure he is more than happy to call it a night.

Jayden comes over and gives both of us a hug. "Thank you for the evening. Cameron and I were talking about going the fair they have going on down the beach in a couple of days. You guys want to join us?"

I look over at Travis with a questioning look.

"I have tomorrow and Monday off," he confirms.

"Monday it is then. I'll text you later, Charliee, and we'll figure out all the details."

Cameron surprises me when after he shakes Travis's hand, he gives me a hug. "Thank you. Just for the record, I'm happy to have finally met you. I'm sorry it took me so long."

I feel the tears threatening to show up again. "Don't apologize, I understand. I'm sorry I couldn't be more help with answering the questions you had."

"Trust me, Charliee, you helped me out a lot tonight."

Watching the two of them walk away causes a flashback of watching Mr. and Mrs. Tovaren walking away to their seat that night. Hand in hand, they were smiling and laughing with each other. A sob sticks in my throat, strong arms wrap around me from behind. I turn to Travis and bury my face into his chest. His arms tighten around me. I inhale his scent and my body starts to calm. When I look back up, he wipes the tears from my cheeks.

"You know, Cameron's right, you are a very tough woman."

I laugh. "Travis, all I have been doing lately is crying."

"Charliee, tears are not a sign of weakness. They are a sign of compassion, healing, and love. Sometimes heartache or disappointment, but never a sign of weakness. Especially with someone like you. From the moment that night when you woke up only worrying about Levi, to tonight with Cameron, I have seen strength pouring out of you. You don't back down, no matter what it's doing to you inside."

"This coming from a man who runs into burning buildings for a career, and have you seen these arms?" I try to tease to lighten the mood.

"My arms are a physical strength, anyone who works hard enough can have that kind of strength. You have a mental strength. You can't build that in a gym, Charliee."

CHAPTER
Twenty-Four

TRAVIS

CHARLIEE HEADS straight for the shower when we get back to her place. Unfortunately Trey, our engineer at the station, had called me just as we pulled up to the house. The more I try to speed up and end the conversation so that I can go and join her, the more he talks. I am starting to think he is doing it on purpose.

I have just thrown my shirt onto the chair in her room when she walks out of the bathroom with only a towel on.

"I was hoping you would join me." She walks right into my arms, the towel dropping to the floor.

"Sorry, Trey wouldn't let me off the phone." Leaning down, I capture her mouth.

Something is trying to nudge in between our legs. I look down, Charliee is laughing, and there sits Levi.

"What do you want?"

Charliee pulls out of my arms, grabs my shirt that I just dropped onto the chair and starts for the door. "Come on, boy, I'll go feed you."

She looks over her shoulder before leaving the room. "Hurry up and take a shower. I'll be right back."

Charliee is just coming back into the room when I come out from my shower. "That was quick."

"I'm a firefighter. The tones always go off the second you get into a shower, we learn to take them fast."

She looks very inviting standing there in my black button-up shirt, sleeves rolled up, the shirt completely unbuttoned. It hangs to just about her knees. Just a hint of her amazing body peeks out teasingly from the folds of the shirt.

"I'm never going to be able to wear that shirt again without picturing you standing there right now."

"I'm hoping that's a good thing."

Nodding, I walk over to her, slipping one hand into the shirt and around her waist, the other to the back of her head, burying my hand in her hair. I pull her hair enough to tilt her head back and devour her lips. Her arms go up and around my shoulders, her fingernails biting into my shoulder blades. Her lips trail from my mouth, down my chin to my neck where she nibbles slightly. One hand comes over my shoulder and rests above my heart. I love it when her hand rests there, I love her.

I bring my hand up and grab hers. I open her hand so that her palm is flat against mine. She looks up, her eyes questioning me. My eyes never leave hers as I push her middle and ring finger down against her palm and mimick the same with my hand. I press our hands together, both signing "I love you." One hand against the other, up against my chest right above my heart.

I hold my breath as I watch emotions change in her eyes. First they question what I am doing. Then they pop open with surprise when she figures out what I am telling her. Last they moisten up with tears and a smile. I may not know the whole language yet but I wanted her to know, that beat she was always looking for when she placed her hand against my chest was created from the love I have for her.

"That night when we pulled up to the devastation of that bombing, I instantly thought it was going to be the worst night ever. The loss of lives was everywhere, but then I uncovered my world, I uncovered you, Charliee. I think I started falling in love with you from that moment."

Tears stream down her cheeks, but she is smiling. "That night was the worst night of my life. I remember waking up the next day and the pain my body was in. The pain my heart felt when I learned of the lives lost. You walked into my room, the pain was still there, but it faded. I instantly felt a sense of security, strength. I have made sure to be independent, take care of myself. A lot of people treat you differently when they find out you are missing something like my hearing, but you never did and never have."

She looks down at our hands. "You have always intertwined our two worlds."

She looks back up, her eyes sparkling from her tears. "I love you, too, Travis."

I watch as she takes a step back and removes my shirt that she is wearing, now proudly standing in front of me completely naked. Her hand reaches out, grabbing the towel I have wrapped around my waist. She pulls on it and it easily comes free of my body. She just lets it drop to the floor.

Her hand comes up in the "I love you" sign again, I place mine to hers. "You know, most women want mushy words when a guy tells them he loves her."

She smiles. "You gave me the mushy words, but you created a way I understand perfectly to actually say the words. My heart fell a little deeper in love with you for that."

I kiss the tips of her fingers. "So is this our thing now?"

She only nods. Her hand leaves mine to join the other one behind my neck. One hand slides up into my hair and she pulls my head down to hers, our lips meeting. She pushes against my body, having me walk backwards. The bed connects with the backs of my legs, I sit down, and she straddles my lap. She is hot against me, causing me to harden more, which presses my tip right against her wet, heated opening. Her body is begging for mine. She has all the control right now, she can have me in her whenever she wants.

Her lips part from mine. When I open my eyes, perfectly rounded breasts greet me. I run my tongue around one nipple and then the other. I hear her soft moan. I bring my hands from her hips to cup under each of her breasts, pushing them up. She watches me as I run my tongue across each nipple a couple more times. I nibble on one, she takes in a sharp breath. Her eyes slant in a warning look. Her hips rotate just slightly in a circular motion, teasing me. I move to her other breast, repeating the same action only a little harder. Her hips rotate a little faster. I'm not even in her yet and I'm not sure how much longer I can hold out with her moving like this.

I suck her breast into my mouth, her hips press down onto me taking me a little further inside of her. Her hands are in my hair pressing my face to her chest. I suck a little harder, she moans and takes me a little more. I twirl my tongue around her nipple, she rotates her hips. I pinch her other nipple between two fingers, her body jumps slightly. I need to be in her, I need to feel her around me. I bring my one hand down and circle her waist. My other one is still on her breast. All at once I pinch her nipple and roll it between my thumb and finger, suck her breast hard in my mouth and pull her hips down, entering her completely.

My name fills the room. She is tight around me, I need her to move. I pull away from her breast, my hand leaves her nipple and I grab the back of her head as I bring her mouth down to mine. She nibbles on my bottom lip and I almost lose it right then. I pull my hand out of her hair and down to her waist. I pull her hips back and then toward me again. I hear myself moan. A couple more times and she takes over the rhythm. I'm more than happy to let her. Every time she pulls me into her, she slightly circles her hips. She's close, her movements are becoming faster. Her head is tilted back, causing her hair to hit my legs. I take a handful of it and pull slightly, she whimpers and quickens her movements. I tug just a little more and she shatters around me. Finally, I can allow my own release and we hold onto each other tightly, our breathing becoming one.

WAKING UP THE NEXT MORNING, I find myself alone in bed. I don't hear the shower running. I grab my phone off the table next to me, it's almost nine. Levi I'm sure has woken up Charliee to let him out. Climbing out of bed I find my jeans, slip them on, but notice my shirt is nowhere to be found. I only need one guess to figure where it may be. I left my bag in the truck last night with my extra clothes in it. Maybe I should just talk to Charliee about leaving a few things here.

Walking down the hall, she isn't in the kitchen. I round the corner and find her sitting on the couch, a glass of juice in her hand, and she looks to be deep in thought. She looks up when I walk over to her.

"Good morning."

I bend down and kiss her, then sit down next to her. "Good morning. Everything all right?"

Nodding, she takes a drink of her juice. "Levi wanted out. Once I was up, I started thinking. I didn't want to bother you so I just came in here."

"You did look pretty deep in thought when I came around the corner, what's going on?"

She twirls the juice around in her glass for a moment. Now I am curious. I rub her knee, bringing her eyes up to me. "What's going on in that mind of yours?"

She glances down at my naked chest and points at it. "I was thinking maybe you should have your clothes here. It seems that you are always missing your shirt."

Laughing, I nod in agreement. "Yeah, my girlfriend has a thing for my shirts, I believe she wears them more than I do. I personally think she just likes to have me shirtless so that she can check out my pecks and arms."

She laughs. "That she does."

Her mood goes back to serious. "What I mean is, I'm thinking since you are here more than at your place, maybe you should just make this your place, too."

I try not to look too shocked, but I'm sure it is written all over my face. She is right, I do spend more time here than at my place. I hate not sleeping next to her at night. I love waking up and having her to say good bye to before I go to work. I feel comfortable here. My place has become more of just a storage location the last month or so.

"You won't hurt my feelings if you think it's all too fast and we should wait a little longer. I just know you spend most nights here anyway. At least you would have other shirts here when I'm wearing one. Although I do enjoy you walking around shirtless."

"If we are being honest, I like it when you wear my shirts."

I notice she only looks at me long enough for me to talk, and then she looks anywhere but at me. She is nervous. She has no idea what I will say to her proposal. She is putting herself out there with our relationship and is nervous to see if I am on the same page as she is.

I take the glass out of her hand and place it onto the coffee table. I trap her between my arms and body, pushing her up against the arm of the couch. Our faces are only inches apart. She has no choice but to look at me.

"Charliee, I love you. I love waking up with you. Going to bed with you. Hearing about your day when you get home from work, or just having you to hold when I've had a crazy shift at work."

I lean forward and gently kiss her, because I can no longer be this close and not have her lips. "If you are absolutely sure about wanting me to move in here, then I'm one hundred percent all right with it."

The shock in her eyes tells me she is surprised I said yes. "Are you sure you want this? You can change your mind, it would only hurt my feelings a little."

She runs her hand over my cheek and then up into my hair. "I like having you here, it feels empty when you aren't here. You have wiggled your way into my life and I like it."

My hand snakes up her shirt. "Does this mean I can have your body anytime I want it?" I tease with her.

"When have you not had it anytime you wanted it?"

She pops the button of my jeans and pushes them down as far as her arms can reach. I pull my shirt up over her head, stand up and finish removing my pants. Grabbing her by the hips, I lay her out under me on the couch.

"When would you like me to move in?"

"When can you get packed by?"

WE ALMOST CANCELLED COMING to the fair with Cameron and Jayden because of us trying to get me moved over to her house. Now that we are here and I see how relaxed Charliee is, I'm glad we came. She and Jayden are walking in front of Cameron and me, laughing and signing. Levi is walking alongside Charliee, his eyes going back and forth. I have never seen him in a large crowd with her, he is on high alert.

"Those two, I have a feeling, could be trouble together." Cameron points at the ladies.

"I hate to tell you this, but I think Jayden is the leader of that pack. She is a spit fire."

"That she is," Cameron agrees with me.

Jayden turns around. "Boys, we are in need of funnel cake, then a ride on the Ferris Wheel."

Charliee just walks alongside of her shaking her head and laughing.

When we join the girls in line for a funnel cake, I stand behind Charliee, wrapping my arms around her. She looks up over her shoulder at me.

"I'm glad we decided to come."

I gave her a small kiss. "Me, too."

Levi begins to growl. Cameron, Jayden and I all look down at him.

"What's going on?" Charliee looks between the three of us and when she notices our attention is on Levi, she looks down at him.

He isn't trying to move away, he just stands there, ears pinned back, growling into a crowd of people sitting down by the funnel cake cart. I look around but I don't see anything unusual.

People are starting to become nervous around us with a growling dog. "Levi, enough. Nothing's there, boy."

He stops growling but he continues to look at something in the crowd. Charliee pats his head, but when she looks up at me she has worry in her eyes.

"Don't worry, he is probably just nervous around so many people," I try to reassure her.

"Travis, Levi doesn't get nervous, he is trained to not be jumpy."

I know this, I just don't want her to stop having fun. I look around once more, but still don't see anything that alerts me to something being wrong. Finally, Levi's ears come back up and he sits down next to Charliee's leg.

"See, he's fine. Something probably just spooked him and he reacted."

Charliee is still not completely convinced, I can tell by the look in her eyes, but Jayden pulls her attention back to her because it is our turn to order.

After funnel cakes and a ride on the Ferris Wheel, I realize everyone has calmed back down. Levi hasn't growled anymore and I am now convinced he just had something spook him. As we come off the ride that spins you around real fast and threatens to bring up all the food you just ate, Charliee points to my right.

"That's Bryce."

I look over where she is pointing and sure enough, there is one of the brothers. I have no idea how she knows which one from this distance. I can barely tell them apart when they are together and up close.

"Looks like he is here with a girl, do you know who that is?" Jayden asks Charliee.

"Nope, but I think we need to go and find out." Charliee smiles over at Jayden, then pulls me along with her to where her brother stands at one of the ball toss games.

When we all walk up, you can tell Bryce is surprised and maybe a little nervous about seeing all of us.

Charliee walks over and gives her brother a hug. "Hey, I didn't know you were coming tonight."

She turns her attention to the woman standing next to Bryce. "Hi, I'm Charliee, Bryce's sister."

The two of them shake hands. "I'm Darryn. This is my daughter, Kendall."

Charliee bends down and waves at the little girl in the stroller, she looks to be a couple years old or so.

"That's Travis, Charliee's boyfriend. Jayden, her best friend." Bryce starts making the introductions but when he gets to Cameron, he doesn't know who he is.

"I'm Cameron." He extends his hand out to Bryce and then Darryn.

"It's nice to meet you guys." Darryn smiles.

"So, how did you guys meet?" Charliee doesn't beat around the bush. Of course her brothers have thrived on giving us a hard time, I think she is just giving a little payback.

I don't miss the uncertain look that Darryn gives Bryce. He clears his throat.

"We actually met the night of the explosion. Darryn was the paramedic who took care of you, Charliee."

I thought she looked familiar. I've probably been on a lot of calls with her. Everyone always looks different when they aren't in uniform.

Charliee's smile falls a little, but she quickly recovers it. "Well then, I guess I should be thanking you."

"Not at all. I'm just happy to know you have fully recovered."

"Everyone here had a part in that."

Just as Charliee stands back up from talking to the little girl, Levi lunges, knocking her off balance and onto the ground. She pulls back hard and yells at him.

"Levi, what's your problem? Sit!"

I grab her hand and help her back to her feet. Levi isn't backing down. He isn't just growling this time, he is barking.

"What's wrong with him? He never acts like this." Bryce comes over to Levi.

I pull the leash out of Charliee's hands, she is having a hard time holding him. "He did this earlier, but I just brushed it off thinking something spooked him."

"Oh my God."

Everyone looks over at Charliee. All the color has drained out of her face.

Jayden comes up to stand next to her. "Charliee, what's wrong?"

She doesn't say anything, but her body begins to shake. I shove the leash into Bryce's hands and quickly go to her. "Charliee, talk to us."

She points across the way, over by one of the children's rides. "That's the guy from the restaurant, the one who ran into me outside. He is standing there in the blue jeans and plaid shirt, he's wearing a backpack."

We all look in the direction Charliee is pointing. Levi's barking must have caught the guy's attention. The second he spots all of us looking at him, he takes off running.

Bryce gives Jayden Levi's leash. "Call 911, let them know what's going on. You guys, get out of here now." He starts running in the direction the suspect went.

"Cameron, take the ladies and head back to the cars. I'm going after him with Bryce."

Charliee clings onto me. "Please, Travis, don't. What if there is another bomb in that bag?"

"Charliee, I'm not going to let your brother go after him alone."

"I'm going as well. That bastard is responsible for my parents' deaths."

Well, I can't argue that with the man, if anything he has the right to be there.

"You three, get that little one out of here and we will meet you at the car."

Jayden is already on the phone with the police. Charliee isn't trying to stop me. Cameron and I take off after Bryce.

WE SEARCHED for a couple hours but we never found the guy Charliee had seen. The fair had been evacuated, police were every-where, and search dogs had been brought in. No bombs were found, thank goodness. Everyone was just assuming that him getting scared and running after we recognized him stopped his plans to set one if that was what he was there for.

Cameron and I head back to where we parked since that was where we told the girls to go. As we walk up, we can see Jayden and Charliee sitting on the tail gate of my truck. Levi is laying down in the bed. Both of them jump down and run toward us when they see us.

Charliee tightly wraps herself around me. I just stand there and hold her for a minute. She looks up at me, worry in her eyes. "Where's Bryce?"

"He had to stay back, he's fine though."

"Did you guys catch him?" Jayden asks.

Both Cameron and I shake our heads no. "Where's Darryn? Bryce wanted to make sure her and the little one got home."

Charliee pulls her phone out of her pocket. "She didn't want to chance anything happening with Kendall here, so she took her home already. I had her text me when they got there. I'll send him a text and let him know."

"Well, there is nothing else we can do here. We should all head home as well," Cameron suggests.

Jayden and Charliee hug, promising to text each other tomorrow. I shake Cameron's hand, then hold the door open for Levi to jump in. Charliee climbs in after him.

When we pull up at the house, I look over and find Charliee asleep. I brush a piece of hair away from her face. I wish we would have caught the guy tonight. I saw the fear in her eyes today when she realized who he was. I know tomorrow she will play it off that she is all good, just another new day, but I know this is going to bother her now that she knows he is actually still out there. Who wouldn't be frightened by that? I will admit that I am.

Levi looks up at me, wondering why we are just sitting here. "You did well tonight, boy." I scratch his head.

Definite lesson learned today for me. If Levi is reacting, there is something to be concerned about.

I jump out of the truck and round over to Charliee's side. Opening the door, I reach over her and unbuckle her seat belt.

"Are you going to throw me over your shoulder and carry me in? If you're thinking about it, I think I would prefer to walk."

Her eyes are half open, that's my girl. No matter what's going on around her, she never loses her sense of humor.

"Make you a deal. If you can stay awake long enough to hold the keys and open the door when we get to it then I'll carry you in the right way."

She smiles and holds her hand out for the keys. I place them in her palm. "I love you."

"I love you, too."

CHAPTER
Twenty~Five

Charliee

I HAVE JUST FINISHED CLEANING the kitchen when the lights begin to flash and Levi comes running in. Someone is at the door. Opening it, I am surprised to see Jayden standing there.

"Since when do you ring the doorbell and not just walk in?"

"Since you decided to get a roommate. I'm trying to be considerate."

Having Travis move in did definitely take a little adjusting. I move aside to let her in.

"Is he home today? I didn't see his truck."

Closing the door behind her, I start following her thinking she is going to sit down. Nope, instead she starts walking down the hall.

"No, he's at work today. May I ask what you are looking for?"

She opens the door to one spare room and then my office.

"I'm checking out the new look to the house. Wondering how much room you gave him and all of his stuff. Nothing up front has changed except the large television."

Travis has been here for a few weeks now and we have managed to go through his stuff and mine to figure out what we needed and didn't.

"Bryan from the station had just moved into his own place and actually needed a lot of what we were going to get rid of, so Travis worked with him on everything."

I follow her back into the living room and sit down with her on the couch.

"So how are things going with having Travis here? I mean, I know you aren't feeling crowded yet because I haven't heard much from you the last few weeks."

What is she talking about? Every time I did text her, she was doing something with Cameron.

"It's been good. Every day he is home all we do is try and finish up around here. When he is at work, I'm still trying to finish the house. All I can say is I'm all right with never moving, it's too much work. I have found stuff that I had completely forgotten that I had. I'm not the only one busy. The last couple times I've asked what you were up to, you had already made plans with Cameron. I'm thinking everything is going good with you two."

Her eyes seem a little sad when I mention Cameron's name and I notice she starts playing with a spot on her jeans.

"Jayden, what's going on? Are things not working out?"

Shrugging, she throws her hands up in the air. "I don't know. One minute we are great, the next we are fighting."

"Are you guys still fighting over Jacob?"

"No, not really since school got out. Actually, Jacob has come and talked to me a few times. Since the last day of school when you were there, he seems to be opening up more around me. Truthfully, I think he likes having someone to talk to, and Cameron isn't that someone. He gets mad anytime I bring up his parents or Jacob needing to talk to him."

"You love him, don't you?"

A sad smile forms on her lips. "Is it that obvious?"

"I can see it, but then again that's part of my job description as the best friend."

She points toward the kitchen. "I hear your phone vibrating somewhere that way."

"Thanks." I go and grab it off the kitchen table and see that I have a text from Bryce.

"Do you have any plans for today?"

Jayden shakes her head.

"Do you want to go with me down to the station? Bryce has asked me to come down."

"Sure, I'll go with you. Did he say why they want you to come down?"

I shake my head no. The last time was to watch the video. *Maybe they found the guy,* I think to myself. We haven't heard much since that day at the fair. I've asked a couple of times but all they would say was they were working on it.

I send a quick text to Travis, letting him know I am going to the police station and that Jayden is going with me. Then I tell him I will stop by after we are done and let him know what is going on.

DERRICK AND BRYCE are waiting at the front desk when we walk in. I give them both a hug.

"What's going on, did you catch the guy?"

"No, but we think we may have a little more to go on," Derrick answers.

"Unfortunately, I never got a good look at the guy that night at the fair. However, we did finally get in touch with an old manager from the movie theater that was able to help us out a lot," Bryce starts to fill us in.

Jayden and I follow the guys down the hall and into a small room. After I sit down, Bryce hands me a picture. I instantly recognize the face.

I look up at my brothers. "This is him. This is the guy from the restaurant and the one I saw at the fair."

"Are you sure?" Bryce asks.

I look back down at the picture. "I'm very sure. Who is he?"

Derrick sits down on the corner of the table and points at the picture. "His name is Steven Finerston. He was actually an employee of both places. It's been a few years, though, since he has worked at either. That's one of the reasons it took someone so long to recognize him. We had to actually start getting a hold of past managers and employees." He makes sure to sign as he speaks, making sure I get everything he is telling me.

Movement from next to me catches my attention. Jayden is signing. "Do you guys have any idea why he would do any of this?"

I look back as Bryce starts to answer. "All we know is he was let go from both of the jobs, so we are thinking disgruntled employee."

"So do you know where to find him?" Jayden continues to ask the questions.

Derrick shakes his head. "All the addresses we have are old ones. We haven't been able to locate where he is currently staying."

I stare down at the picture. He doesn't look like he is very old, maybe early thirties at the oldest. What could go through someone's head to convince them to blow places up and kill innocent people?

"So most likely at the fair he was setting something else up, and since we didn't catch him then, you guys just have to wait around and see what he blows up next," I state matter-of-factly. I know the police are doing what they can, but how the hell does one guy hide so well, but yet still manages to get to places to blow them up? He is literally walking past multitudes of people and no one suspects him. He could be anywhere.

"Charliee, we aren't going to stop until we find this guy," Bryce tries to reassure me.

"But in the meantime, we have to wait and see how many die next."

Standing up, I let the picture drop to the floor. I am ready to leave. I don't want to look at this guy's face any longer. Here is a man who is mad at some past employers and is taking it out on everyone else.

"Do you need anything else from me?" I ask.

They both shake their heads no. Derrick comes over and kisses my forehead. "Charliee, we aren't going to let him get away with what he has done."

"Derrick, my injuries are so minor compared to the eighteen families who lost loved ones, and all those that may be taken. He needs to be stopped before he takes more."

Bryce gives me a tight hug. Over his shoulder, Derrick signs, "We'll get him."

ON THE WAY out of the station, I text Travis and let him know I am finished.

"Hey, you want to grab some lunch?" Jayden signs as she rounds to the passenger side of my Jeep.

I check my phone, Travis hasn't texted back yet, they may be out on a call. "Sure, we can grab something. Where were you thinking?"

"How about that hamburger place down the street?"

As I pull out of the parking lot, my phone vibrates. I pull it out of my pocket and hand it to Jayden. "Can you see who texted me, please?"

"It's Travis," she signs.

"Can you see what he says for me, please?"

She signs to me again. "He is back at the station. Stop by and tell him what happened."

"Can you text him back? Tell him that we are grabbing lunch first and then we will stop by."

We pull into the parking lot and Jayden hands my phone back to me with a huge smile on her face. I start to ask her what she is up to when my phone goes off with another text from Travis.

**I'll be honest I'm smiling from ear to ear and would be more than happy to help you fulfill that fantasy, but I'm a little surprised.

What is he talking about? I scroll up to my, or should I say Jayden's, last text messages.

**I can't wait to see you, strip you out of that uniform that drives me crazy with need when I see you in it, and have my way with you on top of the fire truck.

"Jayden!" I yell at her.

She looks over at me with the innocence of the devil.

"Really? That's what popped in your head when I asked you to text him we would stop by after lunch?"

She throws her hands up in a surrender fashion. "I was helping you out with dessert. Plus, your text sounded boring. I just spiced it up a little."

She turns and walks away, leaving me standing there in the parking lot. I quickly text Travis back.

**Jayden. Do I need to say more?

**Well dammit, I was looking forward to it.

**Sorry it just all sounds a little too movie like. The whole sex on the engine. We need to come up with something a little more original.

I start to follow Jayden into the diner when another text comes through.

**I like the way that sounds. Enjoy lunch see you in a bit. Love you.

**Love you too.

I walk in and find Jayden already sitting at a table looking at a menu. As I walk up, she looks over the top of it at me. "So are you going to make good of your text promise?"

I love her, I really do, but she is way out of control sometimes. "Just remember, payback's a bitch."

"You are no fun."

Smacking the menu that she is holding down onto the table, I glare at her. "You're going to find out how much fun I am. I will get you back."

She blows me a kiss and winks. "I bet he got excited."

WHEN WE PULL up to the station, the truck is just pulling out, lights flashing. I pull over to the side and wait for them to pass us. I see Travis in the window, he sign he will talk to me later and then I love you. I wave and watch as they drive down the street.

A strange feeling hits me in the stomach. I want to chase after them and stop them from going wherever it is they are headed.

Jayden grabs my arm. I look over at her. "What's wrong, Charliee?"

I shrug. I really can't explain it. When I look back down the street, the engine has disappeared around the corner.

I look back to Jayden. "Do you ever get a feeling like something isn't right?"

Jayden rolls her eyes at me. "Charliee, you are just freaking out. Between going to the station today and getting all worked up there and them rushing out of here, lights everywhere, your nerves are just going crazy."

She is probably right. My nerves have been kind of a mess since I was at the station.

"I have to admit, firefighters are already hot, but watching them rush out of here, lights flashing and hearing the sirens. It makes those guys even hotter."

I have to agree. I wouldn't ever admit this to Jayden, because she would never let me hear the end of it, but I could easily strip Travis down and have my way with him on top of the engine with the lights going.

A smack across my arm brings me back to reality. "What put that smile on your face?"

Damn, I am caught. "My firefighter."

"Just for the record, I'm slightly jealous of you over that."

"Jayden, Cameron may not be a firefighter but he is pretty good looking."

Just the mention of his name changes her mood, and not in a bad way. Her eyes take a wicked look to them. "He may be a little moody, but he is mine and the make-up sex we have is amazing."

"Do you always think about sex?"

"When it's good I do, yes." She wiggles her eyebrows.

Nothing, I have nothing else to say to her. I just put the Jeep in drive and head home.

I NOTICE the cop car in front of my house when I turn the corner. I look over at Jayden and she shrugs her shoulders. When I pull into the driveway, both of my brothers get out of the car. Something is wrong, I can see it all over both their faces.

Opening my door, Derrick quickly walks over, his hands flying. "Charliee, we were just about to text you to find out where you were."

I open the back door and let Levi out. "What are you guys doing here?"

Bryce is still back at the car. Derrick looks back at him, then back at me.

"Derrick, what the hell is going on? Why are you guys here?"

Derrick looks up at the sky and then back at me. "Charliee, there has been another bombing."

My heart sinks. Another one means more lives taken. I look at Jayden. "That must be where the guys were headed."

Wait, why aren't my brothers there? Bryce has come to stand next to Derrick now. I look between the two of them. I know these looks and they aren't good.

"There is more, isn't there? Why are you guys here telling me this? You could have texted me."

Derrick looks over at Bryce and then back at me. "Maybe we should go inside, Charliee."

Why do we need to go inside? "Where was it at, guys? What are you guys not telling me?"

"The explosion was at an abandoned building this time."

Oh, thank God for that. Wait, they are stalling. Now I'm just getting pissed. "Dammit, guys, what are you trying to tell me? Just say it already, please."

Derrick walks up to me and places a hand on each of my shoulders. "Charliee, when firefighters went in, a second bomb went off. Two guys from Travis's department are missing. Travis is one of them."

I can't breathe, and I want to puke. "Take me there."

I start for their patrol car, but am stopped by Derrick. "You can't go, we don't even know if it's safe, or if there is another bomb, Charliee."

"I don't care. You two drive us over there now, or I'll drive myself. Either way, I'm going. Travis needs me."

"Charliee, what are you going to do? The crew is doing everything they can to find them. The safest thing to do is stay here. They will let us know as soon as they know something."

"Fine, I'll take my own car."

I turn to head back to my Jeep, Levi right on my heels. Again, I am stopped, only this time by Jayden.

"Hon, what are you going to do there? Your brothers are right, you are safer here."

Jayden, too, really? Is she kidding me? "So you're telling me if that was Cameron out there, you would stay at home and wait for a call?"

She isn't fooling me at all. Nothing would keep her from going and she knows it.

"That's what I thought. Now, I'm going to ask one more time. Are you going to take me there, or am I going alone?" I look between both of my brothers waiting for one of them to decide. They need to make a decision and now!

Derrick and Bryce look at each other. "At least if she is with us, we can watch her," I read Bryce's lips.

"Mom and Dad are going to kill us." Derrick motions to the car. "Come on, let's go. But you need to promise us that you will stay with us."

I'm not promising something I don't know if I can keep. I go straight to the car, open the door and wait for Levi to jump in first. I look over at Jayden.

"I'm coming. Someone has to keep you from doing something stupid and you don't listen to your brothers."

WHEN WE PULL up to the scene, I notice right away all the commotion happening at what looks to be some kind of entrance. They look to be carrying a guy out. I try opening the door but being in the back seat, there are no handles.

"Let me out, hurry."

Bryce opens the door but blocks my path. "You need to promise me you aren't going to do anything stupid, Charliee."

I just stare up at him. Right now he isn't my favorite person. "Promise me, Charliee, or I'm shutting this door and locking you in this car."

I look past my brother and can see they are talking to the guy who they just pulled out. I'll promise him anything that he wants me to if it gets him to move.

"Fine, I promise! Now move!" I yell.

Bryce glares at me and I glare back. I start to get out and he moves out of my way. I run straight to where they are talking to the firefighter, praying it is Travis. The closer I get, the more I realize it isn't Travis, it is Randy. He is talking to the paramedics. That is a good sign, at least that gives me hope that Travis, even though still trapped, has a good chance of being all right as well. I am trying to read his lips but I can't. When I look over at the area they just pulled him out of, all I see are two firefighters talking on radios.

Levi is pacing next to me. He isn't leaving my side, but his eyes stay focused on the opening where everyone is.

Jayden appears at my side. She grabs my hand. "He's going to be all right."

Levi begins to pull on my arm. "Calm down, boy."

Nothing is happening now. No one is coming out or going in, but Levi is still trying to get in that direction.

I look over and see that Jayden's attention is somewhere else. I look down at Levi, he is almost pleading with me to follow him. I signal for him to go and we run over to the entrance, going right past the two men in the front. I believe they are too shocked to react until we are inside. When I look back, they are coming in after us.

Debris and pieces of building are everywhere. I fall once, tearing my jeans and into my knee, but I'm not stopping. Firefighters are pulling back large pieces of debris, Levi runs right past them.

Someone grabs my arm, stopping us. When I turn I find Bryan, the young kid who we just gave all of our stuff to for his new apartment. I think he is trying to tell me something but he has a bandana over his mouth so I have no idea what he is saying to me. "Bryan, I don't know what you are saying."

Levi is pulling my arm hard. I look down, he is trying to move forward, he is barking from what I can tell.

I look back at Bryan. "He is trying to show me something, please let me go."

He looks down at Levi and then back at me, pointing at my leg. I look down, my pants are torn completely open and I am bleeding pretty badly, but I don't care.

"Bryan, please, I'm fine. We need to find Travis."

He pulls the bandana away from his mouth. "I'm going to get into so much trouble for this, but lead the way."

I turn and let go of Levi's leash. He runs about fifteen feet from where the other guys are looking and starts pawing at the pile of building. I run over, my foot once again catching something, but this time when I go down my leg twists. My knee goes, but even through all the pain I can't stop.

I drag myself over to where Levi is. Bryan drops down next to me. "Charliee, you need to let us take you out, you're hurt pretty bad."

I shake my head no. I'm not leaving until we find him. "He found me, Bryan. I'm not leaving until we find him. Levi knows something, start pulling that stuff back."

Bryan runs over to where Levi is and starts pulling stuff back. He looks over his shoulder and yells something, waving his arm. I make my way there and that's when I see an arm. The rest of him is still covered. Levi is pawing as fast as he can. I grab Travis's hand and start yelling his name. His turnout jacket is ripped. *Please be alive.* I feel the tears now, he can't leave me. I sit there feeling helpless as I watch the guys pull large pieces of building off of him.

"Travis, you need to hold on, they are going to get you out." I hope I am talking loud enough, he needs to know I am here.

At first I think I imagined it, but then his hand moves again. I can't say anything, I can only stare as his fingers sign "I love you." I put my hand to his, mimicking the sign. He is alive.

Finally, the shock wearing off, I find my voice through the tears. "He's alive, hurry! He just moved his hand, we need to get him out!"

More firefighters join Bryan. Someone is trying to pull me away. I'm not leaving until Travis is out. I look over my shoulder to see Derrick. He looks pissed and I really don't care, but I see the worry in his eyes as well.

"Charliee, let them do their job. I need to get you out of here, your leg is really bad."

"No, I'm not leaving him, Derrick. He hears me and he knows I'm here." I turn back around, ignoring Derrick pulling on my arm.

They have uncovered most of him and only have his legs left to expose. He is in full gear, air mask and all. His eyes are closed but he told me he loved me, he is alive.

It feels like I am sitting here for hours, feeling helpless as I watch them pull piece after piece of the building off of him. Finally, they have all of him uncovered. The guys quickly grab him and start to carry him out. I try to stand to follow but my leg won't hold my weight. I scream when the pain shoots up my entire leg. Derrick lifts me up and carries me out. Once we clear the building, I see them working on Travis, but Derrick is carrying me away from him.

"Derrick, no, you need to take me over to Travis, please." I beg him but he isn't listening to me.

He ignores my pleas. He carries me over to one of the other ambulances and sits me down onto the gurney. Darryn comes over and starts talking to Derrick. I can't tell what he is saying to her, his back is to me. He turns back to me, he is pissed.

"Pay attention to what I'm saying to you." He is signing and I can tell by his facial expressions there is not going to be any arguing allowed.

"You will stay right here so that they can work on your leg. If you try and get up or give them any kind of trouble, I have given them full permission to tie you down, do you understand?"

I can't walk by myself even if I tried to, but he doesn't need to speak to me like I am a child. I just nod my head and watch as he walks away. I know they are mad at me, but he should understand why I did it.

Levi comes over and places his front paws up on the bed and sniffs my leg. "It's all right, boy, I'll be fine. You did good, boy. You found him."

"This isn't how I wanted to get to know you better, Charliee." Darryn says as she cuts my pants away from my knee.

"I had to go in there, Darryn. I had to find him."

I haven't seen Darryn since the night at the fair. I asked Bryce more about her but he hadn't said much, just that they had been out a couple times.

I look over at where they have Travis. I can't see much past all the people who are around him. They are pulling all of his gear off, but I can't tell if he is alert or not. I close my eyes and send out a silent prayer.

When I open my eyes, I see Jayden running in my direction. "What the hell were you thinking? If you weren't already hurt, I'd beat the shit out of you!"

She stands there looking down at me for a moment. Before I know it, she is laying across me hugging me. I hug her back.

"I'm all right, Jayden."

As she stands back up, she wipes the tears away from her eyes. I look back over at Travis, they are getting ready to load him up into the ambulance. I feel like I am miles away from him right now.

Looking around, I can't believe how many people are here. The media is all here, all trying to get the story out there first. One person catches my attention.

Realization smacks me like a ton of bricks. The bastard stayed and watched. I sit up real fast, throwing my legs over the side of the gurney. Darryn tries to stop me but too late, my leg bends and the pain is so bad, it almost causes me to pass out. I scream again.

Bryce is next to me in a second, trying to help Darryn lay me back down.

"Bryce, the bastard is here."

Bryce looks over his shoulder in the direction I am pointing. When he looks back at me, he has a puzzled expression on his face. "Who's here, Charliee? Who are you seeing?"

Looking past him, the guy is still standing there. "Bryce, he's here. He stayed and watched. Look at the guy standing next to the female reporter. He has on a dark blue sweatshirt. He's the one, Bryce."

Bryce turns around and scans the group of people. I see him bring his radio up but I can't tell what he is saying. He turns to Jayden, says something real fast to her and then heads in the direction of all the reporters. Derrick joins him. They don't run, I want to scream and tell them to hurry before the guy gets away again. This all has to stop, he needs to be stopped. I know what they are doing, they don't want to spook the guy.

I watch the guy, praying they get to him before he figures it out, but no such luck. He starts looking around all frantic, then turns and runs. Police officers come out of everywhere chasing after him, including my brothers.

I hate this, I feel so helpless. Travis is alone, my brothers are off after the man responsible for all of this and I am stuck here with my knee sliced wide open.

Bryan comes up to me. "Charliee, they are taking Travis to the hospital now. He is breathing but they have no idea of what injuries he has."

"I want to go with him."

"You need to get to the hospital yourself, Charliee. This knee is not good," Darryn jumps in as she starts to strap me down to the gurney.

I start to protest but Jayden stops me. "Charliee, you need to get your leg checked. I'll ride with Travis and keep you posted. I already called your parents, they are going to meet you at the hospital."

I don't have much of a choice. Travis is already loaded in the ambulance and Darryn and her partner are ready to load me up. I nod at Jayden. I know if I say anything, I will probably break down in tears. I should be with Travis, not Jayden.

SOMEONE TOUCHING my shoulder startles me awake. I hadn't even realized that I had fallen asleep. I was wheeled into Travis's room around midnight. That was when they finally brought him to the room from running all the tests and the x-rays. Both his parents and mine tried to convince me to go home and get some rest, but I wasn't leaving without him.

Bryce squats down next to me. "How are you doing?"

I am sitting in a chair next to Travis's bed in reach of him. I want to at least hold his hand. My leg has something like twenty-five stitches in it, I think. The meds they gave me when I got here kind of made me loopy so I'm not quite sure of everything they said. They went from just above the knee to the bottom and into my shin. I had split it completely open. I am also wearing a brace that runs the whole length of my leg, because the knee is fractured. They said they couldn't cast it with the stitches.

They had brought a recliner in for me to replace the regular chair that was in the room so that I could elevate it up.

Bryce isn't going to be like everyone and lecture me, which I am thankful for. I've had about enough of everyone scolding me like a child.

"I'm all right, a little sore. Derrick called Mom and Dad, he told them that you guys caught the guy."

He looks my leg over. Levi sits up and places his head in Bryce's lap. "We did, yes, thanks to you."

I see the worry etched across his forehead. "Hey, what's wrong?"

He sits down on the floor, Levi following him down and placing his head back in his lap. Bryce runs a hand from his head down his back. "Charliee, when we saw you run into that building, I know both of us stopped breathing. The night you were involved in the bombing and what you looked like under all the debris kept flashing in my head. We almost lost you that night. We could have lost you tonight. When we caught the guy tonight, they had to hold Derrick and I back. He is the reason we almost lost you, and we may very well lose Travis."

I look over at Travis. He hasn't even flinched. I need him to move or something. Some sign that he is going to be all right. I feel a tear roll down my cheek. Bryce is up off the floor and hugging me to him before I even notice he has moved. I can't hold the tears in any longer. I just hold onto him and cry into his chest.

"I can't lose him, Bryce. I love him."

CHAPTER
Twenty-Six

TRAVIS

WHOEVER IS PUNCHING me in the head needs to stop! My eyes feel heavy, but I need to open them and find out what is causing all of the pain so that I can stop it. The light is bright and the more I open my eyes, the more my head pounds. The room is white, wires and tubes are everywhere. I can hear a faint beeping sound. Where the hell am I?"

All of my memories start rushing back all at once. We received a call that there had been another explosion. We rolled out just as Charliee had pulled up to the station. I hated that I had to leave. I wanted to know why she had to go back to the station, but I was forced to wait.

I remember the chat on the radio, everyone was surprised we were at a vacant building. We hadn't walked in far when one of the guys noticed a backpack against one of the walls. Once we realized what it was, we all started running back out. I remember Randy tripped on some of the already fallen building. I was behind him, helped him up and that was the last thing I remember before everything goes dark.

I remember hearing a dog barking and hearing Charliee's voice screaming my name. She couldn't have been there, so I must have dreamt all of that.

I know with my head pounding like it is, I must have gotten struck pretty good, probably a good thing I had my helmet on. I move my legs, they both move. I go to move my hand and realize it is being held. I look over and that's when I see Charliee. She is asleep in a recliner next to me. I look down at my hand, she has a tight hold on it. That's also when I see the black brace on her leg. What the hell happened to her?

Someone opens the door. When I look over, I see my mom. "Travis, you're awake."

She quickly comes onto my other side and hugs me. When she stands back up, she is crying.

"Mom, don't cry, please. I'm all right."

She quickly wipes the tears away and smiles. "You scared the hell out of us."

"How long have I been out?"

"About two days." She looks over at Charliee. "She hasn't left this room. I was actually stopping in to see if she wanted me to get her anything or if Levi needed to be taken out. The nurses here have been great. They even offered to take him out when we weren't here. He has made all the nurses fall in love with him. He won't leave Charliee's side and she won't leave yours. She is an amazing young lady. If it wasn't for those two, we might not be talking right now."

"What do you mean, if it wasn't for them?"

Mom sits down on the edge of my bed. "I've only gotten pieces of the story. From what I've been told, those two went in after you. Levi was the one who found you."

"What the hell are you talking about? How did they even get there?"

"Her brothers brought her, she demanded for them to take her there after they told her what had happened."

I want to strangle her brothers for even allowing her to be there, but at the same time, I know Charliee. She would have been there regardless of them bringing her or not.

My mom continues. "While they were going to you, Charliee tripped a couple of times. She tore open her knee pretty bad. I think they said something like twenty-some stitches and a fractured knee."

She was there, I hadn't dreamt it. I had heard Levi barking and her calling my name. I was determined to let her know I was alive. She was holding my hand, so I signed I love you, she signed it back against my hand just like the night I told her I loved her for the first time.

"So what's wrong with me? I'm assuming I have a concussion with the way my head is pounding."

"Your gear saved your life, honey. You have a couple broken ribs, but all your tests came back good. They were mainly worried over your head injury. Your back is probably sore from the tank being pressed into it. Actually, you will probably be sore all over, but you were lucky."

I look over at Charliee and squeeze her hand. I really want to pull her over to lay with me, but between her leg and all the wires I am hooked to, I decide against it. She instantly wakes up. She looks around for a moment looking like she is trying to figure out where she is. Her eyes finally find mine.

"Travis, you're awake." She awkwardly gets herself up out of the chair.

"Charliee, I'm all right, please be careful before you hurt yourself more."

"My leg isn't important." She manages, a little wobbly, to get out of the chair and to my side. Then Levi is there looking up over the bed.

"Hey, boy, I hear you are the one who found me." I scratch behind his ear.

Charliee leans over and gives me a small kiss. If my mom wouldn't have been sitting right next to me I probably would have pulled her down onto me and kissed her far more than the little peck she offered me.

"Why don't I take Levi out and leave you two alone for a minute? On my way back I'll let the nurses know you are awake."

"Thank you, Mom."

"Yes, thank you, Anna."

I wait for my mom to leave and then look back at Charliee. Tears are streaming down her cheeks.

"Hey, don't cry, I'm all right."

She wipes the tears away. "I know but I was so scared, Travis. I thought I had lost you."

"You can't get rid of me that easily."

She smacks my arm. "That's not funny right now."

"I'm sorry, I know. I'm trying to not lecture you about going into the building in the first place."

She is playing with my fingers. "You didn't leave me when I was buried, I wasn't going to leave you."

"I heard you when I was under all of it. I thought I had dreamt you being there, but when Mom told me how you ran inside and that's how you got hurt, I realized I didn't dream it."

"They caught the guy. He was there standing by and watching. I looked over and there he was."

Something is wrong, she is acting strange. "Charliee, what are you not telling me?"

Shrugging her shoulders, she sits down on the edge of the bed. Her fingers run back and forth on my palm. "It's hard to explain. I keep seeing him just standing there, just watching. His eyes showed excitement. He has no remorse for the lives he has taken or was trying to take the other day. If they wouldn't have caught him, he would have done it again and again. Yet I still feel sorry for the guy."

That's why she is so amazing. She can't hate. She is feeling sorry for the bastard. Bringing her hand up to my lips, I kiss her knuckles.

"I'm warning you. I'm going to make you marry me."

Her eyes widen in shock. I sign "I love you" with my hand against her palm. Her hand mirrors it back. Then she rests them against my chest right above my heart.

"I hope you know, I'm expecting you down on a knee when you actually tell me I'm marrying you."

Her smile is returning to her eyes, that's my girl.

"Right now I can't get down on one knee, so you are going to have to settle with me laying down."

"So what you're saying is, this is you asking me to marry you?"

"You aren't going to tell an injured man in a hospital bed no, are you?"

She looks up as though she is thinking about it. My heart is beating crazy in my chest. I know she feels it by the little smile on her lips.

She looks back down at me. "Just for the record, I couldn't have imagined a better proposal than this one. For us, I think it was perfect. Yes, I'll marry you!"

Silent Distraction

BOOK 2

CHAPTER
One

"STEVE, just order what needs to be replaced in the morning. This damn deadline can't be pushed back. This is why I hate track homes. I'll call my dad in the morning and let him know what's going on."

I had told my dad I didn't want to take on this project and these last few months reminded me of why. This is the third time we have had these 'pain in my ass' teenagers come through and break out the windows of the houses. I'm starting to think we need to order more security at night. It would be cheaper to do that than to have to keep replacing all the windows.

"Cam, we need to do something about these…"

My phone beeps through with another call, cutting off what Steve is saying. The number isn't anyone I recognize. If it is too important, they will leave a message.

Bringing the phone back up to my ear, Steve is still talking. "What are we going to do about these little shits?"

Steve is my right hand man down here in Texas. He is amazing at his job, but the man is going to give himself a heart attack one of these days.

My dad hired him when I told him I wanted to move down here to Texas and expand Tovaren Construction, our family business. Steve and I handle Texas and my dad runs things up there in Washington. It was great for the business, we have been pretty busy north and south.

"I'm going to call the security company tomorrow morning and hire another officer for the evenings. Maybe we will have a better chance of catching them."

Once again, my phone beeps with another incoming call. Same number, but they didn't leave a message last time, so not really in a rush to answer it this time. I am exhausted tonight and don't really want to deal with business right now. They will just have to get the hint and leave a message.

Steve's voice brings me back to our conversation. "I've thought about staying out there myself to catch the little shits."

I laugh, I can see Steve, the 'good ol' country boy' that he is, sitting out there in his truck, his shotgun in his lap. "Steve, you would have way too much fun scaring the crap out of those kids."

"Yes, I would get a little pleasure out of it, but I could guarantee they wouldn't do it again."

"I would love to see it myself, but let's try the extra security first. If that doesn't work, I'll let you loose on them."

Opening my fridge, I find that I'm ordering pizza for dinner tonight. Tomorrow I think I may need to go shopping. Grabbing one of the last two beers I have, I go and drop down onto the couch.

"Hey, Steve, I'll see you in the morning. I need to order a pizza and then I'm going to bed, I'm exhausted."

"You need a woman. One that knows how to cook. You eat out way too much."

"I don't need a woman who can cook, I can cook for myself. I'm actually a pretty damn good cook, I just need to go shopping for food. We have been so busy lately with finishing this project that I haven't made it to the store."

"Are you still seeing that redhead?"

"Candice? Yeah, off and on, it's nothing serious."

For the third time, my phone beeps through with another call. Same number. Whoever this is isn't giving up. "Hey, someone is trying to get a hold of me, they have called three times now. I should probably see what they want. I'll talk to you tomorrow."

"All right, and just as a reminder, my offer stands to stay on the property one of these nights."

"I'll remember, and I'll keep you posted on what I find out about the extra security. See ya." Hanging up, I find the number and call it back.

It rings a couple times and right when I think it will go to voicemail, a man's voice answers. "Hello."

"Hello. Someone from this number has called me a couple times tonight." That was a lot nicer than I want to be.

"Cameron, is this you?"

"Yes, who is this?"

"I'm glad we finally reached you. Your brother said he texted you but you haven't answered. I'm David Colter. Your brother, Jacob, and my son, Tyler, are good friends."

Pulling my phone away, I find three messages from Jacob that I haven't read. I remember seeing the first one a little earlier but I figured I'd text him back later. Now I have Tyler's dad calling me. Maybe I shouldn't have ignored them.

"Mr. Colter, I believe we have met before. Is everything all right?"

Something isn't settling right. If something is wrong with Jacob, why aren't my parents calling me?

Silence stretches on the other end of the line. "Mr. Colter, are you still there? Is Jacob all right?"

I hear David clear his throat. "Yes, Jacob is fine. I'm, um…"

I'm starting to get impatient. All my nerves are on alert. Something is wrong, and if it's not Jacob, then there are only my parents.

"Cameron, there isn't an easy way to tell you this. This evening there was an explosion at one of our restaurants and your parents were there during that time."

"Explosion?! What kind of explosion? Are they all right?"

Again, silence. I want to reach through the phone and shake the man.

"Cameron, details haven't really been released yet. Search crews are still looking for survivors, but it's not looking very good."

What does he mean, not looking good for survivors?

"How do you know they were there?"

"Jacob came over tonight to hang out with Tyler. He told us your parents had decided to go out for dinner and asked if he could eat with us tonight. I was watching the television when the news broadcast came over the show I was watching. I asked Jacob which restaurant your parents had gone to and he confirmed the same one."

"Are you sure? Has anyone tried calling them?"

"Yes, Jacob and I have tried a number of times. Neither of them are answering."

Something is wrong then. My dad always answers his phone. He always says, "A missed call is a possible missed customer."

My entire body feels like someone injected ice cold water into my veins.

"How long ago did all this happen? How many times have you tried to call them? Maybe something just happened to their phones."

"Cameron, we have been trying since we heard. It happened around five tonight. Every time we call, both phones go straight to voicemail and none of your brother's messages have been answered back."

Five?! My parents wouldn't go this long without contacting someone after something like this happening.

"I'll be on the first flight I can get. Are you good with Jacob staying there until I can get there?" I feel numb. It all feels like a dream; my parents can't be dead.

"Of course! Call me with your flight information and I'll come pick you up. If we hear anything before then I'll let you know. We left our information with the police when we called earlier."

"Thank you." I hit end without waiting for David to say anything else. I can't move, all I can do is stare down at my phone. This can't be happening. Who the hell blows up a restaurant?

CHAPTER
Two

JAYDEN

"ALL RIGHT, guys, time is up for today. If you are still needing help, I'll have another after school session on Wednesday," I sign to the five students who have attended tutoring today.

I watch as they all clean up and start to leave. They each sign thank you as they walk past my desk.

Emily is the last to leave. She waits for everyone to exit and then walks up to my desk. "Ms. Edwards, I want to thank you for all the after school help. I have never been good or liked math. You have changed that. I just wanted to say thank you," she signs.

My heart melts a little. This is why I decided to become a teacher. I had also struggled in math. All it took was one special teacher, Mrs. Morris, my sophomore year math teacher. Because of her, I decided to teach and chose math as well.

"Anytime, Emily! I'm happy it's helping. Your grades are definitely improving. You have a good evening. I'll see you in class tomorrow."

Smiling, she nods and leaves the classroom. Never would I have guessed I would be teaching at a deaf school. I met my best friend, Charliee, who is deaf, my junior year of college. She was in one of my classes with an interpreter. I was extremely fascinated and couldn't stop watching them when they would sign back and forth. It was beautiful to watch.

I have never been shy, and one day after class I ran up to her and introduced myself. After probably a dozen questions, that I shot off so fast I believe the interpreter had a hard time keeping up, we became best friends. Learning sign language seemed to come pretty natural to me. After graduation, we were both offered jobs here at the deaf school. Charliee teaches English and I was offered Math, both of us at the high school level.

Glancing up at the clock, I realize if I don't get moving, I am going to be late for the meeting. Quickly grabbing my purse and bag, I head for the office, locking my classroom door before speed walking to the meeting I was asked to sit in on about Jacob Tovaren.

Jacob is a great kid. Popular, great student academically. He is athletic, loved by all the girls. Tragedy struck his family a couple weeks ago when a popular Italian restaurant was blown up, killing eighteen people. Among those eighteen were both of Jacob's parents.

Charliee was there that night as well. The call I received from her parents that night will forever be burned into my memory. I had just gotten out of the shower and was sitting down to enjoy a little television while grading some papers. I was flipping through the channels, not wanting to watch the news, which seemed to be on every channel. I hate watching the news, it's too depressing.

I had just realized what they were reporting about when my phone rang. It was Charliee's mom, all frantic, asking me if I had seen the news. Charliee had stopped by the restaurant to grab dinner before heading home. She was been leaving the place when the bomb went off. They found her under the fallen building and had just rushed her to the hospital.

Her back was badly burned, she had stitches across one of her shoulders and a broken arm, but she was alive. However, she was still in the hospital recovering from her burns.

Hurrying into the front office, I quickly wave at Cindy sitting at the front desk and rush into the principal's office.

"Sorry I'm late. My tutoring class ran a little over today," I speak and sign as I enter.

"Slow down, Ms. Edwards, and have a seat. We were just about to get started." Mr. Lennerd, the principle, pointed to an empty chair.

Turning around to take my seat, I stumble. There standing against the back wall, arms crossed over his chest, his eyes looking me up and down, is a man I've never seen before.

His mouth slants up at one corner as I quickly regain my balance and take my seat.

"Ms. Edwards, are you all right?" Mr. Lennerd asks, bringing my attention back to him.

"Yes, thank you. I'm fine. Foot just got tangled up." I look over my shoulder, that cocky smile is still there, his eyes are still on me.

"Ms. Edwards, I'd like you to meet Mr. Tovaren," Mr. Lennerd makes the introduction.

"It's nice to meet you, Mr. Tovaren."

He nods, but doesn't move from his spot against the wall. "Call me Cameron. Mr. Tovaren was my father."

My heart skips a little. I'm just not sure if it's from the sound of his smooth voice or the mention of his father.

"I'm sorry for your loss. I met your parents a number of times, they were a very nice couple."

His smile drops, as do his eyes for a moment. I have to fight the urge to go to him and wrap my arms around him. When he looks back up at me, the small smile has returned. It's all for show. I can tell by the sadness in his eyes.

Our eyes stay locked. Nothing is being said, but I feel a pull to this man. It's strange, I have never had this kind of feeling over a guy.

The clearing of a throat pulls me out of my trance and my attention away from the dark-haired god leaning against the wall.

"Sorry, Mr. Lennerd, what were you saying?" I look down at my folder in my lap as I speak, hoping to hide my red cheeks.

What is wrong with me? I don't blush. Guys don't make me react like a high school girl. Embarrassment is a new feeling for me and I'm not liking it at all.

When I glance up at Mr. Lennerd, my cheeks burn a little more. He is giving me a knowing look. To top everything off, I can feel Cameron's eyes on my back. I have to fight the urge to glance back over my shoulder again.

"I was saying that Mr. Tovaren…"

"Cameron," the voice from behind me interrupts Mr. Lennerd.

"I apologize. Cameron has asked for this meeting because Jacob is having some problems with math while he has been out. We had decided, as you know, to put Jacob on home studies for a month while they deal with the family tragedy. Mr…, I mean Cameron, called me yesterday saying Jacob is struggling with math and doesn't want to have him fall too far behind. I figured you being his teacher, and I know you hold study groups for your students pretty frequently, that maybe we can work something out to help him out."

"Ms. Edwards…" The silky voice pours over me as he says my name. What is wrong with me? Damn, I need to pull myself together.

I turn in my chair, facing Cameron again, he hasn't moved a muscle. "Please, call me Jayden. Ms. Edwards is for the children."

His eyes narrow. Yes, Mr. Tovaren, you may have knocked me sense-less for a moment but I bounce back quickly. I speak to him with my eyes. I know he understands by those lips curving just a little more, and his eyes accept the challenge.

He may have knocked me off balance for a moment, but I don't stay off kilter for long.

"Jayden…" he continues.

It's a good thing I am sitting because hearing my name with that voice would have had me down on my knees.

"I don't think my brother is ready to be back at school, even if it's after school hours."

"Actually, we were wondering if you could go to the house and tutor him there. That is if you have time," Mr. Lennerd comes into the conversation.

Looking between the two men in the room, I think about it for a moment. It would probably be hard for Jacob to be around all the kids and their questions. They wouldn't mean any harm but they would smother him with it all, and it would definitely be overwhelming for him. I was emotional answering all of their questions about Charliee when it all first happened.

"You are right, coming here would be difficult I'm sure. I have no problem tutoring him at home."

Pulling a business card out of my bag, I grab a pen off the desk and write down my cell phone number. "Here is my cell number, give me a call and we can set up a schedule."

When I turn to hand it to Cameron, he is standing right next to me and my hand smacks into his very hard stomach. "I'm sorry."

His stomach muscles flex under my touch, but when I look up, he looks cool and collected. Very good, Mr. Tovaren, you played it off well. Your face may show no effect from my touch, but your body speaks loud and clear. He is just as affected by me as I am him.

Cameron takes the card from my hand, flipping it over to where I wrote my number. "Thank you. I'll be calling you soon. I don't want Jacob to fall too far behind."

"Your brother is a very smart kid, but he has struggled with math. I'm sure we can get him caught up pretty quickly."

"Thank you." Cameron turns to Mr. Lennerd, "Thank you for your time and help. I'll stay in touch on when Jacob will be coming back to school." The two men shake hands.

"Miss. Edwards, you will be hearing from me soon." I see the smile before he turns from me to leave the office.

"It was nice to meet you, Mr. Tovaren," I say as he reaches for the handle.

He stops for a moment. I think he will say something in return, but instead he leaves the office without saying another word.

Looking over at Mr. Lennerd, I find my cheeks heating up again with the knowing smile he gives me. "What?"

"There won't be any problems with this set up, will there?"

If only he knew how many times I had asked myself that very question in the last few minutes. "Of course not, why would you think there would be?"

Mr. Lennerd just gives me that knowing smile again. Damn, was I that obvious earlier? "It will be fine, Mr. Lennerd. I'll be very professional. Jacob is the most important person involved here. I don't want him falling behind. There will be no issues, I promise."

Mr. Lennerd sits there studying me. Yes, Cameron is a very handsome guy. True, no one has made me want to grab onto them and not let go until we are both naked and exhausted like I felt when he spoke my name. Besides wanting those lips all over my body, I have no other problems. It will all be fine. I give Mr. Lennerd what I hope is a very reassuring smile.

"How is Charliee doing?"

I almost slump back in the chair with relief when he changes the subject.

"She is doing a lot better. They are hoping she can go home in a couple of days."

"That's good, we miss her here. Please let her know we are happy to hear she is healing and can't wait for her to be back in the classroom."

"I'll let her know. See you tomorrow." I grab my bag and head out of the office.

I am very ready to be home and relaxing in my spa. What a day!

CHAPTER
Three

CAMERON

SHUTTING the door to my dad's truck, a whiff of his smell catches me off guard. I close my eyes, expecting to open them and see him sitting next to me. No one is there, just me, alone, sitting in the parking lot of my brother's school. I need to figure out a way to get my truck up here from Texas and soon.

Turning the key in the ignition, I know I just want to be home. Of course that has nothing but memories either. Before backing out, I catch a glimpse of Ms. Edwards, or should I say Jayden walking through the parking lot.

Instantly my stomach muscles flex again, like they remember her touch. Jayden has fire in her, I could see it in her eyes when she gave me her challenging look earlier. I saw the heat as well. When her hand connected with my stomach and those eyes shot up to mine, desire filled me, and it took everything I had to not grab her hand and pull her up against me. My body wanted to fill more than just her hand. I wanted her body up against mine. Better yet, I would have been good with clearing off that desk and laying her body under my own.

I watch her as she walks across the lot, her eyes down looking at her phone the whole way. She gets to what I figure is her car, gets in and pulls out. Watching her car until it disappears on the street, my stomach jumps again. What the hell is wrong with me? I need to shake this want for Jayden. I don't have time for anything other than running the family business, all the legal matters and my brother.

Jacob and I are eleven years apart. I remember when Mom and Dad told me they were having a baby. Mom was so excited. They had been trying for years. I remember asking why they wanted another kid. Dad smiled and told me, "Don't worry, Cameron, your mom and I have so much love, there is plenty of room for both of you."

Mom just glowed the whole time she was pregnant, even though she had been sick the whole time. I swear she smiled even when she was throwing up every day. Then Jacob was born. They told us he was deaf. As expected, all the attention the new baby received and more because of the added disability, I went through a few years of rebelling.

I didn't spend much time in the first five years with Jacob. Everything changed one night when our family was out to dinner. We had a table next to ours with a couple of older kids with their parents. The kids were making fun of Jacob because of his signing and the sounds he made. I tried to ignore it and could have ignored the ignorance of teenagers, but the father made a comment about my brother being a retard. I told my parents that I had to use the restroom. As I walked by the table, I hooked the father's chair with my foot and pulled it out from under him, sending him and his plate to the floor. I didn't even look back.

The man glared at me as I walked back to our table a short time later. It took a lot to not stop and say something to him as well, but I decided to be satisfied with sending his ass to the ground. Sitting back down, I was expecting the third degree from my parents. Neither of them looked up from their plates, they just sat there eating, but I didn't miss the smiles on their faces.

From that night forward, I made a vow to myself that no one would hurt my little brother, physically or mentally, regardless of what he was aware of. We became attached at the hips after that night. When I decided to move down to Texas three years ago, Jacob tried to talk my parents into letting him move with me. We text almost every day when I'm not homing visiting.

Since our parent's death a couple weeks ago, he hasn't said much to me at all. He eats dinner up in his room. He doesn't go anywhere either. When his friends come over, he sends them away, telling me to tell them he isn't home or busy.

When he had told me he wanted some time off from school, I understood. I didn't see any harm in letting him take a little time away from school as long as he kept up with his work and grades. This might not have been the best idea. I'm starting to think I should have kept him in school.

Living alone in Texas never bothered me. Coming home to a quiet house was relaxing. Coming home to the house I grew up in is a different thing. Standing here on the porch, I almost hate to open the front door. I still expect to hear Mom in the kitchen and see Dad in his office on the phone with a client. Jacob and his best friend Tyler on the couch playing video games. Now all I hear is silence and it isn't relaxing. Eventually I'll get use to this new silence, right?

Shutting the door behind me, I am thrown back a little when I hear a sound coming out of the kitchen. I know it isn't my mom, but damn the memories flood back. Surprisingly I find Jacob looking through the fridge.

I reach around him and grab a beer. I expect him to turn around and acknowledge me, but he doesn't even look over his shoulder. He doesn't talk to me unless I make him.

When he does turn, he doesn't say anything. He begins to walk past me, but I put my hand out and stop him.

"I met with your math teacher today, Miss Edwards," I sign to him.

Still nothing, it is starting to piss me off. "She has agreed to come here to the house and tutor you."

"Okay," he signs back, but that is all. He just stands there giving me the look, like I'm wasting his time.

"Have you done anything today other than sit in your room? Maybe you should see if Tyler can hang out tonight. I'm going to throw some chicken on the barbecue for dinner. Why don't you see if he wants to come over?"

Again, nothing. He just stands against the counter, looking up only to see me sign, then he looks back down at the soda he is holding. I have to fight the urge to throw my hands up in the air and surrender.

"All right, well I'll throw on an extra piece just in case," I sign.

Nothing, Jacob just walks past me and leaves. I have no idea how to handle all of this. I'm supposed to be the older brother, not the parent. There is no manual on what to do with younger siblings after a parent's death.

My phone goes off in my pocket and as irritated as I am right now, all I want to do is take it out and throw it against the wall. Seeing it is Steve, relief floods through me.

"Hey, Steve."

"Hey, how are things going up there?"

"It's going. I'm trying to stay on top of all the projects Dad had going up here. I don't think the man ever slept. How is the track going?"

"It's on schedule, and since we pulled the extra security for the nights, we have had all the windows staying in one piece."

Well, at least some good news from somewhere. "That's good to hear. Are you able to handle everything all right alone?"

I know that is probably a very stupid question. The man probably knows more than I do.

"Cameron, don't worry about anything on this side of things. Everything is under control and running on time. You, I'm sure have your hands full with things up there in Washington."

Looking around the living room, my chest tightens up. It had always felt good to come home. It was warm, loving, and welcoming. Now it only feels quiet and cold. My hands being full is an understatement. Between Jacob, my father's open jobs, piles of paperwork, and the household affairs, I am in overload. I wonder every day how my parents made this all look so easy.

I know the business, I just never realized how much my dad had taken on up here. I think what is driving me over the edge is Jacob. Being the older brother is one thing; becoming the legal guardian of a teenager who just lost both parents, dealing with all of his school issues and trying to get him to talk to me is a totally different thing.

"Cameron, are you still there?" Steve's voice brings me out of my own head.

"Yeah, sorry. I was thinking."

"Do you need me to come up there and handle the job sites for a couple weeks? I can at least take that load off you for a little bit."

"I appreciate it, Steve, but I need you down there more than up here. I have Kevin helping me out on the sites up here while I get the business side all taken care of. We can't afford for something to go wrong down there with both of us being up here."

"All right, but know if you need me, I'm only a flight away."

"I appreciate that."

"Oh, real quick before I let you go. That little redhead stopped by the job site office the other day looking for you."

"Candice?" How did she even know where the office was?

"I'm assuming you didn't tell her you left."

We had been on a couple dates, we weren't serious. "I've been ignoring all of her calls to be honest. Things up here are a little more important than dealing with her right now. Sorry about that. If I would have thought she'd end up there bugging you, I would have talked to her."

"It's no big deal. I wasn't sure what you had told her, so I just said you weren't in at the time."

"I'll call her later today and let her know I'm not in town. Sorry about that."

"Don't apologize, it's no big deal."

"I should be able to come down for final inspection so I'll see you in a couple weeks."

"Sounds good. I would say try not to stress, but from the sound of your voice I believe you have already passed that."

I didn't respond, I just pressed end and tossed my phone onto the couch next to me, which then bounced onto the floor. Bending down to pick it up, I find a business card on the floor. Picking it up, I realize it is the one Ms. Edwards had given to me earlier, it must have fallen out of my pocket.

That warm feeling spreads through my stomach again. Before I really realize what I am doing, I dial the number on the back of the card. Three rings and I think I will be talking to an answering machine, but I'm surprised when her voice says, "Hello."

"Hello, Ms. Edwards, this is Cameron Tovaren."

Silence stretches out for a moment but then her silky voice comes through the line. "Hello, Mr. Tovaren. I'm a little surprised to hear from you so soon."

My skin usually chills when someone calls me Mr. Tovaren, but I find myself smiling at Jayden using the name for me. She is giving back what I am dealing.

"The longer I wait to get Jacob started with tutoring, the more behind he will be."

"Understandable, when were you thinking of getting started?"

Tonight, in my bed is what I want to answer. "What days do you have available? I'll work about your schedule."

"I can stop by tomorrow after school if that works for you. I can be there around four-thirty."

Jayden's voice is very soothing, I can feel my body relaxing as we talk. I need to figure out how to keep her on the phone. "Four-thirty it is! Do you need me to get anything, supplies or anything?"

I hear a small laugh. "No, we won't need anything. He should have his book."

"Okay, well then I guess we will see you tomorrow."

"Wait! I do need one thing from you."

"What would that be, Ms. Edwards?"

"Your address, Mr. Tovaren." Her voice melts through the phone.

I have never wanted to grab someone and pull them through a phone as badly as I want to at this moment. I have to fight the urge to clear my throat. She would take great pleasure in knowing the affect she is having on me, I have a feeling.

"I'll text it to you when we hang up."

"Sounds good."

"See you tomorrow, Ms. Edwards."

"Mr. Tovaren, I can play this name game as long as you can."

I laugh, something I haven't done in a couple weeks. She is forward, says what she wants. I like that!

"See you tomorrow," she adds.

"Goodbye."

Jayden hangs up the phone first. I sit here staring at mine. I save her name with her number, smiling to myself as I type in Ms. Edwards (Jayden).

CHAPTER

Four

Jayden

I'D SEEN Cameron sitting in his truck in the school parking lot when I came out. I felt his eyes follow me as I walked to my car. It took everything I had in me not to look over at him as I walked past. He had started to back out just as I came out of the building. I would have paid good money to know what he was thinking. Funny thing was, usually when I knew a guy was checking me out, I would make sure he didn't miss a move or sway of my hips. When I saw Cameron and knew that he was watching me, all I wanted to do was run for my car, and not in a sexy way. These weren't feelings I was used to. Never has one touch of a guy made me think about him this much. I don't do the relationship thing. Sure, I go out, we have fun for a couple dates, but then I end things before they get serious. Charliee says it's because of what my dad did to my mom.

I remember thinking I was the luckiest girl in the world. All of my friends would talk about their parent's getting divorces or they were already separated. Having to move between houses, or some would talk about how they never saw one or the other. I would just sit there

221

and think to myself how lucky I was that my parents were still in love with each other. I never heard my parents fight. We always took family vacations together. We were the perfect family. Well, that's what I thought any way.

I remember one evening I found my mom crying in the kitchen. I was thirteen, but it still feels like it was yesterday. My father had decided to cheat on my mom with a lady he worked with, and he left both of us for that family. No warning, he never even said goodbye, he just packed his things and left, leaving my mom a note.

I haven't seen my father since that day. He has tried to reach out to me and my mom has tried to convince me that I should talk to him, but I have no desire to have him in my life. I watched what his actions did to my mom.

Somehow, my mom was able to find love in her heart again for another man. She found Todd. He is a great guy, treats my mom like she is the only woman alive. She deserves someone like him. I'm so happy that she was able to find someone who appreciated her.

I have kind of decided that it isn't worth all the pain. That's why I only date and that's where it stays. I can't get hurt if I don't get too close. I go out, meet a guy, enjoy the evening, a little dancing, a few drinks and that is usually where it ends. A few I have taken it further into the night, or on a couple more dates, but that's it.

Cameron, I haven't stopped thinking about. What the hell is wrong with me? Sure, he's good looking. He has a body I won't deny is built like a god, but he isn't the first guy I've met with those features.

I had just stepped out of the hospital from visiting Charliee when my phone rang. I didn't recognize the number and almost let it go straight to voicemail, but for some reason I answered it. The sound of his voice when he said hello and called me Ms. Edwards almost caused me to melt to the ground there in the hospital parking lot. I thought I was being all clever when I called him Mr. Tovaren back, but he didn't respond. I found myself feeling disappointed, why I don't know. He doesn't seem like the type of guy who jokes around. He did, however, accept challenges, and so did I. If he wasn't going to call me Jayden, then I wasn't going to call him Cameron.

Walking into my house, I go straight back to my room and strip out of my clothes. My hot tub is waiting for me. The warm water is calling my name. This is my daily routine: home, strip, hot tub. When I moved in, I had the patio covered so that I didn't have to worry about giving my neighbors a show.

As I sink down into the water, I can feel all of my muscles relax as the water covers me. This is probably my favorite time of the day. Laying my head back, I close my eyes, sinking lower into the water and letting the heated bliss surround my entire body up to my chin. It feels amazing. Why am I so tense tonight? Classes went well. Charliee is doing great, maybe a little stir crazy, but healing fast.

Cameron, leaning up against the wall, arms crossed over his chest and a small sexy smile. This is what I see when I close my eyes, and my body tenses right back up. I can feel my body heat up, and I'm pretty sure it's not from the water I'm sitting in.

Charliee had even asked me today why I was so tense. That woman picks up on everything, damn her for being deaf. Not being able to hear heightened all of her other senses.

Charliee has felt so guilty about being one of the survivors, and all the people who lost their lives. Especially Mr. and Mrs. Tovaren. It is hitting her hard. When she asked about my day, I didn't want to mention Cameron. I was afraid it would dampen her mood today.

What did I really have to tell her anyway? We met for what, a whole ten minutes? Which is one of the reasons it is driving me crazy that I am having the feelings that I'm having. Thinking about going to the house tomorrow and tutoring Jacob isn't helping my nerves either. All right, this hot tub isn't doing the job tonight. I've never wanted to slap myself in the face before and tell myself to get a grip.

My phone goes off with a text message. It is probably Charliee. She has nothing else to do all day except text me. Most of the time it is just little text messages, like come break me out of jail.

This water isn't helping. Actually it is getting a little hot in here, almost smothering. I didn't grab anything on the way home for dinner, which I could smack myself for forgetting. I don't have much in the way of food here at the house. I need to go shopping, but when? Between work, after school tutoring, and visiting Charliee, there isn't much time left in the day, but I am going to have to find it somewhere.

Jumping out of the hot tub, I grab a towel, wrapping it around me as I head back into my room and to the kitchen, grabbing my phone off my bed as I go. Expecting Charliee's name, I stumble when I see Cameron's. It is the text giving me his address.

Going off once again as I am reading that text, I almost throw the phone down the hallway when Cameron's name shoots across the screen.

**Do you prefer I'm home when you come over tomorrow?

Now that could be a loaded question. One side of me wants to play with it a little, the other side, however, the professional side decides on keeping it clean.

**I think a guardian present is the best idea please.

His response comes back quickly.

**All right, see you tomorrow then.

I find myself smiling down at the phone and Cameron's last text. This is so wrong, I'm acting like a high school girl with a crush on the popular guy, who just said hello to me. I'm not in high school. I don't have a crush. I'm a grown damn adult with a job to do and I need to get my head on straight. Damn you, Cameron Tovaren!

Another text message comes through, this one scaring the hell out of me and causing me to jump, my phone flying out of my hands and landing hard on the floor. I swear out loud and then chant to myself, "Please don't be broken. Please don't be broken," as I pick it up.

The breath I am holding rushes out when I flip it over and find everything all good. The screen isn't cracked. Enough is enough, I have to stop thinking about Cameron. This is insane.

I open the screen, expecting to see Cameron's name, but I'm relieved when it is from Charliee.

**I know you were just here, but I love you tons!!

I love this girl. I can only imagine what she is wanting me to do.

**I love you too. What do you want?

**A hamburger and fries!!!

Another message follows it with a picture of what I think may be her dinner that the hospital is trying to get her to eat. I can't make out what it is supposed to be. Underneath the picture she wrote, "I'm begging."

Perfect, now I can grab her and me something to eat.

**Give me half an hour. I'll even go and get our favorite.

**You are the best, I owe you big time.

If anything, I owe her. She is giving me an excuse to go out and maybe that will take my mind off Cameron. I wish I could talk to her about all of it really. It feels a little strange not to say anything to her, we tell each other everything. This is different though. She needs to heal and get over this guilt she's feeling. Talking about the Tovaren family won't help her with that. Plus, there isn't anything to really tell her yet.

CHAPTER
Five

THE DOORBELL RINGS and all the lights begin to flash. Looking at the clock, it is four-twenty. "That is probably Ms. Edwards," I sign to Jacob.

He nods slightly and then looks back down at whatever school work he is working on. Frustrated, I get up from my dad's desk where I have been working on paperwork most of the afternoon and head to the door.

The doorbell rings once again before I reach it. Opening the door, my stomach tightens. She is dressed pretty simple. Tight jeans and a button-up shirt, but those red boots are what catches my attention.

"Are you a Footloose fan?"

Jayden looks down at her boots, a small smile on her lips when she looks back up at me. "I could say I like to express my rebel side a little, but red is my favorite color and I've always had a little country girl in me."

I think I believe the rebel part more than the country girl part, I think to myself.

"I see, so you are telling me you are a city girl that likes to pretend to be a country girl?"

Her eyes narrow at me, she is trying to read me. Good luck with that, Ms. Edwards. Her eyes roam down my body, down to my boots.

She points down at my boots. "Do you think living in Texas for a couple years makes you a country boy?"

"I found out very quickly how comfortable they are. The country music, however, had to grow on me."

Jayden stands there staring at me for a moment, her eyes searching my face. I have no idea what she is looking for and then finally, she breaks her silence.

"Is Jacob home?"

Nodding, I step to the side so that she can come in. "Come on in, Ms. Edwards."

"Thank you, Mr. Tovaren," she throws back at me as she walks past. I don't miss the little smile either.

She walks right into the living room where Jacob is sitting. She signs something but I can't see what. What shocks me is that Jacob responds, and not just a one word answer. They are having a conversation with each other.

I watch as Jacob gives Jayden a small smile and then gets up from the couch, grabbing all of his books. He walks into the dining room, setting everything down onto the kitchen table, then runs up the stairs.

Looking over at Jayden, I'm sure the question is written all over my face.

"He forgot his math book in his room. If you are good with it, we will work at the dining room table, it'll be easier."

When I don't respond, she rolls her eyes and starts to walk past me. My hand goes to her stomach, stopping her before she can get too far. Electricity shoots through my hand, up my arm, right into my chest. I look down at her, she is looking down at her stomach and my hand. My breath catches when her eyes find mine again.

"Is it not all right if we use the dining room table?" she asks me, her eyes questioning me.

I can't move, or maybe I don't want to move. "He talked to you!" It isn't a question.

Her eyes go from questioning to surprise. "Was he not supposed to?"

I have a need to move my hand from her stomach to her waist and pull her in closer against me. I want her lips. What the hell? Quickly, I remove my hand from her altogether and take a large step away from her.

"Of course you can use the table." I answer the first question, but ignore the last question about Jacob talking to her.

Turning, I head back to the office. "I'll be in the office if you need me," I throw over my shoulder as I walk away. I don't look back at her, I can't.

Sitting down at my father's desk, I find myself staring straight at her, our eyes locked. She hasn't moved since I walked away. She just stands there, looking over her shoulder staring at me. This is crazy. I didn't need, nor did I have the time for any of this. But, here we are, staring each other down and all I want to do is grab her, strip her out of every-thing except those red cowboy boots, and have her on this desk. My saving grace is hearing Jacob run back down the stairs. It pulls me out of my own thoughts.

Jayden blinks a couple times, then looks away from me and over to Jacob. She signs something to him, that again, I can't see with her back to me, and then they both go and sit down at the table.

Jacob has probably said more to Jayden in the past fifteen minutes that she has been here than he has to me since I have been back home.

Which just has me believing that he isn't talking to me for a reason. I still have no idea what it is that he is upset with me on, and I have no idea how to find out if he isn't staying in a room with me longer than he has to.

I've no idea how long I have been sitting here staring at the ordering form that I am supposed to be working on, but I'm sure it's been a while. Every time I go to write something down I find myself staring at the back of the woman sitting in the dining room.

What is it about Jayden that is pulling me toward her this much? Sure, she is beautiful, but I've dated beautiful women before. Although those challenges she is always dealing out with her eyes is something new. Most women I've dated say what they think I want to hear, and I'm not one of those guys that shows affection easily. I like to go out on dates, spend a little time with a pretty female, but I have a business to run, I don't have a lot of alone time to have a serious relationship with one person. Steve laughs at me all the time, saying that the women I date are determined to be the one who catches and breaks me. Then he tells me I'm going to fall hard one day. A woman is going to drop me to my knees.

My eyes adjust to the paper in front of me again. I don't have time for all of this. I need to get my head wrapped around what's important. I have the whole business to run now, not just the Texas side of it. *I don't need a woman in my life right now*, I keep repeating to myself.

My phone vibrates with an incoming call, Candice's name appears. Talk about not having time for a woman. I almost push end to ignore the call, but it isn't fair for Steve to have to deal with her stopping by the office at the work site.

"Hello, Candice."

"Cameron, are you home yet?" She is whining, I can't stand when women whine and pout. How didn't I see all of this back home?

"No, and I probably won't back for some time."

"But I miss you."

Miss me, really? We have only been out a couple times, she acts like we have been in a long-term relationship or something. Now that I have her on the phone and I'm listening to her, I'm trying to figure out how I dealt with all the whining and that squeaky voice at all. I find myself starting at Jayden's back again. She doesn't seem like the whining type. Or the type that would beg for a man's attention.

"Cameron, are you listening to me?" Candice's high-pitched voice breaks into my thoughts.

I take a deep breath. "Yes, Candice, I'm listening. I can't tell you when I'm going to be home."

She doesn't need to know the details of everything going on. "Please don't bug Steve at the office anymore either."

"You aren't going to tell me what's going on? Why you are out of town?"

I need to end this conversation with her. Before I do a very rude thing and hang up on her. "No, I'm not. It's a family concern."

Silence stretches over the lines for a moment. I am starting to think she may have hung up on me.

"Well, call me when you get back in town."

I am a little shocked that this is going to end that easily. I'm not going to push my luck though.

"Bye, Candice."

"Bye, Cameron." She hangs up quickly.

CHAPTER
Six

Jayden

A CITY GIRL pretending to be a country girl. He thinks he knows me so well. A part of me wants to tell him how much more of a country girl I am, that I didn't grow up in this city life, but he can go on thinking whatever he wants to about me. I'm just here to help Jacob, not impress his older brother.

When his hand made contact with my stomach and I looked up into those chocolate brown eyes, it took everything in me not to jump into his arms, wrap my legs around his waist and take his lips. When he finally moved away from me, I realized I had been holding my breath. I had to take a couple deep breaths as I watched him walk away from me. Then he turned and our eyes locked again. There he was standing behind the desk and I would swear I saw the want in his eyes. I found myself wanting to follow him in there, clear off the desk and have him take me right there.

Thankfully Jacob came back down the stairs right then, it brought me back to reality and the real reason I was here—to help Jacob, not dream about Cameron. I had to keep reminding myself.

I purposely sit in the chair where my back is to Cameron. I don't need the distraction. Although the whole time I have been sitting here I've gotten the feeling someone is watching me. I can feel Cameron's eyes on my back. I keep wanting to turn around and see if I am right, but I need to pay attention to my job.

My attention is drawn away from my work once again when I hear him answer his phone and say the name Candice, but the rest of the conversation I can't make out. His voice lowers a little and my attention is brought back to Jacob when he taps me on the arm to ask me a question. If Cameron has a girlfriend back home, then I need to stay clear of him altogether.

I catch myself rubbing my stomach as I wait for Jacob to work out the problem we are working on. My skin still feels warm and a little shaky inside from his touch. No one's touch has ever left a feeling behind, a reminder that they had their hands on me.

This isn't staying clear of him, if all I am going to do is think about him the whole time. I'm not going to put myself in the position where I become the other woman. I won't be the cause of some other woman going through the hurt that my mom went through when my dad left her for the "other woman."

Jacob's hands moving bring my attention back again. "Am I doing something wrong?"

"Why do you ask that?" I sign back with a puzzled look on my face.

"You are shaking your head no. I thought you were telling me I was doing it wrong," he explains, signing back to me.

Damn, I got caught not paying attention. "No, you are doing great. Sorry, I was thinking to myself."

Jacob just gives me a small nod and then continues on with his work. I want to slap myself across the face, but I know that would only draw more attention to myself. I really want to turn around and yell at

Cameron to stop. Then I think better of that, what if I am only imaging him staring at me? I can see it now. I throw myself around, yelling at him to stop staring and he is not looking at me at all, or he has left the office. Or better yet, he is still on the phone with his girlfriend and she hears me yell and then that starts a problem. The man has a girlfriend, he probably has absolutely no interest in me and I have just wanted him to. That just makes me sound pathetic.

How the hell is one guy's touch making me go this crazy? Enough is enough, no more ideas, dreams, or fantasies of Cameron Tovaren.

Jacob pushes his paper toward me to check the problems he has been working on. *This is why I'm here, to help Jacob while he is out of school*, I remind myself once again. These two men just lost their parents and Charliee is going to need me more after she gets out of the hospital. I have absolutely no time for school girl day dreams, or woman fantasies.

"They are all correct," I sign to Jacob after correcting all his problems.

He gives me a small smile and pulls his paper back. My heart breaks. I've known Jacob for a while now. In school he was always so full of life. Smiling all of the time. The girls in the school followed his every move. He was on the football team and our school track team.

The small smile he just gave me isn't the same guy, it is full of sadness. I hate seeing all of the happiness gone in his eyes. There is none now, it is completely gone. A forced smile at that. I just want to wrap my arms around him and let him know he has someone to talk to if he needs it, but I think that might make him uncomfortable.

Earlier Cameron had seemed surprised when Jacob talked to me. Well, he didn't really talk to me, he answered the questions that I asked him. It almost seemed like Jacob and he weren't talking at all from what I would guess by his surprise. On the other hand, Cameron doesn't seem like the type of guy who would sit down and let you pour your feelings out to either. Most men seem to be uncomfortable with that kind of stuff, women are usually better in that department I think.

Sitting back in my chair, I watch as Jacob works on the last couple math questions. I wonder if there are any females, aunts, sisters, grandmothers that are around or is it just Cameron and Jacob now?

Jacob pushes his paper toward me once again to check the problems he has finished. I quickly run through them.

"I think you have it," I sign and offer him a smile.

Jacob nods and signs, "Thank you," then starts gathering his books and gets up from the table.

I stop him before he can walk away. "I hope I'm not stepping over any lines, but if you need someone to talk to or anything else, I'm a great listener."

I just sit here watching and waiting as he looks down at the floor. When he looks at me again, my heart shatters. His eyes are glassed over from the tears he won't allow to flow. It is everything I can do not to jump out of my chair and hug this poor kid.

"Thank you, but I'm okay," he signs and then quickly leaves the room, running up the stairs.

I am fighting the tears myself now. He has just lost both of his parents in a senseless incident. He isn't all right, he is hurting and probably very confused. His parents dying wasn't an accident, it was by some crazed man who decided to take the lives of innocent people.

Every time I think about the bastard, I want to find him and beat him. My best friend's life will never be the same, but at least she is alive. Jacob and Cameron's life will never be the same and their parents are gone. I can't imagine what I would have done if Charliee wouldn't have survived.

"Why is Jacob upset?" Cameron's voice booms from behind me.

I jump and quickly stand up. I feel like a kid that just got caught doing something sneaky. I turn and find him storming toward me from the office. When he reaches me, he stops only inches away. Fire is in his eyes when he looks straight down at me. Our chests touch every time we both take a breath, that's how close he is standing.

Nothing is said, we just stare each other down. Daring the other one to be the one to back down. I can't do this, all I want to do is grab the front of his shirt and pull his lips down to mine. Now more pissed off at myself for wanting him than at him for accusing me of upsetting Jacob, I quickly turn and begin placing all my stuff in my bag.

I've only grabbed one book when Cameron grabs my arm, turning me back around to face him. Before I can tell him where I think he can go, his lips claim mine. My knees buckle, his arms going around my waist to hold me up at the same time my hand grabs the front of his shirt to keep myself from hitting the floor. My shock quickly wears off and I find myself kissing him back. I want to climb up his body. His body is now pressed completely against mine, it feels like fire is running through all of my veins. I have a need that can't be described.

Then like cold water is splashed over me, the name Candice flashes through my head. I shove myself from him by his chest, breaking the kiss. I take a step back, hitting the table. My legs feel a little wobbly still so I grab onto the table to hold myself up. My lips still feel his and are begging me to go back to kissing him. Neither of us say a word, we just stare at each other, both of us trying to catch our breath.

After a couple deep breaths, when I am sure that I can let go of the table and hold myself up with my own two legs, I quickly turn, grab the rest of my stuff and shove it into my bag. I can't look at Cameron when I turn back around, I just walk past him and out the front door. I don't even bother to close the door behind me. I need to get out of the house and as fast as I can. I'm not even sure if I even take another breath until I get to my car. Throwing my bag into the passenger seat, I slam my door and start my car. Now I am pissed and turned on. Not two feelings that go well together for me.

I jump when my phone goes off with a text message in my pocket. Pulling it out, I see Charliee's name appear on the screen.

**Are you coming by today?

Crap, I have gone and seen Charliee every day since she has been in the hospital. I had planned to stop by for a while after I was done tutoring Jacob, but now all I want to do is go home and hide.

**Sorry, I'm not going to make it tonight.

I feel like the worst best friend right now, but Charliee reads me too well and I don't have it in me to explain tonight.

**Are you all right?

**Yes, just tired. I had a late tutoring.

I even add a happy face hoping she will accept it and not ask any other questions.

**All right, see you later, get some rest. Love ya.

Worst best friend in the world.

**Love you too.

I text back and then throw my phone onto the passenger seat. When I look up, there is Cameron, standing in the front doorway staring at me.

I sit here for a moment just staring back at him. Neither one of us tries to hide from the other. He doesn't look cocky at the moment either, which I find is his usual expression. The man pours with confidence, he is usually pretty sure of himself I feel. Right at this moment, though, he looks everything but confident. Usually I would say I have the same confidence in myself, but around Cameron I'm not sure of anything.

The name Candice flashes in my head once again. The heat in my body quickly cools. I don't know who she is, but I wouldn't be surprised if Cameron has a girlfriend. I feel almost sick right now. If he does have a girlfriend and he just kissed me...anger begins to take over the passionate feelings. This is a perfect reminder of why I don't get involved, men are not to be trusted!

CHAPTER
Seven

CAMERON

WHAT THE HELL was I thinking? I'd say I wasn't thinking at all when I kissed Jayden. I had just come out of the office and was heading in to see how much longer they had so that I knew when I could start dinner, when Jacob ran up the stairs. He didn't look mad, but I could tell something was bothering him.

When I asked Jayden and she spun on me as fast as she did, I was ready for the battle, but with us standing that close, and the fire in her eyes challenging me, I couldn't help myself. I felt her legs give out and that only gave me the perfect excuse to wrap my arms around her waist and pull her tighter against me. When she grabbed the front of my shirt, I about lost myself. She was holding on as though I was her life support.

Her lips were soft and her kiss was hungry. I don't think I have ever wanted a woman as much as I wanted Jayden just from one kiss.

When she pushed away from me and I saw the disgusted look on her face, it felt like cold water had just been dumped on me. I would put money on the fact that the look wasn't because of the kiss. There for a moment she was just as hungry for me as I was for her. Something else happened to put that look in her eyes. It's the same look I'm getting right now from her as she stares at me from her car.

For a moment when she looked up and saw me in the doorway, I would have sworn I saw the want in her eyes, but it changed to the disapproving look so fast, I'm not sure. It is almost like she is judging me. I'm not the only one who was kissing the other. Sure, I may have made the first move and kissed her first, but she was just as affected as I had been. So why she would judge me and give me that look and not take some of the responsibility is beyond me. Maybe she has a boyfriend. I wouldn't know that though. Maybe she is mad because I did kiss her and she liked it, and if she is in a relationship with someone then being mad at me would be easier for her than to be mad at herself and think she did anything wrong. She could have pulled away, or stopped me altogether. Now I am pissed. Quickly, I turn away from her judging eyes and close the door. I need to check on Jacob.

I take the stairs two at a time and when I get to Jacob's room, I'm not surprised to find the door closed. Staring at it, I try to decide if I should go in or not. When Jacob was old enough to need his privacy, my parents told him if his door was closed they knew not to go in, but if it was open at all they knew they could enter. My dad always said if for any reason he thought Jacob was hiding anything, he had the right to enter at any time.

Jacob was never a problem child. Neither one of us were. We had no reason to sneak things around, our parents were always pretty open and forward with us. I think we both knew it would be Mom we had to deal with and we knew her wrath was much worse than Dad's. Mom never yelled or lost her temper, she always stayed calm, and that's probably what scared us the most. Seeing disappointment in her eyes would have been the worst punishment for me I believe.

I have probably been standing in front of Jacob's closed door for five minutes before I decide that he can't keep hiding himself away in his room like he has been doing. Dad wouldn't have allowed it and neither am I anymore.

Opening the door, I find Jacob laying on his bed. I walk over to stand beside the bed. He doesn't even look at me, he just keeps his eyes up toward the ceiling. If he thinks ignoring me will have me just walk back out, he is wrong. I will stand here until he decides to look at me.

"My door was closed," he finally signs, but still doesn't look at me.

So I wait a little longer. After a couple more minutes, his eyes find mine. My heart slams in the back of my chest. His eyes are red, it looks as though he has been crying.

"I noticed something was wrong when you passed me. You want to talk about it?" I sign, trying to pull myself together.

He doesn't answer back, he just stares at me. "Look, you have been moping around long enough, Jacob. You need to get out, see your friends. Maybe it's time for you to go back to school."

The shift in his eyes is very noticeable, he is mad now. Too bad, if I need to push him a little, I will. I would rather push him than allow him to lay here all the time and get lost altogether.

He doesn't say anything. He just gets up from the bed and walks past me to his door. He is waiting for me to leave. Again, he is pushing me out. This is crazy, does he think this is something only he is going through? I don't know what to do anymore. I can't force him to talk to me.

"Fine, stay up here alone. Keep pushing everyone away," I sign as I walk past him and out of the room.

I stop right outside the door, looking back at him. "Dinner will be ready in about an hour."

I don't wait for a response this time. I turn and walk down the hall. Hearing his door close is like a kick in the chest. Before you head down our stairs, my mom had all of our family pictures displayed on the wall. The one I focus on, Jacob had to have been about seven years old,

I was seventeen. We were all smiling, but my mom's smile seemed to radiate past ours. She was proud of her men. I'm sure right now she isn't very proud of the way I am handling everything. I am failing with my brother. I can almost see the one look I never wanted to see in my mom's eyes when she looked at me—disappointment!

Pain shoots through my hand and up to my elbow as my fist creates a hole in the wall right next to that family picture.

"CAMERON, everything is going great. We are right on track and the final inspection is scheduled for two weeks from today. Hiring the extra security worked, like we talked about before. We haven't had any problems. I still think you should have given me one night though. I would have been just as effective and cost a lot less." Steve laughs on the other end of the line.

"Sorry, Steve, I couldn't risk losing you because their parents pressed charges because of your scare tactics."

Flexing my hand, it is still pretty sore. It has been over a week, maybe I should go and have it checked out.

"Please, they wouldn't have said anything or they would have had to tell their parents why they got in trouble to begin with."

Jayden's laughter in the dining room catches my attention. I don't hear anything else that Steve is saying.

I get up from the desk and walk out to the living room where I can see into the dining room clearly, seeing both Jacob and Jayden.

Jayden has been back a few times since we kissed that first night. She usually doesn't say more than she needs to when I'm around. Basically she answers my questions and tells me when the next time she will be here. That is the end of any conversation between us.

I can see them signing back and forth but Jayden's back is to me like always. She always sits in the chair where her back is to me from where I usually stay in the office while she works with Jacob. Jacob is smiling. I haven't seen him smile since I've been home.

"Cameron, are you still there?" Steve's voice breaks into my thoughts.

"Sorry, Steve. Yes, I'm still here."

Jayden spins around, hearing my voice behind her. Jacob's smile quickly vanishes when he realizes I am here. Damn, I don't understand why he is so mad at me.

"Steve, let me call you back."

"Everything all right?"

Is everything all right? *Hell no, nothing is all right*, I want to say.

"Yeah, everything is fine. I just need to call you back." I decide to go with that instead.

"Not a problem." You can tell in Steve's voice he isn't buying the whole everything is fine thing, but he is being the great guy I know and not asking anymore questions. "I'll talk to you later."

I hang up from Steve and notice Jayden signing to Jacob. "We are good for tonight. I'll see you on Thursday."

Jayden is gathering her stuff as quickly as she can. Jacob is following with all of his books. Like always, he doesn't even look at me. He just walks right past me and up the stairs.

"I'll be back on Thursday," Jayden repeats to me, but she won't make any eye contact.

"Jayden, we need to talk, please." We need to clear the air between us, this silent treatment from everyone right now is starting to drive me crazy.

"There really isn't much to talk about. Jacob is doing great, he is getting all caught up with math. He should be fine when he gets back to school."

Jayden isn't looking at me as she speaks to me, which is driving me a little crazy.

"I'm happy to hear all of that, but that's not what we need to talk about.'

Shaking her head, Jayden turns to leave. "There really isn't anything else that needs to be discussed. I'm here to tutor your brother and that's all, Mr. Tovaren."

It's the Mr. Tovaren thing again, is it? I grab her hand and spin her back to me before she can walk away from me.

"Jayden, I want to apologize."

She just stands there not looking at me, her head is bent down, but she isn't pulling away from me either.

"Please, Jayden, I don't want this to continue being uncomfortable between the two of us."

It takes another minute or so, but she finally looks up at me. Fire is in her eyes, she is pissed.

"Like I said, there isn't anything to talk about. It's in the past, a mistake, we move on."

"Move on? You won't even look at me when I talk to you, Jayden, this is crazy. I didn't mean to piss you off when I kissed you. I'm sorry, trust me, it won't happen again."

She pulls her hand back from mine. I don't want to let go but I am trying to make things right, not piss her off more, so I let go.

"Cameron, you kissing me isn't want pissed me off if you want me to be honest."

All right, now I am confused. "Then what pissed you off?"

"Let me take that back. Yes, you kissing me pissed me off."

Now I am really confused, either I pissed her off because I kissed her or not. She takes a deep breath, I can tell she wants to say more.

"Come on, Jayden, tell me what this silent treatment is all about."

"Who's Candice?" she finally blurts out.

I'm sure she can see the surprise written all over my face. How does she know about Candice?

"I heard you talking to her on the phone last week."

She answers the question without me asking more. She shows no embarrassment about asking about my personal life, I like that. No games, which is a refreshing difference.

"So, you do have a girlfriend!"

It isn't a question, she is stating the fact to me. I almost laugh, but the seriousness in her eyes keeps me from it, so I just shake my head.

"Candice isn't my girlfriend, Jayden. I'm not going to tell you we didn't go out a couple of times, but nothing more."

She doesn't say anything, she just stands there studying me. She is searching for something to tell her if I am telling her the truth or not. Then it hits me, she isn't pissed that I kissed her.

"So you're telling me you weren't upset that I kissed you, you were upset because you thought I had a girlfriend when I kissed you?"

"Not that you just had a girlfriend, but that you kissed me while having a girlfriend back home."

Ahh, so that's what this has been all about. "Jayden, I promise you that I don't have a girlfriend. Candice is just a woman who thinks we are more, and is not getting the hint."

A small smile appears on her lips and I am finding myself having to fight the urge to grab and kiss her again. She might not be mad at me any longer, but I don't want to push my luck this quickly.

"You got Jacob to smile today!"

Shock fills her eyes.

"It's been three weeks and he won't even talk to me. He might answer a question and even that is not guaranteed. You not only get him to talk to you, but he was smiling today."

She shrugs, "We were talking about something that happened in class today."

"Would you like to go and grab something to eat, maybe a drink?"

"Mr. Tovaren, are you asking me out on a date?"

I can't fight the need to touch her any longer, I grab her hand again. This little last name game is doing something to me. How is it when someone else calls me Mr. Tovaren my skin crawls, but when Jayden's says it I want to grab her and carry her up to my room?

"Call it what you would like, Ms. Edwards. I just need some time with someone who will talk to me. Maybe you can tell me how to get through to my brother."

She nods, but says nothing else. She just gives me that smile and I swear it is doing things to me.

"Let me order Jacob a pizza and then let him know we are leaving."

CHAPTER
Eight

JAYDEN

I WATCHED as Cameron walks away into the other room, the phone up to his ear ordering pizza for Jacob. This is a surprising twist of the day. If someone would have told me I would be going on a dinner date with Cameron Tovaren tonight, I would have laughed in their face.

My phone goes off in my bag. Pulling it out, I see Charliee's name on the screen. Crap, I'm supposed to go over to her house tonight. She was released from the hospital last Friday. Her parents, brothers, and myself tried to convince her to stay at her parent's house for a few weeks, but she wasn't having any of it, she wanted to be home. I love the woman, but she is so determined to be independent and so against asking or accepting any help, she drives me crazy sometimes.

**Are you still coming over tonight?

Great, what am I supposed to do now? My best friend needs me, but I saw the look in Cameron's eyes when he was telling me about Jacob's distance right now, he needs someone to talk to.

**Is there anyone there with you right now?

**My mom will be here in about ten minutes. She is bringing dinner.

I feel a little better knowing she won't be alone.

**Do you mind if I skip tonight?

I am feeling like the worst friend in the world right now. Charliee needs me, but she isn't going to be alone. Cameron, right now, has no one.

**Is everything all right?

Her next text comes through. I hate that she worries about me, she has enough on her own plate right now.

**Yes, everything is fine. I just forgot about something I had to do.

I'm not used to all this side stepping with Charliee. We usually tell each other everything, but right now, there isn't really a lot to tell.

**Okay, I'll see you later, have a good evening

I will make this up to her tomorrow. She will understand, because I know my friend so well. I know if I were to tell her what is going on, she would tell me to go with Cameron. Charliee never thinks of herself, she always puts other people first.

"Is everything all right?"

Cameron's voice comes from the stairs. I look up and smile.

"Yep, everything is fine. I just had to rearrange some plans."

"If you already had plans for tonight, I understand, Jayden. We can do this some other time."

Shaking my head, I reassure him. "No, everything is fine."

"All right, if you're sure then we can get going. I already told Jacob I was leaving and that the pizza would be here in about thirty minutes."

. . .

"I'M NOT sure if I've said this yet, but thank you for coming over and helping Jacob."

I watch as Cameron plays with the bottle of beer he is holding.

"I'm a teacher, this is what we do."

"House calls aren't in the job subscription."

"Cameron, my job subscription is to teach children. There is no certain location, it doesn't say only in school or a classroom."

"Why can't you just let me say thank you?"

"You're welcome. Are you and Jacob close?"

I watch as he finishes his beer.

"We were, yes. We texted every day when I moved down to Texas. He tried to convince my parents to let him move with me, of course my mom wasn't having that. Things have been a lot different since losing Mom and Dad, though. He won't look at me most of the time."

The sadness in his eyes has me fighting my own tears. I don't know how far I should go with questions into his and Jacob's relationship. Or what questions won't be crossing the line to ask since I really don't know Cameron too well.

"I can't imagine any of this is very easy for either one of you. Do you guys have any other family?"

He nods, but still keeps his eyes downcast. "We have our grandparents on my mom's side. Some aunts and uncles, a couple cousins."

"Do they live close?"

Again, he nods. "We have an aunt and uncle here in Washington, but mostly everyone else is spread out over the states. My grandparents tried getting me to send Jacob to them down in California but I'm not uprooting my brother. His school and friends are here. Plus, neither one of them really sign a whole lot."

"That would make things for Jacob and them very difficult. Jacob can read lips well, but his speech isn't the greatest."

"I wouldn't send him off to family anyway. Don't get me wrong, there have been quite a few times in the last few weeks I wonder if he would be better with someone else since I'm obviously doing something wrong. But, I couldn't let him go to family. He is the only family I have left. We only have each other."

Seeing Cameron like this is a little shocking. The guy hasn't shown an ounce of emotion since knowing him. Now here he sits, looking like a lost little boy. I want to wrap my arms around him and tell him everything will be all right.

"Today, seeing him laugh with you was great. He hasn't cracked a smile since everything happened. On the other side of it, I feel like I must be doing something wrong."

"Cameron, you aren't doing anything wrong."

He only looks at his empty beer bottle, a look of defeat in his eyes.

"Have you tried sitting down and talking to him about all of this?"

I jump when he slams his beer bottle down on the table, his hands flying up in the air.

"Of course."

"Sorry."

"For what?"

"For upsetting you, that wasn't what I was trying to do," I defend myself.

"You didn't upset me, Jayden, I'm sorry. I'm just frustrated right now. I don't know what to do anymore."

Is he asking me for advice or is he just needing someone to talk to, I wonder to myself. We sit in silence for a few moments. He still looks everywhere other than at me. Finally, Cameron breaks the silence.

"So how did you decide to become a teacher in a deaf school? Is someone deaf in your family?"

A change of topic, that is fine with me.

"Actually, I met my best friend, Charliee, in college, she is deaf. When I saw her signing in class one day with her interpreter, I was fascinated. It was beautiful to watch. We became friends and I asked her to teach me sign language. I picked it up pretty quickly. I've wanted to be a teacher since my sophomore year of high school. My teacher for math of all things helped me with that decision. Charliee and I graduated and the deaf school was hiring, somehow we both got jobs, it was meant to be."

"That's quite a story. So you and Charliee are pretty close?"

I nod. A minute ago, I was thankful for the change of subject, now I'm thinking not so thankful. I'm pretty sure he has heard about a teacher from the school being involved within the bombing. He just probably doesn't recognize her by the name.

"Does she teach math as well?"

I shake my head no. I know he is going to figure this out in a minute. I'm not hiding it, but his mood was beginning to improve. I know the moment this topic goes back around to that night, his mood will disappear again.

"She teaches English."

I wait and watch as the realization hits him. I know the moment he figures it out, you can see it written all over his face and body.

"There was an English teacher from the school that was there the night of the bombing."

"Yes, there was. She actually just got released from the hospital a few days ago."

He doesn't ask, he doesn't need to. I see the question on his face and I'm pretty positive he reads the answer on mine.

"How is she?" He finally breaks the silence.

His tone is sharp, almost resentful. That causes very mixed emotions in me. One side of me wants to ask why he asked if he doesn't seem to really care about the answer. The other side doesn't blame him, when he lost both parents that night.

"She's healing slowly but doing well. She has major burns across her lower half of her back, stitches along one whole shoulder and a broken arm. Some bruised ribs, but all in all she is good. She is strong, she's a fighter and hates having people take care of her, so I believe she will be back on her feet and back to school teaching in no time."

Cameron looks lost in thought.

"Cameron, maybe it would help if you talked about what's on your mind."

"There isn't enough hours in a day to tell you everything on my mind these days."

I can only imagine. His life was turned upside down.

"I have nowhere to be if you need to get some stuff out."

Nothing, again he just sits there staring at an empty bottle.

"Maybe talking to someone who understands a little from that night will help."

Cameron's eyes shoot up to mine, then they narrow on me. "Are you trying to tell me you understand what I'm going through, Ms. Edwards?"

Oh good, we are back to last names, that only means one thing and it's not nice. Cameron is pissed.

"We didn't lose Charliee but yes, I can honestly say I can imagine some of what you are feeling…"

I am cut off when Cameron shoots up from his chair, looking down at me.

"You didn't lose both of your parents. Your friend is alive and home. Don't even attempt to tell me you have even the smallest idea of what we are going through."

His voice booms through the restaurant. I'm pretty sure we've caught the attention of everyone here. I try to understand his anger. Make an excuse for him yelling at me in front of everyone here, but no matter what I try to think about, I can't come up with enough of an excuse for him to make this big of a scene. He is right, I don't understand the loss the way he does. I do, however, understand the way the whole thing changed our lives.

I stand up and look right up at him. I'll be damned if I let people who are watching think he can yell at me and I'll just sit here and take it. We just stand, toe to toe, glaring at each other. Finally, I can't take it anymore.

"You know what, Mr. Tovaren? A lot of people's lives changed that day. Some more extreme than others. Some definitely lost more than others, but all of our lives changed if we had loved ones involved. I just wanted you to know if you needed someone who had some effect from the crazed man's action then I was here to listen."

I'm not going to stand here and have him embarrass me in front of everyone any longer. Walking past him, he stops me before I get too far.

"Where are you going?"

Really, he has to ask that question? Does he really think I would stay and be yelled at?

"Let go of my arm please, Mr. Tovaren."

"Ms. Edwards, you drove here with me."

Does he honestly think that is going to stop me from leaving? I would rather walk all the way home than be with him another minute.

"And I will be leaving on my own. Let me say this, though. If you get this mad with Jacob when he tries to talk to you, it's no wonder he is ignoring you."

Hurt fills his eyes and he quickly lets go of my arm. I feel bad for my words that I just threw at him. I know I'm hitting him where it hurts but I can't take them back now. When he looks away from me, I take that as my chance to walk away. Once outside, I pull my pone out and call Bryce. I'm not sure if this is a great idea since Bryce and his twin brother are cops. These two are Charliee's brothers, which means I am like their little sister as well.

"Jayden, is Charliee all right?"

No hello first? I don't blame him. Both of the boys were there when they found Charliee and Levi, her hearing dog, buried under the building.

"Charliee is fine."

"Oh! Sorry, she told us you were going over tonight. We still kind of freak."

"Don't apologize, I understand. I'm actually not with Charliee right now. I had to change the plans, your mom is with her."

"What's up then?"

"Are you working right now?"

"We just pulled into the station and are heading home shortly."

"Would you mind taking a detour and picking me up and taking me home?"

"Not at all, are you all right? Where are you?"

I can hear the worry in his voice. I am getting ready to explain that I am all right, just out with a hotheaded jackass, but I hear Cameron coming up behind me calling out my name.

"Hold on, Bryce."

I place my phone on mute and then turn around. There is Cameron stalking toward me.

"How are you getting home?"

I hold my phone up. "I'm calling a friend to come and get me."

"I'll take you back to my place to get your car, Jayden."

We are back to first names. "I don't need you to take me anywhere. Plus, you might not like something I say and push me out of the truck."

I swear I see a small smile.

"I wouldn't push you out of a moving car, Jayden."

I arch my brow at him.

"I would at least stop the car first."

I try not to smile, but I can't help it.

"Look, I'm sorry. I overreacted in there. If you would prefer someone to come pick you up and take you home, I understand."

After thinking about it for a moment, I take my phone off mute.

"Never mind, Bryce, I found a ride."

"Are you sure? I don't mind coming and picking you up."

My eyes never leave Cameron's. "I appreciate it, but I'm sure. The guy I'm with just apologized for being an ass, I've decided to give him another shot."

Cameron's eyes slant at me, but he is smiling.

"Jayden, if he is an ass, that won't change. I'll come pick you up."

I hear the concern in Bryce's voice, one of the reasons I love the boys. They would arrest anyone I asked them to without giving them a reason as to why.

"It was more of a misunderstanding."

"All right, but call me if things change. I'll come and get you and arrest him."

Like I said, they would arrest without question. Bryce confirming that makes me smile.

"Keep your phone close. I may take you up on that offer."

"Call or text when you get home, please."

"I will and thank you, Bryce. Bye."

Bryce says goodbye and then hangs up.

"Take him up on his offer?" Cameron's eyebrow shoots up in question.

Is Cameron jealous? I think about giving him something to think about but tonight has already been a whirlwind of emotions so it is better not to.

"Charliee has twin brothers who are cops. That was one of them, Bryce. He offered to come and pick me up and then arrest you."

I can't read his expression but I am pretty sure he is trying to figure out if I am joking or not.

"Protective brothers?" Cameron asks.

"You have no idea."

"I'm starting to get the idea." He takes a step closer.

I have to look up to look at him. I can feel the heat from his body, he is standing that close to me. My body craves to move closer to close the remaining little space between us.

"I will have to remember from now on that you have a lot of power in your hands."

I like this version of Cameron. It is fun and sexy. Although the other version is still in my mind. I know he is going through a lot right now, he has a very full plate, but there is no excuse for his little scene he created earlier. That is the one thing keeping me from reaching out to him right now.

"Don't you forget it!" I tease back.

He closes the space in between us, his arm going around my waist and pulling me into his body. I feel electricity shoot through all of my veins and straight to my core, but earlier is still nagging at me. Why can't I look at him like I usually look at a guy? Maybe a couple of fun dates and then move on, no strings attached. I don't know how to handle this other feeling. It is almost a need, a pull toward him. My mind is saying run from him and fast; my body is saying to tackle him and not let go.

He is going to kiss me again, I can read it all over his face. "Cameron, please don't."

He searches my eyes for a moment before he responds. "You want me to though. You want it as much as I do."

He has no idea how badly I want to kiss him right now. I still feel his lips on mine from the first time he kissed me, which is making asking him to back away all that much harder.

"I'm not going to stand here and lie to you, Cameron. Yes, there is a very large part of me screaming at myself to kiss you, but I'm going with the small part that is still pissed about the little scene you caused inside."

"So are you saying no to just kissing you tonight, or no to anything in the future?"

He is giving me that knowing, sexy smile he has. It is the same one he gave me that first day in the office when we met.

"It's a no, Cameron," I repeat, trying to sound convincing.

I need to step away. It is getting harder to ignore my need to kiss him with his body pressed against mine and that sexy smile looking down at me. My hands are on his chest and I find them gripping the front of his shirt tightly.

"Are you sure?" he asks as he looks down at my hands.

Absolutely not! That small part in my brain of reasoning is fading and almost gone. I release his shirt and push myself away from him. His arms fall to his sides and it takes everything I have not to throw myself back into his chest and take his lips myself.

Cameron watches me for a moment, like he is waiting for me to change my mind. The heat and need in his eyes has me mentally slapping myself for not giving in.

"All right, let's head out of here then." He turns and starts heading back to the truck. "I'll take you back to your car."

I don't say anything else, I just follow him to the truck. The ride back to his house is quiet. When we pull into the driveway, I quickly jump out, say goodbye as I close the door and quickly walk to my car. I need distance from him. I don't look back to see if he is watching me, I just leave as fast as I can. I'm not trusting myself to stay strong with my decision.

As I drive home, I try to figure out what I am going to do about this thing with Cameron. I need to figure this all out before I go back on Thursday for Jacob's tutoring. Maybe I won't have to worry about it. Maybe Cameron won't try anything else. I did just basically jump out of his truck before he came to a complete stop in the driveway, barely said a goodbye and left like I couldn't get away from him fast enough. He might take all of that as a hint that I'm not interested. Problem is, I am very interested, just not sure if I want to go further with all of this. We have chemistry, that is obvious, but the way he went off on me tonight kind of has me pushing away. He is broken right now, and not wanting any help. That alone should have me running, but if I have to be honest with myself, if I am running anywhere, I want it to be back against his chest and those lips!

IT'S BEEN A WEEK! Last Thursday when I went and tutored Jacob, Cameron was nowhere to be seen. I am pretty sure he was there, but the office door was closed and if he was in there then he made sure not to come out until I was gone. I found myself feeling disappointed as I said goodbye to Jacob and left. I wanted to charge into the office and make him talk to me, but what if he had someone in there with him, or he was on the phone with business?

I have done nothing but think about him and what happened last week during dinner. I think I'm using his outburst at the restaurant as an excuse to not get into anything with him. That is my way out. I'm not acting any better than Cameron was, only difference is he acted out in front of everyone, I am doing it all inside and blaming him for it all. I am driving myself crazy. Maybe I shouldn't fight this attraction we have and just see where it leads.

I need to remember Cameron is going through a lot right now. Any normal person would have mood swings and outbursts with everything he is going through. I've spent a lot of time with Charliee since she has been home. She is usually so happy and calm and even she has had an outburst of anger on a couple of occasions. Tragedy and loss can do that to a person. I don't get my feelings hurt with Charliee when she has her outbursts with me, why did I act so differently with Cameron?

Maybe I am overthinking all of this and reading too much into Cameron's actions. Sure, he has kissed me, and yes, he was going to kiss me the other night, but it doesn't mean we are in any kind of relationship. Wait! What the heck am I thinking about? Relationship? How did I go from nothing past a couple dates, no strings attached, to thinking the word relationship and Cameron in the same thought? I want to slap myself, again! Here I am, sitting in my car in front of Cameron's house, thinking about relationships. If Charliee was here right now she would fall out of the car in shock. I don't do relationships, why the hell am I thinking about it now? What has Cameron Tovaren done to me?

CHAPTER
Nine

CAMERON

I SAW Jayden pull up to the house. She has been sitting out there now for about ten minutes. Last week when she came by, I stayed in the office. I figured it would be best for both of us. When we got back from going out last week, she jumped out of the truck so fast, you would have thought she was scared to be alone with me any longer. I know my outburst was wrong at the restaurant, I have scolded myself over it many times. I finally just lashed out, and unfortunately it was at the wrong person. I knew it the moment she turned and walked away from me that night. I also know she wanted to kiss me just as much as I wanted to kiss her that night. The grip she had on the front of my shirt told me she wanted it, but she pushed herself away and I couldn't blame her.

When Jacob asked me today if he could go over to Tyler's house, there was no way I was going to say no. It was the first time in almost a month that he even left the house without me making him get out. I knew today he had tutoring but I didn't care, I told him to go.

I was getting ready to text Jayden and let her know, but I decided not to. This would give me a chance to talk to her. Of course she needs to get out of her car first, and I'm not sure if she is going to. It looks like from here that she may be having a conversation with herself. She may be on the phone with someone, but I have a feeling she is talking to herself.

Another five minutes go by and finally her door opens and she steps out. I'm starting to feel a little guilty over the fact that I didn't call her and tell her Jacob wasn't going to be home. She might have had something else she needed to do. I am being selfish, but I need to talk to her and alone.

The doorbell rings. Well, let's see how much I can piss her off with all of this.

"Hi," she instantly says once I open the door. She looks surprised to see me.

"Hi, come on in." I move to the side and close the door behind her.

"Is Jacob ready?"

"Jacob isn't here."

She looks over her shoulder at me with a questioning look. "Is he going to be home soon?"

I just shake my head no.

She turns around to face me. That spark she gets in her eyes when she gets mad is there. "Did you not think of calling me and letting me know?"

I have to admit, I like it when she gets all fired up. Most women hide their feelings, but Jayden is definitely not like most women. I take a step closer; she doesn't move back, she holds her ground. I take another step, now close enough to wrap an arm around her waist and pull her body into mine. Her eyes never leave mine, but that anger spark she had earlier is now turning to fire and I am pretty sure she is no longer angry.

"Cameron, what are you doing?"

"Hoping you don't tell me no again."

She starts to say something, then stops. Once again, and then again nothing. The fire is still there in her eyes but there is something else now as well, almost a little fear.

"Jayden, what are you afraid of?"

Her hands are gripping my upper arms. "Cameron, I don't do the relationship thing."

"Relationship thing? Jayden, I think you are rushing this a little. I'm only asking to kiss you."

Her cheeks turn a little red from embarrassment, a look I never thought I would see on her. It is cute, then she looks away from me. This is all new domain for her, I have a feeling. I'm pretty sure she is used to being in control.

"So are you saying you aren't looking for a relationship?" she asks, looking up at me slightly.

I swear I see a little disappointment in her eyes this time. Why, I'm not sure, she is the one who just said she didn't do the relationship thing, which to be honest I am all right with. I don't usually do long-term either.

"No! What I'm saying is right now what I'm wanting is to kiss you."

Taking me completely by surprise, she grabs the back of my head and brings my lips down to hers, kissing me. I hear both of us moan a little. Her fingers are digging into the back of my head and she is up on her tippy toes trying to get closer to me. My arm that is around her waist tightens, my other hand I bury deep into her hair at the back of her neck. Our tongues find one another.

What the hell was I thinking when I decided to kiss this woman again? My body isn't satisfied with just her lips, I want more, I could even be all right with begging her for more. She has to be able to feel what she is doing to me. My arm is holding her tightly, our bodies are touching from chest to knees, and I know she feels how hard I am for her. What is it about this woman that is affecting me like this? I am ready, or actually fighting the need to pick her up and carry her up to my room. Maybe skip the walking up the stairs and just have her right on the stairs.

I take that back, I want her up in my bed all night long. My hand has the bottom of her shirt and when she moves slightly, my knuckles brush her skin. Just that slight touch and I am afraid I am going to explode right now. I feel like a teenager touching a girl for the first time.

"What are you doing to me?" I ask against her lips.

Jayden pulls back slightly, her eyes half-closed and looking dreamy. "I was wondering the same thing about you."

"Kissing you isn't going to be enough, Jayden. I thought it would be, but I was very wrong. I want you, all of you." There is that begging I was thinking about.

Again, she brings my lips to hers, the hunger she has very clear. I pull away. "Jayden, I wasn't joking. I want you and if you aren't wanting to do anything other than kiss then I can do that, but we will need to break for a few so I can calm my need for you down a little."

She gives me a small smile and before I can read what she is thinking, she pulls her shirt up and over her head.

"Does this work for an answer?"

"Are you sure?"

She nods. "Only thing I ask is it's not here in the living room. I don't want to risk Jacob walking in. Probably wouldn't be good for my job."

Grabbing her hand, I lead her up the stairs and to my room. I open the door and let her enter first. The moment I shut the door, she slams back into me, again bringing my lips down to hers. All she has on is her bra. Her skin is soft, I can't wait to feel her skin against mine.

I feel my shirt lift up my sides and my chest. She pulls back from me just enough to pull it over my head, and then her lips are back on mine. I unhook her bra and push the straps off her shoulders. Her bare breasts press against my bare chest and again, like the first time we kissed today, we both moan. How in the hell did I think I wasn't going to want all of her? She has all the control. She had it from the moment our lips touched and I am happy to let her keep it.

I feel her unbutton my jeans. I grab her around the waist and lift her up, carrying her to the bed. Sitting her down, I take a step back, I need to slow us down a little. Pulling off my boots and then stepping out of my jeans, I watch as her eyes look me up and down, her green eyes almost turning white. She lays back and stretches out over my bed, her hands going up over her head. She is giving me the control now. I don't mind, undressing her will be like unwrapping a much anticipated gift.

As I slide her pants and remaining clothing down her legs, I find myself fighting the need to kiss every inch of skin as it becomes exposed, but I don't think I'll be able to control myself, I want in her that bad.

Jayden sits up after her clothes hit the ground. She smiles up at me and I wonder what is going through her mind, then her hand wraps around my hardness. Control is back with her. She looks up at me as she strokes me up and down, then up again. Her thumb circles the tip, smearing the beaded moisture around. I don't think I can get any harder, but I am wrong. I am going to lose myself right in her hand if she doesn't stop. I pull myself away from her touch and open the top drawer of my dresser. I pull the square package out and quickly place it on. Jayden has laid herself back down on my bed, watching me with hooded eyes.

"I need to be inside you now, Jayden."

She gives me the sexiest smile I have ever seen. "I need you inside me right now."

I watch as she spreads her legs, an invitation and the sign I need to tell me she is ready, and wanting just as I am. Grabbing her thighs, I pull her legs a little further apart and slide right between them. My tip is at her entrance. Just the slight feel of her wetness and the heat exploding from her body has me fighting to keep myself from exploding. I have to pull away from her slightly and take a few deep breaths. After a few moments, I push forward, burying myself further into her. I watch as Jayden's eyes close and her back arches up off the bed, thrusting her breasts up at me. An invitation I can't deny. I take one hard nipple into my mouth as I bury deep into her. She moans and her hands go to my backside, her nails digging into my cheeks as she tries to pull me even further into her. I gently bite the tip of her nipple, she gasps, and her back arches even more.

"You feel so good, Jayden."

She runs her nails up my back to my shoulders as her legs wrap tightly around my waist, holding me tightly inside of her.

"I need you to move, Cameron. Please!"

Hearing her beg is the sexiest thing I believe I've ever heard. I've never been this turned on by a woman before. I know if I move, I won't last that long. I'm not ready for this to be over, to leave her body. I claim her lips once again. Her legs tighten around me, she is trying to thrust up. Now she's begging me with her body, and I can no longer hold back. I pull out almost all the way then thrust back into her hard and deep, she is tight. We both moan. Her wetness is gliding me easily in and out as I set a steady pace.

"That feels good, but I want you deeper." Her voice is quiet and a little rough.

I fell her tightening around me, she's close. I quicken my thrusts, doing everything to hold myself from my own release, but it's getting harder with each slide against her hot, wet, constricting walls. I pull out, my tip only enjoying the hot center of this woman, and with one last thrust into her my name fills the room and her body shatters around me, and I follow right behind her.

CHAPTER

Ten

JAYDEN

I WAKE UP STARTLED, forgetting where I am, and it's hot. I look around and remember that I'm in Cameron's room. We must have both fallen asleep. He is wrapped tightly around me, which would explain the heat. Looking out the window, I notice that it's dark outside. What time is it?

I turn my head and I'm able to see his face. Cameron always has a look on his face like he's thinking too much. Sleeping, he looks younger, more at peace, not like the world is falling apart around him. My heart breaks for him. I can't imagine what goes through his head these days with everything that has happened.

I try to listen and hear if Jacob is home. I don't want him knowing this happened, but I didn't plan on falling asleep and making this a sleep-over either. I never stay the night with a guy, it seems too personal, too much like a relationship. I've never fallen asleep in a guy's bed after sex either, and here I am finding that not only did I easily fall asleep with Cameron, but I don't want to move right yet. I kind of like laying here. I like feeling his warmth against me, his arm around me. It's like I'm his and he isn't letting me go, protecting me even in his sleep. These are the feelings I have always tried to stay away from and here Cameron has created them inside of me with one night of sex.

Fear starts to spread in my chest. I swore I wouldn't feel this comfortable with a guy. I don't want to ever experience the pain my mom did when she found out about my dad cheating on her. I watched my mom go through a depression, even though she always tried to hide it from me, but I heard her cry herself to sleep every night. I used to go and sit outside her bedroom door and fight a need to go in and hug her. To tell her I was there, she wasn't alone, but she always worked so hard to put a strong face on around me. I didn't want her to feel worse that she wasn't fooling me. Sitting outside of her bedroom door kind of made me feel like I was there for her and still making her feel she was doing her best in front of me.

Looking over at Cameron once more, I make the decision. I need to walk away from him before I become too comfortable. Before I depend on him and these feelings he is beginning to create in me. Slowly I move out from under him, praying I don't wake him. This isn't an easy task when he is wrapped around me like he is afraid to let me go. It takes some time, but finally I am able to get up from the bed. He moves and I stand still, hoping that I didn't wake him. I watch as he settles himself onto his stomach, hugging the pillow under him. I take a deep breath and begin looking for my pants. Pulling them on, I take my phone out of the pocket, it is after eleven. I use the light to look for my shirt. I had it in my hand when we came in so I look by the door, finding it and pulling it on.

Cameron hasn't moved. I stand by the bed looking down at him. I am fighting the urge to climb back in bed with him. I quickly turn and leave the room before I find myself going against everything I have sworn against. As I turn to head down the stairs, a picture on the wall catches my attention. Well no, actually the dent in the wall next to the picture catches my attention first. It looks like someone punched the wall. The picture is of the Cameron, Jacob and their parents. It is easily ten years old. Jacob was so young, and

Cameron's smile looks like he didn't have a care in the world. It is the perfect family. Both Mr. and Mrs. Tovaren were shining with pride. You can see it in their smile and eyes. They were proud of their family.

If I think back to the pictures of my family, my mom always had that smile and look in her eyes. My dad's smile never reached his eyes. It was always forced I realized as I grew up. It's funny what the mind thinks it sees until it's shown the truth.

When I reach the bottom of the stairs, the front door opens, Jacob is home. I see the surprise on his face. I'm sure I'm the last person he expected to walk in and see in his house this late at night. I'm sure you can see the embarrassment on my face. I got caught, by one of my students, leaving their house late at night, obviously from spending time with their older brother.

"It's late," Jacob signs.

I have nothing to say, I just nod my head.

"Why are you still here?"

He doesn't really need to ask that question, I'm sure.

"Are you tutoring my brother now?"

I am in too much shock to answer, but the booming voice behind me causes me to jump.

"Jacob!"

I turn to find a shirtless Cameron standing behind me about halfway down the stairs.

"You need to apologize to Ms. Edwards now," Cameron speaks and signs.

Both guys just stand there staring at each other, and here I stand right in the middle. A place I'm not comfortable in for more reasons than one.

"Is this the reason you were so happy that I wanted to go to Tyler's tonight, so you could do this?" Jacob signs to his brother and then points between Cameron and myself.

"I'm going to go, I'm sorry," I sign to Jacob, but speak as well so that Cameron can hear behind me.

Cameron comes down the couple of stairs and stops me before I can move. "You aren't leaving until my brother apologizes."

Cameron's eyes never leave his brother's as he speaks to me.

"Cameron, it's all right, really. I'm just going to leave," I try again.

I am surprised to see the anger forming in Jacob's eyes. I may only know him from school but I would have never thought I'd see that kind of reaction and anger out of him. He is always smiling and happy. The more I stand between the two men and watch them stare each other down, the more I am beginning to think Jacob's anger isn't because I am here with Cameron, but something between the two of them. I am just his excuse.

Cameron comes around so that he is facing me, his back to Jacob. "You don't need to leave, Jayden."

I look over his shoulder at Jacob, he is shooting daggers into his brother's back. This is definitely between them two, and they need to work it out. Cameron doesn't need an excuse to keep distance between them. We don't need to let this happen again, he needs to fix his relationship with his brother.

"This should never have happened, Cameron. Jacob's right in a way. I was here to do a job, not you."

Cameron flinches a little, almost like I slapped him. Shock shoots across his face, but only briefly, he recovers quickly. Now some of that anger is pointing at me. I can tell he is trying to read me. Good luck with that, Mr. Tovaren.

I expect him to try and stop me when I begin to push past him to leave, but he doesn't. I grab my bag from the floor by the stairs and quickly walk past Jacob. Stopping at the door, I want to turn and apologize.

Tell Cameron it is everything opposite of a mistake, but then I think against it. I need to walk away from this, now before this becomes more to both of us. Opening the door, I almost run to my car. Slamming the door, I take a deep breath, my head going back to rest on the headrest. I know Cameron may never speak to me again. Isn't that what I want? My eyes burn a little. No, that isn't what I want. What the hell has Cameron done to me? I don't cry, especially over a guy!

I need Charliee, but it is midnight. Normally that wouldn't stop me but she is still healing and needs her rest. She probably wouldn't be a whole lot of help right now anyway. She keeps warning me that one day I am going to find a guy who is going to knock all my codes and rules for dating out the door. She would take much pride in telling me, "I told you so."

I need to go somewhere but I don't know where. I don't want to go home, it suddenly seems lonely. I run my hands over my face, looking around. I can't sit here in my car, in front of the Tovaren house. *Dammit, why didn't I just stay away?* I scold myself as I start my car. I have no idea where I am going but I'm not staying here!

IT'S BEEN A CRAZY WEEK. It started with Monday night with Cameron, to finding out Charliee was dating one of the hot firemen that found her that night of the bombing. I am happy for her, Travis seems like a good guy and he is very nice to look at. Charliee doesn't date much, I think she gets tired of guys treating her weird because she's deaf. She can't make it any easier for them, she talks and is usually pretty easy to understand. To top it off she reads lips like a champ, all you have to do is remember to look at her when you are talking. She has a great sense of humor when it comes to someone forgetting she's deaf, which is easily done since she talks so well. She caught me so many times when we first met.

Then Wednesday afternoon, Charliee stopped by the school and had lunch with me. She's been going crazy not being able to work. She told me about her date with Travis. I found myself becoming a little jealous. She was glowing and smiling from one ear to the other while she was telling me. Then she told me I needed a boyfriend. I almost told her about Cameron, but what exactly was I supposed to tell her? "Hey, I met Cameron Tovaren while I've been tutoring Jacob. One day he was not home so I ended up in Cameron's bed. We haven't spoken since." I could imagine the look she would give me.

I'm pretty sure she knows I'm holding something back from her. She gave me the questioning look when it all came up.

Cameron had text me this morning and told me there was no reason to come by for Jacob's tutoring, he wasn't going to be home. Nothing else was said. I thought about texting him back but what would I say? I know he was mad about the comment I made about us sleeping together not being a good idea, but honestly I just wanted out of that house and out from in between him and Jacob. I didn't tell him that the sex was amazing and waking up with him lying next to me was even better.

My phone ringing brings me out of my daze. Looking at the screen, my pulse quickens a little. Why is Charliee's brother, Derrick, calling me? Is something wrong with Charliee?

"Hello," I answer, my heart in my throat.

"Jayden, is Charliee with you?"

"No, I'm still at work, why? What's wrong?"

"There has been another explosion. This one was at the movie theater, no one can get a hold of her."

Normally I would put money on the fact that Charliee wouldn't be at the theater alone, but then again she has been pretty bored and going stir crazy lately so I wouldn't be surprised if she was. Plus, Travis could be off today and they could have gone. My veins go cold.

"I haven't seen or heard from her all day, but I'll text her and see if she responds to me."

"All right, please call me if you hear form her," Derrick's worried voice pleads with me.

"I will and please let me know if you find anything as well."

We both hang up and I immediately text Charliee.

**Where are you?

I wait what seems like forever for her to respond. I swear with each click of the clock in my classroom my heart beats faster. I am getting ready to text her again when I receive one from her.

**Give a person a chance to text back!! What is wrong with all of you??

I take a deep breath. She is all right. She sounds a little pissed, but she is safe.

I know she's feeling a little smothered right now. She has all of us surrounding her making sure she is safe, but she has no choice. She scared the hell out of us, we are keeping her close and she is going to have to get used to it.

I wait a little bit, I'm sure either her parents or her brothers are filling her in on what happened. After about ten minutes, I text her.

**Do you need me to come over tonight? I can stay with you.

She responds pretty fast.

**You have to work in the morning, I'm good. Actually I'd prefer a little alone time right now. I'll be all right. Love you.

Charliee usually doesn't like to be alone. She has always liked having people around her. She doesn't go to restaurants alone, or the movies, or even shopping. Lately, though, I'm sure with all of us hovering over her, she may need some time alone. I don't want to leave her alone tonight, but I need to let her deal with this her own way.

**If you need me for any reason please text me, no matter what time it is. Love you too.

Again, she responds quickly.

**I will, I promise.

My thoughts then go to Cameron and Jacob. This news isn't going to be easy on them either. This lunatic is still loose and still trying to kill people. I want to call Cameron, but I am pretty sure I am the last person he wants to talk to right now.

My plan is to go home and soak in my hot tub. A glass of wine sounds amazing, but I don't want to drink anything that would keep me from driving to Charliee's if she needs me tonight. I'm not sure who is more surprised, myself when I find myself parked in Cameron's driveway, or Cameron when he opens the front door and finds me standing there.

"Hi." He doesn't invite me in, he just stands there in the doorway staring at me.

I don't like these feelings he is creating in me. He has me all twisted up and I'm not sure if I like it.

"I just heard about the bombing at the movie theater and wanted to come by and see how you guys were."

I sound pathetic to myself as I speak. Why would I need to come check on two grown men? Cameron's eyebrow arches a little, I think I surprised him.

"I was just watching about it on T.V. Jacob isn't here, he's at Tyler's house."

I watch as Cameron's muscles flex under his t-shirt when he brings his arm up to the door frame above his head. His shirt tightens across his chest. My hands itch to reach out and touch him and my body heats up with want. I need to leave before I do something to embarrass myself.

"Well, I'll see you later. I'm sorry if I interrupted anything."

I turn to leave, but only make it a couple steps before I decide I need to apologize for the other night. Turning, I find myself plastered against Cameron's chest. I hadn't even heard him move, and here he is standing right behind me. He isn't touching me, but I can feel the heat from his body. My hand comes up and rests on his chest. I can't stop them any longer, not being this close to him. I don't look up at him, though. I'm not sure if I want to see what his eyes may be saying.

"I'm sorry, Cameron," I speak into his chest.

He doesn't say anything back and he isn't touching me back. I am waiting for him to remove my hand and tell me to leave.

"What are you doing to me, Jayden?"

That brings my eyes up to his in surprise. Before I can say anything, his lips claim mine. His arms circle around my waist and pull my body up tight against his. I trail my hands up over his shoulders and to the back of his neck, one hand going into his hair. I hold onto him like a he is my lifesaver and he is keeping me from drowning.

Our lips separate and we just stand there, forehead to forehead. "Cameron, I'm sorry for what happened the other day."

He stands to his full height, pushing away from me a little. "Sorry for what part of the other day, Jayden?"

My mind can't think straight with our bodies touching. I take a step away from him, a chill running through my body with the heat of his missing. "I'm sorry for what I said the other day before I left. About us sleeping together being a mistake."

He takes a step toward me, but I take another one back. We need to have this conversation and I can't do that with him in touching distance, or I won't get anything out that I need to say.

"Wait, please," I hold my hand out in front of me to stop him from stepping closer to me once again. "I need to say this, Cameron."

He only nods and takes a step back, putting more space between us. Now that I have the space and all of his attention, I don't know what exactly it is that I want to say.

"Jayden, why don't we go inside and talk."

I'm not sure if being inside is a good idea. At least out here I will be able to control myself a little where he is concerned. Who the hell am I trying to kid? I lose all control with this man and forget where I am, inside or out won't make a difference I'm sure.

Nodding, I follow him inside, enjoying the view of his backside. *Stop!* I yell at myself.

"Would you like something to drink?"

A beer, glass of wine, even a shot would be great, I think to myself. "No, thank you."

He points over toward the couch. "Have a seat."

I sit and silently hope he will sit in the chair but no, he sits right next to me on the couch.

"So what do you want to talk about?"

How in the blue blazes am I supposed to think, let alone talk with him sitting so close to me? All I want to do is grab him and have a repeat of the other night.

I clear my throat and look down at my hands. "I just wanted to apologize for the way things ended the other night."

"That's what you said outside."

I take another deep breath, he isn't going to make this easy, is he?

"I should never have said what I did. I was embarrassed that Jacob caught me leaving. I don't blame him for being mad that night. I'm his teacher."

"Jayden, that is no excuse for the things he said to you. I understand he has anger in him right now, but that doesn't excuse him for being rude."

"Cameron, really, I understand…"

"No, I think part of the problem right now is that I'm creating excuses for his moods and attitude, but I think that may be the problem. I need to stop babying him. What he said was completely wrong."

"Cameron, have you tried to talk to Jacob?" I finally look up at Cameron and my heart breaks.

His eyes are downcast, he is rubbing his thighs, and he looks worried.

"One day I can't get him to leave the house or talk to any friends, the next I can't get him to stay home."

That brings another thing to mind that we need to talk about. Jacob missing all of his tutoring. Cameron is finally talking to me and I don't want to ruin that, but like he just said about Jacob, I can't keep backing down because I am afraid of how Cameron will react to the conversation. He needs to step up as well.

"That's another thing we need to talk about, Cameron. Jacob hasn't been home for tutoring for a week, this can't keep happening or he is going to fall behind again. You might want to think about putting him back into school."

I watch as Cameron takes a deep breath, leaning back in the chair and running his hands through his hair. "There needs to be a manual on how to raise your teenage brother."

He is getting mad, it is written all over his face. "Raising kids in general doesn't look easy. I can't imagine taking over a teenage sibling after losing both my parents, Cameron. It's not going to be easy, but you can't give up on him either."

He sits back up, his elbows on his knees, his face in his hands. I place my hand on his knee. "Cameron, there are plenty of people willing to help if you just ask."

Still nothing but silence, he has shut down on me. "All right, well I'll be going. I'll be back on Monday for tutoring, please make sure Jacob is here. If you need to talk, Cameron, you know how to reach me."

I wait a second longer, hoping he will say something but no, he just sits there. I stand up, but Cameron moves quickly. Before I know it I am sitting on his lap, his arms tightly wrapped around me, his lips devouring mine. There is a plea behind the kiss. He is holding onto me like I will disappear if he lets go. It is creating all kinds of feelings through me. The feeling of being needed is pulling the strongest.

"Can I have you, Jayden, please?" he asks against my lips.

There is no way I can or want to tell him no. He needs me, and if I am going to be honest with myself, I need him.

"Not down here, Cameron. I don't want to risk Jacob and his friends walking in."

He doesn't even hesitate, he quickly stands up with me in his arms and I swear he runs up the stairs. He sits me down as he closes the door to his bedroom and I am pulling his shirt up over his head, trailing my hands down his shoulders and then over his chest, his stomach and then down to the button of his jeans. I unbutton them all the way down then bring my hands around, sinking them into the back of them, pushing his jeans and boxer briefs down over his waist, grabbing his very nice backside. My hands have itched to grab this man's cheeks since following him toward the house earlier.

His physical strength is obvious everywhere I touch. I don't think I've ever wanted to just stand in front of a man and just run my hands over his entire body, feeling the definition of his muscles.

"Jayden, I need to be inside of you."

His voice is husky in my ear. It sends chills down my very heated body. I step back and quickly remove my clothes, standing in front of him naked, open for him to take me anyway he wants.

He finishes removing his boots and pants. He closes the space between us, then pushes me back against the bedroom door. His lips travel all over my neck, then finally back to my lips. Every time he kisses me, I feel lightheaded. It feels like a quick shot of the best liquor going straight to my core, heating it up. Feeling his hardness between us just ignites that flame working at my core. Holding onto his shoulders, I begin climbing up his body. I feel like I can't get close enough to him.

One of his hands goes under my backside lifting me up, the other one guides himself as he enters me. The feeling of his full length gliding into me is intoxicating. His other hand comes around to my backside and he lifts me up, pulling himself slowly out as I push my hips down, thrusting him fully and deeply back in.

Our pace begins to speed up, my head falls back against the door, which thrusts my hips forward and him deeper. His lips explore my breast. I am close, so very close, and then he stops.

"Jayden, I forgot protection."

My heart squeezes a little over the concern in his eyes. That is the moment it happens. Here I am pushed up against Cameron's bedroom door, my legs wrapped around his waist, him deep inside of me. I am doing something I swore I would never do—I am falling for a guy!

"I'm on the pill, Cameron. I'm clean, I've never had unprotected sex."

"I promise you, I'm clean."

My hands go from his shoulders to the back of his head, burying my fingers into his hair, bringing his lips back down to mine.

CHAPTER
Eleven

"CAMERON, it looks like we will be ready for final inspection on this track in about two weeks."

"Kevin, here is my problem. This track and the one down in Texas are going to be at the same time. So like I told Steve down there, as soon as you have a possible date, I need to know. The other one will have to be set around the first date set."

Silence stretches on the other end of the line. Kevin was my father's second in command up here in Washington. He has worked for our company as foreman for as long as I can remember.

"Cameron, how are you doing?"

The question catches me off guard for a moment but before I can answer him, Jacob comes into the room, signing to me that he is going to Tyler's. It is Monday, he has tutoring today, I sign for him to wait.

"Kevin, I have to go, Jacob just walked in and I need to talk with him. Please let me know of a date as soon as you can, please."

"All right!" You can hear the frustration in his voice that I didn't answer his question. "I'll call you when I have some more information. Cameron, if you need anything, please let know."

"Thanks, Kevin, I'll talk to you later."

After I end the call, I bring my attention back to my brother.

"You have tutoring tonight. You already missed last week," I sign.

Jacob shrugs his shoulders. "I've got it, I don't need it anymore."

"Maybe it's time we think about you going back to school."

"That would make you happy, wouldn't it?" he fires back at me.

Here we go again with the attitude. "Why would you say that? You go over to Tyler's every day now as soon as he gets out of school, maybe you need to be back in school. We agreed on a couple weeks."

"I'm not ready."

"Fine, then you need to continue with tutoring."

"For me or you?!"

I don't think I've ever wanted to punch my brother as much as I want to right now. "You're stepping on dangerous grounds. You have no reason to talk about Ms. Edwards like that."

We stare at each other for what seems like an hour. My brother stands almost at my height, we are eye to eye. Without saying another word, he turns and starts for the front door. I grab his arm before he makes it too far, turning him back to me.

"You aren't leaving today," I sign.

"You can't tell me what to do. You are just my brother, not my dad."

"What is wrong with you? Why are you mad at me?"

Emotions run through his eyes. One thing about the deaf, their faces and eyes are very expressive. He wants to say something, I can see him debating with himself.

The lights began to flash through the house and the doorbell sounds. "That will be Ms. Edwards."

Jacob doesn't make a move to answer it. I don't know what to do anymore. It takes everything I have in me not to throw my hands up and tell him to do whatever he wants to do. I walk over and open the door.

"Hi."

"Hello." She comes in past me and looks over at Jacob. "Hello, Jacob, are you ready?" she signs to him.

Jacob walks over to the two of us. "You can tutor Cameron today since that's what you would both prefer. I'm leaving."

Before I can respond, he runs out of the house and to his car.

"Jayden, I'm sorry. I don't know what's wrong with him.'"

"Cameron, he's hurting and right now he probably thinks I'm taking you away from him as well."

"How can you be taking me away from him? He hasn't said more than a dozen words to me since I've been home."

"You need to start putting your foot down, Cameron, you are letting him walk all over you."

"He is seventeen years old, Jayden. You don't put your foot down like he is five."

What did she want me to do, ground him? Like he said, I'm his brother, not his father.

"Cameron, he is still a kid who needs guidance. He is walking all over you and you are allowing him to. He needs parenting."

"Well, they're dead!" I shout.

Jayden flinches and takes a step back. Her shock quickly changes to anger.

"Then that means you need to step up, Cameron. You yelling and taking your anger out on me isn't going to work. I'm just trying to help."

"I don't recall asking for your help, Ms. Edwards."

"Really, Cameron, back to last names? Maybe you're right. If you are going to act like a teenager, how does anyone expect you to raise one?"

"Who the hell made you an expert? I don't think you have any right to tell me what and what not to do with Jacob. It is absolutely none of your business."

I know I am lashing out at the wrong person. I just can't seem to stop. She is here and I am pissed, she became the target, which isn't fair and I know it. I am getting ready to apologize but am stopped by the hellion in front of me.

"You, sir, are a jackass. Just because you are angry over the situation and frustrated, it doesn't mean you can turn it onto me. No need to worry about me interfering any longer, I'm done wasting my time with the two of you."

She turns and leaves me standing there staring after her. I know I should stop her, but I don't move, I just let her go. Maybe this is the best. I need to concentrate on the business, Jacob, and I still have all the legal affairs, I don't have time for more stress. Whatever we have is causing more problems between Jacob and I, and I definitely don't need all of that right now.

I do see the hurt in her eyes, behind all of the anger. My chest tightens, my anger completely disappears and I realize she is right. I am being an ass, she doesn't deserve that.

My phone rings back in the office. I pick it up and see Mr. Colter, Tyler's father's name up on the screen. My chest jumps, is something wrong with Jacob? I know he left here mad and was driving.

"Hello, Mr. Colter," I answer and hear the insecurity in my own voice.

"Hello, Cameron, please call me David."

"Is everything all right?"

"Jacob is here and safe. I'm sorry, I didn't mean to alarm you with my call."

I take a deep breath and try to calm my racing heart down.

"Cameron, if I'm stepping over lines with what I'm about to say, please feel free to tell me."

His timing couldn't be worse. I have a very strong feeling this is another person giving me their advice on what I need to do with Jacob. This is his best friend's father, though. I need to take a deep breath and listen.

"What's on your mind, sir?" I hope the edge isn't coming through my voice.

Join the party, I think to myself.

"At first Tyler would come home after coming by and would be concerned because Jacob wouldn't talk to him. Now he is here every day."

"I know, I'm sorry…"

"Cameron," David stops me, "we don't mind Jacob being here, he is always welcome. That came out wrong, I'm sorry. We are just catching small conversations, he is angry. Basically the reason I'm calling is I was wondering if you needed any help or advice. I know you're a grown man, but right now you have a lot to take care of. It's hard for parents to handle teenagers, let alone an older brother who has to take care of everything and a teenager because of the loss of their parents."

I don't know what to say. Part of me wants to yell some more and tell him I have everything under control. Another part of me wants to beg the man to tell me what to do about Jacob.

"Cameron, are you still there?"

I have a tight grip on my phone, my other hand fisted.

"Cameron?"

"Sorry, yes, I'm here. I appreciate your concern and your offer, sir. I think for now I've got it. Today I mentioned maybe it was time for Jacob to go back to school. He became mad, saying he wasn't ready."

I'm not going to add the part about Jayden.

"I agree with you, Cameron, I think it's time Jacob starts getting back to what he normally does. School I think is a good idea."

David is going to give me his advice it seems regardless of wanting it or not.

"He says he isn't ready yet."

"I know you just said you were good on handling everything, but I feel I need to give you a little advice, use it as you want. Jacob is going to test you. Do the opposite of what you say. Get mad, even yell and tell you he hates you. You need to remember to hold your ground. Don't give in to him all of the time because of what's happened, he will walk all over you if you keep giving into him."

Everyone today seems to have their opinion on what I need to do with Jacob. Jayden and now David Colter. Someone is pushing me and wanting to see how far I can be pushed. I really don't need all of this right now. I already question myself on if I am doing anything right, all of this is almost showing me I'm not.

"David, I appreciate the call. I will keep all of what you said in mind."

"Just remember, we are here if you need anything."

"Thank you." I quickly end the call before I lose the last of my reserve and tell the man off. I am close to blowing up.

Sitting back in my father's chair, I look around. My eyes land on a picture of my mother my father had on his desk. She always knew how to handle us boys. We never questioned her. I think my brother and I were more afraid of what she would do if we screwed up than our father. She never raised her voice or a hand at us, but she had a look that we knew when we did wrong. I could almost see her giving it to me now. Disappointed in the way I am handling everything. I need to get out of this house. I have no idea where I think I need to go, but I can't be here.

CHAPTER

Twelve

"THIS WAS A GREAT IDEA, Jayden, my toes needed some attention."

All week I have done nothing but think of Cameron. Thursday I didn't even attempt to go by the house for Jacob's tutoring. I am done with all of that. As the weekend came around, I was finding it harder to not text Cameron. So instead I texted Charliee, asking if she wanted to hang out and go get pedicures.

"I'm just surprised you were able to pull yourself away from your hunk of a boyfriend. I feel honored to have a little time with you," I tease her.

I have no room to talk, a certain good looking guy has been taking up a lot of my time until this week as well.

"I know and I'm sorry, but you can only blame yourself. You were the one always telling me I needed to find a guy," Charliee defends herself.

"Well, I'm rethinking it all now. I didn't realize it would take you away from me like this."

"Maybe it's time for you to find someone and we can double date."

Find someone? If only I knew if I had or not. Wait, what am I thinking? Cameron hasn't tried to get a hold of me since Monday night, I think it's safe to say I don't have a "someone". This is why I should stick with my rules of no relationships.

"All right, Jayden, what's going on? Are you seeing someone and not telling me about it?"

No, I'm not seeing someone. I'm having sex with someone, but not seeing them, I think to myself.

"Come on, Jayden. You followed me into the shower literally to get the story about Travis. Who is this guy you haven't told me about?"

Smiling, I think back to the day I found out she had gone to see the firefighter who pulled her out from the bombing. She had gone to the station and he asked her out the next day. I did follow her into the shower to get the details. She wasn't giving any information up and was trying to hide from me with taking a shower. That wasn't going to stop me from getting the details, I followed her in.

I shrug my shoulders. "There really isn't much to tell yet. I'm not sure if there is anything even starting. Honestly he infuriates me more than anything."

"So I'm guessing you like this guy?"

Like Cameron? Right now I'm not liking him very much. Maybe I just need to forget about him, and all of the great sex, and go back to my original dating rules. Or maybe just stay away from men altogether for a little while.

"I haven't said anything because I'm not sure if there is anything to tell." I can tell Charliee is trying to read me. It is hard keeping things from her. She can read me like no one else can.

"So what do you have planned after our toes?" This is why she is my best friend. She knows when to not push me. I know it is killing her to not know who it is, or what is going on, but she knows me well enough to know I am needing more time.

Today has been much needed time with Charliee. I even got her to go shopping after our toes and lunch, and she hates shopping. I had hoped to get Cameron off my mind, but now that I am home again, alone, all I can seem to think about is him. This is crazy. Why am I sitting around on a Saturday night, alone, thinking about someone who obviously doesn't think about or want me? When did I become one of those girls?

I should be out tonight, but Charliee didn't want to go out. She will probably spend the evening texting Travis at work. I have a very strong feeling my best friend is done with her going out days. I saw the look in her eyes today when we talked about Travis. She is in love. I can't blame her, Travis seems like a great guy. I think what convinced me about how much she means to him was today when she told me he was learning sign language. Charliee reads lips better than anyone. I only learned to sign after meeting her because I was fascinated with the language, not because we had a hard time communicating.

Travis is learning her world. There aren't many men out there like him. I'm glad Charliee found him. She, if anyone, deserves a guy like him.

Who am I kidding, I really have no want or desire to go out anywhere tonight either. What I want is to be with Cameron. Damnit, I'm one of those girls. I've actually fallen for a guy. Problem is, that guy doesn't want me.

CHAPTER
Thirteen

CAMERON

THIS LAST PAST week has been hell. First the incident with Jayden. Wednesday, Steve called and informed me we once again had vandalism on the track. This time, though, the group was caught. So hopefully this will be the last time. Unfortunately, the damage is large and will be expensive to repair. Not one that would set final inspection back, which, right now, I don't need. The two tracks are already too close together with dates only a couple weeks apart, the Texas site finishing first. Now they are closer.

Yesterday, Kevin called and one of our workers who was working on the roof fell and had to be taken to the hospital. He dislocated his knee and had some stitches on his forehead. To top everything off, this morning I told Jacob he was going back to school on Monday. He didn't respond at all, but that saying "if looks could kill," yep, I would have been shoved six feet down. He just walked up to his room and I haven't seen him since.

I've had about two hours of sleep each night. Every time I lay in my bed and shut my eyes, I see Jayden spread out on my bed, naked, begging me with her eyes and parted legs to take her. I have no idea how many times I've started to call and text her, apologizing for everything that happened Monday, but never did.

Maybe it is a good thing to keep things this way. Do I really need any more obstacles in my life right now?

Jacob's door slams upstairs, now is the time to prepare for the next round of fun. Last night after he went to bed, I went up and took his car keys. I am done with this anger shit he has been dealing out to me. He isn't leaving to go to Tyler's again until we talk.

"My keys?" Jacob signs the second he comes off the stairs.

I don't respond. Strange, earlier when I thought about all of this, I had plenty to say. Now, I can't figure out where to start.

"Where are my keys?" he asks again.

"I have them."

"You had no right to come in my room and take them."

"We need to talk."

"I have nothing to say."

"Jacob, you need to tell me why, since I've been home, you've acted like you don't want me here."

Instead of answering, he begins to look around. I pull the keys out of my pocket and hold them up until he notices them.

"You want them, then talk. What have I done that has pissed you off so much? I know it's not the whole Ms. Edwards thing, you weren't talking to me before that."

He stands there glaring at me. Tears are in his eyes, which almost causes me to lose it altogether. He is fighting something.

"Jacob, talk to me."

"You weren't here!" He signs it with so much anger, I almost feel like each word punches me in the chest. I wasn't here? What is he saying?

"Wasn't here for what?" I sign back.

Complete silence fills the room. He isn't answering me.

"Jacob, what wasn't I here for?" I try again.

"When they died." His motions are flat and tears fall from his eyes.

I feel like someone has their hands around my throat and bricks are sitting on my chest. Is he blaming me for our parents dying?

"How would I have stopped that?"

"You can go back to Texas." He grabs for his keys but I pull them back. Then it clicks.

"Jacob, I got here as fast as I could. I'm sorry I wasn't here when you found out."

When I moved to Texas a few years ago, Jacob said he was going with me. Of course, our parents would never have let that happen. I knew he wasn't happy I moved away, but I would have never guessed in the time I was gone, he was mad at me for going. We texted every day. We did talk about him coming down after graduation next year, but he never gave me any clue he was that mad that I moved away.

"Why do you think I'm going back to Texas?" Does he honestly think I am going back to Texas and leaving him here?

"None of your stuff is here," he signs.

No, it isn't. I haven't brought my stuff up. I knew I had to go to Texas for the final inspection of the track. At that time, I was going to talk to Steve about becoming one of my partners and taking over the Texas side of our business. I was going to fly down and then drive my stuff back. Did Jacob honestly think I was going to leave him here?

Jacob reaches across, catching me off guard, and grabs his keys out of my hand. Before I can stop him, he is out the door.

Shock is the best word I can think of to describe how I feel right now. That's what this has been all about. He thinks I am going to leave him here and go back to Texas. I know he's seventeen and all. I know the school has boarding, but never did it even cross my mind to leave him here alone. I knew from the moment I got the call from David Colter that my parents were killed in the bombing that I'd be moving back here to Washington. To be honest, I don't know if even my brother had been well into his twenties when all this had happened, I would have gone back. I have even already gotten a hold of a realtor in Texas to start putting things together to put my house up for sale.

Before I can even stop myself, I grab my phone and find Jayden's name and send her a text.

**I need you at my house.

I hit send. I need someone to talk to and Jayden is the only one I can think of to talk to about all of this.

CHAPTER
Fourteen

JAYDEN

WHEN I RECEIVED THE TEXT, I had to look twice at who it was from.

** I need you at my house

Did Cameron text it to the wrong person? I read the text over and over, like somehow it will change. Why does he need me at his house? It is probably a mistake, he probably meant this for another girl. I could text back and let him know, wrong person buddy, but if he texts back sorry, well then…

Wait, what if something is wrong? That must be it, something is wrong. I quickly grab my keys and wallet, running out to my car.

I think I run two red lights, but I make it to the Tovaren house probably in record time. Running up to the front door, I ring the doorbell. My imagination is going crazy. I almost just walk straight in. I swear if someone doesn't answer it soon, I am going to just walk in.

I go to grab for the knob when the door finally opens, and there stands Cameron.

"What…"

Cameron grabs me, pulling me up tight against his chest, his lips taking mine. My body instantly melts. Just this man's lips can cause me to turn to mush.

Finally, my brain turns back on. What the hell is going on? Ending the kiss and taking a step back is one of the hardest things I've done. My body wants to go back, but my brain needs answers.

"Cameron, what's going on?"

He reaches out for me, but I take another step back.

"Again, let me ask, what's going on? Is Jacob all right? Are you all right?"

"Physically, everyone is fine," he finally speaks.

Unbelievable, what is he playing at?

"Seriously, that's your answer?"

Passionate heat is turning to angry heat. Who the hell does he think he is? After the way he yelled at me, he thinks now he can just text and I'll come running? To top it off, he thinks he can just pull me against him and kiss me? Wait! That is exactly what just happened. I came running with a text. Fool me once, my bad, but not anymore.

Shaking my head, I turn to leave. "Jayden, wait, please."

Something in his voice doesn't sound right. His plea stops me, something is wrong.

"Listen, can we just go inside and talk, please?"

Do I really want to go back to this? Sure, earlier I was sitting at home missing him. Now I am still a little pissed that he thought I would just come over and act like nothing happened.

"Jayden, look, I'm sorry. I had no right to take my anger out on you the other day. I have no good excuse. All I can say is sorry."

His eyes are pleading with me. Why can't I stay mad at this guy? I'm not going to make it easy on him though. I will listen, I can't walk away from those eyes. Not saying anything, I walk past him and into the house. I sit down in the chair, this will be safer than sitting next to him on the couch.

"Thank you," Cameron says, sitting down on the couch.

"What did you need to talk to me about?"

"Today, Jacob and I had a little talk. Well, actually I think I did most of the talking. Anyway, I believe I figured out why Jacob isn't talking to me. I'm still a little confused about all of it, but it's nice to have some reason."

I am trying to be patient and listen to where he is going with what he is talking about, but I am running pretty short on patience right now.

"Cameron, what's happening?"

"Jacob is mad at me because I live in Texas."

Live in Texas? Why would Jacob be mad at him for that right now?

"I don't understand."

"Neither did I at first. Today I finally asked him what I did that has made him so angry with me, besides sleeping with you."

I know I blush a little, my face instantly becomes warm. "So you think he is mad because you moved?"

Cameron nods. "When I moved away, he said he was going with me, but of course we all knew that wasn't happening. Anyway, I believe he thinks I'm leaving again and without him."

"You haven't talked to him about any of this before now? Honestly, why wouldn't he think you would be going back? If I thought about it, I would have thought the same thing."

Another reason why getting involved with Cameron probably isn't a good idea. How long can he stay? His home and business are down in Texas.

"No, honestly I haven't really thought about the need to talk to him about it. He hasn't said much to me since being home. I told you that night we went out for drinks he wasn't talking to me. Then he only became more distant after finding out about you and me. Plus, he is a kid, why would I talk to him about my personal life?"

Personal life? Men! I would have thought Cameron and Jacob would have talked about what's happening next. Jacob is probably too worried to ask. Of course he would be worried about what was going to happen to him next. If Cameron was going to push him off to another family member or what.

"Cameron, he probably thinks you are going to leave him again. Then again, why wouldn't he think that if you haven't talked to him about any of the plans? What are you planning on doing?"

"Even if I was going back to Texas, I would have taken him with me, I wouldn't leave him here alone. I decided to move back here anyway. He only has one more year of high school left, I wouldn't take him away from his friends on his senior year."

"Have you told him that now that you have figured out what's wrong with him?"

"No, he never let me explain anything. He took off to Tyler's again. He told me that since I haven't brought my stuff here, my truck and house things, he figured I'd be going back. He is also mad that I wasn't here when everything happened."

Everything happened? Cameron can't even say what happened. His parent's died, by the hand of a very selfish human being, and he can't say it. That can't be good for any of their anger, they both need to talk about it.

"Cameron, you couldn't have stopped the bomb from going off, or your parent's going out to dinner."

"I know that, and Jacob isn't thinking I could. He was with Tyler's family when he found out. I'm thankful for that, but I wasn't here until the next day. I took the first flight I could get, but it took some time for me to get here."

"So what you are saying is that you believe Jacob's been mad at you for leaving in the first place, this just created enough to bring that anger out. Were you two always real close?"

Cameron laughs a little. "No, actually when he was born I was pissed at my parents for having another kid. I was eleven and didn't like that I wasn't getting all the attention any longer. When he was about five, we were at a restaurant and some kids were making fun of him because he was making sounds instead of talking. I got pissed at the kids, but when the father started laughing I got up, walked past him and kicked his chair out from under him. From that moment on, I swore no one would pick on him again and we were always together from that point on. My friends learned that if I was going to be around, so was my brother. He never left my side unless we were in school."

"How mad was he when you moved away? That must have been hard on him."

"He was upset, but we have texted each other every day I've been gone. I always told him he had to finish school and then afterwards he could come down to Texas. He had texted me a couple times the day everything happened. I was dealing with problems with work and had forgotten to read the text and answer him. Finally, Tyler's dad got a hold of me later that night and told me what had happened."

I want to talk to him about talking about what happened with his parents and their death. On the other side of it, I don't want to be yelled at again for telling him what to do. So I decide to let it go for now.

"So you didn't tell him you weren't going back to Texas?"

"He didn't give me a chance. I was a little shocked and before I could explain what my plans were, he ran out. I have to go to Texas for final inspection in a couple weeks and planned on bringing all my stuff back then."

I don't know what I should or shouldn't say. Every time we discuss Jacob and I voice my opinion or a suggestion, Cameron ends up telling me to mind my own business and yells at me. Now he is staring at me like he is expecting me to tell him what to do.

"Cameron, every time I say something, we end up in a fight. Please don't look at me like you are waiting for me to give you a suggestion on how to handle this."

"Jayden, I said I was sorry."

Does he really think that is all it is going to take?

"Cameron, you haven't only yelled at me once, but twice. Once in public. You apologized after that time as well, but that didn't stop this last round we had."

He looks down at his hands. Nothing is said for a good amount of time. I am about to say that I am just going to leave when he finally speaks.

"I needed someone to talk to. You are the only adult I have spoken to since being home. Even Tyler's dad called and tried giving me some parenting advice. I already know I'm not doing a great job with Jacob, everyone telling me what I should be doing is only confirming that. I'm not sure what to do with Jacob. This isn't the kid I know. I'm used to the happy kid he has always been."

Hearing the pain in Cameron's voice makes me want to go over and hold him. I know he basically just told me he wants my advice, but I still feel like I am going to have to watch what I say. He came to me when he needed someone to talk to. My chest expanded some when he said that. I don't trust myself to be sitting next to him but I need to touch him.

Reaching over, I place my hand over his. "Cameron, I wasn't trying tell you that you weren't doing things right with Jacob the other day and I'm sure Mr. Colter wasn't meaning for you to feel that way either.

Your world has been flipped upside down. Losing both of your parents, having to care for your brother, run your family's company and somewhere in there, you need time to grieve. I'm pretty sure you haven't done any grieving. I know I was only trying to help and I'm pretty sure Mr. Colter meant no different. Jacob is a great kid. You are right, he was always happy. Smiling all of the time. He was always in a large group of people. You have to remember his world was turned upside down as well. Like you getting mad at me because you had no one else to get mad at, he is mad as well, and you are the one who he is going to aim his anger at."

Holding my breath, I wait for him to say something, hoping I haven't stepped over a line. His hand just holds mine tightly. His voice is low when he finally speaks. So low I almost don't hear him.

"I miss them so much," he whispers, and it tears my chest wide open hearing the pain in his voice.

I can't stay away from him any longer. Kneeling down in front of him, I place my hand on his cheek, trying to get him to look at me. I feel the wetness, knowing he is crying shatters me. This strong, hard-faced man is crying. I feel the tears well up in my eyes. He doesn't move, he just keeps his head hanging down.

"Cameron, look at me."

Nothing, he almost seems distant. Since my hand is still on his cheek, I push his face up. His eyes look anywhere but at me. Almost like he is embarrassed to show me his pain.

"You should never be ashamed of showing your pain, Cameron. You're not a robot. No one expects you to be strong all the time. Asking for help isn't a bad thing. Showing that your parents' death is affecting you isn't something to be ashamed of."

His eyes finally look at me. The tears are gone, but I can still see the hurt in them. A man who just lost both of his parents that he loved very much. If I wasn't hooked completely on this man before, I am now.

Slowly, he brings his head down to rest his forehead against mine. He is wanting to kiss me. He wants to know if I have forgiven him yet. I circle my hand around to the back of his head, digging my fingers into his hair and bringing his lips down to mine.

Our lips touch and for the first time, it isn't raw. His lips are smooth and tender. He isn't crushing our lips together, eagerly seeking out my tongue with his. Instead, he moves them lightly against mine. There is a tender side to this man and my heart flips in my chest for him. I have officially fallen for a guy!

"Jayden, I have never known a woman like you before."

His voice is husky. I'm not even wondering if what he said is a good or bad thing. Everything right now is good. The feelings racing through my body, the way my heart trips every time his lips tenderly touch mine, everything is good.

"You are one of a kind as well."

"I want to take you upstairs now."

"Are you asking me if I forgive you?" I smile against his lips.

"I'm really hoping you forgive me. I hear make up sex is the best kind of sex."

I think I like playful Cameron. "Is that all you want me around for, my body?"

His smile fades. "Is that what you think?"

I don't want the playful Cameron to leave. I bring my hands down to the top of his jeans, unbuttoning the fly of his pants. I run my hands up and under his shirt, running them up his stomach to his chest.

"I'm using you for your body!" I smile up at him, looking through my lashes.

His smile returns. Or maybe it is more like a cocky grin. Before I can guess what he is going to do, he is up on his feet with me slung over his shoulder and heading up the stairs.

"This is so caveman," I say as my hands smack his backside.

"I could drag you up the stairs by your hair, woman."

"Hair pulling sounds fun, just in bed though, not being dragged by it up the stairs."

We reach his room. Cameron sits me down and starts working out of his clothes. I quickly discard my own. We are standing in front of each other naked in no time. He takes a step closer to me, our bodies barely touching. His arm goes around behind me. I feel him grab my hair and twist it around his hand. He pulls down, forcing my head back, his lips instantly going to my neck.

"I like your hair, Jayden," he whispers.

Electricity shoots through my body. He pulls a little harder and I moan. I feel him smile against my neck.

"You like it a little rough, do you?"

He starts walking me backwards toward the bed. The back of my legs hit the softness of the mattress. Without releasing my hair, he turns me around, now my back is against his chest. His other hand starts at my thigh and slowly runs up my leg, over my hip, to my back. Once his hand makes it to my shoulder, he gently pushes me forward, my chest now against the bed. I can feel his hardness against my backside. Cameron's hand comes back down my back, once he comes to my hips his hands come around to my front and two fingers slide deep inside of me.

"You're so wet, Jayden. So ready for me."

"Cameron, please," I beg and push my backside against his hardness.

He removes his fingers, I moan again. At once he pulls my hair again and enters me with one quick thrust. I bite my lip to keep from yelling. I feel him slide out almost all the way and then once again thrust into me, again pulling my hair. The sensation is like nothing I've ever felt before. The pleasure of him filling me so completely and deep, with the sting of my scalp from where he pulls my hair. It takes no time at all to lose myself. My insides tighten around Cameron's hardness, my body begging him to release with me.

CHAPTER
Fifteen

CAMERON

THIS WOMAN IS CAPTURING my heart. I never thought that would happen. I was always too busy with work to open enough time in my life for a relationship. Or maybe I just never found someone who made me want to create extra time for them. Now here when timing is crazy with both sides of the business to run, dealing with Jacob and still finishing up with business from my parents' deaths, Jayden appears in my life.

Jayden is still asleep, her head resting on my chest, her leg slung over mine. She had said she didn't do the relationship thing as well. Now I wonder what she meant by that.

Hearing the door shut downstairs, I figure Jacob just got home. Looking over at the clock, I'm shocked that it is only seven, he's home early tonight. I hate to wake Jayden, she is sleeping pretty sound, but Jacob and I need to talk. I need to clear things up with him, we can't keep going the way it has been. I try as soft as possible to move out from under Jayden, even though my body right now only wants to stay where I am. She can stay up here and sleep while I go and talk to Jacob, we aren't going to hide whatever this is between us.

Once I move away, Jayden stirs and quickly settles back to sleep. Throwing my jeans back on, I grab my shirt and leave her sleeping there in my bed.

I find Jacob in the kitchen, looking through the fridge. I lean against one of the counters and wait for him to turn around. A few moments pass and finally I have his attention. I wait for him to roll his eyes and try to jet past me but instead he surprises the hell out of me and matches my stance against an opposite counter.

"You are home early," I sign after a few moments of both of us just standing there staring at each other.

He only nods his head.

"Jacob, we need to talk and clear a few things up."

Again, he only nods with agreement. It seems like I'm going to be the one doing all the talking, which is fine, he needs to know what I have to say.

"Let's start with the school issue. I called the principal yesterday and told him you would be back on Monday. I think it's time to start getting back to life."

Jacob stares down at the coke can he is drinking out of. After a minute, he sets it down on the counter and then finally looks back up at me.

"I'm not sure what exactly a regular life is anymore, but I will go back on Monday."

A little shocked, all I can do is stare at him in surprise. He has gone from a very angry, almost childlike temper tantrum earlier today to my seventeen-year-old, mature brother. What happened in between to change him that fast?

"Jacob, we are going to have to adjust to a new life, both of us. Mom and Dad are gone, we will have some changes, which brings me to the next thing. I don't know why you thought I would leave you here alone and go back to Texas, but I never even thought that. In a couple weeks, I will have to go to Texas and go through the final inspection on the track home down there but afterwards, I'm packing everything and coming home here. I have already looked into selling my house there, it's on the market already."

"What about the business down there in Texas, how are you going to run that from here?"

"I can do most of the work from here, paperwork wise. I may have to make a trip down there every once in a while but Steve will actually run the projects."

"Tyler's dad told me today that I needed to talk to you."

So that's what changed in the last couple of hours. It pisses me off a little that Jacob will listen to Mr. Colter, but wouldn't give me a chance to talk to him. I instantly cool my temper, at least someone was able to get through to him, now maybe we can start fixing things from this point on.

Jacob looks down at my bare feet, "I saw Ms. Edwards' car outside."

It isn't a question. I just nod, now we need to figure out this problem. Get everything out in the open and start fresh.

"I'm not sure how I feel about you sleeping with my teacher."

I understand his feelings, if I am honest with myself I'm not sure how I feel about sleeping with his teacher. Obviously not for the same reasons as his, but all the same.

"I'm not just sleeping with her, I think I'm starting to like her more than that," I confess to him.

As he stares at me, you can see him thinking about it.

"Just don't push it on me."

Push it on him? I haven't pushed anything on him, especially Jayden and me. I'm not going to tip-toe around him, though, he needs to know she is going to be around.

"Look, first off you need to apologize for the things you have said to and about her. You were completely out of line to attack her like that. Second, I'm not going to push you to like the situation, but I am letting you know now that I'm not ending anything with her. She will be around and you need to get used to it."

He doesn't say anything else, he just nods. Pushing off the counter, I walk over to him. "Jacob, you're my little brother, I will always be here for you, even when we grow old and have lives of our own."

For the first time in a long time, Jacob smiles. "When we grow old? You are already old."

"Not too old to kick your butt still." Laughing, I hug him. This is my brother, I'm glad to have him back

"You could try, old man, you could try," he signs as he walks past me and out of the kitchen.

QUIETLY OPENING MY BEDROOM DOOR, I find Jayden fully dressed and sitting on the edge of the bed.

"Everything all right?" she asks.

Walking over to her, I grab her hand and pull her up onto her feet, claiming her lips.

"I'll take that as everything went well," she answers her own question, a little breathless.

"I guess Mr. Colter had a little talk with him and convinced him to finally talk and listen to me."

"How do you feel about that?"

"At first it pissed me off. After thinking about for a minute, I realized as long as it got us talking, why do I care if it took someone else to get through to him as long as someone finally did?"

"So everything is good now?" Her eyebrow rises up in question.

She isn't talking about between Jacob and me, she is talking about how Jacob feels about her being here with me.

"I'm sure we will have some bumps here and there, I'm not expecting everything to go perfect, but I think it will definitely be better between us now."

She doesn't say anything. She just looks up like she is waiting for me to continue. She wants to know about how he feels about us.

"He knows he owes you an apology."

"Cameron, don't force him on that. I understand his reaction."

"Jayden, for one he was raised better than he treated you. Second, he had no right to say the things he did. He should be respectful, and he was anything but that."

"A lot has happened, Cameron. He was going through an anger stage."

"Jayden, don't make excuses for him being rude. He needs to apologize."

She wants to continue arguing with me, I can see it in her eyes, but what he did there was no good reason to excuse. He should never have said what he did, regardless of how he felt about the two of us being together.

"So he's all right with this?" She gestures with her hand between the two of us.

"What are we saying this is?" I mimic her gesture between the two of us. "Jayden, you are the one who said you don't do the relationship thing."

Shrugging, she looks down. "I've never done the relationship thing, Cameron."

Well that is a surprise to hear. "Was that a choice of yours?"

I have a hard time believing she has never been in a solid relationship due to no interest. I have a feeling it has to be a choice she has made, but why? I watch as she sits down on the edge of the bed, her hands between her thighs, eyes looking down.

"It's a long story, but I'll give you the short version." She looks up at me, "I thought my parents had a perfect marriage. A couple completely in love. One day I came home from school to my mom bawling in the kitchen. She had been completely in love with my father. My father, however, was sleeping with others. I watched my mom almost completely fall apart from a broken heart. I never wanted to feel that broken. I decided as long as I didn't let anyone in, then they couldn't break me when they decided they wanted out."

"You haven't been in a relationship because you think whoever you decide to be in a relationship with will cheat on you?" I don't even try to hide my surprise. Jayden seems like too strong of a person to allow someone to break her.

"Cameron, I watched my mom hurt and go through hell because of how much she loved my father and he didn't return the same love to her. She tried to act strong around me, but at night I would hear her crying, alone in her room. I would sit outside her door and listen to her. My dad did that to her."

"Jayden, not everyone cheats. How is your mom now?"

"Great! She is remarried to a great guy that she met here in Washington. I grew up in Tennessee, but once everything happened, Mom and I moved here. My mom has family here."

"So your mom remarried and is happy. That should prove to you that there is love in a relationship. Not everyone is like your dad."

She doesn't say anymore. She just sits there playing with her nails. Kneeling down, I grab her hand. She looks me in the eyes, I see the fear, and it tears at my chest. This strong woman is showing fear, showing me her weakness.

"What is this we have going on here, Jayden?"

"Cameron, earlier today before you sent me the text, I was sitting at home, thinking about you. I was having very mixed feelings. I haven't stopped thinking about you since we met. From the moment I walked into Mr. Lennerd's office, you have had an effect on me. Then you basically told me to step away. No one has affected me the way you have, and honestly it scares the hell out of me."

"Jayden, I can't tell you what the future will hold. I have definitely learned that life can change in a second. One thing I can say is I'll never cheat. One woman at a time is all I want or can handle."

Laughing, she smacks me on the arm. "We aren't that bad. Trust me, you guys aren't as easy as you think you are. You said yourself you don't really do the relationship thing either. Why has that changed?"

"Because a few weeks ago, this fireball fell into an office I was at for a meeting and I haven't been able to think straight since."

I wait as she searches my face. She is thinking, you can see the wheels turning behind her eyes. She leans forward, I think she is going to kiss me but she stops close enough that I can feel her lips against mine when she speaks. "All right, let's try this relationship thing."

I gave her a light kiss. "I'm not going to promise I'll be easy to deal with, I'm kind of cranky."

"Kind of cranky?! That's putting it nicely."

Moving quickly, I stand back up but push her back so that she is laying on the bed, leaning over her. "Does this seem cranky to you?"

She laughs, pushing against my chest. "As much as I'd like to see this cranky side, I'm starving, for food. Some cranky guy has been playing with my head, which has played with my appetite."

Pushing up off the bed, I grab her hand to pull her up to her feet in front of me. "Come on then, let me feed you."

AS WE COME DOWN the stairs, I find Jacob sitting on the couch. He looks up as we hit the bottom of the stairs.

"We are going to go grab something to eat, do you want to join us?" I sign.

I watch as he looks behind me and Jayden. "Ms. Edwards, I'm sorry for what I said to you the other day," he signs.

"It's all right, Jacob, I understand," I hear her say behind me.

She is letting him off too easy I think, but I'm not going to push it tonight. He apologized, I am going to be happy about that.

"So did you want to go?" I sign once again.

I watch as he looks between Jayden and myself, then shakes his head no. "I had pizza at Tyler's before I came home."

"All right, I'll be home later then. If you need anything, text me."

He nods and then looks back down at his phone.

When I look back at Jayden, I see the concern in her eyes. She doesn't miss the looks from Jacob, which they are hard to miss. He did apologize but his face speaks of his concerns and disapproval of the two of us. He is going to have to get used to it.

"Jayden, he will be fine, don't worry." I grab her hand and lead her out of the house.

I WAS EXPECTING some issues from Jacob Monday morning but there were none. He was up and ready in plenty of time. He almost seemed happy to be going back to school.

An hour after school starts, my phone goes off with a text from him. Maybe he isn't ready to go back to school? I let go of the breath I am holding when I read it and all he wants is for me to come down to the school and sign forms for track that the coach needs. He is putting himself back into sports, this has to be a good thing.

I have no idea what Mr. Colter said to my brother, but it completely turned him around. Not only are there no more issues with going back to school, he is going back to sports as well. I need to call Mr. Colter and tell him thank you.

Walking down the hallway of the school, I look into each class as I pass wondering which room is Jayden's. I almost asked the coach before I left, but then thought better of it. I don't want to cause problems for Jayden.

I have just passed a row of rooms and am getting ready to go out the door, when I hear Jayden's voice behind me.

"Cameron."

I turn to see her standing in the doorway of one of the rooms. "Hey, I was just wondering which one of these rooms you might be in." I make my way back over to her.

She points up above the door, it reads Room 12. "This would be mine. I saw you pass by, is everything all right with Jacob?"

She is always concerned about him, even after he has been a jerk to her. He doesn't deserve her worry after the way he treated her.

"Yeah, everything is good. He wants to get back on the track team, I had to sign some papers."

The lights flash through the hallway and before you know it, all the kids are piling into the hall all heading in different directions. I watch as she says goodbye to the kids from her class and when she looks up at me, I notice her looking past me to something or someone behind me. When I look over my shoulder, I see another teacher around Jayden's age standing at the last door of the hallway.

Jayden speaking brings my attention back around to her. "Are you by any chance interested in maybe going on a double date? I would like for you to meet Charliee. She has just started dating one of the fire-fighters who helped with the rescue."

Jayden had mentioned before that her friend was there that night of the bombing as well.

"I don't know, Jayden. I'm pretty busy with both tracks getting ready to be finished here real soon, time isn't something I have a lot of extra right now."

I try to keep eye contact with her but can't and she is seeing right through my crap, I can see it in her eyes.

"Cameron, what's going on?"

"Jayden, I really don't want to talk about this now or here."

"What's the problem? If we are going to do this, you should meet one of the most important people in my life."

"Jayden, what part of I don't want to discuss this right now was I not clear on?" I know the tone in my voice is harsh, and I shouldn't be talking this way but she isn't letting up.

"Is it because she was involved that night?"

"Jayden, enough!" I hiss at her, trying to keep my temper at bay. I need to leave before I say something I am going to regret. I don't wait to give her a chance to say anything else, I turn and walk away from her. Jayden is pissed and honestly, I can't blame her, but I don't want to talk about this in the middle of a hallway in the school with people all around. Right now I need air.

CHAPTER
Sixteen

JAYDEN

CAMERON JUST WALKED AWAY from me, what the hell? He isn't even willing to talk to me about this. I know I'm new at this relationship thing, I haven't had a lot of experience with them at all, but I'm pretty sure if the guy you're seeing won't meet your best friends, that can't be a good thing.

I watch until the door closes behind him and Charliee starts walking up to me. How am I supposed to explain this to her? I can see the questions in her eyes as she nears me. This is going to be fun.

"Are you ready for lunch?"

No twenty questions, really? What happened to my best friend? I know she's curious, it's written all over her face. However, I'm not going to push my luck, I let the conversation go for now.

"Yeah, let me go and grab my lunch."

. . .

I'M NOT HUNGRY, thanks to Cameron.

"So when are you going to tell me who the guy was?" Charliee finally asks the question I have been waiting for her to ask.

I can't keep this from her any longer. We are best friends, we tell each other everything. I followed her in shower to get the story about her and Travis.

I take a deep breath. "That was Cameron Tovaren."

Charliee's eyes get large. "How is he related?"

"Cameron is their oldest son. He moved back to take care of Jacob."

"You guys seemed to be arguing."

It isn't a question, Charliee is great at reading situations. I just nod my head.

"What were you two arguing about?"

"It was nothing really."

She studies me for a moment, she knows I'm holding something from her.

"Were you guys arguing over Jacob?" she asks when I don't say anything.

Oh, how I wish that was what it was about. That would be easier than telling her he didn't want to meet her.

"How close have you two become?"

Again, words aren't needed, she is reading all of the answers from my face.

"How long, Jayden?"

"We met about two weeks after the bombing. Jacob had taken a few weeks off from school. They didn't want him to fall behind, I told Cameron I would tutor Jacob while he was out. I ended up going to the house to tutor him. After a couple of times, Cameron asked me out for drinks. He said he needed someone to talk to, so I accepted. He's a great guy, we have a lot of chemistry. Things are great as long as I don't interfere or say anything about Jacob."

"So you guys were arguing about Jacob?"

Right now, I wish I could say yes. "Today surprisingly wasn't about Jacob."

I take a deep breath, I can't keep all of this from her any longer.

"Charliee, the other day when we were getting our toes done, you mentioned double dating. I asked Cameron about getting together with you and Travis. That would be what we were arguing about. It's you!"

"Wait, what?" You can see the shock all over her face, I know she wasn't expecting that answer.

I hold up my hands before she can say anything. "Let me explain."

"Please do," she signs only.

Charliee usually talks when she signs, but when she is mad or frustrated, she only signs. I think she messes up words more during those times so she just reverts to what she doesn't have to think about.

"I asked him about us all getting together. He isn't sure if he's ready to meet you."

"I didn't blow up the place, what does he have against me?"

"Charliee, it isn't like that."

The lights flicker, telling us that lunch is over. I don't want her leaving now and being upset for the rest of the day.

Charliee quickly stands up and collects her lunch, then turns to leave. Grabbing her arm, I turn her around to me.

"Charliee, please believe me, it's nothing like that. Cameron has a lot of mixed feelings right now. He needs to mourn his parents, but won't because he is staying strong for Jacob. I think he is afraid that if he meets someone who was so closely involved, it will create or open up those emotions. He refuses to be weak, no matter how much I try to convince him that sadness isn't a weakness. It's not really you, it's what you may open up in him."

I am defending him even being mad at him for walking away from me earlier. I don't want Charliee to be upset either. I'm hoping Cameron comes around and if he does then I don't want Charliee not to like him because of all of this.

I watch as Charliee's face softens a little. She is coming around, I knew she would. Charliee, for one, never stays mad at people, she is always looking for the best in a person. I don't think the woman has a mean bone in her body.

"I understand, you just caught me off guard is all. If he changes his mind or you talk him into going out one night, just let me know."

This is why I love this woman. She always understands and forgives.

AFTER SCHOOL I sit in the parking lot trying to decide if I want to go to Cameron's house, text him or just go home. Cameron hasn't texted me at all since he left earlier today. The pissed off side of me wants to go home. Is this relationship always going to be about fights and apologies? I know it's common to argue but I'm pretty sure the arguing isn't supposed to be more than not. He needs to talk to me, not get mad and walk away and then think he can just apologize when he cools down and everything will be all right. It is going to get old fast. Today at lunch with Charliee, I made excuses for him, I shouldn't have to do that.

I can't go home, all I will do was sit there and keep going over all of this and become more pissed off. He may not want to talk about it, but we need to. He can listen and I'll talk but then he will be given a choice on how he wants to proceed with this relationship.

Pulling up to the house, I don't see any vehicles here. Well damn, there went my whole get it all off my chest speech I have been perfecting all the way over here from the school. Now I have to go home and dwell on it.

Just as I'm about to pull away from the curb, I see Cameron coming around the corner in his father's truck. I throw my car back into park and sit and wait. Damn it, my speech that I was all ready to lay into him with is gone from my brain and my nerves are jumping all around. Why does this man jumble everything up inside of me?

Watching and waiting, Cameron pulls into his driveway and is just sitting there. At first I think he is on the phone. I get out of my car and can now see that he isn't talking, he is just sitting there. I walk past the truck and up to the front porch. He hasn't even acknowledged that I'm here. I swear I've been standing here for a good five minutes. Is he hoping I'll just leave? Well, he is going to be disappointed because I'm not leaving and I'm not standing here any longer waiting for him either.

Walking up to the truck, I open up the driver side door. "Are you ready to talk to me yet?"

Cameron shakes his head. I'm about to lose my temper completely until he looks at me and I notice how red his eyes are. He's been crying. Now all my anger is gone, I have to fight the urge to jump onto his lap and wrap my arms around him, letting him know everything is going to be all right.

"Cameron, you need to open up to someone."

"Jayden, I think I'm losing my mind. I can't do all of this."

I close the space between us, my hands going to rest on his thigh. "You need to lean on someone, too, Cameron. You haven't even mourned your parents. You've been dealing with Jacob and the business. Your whole life turned upside down without any warning, Cameron, that's not easy for anyone to deal with."

"Jayden, I've disappointed or screwed up everything lately. I have two developments finishing at the same time in two different states. I can't do anything right with Jacob, it takes his best friend's father to get through to him and then I do nothing but piss you off."

"Why don't we go inside and talk about this, Cameron?" My heart feels like a vice is around it squeezing. Here is this tough, nothing bothers me guy sitting in his truck, broken. How do you help the one who's strength everyone else depends on?

He isn't getting out of the truck. "I went by the cemetery. I think I sat there for two or three hours, but couldn't get out of the truck. It still seems like a sick joke. I still walk in that front door," he points up toward the house, "and expect to see my mom in the kitchen or sitting on the couch and my dad sitting in his office working. I sit in this truck and expect to look over in the passenger seat and see my dad sitting there. I smell him every time I get into this damn truck. It takes my breath away every single time, it's like a punch in the face."

His one hand is on top of mine on his thigh. He squeezes it more and more with every word he speaks. I'm fighting the tears now, but I need to keep them from falling. Cameron doesn't need me crying for him, he needs the strength of someone to lean onto right now.

"This isn't something that you get used to in a couple of weeks, Cameron. It's going to take a long time to feel normal again, if ever. I'm pretty sure you will always expect to see them when you walk into that house. It's home! Your parents were home for you boys, they are part of that house and all the great memories you have of growing up. Talking about them and what's going through your head or maybe even asking for help every once in a while might help. Problem is you are still pushing everyone away who wants to help you. You are shutting everyone out."

He doesn't say anything in response. He just keeps staring at the house, but he does keep the tight grip on my hand. I just stand there and wait. There is nothing else I can say, he has to make the next move.

"I know you are mad at me about today," he finally speaks.

"I'm upset that you shut me out, Cameron. One minute you want a relationship, the next you are walking away from me. If you aren't ready to do something like meet my best friend because it ties into your parents' death, I'm not going to be mad at you. What pisses me off is when you say nothing and walk away from me. I can deal with you yelling at me, before dealing with you giving the silent treatment and walking away."

"I saw her and wondered why my parents died but she didn't. What did she do so different in her life that rewarded her to live?"

I am speechless for a moment. He is trying to figure out what happened in life for certain people to have been taken and others not.

"Cameron, it was timing. Wrong place at the wrong time. Your parents didn't do something wrong. They were just in the wrong place at the wrong time."

This is the only explanation I can think to give. Aside from being taken back on the fact that he thought his parents did something wrong and that's why they died. I think about it all of the time. If Charliee would have been only five seconds slower about walking out that front door. I am still amazed that she lived through having the entire front wall of the building burying her.

"I'm not mad that your friend lived, I'm just mad that my parents didn't, Jayden. I'm not ready to meet her. I don't have a great excuse, but it will have to be enough for right now."

"There doesn't have to be an excuse, Cameron. I just need to know what's going on."

He finally looks over at me. "I'm not making your first relationship a good experience, am I?"

I can't hold the small laugh from bubbling out. "I'm not expecting only happiness but yes, this has been an experience."

"Are you still wanting to stick around?"

"Cameron, I'm a fighter. I'll be able to handle it all for now. Just don't keep shutting me out."

Leaning forward, he kisses me gently. "How about I take you out to dinner. I know it's not a double date, but it's a date."

I can't wait for him to meet Charliee. He is becoming a piece of my life and she is my other half, but for now I will wait.

"Sounds nice, how about I drive?" I will at least try and get him away from the memories for a few hours.

"We can take your car, but can I drive?" he asks.

"What's wrong with my driving? You have never been in a car with me while I drove."

"I hate being the passenger," he states calmly but with a hint of a smile.

Smart answer, I think to myself. He doesn't trust my driving but isn't going to say it. I hold the keys out to him. "Fine, you can drive!"

CHAPTER
Seventeen

CAMERON

THE LAST COUPLE of weeks have gone in a blur. It hasn't been perfect, but what in life is? Even after Jacob said he wanted to go back and do track, he ended up not running. I think everything was too much and that's why I didn't push the issue when he told me he had changed his mind. Now with the summer here, maybe he can work on getting the rest of what's going through his mind situated and then by next year, he will want to go back to the sports for his senior year. He and I have been doing a lot better. He still doesn't talk to Jayden a lot when she is over at the house but he is respectful and that is all I am asking for. He even offered to help us today in Jayden's room with cleaning it all out for the summer break, which is where we are at the moment.

It is the last day of school and all the teachers are cleaning out their classrooms. When Jayden told me she would be staying after to finish, I offered to come and help. I am surprised when I walk in and find Jacob helping her. When I ask her about it, she just tells me he stayed after class and asked what she needed help with. I don't ask any other questions than that.

Jayden hands me the last two books on the shelf we have been emptying. "Hey, I have to go down to Texas next week for the finalization of the project I have going on down there. I'm flying there but driving all my stuff back. Do you think maybe you would like to join me?"

I do believe I just shocked her I am guessing from the look I am getting from her at the moment.

"Really, you want me to go with you?"

"Why does this surprise you so much?"

I watch as she shrugs her shoulders and then starts closing the box we have just finished filling with books. "I don't know, you just caught me off guard asking I guess."

Before I can say anything else, the classroom door opens and a small petite blond comes in with a beautiful German Shepherd following her. This has to be Charliee. Jayden talks about her all of the time and about her dog.

"I'm sorry, I didn't know you had people in here with you. I was finished in my room and just wanted to say bye before I headed home. I will text you later," she speaks and signs at the same time.

I am surprised at how well she speaks. Jayden told me she was completely deaf but spoke, I just wasn't prepared for how well she spoke. My parent's had put Jacob into speech therapy and he spoke on occasion, but nothing like this woman in front of me. I have to admit, I am impressed. The whole time she speaks, her eyes go between Jayden and myself. She knows who I am, I'm sure of it.

She turns to leave, that's when I am surprised to see my brother go up to her and stop her before she gets out the door.

"Ms. Brooksman, I would like you to meet my brother," Jacob signs.

Charliee's eyes meet mine, I have very mixed emotions right now and I believe she reads that in me.

"Jacob, what are you doing?" I ask before I think about it.

Jacob walks over to me. He stands my full height. My brother is a man now, not the little boy I wanted to protect.

"You need this, Cameron, trust me. If you are that stubborn to admit it then do it for Ms. Edwards," he signs to me, basically telling me to get over myself.

Before I can respond to anything, Charliee surprises me by walking over to me. "Hello, Cameron, it's nice to finally meet you. I'm Charliee."

I look down at her hand that she extends out to me. I need to get over this. It isn't Charliee's fault our parents were killed that night and she was lucky to survive. I'm not mad at her. I think my problem is more the why, not who died and who didn't. Meeting someone who was lucky to survive, you felt like you needed to talk about it, and I'm not ready to talk about it.

"Charliee, it's nice to meet you."

We shake hands, I hear Jayden take a deep breath behind me and release it slowly. Jacob is right, I should have done this way before now. If for no other reason than for Jayden. This is her best friend, the boyfriend should have to meet the best friend, but I've been too stubborn to put Jayden before myself. No more, she comes first.

"I have one thing to say, I feel I need to anyway, and then I promise not to bring it up again unless you want to. If you ever want to ask questions, I'm more than happy to answer what I can. I'm sorry for your loss, your parents were great people. You are becoming a very important person to my best friend over there," she points behind me, "which means you need to realize I'm going to be around. I gave space because I understand, but we are part of each other and with you being part of her now, I hope we can be friends."

Now I see why these two are such good friends, they are both full of fire.

"If you aren't already busy tonight, maybe we can all get together. Jayden has been bugging me for weeks to go on a double date with you and this new boyfriend she says you have," I offer, surprising myself.

Jayden appears at my side, her arms wrapping around my waist. The smile she is wearing is well worth the decision to step forward.

"Tonight would be great. I'm going to go let Travis know." Charliee looks over at Jayden, "I'll text you in a while and we will plan something."

I watch as Charliee quickly turns and leaves, her dog following close behind. I look over at Jacob. He isn't looking at us but he is smiling, almost a little shyly. Looking back down at Jayden, her smile falls a little, and the question is in her eyes.

"It's all good. I guess I just needed to be forced to move forward," I answer her question.

"I'm so excited, I have been wanting you two to meet. You will love her and Travis is a great guy, I think you two will get along great."

"I'm sorry it took so long."

She stretches up onto her toes and gives me a small kiss, which surprises me. Usually when Jacob is around, Jayden doesn't even hold my hand, let alone kiss me. Things are changing and for the better, hopefully this will make our relationship smoother as well.

THE FOUR OF us end up at the beach, around a fire after dinner. Travis and Charliee are nice to hang out with, both very down to earth. Jayden wasn't kidding when she told me Charliee was a ball of energy, she never stops. To top it all off, she brought s'mores for us to have tonight. It brings back great memories of being on the beach with family and friends growing up.

Earlier tonight, before we met up with Charliee and Travis, I told myself I wasn't going to ruin our evening with talk from the night of the bombing. The further we got into the evening, the more questions I found I wanted to ask. Jayden mentioned Charliee had spoken to my parents that night, she was the last one to talk to them really. The fire is calming to sit back and watch, but the more I sit here listening to everyone talk, the more I want to know some answers.

"Can you tell me anything about that night and my parents?" I sign to Charliee. I don't say a word, I still can't find my voice to ask the questions.

Jayden's eyes swing over to me in surprise; Charliee, however, looks over at Travis. He is her anchor, you can see it all over her face. She begins to tell Travis what I said and he stops her.

"I picked up enough to know what he asked. I've been studying," Travis explains to Charliee.

"I'm sorry, that was rude of me. I just wasn't sure if I could find actual words to ask so I signed them, forgetting that not everyone here probably signs," I explain.

Travis waves it off. "Don't worry about it, I started learning the language because all of Charliee's family and Jayden over there would only sign when they didn't want me to know something."

Poor guy, I think to myself. He had both of these women to deal with when he started dating Charliee.

"Well, that's good to know now. Note to self, Travis knows sign language now," Jayden says next to me, lightening up the mood a little.

"That's right, no more talking about me right in front of my face," Travis easily teases back to Jayden.

Feeling bad isn't even covering how I feel at the moment watching Jayden and Travis tease with each other. They are friends, she is part of their lives. I didn't want to get to know Charliee, Jayden had to keep this part of her life separate from our relationship, that couldn't have been easy.

Charliee's voice brings my attention back to her. "I'll tell you the same thing I told Jacob when he came to me about a week ago. There isn't much I can tell you that the police report doesn't already cover. I'll do my best, though, I want you two to find some peace with all of this."

"Jacob talked to you?" I ask, completely shocked. He hasn't said a word to me about the whole thing. To be honest, though, I am happy to hear he is talking to someone.

Charliee nods her head. "Trust me, I was just as surprised as you are now."

One thing I have learned the last couple of weeks is I don't have to be the one there for everything. Don't get me wrong, I wish he would talk to me, I still feel that distance between the two of us, but I'm not going to push it.

"I don't even know what exactly I want to know really," I admit. What do I want to know? What am I expecting her to tell me that will help?

"Cameron, I was waiting for my dinner that I had ordered to go when I saw your parents. They passed me when they were following the hostess to be seated. I only got to say hello," Charliee starts explaining to me.

The fire is dancing in front of me. That was my main question. The fire, the explosion, how much did my parents suffer, what did they feel? The tears I can't hold back, just thinking of them suffering and hurting, I can't handle it.

"Did they go fast, or did they suffer?" I finally find my voice to ask.

I watch as emotions run across Charliee's face. The tears spring from her eyes instantly, running down her cheeks.

"I have no memory of that night past the part where I said hello to your parents. I was walking out the front door when the explosion happened. I remember a lot of heat behind me and that's all. I'm sorry. I pray every day for those who lost their lives that night that they all went quick and no one suffered." Charliee looks over at Travis, pleading with her eyes for him to add something that may help.

Travis leans forward in his chair, Charliee's hand tightly in his own. "Cameron, I was one of the firefighters who first responded that night. I don't believe your parents suffered. The blast was centered right there in the dining area, we found no survivors in that area of the restaurant."

It is strange to feel relief rush through me. Thinking of them lying there, hurt, burning and needing help and not getting it in time bothered me more than anything.

"I'm sorry for ruining the evening, we were having a great time," I apologize.

No one is laughing or smiling any longer like we were moments ago. Both women have tears streaming down their cheeks and Travis looks like he would like to know how to help everyone but can't. He looks over at Charliee, helpless and troubled. I'm sure that night wasn't easy on him either.

Charliee finally breaks the silence around the fire. "I know I can't sit here and say I know what you are going through, Cameron. Yes, I may have been part of that night, Travis may have been there and seen all the destruction, but you lost loved ones, and not just one but two of the most important people of your life. Please don't ever apologize for talking about it or wanting to ask questions. I've learned that talking has helped me heal. It's hard sometimes. You wonder if you want to know the answers to certain questions, but keeping it all bundled up will only hurt you and those around you, trust me on this."

Charliee pauses for a moment, looking over at Travis. She doesn't break eye contact with him as she continues, "I know what it's like to have to put the smile on your face and be strong around the people you love to assure them everything is all right. You are the one who went through it all, yet you need to make sure the people around you are healing." She looks over at me once again, "Find that one person, be it Jayden, an old friend, whoever, and talk to them. Believe me when I tell you it will help you heal and it will help those around you heal."

Charliee is amazing. Her strength isn't something many people have. Travis has his hands full with her, I'm sure she keeps him on his toes. It makes me smile a little to imagine an argument between the two of them, I'm sure he doesn't win often. Charliee, this sweet, little petite thing telling you how it is and is going to be has to be entertaining.

"You are one tough woman, Charliee. Jayden has told me about how they found you and about your injuries from that night. I wish I had half the strength you possess. Thank you for answering my questions, I know this isn't easy on you either."

Travis just sits there staring at his woman. He is a very lucky man and he knows it, you can see it written all over his face, he worships Charliee. Jayden brings my attention back to her when she stands up next to me, holding her hand out to me.

"I'm ready to go if you are."

Travis isn't the only lucky one here. I have this fireball next to me and I need to start making sure she knows how lucky I am to have her in my life. This woman has handled a lot of crap from me and I have said things to her that should have had her walking the other way, flipping me off as she walked away and forgetting my name with every step, but no, she always comes back, telling me how it is and to man up.

Getting up, I follow Jayden over and wait as she hugs Travis and then Charliee. "Thank you for the evening. Cameron and I were talking about going to the fair that they have going on down the beach, do you guys want to join us?"

Charliee looks up at Travis. "I have Monday off," he answers her questioning look.

"Monday it is then. I'll text you later, Charliee, and we will figure out all the details." Jayden turns to me.

I walk over and give Charliee a hug. "Thank you. Just for the record, I'm happy to have finally met you. I'm sorry it took me so long."

"Don't apologize, I understand. I'm sorry I couldn't be more help with answering the questions you had."

"Trust me, Charliee, you helped me out a lot tonight."

Jayden leads the way as we walk away. I don't realize how tightly I have been holding her hand until we get to the car and she turns before getting in and looks up at me. I see her rub her hand a little when I let go.

"Are you all right?"

Am I? I think to myself. Actually, I think this is the first time my chest doesn't feel heavy. Kissing her lightly, I smile. "I'm good actually. I'm sorry it took me so long to do this, meeting Charliee I mean. Her strength and her advice was good to hear. I've sat around since all of this happened and listened to you tell me all about her. I've wondered why she survived and my parents didn't and I know that makes me a huge jackass. Then I would be mad at myself for wondering why a person didn't die. It was a lot of mixed emotions to deal with. After meeting Charliee, I feel like a bigger ass than before. It was my parents' time to go, and not hers. It's the whole 'Everything happens for a reason' thing I'm starting to believe. I don't do the mushy words thing well, Jayden, but out of all this bad, something very good came out of it. You!"

A single tear springs from her eye and rolls down her cheek as she brings my lips down to hers. This kiss is different, it is saying what neither one of us are ready to say out loud. I am falling in love with her.

Eighteen

Jayden

IT IS a perfect evening for the fair, the weather is great, which also means it is very busy. Everyone is taking advantage of a perfect evening on the beach and a good fair. It isn't a surprise we run into someone we know, but what is a surprise is it is Bryce with a woman who he introduced to us as Darryn and her little girl. No one knew about these new girls in Bryce's life I would guess from the look of surprise on Charliee's face. I can see the questions twirling in Charliee's head over all of it. She and her brothers are very close so not knowing who this is bothers her. All introductions and questions that Charliee may have are cut short when Levi, Charliee's hearing dog, lunges out at a crowd of people, knocking Charliee onto her butt.

Levi is a great service dog, he never acts out of sorts. He never leaves Charliee's side, but right now he is doing everything he can to get away from her and after something, which puts us all on alert. This is the second time tonight, earlier he started growling at a crowd around us. He is barking now, however, and that is not normal, something is wrong. He isn't backing down, no matter what Charliee does and for him not to listen to her, my nerves start up.

"What's wrong with him?" Bryce asks as he goes to Levi and tries to calm him down, but nothing is working.

All of his barking is drawing the attention of everyone around us. He isn't a small dog and you can tell some are getting nervous to be around him. Travis grabs Levi's leash from Charliee and then helps her up off the ground.

"He did this earlier but I brushed it off thinking something spooked him," Travis says, making sure Charliee is all right but keeping a tight hold of Levi.

"Oh my God." Charliee's voice brings all of our attention to her. All of the color has drained from her face, she looks terrified.

I look in the direction she is looking in but I don't see anything unusual. She doesn't answer, but now her whole body is shaking.

Travis shoves Levi's leash into Bryce's hand and stands directly in front of Charliee, concern etched in his eyes. "Charliee, talk to us."

Charliee finally points across the way at one of the children's rides. "That's the guy from the restaurant, the one who ran into me outside. He is standing there in the blue jeans and plaid shirt. He's wearing a backpack."

Charliee's brothers had her come down to the station a few weeks ago after some video they had found led them to believe the guy that ran into Charliee just before she entered the restaurant that night of the bombing was responsible for leaving the bomb. Charliee was the only survivor who had seen him.

Levi's barking catches the attention of the guy Charliee has pointed out to us. Once he looks over and sees all of us staring at him, he takes off running. That completely yells, "Guilty!"

Bryce shoves Levi's leash into my hands. "Call 911, let them know what's going on. You guys get out of here now!" he yells as he starts running after the guy.

"Cameron, take the ladies and head back to the cars. I'm going after him with Bryce." Travis starts to go after Bryce until Charliee grabs his arm.

"Please, Travis, don't. What if there is another bomb in that bag?"

"Charliee, I'm not going to let your brother go alone."

"I'm going as well," Cameron speaks up.

My eyes fly to him now. I'm sure he knows I am asking him if he is crazy without a word being said.

"That bastard is responsible for my parents' death," he answers my unasked question.

I can only imagine what he must be feeling, but if something happened to Cameron, Jacob would have nothing left. I wouldn't have him! The 911 operator keeps asking me what my emergency is. Cameron is telling me I can't stop him with his eyes.

"You three ladies get that little one out of here," Travis yells as he and Cameron take off in the direction Bryce has gone.

Finding my voice finally, I explain what is going on as we all quickly walk back to the parking lot to wait. Darryn didn't stay, she had her little girl with her and wanted to get her out of here just in case some-thing happened. She told us to tell Bryce to call her later to make sure he was all right. If this situation wasn't so serious, I believe Charliee and I would have both shot off a million questions after seeing the look in Darryn's eyes. She cared for Bryce. How had Bryce kept this from all of us and why?

Charliee and I sit in silence as we watch everyone being evacuated from the fair. The police tried to tell us we had to leave. We weren't going anywhere, and after we explained to one of them who we were, they left us alone. However, I do notice we always have one officer very close by. If that is planned or not, it helps calm my nerves a little. I'm pretty sure Charliee never notices they are there. I sit here waiting to hear anything that will tell me if things went very wrong. Charliee can't do that. Every time I look over at her, I can see her eyes focusing on certain officers. As they are talking into the radios or to each other, she s reading lips—a very useful talent at times like now.

I'm not sure how long we have been sitting here but I am getting restless. I want to get up and go look for Cameron, honestly I am surprised Charliee is still sitting here. Levi quickly stands up from where he is laying down which gets both of our attention. When we look in the direction he is looking, we see Cameron and Travis walking back to us.

Both of us jump up and run to them, launching ourselves into their arms. Charliee speaks first.

"Where's Bryce?" You can hear the panic in her voice.

"He had to stay back, he's fine though," Travis answers her.

"Did you guys catch him?" I ask, but I know the answer the second I look up at Cameron and see the anger in his eyes. I can feel the tension in Cameron's body.

"Where's Darryn? Bryce wanted to make sure her and the little one got home safe," I hear Travis ask.

My eyes don't leave Cameron, he is irritated and tense. He looks everywhere but at me.

"She didn't want to chance anything happening with Kendall here so she took her home," Charliee explains to Travis.

"There is nothing else we can do here, we should all head home." Cameron's angry voice breaks through to all of us.

I quickly give Charliee a hug and when I turn back to Cameron, he has already walked away and is getting into the driver's side of my car. I look back at Charliee to apologize for him not saying goodbye but neither of them seem to care that he didn't so I quickly follow after him. The whole ride back to Cameron's house is quiet. He is shutting down again. When we pull up to the house, he just gets out of the car and leaves me sitting here.

This is crazy. I want to follow him and make sure he is all right but then I think about it for a minute and my anger starts to boil. I understand he's upset, disappointed and I'm sure pretty pissed off, but that doesn't give him the right to act like I'm not here. We are supposed to be a team. Lean on each other when we need an extra shoulder, not shove each other to the side. I am always making sure he is all right. Taking his outbursts and accepting the apologies. Or ignoring it altogether and moving on like nothing happened. I've been sitting here a little time now. He has gone into the house and shut the door behind him. I'm not saying he doesn't need me, but he needs to realize I'm not always going to just be here to be the wall. If I want him to quit pushing me away, I need to walk away and make him come to me. My mind made up, and before I get soft and change my mind, I quickly get out of the passenger side and round to the driver's side of my car.

I'VE BEEN HOME for probably an hour or so. Enough time to take a shower and dry my hair. I have to keep myself busy. I wash the couple of dishes I have in the sink. I've even put in a movie and am getting ready to turn it on when I get a text.

**Where the hell did you go?

Really, an hour later he realizes I didn't follow him into the house? Screw him, I'm not even going to answer that question. Where did he think I went? Throwing my phone on the couch next to me, I push play. It goes off a couple more times but I ignore it, I know who it is.

He must have given up, my phone hasn't gone off in a while. I try to pay attention to the movie, not think about Cameron, but it isn't working very well. This is crazy, flipping the television off, I decide going to bed is sounding like a better idea.

I've just started walking down the hall when someone pounding on my front door scares the crap out of me. Whoever it is isn't just a heavy knocker, they are using their fist and pounding on it.

I am getting ready to look through the peephole when the door shakes again from the pounding and Cameron's voice booms through. "Jayden, open this damn door!"

Why is he so pissed off? He left me in the car. Better question, how in the heck does he know where I live? We have only met at his house, he hasn't been here yet.

"Jayden!" he yells again.

Flinging open the door, I yell back, "What the hell do you think you are doing? My neighbors are going to call the cops because of all the commotion you are making out here!"

"I don't give a damn what your neighbors do. Why did you leave tonight? Why didn't you answer my texts?"

He is mad I can see that, but I can see a little fear in his eyes as well. He has been worried. That cools my temper quickly. Now all I want to do is throw myself into his arms, but I need him to understand what he did hurt.

"Would you stop yelling at me?"

Cameron takes a couple deep breaths. When he looks back at me, all I see is relief in his eyes. Before I know it, he grabs me, pulling me up against his body and devouring my lips, all while he walks us both into my house and shuts the door.

Any anger left melts away, along with any resistance. It kind of bothers me knowing that just his kiss can change me so quickly. I can't let him get off the hook this quickly and easily this time. I push away from him and take a step back. He takes a step toward me again and I hold up my hand to stop him.

"Cameron, how did you find out where I lived?"

"I got Travis's number earlier tonight so I texted him and asked."

Crap, now Charliee will be wondering what's going on.

"Don't worry, even due to the fact that I was pissed and worried, when I asked I made sure not to worry them," he answers without me saying a word.

"Pissed and worried about what, Cameron?"

"Really, Jayden? You just left and then when I texted, you didn't answer. I didn't know where you were or if something had happened."

"Wait! You aren't turning this around on me. Did it take you an hour to realize I didn't follow you into the house, Cameron?"

"Jayden, really, that's why you're mad? Because you think it took me an hour to realize you weren't around?"

"No, Cameron," I am shouting now. "It wasn't that you took an hour. What pissed me off was the fact you closed me out again. I understand you were upset about that guy getting away, but you can't keep putting a wall up in between us. You got out of my car, didn't say a word and walked into the house, shutting the door behind you. It may be just me, but that doesn't say 'Please come on in'. You wanted to be alone, I left you alone."

"Damnit, Jayden…"

I put my hand up to stop him. "No, Cameron, this isn't going to be my fault, so don't start with the whole 'Damnit, Jayden' thing."

Cameron stands there with his hands on his hips. "I have no idea what you want me to say!"

Want him to say? Really?! He really had no clue, did he?

"Cameron, you need to go, there is obviously nothing we are going to figure out tonight. I will tell you this, though, I can't keep being the person you push away. We are together, we are supposed to lean on each other. I understand not everything is going to be smooth, but right now your mood is all over the chart and I seem to be the one you take everything out on. I've tried to understand, be here for you when you are hurting, but I can't just be here when you are happy and take the crap when you're pissed. I understand you are disappointed about tonight, but you left me sitting in the car, Cameron. You didn't say a word. You got out, went into the house and shut the damn door, only to finally wake up to the fact I wasn't there an hour later. To top it off, you come here and blame me for all of this. I think that hurts the most."

The anger and fear I saw earlier in his eyes are now gone. Nothing, I see no emotion in his eyes right now. He isn't saying anything, he isn't doing anything, he's just standing there. He is great at being quiet, that is one thing I do know.

For the second time tonight, he turns and leaves me alone without a word. He is walking away from me again. I watch as he turns and walks out of the house, this time he doesn't shut the door. He leaves it open so that I can watch him walk to his truck and get in, driving away without a look back. It is like a scene from one of those sappy girl movies.

Slamming my door, I walk over and grab my phone, quickly typing out a text to Cameron.

**Thank you for proving me right.

Throwing it back on the couch, I don't want to know if he responds or not. I am going to bed, although I am pretty sure I won't be getting much sleep tonight.

CHAPTER
Nineteen

CAMERON

**THANK you for proving me right.

I had heard my phone go off right after I pulled away from Jayden's house, but I ignored it until I got home. Proving her right? I guess I did. I left without saying a word. She did tell me to go though. I'm still trying to get over the fear and worry I felt earlier when she wouldn't answer me. I wasn't used to all this "talk to me" stuff. I didn't want to talk earlier. I was pissed the guy wasn't found. He was so close, he wasn't impossible to capture. The bastard got away, though. The man who killed my parents was there and I let him get away.

How do you talk to someone when the last thing you want to do is talk? What pissed me off more was when I noticed Jayden had left. She thinks it took me an hour to realize she was gone. It didn't! I realized it right away. I actually watched her pull out of the driveway. I realized I just walked in and she wasn't with me. When I opened the door and saw her starting down the street, I grabbed my keys and tried to go after her but she had a head start on me and I lost her. I had never been to her house so I didn't even know which direction she would have gone. I immediately texted Travis and asked where she lived. His first question back was if everything was all right. I assured him it was. Told him we had a little fight, she left and I wanted to make things right. I didn't want to alert either him or Charliee that I couldn't find her and she wasn't answering my texts or calls. He sent me her address. After texting and calling her with no response, my anger started turning into fear. I was worried something had happened to her on the way home and we had no idea where she was.

When she opened her door, I wanted to shake her. All she did was tell me how I was closing down on her again. All I wanted to do was yell at her for scaring the hell out of me. I almost pull back out of my driveway once again and go back, but that wasn't going to do any good tonight, we were both in moods and it would only end up with things being said we didn't mean. Now that I know she is safe at home, we need to both take the night to breathe. I'll call her tomorrow and maybe we will both calm down enough to talk.

Walking into the house, I see Jacob and Tyler sitting at the dining room table eating.

"Did you find her?" Jacob signs as I pass him and head into the kitchen.

I nod and continue through the door, I need a beer. I don't want to talk to him or anyone right now. When I turn from the fridge, Jacob is standing behind me.

"Everything okay?"

Again, I nod as I take a long drink of my beer.

"You guys fighting?"

I'm starting to think I may have liked it when he didn't want to know anything about my relationship with Jayden. Ever since he went back to school, the old Jacob seems to be resurfacing. Don't get me wrong, I am happy about that, I have my little brother back, but right now I want to be left alone.

"Jacob, I'm tired. I'm heading upstairs and to bed."

"What happened tonight?" He isn't letting this go.

I don't want to tell him about the guy tonight at the fair. I don't want to tell my brother that I was that close to the man responsible for turning his world upside down and he got away.

"Nothing major, just a misunderstanding. It will be fine."

He stands there staring at me. I can tell he isn't buying it. I really don't want to see disappointment in someone else's eyes tonight.

"I'm not a child, Cameron."

No, he isn't, but I let him down. "It has nothing to do with you being a child. It's between Jayden and me," I sign.

Again, he just stands there for a moment staring at me. "If you don't wake up to all of it pretty soon, you are going to lose her."

I didn't have time to respond, he turned and walked out. Since when did he care if Jayden walked away from me or not?

If this is the kind of crap relationships are about, I'm not real sure they are for me. Why can't Jayden just understand I'm not ready to talk about it? I'm not wired the way she wants me to be. Grabbing my phone from my pocket, I open the message screen to her name and again read her text.

**Thank you for proving me right.

Right about what? Having a relationship or the way I acted? Here is one problem I have though. If I don't open right up to Jayden and spill my feelings or thoughts, she automatically goes to me putting up a wall and shutting her out. Just having her next to me calms me down. We don't have to talk, I just like knowing she is there. It shouldn't have to always be about talking.

Maybe trying to work on a relationship at a time when my world is spinning on super speed isn't the best idea. It's Jayden though. Even now with wondering if this will work, I can't imagine not being able to call her or touch her. The minute I see her, all I want is her in my arms. That woman does something to me. She has ever since she stumbled into the principal's office. It's not just her looks that draw me to her, it's the challenging look in her eyes, she doesn't back down. She's strong and won't take my crap. She has put me in my spot a few different times. She doesn't show weakness very often but there is an insecurity in her that pops out through her eyes. It makes you want to wrap your arms around her and let her know everything is good.

I want to text something back, but I can't figure out what. Everything I start to text, I delete. I'm just going to wait until the morning. I'll call her or drive over, see if she wants to grab breakfast and talk.

SLEEP NEVER HAPPENS. I look over at the clock and it reads six-thirty. I can't lay here any longer. The whole night I thought I should have texted back last night and not waited. I almost texted her a few times through the night but didn't want to wake her. Now all I want to do is call her but it is early. I can't wait any longer, we need to talk and not over the phone.

I grab a quick shower and am out of the house. On the way to Jayden's, I stop and grab a couple of coffees and breakfast sandwiches. I would rather talk in private rather than in a restaurant with a lot of people around us. By the time I pull into her driveway, it is eight. Just as I am opening my door, my phone rings, it is Steve. I want to ignore the call but we are at the finish line of the track down there in Texas. If it is something important, I shouldn't make it wait.

"Hey, Steve, what's up?"

"Cameron, just making sure everything is good for Monday. You are all set to be here, right?"

Steve worries too much. He has already called me a least once a day this week to make sure I will be there, it makes me chuckle a little.

"Yes, Steve, everything is good to go. I will actually be flying in Saturday. Since I have you on the phone, are you and your wife free for dinner Saturday night? I would like to take you guys out as a thank you, plus I have a couple of things I would like to discuss with you."

"Sure, not a problem. Wait, is everything all right?"

"Steve, I swear, man, you worry too much." I am laughing.

"It's not worry, it's being prepared."

"No, it's worry, Steve. Everything is fine."

I look up at Jayden's house. "Steve, if that's all, I have to go. Can I call you a little later to clear up any details?"

"Sure, I'll talk to you later."

Hanging up with Steve, I grab the bag with the food and pick up both coffees, take a deep breath and head up to the front door. I knock a couple of times and no one answers. Should I call and see if she is even home? Her car is here, but that doesn't mean she is here.

Knocking one more time, I step back in surprise when the door flies open. I am met with Jayden, still looking half asleep, glaring at me, wearing a pair of short cotton shorts and a tank top, no bra underneath and her nipples are perked up. It takes everything I have in me not to drop everything I am holding, grab her up in my arms and carry her back to bed, waking her up in a much more fulfilling way.

"Good morning." I smile down at her.

She glares back, then quickly turns away from me, trying to shut the door behind her, but I stick my foot in the way. She doesn't stop so I follow her in and shut the door behind me. I'm starting to believe she is still pissed about last night.

"I brought breakfast." I hold the bag and coffee out to her.

Jayden turns around, arms crossed over her chest. "What do you want, Cameron?"

At least she is talking to me. "I thought maybe we could talk this morning over breakfast."

"So since you are ready, now we can talk?"

Her arms are flailing around as she talks, bringing my attention back to that damn tank top and how little it is hiding. "Could you please go and put on a robe or t-shirt, something? That tank top is doing nothing but distracting me right now.

She looks down at her shirt and when she looks back up, she is smiling, and not angelically either. Her hands go onto her waist, which thrusts her chest out more.

"What do you want to talk about, Cameron, since we seem to be on your time schedule?"

"What the hell does that mean?" On my schedule? Screw the tank top, we need to clear some stuff up.

"Cameron, I tried talking to you last night. You left without saying a word. However, now you seem to want to talk, so talk."

"Jayden, look, last night I had a lot going through my head. I was trying to sort it all out, including the fact that I let the bastard get away who killed my parents."

"Cameron, you weren't the only one who was going after the guy last night, there were a lot of people who wanted that man caught. My problem last night was you were shutting me out." She crosses her arms over her chest, you can see her temper cooling.

"I wasn't ready to talk. Not just to you, but I didn't want to talk to anyone. I needed to sort things out in my own head first. Just because I'm not talking, it doesn't mean I don't need you or that I am shutting you out. I needed you last night, trust me. Just sitting next to you or holding your hand calms me down, helps me think clear."

For a moment she stands there, neither of us saying a word. After a while, she goes and sits down on the couch, grabbing coffee out of my hand on the way. I sit down next to her, setting the bag with the food in it on the table in front of the couch.

"Cameron, you left me sitting in the car. Walked into the house and shut the door. You never even looked back, you shut me out. There was nothing in your actions last night that said to me 'please stay, I need you with me.'"

"I know and I'm sorry. I actually realized what I had done pretty quickly. When I went back out, you were pulling away down the street. I ran inside, grabbed my keys to follow you but by the time I got into the truck, you were nowhere in sight. It didn't take me an hour to notice you weren't there, I promise. It did take me about an hour to find out where you lived though."

I wait as she stares down at the cup of coffee in her hands.

"Jay, look at me."

Her eyes come up, a small smile on her lips. What's that all about?

"I'm sorry. You are right. I shouldn't have walked away from you, but you need to relax a little. I'm not used to all of this relationship openness stuff. I can't even tell you when the last time was that I had a steady girlfriend where I had to worry what was going on between us. I don't talk openly. I deal with it inside my head."

"Cameron, I'm sorry, too. I know all of this is a lot to deal with. You have a lot going on. I remember overhearing my mom one night, honestly I don't even remember who she was talking to. Anyway, she said my father never talked to her. She thought if he had, she wouldn't have been so surprised by all of his actions or maybe he wouldn't have found someone else to talk to."

"You can't keep comparing our relationship to your parents'. For one, I'm not your father. You need to figure out me and how I deal with stuff. We need to have our own relationship, not one based on what happened to your parents or mine."

She rolled her eyes. "I'm trying but if you aren't talking to me then how am I supposed to know?"

"All right, I'm hearing you. We need to work together a little more.

You need to quit being so fast to compare what we have with what happened with your parents. I need to learn to communicate more."

"I liked it when you called me Jay."

I didn't even realize that I did, I think to myself.

"It's much better than when you call me Ms. Edwards."

"I kind of like the Ms. Edwards. Every time I call you by your last name, you get a spark in your eyes. Almost like a challenge. You become feisty and I like that."

"You like feisty, do you?" She is laughing at me.

"On you I do, it's one of the things that attracted me to you that first day. Are we good?"

She leans over and lightly kisses me. "We are good. Which I'm happy about. When we fight, I don't sleep. It's exhausting."

"How about I take you back to bed, tire you out a little more and then hold you while you take a nap? I'll probably even join you on sleeping. I didn't sleep much last night either."

"Why didn't you get sleep last night?"

There is that insecurity look she gets in her eyes every once in a while. That side of her she doesn't like to show. It is the tough Jayden she likes to make sure people see.

"Jay, trust me, I didn't leave here last night feeling good. I know there are things I did wrong. I hated that you were mad at me. I almost called you a couple of times throughout the night. My parents had a rule with each other. Never go to bed mad. No matter how long it takes to talk it out, you do it before going to sleep. I know why now. You're either up all night fixing it or up all night worrying about it. Might as well fix it."

Jayden puts her coffee down on the table and scoots over to me. "I hate to say that I'm glad you were as miserable as I was last night. I would have much rather been tired because we did this instead."

She grabs the back of my neck and brings my lips down to hers. Her tongue darts in to find mine. I can feel her nipples harden against my chest through that very thin tank top.

"Jay, if you don't stop, I'm stripping you right here and taking you now."

She stands up and I am getting ready to stand up with her to follow her to her room when she quickly pulls her tank top off and lets her small shorts fall to the floor.

"You see, here we can do this anywhere, no one will walk in on us." She smiles down at me, then leans over, grabbing my t-shirt and pulling it over my head.

"Being here will definitely have its advantages." I stand up and remove my boots and remaining clothes as quickly as I can.

Once I am naked, Jayden pushes me back down onto the couch, climbing onto my lap straddling me.

"Just to let you know for the future, I have a spa in the backyard we can use as well."

She lifts her hips and guides herself over my hardness, taking me deep inside of her. Those teasing nipples are now directly in front of my face. I can finally do what I've been wanting to do since she opened the door. Sucking one deep into my mouth, I twirl my tongue around the hard peak.

Jayden moans, her hands in my hair, pushing my face into her chest as she grinds down onto me. My hands on her hips, I lift her up and pull her back down. She is so tight around me that I already feel like I'm going to lose myself inside of her.

Jayden quickens the pace. "Cameron," I hear her whisper as she guides me deep inside of her.

She is close, I can feel her tightening around me more and more with each time that she slides me into her, a little deeper each time. Her movements have become faster and faster. I'm not going to be able to hold back much longer.

I bring one hand away from her hips to her to other breast. I find the nipple and roll it between my finger and thumb.

"Jay, come on, babe, I'm about to lose all control. I need you with me."

I pinch her nipple, suck hard on the other and thrust my hips up. Jayden loses all control. Her body shakes around mine, with each contraction she pulls me deeper and deeper inside of her. Finally, I lose myself inside of her, bringing her breast deeper into my mouth. Jayden calls out my name, tightening her arms and legs around me.

I hold her as she comes down from her release. Our bodies both moist, her head is laying on my shoulder.

"I like it so much more being exhausted like this, than not sleeping because we are fighting," I hear her whisper into my ear.

I laugh. "I agree. You ready for a morning nap?"

I feel her head nod against my shoulder. I gently slide from her, then stand up. "Which way?"

"Down the hall, the door at the end," she answers so low I almost don't hear her.

By the time I lay her down, she is asleep. When I lay down next to her, she turns herself over and lays her head on my chest, her leg over mine. It feels natural, like we have slept like this every night. I have a feeling my bed is going to feel empty from now on.

CHAPTER
Twenty

JAYDEN

I HAVE no idea what time it is and I don't care. If I could stay all day in this bed with Cameron wrapped around me or maybe in me, I would. I smile to myself.

"I'm hungry." His deep voice vibrates in his chest against my cheek.

"I'm still sleeping."

"I'll be honest, I wasn't sure if you were ever going to wake up. You snore!"

I slap his chest, rolling off of him. "I don't snore."

Grabbing me around my waist, he pulls me back, my back now against his chest, his hardness pressing against my backside. "I hate to tell you, but yes you do," he whispers in my ear.

His hips move against mine. "Are you hungry or not?" I ask, smiling to myself. Yes, definitely could stay here all day with this man inside of me.

The pulse in my center starts to wake up. My nipples harden, and my core heats up instantly.

"Food was sounding good earlier, but right now I have a hunger for you," he whispers in my ear. The soft touch of his breath in my ear sends tingles throughout my body.

I turn myself around so that I am facing him, taking his hardness into my hand. I stroke down then up the entire length slowly, running my finger over his tip, spreading the beaded moisture around. I barely touch him and I hear his moan, his hips thrusting up begging for my touch.

"Do I snore?" I tease him with circling my finger around his tip. I hear his sharp intake of breath and smile to myself.

Before I can react I am flipped over onto my back, Cameron's body covering mine, his hardness pressing into my center. He kisses me deeply, my hips thrusting up trying to get him inside of me.

"You snore, and it's not a cute snore," he says, smiling, and then enters me in one deep thrust. My back arches up off bed, taking him as deep as I can.

"No more sleepovers then. I wouldn't want to keep you awake all night with my snoring."

He pulls out and then thrusts deep back in again, my eyes never leaving his.

"Jay, as long as you wake up like this, I'll manage through the snoring."

I slap him against the chest and he laughs which vibrates through my whole body, doing amazing things to my core. I hear myself moan. Cameron's lips claim mine and together we find our release.

"IT'S ALMOST three in the afternoon. I need food, Jayden."

I must have fallen back to sleep again, Cameron's request for food wakes me up. "Three in the afternoon, really?"

"Yes and as much as I would like to lay here and repeat activities from earlier, I need food. We skipped last night and the food I brought this morning is still sitting in the living room and not sounding as good as it did earlier today."

"What would you like to eat?" Problem is I haven't been shopping and I have no idea what I can make. I wasn't expecting company.

"Why don't we grab a quick shower and I'll take you out to an early dinner. Jacob texted me earlier and told me he is staying at Tyler's house tonight. So we can come back here afterwards and use the spa you told me you have."

"You mentioning the spa is giving me ideas that do not include getting up right now and taking a shower and going anywhere."

Cameron smacks me on the backside and jumps out of bed. "Get up, woman, I need food, you need food, then we will come back and start up on whatever lit up your eyes talking about the spa."

I watch as he walks into the bathroom as though he has been in there many times before. I hear the water go on. Quickly I get up and follow him, joining him in the shower.

"What are you doing?" he asks as he runs my shampoo through his hair.

"Taking a shower." I rub my body up against his.

"We need food. I need food. You doing this isn't helping with getting us out of here and to a food establishment."

I pout up at him. "Are you telling me no?"

He finishes rinsing off. I watch as his muscles flex with each of his movements. How can I need him again? I run my hands down his chest. Before I know what's happened, my arms are pinned above my head and my back is against the wall, Cameron's body pressed hard against mine. He takes my lips in a kiss of pure hunger, and not for food.

His lips move along my jawline up to my ear. "As much as I would love to take you right here up against the wall with the water cascading over your very tempting body, I'll have to restrain myself and settle for food."

Before I can respond, he shoves away from me, leaving me alone in the shower, using my towel to wrap around his waist.

"Hey, that's my towel."

Before leaving the bathroom, he looks back at me. "You didn't grab me one. This one was free." He gives me that cocky smile he gave me the first day we met in the principal's office, the one that almost knocked me onto my butt. "Now hurry up or I'll go without you." Turning, he leaves the bathroom.

WE PICK a small little diner we all like to eat at that has the best chili fries. Travis's sister had brought Charliee here a while back and she got me hooked. I don't realize how hungry I am until my chili fries are placed in front of me. It's usually enough for two, but I am handling them pretty good on my own.

"Are you still coming down to Texas with me this weekend?" Cameron asks in between bites of his cheeseburger.

"As long as you still want me to go."

"I bought the tickets already so yes, I still want you to go. I just didn't know since everything last night."

"Cameron, I think we both just need to talk more. That will keep last night from happening again."

"I'm not the best at all of that, especially at first. I told you I need to sort things out in my own head first."

Nodding, I know this all now. That's what I meant when I said we needed to talk. Maybe I should say we need get to know each other more. "I know and I understand, but that's what I meant. We need to just learn a little more about each other. I'm sure last night won't be our last argument, but hopefully there will be less of them."

"We will be meeting up with Steve and his wife Saturday night for dinner."

I know Steve is the guy who works with Cameron down in Texas, but that is really all I know. "That's fine, I'd like to meet him. I know you have a lot going on this weekend, I'm going along to help with whatever I can."

The waitress stops by and sets our check down. "Thank you for coming in. Have a good evening. You can pay up front on your way out."

"If you are ready to go, we can go back to your place and try out that spa."

"After what you did to me in the shower, I think you should go home and sleep alone."

Cameron reaches across and grabs my hand, running his fingers over the inside of my palm. Damn him. "Do you really want me to go home alone?"

I feel the tingle from my palm straight to my core. My body temperature rises quickly, and from the look in his eyes he knows what an effect he is having on me. No one is going home alone tonight!

WE LAND in Texas around two in the afternoon. We grab a cab and go straight to Cameron's house.

"It will probably be a little stuffy, sorry," Cameron explains as he unlocks his front door.

He is cute being all worried what I am going to think of his home. "Cameron, stop worrying how the house may look."

He opens the door and stands aside so that I can enter first. Just what I thought, a clean freak. It isn't fancy but it is a guy's place, I wasn't expecting fancy décor. Nice furniture, some pictures on the wall, the simple stuff. It screams Cameron, though. I am impressed.

"You should really dust more often." I turn and smile up at him, teasing him.

Rolling his eyes, he walks past me with my bag. "Get out of my way, or you can carry your own bag."

Laughing, I move to the side and then follow him into his room. This room, just like the rest of the house, is clean, the bed made.

"What are you going to do with all of your furniture since your parents' house is already furnished?"

He looks around then shrugs his shoulders. "Honestly, I have no idea. I'm not sure if I even want to stay in my parents' house, but until Jacob graduates I'm thinking to just get a storage unit for all of it."

"Why not just keep your parents' house?"

"I'm not sure what to do with it, to be honest. I don't think I can change their bedroom, Jacob will be going to college, why do I need something that big? I thought about selling it and getting something else since Jacob will be going off to college."

"What if Jacob decides to go to a local college?"

Again, Cameron shrugs. "I haven't thought much past getting all of my stuff moved back to Washington, and this place up for sale. Jacob will always have a place with me if he wants it. If we sell the house, he might want a small place of his own. We'll figure all of that out."

The smile is gone. He is pulling back again. He usually does when conversations have anything to do with his parents. It is fine, I'm not going to push anything this weekend. He has a lot to do and worry about in the very short time we are here. We are leaving early Tuesday morning to start heading back to Washington. The drive will take us the rest of the week to get home. We will have plenty of time on that trip to talk.

"What time did you say we were going to dinner tonight?"

"We are meeting them at six." Cameron looks relieved the conversation has changed.

I kick off my shoes and close the space in between us, and unbutton the fly of his jeans. "I think I have a pretty good idea of how to spend our time until then if you would like to hear it."

"I believe I like the way your mind is working, Ms. Edwards."

CHAPTER
Twenty~One

CAMERON

"SO STEVE, there's no way to repay you for everything you have done with finishing everything since I have been in Washington." I look across the table to the man who is tough as nails and would swear he blushed a little. His wife, Carol, just sits there beaming at him. You can see her pride through her eyes.

"Cameron, I wish there was more I could have done to take some of the load off your shoulders. I only met your mom a couple of times but she was a very nice woman. Your dad was a great guy. I'm sorry for you boys' loss." Steve looks a little choked up as he speaks.

My chest tightens for a moment, but I almost lose it completely when Steve looks straight at me and adds, "Your parents would be proud of how well you have done through all of this. I know I'm proud of you."

It feels like a punch to my chest, my breath catches in my throat. Jayden's hand is resting on my thigh and she squeezes it. I grab her hand under the table and squeeze. It helps.

"Thank you, Steve, that means a lot."

It is quiet around the table for a moment. Then Steve clears his throat. "I hope I'm not pushing you, so please don't take this that way, but are you coming back down or what's happening with this side of the company?"

I see a little fear in his face. Steve is worried that I'm not coming back and am going to close this side of things. Now I feel bad that I waited until now to talk to him. He has probably been worrying about this for a while.

"Steve, that's what I wanted to talk to you about actually. I'm sure you know my brother has one more year of high school. I couldn't pull him away his senior year so I have decided to move back to Washington."

I see Carol's shoulders slump a little and her eyes well up with tears. Steve just nods. "Cameron, I figured that you would. It's what needs to be done. I understand."

"Actually, I don't think you do. I have, or should I say we have worked so hard to build this side of the business down here. We have projects lined up. I actually wanted to offer you a partnership with me. You run Texas, I run Washington. We continue to build Tovaren Construction in both states."

Carol's smile can't get any bigger and the sad tears from earlier now spring from her eyes but they are no longer sad tears, they are happy tears. Steve keeps looking around, like he is expecting someone to say "Gotcha" or something.

"Cameron, as much as I appreciate the offer, there is no way I could buy into half of this company. I don't have that kind of money."

"Steve, you aren't needing to buy anything. I'm asking that you take my spot down here. We can talk all the shop talk later, I just need to know if you are interested. I don't want to lose this side of things, you and I have worked hard and I don't want to see that all go to waste. I know you can handle all of this, we can even look into hiring someone if you think you need the help."

"Hell yeah, I'm interested," he yells a little louder than is needed inside a restaurant. The tables around us all look, giving us curious glances.

Again, it's the good ol' cowboy, and I wouldn't change a thing about him. "That's the answer I was hoping you would give me. Monday before the inspection, we will meet and talk everything over. For now, let's enjoy the rest of this dinner and our ladies."

The rest of the evening goes great. We spend the entire evening with Steve telling Jayden stories about me. It is almost like a father meeting the son's girlfriend for the first time. It is a great night and for the first time in a while, I feel completely relaxed. Things feel like they are finally getting back to as normal as it is going to get, I think. Since the news of my parents, tonight is the first time I am ready to start looking forward again.

I look over to the passenger seat, Jayden is asleep. *Asleep, her feisty side looks innocent*, I think to myself. I know all of this hasn't been easy on her. Not only did she almost lose her best friend, but then she met me. I push a piece of hair off her face. Things with me haven't been easy, I know. Why she has stayed around is beyond me. In each of our arguments, I did see the challenge in her eyes, which was one thing that drew me to her. She gave me that look in the principal's office that first day we met, I think she hooked me from that moment.

After tonight and talking with Steve, knowing he is all on board with my plans of him taking over down here in Texas, I realize it is time to move on with our lives, Jacob's and mine. Our parents would want us to. I know this is going to be easier said than done but it is time. I am ready to work harder on this thing between Jayden and me. My parents would have loved her. My mom always said it was going to take a feisty woman who would challenge me and not take my crap to tie me down. Maybe not in those exact words, but it meant all the same. Jayden definitely did all of that. There is a very insecure side to her, however.

"Hey, are we back at your place?"

I didn't realize she had woken up. "Yeah, we are."

"Sorry, I didn't mean to fall asleep."

"It's no big deal, just means you're comfortable. I'm good with that." I smile at her.

Jayden smiles back, she looks like she could easily fall back to sleep. It has been a long day.

"Let's go inside and get you in bed."

I think she tries to give me her sexy smile but she isn't pulling it off with those sleepy eyes.

"Come on, beautiful, let's go in and get some sleep." Laughing, I get out and round the truck to her side. She hasn't even moved to take off her seatbelt I notice when I open her door.

I reach across and unbuckle her and pick her up out of the truck.

"I can walk."

"You can, but you hadn't even taken your seat belt off yet, you're tired. If I wait for you, we will be out here all night. I don't know about you but I would rather sleep in the bed tonight, and I'm not talking about the truck bed.

"Ha ha." She doesn't fight me, though. Instead, she lays her head down against my shoulder.

Walking straight back to my room, I lay her down on my bed. "Do you want me to change you, too?" I start to pull her boots off.

Sitting up, her second boot falls to the floor. "As much as I'd love to allow you to finish this job, I think tonight I'm going to have to pass."

Laughing at her pouty face, I grab her hands and pull her up onto her feet. "Get changed and we'll go to bed." I watch as she grabs some of her stuff and disappears into my bathroom.

. . .

THE CONSTANT RINGING of my doorbell wakes me up. Picking up my phone off the nightstand, it is about nine-thirty in the morning. I am surprised I slept in this long. Six-thirty, maybe seven is the usual for me. Looking over at Jayden, I realize how relaxed I feel. That is until the doorbell starts ringing again. I quickly get out of bed, pulling on my jeans as I walk down the hall.

Who the heck even knows I am home? Opening the door, I hear myself groan. "Candice."

"It's about time you answered the door. What took so long?"

What had I seen in this woman? She looks up at me like she is waiting for me to move, but I keep my stance, my arms stretched out across the doorway casually.

"I was asleep, what can I do for you?"

"Why aren't you letting me in? Aren't you happy to see me?" She places her hand on my bare stomach but I step away from her touch.

"Candice, I know we have been out a couple times, but that's all it was. I'm sorry. Now if you will excuse me, I'm going back to bed."

I go to shut the door and she stops it. "Do you have someone else in there with you?"

What right does she think she has to even ask me that question? From the look on her face, she is fully expecting me to answer it. I'm starting to lose my patience though.

"I can't see why who I have and don't have in my bed is your business."

She pouts and it takes everything in me not to yell, "Really?!"

"Cameron, you know I love you."

I roll my eyes. I must have had too many to drink the night I met this one. Either that or meeting Jayden has shown me what I want. "Candice, you don't even know me. Look, again I'm sorry, but I'm going to ask you to leave now."

I don't wait for her to respond, I push the door closed, locking it just in case. I wait a minute, I wouldn't put it past her to start ringing the doorbell all crazy again. When I hear a car door slam, I figure it is safe to say she has left. I hadn't dated much, work kept me pretty busy, but I go and find the crazy one.

Walking back into the room, Jayden is still asleep. She must be exhausted to sleep through all of that, Candice hadn't kept her voice down. I am relieved she hadn't come out. Jayden is strong on the outside appearance but very insecure inside. She would ask questions, I would answer all of them but she would play out all kinds of stuff in her head. There is no comparison between the two women, but convincing Jayden would be a chore I had a strong feeling. Ever since her father cheated on her mother, she thinks that is going to happen no matter who the man is.

I'm not one who normally likes lounging in bed, but looking at Jayden sleeping in my bed, all I want to do is climb back in and wrap my body around her. I quickly strip back out of my jeans and slide back in bed. Jayden stirs next to me, her eyes opening slightly. She has the sheet half on and half off. She is only wearing a tank top and underwear, so I have full view of one very nice leg.

"Hey, what time is it?" she asks in a very sexy, half asleep voice.

I crawl over her, claiming her lips in a good morning kiss. Her body instantly becomes awake. I can feel the heat from between her legs, and feel her nipples tighten against my chest. Her fingers go into my hair, tugging slightly, which makes me harder.

"It's almost ten," I finally answer her.

Her eyes go wide. "Are you kidding?"

I kiss a trail across her neck and then back up to her lips. "I'm thinking of something pretty sweet for breakfast."

Her eyebrows shoot up, but she doesn't move. I begin my journey to her sweetest spot. Her eyes never leave mine as I work my way down her body. Pulling her tank top up and exposing her breasts, I take turns sucking each one into my mouth. As I make my way further down, I slide her underwear down her legs. She kicks them off for me. She watches me with those sexy, half asleep eyes as I work my way down her body to the sweet heat in between her legs.

Keeping her eyes with mine, I lick her and watch as her eyes roll back and her back arches, pressing herself onto my tongue. Her fingers are in my hair, pulling. I about lose it right here watching her. I can feel her body tightening up, she is ready for her release. I think she is about to when she surprises me by pushing me away from her and quickly rolling us over so that she is straddling me. No longer looking half asleep, but fully awake, her hand now wraps around my base guiding me into her very wet, very ready body.

I sit up and Jayden wraps her legs around my waist. Her breasts beg for attention, I suck one begging nipple into my mouth. Her back arches, pushing me further into her, and her hands are back in my hair, pressing her breast further into my mouth. With my hands on her hips, guiding her hips as she rides me and my mouth working on her breast, it doesn't take long for either of us to lose ourselves.

CHAPTER
Twenty~Two

JAYDEN

SINCE WE ENJOYED breakfast in bed, we decide to go out for lunch. Today is the only day we have to drive around and enjoy the day. Cameron wants to show me around. Tomorrow, he has to work most of the day with the inspectors and packing up the rest of the house. Cameron is hoping to be on the road back to Washington pretty early Tuesday morning.

We have just sat down and ordered when his phone goes off once again, all morning it has been going off. I notice that he looks at it and then roll his eyes and presses ignore. Then shortly after, he gets a text message and he says something under his breath. He never says who they are from and I don't ask, but it is driving me crazy.

We have just received our food when his phone rings again. "Cameron, answer it. Ignoring it isn't working."

"Fine, I'll be right back." He scoots out of the booth. I hear him answer it as he walks out the front door.

I don't expect him to leave to answer it, now I am even more curious about who it is. He doesn't want me to know, that is for sure. When he sits back down, I can tell he is pissed. I am trying very hard to seem like I'm not bothered but it is difficult.

"Everything all right?" I finally ask after some time of eating in silence.

Cameron just nods. He is shutting me out again.

"Are you sure you don't want to talk about it? You seem pretty bothered by who or whatever it was," I try one more time.

Cameron rolls his eyes and takes a deep breath, but then his attention goes back to his plate of food that he really hasn't touched. I know that look, I have seen it a couple times. Usually each of those times had him telling me to mind my own business and yelling at me, and then me leaving, pissed. We are in Texas, I can't just drive home.

"Never mind, forget I asked," I tell him before he yells or snaps.

Another ten minutes or so goes by and still nothing, I just sit here eating my fries waiting for him to explode. This is crazy, why do I have to walk on glass because he is pissed off at someone else? He either needs to get over it or talk about it, but I'm not going to get the silent treatment from him all day long. He told me he needs some time to think things through before he talks things out. I thought I had given him that time, I mean what could be that bad? I am about to tell him all of that, too, when he finally speaks.

"Look, Jayden, I'm sorry. I think I'm just stressed about tomorrow. I didn't mean to get upset and ruin our afternoon."

"Are all those calls and texts about tomorrow?" I ask, pretty sure they have nothing to do with the inspection. If they would have been from Steve, I don't think he would have ignored them. This is his excuse so that he doesn't need to talk about what is really the problem.

He shakes his head. "No, those are another problem that isn't taking a hint."

Well, if that didn't scream another woman then I don't know what does. My heart leaps into my throat for a second. Then I tell myself to relax. Cameron said I had to stop comparing our relationship to my parents' and he is right. Not every man is a jerk like my father.

Cameron finally takes a bite of his hamburger. "Let's just forget about that and I'll try to relax about tomorrow so that we can enjoy the rest of the day."

So I either push this issue and risk a really bad day, or let it go. Trust that if it's something that I need to know about, he will tell me. In other words, pick my battle. Cameron has really never given me a reason to not trust him, even if it has to do with another woman. I need to let this go and trust him.

"So what were your plans for the rest of the day?" I ask. I watch as his shoulders relax a little when he realizes I am letting it go.

THE DAY HASN'T BEEN bad. We drove around and he showed me more of the town. We went by the housing track that he has been working on down here and we went out for dinner. I could tell that Cameron wasn't himself though. He had turned his phone down so that I couldn't hear it when it went off. I saw him checking it every so often, I think more out of making sure Jacob didn't text needing something than any other reason. I didn't bring it up though. I needed to trust him.

When we pull back up into the driveway of Cameron's, I see someone sitting on the porch. It is a woman, all I can make out is she has red hair. Cameron throws the truck into park, cursing a whole string of words. I am about to ask who she is, but Cameron jumps out of the truck before I can, slamming his door shut.

Once again, I am left sitting alone in a vehicle. I watch as he goes up onto the porch talking to the woman. She has her hands all over him and all the while he is trying to keep her from touching him. Now I am getting pissed, why am I sitting here? This lady thinks she can touch my boyfriend? She has another thing coming. Getting out of the truck,

I walk up to the house getting ready to give this woman a piece of my mind if she touches Cameron once again.

"Candice, you need to listen to me."

I stop on the step. Candice! I recognize the name right away. This is the woman who Cameron was talking to that day after he first kissed me.

"Is everything all right?" I ask as I walk up to stand next to Cameron. I need to trust Cameron when he told me nothing was going on between them, but it is hard at the moment. I go to grab his hand, kind of claim my status as his girlfriend I guess you could say, but he moves away from my touch. My heart leaps into my throat.

"This has nothing to do with you, you don't need to include yourself," the redheaded woman in front of me spits out.

"Who are you?" I ask, standing my ground.

"I'm his girlfriend," she answers, arms crossed over her chest. She looks at me like she can't believe I asked her such a question.

I look up at Cameron, he is rubbing his forehead. I wait for him to say something but he doesn't. This woman in front of me looks at me like she is waiting for me to get the hint and walk away. I stand there waiting for Cameron to say something to clear everything up, but no, he just stands there looking down at the ground. Am I missing something here?

"Cameron?" I ask, looking at him, waiting for him to say something.

"Jayden, just go inside." He sounds tired.

I don't care. Did he just ask me to go inside? "Excuse me?"

"Jayden, please, let me deal with this," he points over at Candice, "then I'll deal with this," he points between him and me.

Deal with this? Is he serious, he had to deal with me? Screw him. I'll leave him to deal with Candice. I am pretty sure Candice isn't his girlfriend, but I am done with him. I walk into the house, pulling my phone out of my pocket and calling the first cab company that is listed on the search I found. Cameron won't have to worry about dealing with me next. No matter how much I am falling for him, I am done having him shut me out. Tonight is the worst though. He pushed me aside and for another woman. This woman might not mean anything to him, but that almost makes it worse.

I quickly grab all my stuff, putting everything in my bag as fast as I can. I quickly look up flights, finding one leaving tonight in a couple of hours. I feel the tears burn my eyes, but I'm not going to cry. I won't walk in front of that woman and give her the satisfaction of knowing I am upset because of her.

One last quick look around, I make sure I have grabbed everything. As I am walking back out to the living room, I hear the horn outside letting me know the cab is here already. I hate that I have to walk past the two of them outside to leave, but I'm not going to hide in here until Candice leaves and then have to listen to Cameron yell at me.

Cameron and Candice are both still on the porch when I walk back out. Cameron has a puzzled expression on his face as he looks over at the cab pulled in front of his house. When his eyes swing to me coming out the front door, I know the exact moment when he realizes what is going on.

He grabs my arm as I walk in between the two of them. "Where the hell are you going?"

I look between him and Candice and then back up at him. I can see it in his eyes he has read the situation wrong. He thinks I am leaving because I believe this woman is more to him. He doesn't even think for a second it is because of how he treated me.

"Jayden, this isn't what you think it is." He confirms what I believe he thinks is the reason why I am leaving.

The tears burn once again. I think it almost hurts worse to know that he hasn't figured it out. That his words and the way he talked to me was wrong. I'm not a child, I'm his girlfriend.

"Believe it or not, I'm not upset about Candice. I can see desperation when it's pouring out of someone like it is her."

I hear the sharp intake of breath from Candice but I don't care. I want to turn to her and yell at her, "Yes, I called you desperate," but I control myself.

"Jayden, don't do this right now, just go back into the house."

Why do I always feel like a child being scolded when Cameron is mad at me? "You know what, Cameron? You need to finish up with all your loose ends and business here. I'm going home."

"Jay, don't do this right now," he repeats again.

Calling me Jay almost has me turning back around and waiting for him inside. I take a deep breath, if I give in now this will never change.

"You know what, deal with things here and maybe once you get back, we can talk but right now I need to go home."

I think what hurts more than anything is he doesn't fight harder. I'm not mad, just hurt. I quickly walk down to the cab and don't look back. I don't want to let Cameron or Candice see me cry. There is no holding back the tears this time.

ONCE ON THE PLANE, and I realize Cameron isn't going to stop me, I break down. I wait to see him come running into the airport, stopping me at the boarding area, something. I need to go, I need him to let me go, but I want him to care enough to come after me and stop me. I think I'm a complete mess. Maybe the whole problem isn't Cameron, but me as well. Cameron's problem is communication, mine is reacting without thinking. I jump instead of sitting down and thinking. That is one of the things that keeps me from calling Charliee to come and pick me up at the airport. I sit here and actually think about it. If I call her, she will instantly take my side and get very mad at Cameron. I'm not sure if I want that. I'm not even going to let her know I am home early. I don't want her mad at Cameron. Even leaving him, I can't help but want to protect him.

CHAPTER
Twenty~Three

CAMERON

"IT'S ALL DONE. Papers are signed, inspection over, out of our hands now. Damn, that feels good." Steve sits back in his office chair and smiles.

I feel a huge weight lifted from my shoulders. I know Steve can handle everything here. He could have handled the inspection without me, but I started all of this with him, I wanted to make sure I was with him to finish it. That was the only thing that kept me here last night after Jayden left. I wanted to run after her, go to the airport and stop here, fly out and go back to Washington, but I had other responsibilities I had to think of.

"Hey, why don't we take the ladies out tonight to celebrate?" Steve suggests, having no idea of last night's mess.

"I have a couple more great stories I thought about to tell Jayden I think she would appreciate hearing," he adds.

"You, my friend, will have to wait and tell those stories at another time." *That's if there is another time,* I think to myself.

"You two already have plans to celebrate tonight?" he asks, raising his eyebrows up at me with that "I know how you guys plan to celebrate" look.

"No, Jayden went home last night."

"Wasn't she supposed to drive back with you?" Steve asks, confused.

I nod, playing with a paperclip on the desk.

"Do you want to talk about it?"

"Not really," I state plainly.

"All right, well then how about you and I head out and grab a final beer?"

"Steve, you act like we aren't going to see each other again. We'll be talking so much you are going to throw your phone when you see my name pop up on the screen."

"Probably but since we saw each other every day here, talking on the phone shouldn't be too bad. Do you want to go for that beer or not?"

I hate saying no, but I am planning on pulling out tonight instead of in the morning. I need to get home and straighten things out with Jayden. "Actually, Steve, I was thinking about starting out tonight so I'll have to take a rain check on that beer until the next time I'm here."

Steve stares at me from across the desk for a moment. I'm not fooling him, he knows why I am in a hurry to leave tonight. I've already been up all night. I watched the taxi pull away with Jayden and I lost my temper altogether. I had been trying real hard with Candice to get her to understand there wasn't and never would be anything between us, but she wasn't letting up. After Jayden pulled away, I came unglued. I am now pissed at Candice, Jayden and myself. I was trying to handle the whole situation without hurting anyone, but I obviously didn't do it right. I think I may have screwed everything up completely with

Jayden this time. I saw the look in her eyes, it was that look that kept me from sleeping all night.

"Cameron! Hey, are you all right?" Steve breaks through my thoughts.

"Sorry, I didn't get much sleep last night. I think between that and everything today, I'm just tired."

"And you think driving tonight is a good idea? Why don't you get some rest tonight and pull out early in the morning? You can't make things better if you don't make it to Washington alive."

The dad side of Steve is coming out, I smile. "I won't sleep anyway."

"I was going to let it drop but now I can't. What's going on with Jayden? Obviously she didn't leave on a good note last night."

Pulling the paperclip apart, I sit quiet for a moment. No, she didn't leave happy, but I hold on to the part where she said we could talk when I got back to Washington. That is the only thing giving me any kind of hope that I didn't completely mess it all up. I look up at Steve, who is reclined back in the office chair just waiting for me to answer.

"Candice showed up at my house last night when we got home. She was waiting on my porch when we got there. She had showed up yesterday morning and I thought I made it clear I wasn't interested. Then she either called or texted all day long. When the calls stopped, I thought she got the hint, until I pulled up and there she was."

"So what, Jayden thinks you guys are a thing or something?"

I shake my head no. "I think she knows there is nothing going on between the two of us."

Which to be honest, I was surprised about. She is usually so hung up on what her father did to her mom, I figured she would have jumped right to that conclusion.

"I'm lost. Then why did she leave?"

"I think it has something to do with the way I handled everything last night. Long story short, I'm pretty sure it has to do with me getting frustrated and telling her to go inside and I'd deal with her after I dealt with Candice."

After I finally got Candice to leave and I had been sitting down trying to figure out what I had said to piss her off so much, that comment came running back to memory. I don't blame her for being upset, I am pretty mad at myself for saying something so stupid.

Steve whistles and shakes his head. "You made a few mistakes there, buddy."

Throwing the clip onto the desk, I stand up and walk over to the window. "She did say before she left that we could talk when I get back to Washington."

Steve chuckles behind me. I wish I still had the paperclip in hand so I could throw something at him. "I'm happy to see you are finding the humor in this."

Steve throws his hands up in a surrender. "Sorry. Every man who has been in a serious relationship has been where you are now, my friend. We men learn very early we will put our foot in our mouth a lot. I just wish I could have been there when you told her to go inside and you would deal with her after Candice. I'd put money on the fact that Jayden doesn't give a crap about Candice, anyone can see that woman is just needy and desperate, telling her you would deal with her later I'm sure is what got her all riled up."

Steve is laughing and I am getting pissed. "Candice was driving me crazy, I wasn't thinking," I try to defend myself.

"Women don't care what's going on before you speak, they only hear what's coming out of your mouth when you are talking to them. You'll learn, trust me," Steve continues laughing.

I'm glad he is finding this situation funny. I may have lost Jayden because I was trying not to be rude to Candice. I'm not finding any of this funny.

"Learn what? I'm not even sure if I want to try and work all of this out.

I have a lot going on right now. I'm not sure what to do with all of this, maybe I should let it go. Let Jayden go."

Even as I say it, I know I'm not leaving it alone. I hate to admit this but I already miss having Jayden here. I don't want to wait an extra night to get home. If I could leave now, I would.

"I don't know who you are trying to convince, me or yourself. I see that look in your eyes, you are hooked. Can't say that I blame you, Jayden seems great."

"Does this relationship thing ever get easier?"

Laughing again, Steve shakes his head. "You learn, trust me."

"Right! Well I'm learning to apologize well."

"That's a start, son."

IT DOESN'T TAKE LONG to clean up my side of the office here in the portable for the track housing. I make sure to clean out what I can so that Steve doesn't have to take care of all of it. The trailer will be moved to the next site soon. I didn't sleep last night, so I made sure everything was ready to go for the movers to come get all my stuff. I got on the road around six-thirty this morning. I've tried to call Jayden a couple of times but all I get is her voice mail. All of the texts I've sent have gone unanswered. She said we would talk when I got home but now I am wondering if she has changed her mind.

Once more I try to call, and like the last three of four times, her voicemail is what I get. "Jay, I'm sorry. I'm on my way home. Hopefully in the next couple of days you will decide to talk to me when I get home. I know I apologize a lot to you and I keep saying it won't happen again, but I'm a work in progress and I'm sure I'll mess up again if you decide to give this thing between us another shot. Call me back if you want, but if I don't hear from you before, I'll see you when I get home."

Throwing my phone in the seat next to me, I take a deep breath. She will talk to me even if I have to sit outside of her house. Things are coming around to normal again. I want to work on this relationship with Jayden, I don't want her giving up on us. I have a long drive home, lots of time to think, and by the time I reach Washington I should have a pretty good idea on how to fix all of this.

CHAPTER
Twenty~Four

IT'S BEEN A LONG WEEK. I haven't heard back from Cameron since his voicemail he left the day he left Texas. He should be back in Washington by now, but I haven't heard anything from him. I am expecting him to show up at my front door at any time now. I have to admit, I miss him. I missed him the moment I sat down in the cab to leave his house back in Texas. I haven't answered any of his calls or the texts he has sent me. I know if I do, I will instantly forgive him and right now, I'm not real sure what to do with this thing between us. He will apologize, I will forgive him and then things will go good for a little while, then something will happen and he will take it out on me again. I can't sit here any longer, I need my best friend.

"SINCE WHEN DO you ring the doorbell and not just come in?" Charliee answers the door, surprise written all over her face.

"Since you decided to get a roommate. I'm trying to be considerate. Is he home today? I didn't see his truck."

Walking past Charliee when she moves aside to let me in the house, I head down the hallway. I am curious how much room my friend gave up for her man.

"No, Travis is at work today," Charliee answers, following behind me down the hall. "May I ask what you are looking for?"

I open the door to her spare room and the office. Turning to her, I laugh. "I was checking out the new look to the house. Nothing has really changed except the large television in the living room. I figured you would have had to clean out a least one room maybe for a gym or something."

Charliee laughs. "Bryan from the station has just moved into his own apartment and needed a lot of what we were going to get rid of, so Travis worked with him on everything."

"So how are things going with having Travis here? I haven't heard much from you the last few weeks."

"It's been good. I'm not the only one who's been busy. The last couple times I've asked what you were up to, you had already made plans with Cameron. I'm thinking everything is going good with you two."

Damn, I shouldn't have brought this conversation up. I was just trying to give her a hard time. That completely backfired.

"Jayden, what's going on? Are things not working out between the two of you?"

There is no reason to try and keep everything from Charliee, plus I don't think I want to anymore. I don't know what to do anymore, I mean I came here to keep from seeing Cameron just in case he showed up at my house.

"I don't know. One minute we are great, the next we are fighting." I need my friend. I need her advice on what to do, but I don't want her mad at him either.

"Are you guys still fighting over Jacob?"

I wish, I think that was easier times, I think to myself. "Not really since school got out."

"You love him, don't you?"

No reason to hide it from her or try to deny it with Charliee, she will see right through me. "Is it that obvious?"

I watch as she shrugs her shoulders. "I can see it, but then again that's part of my job description as the best friend."

I hear a vibration coming from the kitchen. Saved by the phone. I point to the kitchen. "I hear your phone going off somewhere that way."

"Thanks," she signs as she quickly heads over toward the kitchen.

Charliee is happy, it is written all over her face. I pull my phone out of my pocket. No calls, no texts. Maybe I should just call him. Maybe he thinks that since I haven't returned any of his calls or texts, I don't want to talk to him.

Charliee walks back in holding her phone. "So, you have plans for today?"

I should call Cameron, but maybe he isn't home yet. I'll give it until tonight. If I don't hear from him by then, maybe, just maybe I'll call him. I just shake my head no to answer Charliee.

"You want to go with me down to the station? Bryce just asked me to come down."

Perfect, maybe this will keep my mind off things for a while. "Sure, I will go with you."

IT KILLS me to see Charliee's disappointment leaving the police station. Sure, they had a little more information on the person who is responsible for so much pain. After seeing him at the carnival, I've noticed a change in Charliee and Cameron.

Charliee is a type of person who always looks at the positive, but today you can see Charliee losing hope, getting frustrated. She is getting mad. I can't say I blame her but it is still a different side of Charliee, one I really hate seeing on her.

"You want to grab some lunch?" I ask as we jump back into the jeep

She checks her phone. "Sure, we can grab something. Where were you thinking?"

"How about that hamburger place down the street?"

She nods then pulls out of the parking space. Before pulling out onto the street, she pulls her phone out of her pocket and hands it to me.

"Can you see who texted me, please?"

"Travis," I sign to her. "He is back at the station. Stop by and tell him what happened."

She asks me to text him back that we will stop by the station after lunch. So I do, of course it isn't going to be that boring. If I was dating a hot firefighter, my messages wouldn't be as boring as the ones on her phone. Best friend privileges in full swing working.

As she parks, I hand her back her phone but I can't control the huge smile on my face. I know I look guilty.

"Jayden!" Charliee yells behind me, stopping me as I walk toward the diner.

I turn around with a questioning look, hopefully looking innocent. Although I'd love to know how he responded to Charliee's text.

"Really? That's what popped in your head when I asked you to text him?"

I throw my hands up in surrender. "I was helping you with dessert. Plus, your text sounded boring. I just spiced it up a little."

I leave it at that, turning and heading inside before she can yell at me some more.

Charliee follows in shortly after. I keep my eyes on my menu as she sits down. When she doesn't say anything, I put the menu down.

"So are you going to make good on your promise?" I smile innocently at her.

"Just remember, payback is a bitch."

I blow her a kiss and wink. "I'll bet he got a kick out of it."

AFTER LUNCH, we head straight to the station. Charliee basically shovels her food in and finishes in record time. I know she wants to see Travis and tell him what happened at the station. Travis calms her in a way none of us can when it comes to anything with the bombing.

Turning on to the street of Travis's station, the engine comes out of the driveway, lights and sirens on. Charliee pulls over, giving them room on the road. We see Travis in the back cab window and as he passes, he signs that he will text Charliee later and that he loves her. I have to admit, I am a little jealous over their relationship. It is always so comfortable between the two of them. That perfect match you hear about, or true love, the happily ever after, that's what Charliee and Travis have. I don't think they have ever had an argument. Travis worships Charliee. She deserves it, though, she deserves to be treated the way he treats her. Like she walks on water.

I look over and see her hands tightly gripping the steering wheel. I grab her arm to get her attention. "What's wrong?"

She shrugs, but her eyes look worried. She looks back down the street but the engine has already disappeared around the corner.

Charliee looks back over at me. "Do you ever get a feeling like something isn't right?"

"Charliee, you are just freaking out. Between going to the station today and getting all worked up there and them rushing out of here, lights everywhere, your nerves are just going crazy."

Charliee looks like at any moment she is going to drive after the engine, following them onto whatever call they are headed to.

"I have to admit, firefighters are already hot but watching them rush out of here, lights flashing and hearing the sirens, it makes those guys even hotter."

There is the smile I was hoping for. She is calming down. The worry is still in her eyes, but she takes a deep breath and nods her head in agreement with me.

I AM LOOKING for a distraction to keep my mind off of Cameron and today doesn't disappoint. We turn onto Charliee's street to find a squad car sitting along the curb in front of her house. As we pass by to pull into her driveway, both of her brothers step out of the car. I am hoping this has to do with us being at the station earlier, maybe some good news from everything, but I am pretty sure they wouldn't drive over here for any of that. Charliee parks the jeep and we both jump out. I come around as Charliee opens the back door to let Levi out. I look over at the boys, this isn't good. I can see their faces from here and all I see is dread and seriousness. They have on their police faces.

"What are you guys doing here?" Charliee asks when neither brother makes the move to approach us.

Derrick looks over at Bryce and then starts toward us. You can tell he is even less happy to have to be the one to do whatever they are here to do.

"Derrick, what's going on? Why are you guys here?" Charliee is losing her patience, I can hear it in her voice, plus she is talking and signing, never a good sign with her. That usually means she is pissed or upset, something. She always leans back onto signing when she is emotional. I think that is because she doesn't have to think when it comes to sign-ing. Plus, it always seems to get her point across a little better. You know that saying "Actions speak louder than words."

I watch as Derrick looks up at the sky, like he is looking for the easy way to say something. I am about to yell at him myself when he finally speaks. "Charliee, there has been another bombing."

A chill runs through my body. Charliee looks over at me. "That must have been where the guys were going when we pulled up."

A puzzled look comes over her face. Charliee turns back to her brother. "There is more, isn't there?"

"Maybe we should go inside, Charliee." Derrick makes a move toward the house, but no one follows.

"Where was it, guys?" Charliee asks, not moving from the side of the jeep. "What are you guys not telling me?"

"The explosion was at an abandoned building this time," Bryce answers, finally speaking up.

Well that is good news I'd think. Why all the seriousness? I am about to ask but Charliee beats me to it.

"Damn it, guys, what are you trying to tell me?"

Derrick walks up to Charliee and I come around to stand next to her. Something is very wrong, I can feel the tension. This isn't going to be good news.

"Charliee, when the firefighters went in, a second bomb went off. Two guys from Travis's department are missing. Travis is one of them."

Charliee looks pale, like she is going to pass out or be sick.

"Take me there." Charliee starts over to the squad car.

Derrick grabs her by the arm to stop her when she starts to walk past him. "You can't go, we don't even know if it's safe or if there's another bomb, Charliee."

"I don't care. You two drive us over there now, or I'll drive myself. Either way, I'm going. Travis needs me."

Charliee turns around and starts back to her jeep, Levi close on her heels.

I put my hands up to stop her after Derrick pleads with me to help.

"Hon, what are you going to be able to do there? Your brothers are right, you are safer here."

Derrick is right, there may be another bomb and she doesn't need to be anywhere near there if another one goes off. There have already been two, why not a third?

"Jayden, you are telling me that if that was Cameron out there, you would stay at home and wait for a call?" Charliee challenges me.

Hell no, I wouldn't sit around and wait for a call and she knew it.

"That's what I thought," she says after I don't answer her, but I don't need to, she reads my answer through my eyes.

Charliee turns back to her brothers. "Now, I'm going to ask one more time. Are you going to take me there, or am I going alone?"

I can see the moment when her brothers give up. Bryce opens the back door of the squad car. Charliee runs over, lets Levi in first and then follows him into the back seat. She looks over at me. I can't stay back and worry, waiting to hear from someone on what is going on.

"All right, I'm coming. Someone has to keep you from doing something stupid and you don't listen to your brothers."

WHEN WE ARRIVE, I can't believe the amount of emergency vehicles and personnel that are there. The front part of the building is all rubble. You can still make out the front wall and what looks to be maybe where the door was, but you can see all the walls down inside.

After convincing Bryce she would stay back and not do anything stupid, we are all let out of the back of the car. Someone is being carried out of the building, they have found one of the firefighters. We quickly learn it isn't Travis. Charliee just stands there watching the building; Levi, however, won't stop pacing.

I grab Charliee's hand. She looks over at me, tears in her eyes. "He's going to be all right," I try to reassure her.

My attention is brought to where they are working on the firefighter they just brought out. They are shooting off questions to him and checking for his injuries. The good thing is you can hear the firefighter answer the paramedics.

I feel Charliee's hand being tugged away from mine, but I hear her tell Levi to calm down so I keep my attention on the firefighter, hoping to hear something that I can tell Charliee to give her hope that everything will be all right.

Turning to update Charliee, I panic. She is no longer next to me. Looking around frantically, the only faces I recognize are Derrick and Bryce and they are both deep in conversation with other officers. Where the hell did she go?

Yelling and commotion at the building catches my attention. My heart stops. Charliee and Levi are running in. A thousand images run through my mind. I don't even notice I have started running in after her until someone grabs my arm to stop me right before I get inside.

"What the hell are you doing?" I turn to see Derrick has my arm.

"Charliee ran inside, we need to get her out, Derrick. What if there is another bomb?"

The words that stream out of Derrick's mouth has all ran through my head. Before I know what is going on, Derrick pushes me toward the other way. Another pair of hands are holding me now and I watch as he runs inside after his sister.

"You were supposed to be watching her," Bryce says from behind me. He must be the one that Derrick handed me off to.

I turn around and glare at him. "Do you know your sister at all?" I yell up at him. "I looked away for a minute trying to hear some informa-tion for her and when I turned back around, she was gone."

Bryce starts pulling me back from the building. Emotions are running wild through me. I want to pull out of his grasp, run inside and pull Charliee out before anything else blows up. I want to turn around and smack Bryce for yelling at me for allowing Charliee to get inside. I am mad at myself for allowing her to go inside. I want to sit on the ground and cry!

Neither one of us says another word, we just stand there staring and waiting for Derrick, Charliee and Travis to come back out. I can't stand here and wait much longer, I feel helpless. It feels like I have been standing out here staring at the building for an hour, but I'm sure it is only minutes, waiting to hear the boom. I'm not even sure I am breathing.

A bunch of commotion starts going on, and firefighters start running into the building while police officers start gathering at the entrance. What is going on? I look up at Bryce, he has his radio up to his ear as he listens to the chatter. His eyebrows are drawn together as he concentrates on what he is listening to.

"They found Travis," Bryce yells at me, even though I am standing directly next to him.

"Is he alive? Where is Charliee?" I shoot the questions at him.

Bryce just shakes his head. "That's all I'm hearing right now."

The waiting game again. I am getting antsy. I need to know what is going on. Is everyone all right? Every once in a while Bryce puts the radio back up to his ear, but he won't tell me what is being said.

I can't take it anymore and am about to pull my arm away from Bryce and go in myself when I see Derrick exiting the building carrying Charliee, Levi following close behind. He heads straight over to one of the paramedics. That can only mean one thing, she is hurt. A group of firefighters carrying Travis follows out shortly behind them and rushes him directly over to another waiting ambulance. I can't tell from here if he is alive or not.

Bryce and I run over to where they have taken Charliee. Running up, I notice Darryn, the girl who was with Bryce that night at the fair, working on Charliee's leg. Her knee is cut wide open. I look her over to see if I can see any other injuries.

"What the hell were you thinking?" I yell at her. "If you weren't already hurt, I would beat the shit out of you right now." I lay across her upper body and hug her.

"I'm all right, Jayden," she reassures me.

Standing back up, I wipe the tears away. I hadn't noticed I had started crying. My phone vibrates in my pocket. Pulling it out, I see Charliee's mom's name on the screen. I show it to Charliee and then answer it. I don't get to say a word before she starts shooting off questions and crying.

I step away for a moment while I calm Mom down and explain as quickly as I can what has happened. She just keeps telling me that she can see Charliee being worked on by paramedics on the television. The news crews are everywhere. I explain she is all right and where they will be taking Charliee. She tells me they will meet us there.

I turn back to Charliee and am putting my phone back in my pocket when I hear Charliee yell.

"Bryce, the bastard is here!" We both look in the direction that Charliee is pointing.

"Who's here, Charliee, who are you seeing?" Bryce asks, scanning the area.

I start scanning the area looking for someone who looks out of place. I know Charliee says something else behind me but I don't hear what it is. Bryce, walking toward all of the news personnel quickly and talking into his radio, has caught my attention. Along with the guy in a hoodie who takes off running as soon as he spots Bryce coming at him. There are too many cops here, he isn't getting far this time.

I turn back to Charliee just as another firefighter comes up to her. "Charliee, they are taking Travis to the hospital now. He is breathing on his own, but hasn't woken up. They have no idea the extent of his injuries so they want to get him there quickly as possible."

"I'm going with him." Charliee tries to sit up.

Darryn quickly gets to work on strapping her down to the back board. Smart lady, get her down before she can get up and hurt herself more.

"We need to get you to the hospital yourself and get this leg checked out, Charliee. You need to sit still," Darryn explains to her.

Charliee is about to argue when I cut her short. "Charliee, you need to get your leg checked. I know you want to go, but you need to take care of yourself first. I'll ride with Travis in the ambulance if they will allow it and keep you posted. I have already spoken to your parents, they are on their way. There is nothing you can do until they check him out, so get yourself treated first."

She wants to argue with me and I can't say I blame her. We don't know exactly the extent of Travis's injuries, or if he will make it to the hospital. She, however, isn't going anywhere. Her knee has bone showing out of it and she needs to get herself fixed first. Finally, she lays back down and nods.

"Come on if you are going with him." The firefighter leads me away by the arm.

They have already loaded Travis into the ambulance so I quickly jump in and sit on the bench next to him. Just as we pull away, my phone goes off again. I am expecting it to be Charliee's mom again, but it isn't. It is Cameron. I don't have the time for that conversation right now. I push ignore and slip my phone back into my pocket. I'll call him back later.

I look down at Travis, and my heart hits my feet. He just lays there. I grab his hand. "Come on, Travis, you have to pull through this, you can't leave her now. She is strong, but if she loses you it will destroy her. You are her strength now and she leans on you, please don't let her fall."

My phone goes off once again, but I ignore it. I just sit here listening to the sirens of the ambulance as we are rushed through the streets and pray.

Everything happens pretty quickly once we arrive to the hospital. The staff goes right to work on getting Travis unloaded and quickly taken back to be examined. I am asked to wait in the waiting room while they take him back.

I have just sat down in one of the chairs when the doors open again and in comes Charliee. She isn't saying anything, all I see is her lying there. My heart falls again, what happened on the way over? Jumping up, I run over to them. I look up at Darryn with the question in my eyes.

"Don't worry, she is fine. I gave her something for the pain and to calm her down a little. It knocked her out, which is probably for the better," Darryn explains.

Two nurses and a doctor come over and I listen as Darryn explains to them Charliee's injuries. Like with Travis, I am helpless, all I can do is stand there and watch as they take my best friend back behind the same doors that Travis was taken through. Hospitals are becoming a place I don't ever want to see again.

I wait for Darryn to finish up with the nurse behind the counter and when she turns back around, I ask, "Have you heard if they caught the guy or not?"

She shakes her head. "No, we haven't heard anything. I was about to ask you the same question."

"Jayden!" My name is shouted from behind me.

I turn and see both of Charliee's parents, along with another older couple running into the hospital.

"Have you heard anything yet?" Charliee's father asks.

I give Charliee's mom a quick hug and am slightly taken back when she goes straight over to Darryn and hugs her next. "They just took both of them back, they said they would come out as soon as they have something for us."

"Darryn, what's wrong with Charliee?" her mom asks.

"I'm not sure exactly what is all wrong with her leg, but she will need stitches, that I know for sure, and I'm sure she broke it but we will have to wait until they examine her to let us know if she'll need surgery or not," Darryn explains Charliee's injury.

"You two know each other?" I ask, a little puzzled.

Both Darryn and Charliee's mom look at each other, Charliee's mom answers, "We have been introduced by Bryce. They have been seeing each other," she explains like I should have already known that.

I feel like something isn't being said and I would have asked more questions but the other lady steps forward.

"How is Travis?" I see the tears in the woman's eyes. This must be his mom.

I look between the lady in front of me and Charliee's mom. "Sorry, Jayden, this is Anna and Kevin, they are Travis's parents."

"Oh, sorry. They both just went back right before you guys came in so we haven't heard anything yet. They just told me to wait here and they would come and let us know when they have something to tell us."

"Did you ride over with Charliee?" Steven, Charliee's dad, asks.

"No, I rode in the ambulance with Travis. Charliee was worried about Travis and giving everyone a hard time about not being with him so I rode over with him to calm her down."

"Was he awake?" Anna asks.

I shake my head no. "I'm sorry I can't give you more information. They didn't tell me anything on the way over here."

The sliding doors to the hospital open again and a very pissed off Cameron comes charging in. How did he even know where to find me?

CHAPTER
Twenty-Five

I HAVE JUST WALKED into the front door from driving since Monday night when my phone rings. It is David, Tyler's dad. I know Jacob stayed with them while I was gone so I have to answer it.

"Hello."

"Cameron, are you home yet? Have you heard about what's going on?"

"I literally just walked in the door. Is Jacob all right?" Fear slices through my veins.

"Jacob is fine. Sorry, I didn't think, I should have told you that before worrying you. I do think you need to turn the television on to the news. There has been another bombing."

I grab the remote and turn the television on. "What channel?"

"Pick any one of them, they are all covering it. Two firefighters are buried in the explosion. They haven't mentioned names of them yet, though."

David isn't joking. It is breaking news. "Thanks for calling. I already texted Jacob that I was home."

"All right, I'll have him text you on what they are doing tonight."

"Thanks." I place my phone on the table in front of me. When I look up, I see Jayden standing with a police officer. I think it is one of Charliee's brothers. What is she doing there? I don't see Charliee. David said two firefighters are buried. Is Travis one of them? I turn up the volume to listen.

The reporter announces that the first explosion happened at the empty building around one. Shortly after, firefighters arrived and entered the building before another explosion went off. Two firefighters had been caught inside the building. One has already been rescued, but no word on the second one.

As the reporter finishes with his update, the camera is quickly directed back to the rescue. The reporter starts going on about a commotion and people being brought out again. An officer comes out carrying what I think is a woman, but it is hard to see. I thought they said the building was abandoned. Why the hell would they be carrying out a woman? She wasn't dressed like a firefighter. Shortly after they exit, a whole crew of firefighters come out carrying what looks like another person. This one has gear on, he must be the second firefighter. I pick up my phone and dial Jayden, it goes straight to voicemail.

I sit and watch for another couple minutes, hoping to catch a little more information on the people involved, but nothing. I am about to turn it off, I am tired of listening to the reporter just stand there repeating everything because they have nothing new, when all of a sudden all the cameras and reporters are pushed aside. Cops fill the area, all running toward the crowd of news crews. After a moment, a rattled reporter comes on air reporting that the cops are in pursuit of a man who they believe is in connection with the bombings.

The camera scans back to the area of where the ambulances are and that's when I spot her. Jayden is climbing into the back of one of the ambulances. She doesn't look hurt, which brings me to believe something has happened to Travis and possibly Charliee.

I dial her number again. It rings this time, a couple of times actually before I am sent to voicemail again. I send her a quick text asking her to call me and then run out of the house. My truck is still full so I jump into my dad's, his smell once again smacking me in the face. My body runs cold, the irony of the whole situation not going unnoticed.

At a stop light, I once again dial Jayden's number, only to be sent to voicemail again. Once in the hospital parking lot, I find the quickest spot I can and then run to the entrance. I immediately see Jayden standing there talking to two other couples and a paramedic. I take the first deep breath since I got home, she is all right.

I don't move from the entrance, I just stand there and watch as she excuses herself from the group and walks over to me.

"How did you know I was here?" she asks as she walks up.

No hi, hello, happy to see you? Just how did I know she was here? Anger is now replacing panic.

"It's all over the news. I saw you get into one of the ambulances, it didn't take much to figure out where you were headed."

She just nods. I want to wrap her into my arms and assure myself she is all right, or maybe shake the crap out of her for not answering my calls.

"I tried to call you but you sent me to voicemail."

"I was a little busy, Cameron."

"You couldn't answer long enough to tell me you were all right?" My voice starts to raise and brings the attention of those in the waiting room to us.

Jayden closes the space between us, but instead of stopping, she grabs my arm and drags me outside away from the eyes of those inside.

When she turns back to me, there is fire in her eyes. Good, we need to have this out. I have been driving for days thinking of nothing but her, only to come home and find her life in danger by the crazy man who killed my parents. She wants a war of words, then I am all in for that.

"Cameron, honestly, I had no idea you were calling because you were worried."

"Jayden, I've call you a couple of times and left you a text. It never crossed your mind that maybe you should call me back? Damn, you could have even just answered the phone, said hi and said you had to go. Anything would have been better than nothing and not knowing what the hell was going on."

"Cameron, right now all of this isn't about you and me! Charliee is injured and Travis, we have no answers on how he is right now. I didn't think a conversation about our relationship was good timing at the time."

Is she being serious right now? She really thinks the only reason I was calling was to talk about what happened in Texas? Unbelievable!

"They are my friends as well, Jayden, and you didn't think I needed or would want to be here for them? Even if I didn't know Charliee and Travis, I would have wanted to here for you."

She just stands across from me, rolling her eyes, arms crossed at her chest. I am trying pretty hard to remember she is stressed right now, but the attitude I am getting is pretty hard to ignore. I have to keep reminding myself that I am lacking in the sleep department and I have been through the emotions of worry, anger and relief. Neither one of us are in a great spot for this conversation. It is probably pretty safe to say if we keep any kind of conversations going, it won't end pretty.

"Look, I didn't come here to fight or piss you off or anything else. I was worried about you and Travis and Charliee. I'm sorry you thought I would think anything would be more important right now than how those two are doing. Go back inside, I'll wait out here to hear anything and then take off to go home."

I don't wait for her to say anything back. I turn and head back to the truck. I'll admit, I am disappointed when I reach the truck and look back to see she has already gone back inside. Damn, I have never had a woman make me want to shake them as much as Jayden does.

I'VE BEEN SITTING HERE in the parking lot for almost two hours now when the text from Jayden comes through.

**Travis still hasn't woken up, but is in a room now. They are done running tests on him for tonight. Charliee had to have fifteen stitches on her knee and has a fracture. Haven't seen either yet. Charliee was wheeled right into Travis's room and won't leave. We are hoping in an hour or so they will let us in to see him.

It isn't a lot to go on about Travis but a least he is in a room now. I'm still a little confused on how Charliee got hurt. I have questions but I don't ask any of them. Sitting here for two hours has given me a lot of time to think. It is amazing how fast life can change. I can't believe how fast mine has changed. First losing our parents. Coming back to Washington. Raising a teenager. Meeting Jayden. Bringing Steve on as a partner. My life went from all work and only having myself to take care of to being completely flipped the other way and not having a second of time to myself.

When I first got back to the truck tonight after talking to Jayden, I had convinced myself I was over trying to make this thing between us work. I was pissed. How could Jayden think I would come here at a time like now and be shallow enough to not be worried about our friends and only thinking about our little fight? Sure, we have things to talk about. I would hope she knows me better than to think that is what I thought was more important right now.

Were things between us ever going to be easy? It always feels like we would have things going great, but then there would be that one moment and everything would blow up. We never just argued and talked things out, our fighting world usually has Jayden storming away from me and me chasing her down to apologize. I know relationships have ups and downs but ours is getting a little crazy. I've asked myself many times this week and a few times in the last couple of hours sitting out here if this is all worth it.

Then I think back to this week without her. I hated not having her with me on the drive from Texas. I would drive longer than was probably safe for myself and others around me before I would finally pull over and get a little sleep just because I wanted to get back and clear things up with her.

Today when I saw her on the news, my world stopped. Sure, I saw her jump into the back of that ambulance, but I didn't know if she was hurt or if another bomb would go off while she was there. All I knew was I wasn't there to protect her and that was a feeling I didn't like. There are no words to describe how I felt when I entered that hospital and saw her standing there in the waiting room. She was safe and unharmed. I don't think I took a solid breath until that moment.

Then she attacked. Accusing me of being selfish basically. After the first hour of sitting here had passed, I thought about just going home and waiting there to hear how Travis and Charliee were doing. I figured I could just come back later if I needed to. Then I realized that no matter how mad I was at Jayden for thinking so little of me, if something would happen to either of our friends, I wanted to be here for Jayden. I may not be sitting inside with everyone else, but Jayden knew I was here if she needed me.

My phone goes off once more, notifying me of a text.

**Going in to see Charliee. Do you want to come with me?

I have to read it a couple times to make sure I am reading it right. Jayden is asking me if I want to go with her. One thing it does confirm is she does in fact know I am still here if she needs me.

**Go ahead without me. Tell Charliee I'm here if they need anything. Call if you need or hear anything else about how Travis doing. I'll come and visit them when things calm down. Their family being with them is more important right now.

That was hard! I'm sure me saying no about going in with her has Jayden's mind spinning. She probably thinks I'm still mad at her and sitting here pouting over it. I do want to make sure family can spend all the time they can with the two right now, that's more important than me going in. Before I can change my mind because of worrying what Jayden is thinking, I start up the truck and pull out of the driveway.

CHAPTER
Twenty~Six

JAYDEN

I MUST HAVE READ Cameron's text at least three times. Maybe I thought the words would change if I just kept reading it. He is mad at me. Can I blame him? I basically accused him of being selfish and unfeeling. I'm worried, tired, and if I'm being completely honest right now, very frustrated at Charliee for the stunt she pulled today, and I took it all out on Cameron when he showed up.

When the nurse came in and told us we could go up and see the two of them now, I texted Cameron right away. I knew he was still in the parking lot waiting to hear any news. Travis's and Charliee's parents had all gone up right away. Charliee wasn't leaving Travis's side so they told both parents they could go up together. I told them I would go up after they were done.

We are still waiting to hear more from Bryce and Derrick about the guy who is responsible. Bryce had been able to send a quick text out, but all it said was everything was under control. Hopefully that means they caught the guy. I'm sure it is still going to be a while before either one of them are going to make it here to the hospital. I did send them a text whenever we got any news from the doctors just so they didn't worry.

I am alone in the waiting area now. I'm sure the parents will all be up there for some time. Cameron is out in the parking lot. Maybe I should go out and talk to him, clear things up. Apologize for how I treated him earlier.

Walking outside, I scan the parking lot for his truck. I even walk around a little, but I don't see Cameron's truck or his father's company truck. He left! My heart drops. I think I may have screwed things up pretty good between us this time. I fight back the tears, maybe I should try and call him.

Pulling out my phone, I am searching for his number when someone touches my shoulder from behind. Jumping and almost throwing my phone across the parking lot, I turn to find Karen and Steven, Charliee's parents.

"Jayden, I'm so sorry. I didn't mean to scare you. I called your name a couple of times but you didn't answer." Karen looks at me concerned.

"Sorry, I was in my own head. How is Charliee doing? Is Travis awake?"

Karen shakes her head. "No, Travis isn't awake. Charliee looks exhausted. I'm sure she is in pain, but you know how she is, she won't say that she is. Are you all right?"

Nodding is all I can do to answer her. I am pretty sure she isn't buying it though. Karen knows me probably just as well as my own mom knows me.

Karen searches my face for a moment, but I am relieved when she doesn't ask anything else about it. "Go up and see Charliee. We are going to her house and grab some stuff since she isn't leaving."

"Do you want me to go instead? That way you guys can be here with her just in case anything changes," I ask.

"No, we will go, you go and see her. Travis's parents are back in the waiting room making phone calls to the family with updates. Charliee needs to see you and I'm thinking you need to see her."

I need to choke her is what I need to do, I think to myself. "All right, I'll head up. If you need anything, call me. If anything changes while you are gone, I'll let you know."

Karen gives me a hug, Steven waves as they walk away hand in hand.

CHARLIEE HAS her eyes closed when I walk in to the room. The wheelchair she is sitting in is pushed as close as it can get next to the bed Travis is laying in, her hand holding his. I stand just inside the doorway watching them for a moment. You couldn't have put a more perfect couple than these two together. Both of them are very caring of others and giving. I'd put money on the fact that they have never had a fight. They are a complete opposite couple than Cameron and me.

Charliee looks exhausted. I am about to leave and let her rest when Levi sits up. His movements cause his leash that Charliee is holding to move, which in turn wakes her up. Her eyes instantly go to Travis. She takes a deep breath and sits back in her chair when she realizes he is still asleep. It breaks my heart to see the pain in her eyes. It makes all the frustrations I have been feeling over her risking her own life today just disappear.

She looks over at me, giving me her best effort of a smile. "Hey, how long have you been standing there? Why didn't you wake me?" she signs.

She must be tired if she is only signing. It seems easier for her than talking sometimes. No thinking required, I guess you can say.

"You are tired, you need your rest. Go back to sleep, I'll come back later. I just wanted to check on you myself," I sign back.

She sits there for a moment just staring at me. "What's wrong?"

She doesn't need to hear about my petty problems with my boyfriend when her boyfriend is lying in a hospital bed.

"I'm good. Just been a long day," I sign.

She gives me that look. The one that says, "You're lying through your teeth."

"Don't worry about it. I'll figure it out later. How are you doing?" I try to steer the conversation away from me.

"I'm on some strong pain medications, so the pain isn't that bad right now. I keep falling asleep though."

"You probably need sleep, Charliee. How about I take Levi outside for a small walk, and you get some rest?" I walk over and hold my hand out for Levi's leash.

Charliee just shakes her head no and eyes the chair next to her. "Have a seat."

I'm not getting away from her, so I plop down in the chair. "Really, it's not important right now."

"Jayden, you look defeated. I'm not doing much right now and I need my mind distracted from all of this." She waves her hand between her leg and Travis laying in the bed.

She is talking more now, but still signing, which means she is waking up a little more.

"I think I screwed things up with Cameron pretty good today."

"What happened?"

"I should probably tell you the whole story." I start back at the beginning with what happened in Texas and me coming home early, and then finish it with our fight downstairs today.

"Before I came up here, I asked if he wanted to come up with me to see you guys. He said he would come by later when everything with the parents settled down," I sign as I speak. Charliee looks ready to fall back to sleep, I'm not even sure if she caught much of what I was telling her.

"So you have been home since Sunday and didn't call me with all of this?"

Well, so much for thinking she wasn't catching the story. She is awake enough.

"I didn't want to complain about Cameron and get you all pissed at him because let's face it, you would have taken my side, then clear everything up with him and you be mad at him."

"What else has happened that you haven't told me about?" Charliee asks, looking a little disappointed.

I can't take anymore disappointment from people today. First Cameron and now Charliee.

"Come on, Charliee, you have been crazy busy with your perfect relationship. You don't need to hear about my crazy confusing one."

The confusion and hurt that shoots across Charliee's face makes me want to slap myself. I am lashing out again, like I did at Cameron earlier today. What the hell is my problem?

"Charliee, I'm sorry. That came out wrong."

She doesn't say anything. She just looks at Travis, then back at me. She looks around the room. She is fighting the tears.

"Don't cry, I'm sorry…"

She cuts me off. "No, I'm the one who's sorry, Jayden. You're right. I have been very wrapped up in Travis and our relationship. I haven't paid enough attention to what's going on around me with everyone else. You're my best friend, actually more like a sister. I should have been paying more attention. No, actually I should have made you talk to me more. I noticed you've been distracted, not fully yourself. I knew something was going on. I just didn't want to push you. I figured you would tell me when you needed me. I should have known better with the way you are and for that, I'm sorry."

"Charliee, I haven't exactly been calling you with all of the stuff going on either. We have both been distracted lately."

Leaning over, I give her a hug. My heart breaks when I notice she is hugging me with one arm, the other hand still tightly in Travis's. How selfish can I be? Here she is sitting next to her boyfriend, who is unconscious and we have no idea if and when he will be waking up, and here I am complaining about my relationship. What kind of friend am I?

"For right now why don't we concentrate on Travis and you getting better and not my crazy love life?"

She is shaking her head no as I speak. "We aren't going anywhere." She points between herself and Travis. "And you aren't leaving until we have everything figured out, so start talking, my friend, and I mean start from the beginning. If I start to fall asleep, don't take it personally and just nudge me."

CHAPTER
Twenty-Seven

I HAVE BEEN DRIVING for at least an hour before I pull into the cemetery. Pulling up alongside the curb, I take a couple deep breaths. I haven't been here since the day I drove here and just sat in my truck. I haven't been up to the area where they are buried since the day we laid them to rest. Walking up to their area, I bend down and wipe off their headstone. Only one, with a picture of the two of them on it. There was never any other thought of two different headstones. My parents meant the world to each other. I remember catching my dad staring at my mom like she was the most beautiful woman in the world when she would be cooking in the kitchen or talking to someone else. Every time my mom would look at my dad, she had a spark in her eye. Their kind of love not everyone finds. They weren't perfect, I'm sure they had bumps in their marriage, they just never showed it to us boys. Sure, they had their little arguments, but I can honestly say I never saw my parents fight.

I remember back when I was probably sixteen or seventeen. We were getting ready to eat dinner. Jacob and I were already sitting at the table,

Mom had just brought a plate over of some kind of dish, and Dad had just come in to join us. Before he sat down, he came up behind Mom, wrapping his arms around her and kissing her. Not a peck, nothing deep, just an "I love you for everything you do to take care of us" kind of kiss.

Jacob had signed to me, "Gross." I just laughed, but I remember asking them that night if they ever fought. My dad smiled, gave my mom one more quick kiss on the cheek and sat down. My mom said, "Nothing is ever perfect, hon, but we keep it between us. We never go to bed mad at each other and we always tell the other, or show," she laughed and pointed at my father, "each other how much we love the other as often as we can. You never know what life will bring, you don't want to regret or wonder if that person you love questions your feelings."

I stare down at the picture of the two of them. I find it funny how that is the memory I am having at this moment. I know I've changed in the last few months. Who wouldn't have with all of this? I've never been the emotional kind of guy. Mom use to tell me it was all right to not always be the strong one. Women like to see a softer side of guys some-times. Lately I feel like a damn time bomb. I feel like everything is being thrown at me and every one of them I'm throwing back messed up or I missed catching altogether.

"I'm a twenty-eight-year-old man who needs his parents right now."

"We always need our parents, there isn't an age limit to that need." The soft voice comes from behind me.

I feel myself jump a little. I had no idea anyone was around. No one was here when I got here. I turn around to find a lady who looks to be about my mother's age.

"I'm sorry, I didn't mean to eavesdrop on your conversation."

I hadn't even realized I had spoken out loud. She is standing in front of two headstones. One looks to have been there for a while. The other, however, is new, along with the plot in front of it. You can still see where the grass was pulled up and set back in place.

She points over at my parents' headstone. "I'm sorry for your loss. The other day when we buried my father, I must have stayed here for three or four hours after everyone left. I couldn't leave, I felt like if I did he would be gone to me forever. I walked around a little and your parents caught my attention. They were young and just from that picture you could tell very much in love."

I am at loss for words. I just stand there staring at the woman.

"I'm sorry, I shouldn't have interrupted or butted in." She starts to turn and walk away.

"Don't apologize." I finally am able to speak.

She turns back to me. "I'm sorry for being rude, you kind of caught me off guard. I didn't know you were there. I'm sorry for your loss." I point down at her father's headstone.

"Thank you. Dad and I lost my mom when I was very young, car accident. My dad was my everything." She points at the newer looking headstone. "I couldn't have imagined losing both of them at the same time." She points over at my parents' stone.

"Yeah, it's definitely a life changer." I turn to look at their picture again.

"My dad used to tell me when I was having a rough day over my mom, to always remember she is never gone. She is with me every day because of the things she taught me and the love she had for me. I may not see her but she will be walking next to me guiding me for the rest of my life. Our parents may allow us to stumble. They have to so that way we learn to stand on our own two feet, but never fall. That goes for them being here physically or in our hearts." She smiles sadly.

I watch as she blows a kiss to each of her parents' stones and then just turns and walks away without saying another word. Turning back to my parents, that's when something my father once told me comes to me.

"Nothing is meant to be easy, son, in life, love or work. You need to work hard to get it and you need to continue working hard to keep it."

The woman's words hit me. "The lessons they taught me and the love they showed."

"I love you guys." I turn and head back to my truck. I know where I am going this time and what I want to say.

This is the first time in a while my chest feels lighter. Funny how people can come into our life, be it for five minutes, a few months or a lifetime, and change everything you are looking at to be more clear. Fighting and loss is never going to be easy, but neither is loving and gain. Learning something from all of it is what it is all about.

CHAPTER
Twenty-Eight

JAYDEN

I HAVE TO ADMIT, talking to Charliee and getting everything out helps a lot. I need my best friend. Why I thought to keep her in the dark about all of this was beyond me. Plus, she always knows how to tell me when I'm wrong. When I tell her I am going home to change and grab something to eat, she tells me not to come back without Cameron. That is her way of telling me to go and apologize, and to not come back until I do.

Reaching the front entrance is when I realize I don't have a car. It is still at Charliee's house. I guess I'm not going anywhere. My phone goes off in my pocket. I am hoping it is one of the boys with some news. Nope, it is my mom.

"Hi, Mom."

"How is Charliee and Travis doing? Would this be a good time to come by? I wanted to give their families room."

"Mom, you are Charliee's family, too, you don't have to wait to come down. Charliee is doing all right. Broken leg, stitches, but not admitted which is good. Travis is in a room but hasn't regained consciousness yet. They are still waiting on some test results. Charliee won't leave his side. She was falling back to sleep when I was leaving."

"I'll wait a little longer then to come down and visit. I'm sure she is exhausted."

I walk outside, the air feels really nice. It has cooled down for the evening. "Actually, Mom, I need a favor."

"Sure, honey."

Looking around, that's when I notice the truck. It looks just like Cameron's. Is he still here? It is pretty dark in the parking lot.

"Honey, are you still there?" My mom's voice reminds me she is still on the phone with me.

"Sorry, Mom. Yeah, I'm here. Can I call you back in a minute?"

"Is everything all right?"

I notice the writing on the side of his father's work truck. The driver side door opens and Cameron steps out.

"Everything is fine, Mom. I just need to talk to someone real quick. I'll call you back in a few minutes."

"Okay, if you are sure everything is all right."

"Yep, everything is fine. I'll talk to you soon. Love you. Bye." I hang up my phone before my mom can say anything else.

Walking over to the truck, I stop a couple feet away. "You are still here!" It isn't a question, more of a surprised fact.

"Actually, I just pulled back in."

He doesn't move toward me and he isn't saying much. I can't read his expression. My heart falls a little. This isn't going to be an easy conversation, I have a feeling.

"Charliee may be asleep right now, but I'm sure she would be happy to see you."

Nothing, he isn't moving or saying anything. I am going to say what I need to say and then call my mom back to come and pick me up.

"Cameron, I…" Before another word can come out of my mouth, he is right on me, his lips devouring mine. What the heck just happened?

His lips are soft on mine. Nothing demanding about this kiss. It isn't the kind of kiss that makes me want to climb up his body, but the kind that makes me want to melt at his feet.

He pulls away just enough to look into my eyes. "Jayden, I love you."

What?! Did I hear him right? I pull back a little more so that I can see his whole face, but he isn't allowing me to go too far.

"What did you just say?" I can't have heard what I think he just said.

He smiles one of the sexiest smiles I have ever seen down at me. "I said I love you."

Something is different about him. He looks relaxed, calm. Two things that I just realized I have never seen with him before.

"Where were you?"

Cameron laughs. I'm not sure if I've ever heard him really laugh like this before. What is going on? He hasn't been drinking, I think I would have tasted that when we kissed.

"Let's just say I had an eye opening conversation. I met someone I needed to meet," he kind of explains, I guess.

Something inside of me tells me to just go with it. I don't need to ask questions. Well, maybe just one question.

"Does this mean you forgive me?"

"Jay, we have both said things and reacted to things we wish we hadn't. I know the last few months I haven't been the easiest guy to be around and get to know. We have both had a trying few months. I'm not saying I'm going to change overnight. I'm sure I'll still open my mouth and say things I shouldn't, and overreact to situations without thinking first. I will be fully expecting you to tell me where to go when I do and put me back in my place. But, I'll love you deeply through all of it. You are like no one I've ever had in my life and I want to keep you in my life and just to warn you, I'm not letting you decide any other way."

Tears, damn it! I am crying. Cameron runs his thumbs over my cheeks to catch them as they roll down.

"Are these happy tears?" he asks.

I nod yes. *They are very happy tears,* I think to myself. For the first time in my life, I find myself speechless.

My phone vibrates in my pocket. My mom and her timing. "I have to answer this, sorry."

I pull it out of my pocket, but make sure I don't pull out of Cameron's arms. "Sorry, Mom."

"Are you all right, honey?"

"I'm fine," is all I say as I stare up at the man I love in front of me. I am much better than fine, but don't want to get into that with my mom at the moment.

"Are you sure? I'm not very convinced."

I laugh. "Mom, can I call you back later? I'm kind of in the middle of something."

"All right, if you are sure you are all right. I'll talk to you later."

I shove my phone back in my pocket. Looking up at Cameron, I say, "You should have let me talk first. I had a great apology all figured out. I may have even groveled a little."

He kisses me again. "We both have things to apologize for, but I think we need to move past all of it and move forward."

"You know when I was up there talking to Charliee, she told me I had to find you, apologize and tell you how I feel about you before I was allowed to come back. Then she informed me I wasn't allowed to come back without you."

One eyebrow shoots up. "So how do you feel about me?"

"Somehow between the arguments and sarcasm, I fell very much in love with you."

"Really, only the arguments and the sarcasm?"

I shrug my shoulders. "Well, I guess we had a couple of fun times in between there, too."

"Sarcasm, you're one to talk." He pulls me in close.

"I love you, Cameron."

"I love you, Jay."

Silent Protection

BOOK 3

CHAPTER

One

DARRYN

"SO, are you ever going to say yes when I ask you out?"

The voice comes from behind me. It flows over me like hot liquid, warming my entire body. My knees almost buckle. Bryce Brooksman has been asking me out for the past month.

We met the night of the bombing. His sister, Charliee, was a victim that night, when a popular Italian restaurant was blown up. My partner, Tom, and I were the paramedics that took care of Charliee when they uncovered her. Bryce pissed me off when he basically pushed me away trying to get to Charliee, but my anger had quickly vanished when I witnessed the tenderness he used toward his sister. Charliee is deaf and she has a hearing dog that was also involved in the explosion. She was going crazy wondering about where he was and watching Bryce calm her down was amazing. He was so gentle and caring. On the ride to the hospital, he kept her calm, signing to her the whole time. No words were spoken between them, it was beautiful to watch. As we approached the hospital, Charliee had gone unconscious again. I will never forget the look in Bryce's eyes when he looked back at me, the fear that was behind those deep green eyes.

Before that night, I don't remember ever seeing Bryce on a call or at the hospital, but since then I swear we run into each other at least twice a week. Tonight, again, here I am finishing up from dropping off a patient and there he is.

"You haven't asked me out this time." I smile to myself, keeping my attention on the paper I'm filling out. I know if I turn around, I'm going to get lost in those eyes. It's been extremely hard saying no to this man because of those eyes.

My body goes from warm to hot when he takes a step closer to me and I can now feel him against my back. He is working today, I can feel his bulletproof vest against my back. My heart skips knowing why they wear those vests. The meaning behind them, the danger they imply that this man puts himself into every time he goes to work.

"If I ask, will you say yes?" He speaks into my ear, causing my body to shiver.

How can I feel this hot and shiver at the same time? The way my body reacts to this man scares the hell out of me. No man has ever had this kind of effect on me.

Reaching around me, Bryce takes the pen out of my hand and turns me around to face him. "Darryn, would you like to grab a drink with me one evening?"

Damn it, there are those eyes. Maybe I should just tell him the truth and then he will finally stop asking me out every time we run into each other. It's a sure method, works every time. Placing my hand onto his chest, I push him back a couple steps. We are both in uniform and we don't need to be that close, plus I can't think straight with him standing that close to me.

"Bryce, here is the problem. I know I'm always saying no, but it's not because I'm not interested." I watch as the corner of his mouth slants up in a smile. "Hold on, this isn't me saying yes, I'm sorry. I'm just going to tell you the reason I keep saying no, that way you don't keep wasting your time asking and I don't have to keep telling you no. I'm not unattached."

I watch his eyebrows shoot up. "Darryn, all you had to do was tell me you had a boyfriend and I wouldn't have kept asking. I'm not like that."

He starts to walk away from me. I should just let him go, let him think whatever he wants to think. What do I care if he thinks I already have a boyfriend? But, I can't. I don't want him thinking I've led him on or something.

"Bryce, wait, you don't understand."

He just keeps walking in the other direction. "I don't have a boyfriend, Bryce, I have a daughter!" I yell after him, drawing attention from everyone in hearing distance.

It does stop him, though. Turning around, he stares me down for a moment. Why does he look mad? "You have a daughter?"

Nodding, I want to crawl behind the counter and hide from all the attention we have now. "Look, I should have said something earlier."

I watch as he walks back toward me. "I have said no because I can't just go out for a night 'out on the town.' I have no one to watch her."

"Is that the only reason you have said no when I've asked you all of those times?"

"Yes!"

"Bryce, we have to go," Bryce's identical look-alike says as he comes through the emergency room doors in a hurry.

Bryce has a twin brother, Derrick. The two look exactly like each other. The first time I thought I saw Bryce here at the hospital, I made a little bit of a fool out of myself when I accused him of ignoring me. Saying he was still mad at me for the night we met and I yelled at him when we were working on his sister. I basically told him to get over himself.

Lucky for me, Derrick has a sense of humor. He figured it out pretty fast that I was thinking he was his brother. I think he liked it even more that he got to tell me I had the wrong brother. I wanted to slap them both when Bryce walked up a short time later and Derrick had to clue him in to what was going on, and they both just stood there laughing at me. Bryce asked me out the first time that night. I had no trouble then telling him no, I just wanted to slap the smiles off both their faces. From that night forward, I didn't make the mistake again. I can tell the two of them apart no matter if they are together or not. It's all in their eyes. Bryce has kind eyes, they are soft. Derrick has mischief in his eyes, they are more playful or flirty. They may be identical in looks, but their personalities are complete opposites.

"Can I have your phone, please?" Bryce holds out his hand to me.

I don't even ask why, I pull it out of my pocket and hand it to him.

I watch as he types on it and then hands it back to me. "You now have my number. Call me when you have a day off." He turns and walks away, following his brother outside.

"What was that all about?" Tom, my partner, asks, now standing next to me.

"Nothing." I quickly shove my phone back in my pocket.

"Well, if you are done flirting with the police officer, I have everything restocked and we are ready to roll."

"I wasn't flirting with him." I keep my eyes down, hoping he doesn't see the redness in my cheeks.

Tom is a great partner. He and his wife are the only people I can call friends since I moved here to Washington a year ago. They are both always trying to set me up on dates though. His wife has even offered to watch Kendall for me so that I could go out. If only it was all that simple. So many times I have almost opened up to them and told them everything, but the fear is still there. I have to keep my daughter safe!

CHAPTER
Two

"SO, did you ask her out again only to have her turn you down?" Derrick smiles over the hood of the car and then disappears as he takes the driver's seat.

"This time she didn't really turn me down," I inform him as I slide into the passenger seat.

"So she said yes?" He quickly starts the engine and pulls out of the parking lot, sirens now blaring.

"Where are we off to?"

"Car accident, don't change the subject." Derrick gives me that knowing look he has, the one that tells me he thinks I'm dealing him a bunch of crap.

"This is the third one this morning." I have no hope of seeing Darryn on this call, or they would have been called out the same time as us.

"Focus, brother. Did the paramedic finally put you out of your misery and say yes to going out with you?" Derrick keeps probing.

He isn't going to shut up until I tell him. I just know what he is going to say when I tell him she has a kid. "She told me she has a daughter. That's why she keeps telling me no, not because she isn't interested."

"A daughter?" Derrick gives me that look. The one that tells me he thinks I'm crazy.

"Yep!" I confirm, nodding my head.

We may be identical in looks, but we are nothing alike when it comes to women or relationships. Derrick is still good with playing the field. Nothing serious, in no way ready to be "tied down" as he would say. Where I'm the one who wants the relationship. One person to get to know, and maybe have a future with. Commitment doesn't scare me in the least. I've never dated anyone before with kids, but it doesn't scare me away.

There is something about Darryn that pulls at me. I've watched her as she works a scene, helping the injured. She is strong, in control. Even her partner kind of backs up and lets her run the show I've noticed. But when you are talking to her, there is something there behind her eyes. She's not as tough as she seems on the outside. Like she is carrying the world on her shoulders and she is ready to fall.

"So did she say no again?" Derrick breaks through my thoughts.

"I gave her my number and told her to call me when she has a day off."

"Are you sure you want to get involved with someone with a kid? That takes relationships to a whole new level, man."

"It's a date, Derrick, let's just start there first."

Pulling up to the accident, I'm saved from any further questions about Darryn. This one is bad. Multiple cars, firefighters are already on scene. Derrick and I instantly go to work, controlling traffic around the scene.

. . .

"**CHECK** out this text that I just got from Charliee." Derrick throws me his phone.

"Is she all right?" I ask before looking down. Panic shoots through my chest for a moment. Since that night of the restaurant bombing and almost losing her, I will admit we have all been a little more protective over Charliee. Seeing her laying on the ground, blood everywhere, clothes burnt, it's an image I don't think I will ever get out of my head.

I know since then we have all smothered her a little. She has been out of the hospital for a couple weeks now, but she is home alone. We tried to get her to go to Mom and Dad's for a while but no, our stubborn, very independent sister wants to be home. Between Derrick and myself, our parents and her best friend, Jayden, she isn't alone for long. Charliee is trying to be a good sport about it, but I can tell she is over us all hovering around her all the time.

I read the text and then glare over at my brother. "I'm sure this has nothing to do with thanking the guys from that night and a lot to do with that firefighter, Travis. He went a couple times to visit her at the hospital."

"Look who is on call with us." Derrick points over to one of the fire engines that is on the scene. Everyone is mopping up right now.

Looking over, I spot Travis. He and one of the other firefighters were the ones who found Charliee that night, buried under some of the fallen building.

I throw Derrick back his phone. "She asked you."

"Thanks, man. That way I look like the bad guy for not helping her out."

I smile. "He isn't a bad guy," I defend Travis. If Charliee is going to be interested in someone, he seemed like a decent guy. I wouldn't tell her that, of course. No one is going to be good enough for our sister.

"So you're saying give her the information?"

"Give her a little bit of a hard time first. Then a warning and then give her the information. Don't just hand it over. Definitely don't make it easy on her." Charliee thinks she has us wrapped around her little finger. Maybe she does.

Charliee was born deaf. Derrick and I were only three when she was born. Learning sign language was part of learning how to talk for us. She learned how to talk just as fast as she learned to sign as well. Mom and Dad wanted to make sure nothing held her back and put her in speech therapy at the age of two. Whatever you do, don't talk around her and think just because she can't hear, she doesn't know what you are saying. As long as she can see your lips, she can read them. She has never wanted people treating her differently just because she can't hear. Half of the people who meet her have no idea she is deaf. Levi, her hearing dog, came into the family when she was a senior in high school. They haven't been apart since.

"Hey, you ready to head out of here? I'm starving." Derrick slaps me on the back, heading toward the car.

It's been nonstop all morning. Looking at my watch, it's hard to believe it's already after 2:00 in the afternoon. Pulling my phone out, I check to see if I have any missed calls or texts. Nothing, did I really think she was going to try and get ahold of me? Maybe I should have gotten her number. I saw the look in Darryn's eyes when she told me about having a kid. She figured that was a sure way to scare me away from asking her out any more. The reason I put my number in her phone instead of hers in mine was to show her it didn't make me change my mind about wanting to go out with her.

"Are you coming?" Derrick yelled at me from the car.

Shoving my phone back into my pocket, I walk over and get into the passenger side of the car. "Where do you want to eat?"

CHAPTER
Three

DARRYN

"SO DID Bryce asked you out again?" Tom asks as we sit and eat lunch.

I shrug my shoulders.

"Come on, Darryn, how many times are you going to turn that man down? Do you want me to talk to him? Tell him to back off?" Tom offered.

This is one of the reasons why I love Tom, he is like a big brother. "No, I don't need you talking to him. Today I told him I have a kid, thinking that might scare him away. It usually works."

"Usually? I'm guessing not this time," Tom said, laughing.

I shake my head. "No, instead he put his number into my phone and told me to call him on my next day off."

"Well, I have to give it to the man, he is persistent. So, are you going to call him?"

I shrug my shoulders and stare down at my half-eaten sandwich.

"Look, Darryn, I've known Bryce and Derrick for a few years now. They are good guys. You have been here about a year now and not gone out once. Why don't you give him a chance?"

Well, so much for being the big brother. *Most brothers wouldn't be pushing you to go out with someone, they would be threatening to do bodily harm if they touched you,* I think to myself.

"Why do you keep on me about going out?"

"Because you are a young lady who needs to meet someone nice. You act like just because you have a daughter, your life is only about her. I believe your kid should be first, but you need a life, too, Darryn. You deserve to find someone to go out and have fun with," Tom explained.

Again, I find myself debating on telling Tom what has happened. Maybe then he would understand more of why I'm so hesitant. There is still a part of me scared that somehow my secret will get out. I can't afford that. It's more about Kendall than myself. I have to keep her safe.

"I'm just not sure if I'm ready to trust anyone yet," I explain, without giving the whole story. Maybe it will be enough to get Tom to stop pushing.

"Whatever that little girl's dad did to you, you can't use that to push away all men altogether. Not all men are jackasses, Darryn. Plus, you need to look at it as his loss. That little girl is adorable. Now you can find her someone who would love to be her dad, and I promise you there is someone out there, be it Bryce or someone else, who will love the both of you. You just have to put yourself out there to find them." Tom crunches up his sandwich wrapper and shoves it into the bag.

Not all men are bad! I know this. I just haven't had many in my life that haven't been, as Tom calls them, "jackasses." My parents died in a car accident when I was two. My mom had no family and my dad's parents' health wasn't good enough to take care of me. I was pushed around from foster home to foster home most of my life. Most of the homes I was put into, the men either didn't have anything to do with the kids placed in the home, or they were abusive, mostly verbally. I couldn't wait until I was eighteen. I got a job and shared an apartment with a friend from high school and put myself through college to become a paramedic, with the help of student loans. I have been taking care of myself most of my life.

"Hey, come back to me." Tom's voice breaks through my thoughts.

"Sorry." I wrap the rest of my sandwich up and shove it in the bag, I'm no longer hungry.

"What's going on, Darryn? Why do I get the feeling there is more than you are telling me?" Tom asks, concern written all over his face.

"Like you said, bad relationships from the past. Let me tell you, those can really screw with you in the future. Let's just say my last relationship was not a good one." I know this may be opening a door for a lot of questions.

Nothing but silence. I look over at Tom and he is just sitting there staring at me, waiting for me to continue. No questions, just the chance if I want to open up and tell him more. I need to have someone to talk to, it's eating me up inside to have no one, but at the same time I'm just not ready. It's more like a fear. Not that I can't trust Tom, I know if I told him anything it would stay between him and me, but I think I'm more afraid that if I start talking about him then somehow, someway, he will find me.

"I'm not going to push the issue with you on this, Darryn. Just know that if you need anyone to talk to, Heather and I are here for you," Tom offers.

"I know and you have no idea how much I appreciate your friendship, both of you. I'm glad I can call you both friends. I don't have any other friends here. One of these days I will probably take you up on that offer, but right now I'm just not ready," I explain, hoping he understands it's not because I don't trust him, just that I'm not ready.

A call comes over the radio, saved by the emergency. Sounds kind of warped I know, but it cuts this conversation off and I'm good with that.

IT'S BEEN A VERY long day. I have the next two days off and I am ready for them. I've been on a four-day stretch, taking a day of over-time yesterday. All I want to do now is go pick up Kendall from daycare and go home and relax a little.

Walking into the building, Kendall spots me and runs. I kneel down and catch my little girl in my arms. "Mommy."

The guy and the relationship might have been disastrous, but this little girl is the angel that came out of it. I never thought someone could love another human this much. Kendall is my world and my saving grace. The only reason I think I'm here today is because of this little girl. The moment I found out I was pregnant I realized I had to think of someone else, that was what gave me the courage to leave and change my life completely.

"I'm so sorry, Carrie, I didn't mean to have to do this again." The last call we were called out to caused me to run an hour late picking up Kendall from daycare.

"Darryn, don't worry about it, I don't mind really." Carrie handed me Kendall's bag with an understanding smile.

I couldn't have found a better daycare than this one. It's small, Carrie and one other run the program here. It was what I could afford. When I first walked in I was a little worried, the building is a little run down, not a lot outside, but it's clean and Carrie is amazing with the kids, and my crazy schedule.

"I have no idea how I got so lucky to find you. I'm sorry I didn't call." By the time we cleaned up from the last call, I was already twenty minutes late on picking up Kendall. We pulled back into the office, I ran straight to my car and flew over here.

"Darryn, please stop worrying. You told us what you did for a living at the beginning. Trust me, I understand emergencies don't run on a schedule." Carrie spoke softly, then bent down to Kendall, "We will see you in a couple days, little one."

Kendall pulled away from me and gave Carrie a hug, then turned and raised her arms for me to pick her up.

"Thank you again, Carrie." Turning, I quickly walk out, not wanting to take up any more of her time with apologies. I'm sure she is just as ready to head home as I am.

I decided grabbing a small pizza on the way home for dinner would be better and quicker than trying to figure out what to cook, plus it's one of Kendall's favorites. Dinner, quick bath, a story and Kendall is asleep by 8:30 tonight.

I jump into a quick shower and with sweatpants and my favorite comfy t-shirt on, finally plop down on the couch and click on the television. The news is on, covering an accident on the freeway from earlier today. I am getting ready to change the channel when one of the police officers on the accident catches my attention in the background behind the reporter. It's Bryce! Actually, it could be either one of them. I can't really tell. Picking up my phone, I hit the button and the screen lights up. I open up the contacts and right on top under new contacts is Bryce's name and number staring back at me. He left it completely in my ball park to contact him. My thumb hovers over the call button. What would I say? Instead of pushing call, I turn the screen off, throwing the phone on the couch next to me. Now I'm just pissed at myself. I'm still letting him run my life.

"DARRYN, we are good to go here. That guy we were just with signed the waiver to not accept transportation to the hospital." Tom comes up behind me with the gurney.

Quickly we clean up and secure everything back down. I round the rig and just about to jump into the passenger seat. "Darryn." I hear my name from behind me.

Turning around, I see Bryce walking toward me. It's been almost two weeks since I saw him at the hospital and he gave me his number. I turn to look at Tom in the driver's seat. He is sitting there, looking down at some paperwork on his clipboard, with a huge smile on his face. I turn my attention back to Bryce and find him now standing just a couple feet away from me.

"How are you?" Bryce asks. The smile he gives me almost causes my knees to buckle. I lean back against the passenger seat just in case.

"I'm good, how are you?" I ask back, wanting to turn around and yell at Tom to stop smiling like I know he is right now.

"Good, thanks. Hey, Tom, how are things going with you? How's Heather doing?" Bryce surprises me when he asks how Heather is doing. I didn't know they knew each other that well.

"We are good. How is Charliee doing?" Tom asks in return.

"Good. I think we are all driving her crazy. It's hard for any of us to leave her alone since she has been home." Bryce laughs and I about melt to the ground.

"Understandable, happy to hear she is home and doing well."

Bryce looks back at me. "So I have now asked you out I don't remember how many times. I have given you my number, but you haven't called. Most guys would take that hint and leave you alone, I'm sure. I was going to, but I want to give it one more shot. So, Darryn, would you please allow me to take you and your little one out to dinner?"

One more shot! That's what he just said. This is going to be the last time he asks me out. I can tell him no and he won't ask me again. You would think that would make me happy to hear, but surprisingly it doesn't. I have to admit, I have liked all the playful times he has asked me out. What do I expect him to do, though, when I keep telling him no, or not answering at all? He will get tired of the game and just stop talking to me. I don't want that, I realize.

I hold my hand out to him. "Can I have your phone please?"

He doesn't even hesitate. I watch as he reaches into his pocket, pulling out his phone and puts it into my hand. I quickly type my name and number into his contacts and hand it back.

"I'm off tomorrow." Before I can change my mind and grab the phone back out of his hand and erase my number, I jump into the passenger seat and shut the door.

Tom is laughing next to me as he starts up the engine. "Shut up, Tom, or I will find something to throw at you."

"I can't believe you finally told him yes."

That makes two of us right now. I look out the window as we pull away and Bryce is walking back toward his car. Excitement and fear race through me together.

BRYCE

"I'M GUESSING from that smile on your face, she finally said yes." Derrick starts up the car as I shut the passenger door.

"She gave me her number and told me she is off tomorrow, so I'm going to take that as a yes." I want to call the number now and make sure it's hers and not a fake one to make me go away.

"Are you sure you want to get involved with someone who has a kid?" Derrick asks.

"Look, it's one date, I'm not marrying her. Kids don't scare me like they scare you." I'm starting to get a little annoyed with his constant questions about her having a kid.

"Calm down, man. I'm not trying to piss you off, just making sure you know what you could be getting yourself into, that's all," Derrick defends himself. "I don't have a problem with kids. I love kids, just don't think I'm ready for any right now."

"I don't know what it is about Darryn, but I want to get to know her more. Her being a mom doesn't change that at all," I reassure my brother.

"All right, well I will only say this then. I'm happy that she has finally stopped turning you down. It was getting a little embarrassing to keep watching it happen."

"Shut up."

THE DAY FELT like it dragged by. It wasn't real busy, which is a good thing in this profession, I know, but it makes for a long day in a car with my brother. We handed out a couple tickets, one small accident where we spent more time calming down both parties than we did writing the report. There was no visible damage to either car, but of course to both parties their car was totaled and it was the other's fault.

Before leaving, I put in for a day off tomorrow. I told the captain I had a last-minute change of plans and needed it off. He didn't ask any questions, just granted the time off and I left before anything could change.

Running through a drive thru for dinner on the way home and grabbing a quick shower, I finally sit down and realize it's after 9:00. Instead of calling, I decide to send a quick text.

**Is it too late to call you?

I am a little surprised at how fast she responds back.

**No, it's a good time.

I push the call button on the screen and listen as it rings. I'm surprised when the third ring goes off in my ear. Didn't she just tell me it was all right to call now?

"Hello." Her voice comes over the line. She sounds a little out of breath.

"Is this a bad time?" I ask

"No, not at all," she answers, but still sounds busy.

"Darryn, if you are busy you can call me back when you get a chance, it's not a problem."

"Really, it's all right, Bryce. After you text me, I had to run in and give a bedtime bear I forgot to put in bed and was reminded." She laughs, sounding a little nervous. "When I heard my phone ringing, I ran down the hall to answer it, sorry."

"Don't apologize, I just wanted you to know you could call me back if you were busy, I would have waited," I reassure her.

"I should be in the clear to talk right now, but can't make any promises." She is definitely nervous, I can hear it in her voice.

"So is it all right to ask what your daughter's name is, or too soon?" I ask, laughing, trying to put her at ease a little.

"Her name is Kendall. She is two. I'm sorry."

"Darryn, stop apologizing for everything." I'm not sure what she is even apologizing for.

Silence stretches over the phone. When I'm not asking her out, I have no idea what to talk about.

"What would you ladies like to do tomorrow? I have the day off, so we can plan a day out, or if you just have time for dinner, we can plan for that. You just tell me what you two like." I decide to skip the small talk and go straight to date conversation.

"Why don't we start off with either lunch or dinner?" Darryn suggests.

I sit here for a moment silently trying to figure out what we could do since we have a child with us. It's not like I can invite her out for a drink or anything.

"All right, I'm going to be very honest with you, Darryn. My experience with taking out a little one is very limited. What would you two like to do? You name a place and time and I will either pick you up or meet you there. Whichever makes you more comfortable." Why act like I know what I'm doing? Just being open and honest with her I figure is the best idea.

Again, silence. I am about to ask if she is still on the line when she finally speaks up. "How about we meet for pizza around 12:00? It's Kendall's favorite."

"A kid after my own heart. Pizza I'm good with. Would you like me to pick you guys up, or meet you there?"

"I think it's best if we just meet there." Darryn gives me the cross streets of the place, which I know well.

"Sounds like a date. I will see you two tomorrow. Have a good evening."

"See you tomorrow." Darryn quickly hangs up.

I could hear how nervous Darryn was on the phone. I was a little surprised she didn't tell me that she had changed her mind. I think I will be surprised even more if she doesn't call sometime tomorrow and cancel.

WALKING into the pizza place we agreed to meet at, I look around and don't see Darryn. I've been waiting all morning for the call from her saying that she has changed her mind. Now that I'm here and don't see her, I'm wondering if she just brushed me off without a call. Looking down at my watch, I see it's only five past 12:00. Maybe I just need to give her a minute to get here.

"Are you waiting for us?" I hear from behind me.

Turning around, Darryn is standing there holding a little girl with the biggest green eyes, and dark curly hair. She instantly gives me a huge smile, holds her arms out and leans forward for me to take her from Darryn.

I don't want Darryn to feel uncomfortable, so I raise a questioning eye to her. I watch as she looks between her daughter and myself. She looks a little surprised. After a moment, she nods the all right to me and passes her into my arms.

"You must be Kendall," I say to her as she looks me straight in the eyes, the smile still huge on her chubby little cheeks.

"She never does that, she is usually pretty shy around new people, especially men," Darryn informs me.

The last part about, about her not trusting men, doesn't go unnoticed by me. Being in my profession, that statement sends an alert in my head. I know nothing about Darryn's past relationships or the father of this child, but words will tell you a lot.

"They say kids are a great judge of character," I make sure to point out to Darryn. I want her to trust me, give me a chance. I can see the fear and uncertainty in her eyes.

"They do? So you are saying just because my daughter thinks you're cute, I should trust you?" Darryn smiles and I feel my heart jump in my chest.

I look down at Kendall, who is just staring back up at me. "You think I'm cute, little one? I'm thinking that is your mom's thoughts and she is using you so that she doesn't have to admit it."

"You wish." Darryn walks past me and up to the hostess.

"Mommy thinks I'm cute," I whisper to Kendall, but loud enough that I know Mom heard me. Then I turn to follow Darryn and the hostess to our table.

DARRYN WASN'T KIDDING when she said pizza was Kendall's favorite food. I didn't know a two-year-old could put away that amount of food. From the amount on her face, it's safe to say she loved it.

"So how long have you been a paramedic?" I ask.

I haven't asked much through eating. I've let Darryn control the conversation. I'm hoping that now that we have sat here for a while and I have answered every question she has asked, she will be feeling a little more comfortable to open up to me.

"For about four years. I was one of those kids right out of high school that didn't know what I wanted to do, so I went and just took some prerequisites at a local junior college, finally deciding on paramedic," she explains, but she seems to be holding something back.

"So I'm going to guess something happened that led you to choose that line of work," I probe.

She shrugs her shoulders. "I'm not sure if it was any one thing really. I wasn't part of some bad accident and owe my life to a paramedic or anything like that, I just knew I wanted to help people. I've never been good with being inside all day, so I knew I didn't want to work in a hospital. I didn't want to run into a burning building, or go in with guns blazing, so firefighter and police officer was off the table. I pulled over one day for an ambulance to pass and it just hit me, that's what I want to do."

"Go in with guns blazing?" I'm laughing. I can't help it. "You make us sound like a western movie or something."

"Is that where you quit listening? You are such a guy. Hear what interests you only and ignore the rest of the conversation?" Darryn rolls her eyes.

"I heard the rest of what you said. It's just that part was pretty funny. Just for the record, we don't go into every situation with 'guns blazing.' I prefer to keep my gun holstered if I can," I explain.

I watch for a moment as the expression on her face changes. The easy, laid back look in her eyes is gone and I want to slap myself for that. I was only teasing with her. Her eyes move to my chest for a moment and then back to my eyes. What's she thinking?

"Do the vests you guys wear actually stop the bullet?" Darryn asks, her hand going up and waving in front of my chest.

I see the worry in her eyes. Her eyes actually speak more than she does. If you pay attention, they will tell a person a lot. "I'm not going to say it's 100% going to save my life, but it will definitely help, but nothing is guaranteed. Of course nothing is in life, right?"

"That doesn't scare you? You go to work every day not sure if you will come back."

"Darryn, your job can be considered just as dangerous. You put your life at risk every day you go to work as well. Don't get me wrong. Yes, I have a larger possibility with my job, but you can be called out to someone on drugs and he can have a needle you don't know about and stick you with it. You still do your job. It's all about helping someone in trouble. We don't do our jobs because we are worried about our safety, we do it because we live to help those in need." I watch as she looks over at her little girl.

I'm not a parent. Things may change a little when I have children and I have to think about a family when I go to work. Darryn is a single mom. I'm not sure if the father is in the picture, but she has to worry about what will happen to Kendall if something happened to her. I would think that would make her job very difficult.

"You are right. I guess I don't think of it like that."

"Will you now change your profession?" I asked.

Again, she looks over at Kendall, who is watching the kids in the booth next to us. "I know it might sound selfish but no, I can't change my profession."

"It's not selfish at all. If we didn't do what we do for a profession, people would die because they didn't get help. In the backs of our minds, yes we know what can happen, but it's our need to help others that drive us to go to work."

I want to change the subject, this one has gotten a little deep. "Okay! So what do I have to do to maybe convince you to take me up on an offer to head over to the beach for a little bit. It's a great day for a little sand play, maybe play on the playground there.

She is thinking about it. That's a good sign, she didn't say no right off. "If you have other plans, I understand and we can do it another day," I add quickly, wanting her to know if she does say no, I'm going to try for another day.

"No, we have nothing else planned for today, just hanging out at home," Darryn confesses.

"Why stay inside? I'm sure Kendall here would love some playground fun," I try to convince Darryn while I tickle Kendall on the belly, which makes her giggle.

"Bryce, why are you doing all of this?"

The question throws me off. What does she mean why am I doing this? What am I doing? "What is that supposed to mean? Why am I doing what? Am I making you uncomfortable? If so I'm very sorry, I had no intentions of that."

"No, I'm sorry." Darryn scoots out of the booth and quickly grabs Kendall out of the highchair.

I'm speechless, I have no idea what just happened or what I did to cause Darryn to just want to leave.

"Darryn, wait." I throw money down on the table and hurry after her.

As I run out the front door, I spot her quickly walking across to parking lot, heading to what I assume is her car. Kendall, being so innocent, spots me and is waving goodbye to me with a big smile on her face. The innocence of a child.

I catch up to them just as she opens the back door to a white Jeep Cherokee. "Darryn, stop and talk to me, please."

She completely ignores me and starts to open the driver door. My hand against the door, I stop her from opening it. "You need to tell me what just happened."

CHAPTER
Five

I'M SCARED! How the heck do I explain that to Bryce? He scares me, not physically, but emotionally. I watch him with Kendall and her reactions to him. It's all too perfect. No guy can be this good. I've been fooled by that kind of guy before. All sweet and fun. Says all the right things, makes you fall head over heels for them, then one day it begins, and slowly you realize you have fallen in love with a monster. Someone who wants to control your whole life, what you eat, wear, the friends you hang out with, the money you spend. I'm not going back to that. I'm going to control my life, not a man.

"Bryce, just let me go, please. This was all a mistake, I'm sorry." I try the door again, but he isn't moving.

"No, if I said something that bothered you or did something, please let me know." His hand stays firm on my door.

"It wasn't anything you did."

"Really? For some reason I don't believe that. Whatever it was has bothered you so much and put you in such a hurry to get away from me that you didn't even strap Kendall into her car seat. I'm pretty sure that's not a habit for you, so I'm going to ask again, what's wrong?"

I look into the back seat and Bryce is right. Kendall is sitting in her seat, not belted in. What the hell is wrong with me? I open her door and quickly belt her in. Shutting her door, I turn to find Bryce leaning against my door with one hip, his arms crossed over his chest, a questioning look on his face. He isn't going to let me go without an explanation.

"Listen, Darryn, if I did something, please tell me and I will leave you alone."

"It's nothing you did or said, Bryce. Kendall seems to love you. You have been great to talk to, very caring, very nice, but the nice guy act I have been fooled by before."

"Excuse me?! The nice guy act? Do you care to explain that for me?" Bryce is mad. I can see it in his eyes.

"Look, this is all coming out wrong. I can't explain it to you…"

"What can't you explain? Darryn, what are you not telling me?" Bryce interrupts me.

It's been almost three years! Three very long years of secrets! I never expected it to be so hard. Actually, only this last year has been hard. I've moved twice, and I really don't make friends. My last partner was all business, no fun, so it wasn't hard to not become friends with her. Tom is completely different. He is very friendly and so is his wife, I would say they are the first friends I have had in almost three years. Now there is Bryce, too. He deserves the truth, or at least someone who isn't living a life of secrets.

"Bryce, just take my word when I say this isn't going to work out." I stare up at him, pleading with him with my eyes to let it go.

He takes a step closer to me. His eyes turn to a hazy blue, and my stomach knots up. He's going to kiss me! I want to take a step back but my feet won't move. Placing my hand on his chest, I intend to push him away, but instead I end up clutching his shirt in my fist. His face moves in closer to mine. He stops just before our lips touch.

"Your words and your body are speaking very differently, Darryn." His warm breath rushes over my lips.

It takes everything I have in me not to pull his shirt that I'm clutching onto, so that the little space between our lips is no more. I hold my breath as I feel him lean forward and my eyes close. I wait to feel those lips on mine, but instead his lips move to my cheek. When he pulls away, my hand drops from his shirt.

"Thank you for the lunch, I had a great time. We will talk later." Bryce turns and just walks away.

I watch as he walks over to his car and gets in. He never looks back, and he doesn't wave as he drives past me. What just happened? My legs are still a little shaky and disappointment is heavy in my chest. I wanted him to kiss me. I had a death grip on his shirt, basically begging him to kiss me, after telling him nothing could happen between the two of us. After I basically accused him of putting on a nice front. What is wrong with me? Better question, what is wrong with him? I had turned him down many times before I finally agreed with going out with him today, and then today I treat him like a bad guy and he still tells me we will talk later. Of course, that could mean he will say hi when we see each other on a call or in the hospital.

Getting in my car, I sit here for a moment. I want to slap myself for the way I treated Bryce. He didn't deserve it. He was great today. He was fantastic with Kendall, and she likes him. She doesn't go to anyone. It took her forever to go to Tom and Heather. With Bryce she didn't even hesitate, she held her hands right out to him. This isn't right. I swore to myself I wouldn't allow him to control my life anymore. I made a pact with myself that I wouldn't stop living just because of the decisions I made. All of that is exactly what I have done today. I need to stop it.

Picking up my phone, I find Bryce's number and click on the text message icon. I need to apologize, tell him he was right. I want to see him again. My fingers sit over the letters to text it all out, I just can't get them to move. Throwing it on the seat next to me, I quickly start up the car and head for home.

WALKING up the two flights of stairs to our apartment, my steps slow as I come up to our front door. It's open! My steps slow down some more and I mentally go through my actions as we left earlier. I remember walking out and shutting the door for sure. I remember locking the top bolt. Now I'm standing in front and I notice the door has been kicked in. Quickly, I pull my phone out of my pocket as I balance Kendall on my hip and hurry back down the short walkway to the stairs. I don't want to scare Kendall, but I'm starting to feel myself shake. My veins feel like ice is running through them. Without hesitation, I find Bryce's number and push call.

One ring, two rings. "Come on, Bryce, answer please."

Nothing, I get his voicemail. I try one more time, quickly pushing the call button once again. Again, his voicemail. Damn it, I quickly dial 911.

"911. What's your emergency?"

"I just got home and my front door has been kicked in, please send the police." I quickly tell the operator my address.

"Okay, we are sending out an officer, are you in the house?" she asks.

"No, we are back down in the parking lot."

"All right, officers are en route, I will wait with you on the phone until they get there. Did you see anyone in the house?"

"No, I didn't enter," I confirm and listen for the sirens.

It feels like it takes hours, but I know it was only maybe five minutes when I hear the sirens and shortly after, see two police cars fly into the apartment complex parking lot. The four officers run up to the apartment. A third patrol car pulls up next to the other two. The officer in the passenger seat runs out and up the stairs, the driver steps out and I recognize him instantly. "Derrick."

He turns and runs over to me. "Darryn, what are you doing here?"

"It's my apartment," I answer, pointing up in the direction of my apartment.

He heads up without another word. I just stand there and wait as they are all inside. I don't hear any commotion, so I hope that means whoever was here is no longer, but again they have been in there for quite some time now and my place isn't that big. What's going on? I watch as two officers come out and head down the other end of the walkway toward the other apartments. Why isn't anyone coming down and telling me what's going on?

The sound of tires skidding behind me has me turning around fast. I swear Bryce jumps out of the driver's seat before the car comes to a complete stop.

"Darryn, are you guys all right? What happened?" He runs up to me, his eyes searching Kendall and myself.

"Why didn't you answer my calls?!" I yell at him. I am angry and scared and taking it out on the only person here right now, Bryce.

Kendall starts to cry and puts her arms out to Bryce. He instantly takes her from me, which only seems to frustrate me more. I want to pull her back to me but her little arms are wrapped around his neck and he is rubbing her back, calming her down.

"I called you twice and you didn't answer!" I yell at him again, this time I can feel the tears starting to fall down my checks.

"I'm sorry," is all he says, but wraps his free arm around me and pulls me against his chest, now rubbing my back just like he rubbed Kendall's.

I take a couple deep breaths, breathing in Bryce, which seems to calm me quickly. My body begins to warm up, I feel safe in his arms.

"Darryn, why don't you and Kendall go and sit in my car, let me find out what's going on." Bryce pulls back from me slightly so that he can look at me.

He looks up over my head, I turn to see his brother walking back down the stairs and heading toward us. "I want to stay and hear what he has to say."

"Did you see anyone at all when you walked up, Darryn?" Derrick asks as he walks up to us.

Shaking my head, I try to think back to when I got here, and when we walked up the stairs. I don't remember seeing anyone. "No, I'm sorry. I didn't notice anything wrong or out of place until I was walking up to my door and found it open. When I noticed it had been kicked open, I turned around and came back down here."

Derrick is writing everything down as I answer his question, nodding his head. "All right, well whoever it was isn't in there now. We have a couple guys walking around seeing if they can find anything, and we have contacted the apartment office to let them know they will need to repair the door frame."

I can feel Bryce's hand on my lower back. Strangely it helps, but unsettles me all at the same time. For the past three years, it's been me taking care of Kendall and myself. I haven't needed a man to lean on, but now that there is one to lean on, it feels nice.

"Darryn, while we are here finishing up, why don't you go inside and see if anything is missing so that we can put it in the report?" Derrick suggests and then turns and heads back to the stairs.

I start to follow after him when my name being called from behind stops me. "Ms. Carlsen, Ms. Carlsen."

Turning, I find our apartment manager running over to us. "Yes?"

The middle-aged apartment manager is breathing heavy when he reaches us. He puts his hand up to signal to give him a minute. He takes one deep breath and straightens up. "I'm sorry about the break in, first off. I just got off the phone with our property's handyman and he said he can come and put some sort of barrier up for the night, but will not be able to get the supplies to fix the door until tomorrow, so you might want to make arrangements to sleep somewhere else for the night."

Other arrangements for tonight? Where am I supposed to go? "There is no way he can fix it today?"

The manger shakes his head no. "Sorry, he is at the other site on some kind of plumbing emergency and says he won't be able to get supplies until morning. I'm very sorry."

"All right, thank you." I turn and head for the apartment.

I feel numb and I have a sick feeling in my stomach as I walk in the front door. It may sound strange but I was really hoping things would be missing out of the front room and stuff thrown all over. If it wasn't for the front door being broken, you would never know anything was wrong. I walk into my bedroom and that's where my breath catches. Papers are thrown everywhere. My drawers are all pulled out, the closet is all pulled apart. Nothing looks to be missing, which just confirms my worst fear.

A strong hand on my shoulder causes me to jump. "Hey, it's all right. I'm sorry, I didn't mean to scare you." Bryce's voice comes from behind me.

"I'm just a little jumpy, I'm sorry."

"Kendall is in the living room playing with some toys on the floor. Derrick is keeping an eye on her so she doesn't go out the door. Does anything seem to be missing?" Bryce comes around me and starts looking around, flipping the bed mattress back upright on the box springs, closing drawers.

"I don't have much someone would want to take. I'm sure whoever this was realized this after going through my room." I try to sound normal, but even I can hear my voice shake.

"This is the only room touched. Kendall's room is all good, I checked before I came in here." Bryce looks around. I watch, he is looking for something. "Where are you staying tonight?"

Shrugging, I try to smile. "Maybe I'll just go to a hotel or something."

"Don't you have a girlfriend you can ask or something?"

"No, I really don't have any friends here. Only person I talk to is Tom and his wife. They have a full house, though, so I don't want to bother them. It's no big deal. It should only be for one night." My stomach is all knotted up, what a way to end this day.

CHAPTER
Six

BRYCE

LOOKING around the room and watching Darryn's reaction to everything, I realize something isn't adding up. She looks upset, but not surprised. Looking back at our conversation from earlier, and now all of this, Darryn isn't telling me something. I want to keep pushing her for some information, but I want her to feel comfortable enough with me to tell me without me asking. I need her to feel like she can trust me and open up.

"You two can stay with me tonight." I speak before really thinking. Derrick comes through the door at the same time, surprise written all over his face.

When I look at Darryn, the same surprise is in her eyes. A shirt she was holding in her hand drops to the floor. I watch as the surprise changes to a "really" look.

"Look, I have an extra bedroom at my place, you and Kendall can stay in there tonight. Why spend the money on a hotel? That's not going to be cheap."

Derrick's back is to Darryn, thank god, because the look he is giving me right now would have had her slapping the both of us and then throwing us out of her apartment. "Aren't you supposed to be watching Kendall in the living room?" I question him before he does something to embarrass both of us.

"I didn't leave her alone, I have a question for Darryn and then we will be heading out." He is laughing at me. He turns his attention to Darryn, "Is there anything else you need to add to the report as missing or anything?"

Darryn just shakes her head.

"All right then. Well, you know how to get a hold of us, or at least Bryce if you find anything else is missing or anything you think we need to know." Derrick turns back to me and nods, then he turns and leaves the room.

Darryn is over by her dresser, a piece of paper in her hands, and she is shaking. "What's that?"

Quickly she folds the paper and shoves it in her back pocket. "Nothing."

She is lying. She looks like she is ready to break down. I know all of this must be overwhelming but something just changed in her, a different kind of scared. What was on that paper?

"All right, Darryn, what's going on? You look like you just saw a ghost or something."

Her body is shaking and tears are forming in her eyes. "I'm just scared."

I walk over to her, half expecting her to push me away when I wrap my arms around her, but I'm surprised when she wraps her arms around my waist and lets me hold her.

"Hey, it's going to be all right." I rub her back. "Darryn, look, why don't you and Kendall come and stay at my place tonight? I promise I'll behave myself. You don't need to be alone in a hotel with Kendall right now this upset. I would like to think we are friends and as a friend, I would like to help."

She takes a deep breath, her arms are tight around my waist. She fits perfectly against me; it feels good to hold her, it feels right. I feel her head nod against my chest. I push her back a little and look down at her.

"Is that a yes?"

She looks up at me and I see the tears are now flowing down her cheeks. I have to fight the urge to wipe them away.

"Yes, and thank you, Bryce."

"It's no problem. You gather some stuff up for the both of you and I'll go back out and watch Kendall until you are done. I have tomorrow off, too, so we will come back after they fix the door and I will help you finish cleaning up all of this stuff."

Darryn takes a step back, pulling out of my arms and I have to fight to not pull her back to me. She doesn't say anything else, she just starts gathering clothes. I walk out to the living room and find Derrick on the floor with Kendall.

"Thanks for watching her."

Derrick picks Kendall up off his lap and sits her on the floor next to him, telling her goodbye, then stands up. "It's no problem, is Darryn doing all right?"

"She's a little shaken, but that's to be expected. Who wouldn't be coming home to all of this?"

"So is she staying with you tonight?" he asks, sounding a little concerned.

I just nod. "Man, be careful, something isn't right here and I know you know what I'm talking about. We have both been doing this job for a while now and we know the signs."

He is right, I can't argue with him on any of it. "I know what you are saying, I think the same thing, but whatever it is, I need to protect her and this little one," I point down at Kendall. "I'm hoping she will start trusting me and tell me what's going on."

Derrick stands there staring at me for a moment. He wants to say more, but he doesn't. "All right, well if you need me, you know where I'm at. I'll see you later." He turns and waves down at Kendall who is looking between the two of us. "I think she thought I was you."

We both watch as Kendall stands up and walks over to the two of us. She looks at Derrick and then over at me. You can see her little mind working around the fact that she is looking at two people who look exactly like each other. After going between the two of us for a moment, she looks at me and puts her arms up. "Up."

Picking her up, she wraps one little arm around my neck and with the other she waves to Derrick. "Bye."

Derrick laughs. "Bye, little one. I think she has us figured out." He turns and heads out of the apartment.

After making sure the door to Darryn's apartment is boarded up, we finally head back to my house, grabbing a quick something for dinner on the way. I pull into my driveway, Darryn parks next to me. Jumping out of my truck, I go around to Darryn's car and grab the bags she packed for Kendall and herself, while she gets Kendall.

"Bryce, are you sure this is all right?" She is standing next to her car looking scared to move.

I swear she is begging me with her eyes to tell her she really isn't welcome and she should leave.

"I wouldn't have offered if it was going to be a problem, Darryn."

With her bags in hand, I head to the front door. I unlock the front door and turn to let them in, but Darryn is still standing by her car. She looks scared.

"Darryn, if you feel more comfortable staying at a hotel, or somewhere else, you aren't going to hurt my feelings. I understand," I try to reassure her.

CHAPTER
Seven

Darryn

WHAT THE HELL is wrong with me? I haven't always been the type of woman who cowers from everything, always looking over my shoulder. I hate the person I have become in the last couple of years, I need to get back to myself. I know I can trust Bryce, he has been nice to me and Kendall, and was very generous offering for us to stay here tonight. I really didn't have the extra money for a hotel tonight, but I wasn't calling Tom and asking him if I could stay there either.

Walking up to the front door, I smile at Bryce. "I'm sorry, I think I'm still a little shaken up from this afternoon. I appreciate you offering for us to stay here, you didn't have to go out of your way today to help us and I know you have. I apologize for the way I have been acting."

"Darryn, I don't know too many people who wouldn't be shaken by what happened today. Just for the record, it's my job to do what I did today."

Disappointment soars through me when he says it is his job to do what he did today. I know we have only had the one date and all, and I have fought this attraction between us since the first time he asked me out, but him stating it was his job to help made me wish he would have done it just for us, not because the job called for it. What did I expect, though? I have done nothing but push him away.

"Well, thank you all the same," is all I can find to say, then walk past him into the house. I don't want him seeing the disappointment in my eyes.

Observing my surroundings as we walk in, I'm surprised at how clean and organized his house is. It is simple, nothing on the walls, a couch against one wall, a loveseat next to that with a coffee table in front of them. A big screen television with a game system and radio sitting below it on some shelves. Men and their games. It's set up as a large great room, the dining room and kitchen all attached. Carpet in the living room but wood tile floors through the rest.

"Follow me and I will show you to the spare room, it's down here." Bryce walks past me and I follow him down the hall.

The first door we come to is closed and the one across from it is where we go in. "Sorry, it's not much in the way of decorated."

I laugh. "Really, you think I'm worried about how your spare room is decorated?"

Bryce shrugs his shoulders and puts the bags down on the bed. "The bathroom is the next door down the hall. Clean towels are under the sink, if you need anything let me know. The kitchen is yours to use as you need, please feel free to help yourself to anything in there. I will let you and Kendall get settled."

I watch as he walks out of the room and closes the door behind him. Kendall wiggles out of my arms. Once I sit her down on the floor, she runs to the door, opening it and yelling at Bryce. "Wait for me."

"Kendall, come on, leave Bryce alone," I call after her as I follow her out of the room. I find them both in the kitchen. Kendall is back up in Bryce's arms.

Kendall's trust of Bryce should tell me that he is the real thing. Actually, I should know that without my daughter's constant want to be held by him.

"I'm sorry, I think she has her first crush."

Bryce goes over to one of the cupboards and pulls out a bag of cookies. "Do you mind?" he asks.

I shake my head no.

"Why don't you go get settled and Kendall and I will sit here and have some cookies."

"Bryce, you don't have to take care of my daughter, she can come with me. You have already given us a place to stay for the night, you don't have to babysit as well."

I walk over to take Kendall from him, but she wraps her arms tightly around his neck and turns her face away from me. "Bryce."

"Darryn, she is fine, she isn't bothering me. I like having a little buddy to eat cookies with." He sits her down onto the counter and hands her a cookie, then he turns and offers one to me.

"Thank you." I take the cookie from him and lean up against the counter opposite of him.

FINALLY, Kendall is asleep. I think the cookies gave her a little sugar rush, it took two stories tonight to settle her down and get her to sleep. I change into my yoga pants and a t-shirt, and wrap my hair up in a messy bun, finally feeling relaxed for the first time today. Looking at my phone, I realize it's only a quarter after nine, and I know I should be exhausted, what with all the emotional roller coasters I have been on today—first time date, house being broken into and now staying the night at a guy's house I barely know. I feel like I should already be passed out next to my daughter, but I'm surprisingly very awake. I have already called work and asked for tomorrow off. They didn't even hesitate to give me the time off after I explained what happened. I don't want to risk waking Kendall, so I grab my tablet and head for the living room. Maybe if I read for a little while it will relax me enough to get some sleep.

Coming around the corner from the hallway to the living room, I find Bryce sitting on the couch with his phone in hand. He looks like he is texting someone.

"Sorry, I didn't know you were in here, I will leave you alone." I turn to head back to the room.

"Darryn, you don't have to stay in the room all night. Please, make yourself comfortable. I was just texting Charliee. I was supposed to go over tonight, but sent Derrick instead. I just wanted to check on her."

Great, because of my messed up life, Bryce is stuck taking care of us instead of his sister, who really needs him right now. "I'm sorry."

He looks up at me, puzzled. "What are you sorry for?"

"You should be with your sister, not having to deal with house guests you weren't planning on having."

"Darryn, stop! If I didn't want to help, I wouldn't have. You needed a place to go and I have an extra room. Derrick doesn't mind going over to Charliee's tonight, that's what family is for."

I stand there for a moment and we stare at each other. He is getting frustrated with me, I can see it. "I'll head to bed, see you in the morning."

"Darryn, come on, stop hiding from me whenever you can. Come sit down. We can watch a movie, talk, or you can sit here and read and I'll leave you alone."

I'm not hiding from him, I just don't want to put him out in his own home. "Fine, what movie do you have in mind?"

I HEAR the front door open and my heart stops, he is home. Looking at the clock, it's after two in the morning. I was hoping he wouldn't be home tonight. Coming home this late means he is probably drunk. I make a quick mental note of the house, making sure everything is clean and put in place. Of course if he is drunk it won't matter, he will either find a reason to become outraged and he will take it out on me, or he will be wanting sex. Nothing pleasurable for me, all for him and only him. Jumping out of bed, I quickly undress, maybe I can at least teeter it more toward the sex and not the hitting. I rub my now rounding stomach, I need to protect this little one.

It's dark but I know the moment he enters the room, I can hear him stumble around. My stomach becomes nauseous as I hear his clothes hit the floor. I'm trying to keep my breathing even and not move. Maybe, just maybe he will just lay down and go to sleep. The bed dips and his arms snake around my waist. So much for just going to sleep. It is wishful thinking, it never happens that way.

He begins to grind into me from behind, his hand is on my stomach. I can feel his hot breath in my ear and I can smell the liquor on his breath as he begins to breathe heavier. I want to leave him, run to a place he can never find me, but like he reminds me every day, where will I go? I have no job, he made sure of that. I have no friends, again something he made sure of and no family. I have a baby on the way, how would I take care of the two of us?

"I have a secret." His voice brings me out of my own thoughts.

I don't respond, I have learned that he talks more if I stay quiet.

"You will never see this baby, Serina."

MY EYES FLY open and I sit straight up. Looking around, I have to remember where I am. The television is off and as I look to my right, I see Bryce. He is awake now as well, looking around. I must have startled him.

"What's wrong?"

I stand up quickly and look anywhere but at him. "Sorry, I think we fell asleep. When I woke, it took me a minute to remember where I was."

I'm a little afraid to turn and look at him, he will know there is more to it than just waking up in a strange place. I would put money on the fact that Bryce already knows more is going on than I am telling him, I think he is waiting for me to tell him first. I wish I could, everything is starting to weigh on me now, and with today happening I need to decide what I want to do. Run or stay and fight.

CHAPTER
Eight

BRYCE

SOMETHING IS WRONG, more than just not remembering where she is. She isn't looking at me, and is making a point not to. She is shaking and looking around like she needs an escape.

"Darryn, what's wrong?"

She doesn't look at me, she just stands there, her arms wrapped around herself. All right, I can't do this anymore. I can't keep acting like I believe her when she tells me nothing is wrong. Something is very wrong.

Standing up, I stand in front of her and close the space in between us so that she can't look anywhere other than at me. I'm standing so close that her crossed arms are against my chest. She looks down, that's the only place she can look. One hand under her chin, I bring her eyes up to look at me. Seeing the tears in her eyes, my chest tightens and it feels like someone is punching me in the gut. How has one woman affected me this quickly? I want to take her pain away. Destroy the reason that is creating those tears. I intended to question her, but I find myself wrapping my arms around her and pulling her into a hug instead. At first she goes very stiff, but I don't back away and after a few moments, her arms move around my waist, and that's when I realize she is crying. I feel her hands grab onto the back of my shirt like I am her lifeline, keeping her from drowning.

We don't move, I don't attempt to calm her down with words, I just hold her while she cries. I can feel the front of my shirt becoming wet as I tighten my arms around her. If this is what she needs, I am going to be here to give it to her.

Her shaking is starting to subside so I lean back to see if she is ready to talk. She still won't look up at me. I place my hand under her chin and tilt her face up to mine. My heart flips in my chest. Here Darryn is, red eyes and nose from crying, tears still falling down her cheeks, and she looks beautiful. I can't help myself, I need to feel her lips, and before I can really think about what I am doing, I bend down and claim her lips with mine.

It is a simple kiss, I taste the saltiness from her tears. I can feel her breathing against my lips as I look down at her. She is searching my eyes and before I can guess what she will do, her hand goes into my hair at the back of my head and she is up on tip-toes claiming my lips in a kiss that is anything but gentle. She isn't wearing a bra, I can feel her nipples harden and rub against my chest through our shirts. A little moan comes from her and I'm pretty sure just that little sound causes me to about lose myself. I kind of feel like a teenager getting kissed for the first time again. I need to stop this, she isn't in the right frame of mind and I don't want her mad at me for letting this happen. I am trying to get her to trust me, this isn't the right direction for that.

Gently I pull away from her, ending our kiss. "Darryn, we need to talk."

I watch as she goes from a dreamy look in her eyes to the realization of what just happened between the two of us. She tries to pull away from me but I'm not going to let her go and start closing up on me again.

"Darryn, I'm not letting you run and hide."

"Let me go, Bryce."

"No, you need to talk to me." I tighten my hands around her forearms and terror fills her eyes.

I instantly let go of her so quick, she stumbles back. She looks terrified of me. "Darryn, I'm sorry, I just want you to talk to me. I didn't mean to scare you."

She is physically shaking, her arms are wrapped around her middle, and she won't look at me. I know all of these signs, I see it more than I care to in my line of work. It confirms what I have been wondering about all day. Someone in her past was abusive to her. I'm pretty sure there is a lot more to the story, but I would bet my next paycheck that I'm correct about the abuse.

"Darryn." I take a step toward her.

Holding up a hand, she stops me but still won't look at me. "Don't touch me." She walks quickly past me and to the room she is staying in with Kendall.

It takes everything in me not to follow her and make her talk to me. Or to at least apologize for what just happened. The last thing I wanted to do was scare her away. I've been trying to get her to trust me, now I'll be lucky if she ever talks to me again.

For the past month, I have been asking her out. She always seemed strong, independent, not afraid to tell a man no. Then today it's been the complete opposite. She looks like she is ready to run and I'm not just talking about from me. This afternoon during lunch, things seemed off. She accused me of basically being fake, saying she had fallen for that before. That was my first clue that someone in her past had hurt her in some form. I wouldn't have said then it was abuse, but she had been hurt emotionally. I just figured she was worried about being hurt again. Now I'm pretty sure it goes way past just a bad rela-tionship, and to top it off I would bet she is hiding from someone. Today at her apartment, she didn't seem surprised about the break in. She didn't seem relieved that nothing seemed to be missing. In my line of work we learn to read people, watch reactions, body language, facial expressions.

Ten minutes have passed since she went into the bedroom. I'm about to go and knock on the door, if for no other reason than to make sure she is all right, when she comes out of the room. She is carrying a sleeping Kendall in one arm and their bags in the other hand.

"Darryn, where are you going?"

She still won't look at me, this is becoming ridiculous. I grab her arm as she walks past me. Darryn freezes and I hear her sharp intake of breath. I almost let go, then think better of it. If she is ever going to trust me, I have to stop tip-toeing around her, so I hold onto her arm.

"Please let go of me?" she asks through clenched teeth.

"Not until you promise to stay and talk. You are running and you need to stop. It's after one in the morning, where do you think you are going?"

"Please let go of me," she says again, this time with a little anger in her voice.

That a girl, get mad. I can handle mad, it is a lot better than scared. She needs to be strong for herself and for Kendall.

"I'll let go if you promise to walk back into that room and stay until morning. You shouldn't be driving around town with a two-year-old by yourself this late at night. Where do you think you are going at this time of night?"

"What does it matter to you where we go?"

"Darryn, this is crazy. Come on, look, I really don't want the two of you driving around this late at night. If you are set on leaving then I will drive you to a hotel and make sure you are set for the night, at least that way I know you will be safe."

Something changes in her eyes. It isn't fear, or anger. It almost seems like a light bulb came on for her. She takes a deep breath and I feel her body relax under my touch.

"Fine, we will stay, but I'm going to bed." She moves to walk past me again, this time I release her arm and watch as she walks back down the hallway and into the room, shutting the door behind her.

I'm not going to push anything more for tonight. I'll talk to her in the morning, maybe after some sleep she will open up a little and let me help her.

MY PHONE RINGING is what wakes me what seems like only minutes after I finally fell asleep. Reaching over, I grab my phone off the nightstand. It is Derrick, no surprise there. What does surprise me is the time, it is after ten in the morning. I can't even remember the last time that I slept any later than maybe seven.

I tap the screen to answer and Derrick's voice comes through the phone before I can even say hi. "Hey, man, what are you doing?"

Rubbing my eyes, I fall back against my pillow. "Sleeping."

"Sleeping, it's after ten."

"What do you want, Derrick?"

"Man, you are grouchy this morning. Go back to sleep and call me later."

I don't even respond, I just hit the end button and throw the phone on the bed next to me. I don't hear any sounds through the house. I was expecting to hear some kind of movement. I'm pretty sure Kendall wouldn't sleep in this late. Knowing Darryn, she is keeping Kendall and herself in her room until I come out. She hates putting people out, so I can see her doing whatever she can to make sure I'm not disturbed by them. That gives me the energy to get out of bed. I think last night I was afraid that once Darryn thought I was asleep, she would try and sneak out of the house. I know one of the last times I looked at the time was about four thirty this morning. I must have fallen asleep shortly after that.

After a quick shower, I decide that I'm going to make some breakfast for us and then call the apartment manager to find out when the door to Darryn's apartment will be fixed. Walking up to the spare bedroom door, I knock and wait. Nothing, I don't hear any sounds coming from the room. Kendall is a two-year-old, it can't be easy to keep her quiet. I knock again and still nothing.

"Darryn, are you guys awake?"

I try the handle and it's not locked, opening the door I find an empty room. Darryn and Kendall are gone along with their bags. I go to the front door, opening it to see her car is no longer in the driveway. She left either while I was asleep or when I was in the shower. I pull my phone out of my pocket and look to see if she left any messages that I may have missed, but there is nothing. Finding her name in my contacts list, I hit send. It doesn't even ring, it goes straight to voicemail. I'm not going to even bother with leaving a message, if she left without telling me then she isn't going to call me back.

Frustrated, I don't know what to do anymore. Darryn obviously doesn't want my help, maybe I need to take the hints and just leave her alone. Shutting the door, I walk down the hall and into the living room, flopping down onto the couch. This is crazy, she is driving me crazy! I'm not one of those guys that can't take a hint. Sure, she turned me down a number of times when I asked her out. It was more a game between the two of us. She never acted disgusted that I was asking or insulted. She would have that playful gleam in her eyes. She finally says yes and the playful look is gone. On our date yesterday she seemed nervous, which I didn't take personally. Well, at least not until she accused me of being fake. Then at her apartment yesterday, she looked defeated, like she was ready to surrender over the fight.

Then last night when we kissed, something happened. The first kiss was soft, and with just that one touch of her lips it felt like something slammed into my chest, opening it to feelings I have never felt for a woman before. Then she claimed my lips in a kiss that shook me to my core. She held on like I was her security and all I wanted to do was wrap her in tighter and protect her from all that was making her run.

Now I sit here and know I should just let her go. She left without a word, she turned off her phone. How many clues do I need to know that she doesn't want to talk to me? I'm not going to beg her to accept my help, or me, no matter the feelings I'm having for her. There is another factor in all of this, Kendall! I love kids, I have always wanted a family with a few of them. Dating a girl with kids never bothered me, I just never dated one with any. Kendall's little arms around my neck and her head resting on my shoulder melted my heart. In a very short time these two ladies have wiggled their way into my life and my heart, how am I supposed to walk away from that?

Picking up my phone, I text her.

**I'm here if you need me.

I'm leaving it at that, I'm not chasing her, no matter how much I want to, but I want her to know I will be here if she needs someone. I really don't expect her to use it, but at least I know it's out there.

CHAPTER
Nine

IT'S BEEN a week since the break in and I'm starting to think it was just a simple break in. Maybe they just got scared by something before anything could be taken. I don't have much to take anyway. I have nothing of value in the apartment, and the television in the living room is nothing to get excited over, it's small but it does the job. Nothing seems out of place, I haven't had any other problems. Sure, there was the letter I found, but rereading it I probably overreacted to it, going to the worst case scenario like always.

I haven't talked to Bryce at all in this past week either. We left around eight in the morning that day. His door to his room was shut, I took a chance that he was asleep and as quietly as possible left without bothering him. I was so embarrassed about throwing myself at him the night before. What he must think of me, I don't even want to try and imagine. One minute I'm all right, then mad, then scared and yelling. He must think I'm unstable, he would probably be right. In one day I accused him of being fake, and then yelled at him like he would hurt me, and then kissed him like some out of control woman. The man probably has whiplash from all of my mood swings that day. Then I turned my phone on later that day and his text popped up, telling me he was there if I needed him. Bryce was definitely someone special and I was letting him get away, but it was all for the best.

"Hey, are you listening to anything I have to say?" Tom's voice breaks through my thoughts.

"What?"

"That's what I thought." He rolls his eyes and takes a bite out of his sandwich.

"I'm sorry, I have a lot on my mind." I look down at my lunch that I haven't even touched.

"All right, what's going on? Everything all right at home? No more problems, right?"

I shake my head no.

"Good, because I'm still a little pissed at you for not calling me that day and letting me know what happened. Or asking for a place to stay the two nights you stayed at a hotel."

I called my complex manger after leaving Bryce's house and he assured me that the door would be fixed that day, but I still didn't go home that night. I decided to stay in a hotel for a night while I thought about what I was going to do. I didn't tell Tom that I stayed at Bryce's house the first night.

I was ready to leave altogether. I was going to go and grab our stuff and just start driving, like the last four times, but something stopped me. I can't say what it was but I couldn't leave. It might be because I'm getting tired of running, I'm tired of the person he has changed me into. I want my life back, I want to be able to think about having a life. How can I do that if I'm always running?

"Darryn, what is going on with you? All week you have been distant."

I take a deep breath, "I'm sorry, I guess this whole break in thing is affecting me a little more than I realize."

"You know we are here for you if you need us, right?"

I nod and smile up at him. Tom and his wife are a little of the reason I want to stay. I like having friends. I usually try and stay away from getting close to anyone because when I have to leave it makes it that much harder, but I fell in love with Tom and his family pretty fast. They left me no other choice.

"Let's change the subject, how are things going with Bryce?"

Not a better subject, I think to myself. "Nothing is going on with Bryce."

"Don't try and pull that blinder over my eyes. I saw the way he watched you yesterday while we were on that accident."

What is he talking about? Every time I looked at Bryce he was doing his job, I didn't think he was even aware I was there. "I think you were seeing things."

"Didn't you guys go out, how was it?"

"Yes, we went out for lunch, it was all right. We haven't talked since that day, though, so whatever you thought you saw, I think you were imagining it."

It was the only time this week we had a call together. Every time we are dropping off a patient at one of the hospitals, I swear I hold my breath until we leave. I'm always waiting to go around the corner and have him standing there. When we rolled up onto the call yesterday, he was already there. My chest felt tight the whole time. I tried to not look in his direction but found I couldn't help myself. Kendall has said his name a couple times this week. How did he wiggle into our lives this quickly?

"Really, only one date? As many times as that man asked you out, I was pretty sure he was hooked on you. Men don't keep asking after being told no that many times unless they see something they really want."

"Well, I guess you were wrong. Can we please talk about something else?" I snap a little.

"Oh, I'm not wrong and that reaction confirms it."

A call coming over the radio has the two of us quickly putting our lunch away and getting on the road, saving me from anymore of Tom's questions.

Pulling into traffic, lights and sirens going, Tom looks over at me from the driver's seat. "This isn't the end of this conversation, just to warn you."

I don't even respond, I just turn my head and watch the city quickly pass by out of the passenger side window.

IT HAS BEEN A LONG DAY, and not enough calls for me. I know that makes me sound bad, but every time we pulled over to wait for the radio, Tom would start back up about Bryce. I thought guys didn't like girl talk. Pulling out of the driveway from work, I make my way to go pick up Kendall. All I want to do is get home, spend a little time with my little girl, and then maybe sit down with a book tonight. I love to read, just haven't made much time for it lately. It relaxes me to sink into a story that I can forget about my own story with.

I'm at a red light, getting ready to turn onto the street with the daycare when I look into my rear-view mirror and notice the same silver sports car that has been behind me since I left work is a couple cars back. The hair on my arms stands straight up. The daycare is only a little ways down the street once I turn. The light turns green and even though I'm in the right turn only lane, I go straight. The driver I cut in front of blares his horn telling me how "happy" he is about the fact that I can't follow traffic laws but at the moment, I don't care. My blood turns cold when I notice that the other car does the same thing.

I try not to panic, a person can't think straight when they are panicking. I try and talk to myself like we talk to patients when we are trying to calm them. It's not working, though, it's a little annoying actually. I need to remember that the next time we are talking to a patient. After a couple more random turns I realize my worst fear has come true, I'm being followed.

Reaching over to my bag on the passenger seat, I search for my cell phone inside. I need to stay calm. As long as I'm driving, I'm safe, right? Finally, my fingers find my phone. I hit the number I'm looking for.

"Hello." His voice comes over my speaker in my car.

"Bryce, I'm being followed!"

CHAPTER

Ten

BRYCE

WHEN DARRYN'S name and picture flash on my phone, I am so shocked I probably answer it a little too fast.

"Bryce, I'm being followed!" Her voice is shaking.

I am just leaving work. I just left the building and was walking out to my car, now I am running. "What do you mean you are being followed? Where are you?"

"I was around the corner from Kendall's daycare when I noticed a car behind me that I had seen since I left work. Instead of turning, I went straight, I've made a couple random turns and the car is still there. I'm sorry, you were the first one I thought to call."

She sounds scared, but she isn't freaking out. She is doing everything right actually. "How far behind you is the car?"

"They usually stay about two cars behind, I'm not sure how many more turns I can make before they figure out I know they are back there."

"Where are you exactly?"

She tells me her location and I realize she is headed straight to the station, good girl. "Keep coming this direction, Darryn. When you get here park on the curb next to the front door and go inside, I will meet you in there."

"Don't hang up, Bryce, talk to me until I get there," she pleads with me.

Her voice slams into my chest like a sledge hammer. I need to have her by me, in my arms so that I know she is all right. I need to stay calm for her. "I'm not hanging up, Darryn, I'm here with you. I'm always here for you!"

I hear her take a couple deep breaths over the phone. "Where are you now?"

"A block away. Bryce, I'm sorry."

I just walked back into the station when she says I'm sorry, I stumble back a little. This call shouldn't be affecting me like it is right now. This is my job, I'm supposed to be the calm one, but right now I feel like someone is tearing my heart out of my chest.

I was parked in the back of the building behind our locked gate and I quickly ran to the front. I come up to the front desk. "Darryn, describe the car to me." I tap on the desk to get the officer behind the desk's attention, "We need a car out front and ready to follow a car coming up to the station." I repeat the car's description that Darryn is giving me.

"They know where I'm headed. They just turned around, heading back in the direction we just came from. They just U-turned in the middle of the road."

I have Darryn on speaker and the officer sends the report over the radio to the officer waiting. I look up as the front doors open and Darryn comes running in, right into my arms, her head buried into my chest.

"Do I need to call for medical attention?" Carly, one of our female officers, asks.

I shake my head no. "I'm taking her to the breakroom, let me know if they find the car."

Darryn lets me lead her back, she is shaking. We walk inside and luckily, no one is in here. "Darryn, you need to call the daycare and let them know I'm coming to pick up Kendall."

She shakes her head no. "I'll go get her."

"After you calm down, you will leave with me. My car is parked out back, we will go and pick up Kendall, but you are staying in the car. Then we are going back to my place and you are going to tell me what the hell is going on."

I watch Darryn nod her head, but I hate the defeated look in her eyes. She isn't being given any choice on trusting me any longer. Being followed makes this a problem that I am no longer going to ignore or give her space on. She needs help regardless if she wants it or not, and I am going to help her if she wants me to or not.

Carly, the officer from the front desk, opens the door and motions for me to join her out in the hallway. "I'll be right back, then we will leave."

Again, Darryn just nods. She keeps her face down and her hands folded in her lap. I follow Carly out into the hall. "What's up?"

"They weren't able to find the vehicle."

It doesn't surprise me. I'm a little pissed at myself for not getting in here faster and getting a squad car out and headed in her direction sooner. I wanted to make sure Darryn was safe, keep her calm on the phone and get her to the station and out of danger.

"Thanks." I head back into the room with Darryn. "They weren't able to find the car."

"I should have gotten a plate number, but they stayed far enough back and with cars in between us, I never could see the plate or if it even had one."

"I need your apartment keys and a list of what you want an officer to pick up from your apartment for a couple days for you and Kendall. They will bring it back here to the station and I'll come back and pick it up tomorrow."

"What about for tonight?"

"I have sweats and a t-shirt you can borrow for the night, I don't have anything for Kendall, though."

"She has extra stuff and pajamas in her bag at daycare, I always tend to pack too much for her." She laughs a little, shrugging her shoulders.

I want to pull her into my arms and promise her everything is going to be all right. Let her know I am here and I'm not going to let anyone or anything hurt her or Kendall, but I need her to open up to me. She needs to tell me what is going on and all of it. I need to stay strong with her right now. She needs to know I'm not letting her run from me this time.

"Come on, let's go pick up Kendall."

WALKING INTO THE DAYCARE, Kendall notices me right away, running over to me. I kneel down and catch her in my arms, standing up with her in my arms.

"You must be Bryce." A middle-aged woman holds her hand out to me. "I'm Carrie."

"It's nice to meet you. Sorry we are late getting this little one picked up tonight."

"It's no problem. Is everything all right? Darryn sounded different on the phone tonight."

I notice the real concern in Carrie's eyes. "Everything is good, thank you, though."

Carrie doesn't believe me and that is fine. I turn my attention to Kendall, tickling her on her side. "Are you ready to go?"

Carrie hands me her bag. "If Darryn needs anything, please tell her to call me."

"I will, thank you. She did tell me to tell you Kendall won't be here tomorrow, she took the day off."

Carrie just nods and smiles. I return the smile and turn to leave.

CHAPTER
Eleven

I WATCH as Bryce comes out of the little daycare with a smiling Kendall. I can't remember ever seeing her smile like she is. She likes Bryce, who could blame her, and Bryce is great with her. When he asked me out and found out I had a daughter, he went right into trying to do something that would include her. I wanted to believe there were men out there like him. Never thought I would actually find one. All I have done is fight him, from the moment he asked me out the first time, to the morning I snuck out of his house, and yet here he is helping me again. I have never felt as safe as I did that night in his arms. All I want right now is to be back in those arms.

The door behind me opens and my little girl's voice makes me smile. "Mommy."

Turning around, I turn on my best smile. I never want her to know how unhappy and scared I am. "Hi, my angel. How was your day?"

She points at Bryce who is strapping her into her car seat. "Bryce."

I watch as he kisses her on the forehead before shutting her door and rounding the car to the driver's side. What the hell is wrong with me, why do I keep pushing this man away? "Thank you," I tell him as he settles back into the driver's seat.

He just nods. He's mad and I don't blame him. I sneak out of his house and never return his calls or texts, but the moment I'm in trouble I call him. Was I expecting him to be forgiving and happy to hear from me? Most men would tell me to go take a flying leap off a building, but Bryce can't, it's his job to help people and now he is stuck with us, at least for the night.

I watch him as we drive to his house. He is tense, always looking in his mirrors. I have now brought my problem into Bryce's life. I should have left last week, but no, I decided to stay because everything was a fluke. I should have known he would find me again, somehow he always does. Nothing is a fluke in my life, he has made sure of that.

I SIT with Kendall and read to her until she falls asleep. Usually it is one book and then I leave the room, but I wasn't ready to face all of Bryce's questions yet. If I could get away with staying in here all night and reading I would, but I know if I stay too much longer he will come looking for me. He isn't letting the questions go without answers tonight, and I don't blame him.

I look down at my little girl. What kind of life am I giving her right now? Always moving, never making any friends. Sure right now it's not too important to her, she is too young, but when she is older she will start hating me for always pulling her away from her friends. Or one of these days, he is going to catch up with us. It's time I trusted someone.

Walking out to the living room, Bryce is sitting on the couch. "Is she asleep?"

Nodding, I sit across from him on the loveseat.

Bryce takes a couple of deep breaths. "Bryce, I know you are mad…" I speak first. I want him to know I'm not proud of what I have done.

"Darryn, I'm not mad," he interrupts me. "I'm frustrated. I have tried to be patient with you. I want you to trust me, to tell me what is going on. I didn't want to push you. You didn't really know me and I don't blame you for being careful. Then your apartment got broken into, you didn't seem surprised. You telling me I was faking being nice. The reaction you had after we kissed, or when I grabbed your arm that night. I know what all that means, but then today you have someone following you. I thought there may be more, now I know for sure there is more, much more, and I'm done being patient. Both of you are in danger and you are going to tell me everything so I can do everything I can to make sure you and Kendall are safe."

"Bryce, this isn't your fight," I try to argue.

There is that look again. The one that tells me he wants to grab me and shake me. I watch as he gets up from the couch and walks over to the window.

"Damn it, Darryn, tell me what the hell is going on." He turns on me and tries not to yell, I know he is trying not to wake Kendall.

I need help. I trust Bryce, if not for myself, then for Kendall's sake. "His name is Brett Hammonds, he is my ex and Kendall's father."

I look up and he is standing there, no expression on his face, just waiting for me to continue. I might as well start from the beginning.

"We met while I was in college finishing up with my paramedic class. He had been persistent on asking me out. The paramedic class doesn't really allow much time for a social life, for a year the class pretty much owns you. I would explain that to him, and he would always tell me he would wait. It was very flattering. Some friends and I from class went out one night after graduation and Brett and some of his friends happened to be at the same club. He informed me that night I had no more excuses to say no when he asked me out yet again and he was right, I didn't. At least none that I could think of. Well, long story short we ended up dating. It's your typical story, everything was great at first, one of those too good to be true stories. He spoiled me like crazy and I was a young stupid woman thinking I had found my prince charming."

Now that I was talking it felt like it wasn't going to stop coming out of my mouth. I haven't told this to anyone, it's been my horror story to live, remember and run from. I can't bring myself look up at Bryce. I don't want to see the look on his face telling me I should have known better.

"One day I had received a call saying I got my first job, I was excited. He took me out to dinner to celebrate, we had a couple of drinks, went home and that night was the first time I saw the real side of Brett. I won't give you all the details, trust me, you don't want to hear them, it's your typical abusive relationship stuff. Before I knew what was happening, he had complete control of my life. My friends were gone, we did what he wanted to, when he wanted to and I didn't dare complain or suggest something or he took it out on me with his fist. Never where you could see the bruises. I even quit my job after only two months of working.

"When I became pregnant, I was surprised how happy Brett was, his parents were even more excited. On the plus side, the hitting stopped. Don't get me wrong, he found other ways to control me and hurt me. I'd always wondered how women could allow their lives to be controlled by a man, how they could allow themselves to be so weak and their confidence to be so low. Then, I became one of those women."

Now I know why I never told anyone this story, it's humiliating. Telling another person about the weakness you had to not be able to control your own life. Allowing someone to change you into someone you hated when you looked in the mirror.

CHAPTER
Twelve

BRYCE

IT IS TAKING everything in me to stay where I am standing. I want to go to Darryn and wrap my arms around her. She looks embarrassed and ashamed of what she is telling me about herself. I want to let her know I don't see her as the weak woman she is telling herself she is, but I need her to finish telling me everything. If I go to her now, then most likely she will stop talking.

"Darryn, why is he after you?"

"One night he came home really drunk, he kept telling me he had a secret. I just laid there, I realized early on when he came home that drunk if you just let him talk, he will tell you just about anything. I just wasn't prepared for what he said that night. He told me that I would never see my baby, he had the plan all laid out. He never told me exactly what he had planned, he just kept repeating that he wouldn't need me after our baby was born. That our child didn't need a mother who would raise it to be weak and useless."

I am waiting for the tears to start, but she never starts crying. That shows her strength right there, she doesn't see it, but she needs to.

"I laid there for a couple of hours running his words through my head. Something that night changed. I realized what was happening to me, I realized I didn't want my child growing up thinking I was weak, or anything like their father. I wasn't sure if we were having a boy or girl yet. I didn't want my son growing up treating women like his father did, or my little girl growing up thinking it's all right to let men treat her like he treated me. Brett didn't know it, but his words gave me the strength to leave. If he would have never said that stuff that night, I hate to think where Kendall and I would be today. I had some money saved in an account Brett didn't know about. I knew he was out cold for the night, a marching band could play through that room and he wouldn't have moved. I knew that was going to be the only time I would have to get away. I grabbed only what I thought I would need and I left. I waited outside of the bank until it opened, pulled out all of my money, closed the account and left town."

She is looking down at her hands, I need her to finish the story. If I am going to be able to help her, I need to know everything. "Where were you living at the time?"

"A small town in Colorado, I went to California first. When I got there, I had my name legally changed. It took a little time to get my paramedic stuff changed over, but as soon as I did I found a job. I played off not knowing I was pregnant, I was lucky the company was understanding."

"You legally changed your name?" I am surprised, most people wouldn't even think of that.

She nods. "Yeah, I figured it would be harder for him to find me if I changed it. I went with my mother's maiden name for a last name and changed my first name to Darryn. I met a girl with the name and spelling and loved it."

"What was your name before?"

She looks up at me, thinking. She needs to trust me and this is the test to see if she does. After all of the stuff she has told me so far, I am pretty sure the person following her today is her ex.

Darryn takes a deep breath and that's when I see the last wall fall away from her eyes. "Serina Alcove."

I think about it for a moment. She doesn't look like a Serina. Darryn fits her much better.

"For a while I thought he wasn't looking for me. When Kendall was about six months old, he showed up at my work. He was at the front desk one day asking for me, but he was still using my old name. How he found out where I was, I have no idea. I moved that night, giving the company I was working for an excuse of a family emergency that was making me have to move back to my parents'. I didn't want to leave on bad terms, I would need them for a reference later. Long story short, I moved to Minnesota, and then here. I thought we were good, until my apartment got broken into. It's him, he is looking for some kind of paperwork or pictures to confirm it is me, I believe that's the only reason my room was messed in. I don't keep anything out, I have a safe deposit box that has all my legal paperwork and pictures, believe it or not."

Now that I think about it, I didn't see any pictures in her apartment of Kendall. That should have been something I noticed. "So what are you going to do now?"

"I'm tired of always moving. I don't know what to do. I won't let him take Kendall from me. I don't want to spend my life running. I have friends here. Tom and his wife are the first friends I have had in years. I want Kendall to have a home. I want us to have a life, I want to stop fearing for my life. I save lives for a living, but I can't help myself."

There are the tears and I can no longer stand here. I go to her and pull her up and into my arms. She doesn't fight me, her arms go around my waist and she buries her face into my chest. We just stand here in the middle of my living room, her crying and my chest feeling like someone just punched me in it. That's when it hits me, I have completely fallen for Darryn and Kendall. Sure, it's my job to serve and protect, but this is different. The feelings I'm having right now are different. I don't want to arrest this man and have the system punish him, I want to find the guy and beat the shit out of him. Let him feel some of the pain that he put Darryn through, physically and mentally.

I give her a few moments, then sit her back from me so that I can look down at her. "Darryn, you no longer have to run. You not only have Tom here, you have me, and I will make sure Brett no longer harms you or gets anywhere near Kendall."

"This isn't your fight, Bryce."

The way she is looking up at me, her lips a little swollen from crying, her cheeks wet from tears, I have to fight the urge to bend down and kiss her.

"Are you supposed to work tomorrow?"

She nods.

"All right, well call in sick tomorrow, I'm calling in at the station. For now, why don't we get some sleep and then tomorrow we will figure some stuff out and how we are going to deal with all of this, but you aren't running, Darryn."

"I have nowhere else to go, Bryce. He knows where I live."

"Move in here with me then." The words are out before I even think about them. What surprises me isn't that I offered it without thinking about it, but the fact that if she says no, I know I will be disappointed.

Darryn, on the other hand, is very surprised by my offer, but she covers it quickly. "Bryce, that's very nice of you but for a couple of reasons, I would have to say no."

"What are those reasons?"

She pulls away from me and takes a couple steps back. "Well for one, this is my fight, not something you need to be dragged into. Second, after I left Brett I swore the next time I lived with a man, if I ever found one I could trust, I would be married. I did so many things wrong when it came to Brett, and even though Kendall is very young, I don't want to do anything that I wouldn't want her to do. I live my life now to show her how she needs to expect to be treated when she gets older. To understand she doesn't need anyone to take care of her, she needs to be able to take care of herself. Don't take this the wrong way, please, but we have been on one date and you are asking me to move in? That's seems a little fast if you ask me."

If the situation wasn't as serious as it is, I would have laughed. I understand what she is saying, after all that Darryn has been through, she wants to make sure her daughter doesn't make her same mistakes. "Then what is your plan?"

She shrugs her shoulders. She isn't running, I will do whatever I need to make sure of that. Not only because that is no way to live, but because I'm not going to lose her. I can't say I believe in the whole love at first sight, but since the first time I met Darryn, I was taken by her.

"Why don't we get some sleep, clear your mind a little and we will figure this all out in the morning."

"That sounds like a good idea."

"This means you can't take off in the morning without a word, Darryn."

She gives me a shy smile and shrugs her shoulders again. "I really can't go far. I have no car, remember, we left it at the station."

"Something tells me that wouldn't stop you."

"True." She closes the space between us once again. Her hands go up onto my chest and then she shocks the hell out of me by stretching up and kissing me.

Her warm lips against mine is all it takes. I can't resist her any longer. My one hand goes into the hair at the back of her head and my other around her waist, pulling her tightly against me, deepening the kiss. Dipping her back down onto the couch, I hold my weight above her with one hand on the arm rest of the couch, one knee in between her thighs, my other foot still on the ground and with my other hand I grab her hips, thrusting her up against me. I expect her to push me away, but nothing could have prepared me for the feelings that shoot through me when I hear a soft moan escape from her instead. It almost undoes me all together. She has to feel how hard I am for her, with how tightly we are pressed together. Her hands slide up and under my shirt and it is like cold water being splashed all over me. We can't do this right now. I need her to trust me, not think the only reason I want her around is physical.

Pulling away from her is one of the hardest things I have ever done. Looking down at her dreamy and a little confused look almost has me saying screw being a gentleman, but if I want any chance of her staying, I need to prove to her that it is because I care for her and Kendall, not just because I am a man who wants only sex.

Standing up, I grab her hand and pull her up off the couch with me. If I look down at her laying there, I can't promise I would be able to go to bed alone tonight. "We need to get some sleep."

She just nods her head, but she won't look directly at me. She looks a little embarrassed. With a finger under her chin, I lift her chin up so that she has to look at me. I give her a small kiss and smile down at her. "Good night."

She doesn't say anything, just turns and heads to the room that she is sharing with Kendall. Once the door is shut, I flop down onto the couch, my head falling back. I take a couple deep breaths. That had to be one of the hardest things I have ever done. I would have liked to have her next to me all night, after spending some time inside of her, but it isn't the right time. I want to prove to her I don't want her only for her body, but for her heart as well.

CHAPTER

Thirteen

DARRYN

SHUTTING THE DOOR QUIETLY, I don't want to wake Kendall. Leaning up against the door I take a couple deep breaths. What the hell has gotten into me? Something draws me to this man and it's kind of scary how I can't seem to control myself with him. Running my fingers over my lips, I can still feel his against mine. My fingers are still pulsing where I touched his stomach, skin to skin. He was warm and well built, I could feel his muscles flex under my fingers when I first touched him under his shirt. I can't remember ever wanting a guy as much as I wanted Bryce tonight. When he pulled away from me and stood up, I felt the cold air between us rush over my body, showing me how warm he had made me. Just thinking about it is making my legs shake. Sliding down the door, I sit down on the ground before my knees buckle under me. This is crazy, right? How can he be affecting me like this? We have had one date, how could I be having these feelings for a man I don't really know? If I'm being honest with myself, one of the reasons I don't want to run anymore is because of Bryce, but that doesn't mean I need to jump into bed with him, I scold myself.

Before Brett showed his true side to me, I thought I was in love with him. I can't say I'm in love with Bryce, but with the feelings I'm having around him, I can honestly say I wasn't in love with Brett, it was more like infatuation. I see that now. My heart skips a little every time I see Bryce. Even through this week when we weren't talking, when I spotted him at one of the calls we were both on, my chest tightened. Every time he smiles at Kendall, my heart feels like it flips over. When he kisses me, he makes me feel like I'm the only woman alive that can kiss him like that. He holds onto me tight, like he is afraid I'm going to disappear if he doesn't hold onto me tight enough. I feel needed, wanted, desired. I thought those were only feelings that happened in a movie or book, not in real life.

When he suggested I move in here with him, it took a lot to say no. No matter how I feel when we are together, or how great he is with Kendall, and how much she obviously likes him, I can't and won't go back on that one promise I made to myself when I left Brett. I stayed all that time with him because I didn't believe in myself enough to leave. I would listen to him when he told me that no other man would love me, that I wouldn't be able to take care of myself without him. The only way I can explain the feeling is like being under a spell. Like you have no control over your own body or mind. I knew he was wrong, but I couldn't say no to him or leave him, until that night when something just clicked.

Getting up off the floor, I walk over to the bed and sit down next to Kendall. She is the most amazing thing that has ever happened in my life. I was given one amazing thing from Brett and that's this little girl. I want to hate the man, but I can't. He gave me this loving little gift, he gave me a reason to fight. Laying down, I stare at her. I smile just looking at her. Pushing a little piece of hair off her face, she moves a little, placing her little body up against mine. I will do anything I have to to keep her away from Brett, even if I have to leave Bryce and my feelings for him. She comes first, always.

. . .

OPENING MY EYES, I see the sun is up and shining through the window into the room. I reach over to the nightstand to grab my phone to check the time and that's when it hits me, Kendall. Flying out of bed, I look around the room, but she isn't in here. That's when I hear the voices coming from down the hall somewhere and her little giggle. I take a couple deep breaths trying to calm my heart back down as I listen to Bryce's deep voice and Kendall's higher-pitched but little voice. I didn't even hear her get out of bed. My ears perk up when I hear another voice, it is a woman's voice.

I don't even bother to check on how I look before I head out of the room, I just want to know who is here and why. Maybe it is one of the officers with news about Brett, maybe they found him. That would solve so many problems. Walking quickly down the hall, I find Bryce in the kitchen, at the stove, making what looks like pancakes. Kendall is sitting on a bar stool up at the counter and an older lady is sitting next to her. I've never seen this lady, and I'm pretty sure she isn't an officer.

"Good morning." I walk over and pick up Kendall, sit down on the stool she was on and place her in my lap, kissing her on the top of the head.

"Pancakes, Mommy." Kendall points over at Bryce.

"Good morning, sleepy head," Bryce teases me, flipping a pancake onto the plate next to him on the counter. He points over at the woman next to me. "Mom, this is Darryn."

"Good morning, Darryn, I'm Karen."

His mom, my cheeks instantly warm. How must it look to her to have myself and my daughter here in the morning at her son's house? She wouldn't know I slept in the guest room. To top it off, I'm wearing Bryce's t-shirt and sweatpants.

"It's nice to meet you." I look at her only long enough to not be rude while talking to her and then look away. "What time is it?"

"It's almost ten." Bryce brings a plate over with a pancake all cut up and places it in front of Kendall, and then brings another over to me.

"Oh no, I haven't called work yet." I start to get up and go grab my phone but Bryce stops me.

"Don't worry, I already called in for you. I just told them there was a family emergency."

Part of me is relived he thought to make the call, another part is a little upset. I don't want work thinking I'm slacking with not calling earlier, so for that I'm thankful he called for me, but on the other hand I don't need him taking care of me.

"Don't give me that look, Darryn, I'm not trying to be in control." It's like he is reading my mind. "I knew you had a long day yesterday and I wanted you to get plenty of rest, that's the only reason I didn't wake you to make sure you called in early enough."

Well now I feel like an ass. I have to stop going straight to the worst, I should be thankful he thought about it at all. So instead, I try to play it off like I have no idea what he's talking about. "I'm not mad, Bryce, just surprised. Thank you."

"Yeah, right," he says and then turns back to the stove.

"Sorry if Kendall woke you up this morning." I'm really hoping she didn't go into his room and wake him this morning instead of waking me.

"She didn't wake me up, I was already up. She was talking away in the room, but I didn't hear anyone talking back. I knocked and she opened the door. I saw that you were still a sleep so I brought her out here with me. We watched a little cartoons and then came in here and started breakfast when my mom got here," he explains.

How the heck did I not hear her this morning if Bryce could hear her from the hallway? I'm not looking like the best mom in front of his mom this morning.

"Stop worrying and overthinking everything," he scolds me. How does he do that? How does he know everything I'm thinking?

"I pay attention," he answers my unasked questions again, laughing as he goes back and turns off the stove.

"So I have something to run by you. Hear me out before you say no," Bryce adds as he leans across the counter and steals a bite of Kendall's pancakes.

"Hey mine, Bryce." She giggles.

"Kendall, you can share," I correct her.

She looks at me and then her pancakes with a little pout on her face. After a moment, she looks up at Bryce with a smile. "I share."

"Thank you but I'm full." Bryce rubs his stomach.

My hand twitches remembering what that stomach felt like last night. *Damn, stop that*, I scold myself. "What do you want to run by me?"

"Well, we have a lot to talk about and figure out today, I asked my mom here if she wouldn't mind taking Kendall for the day so we can get things figured out. This way you won't have to worry about her at the daycare all day, and we don't have to worry about getting the things done that need to be done with her around. She needs to stay away from all of this."

He is talking in code. I understand what he is saying but I'm not sure about Kendall staying with a woman I don't even know, or that she knows for a matter of fact. "That's very nice of you, Mrs. Brooksman, but Kendall is shy, and I'm not sure how she would do with someone she doesn't know without me."

"Please, call me Karen." She puts her arms out to Kendall, who basically jumps out of my lap and into her arms to my surprise. "I don't mind at all keeping her for the day while you guys take care of everything. I love children and since I have no grandchildren of my own, I will have to borrow your child for now." She tickles Kendall on the tummy and she laughs.

My daughter is making me out to be a liar. She is usually shy and connected to me, but with this family she seems to not be bothered if I'm here or not. I look up at Bryce, he nods his head at me. He is right, she doesn't need to be towed around all day, or around any conversations that might be happening. She may only be two, but she is smart. "All right, if you are sure you don't mind, I would appreciate you taking her for the day."

Karen looks down at Kendall and claps her hands. "Then it's a play date. We are going to have so much fun today, little one."

I watch as Kendall claps her hands along with Karen. I have instantly fallen in love with his mother. Her eyes are so kind. She is the grandmother I always wished Kendall would have. Losing both of my parents, and with Brett's parents thinking their son was an angel, Kendall would never have any. I feel my eyes water up, but blink them back quickly. I don't need to make a scene that I am going to have to explain to this woman who probably already thinks of me as a mess anyway. I know I shouldn't be worried how Karen sees me, it's not like Bryce and I are in a relationship. Why do I think I need to impress her, or worry about how she thinks of me?

I look over at Bryce who is studying me. He shakes his head no at me. Why? He knows I'm upset and judging myself again, I see it written all over his face. He may not know exactly, but he has read enough through my eyes to see it. It's exciting and scary all at the same time to know this man has figured me out that quickly, yet there isn't one time that I can say that I have been able to do that about him.

"Well, I better go and get her dressed." I pick Kendall up off Karen's lap and quickly leave the kitchen before I make a complete fool of myself. I'm either going to cry or get up and round the counter to kiss Bryce, neither is something I want to do in front of his mom.

Walking down the hall, I hear his mom say, "Are you sure about this, Bryce?"

I stop for a moment, I need to hear what he has to say. What is she wondering if he is sure about? I'm sure he has told her about offering for us to move in, but I'm pretty sure I made myself pretty clear last night that I wouldn't be moving in. I expect him to try and change my mind today, but I'm standing strong on this one.

"Mom, I have known since the first day, even with all the hell going on that day, all the panic and worry over Charliee, I knew. So yes, I am sure."

That is cryptic. What has Bryce and his mom been talking about this morning? Now I feel bad about eavesdropping. Here I thought she was talking about me and now I'm pretty sure I'm listening to a conversation I have no business being nosy about. Kendall starts singing at the top of her lungs, giving me away. I don't want to get caught standing in the hallway listening to a conversation I shouldn't be listening to, so I quickly run the rest of the way to the room.

CHAPTER
Fourteen

BRYCE

I HEAR Kendall in the hallway. Darryn is listening to our conversation, I'd put money on it. This isn't really the way I want her to hear about my idea. Moments later, the bedroom door closes.

"Bryce, if you are sure then you know your father and I will support you."

"Thanks, Mom, I knew you would."

"I just want you to make sure you aren't jumping into this without thinking it through. This is a lot to take on."

I know what my mom is saying, but I have been up all night thinking of nothing else. I need to make sure Darryn and Kendall are safe. I had called my mom this morning and asked if she could come over. We have always been close, my parents always made it easy for us to talk to them and be open. They were smart about that, we never kept things from them and they never corrected us if we screwed up as long as we were open. We had to fall a couple times, but they would give us their opinion and then let us decide from there. She was doing that now.

"Mom, there is only so much the badge will allow, this will give me a little more room beyond the badge. Plus, if this doesn't work then I think she will run and I'll be honest, I don't want her to do that. I wish I could explain it to you, but there is something there and I don't want to let it go."

"Bryce, I love you and I will support you like I said, but maybe you should talk to Derrick as well."

I shake my head no. This is going to be very difficult to keep from Derrick, we always work things out together. That whole saying "two brains are better than one," we depend on each other for pretty much everything. I'm not sure if there has ever been a time I haven't talked to Derrick, but this is different. If he knew, he would go beyond the badge to help and I don't want him in that spot. I am going to talk to him about Darryn's ex, let him in on what is going on, I need his help along with Tom's, so this isn't going to be a secret for her to keep any longer, but this part of the plan isn't something I plan to bring anyone else into right now.

"No, Mom, just you and Dad need to know right now. Trust me, it will have to come out at some point because even after it's all over, I don't plan on letting her go."

SHUTTING the back door to my mom's car with Kendall all ready to go, Darryn is waving to her through the back window looking like she is going to cry. This is difficult for her, I know. She isn't used to trusting people and within a couple days she has had to learn to do it fast. I take her hand in mine, hoping to reassure her that everything is all right.

My mom rolls down her window. "Don't worry, Darryn, we are going to go do a little shopping, maybe stop by the park for a little while, have some lunch. You know, a little girl fun."

This is why I love my mom, she even knows Darryn is panicking and is trying to calm her down. I look over at Darryn who is smiling now at my mom.

"Thank you, Karen, for all of this."

"Don't thank me, honey. Like I said earlier, none of my children have graced me with any grandchildren yet so I'm excited about today." My mom looks over at me. "Let me know when you need us."

I just nod and wave as she pulls out of the driveway. I can feel Darryn looking at me with a questioning look. "Let's go inside and I will answer the questions flying through your head right now."

I don't let go of her hand as I lead her back to the house. Once inside, I figure there is no reason to not get everything out and in the open. I almost woke her up real early this morning when I made up my mind to talk to her, but I knew she needed sleep and talking to my mom this morning helped me realize I was doing the right thing.

Sitting us both down on the couch, I am surprised I'm not nervous. I am sure about what I'm going to ask Darryn, but I still expected to be nervous. Instead it just feels right. There are a few questions I need answered first.

"All right, so I have a few questions for you before we go into anything else."

Darryn just nods and waits.

"Darryn, where are your parents?" I start with.

"Um, they died when I was Kendall's age in a car accident. We were on our way home from visiting my mom's parents one night and it was raining. A lady hydroplaned, losing control of her car which went head on with us. My dad died instantly, my mom died later at the hospital. I had a broken leg and arm but other than that, I was fine."

My chest constricts, I can't imagine not having my parents, and thinking that Darryn could not have made it through that accident as well, that's something I can't and don't want to think about.

"So did your grandparents raise you then?"

"No. They were both old and unable to take care of themselves, they were in a nursing home together. My dad's parents died long before I was born. Neither of my parents had siblings so I was put into the system. Pushed around from home to home. Some weren't that bad, others were bad, only out for the money they received from homing a foster child. I'm sure you know what I mean. I was put into homes with so many other children and watched as so many of them took the wrong paths, or ran away, I decided I wasn't going to be like that. I stayed out of trouble and out of the way if I could. I tried to be invisible. Graduated high school and put myself through college to become a paramedic. I wanted to help people. I don't blame the emergency crew for my parents' deaths, but I wanted to be the person to help others if I could, save a life. You never know whose life you are changing when you work hard to save a life from ending."

I understand what she is saying, one of the reasons I became a police officer was to help save lives. My reasons just aren't as deep and personal as hers are. Hearing all of this just confirms how strong Darryn really is.

"I never expected myself to be one of those women I had been called out to help so many times. Unfortunately, more times than I would like to say, we couldn't save those who had gotten into relationships with the wrong person. I didn't want to admit I was one of those women. I told myself I would never let it get that bad with Brett, but it did. If I would have stayed, I'm not sure I would be alive today."

Hearing Darryn talk about Brett isn't helping my need to find the man and beat the hell out of him. I myself see a lot of abuse in my line of work and just knowing Darryn was in that kind of situation has me clutching my fist.

"You left, though. You got yourself away and your child."

"Sure, but look at where I am now. I can't even go home because he knows where that is. I'm going to spend my life running, moving Kendall all around, trying to stay one step ahead of Brett so that he doesn't get his hands on her. I won't let him anywhere near her. I will do whatever needs to be done to make sure that doesn't happen."

This is the time. "Marry me."

Darryn's eyes go wide, she even moves herself away from me a little more on the couch. "Excuse me?"

"Darryn, you have said it yourself, you don't want Kendall spending her life on the run. Never being able to make friends. It's not healthy for you either to always be looking over your shoulder waiting for Brett to find you again. What are you going to do, keep changing both of your names in hopes that one day he may give up? What happens if a day comes that you don't see him coming and you are alone, no one around to help keep Kendall and yourself safe? I know you are going to run, you don't see any other way around this right now. I see it in your eyes. I offered for you to move in here, I can keep you both safe while we find this guy. You said no, I understand that and your reasons, I don't want to force you into anything you aren't comfortable with, but I also know you don't want to leave. You are tired and it's understandable, no one should have to live in fear all the time and you definitely don't have to do it alone anymore, Darryn."

She gets up from the couch and starts pacing the living room. I watch her for a moment, giving her a minute to soak it all in. I watch as she goes through the emotions in her head, shock, denial, disbelief, back to shock, and then anger, that's the clue to step back into this conversation.

Getting up from the couch, I stop her pacing by getting in front of her and placing both hands on her arms. "Don't get mad at me, Darryn, I'm not trying to take control of you by marrying you."

Her eyes fly up at me, anger flaring. "How the hell do you do that? I think that scares me more than anything with you, Bryce. You answer everything I'm thinking, like you can read my mind or something. I don't have even a free thought around you."

I am going to have to tread around this carefully, choosing my words so that I don't piss her off even more and then have her run, because right now she is very close to doing just that.

"Darryn, anyone who pays attention to you would know exactly what you are thinking, your eyes say everything anyone would ever want to know if they just paid attention. I knew from our lunch together there was something you were hiding. If I wanted to know, I needed to pay attention. You were scared and I needed to know why. I don't want you scared of me, I want you to trust me. I'm sorry if you think I am trying to control you, I'm not. I understand everything you are telling me, even down to the reason why you won't move in unless you are married. I get it all, I swear. My job is to protect, but I can only do so much behind the badge. I want you to be able to give Kendall the type of life you want to give her. A place to grow up and call home and friends, but you know you can't do that if you are running and hiding. How free are you if you are running? That's not freedom, Darryn, that's letting Brett still control your life."

Shock, that's what shoots into her eyes and she takes another step back, keeping herself completely out of my reach. I don't make a move toward her, I want her to have the space to think.

"You think me marrying you is freedom?" she shoots at me.

"Darryn, it's not like I'm going to lock you up in the house. I want to help you and Kendall have a life without fear. You have to stop running." I have to take a different approach to this. I can't blurt out my feelings for her, she won't believe me right now. She would think I'm only saying things to get her to agree.

"Look, as soon as this is all over, you can divorce me and move anywhere you want to go and live the life you want and deserve."

CHAPTER
Fifteen

DARRYN

THIS MORNING when I woke up, I knew Bryce and I would have to talk. He offered for me to move in with him until Brett could be stopped. I expected the conversation to come up again today, but not in the form of a marriage proposal. I am having a hard time breathing, everything is moving way too fast, but what did I expect? This is my life. In a moment, it could change. Damn, why did I have to meet him now? Then again, when would have been a good time? My life is never going to be easy or mine if I am always running from Brett. Bryce is right, Brett is still in control of my life. He will always be unless I do something to change it, but is marrying a man I don't really know the answer to that? I'll admit, I have feelings for Bryce that I have never had for anyone else, but is it love? That I can't answer yet. I'm pretty sure marrying him isn't going to answer that question either. What other options do I have right now? Brett knows where I am, so it is either stay and fight, or run. I'm not only running from Brett this time. I am running from friends and Bryce. How long can I run? Bryce is right and I know it, one day Brett is going to catch up

"

with me and I'm not going to see it coming. He will get to Kendall and how will I stop him alone? Then he would have Kendall and that alone is something I can't allow to happen. I swore I would do anything to keep her safe!

Taking a deep breath, I try to settle my nerves. I look up at Bryce who is standing there in front me giving me time to think it all out. He is even giving me an out after all of this is over. Oddly, that doesn't make me happy. A part of me, even when angry, was hoping he made the marriage proposal because he has some kind of feelings for me. He is offering me a divorce once it is all over; this proposal isn't because he has feelings, it's his way of protecting us. He is giving up his freedom to protect my daughter and me. He may not have deep feelings for me, but I think I just fell in love with this man.

Is what I am about to do fair to him? Taking over his life in order to keep my daughter safe? I know his job is to serve and protect, but I'm pretty sure this isn't in the job subscription. "Bryce, I can't let you sacrifice your life for our safety."

He takes one small step closer, close enough for him to cup my face with one hand. "Darryn, please let me help you. Let me help you get your life back, help keep you both safe. Marry me?"

He isn't demanding it, he is asking. I'm tired of running and I want to stay. Who knows where this will go, maybe our separate ways, but for now I'm going to take Bryce anyway I can. "All right."

"Really?" His hand falls from my face and his eyebrows raise in surprise. That makes two of us.

"You are right, Kendall is who I need to think about right now. I don't want her growing up on the run. How do I explain that anyway? I just have one request."

"What would that be?"

"We don't announce this to anyone. I don't want to have to explain why my marriage is for protection only." I don't want people to pity me.

"My mom and dad are the only ones who will know besides us. We will need witnesses so I had my mom come over this morning so I could talk to her."

His mom already knew! Great, what that woman must think of me. The conversation I heard in the hallway earlier is making complete sense right now. His mom questioned if he was sure this was the right thing to do. She didn't sound completely supportive, and I can't say I blame her.

"Stop that, Darryn, my mom isn't like that. I explained the situation to her this morning. Sure, she wants to make sure I'm doing this all for the right reasons and I wouldn't expect her not to ask, but she and my dad trust my decisions so they are supporting both of us."

"Damn it, Bryce, quit doing that, it's really starting to freak me out."

"What am I doing?"

"The whole answer my questions without me actually asking them thing. It's kind of freaky."

Bryce closes the space in between us, wrapping an arm around my waist, pulling our bodies together. His eyes turn that crystal color, it's the color they turn right before he kisses me. I'm not the only one with eyes that speak.

"Darryn, with this marriage I'm not going to push you. You can still sleep in the spare bedroom. I don't expect anything a married couple would be able to share, but right now I really want to kiss you," he basically whispers against my mouth.

Still sleep in the spare bedroom? He was marrying me to keep me safe so why did it disappoint me so much to hear I would still be in the spare room? What did I expect, to move into his house, into his bed? Right now, though, he is wanting to kiss me and waiting for me to answer him. How can I say no when he is this close? I know what those lips feel like against mine, it's a tease to have them so close and not quite feel them. My hand goes to the back of his head and brings his lips to mine. I hear his moan and my knees buckle. Bryce's arm tightens around my waist to keep me up on my feet. My other arm goes up and around his shoulders, holding myself close to him.

I can't seem to get close enough to this man. His body against mine elicits sensations I have never experienced and we have our clothes on. My walls are all down where this man is concerned and I'm going to have to be careful. This isn't a real marriage, this is a protection detail for him. I need to remember that.

Our lips part and he leans his forehead against mine. He is breathing hard, at least I'm not the only one affected by this kiss. I need some space from his body, his lips and the man in general.

"So what is the plan from here?" I ask, keeping my eyes closed. I don't want him to know exactly how affected I am by him. As long as he can't see my eyes, my thoughts stay to myself, right?

Bryce takes a deep breath and then a couple steps back. I take a deep breath myself and level my eyes to his, hopefully my eyes show calmness because my body feels anything but. Right now, all I want to do is throw myself back into his arms and claim his lips with mine. This is going to be a lot harder than I thought.

"I need to make a couple of phone calls. We need to get movers over to your apartment, figure out all of that. I need to talk to my brother, and you to Tom. I think it's time to tell him what's going on."

"I can't quit my job, Bryce." How can he even think to expect that of me?

"I'm not telling you to. If Tom knows what's going on then I will feel better about you being at work. I will know someone else is watching after you. Another thing I spoke to my mom about is Kendall and daycare. I want to keep her with family and friends while all of this is going on. I spoke to my mom and she was very excited to help, she would be more than happy to watch Kendall while we both work, and then on our days off she will be with us."

My head is starting to spin. There is so much changing and very quickly. "Speaking of Kendall, what do we tell her about us and your mom? What does she call your mom?"

"I'm leaving that up to you. She can call me Bryce, I know you don't want to confuse her with all of that. As for my mom, she can call her Karen or Grandma Karen, whatever you feel comfortable with. I had lots of moms and grandmothers growing up. If they were your friend's parents and grandparents, they were yours as well."

That's one thing I missed the most growing up. My mom's parents didn't live long after my parents died, I was told. I had no family. I wasn't in one home long enough to make a best friend, or any friends for that matter, to call their parents anything. I stayed to myself, it was easier when I had to leave.

"I'm fine if she wants to call your mom Grandma Karen. Tom's wife has her call her Aunt Heather, so I see no harm in any of it."

"Next, we need to decide what you want to bring here from the apartment and what we need to put in storage for right now."

I think of our stuff at the apartment. The spare room is a nice size, plenty of room for Kendall's bed and dresser, I will just use the bed that is in there and bring my dresser in. The closet isn't huge but we will make it work. I'm getting a headache, this is all happening way too fast. I sit down on the couch and take a couple deep breaths, then ask the big question.

"When were you planning on the wedding?"

CHAPTER
Sixteen

BRYCE

WHEN SHE PLOPS down onto the couch, she looks defeated. I can only imagine what is going on in her head. Even though she thinks I can read her mind, there is still a lot of mystery behind those eyes and sighs.

I kneel down in front of her, placing my hands on her knees. "Darryn, take a couple deep breaths. We will get through all of this together, all right? Later this afternoon, I will call my parents and they will meet us over at the town hall for us to get married."

"Today?!" Her eyes fly wide open again.

I nod. "We can't wait on this. He is out there now, and you are staying here. Your stuff will be moved out of your apartment by tonight. I want to get Kendall's stuff here so that she has some familiar stuff around her, we don't want to stress her out. She is going to have enough changes."

"Are you for real?" She looks at me in disbelief.

"What?"

"Men like you don't happen outside of books and movies, Bryce. You are marrying someone you really don't know to keep them from a crazy ex. You worry so much about Kendall, you would think you were her father. You are turning your life upside down for us. Why?"

There is the famous question I have been waiting for her to ask. I can tell her it's because I have fallen in love with her and Kendall has taken my heart as well. That if anything happened to either one of them I wouldn't stop until I killed the man that hurt them. I actually wonder how she doesn't already know all of this, but I know she isn't ready to hear it from me.

"I promised you I would help at any cost so that you didn't have to run anymore, to give Kendall the life you want her to have. Let's think of it as a witness protection detail. Going undercover. Whatever you want to call it. I will make sure you don't have to look over your shoulder for the rest of your life, running."

I watch as she studies my eyes. There are tears in hers. She leans forward and kisses me softly on the lips. "Thank you, Bryce, for everything. I don't deserve someone in my life like you."

"You are so wrong, Darryn, and I plan to prove it to you." Leaning forward, I place one more kiss on her lips but know if I don't end it there, it may go further than it should right now.

DARRYN IS in the living room talking to the movers on the phone, I need to call Derrick. I have never kept anything from my brother, we tell each other everything. Well, that's important anyway. Not telling him that I am getting married today is going to be hard, even before Darryn asked me not to tell anyone I had decided not to say anything to anyone else other than my parents. I need her to trust me even if it means me keeping this from Derrick.

Sitting on my bed, I dial up my brother's number. I called in earlier today for the day off, but he is on shift today. I'm hoping he isn't on a call right now.

"Hey, man, what the hell is going on?" Derrick answers the phone.

"I'm guessing you talked to someone at the station." I figured he would have heard about last night the moment he got to the station today.

"To someone, no! The whole station was talking about it this morning. Do you know how stupid it looks when your partner and twin brother has no idea what they are talking about? Why the hell didn't you call me last night and tell me what was going on?"

If Derrick is this mad about me not calling about last night events, he will be a lot of fun when he does find out I got married without him knowing.

"Look, it was kind of a crazy night, we had a lot to deal with and are still dealing with. If you can talk for a minute, I'll give you a heads up on what's going on."

"Talk fast because you know how the calls go, it's like they know it's not a good time."

I laugh, that is very true, you can go all day without a call and as soon as you think you have a moment, the city goes crazy. I quickly fill him in on the events from last night.

"Leave it to you to find a girl with a crazy ex. So what are your plans? Obviously she can't stay at her place without protection."

"Well, I guess you can say I'm going to be her protection, she and her daughter are moving into my spare room until this is done."

I'm not going to talk about the marrying her part, but I know he would find out about her living here so I might as well tell him now.

Silence stretches out on the line. "Derrick?"

"Yeah, I'm here. Are you sure this is the right move? Couldn't we put her in a safe house or something? You are talking about moving in not only a girl, but her daughter, too."

"I need to make sure they are safe, I can assure that if they are here."

"You really like this girl, don't you?"

"I can't explain it, something about her has just stuck with me, and her little girl is amazing. I'm not going to lie to you, Derrick, I've fallen hard for this one and I'm going to do whatever I need to do to make sure they are safe."

"Well, you know I have your back, but you need to keep me in the loop on what's going on. I don't want to hear about it from the station."

I expected a little more from him about the girls being here, it surprises me how easy he let me off about it all, but I'm not going to ask questions.

"Why do I feel like you aren't telling me something?" Derrick's voice breaks through my thoughts.

Why, because I'm keeping a secret about one of the biggest events of my life and it's driving me crazy, I think to myself. Derrick will forgive me, it might take some time, but he will forgive me. If Darryn finds out I said anything, she may leave and that's a risk I can't take.

"I've told you everything there is. I will be back tomorrow so I'll file my side of the report then. We sent out an officer last night when Darryn called, but they didn't find the car, so we don't have much to run on right now but a description of it. Can't really go after the guy yet without some proof it's him. Darryn didn't get a good look at the driver, and no one saw anyone in her apartment. None of the security cameras picked up on the face of the guy, he kept it hidden, so we really don't have much to go off of."

"Definitely not the ideal case. Just let me know what you need help with."

"One thing, I don't want Charliee knowing about any of this. Mom and Dad know, Mom is going to start keeping Kendall on the days we are both working. Charliee needs to worry about healing, not worrying about all of this."

Charliee has been out of the hospital for a while but she needs to worry about herself, not all of this, and she is the one who will worry the most. She has dealt with enough in the past month or so, she needs no involvement in this. We almost lost her once, I will not put her into the middle of anything that may put her in danger again.

"I agree, but you know when she finds out you have your girlfriend, much less a girlfriend with a daughter, living with you and she is the only one who doesn't know about it, she is going to be pissed. You know she hates being left out."

"Darryn's not my girlfriend." It's not a lie at least.

"Whatever you want to call her, be prepared for the wrath of Charliee when she finds out."

Wrath of Charliee, wrath of Derrick, damn the things we do for the people we love. I need to get off the phone before I break down and tell Derrick everything. I never realized it would be this hard to keep something from my siblings.

"Hey, I need to get going, I'll see you tomorrow."

"All right, call me if you need anything." Derrick ends the call.

I sit here for a moment. I'm not nervous about marrying Darryn today, something just tells me it is right, but what if she doesn't want this after everything is over? When I think about marriage, I think about sharing a life with a woman I love. Creating a home together, a family. Sharing my bed, my life, and our ups and downs together. Today, I'm getting married and coming home to an empty bed, a secret love for the woman and child, and no future plans. To top it off, I'm keeping a very large secret from half of my immediate family. For the first time I'm wondering if it's all worth it.

A soft knock on my door brings me back. "Come in."

Darryn opens the door and stands in the doorway. My breath catches like it does every time I see her, and like it has every time since the first time I saw her. She has absolutely no idea what kind of control she has over me. Is it all worth it? Most definitely!

CHAPTER
Seventeen

DARRYN

I **DON'T KNOW** if I should bother Bryce, I know he is in his room making some phone calls, but he told me to let him know when I was done with the movers. On top of that, I called Tom and told him everything. Well, at least the short version of everything. He promised me a good scolding when I get back to work tomorrow. When I open the door to Bryce's room, I almost stumble back. There he is sitting on the edge of his very large king-sized bed, leaning down with his arms on his legs looking defeated. It is only a second, his expression changes fast, but I still noticed it. What am I expecting from him? He is being forced to marry to keep someone safe from their psycho ex. Who wouldn't be happy about that?

"Sorry, I didn't mean to interrupt. Movers are all set, I even called Tom and told him what's going on. I figured you wouldn't let me go back to work until I did." I laugh, trying to lighten up the mood in the room.

He doesn't laugh, he just stares. I can't read anything in his eyes. Standing here, I don't know what to do. "Well, you just asked me to let you know when I finished on the phone, so I'll just be out in the living room when you are ready."

I turn to walk away. "Darryn."

I turn back to find him now standing right in front of me, I didn't even hear him get up from the bed. Before I know what is happening, he hooks a hand behind my head, claiming my lips. My knees buckle, he turns us, my back now against the door frame which is serving to keep me standing, with his body pressed tight against mine. This kiss isn't soft, it is raw. His tongue instantly finds mine, one of us moans, I'm not sure who, maybe it's both of us. His leg is pressed between my thighs and I can't stop myself from pressing my hips into his, my center instantly heating up. I can feel his hardness against me. I have never wanted a man as much as I want Bryce at this moment. His kisses aren't gentle, not this time. Usually when he kisses me I feel like he is holding back, afraid to break me. He is gentle, in control, but not this time. My hands go under his shirt and contact with his skin. This time I know the moan that fills the room is from me. My hands have been aching to touch him again since the other night. My hands tingle every time I think about the last time I touched him.

He stills the moment I touch him. He doesn't pull back, he just stops kissing me, breathing hard against my lips. "I'm so sorry, Darryn, I need to control this impulse around you."

No, no you don't! I want to yell at him. I want to take his lips back and finish what we started. Then something clicks inside of me. More like I came out of the trance he puts me in every time he kisses me. I want him, no question in my mind, but we don't need to complicate the situation by becoming physical with each other.

I can't speak, all I can do is nod. Bryce takes one deep breath and then pushes himself away from me using the frame of the door behind me. A chill runs over me the second his body leaves mine. It is so intense, it takes everything in me not to grab him by the shirt and pull him back to me.

"We need to get going," Bryce says as he walks away from me and down the hall.

THE DRIVE over to city hall is quiet. Bryce's parents are meeting us there with Kendall. My hands are shaking in my lap. I can't believe I'm on the way to get married right now. If someone would have told me even this morning when I woke up that I would be marrying Bryce, I would have laughed in their face. I guess this isn't a real marriage though, right? Sure, we will say our vows, be pronounced husband and wife, but there will be no rings, sleeping in separate rooms, basically in name only. Probably a divorce in a couple months at the most.

Bryce grabs my hand and I jump. "Are you all right?" he asks.

"Yes, sorry. I was thinking, you just surprised me is all." He hasn't said a word to me since we left his house.

"Darryn, I'm sorry about earlier. I don't want you to get the wrong idea."

In other words, he doesn't want me to think he wants me, I think to myself. Why would he want to get any more involved with me than he already is?

"Bryce, don't worry about it, it's fine. I'm really sorry about all of this. You have no idea how much I appreciate everything you are doing for me, including giving up your freedom."

"Stop, Darryn! For one, I'm not giving up my freedom. I have told you I will do anything to make sure Kendall and you are safe. Remember, I'm the one who asked you to marry me." He smiles over at me.

I can feel the tension between us start to melt. My shoulders relax, and my body warms by just him holding my hand. I'm waiting for him to move his hand but he doesn't, we drive the rest of the way, our fingers tightly entwined. This may not be a real marriage, but we are both still very nervous. Who wouldn't be on their wedding day?

Pulling into the parking lot, Bryce finds a spot quickly and turns the car off. I start to get out but he stops me.

"Darryn, I know every girl dreams of a big wedding, family and friends there to help celebrate two lives becoming one, I'm sorry this isn't going to be like that."

He looks upset for me which tugs at my heart. He is worried he isn't giving me the wedding of my dreams. That gesture does it, the last wall is down. This man may never know it, but he has my heart completely.

"I guess it's a good thing I didn't grow up like most girls then. I have no family or friends, well, maybe Tom and Heather, but other than that no one else." I laugh, trying to lighten the mood, but instead I see pain shoot across his eyes. Pain for a little girl who had nothing growing up.

I place my hand against his cheek. "Don't look at me that way, please. Don't feel sorry for me. I don't want people to feel sorry for me, that's why I don't tell many people about my past. Sure, I was passed around, and there were homes that weren't that great, but there were a few that were good."

Taking my hand, he kisses my palm. "Sorry. I'm glad you told me."

"I'll be honest, it felt good to talk about it finally, about all of it. You are an amazing man, Bryce, I just wish my life wasn't so screwed up."

We sit here staring at each other for a few moments. I wish I knew what he was thinking about, it's like he is wanting to tell me something, but instead he gives me a smile and then gets out of the car. I take a deep breath, this is it, it's time to go and become Mrs. Bryce Brooksman.

Bryce's mom and a man I assume is his father are already here and waiting for us when we walk up.

"Mommy, Bryce." Kendall's little voice echoes through the building when she spots us.

She wiggles out of Karen's arms and runs right into mine. "Hello, my angel. I've missed you today. Were you a good girl?"

Kendall nods her little head up and down, I look over to Karen for confirmation.

"We had a blast today. She may be a little hyped up, there was ice cream and candy involved with today's activities," Karen explains.

"Bryce." Kendall leans toward him with her arms out, signaling for him to take her.

"How's my girl?" Bryce takes her from my arms and gives her a raspberry kiss on her cheek. My heart melts watching the two of them interact.

Karen walks up and hands Bryce a box. "Everything is in here that you asked for."

I won't lie, my curiosity piques. Bryce looks over at me as his mom hands him the box, a small smile on his face. Damn it, he caught me being nosey.

"Darryn, this is my dad, Steven. Dad, this is Darryn." Bryce makes the introduction.

Nothing like meeting your father-in-law on the day of your wedding. "Mr. Brooksman, it's nice to meet you."

"Please call me Steven, or anything else other than Mr. Brooksman." He smiles at me and then winks.

I get his meaning, what I like is he didn't come right out and say I could call him Dad, but I picked up on the meaning of his words. "It's nice to meet you, Steven." I'm not ready for the Dad title yet.

"Come on, we need to get going, we have our appointment in fifteen minutes." Bryce takes my hand, still holding Kendall in the other arm, along with the box in hand.

· · ·

IT IS STRANGE, here I am standing in front of a man I have only really been on one date with, his parents and my little girl, along with the judge as he speaks the words that will marry us. It is like being in a tunnel, everything seems kind of far away. I answer and repeat when I am instructed to, feeling like I am in some kind of trance.

"Bryce, do you have the rings?" I hear the judge ask.

My cheeks begin to burn from embarrassment. How do we explain that there isn't any rings?

My embarrassment quickly turns to shock when Bryce speaks up. "Yes, sir."

My eyes fly wide open, looking at Bryce puzzled. He got me a ring? Why didn't he say anything? I would have gotten him one. How, I'm not sure, I haven't been out of his sight since last night, but all the same. I watch as he opens the box he has been holding the whole time. He pulls out three chains.

"Darryn, I know you wanted to keep this marriage between us." My eyes shoot over to the judge and my cheeks heat up again, what that man must think about all of this. "Even as untraditional as all of this is, I couldn't let this one tradition go. So I bought us both rings and placed them on chains. This way we can wear them, but not in sight for everyone to question."

Bryce places my necklace around my neck as he repeats the vows the judge is reciting and then hands me the one meant for him. The bands are simple white gold bands, but the meaning behind them moves me to tears. I don't try to stop them from falling as I repeat my vows and place the thicker chain around his neck.

I look down at his hand and see the third necklace. A much smaller chain with a little silver heart.

"Judge, if you don't mind, before we continue." Bryce points over at Kendall who Karen is holding.

"Of course." The judge smiles at Bryce.

Karen puts Kendall down and when Bryce bends down, Kendall walks over to him. "Kendall, I promise to protect you and your mommy with my life and to cherish you both." He spoke to her like a little adult, as though she is understanding it all. She may not be but I am fully understanding it.

Kendall looks down at the little necklace and smiles. "Mine?" She looks up at Bryce.

"Yes, little one, yours. Now and forever," Bryce answers, not only to her, but to me as well. His eyes don't leave mine as he speaks to her.

I have already admitted to myself that I am falling in love with Bryce, but if I had any doubts about it, this scene I am watching right now would have sealed the deal.

"I pronounce you man and wife, you may kiss your bride." The judge finishes the ceremony.

Bryce places his hands on each side of my face and claims my lips. It is soft, one of those kisses that make you want to curl up against him and stay forever. One that says I will be safe at any cost to him. Guilt washes through me once again. He is putting his life and his family's lives in danger for me. What have I just agreed to do? This is so selfish of me to do to Bryce, he should be out living his life, finding someone who could give him a normal family, not babysitting me and my daughter. Our kiss ends and I bury my face into his chest. Yes, I am crying. There is no way I'm ever going to be able to pay him back for all of this.

"Congratulations to the both of you," the judge says.

I feel Bryce extend his arm out to shake the judge's hand. "Thank you, sir." He starts rubbing my back, trying to sooth me.

I need to snap out of this. It happened, we are married. I need from this point on to make sure nothing happens to this family and to make sure Bryce doesn't regret all of this. When the time comes, no matter what my heart is feeling, I will let him go.

. . .

WALKING OUT OF THE BUILDING, the sun is setting. What a day. Bryce is carrying Kendall with one arm and has my hand with his free one. I look up and notice the smile on his face. Anyone passing by would think he is a happy groom who just attached himself to the woman of his dreams.

"So why don't you let us take Kendall for the night? You guys can go out to a nice dinner, spend a little down time before getting back to the real world tomorrow," Karen suggests.

"What do you say, Darryn?" Bryce looks down at me, giving me a slight nod saying he thinks it sounds like a good idea.

"I don't know, I have never been away from her overnight, plus I didn't bring anything extra for her."

"Don't be upset, Darryn, but today Kendall and I did a little shopping." Karen holds her arms out and Kendall goes right to her.

"Trust me when I say, she won't be needing extra clothes when she is at our house," Steven adds, rolling his eyes.

"All right, all right. I went a little crazy, but we had fun, didn't we?" Karen tickles Kendall's tummy and she giggles, then wraps her arms around Karen's neck in a tight hug.

"Do you want to stay with Grandma Karen tonight?" I ask her.

Karen's head swings toward me, tears shining in her eyes. "I hope you don't mind?" I ask.

The smile on her face answers for her. "No, of course not, I'm honored you even suggested it. So does this mean we can have a sleepover tonight?"

I look up at Bryce, he nods his head. "It will be all right."

"All right, we can try it," I agree, but my stomach is in knots. Today has been a whirlwind of changes.

CHAPTER
Eighteen

BRYCE

"SO DO you have any preferences on what you would like for dinner?" I ask, needing to break the silence in the car.

I know her head must be spinning. If I am being honest with myself, mine is a little as well. We just got married. Strange how all day I was fine, sure a little nervous, but that was expected. Right now, driving in silence, it all seems to settle in. Darryn just sits there, looking out the passenger window, her elbow on the door's arm rest, her chin resting in her hand. My nerves probably aren't from realizing I'm a married man now, but more from wondering what is going through her mind.

Her shoulders shrug and she takes a deep breath. She doesn't face me, but she does turn her head to look out the front windshield. "I know your mom took Kendall so we can have a nice dinner and all, but really, Bryce, I'm not expecting anything special. We can just grab something fast on the way to your house."

I want to pull over and shake her. I'm pretty sure that wouldn't do any good. She looks defeated and that is bothering me. I know this isn't the ideal way for her to handle things, marrying a man she didn't know that well in order to be protected from her psychotic ex. There is a small part of me hoping that when this is all over, she will want to stay with me, but watching her right now is not giving me much hope of her wanting to stay. Just the thought of her leaving feels like someone punched me in the chest. I need to use this time to convince her that my feelings are more than just to protect her and Kendall. They both have my heart fully. Now I just need to figure out a way to make her see that.

I know the perfect place to eat. It is one of my favorite restaurants along the boardwalk. Turning into the parking lot, I notice the puzzled look on Darryn's face. "Look, we haven't had a real date, just the two of us yet. What more of a perfect time than our wedding day?"

Darryn just sits there for a moment looking out the front window. Her laughter shocks me when it bubbles out of her. Her head resting against the headrest of her seat, she turns and looks at me for the first time since we got into the car with a smile on her lips. "You can always make me smile, thank you."

"Well what are husbands for?" I grab her hand and kiss it. "Would you please honor me by joining me for dinner tonight, Darryn?"

"How is a girl supposed to say no to that?"

"I'm hoping that you can't say no."

"It seems that I have a very hard time telling you no, my husband."

It shocks me to hear her call me her husband, but I think it surprises her more to say it by the look in her eyes. She almost seems embarrassed. She tries pulling her hand away from mine, but I don't let go, I need her to stop wanting to pull away from me physically and mentally. I know the word was used to prove her point of saying yes when I asked her to marry me, but just hearing it out of her mouth catches us both by surprise I think. Personally, I like the way it sounds coming from her.

"Would my wife please join me for dinner tonight?" I ask again, hoping to help her feel a little more comfortable with her earlier choice of wording.

"I would love to." She squeezes my hand and it takes everything in me not to pull her over onto my lap and kiss her.

DINNER HAS GONE WELL but when Darryn asks me for the tenth time to check my phone to make sure my mom hasn't called, or looks at hers for the hundredth time, I am ready to throw them both on the tray of the next passing server.

"Darryn, I know this must be stressful for you, the first time away from Kendall, but trust me, she is in good hands. My mom has the largest collection of Disney movies you have ever seen. They are probably having a movie marathon, complete with popcorn and candy," I try to reassure her.

Darryn puts her phone down on the table, face up, so that she can't have any chance of missing a call from my mom. "I'm sorry."

"Don't apologize, just try and relax a little. By the way, when you called my mom Grandma Karen to Kendall today, you made her day." I remember the way my mom's eyes beamed when she heard her new title to Kendall. All she has talked about the last few years is when either of us were planning on settling down and giving her grandbabies to spoil. Now that she has one, there will be no holding back for her.

"Like you said earlier, a child can't have too many grandparents in their life. Kendall has none, so if she were to ever have one, I would want them to be as sweet as your mother."

"I'm going to warn you, there is going to be a lot of spoiling, just prepare and before you can argue about it, there is nothing any of us can do to stop it, so just let it happen. Trust me, we would be in a lot more trouble with the spoiling if Charliee knew about all of this, she loves children."

Darryn's smile drops and she looks down at her plate. "I'm sorry."

"For what?"

"I know this can't be easy to keep from your brother and sister." She is playing with her napkin and again, she won't look at me.

"I didn't tell Derrick about us getting married, but I did tell him you were moving into my place. He has a tendency to stop by a lot, so I figured I'd let him know you will be there. We have both agreed it would be better to keep Charliee out of everything. She is still home recovering and she needs to concentrate on that, not worry about all of us right now."

"Another thing I'm sorry about. Your family should only be concentrating on Charliee, not having to be pulled into my problems."

Reaching across the table, I take her hands in mine. "Darryn, stop, all right! We are all taking care of Charliee. I don't want to spend this evening with you worrying all night and me trying to convince you everything is going to work out. It's a nice night, why don't we go for a walk on the beach before we head home. Trust me, starting tomorrow there will be plenty of time to worry about everything and work out all the details; for tonight, let's just relax and enjoy the evening."

When she looks up at me, I see that she wants to argue with me and I'm ready for it, but instead she surprises me by taking a deep breath and just nods her head.

"Does that mean you are good with the walk on the beach?" I ask, hoping so because I have something in mind.

"Yes, that sounds nice."

I get the attention of our waiter and pay the bill. I take her hand as we leave the restaurant and lead her down to the water. There is still a chill in the air, which is nice because that means there aren't a lot of people down here. We walk a little distance and when no one is around that I can see, I stop and pull my phone out of my pocket.

"Is everything all right? Is your mom calling?" Darryn tries looking over at my phone's screen.

"Darryn, breathe, no one is calling me." I flip through my phone to find my music, and finding the song I want, I hit play.

"Every bride should be able to have a first dance on her wedding day." I hold my hand out to her as the song begins to play.

She doesn't move, she just stares down at my hand. "Come on, Darryn, dance with me."

Looking up at me, there is enough light from the moon that I can see the shine in her eyes from her tears. No longer waiting, I take her hand in mine, wrap my arm around her waist and pull her into me. She doesn't resist, but it does take a moment for her to move. Finally, her arms wrap up around my shoulders. I wrap my other arm around her waist, pulling her tight against me, and she surprises me when she rests her head against my chest. At that moment, I know I'm not going to be able to let her go when all of this was over.

CHAPTER
Nineteen

DARRYN

WHAT HAVE I done to deserve a guy like this in my life? Actually, this is more like a cruel joke being played on me. I'm being given this amazing guy only to have him be pulled away from me later. As soon as this is all over with Brett, Bryce will want a divorce and I will have to let him go. He pulls me closer into him when he wraps his other arm around my waist and I just want to melt into his chest. It's a little unnerving on how safe I feel when I'm in his arms. I don't feel the need to look over my shoulder, I don't have the feeling like someone is watching me. I don't really have any cares to be honest. Right now, all I want to do is get closer to Bryce.

"Are you all right?" Bryce's voice breaks through my daze.

I nod against his chest. "Yeah, I'm good. This is sweet of you."

Bryce pulls back to look down at me. The heat cools in my cheek instantly without his body against my face. "Well, your wedding day should be something you always remember."

I laugh, always remember! How could someone forget a day like today? "Bryce, I can promise you I will never forget today. I woke up this morning and agreed to marry a man I've only really known for a couple weeks. Someone I have only had one date with, someone who is protecting me against my crazed ex. Trust me, I will never forget today."

He reads me like a book, however I can never guess what is going through his mind. Like right now, he is staring at me like he really wants to say something, but what I have no clue. I can see he is debating with himself.

"Bryce, what is it, what's going through that mind of yours?"

I watch as his eyes change to that crystal color again. I know what that means, my whole body heats up in anticipation. There is a look of questioning in his eyes; he isn't going to make the first move, he doesn't want to push me. He is afraid of how I may react, too much too fast.

Pushing up onto my toes, I bring his head down to mine, our lips lightly brush against each other's. Bryce takes a deep breath.

"Please kiss me, Bryce." It comes out sounding like I am begging, but right now I don't care. I will be more than happy to beg this man to kiss me.

"Darryn, don't do anything you don't want to, I'm not expecting anything from you."

"Bryce, kiss me!" This time I demand it, bringing his lips back down to mine, not giving him the chance to try and talk me out of it.

I'm surprised when he groans and pulls me up tight against his chest again. Almost like he is afraid I will change my mind and pull away from him. How wrong he is. All I can think about is a way to get closer. The kiss is deep, when his tongue finds mine I hear myself moan. I want more of him, I want all of him, not just his lips. Sliding my hands under his shirt, my knees buckle when I feel his skin, warm and toned under my hands. Something snaps inside of me, I need this man and I want him now.

Pushing his shirt up, I'm shocked when he quickly pulls away from me and out of my reach. Instantly I realize what I was about to do. My cheeks instantly burn and I can't look up at him. What the hell is wrong with me? Here is a guy who is trying to protect me in any way that he can and here I am trying to strip him on a public beach. Grabbing my hand, he leads me off the beach and back toward the restaurant. I hadn't even noticed the group of teenagers until we passed them walking back. Now I'm mortified. Not only did I throw myself at him, but I caused a scene in public while doing it. No wonder he is pissed at me.

He hasn't said a word, he basically drags me along as he quickly makes our way back to his car. He opens my door, shutting it as I sit down in the passenger seat. I want to crawl in the back seat and hide, or jump out and run as far away from Bryce as I can get. Folding my hands into my lap, I curl myself into the door, looking only out the window, wishing I had the strength to just jump from the car.

Not a word is said all the way back to Bryce's house. Can I blame him? When we pull up to the house, I quickly get out of the car and run up to the front door. All I want to do is go to my room and hide. Turning the door knob, I swear under my breath. Damn it, it's locked. All I can do now is wait for Bryce.

Before I know it, he is by my side, quickly unlocking the door. He opens it and I push myself past him only to be stopped by him. Grabbing my arm, he stops me at the same time he slams the front door shut. Before I know what's happening, my back is against the door. Bryce's arms have me trapped, one on each side of my head, his body tightly against mine. His breathing is heavy; I can't look at him though.

"Look at me, Darryn."

All I can do is shake my head no. I can't look at him. I just want to go to my room and hide until Brett can be found and I can leave.

"Damn it, Darryn, look at me please."

My eyes fly up to his. This is a tone I haven't heard from Bryce. When our eyes meet, I'm surprised to find his eyes are crystal again. "I'm so sorry, Bryce, I don't know what came over me."

"I'm not sorry, Darryn, and I don't want you to be sorry. I want you, I'm not hiding that from you, but I'm not going to do that in a public place and in front of a bunch of teenagers. Tell me no, and I will let you go to bed right now. Tell me yes, and I'm taking you to my bed tonight, and I can't make you any promises that if I have you tonight, that I'll be able to not have you in my bed every night."

I don't know what to say. He isn't pissed at me. I can see that now in his eyes. He is giving me a choice, but along with that choice is a promise. Every night in Bryce's bed sounds very tempting, but it will make it all that much harder when I have to say goodbye. His lips are only inches away from mine. I can feel his chest rub against mine with every breath he takes. My brain is telling me to run and fast. My body is begging me to have this man. I'm so tired of always being cautious. Always doing the right thing hoping to fix all the mistakes I have made in the past. I don't want to think anymore; I want to live.

Looking up into his pleading eyes, I bring my hands up and under his shirt. His breath hitches the moment my hands touch his skin. Running my hands up his sides, over his chest, I bring the shirt up as I go. He pushes away from me and removes his shirt, letting it fall to the floor. Before I have a chance to enjoy the vision in front of me, one of Bryce's arms links around my waist pulling me tightly against him, his lips claiming mine with a hunger that's hard to deny, along with his hardness pressing into my pelvis. My center heats up instantly, begging for what he is offering. Before I know what's happening, he hooks an arm under my knees, picking me up without breaking our kiss. I know where we are headed and I find myself becoming nervous.

Feeling the softness of Bryce's bed sends a shock through me, so much so that I break our kiss.

"Are you all right? You can stop me, Darryn, I'm not going to force you into anything." Concern is etched in his eyes.

I know he will never force me, I have never feared Bryce. Can I do this and not fall for him more than I already have? I already know it's going to tear me apart when we have to part ways, if I add a physical relationship into the deal it may destroy me. Looking up into his eyes, I find myself melting. There is a need and want in those eyes. He wants me, maybe he won't want to end this. Just maybe we can make it work. I'm always having to look into the future. Worrying and having a plan for if Brett finds us. I can't live in the moment or let my guard down. Right now, I want to live in the moment. Not worry about what will happen tomorrow, just enjoy the now.

"I don't want you to stop, Bryce," I tell him before I can change my mind again and become the sensible person I usually have to be.

Please don't ask me again if I'm sure, I think to myself. I don't want to think any longer, the more I think about it the better the possibility I will chicken out and go to my own room tonight.

Bryce stares at me for a moment, I'm afraid he may be the one to pull away now. I hope my eyes aren't telling him how scared I am, but how much I want and need him as well. Hooking my hand around the back of his neck, I pull his lips back down to mine. He doesn't pull away, his lips start out tender. Running my fingers up into his hair, I deepen the kiss and am rewarded with a deep moan from him. At that point my mind clears from all doubt and my body takes over.

Bryce works us up so that I am now sitting in front of him, but never breaks our kiss. I feel his knuckles skim across my ribs as he pulls my shirt up and over my head, letting it drop to the floor, my bra quickly following. My hands travel down to the waist of his pants. Unbuttoning them, I can feel his hardness begging to be released from the tight denim. I slip my hands into the backside, under his boxer briefs, and push them all down over his legs.

Bryce steps out of his pants and before I can sit here for too long and enjoy the breathtaking man in front of me, he gently pushes me back against the bed. My hands on his chest, I move them down, exploring the many muscles running along his chest and stomach. Bryce's lips start on my neck, placing small kisses as he moves down my throat to the top mound of one of my breasts. I can feel my nipple tighten with want. He trails small kisses from one breast, to the valley in between my breasts to the top of the other, and then all around the nipple, taking care not to touch the nipple begging to be touched. I dig my nails into his backside and arch my back, hoping he will end the torturous teasing. I can feel the moisture and heat from my center and I am yet to feel his naked body against mine. It's all part of his slow tease he is torturing me with right now. I want to beg him, but part of me wants him to continue. It's a very confusing feeling, one that only drives the need that much more.

His lips move down over my ribs and down my stomach to the waist of my pants. It takes everything in me not to push him away and strip the rest of my own clothes off and then push him back down onto the bed. His tongue lightly skims over my skin from one hip bone to the other, my hips thrust up on their own, begging. When he pulls back, I almost scream out, no!

His eyes never leave mine as his hands go to work on unbuttoning my jeans. I know he is watching for any signs that I am changing my mind and want him to stop. He is still worried that I may not be ready or wanting this. No words I can say will convince him that I'm completely ready and having no doubts, so instead I'm going to have to show him.

Sitting up, I push him back a little and stand in front of him. I finish removing the rest of my clothes, stepping out of them, my eyes never leaving his. We both stand here for a moment, not a word spoken, eyes locked with each other. I need his touch; it's not a want, it's very much a need at this point. I'm going to drop to my knees and beg for his touch in second. Not being able to stand it any longer, I close the space between us and hear both of us moan the moment our bodies touch. Fire shoots through every vein in my body and slams into my core all at once. My lips find his in a hunger I have never experienced before. I want to climb up his body and wrap my legs around his hips. I can feel his hardness pressing against my stomach, my core is begging for it. I'm ready, I can feel how hot and wet I am.

I swear I hear a deep growl come from Bryce, but before I have any time to think about it, I'm picked up and we are both now on the bed, myself laying under Bryce. Something has changed, he is no longer holding back or being cautious. His hungry mouth finally takes one very hard nipple and he sucks hard. I almost lose myself right then. My core pulses with need. I arch my back and with my hands at the back of his head, press his head down, begging him to suck harder. His mouth moves from one breast to the other, I hold back the scream that threatens to escape.

Lost in a daze of need, I don't realize he has moved his way down my body until I feel his hot breath against my hot center. I shoot up off the bed, my eyes flying wide open. He just smiles up at me and his eyes never leave mine as I watch his tongue dart out to taste my very wet center. He moans, and I try to hold it together. My head falls back, my arms are shaking trying to hold me up. Bryce spreads my legs so that he can taste me deeper and I can't hold it in any longer, I fall back against the bed, my hands clutching the bed sheets and my body shaking uncontrollably with release. Before my head clears enough to think, I feel Bryce quickly bring himself back up, his lips take mine and he quickly enters me. I scream against his lips. I'm so tight and he is now filling me completely, I can already feel another release. How is that even possible? He pulls out and thrusts back in, I can feel myself convulse around him, pulling him deeper and deeper inside with each thrust. I wrap my legs around his waist, needing him even deeper. He quickens the pace and I'm not sure how I'm going to make it through this release that is building, I try to hold it back, but I think that just might make it more intense.

"Come on, Darryn, let go, I can't hold back much longer," his husky voice begs me and that is my undoing. My body explodes around him. I feel Bryce's body tense and his mouth crushes against mine as we share our release.

BRYCE IS STILL KISSING me gently as my body relaxes from what

I would say is the most intense sexual experience I have ever had. I didn't know sex could feel like that.

"Are you all right?" Bryce whispers in my ear.

I shiver from the feel of his warm breath in my ear. I feel that stirring in my core again. There is no way I can make it through another experience like the last one again tonight. My body obviously is thinking differently. Bryce is still inside of me, and every time he kisses the side of my neck and then up to my ear, his body moves against mine, and inside of me. I'm exhausted, but my body is very awake and alert. My hips begin to move with his, Bryce groans against my neck and it vibrates through my entire body.

"What are you doing to me, Darryn?"

What am I doing to him? I think I should be the one asking that question to him.

CHAPTER

Twenty

BRYCE

I FEEL Darryn's body starting to move with mine. I didn't intend to go for another round, but I am still hard inside of her. Even after a release like I just experienced with this amazing woman, I'm ready for another. I can't seem to get enough of her.

Earlier I told her if she came to bed with me tonight, I wouldn't be able to let her sleep in the other room afterwards. I knew if she said that was where she was staying, I would have put the white flag up and slept alone, but now after having her, I'm pretty sure I am going to do whatever is needed to make sure I have her in my bed every night. This just sealed the deal with me. I know I'm going to do what needs to be done to try and keep her from wanting to leave after we ended this thing with her ex. I'm in love with this woman, hands down, no questions asked, there are no doubts in my mind. Now you add the chemistry between us in the bedroom and it's a sealed deal as far as I'm concerned.

We both need to be up early in the morning for work. It's been an emotional and very busy couple of days, I know she needs her rest. I should let her get some sleep, but now with her body starting to sway with mine again, sleep is going to have to wait just a little longer. If it means being exhausted tomorrow at work because I spent the evening inside of this woman, then it will be completely worth it.

That's when I realize it, one of the reasons why I'm pretty sure this feels so much different and better, I used no protection! The realization feels like cold water being dumped on my entire body. What the hell has gotten into me?

"Bryce, what's wrong?" Darryn's voice sounds concerned.

How can I have been so negligent? I know how, it is this woman in my arms. I can't think of anything else other than being inside of her.

"Darryn, I forgot protection." I have never slept with a woman without protection, even if she told me she was covered.

Silence stretched throughout the room. I'm ready for her to push me away, but she hasn't moved.

"Darryn, I'm so sorry. That's not like me at all. I promise you I have never had unprotected sex, and I have a physical with work yearly. I'm clean."

Still nothing from her. I start to pull away from her, the silence from her I assume means she is completely pissed off and I can't blame her for being mad at me. She surprises me when her hands slide down to my backside, stopping me from pulling out of her.

"Bryce, don't put all the blame on yourself. I should have asked. I'm on the pill so we are covered in that sense. I just had my physical with work and everything came back clean."

I can't see her face in the dark room, but she doesn't sound mad. If I had any doubts, they are quickly dismissed when she pushes me over onto my back, now with her straddled on top of me, which pushes me even deeper inside of her. Sitting myself up, her legs wrap around my waist and her arms go around my shoulders. My hands travel down to her hips and I claim her lips. Sliding her body back just enough to where only the tip of my hardness is still inside her, I thrust deep back into her. Her legs tighten around my waist, her nails digging into my shoulder blades. It doesn't take long before we are both tightly holding onto the other in a release so intense, I swear I might have blacked out for a moment.

Sitting here for a moment, neither of us move. We just stay wrapped tightly around the other. Her body begins to relax against mine and her arms loosen around my neck, but her body stays pressed against mine, her head resting on my shoulder. After a moment, I can hear her even, soft breathing. Smiling, I realize she has fallen asleep. Carefully, I pull her arms from around my shoulders and maneuver us apart, not a very easy task from this position. Stretching out on the bed, I pull her down with me and instantly she snuggles up against my side, and tugs at my heart with the little sigh of contentment that releases from her lips. I have never had a woman sleep with me in my bed, but with Darryn it feels right. This is where she belongs, now all I have to do is convince her to stay.

"MAN, you look exhausted, but oddly very content, if that makes any sense." Derrick smirks over at me from the driver's side of our patrol car.

He is searching for information. It is killing him not knowing everything about the situation between Darryn and myself. If I'm being honest, it is killing me not being able to tell him everything. I want to tell him how amazing she is and her daughter, but that would start too many questions and I made a promise to Darryn.

I am exhausted, even though I think last night was the best sleep I have ever had. Sleeping next to Darryn was comforting. When the alarm went off this morning, she jumped out of bed, which made me jump out of bed. She ran into the room that she and Kendall have been sharing without even a word. I wanted to go after her and make her talk to me, but I decided to give her a little time instead. When I walked past the bedroom door to head to the kitchen for some coffee, I heard her talking in the room. I assumed she called my mom to check on Kendall. When she finally came out to the kitchen, she was dressed and ready for work. Our conversation this morning before we left the house consisted of her meeting me at the station after work, leaving her car there, and the two of us heading to my parents' house to pick up Kendall. She wouldn't even look me in the eyes, she just moved around the kitchen, pretending to be busy as we talked so that she wouldn't have to look at me. She did text me when she got to work this morning like I asked her to before she left.

"It's been crazy the last couple of days trying to help Darryn with this ex-boyfriend situation."

"Are you sure you haven't gotten too invested in this situation?" Derrick gives me that smirk, he isn't talking about the ex-boyfriend. He is fishing for information about the living situation between Darryn and myself.

"Why is it so hard for you to believe that I'm just trying to help her? Why does it have to be a sexual thing with you? Maybe that's you, but not me," I say, feeling a little guilty because after last night, it became a personal thing as well.

"Because, I was there every time you asked her out, and you just don't move a woman and her daughter into your house to protect them. You could have gone through the department and put them in a safe house or something. Instead, you have decided to play the hero and take care of all of it yourself. The only reason there is a report is because she ended up at the station the other night because she thought she was being followed. So, do you want to tell me what is really going on here?"

I need to give him something, he knows me too well and obviously I'm not fooling him. I should have known it wouldn't be that easy. If the situation was turned then I wouldn't believe him either.

"Honestly, our main focus right now is her ex. I'm not going to say I'm not still interested in her, but if you think I only moved her in for that reason you are wrong. I do care about her and her daughter, trust me, once you meet that little one you are a goner. After her telling me everything he has done to her, I just want to make sure nothing happens to either one of them. Everything kind of happened fast, but I don't regret any decisions that have been made."

Hopefully this is enough info for him to lay off the subject for a little while. I admitted to it being a little more than just a protection detail, that's what he wants to hear. He just wants me to admit that I like Darryn.

Derrick sits there staring at me, like he is trying to look into my head and see if there is more or something. "Well, at least you are admitting to it being a little more than just being the cop protecting the girl." He laughs at me.

"I see that you have Mom watching her little one?" Derrick asks next.

How did he know it was Kendall? I almost ask, but then remember the night Darryn's apartment was broken into, Derrick was there. "When did you go over there?"

"Last night after work, I stopped by for a minute. I walked in and she came running out of the living room when she heard my voice, but she was calling me Bryce. It took me a minute to figure out who she was at first, the day of the break in at their apartment had a lot going on, and then I remembered you telling me Mom was going to be watching her. She almost ran right into me but stopped right before she wrapped her arms around my legs and just stared up at me, like she knew I wasn't you.

"Smart girl."

My heart skips a little. Kendall may have been confused but she knew something was different, she sensed that Derrick wasn't me. There are adults who have known us our entire lives that can't figure out who is who.

"Ha-ha! Do you think having her with Mom and Dad is safe? I mean if there is someone following Darryn, and she goes to their house to pick up her daughter, what's to stop them from going back there later?

Don't get me wrong, she needs to be in a safe place, and Mom will do anything to keep that little one safe, but isn't that kind of bringing trouble to Mom and Dad?"

I know what Derrick is trying to say. It is something I thought about a lot actually. This is my choice to be involved as much as I am, and I'm possibly bringing danger to our parents.

"I have hopefully created a solution to that problem. Either I will go and pick up Kendall and drop her off, or if Darryn does go she isn't in her car, she is with me. Trust me, this whole situation has been very thoroughly thought out, I hope. It's complicated, I'll admit to that, and hopefully it's all over fast and we find this guy and put him away before anything gets to that."

"Bryce, I'm not trying to say you haven't thought of everything, I'm sure you have a pretty good plan in order, but something is always missed, or someone slips up. I don't want to sound like an ass and say Mom and Dad are more important than this little girl, but..."

I stop him, I know what he means. "Derrick, trust me, this is the last thing I wanted. I was talking to Mom and she offered."

"Come on, Bryce, you know if you tell Mom anyone is in trouble, especially if you are adding a child into the equation, she is going to jump in and offer to help. We have been through so much with this whole situation with Charliee and almost losing her, now we are going to add this to everything."

Derrick is getting mad. I really can't blame him. "Derrick, I have Darryn meeting me at the station and parking her car in the back behind the gates at night after work and then she leaves with me, we then go and pick up Kendall. My windows are tinted, you can't even see the passenger in my car. He has no idea who I am or if we have any kind of connection. Mom and Dad are going to be fine."

"Famous last words!"

The call over radio cuts our conversation short. Probably a good thing, any longer and I would have had to take the side of my new family against my brother, who has no idea I have a family now, and piss him off thinking I'm endangering my own family for a girl and her child. If he knew this guy was after his sister-in-law and niece, this conversation would be going in a completely different direction. Not that my brother doesn't care. He does and I know that, I understand what he is saying, it has run through my head a million times and I have done everything I can think of to make sure my parents never have any trouble.

We pull out onto the street, sirens blaring, on our way to a traffic accident. The drive there is in complete silence. Just before we reach the scene, I can't take it any longer.

"Derrick, I need your help finding this asshole."

"I may not agree with everything you have chosen to do, and I'll be honest with you, Bryce, I feel like you are keeping something from me and it bugs the hell out of me, but I would never not have your back. If you need me I'm here, you should never question that."

Before I can say anything back, we approach the accident and have to get to work. I've never questioned if my brother would help if I asked for it, but I have to admit it is nice to hear him say it.

CHAPTER
Twenty-One

Darryn

"ALL RIGHT, Tom, I can't take the silent treatment any longer. Talk to me."

All day, Tom has only answered the questions asked to him. I have gotten the silent treatment other than that.

"What would you like me to say, Darryn?"

"Right now I really don't care. Yell at me if it makes you feel better, just don't keep giving me the silent treatment, I can't take it."

I had called Tom and told him about Brett and everything that has happened, up to when he was following me the other day. Bryce asked me to. He wanted to make sure I was watched when he wasn't around.

"What do you want me to say?" he asks, his tone flat.

"Anything right now would work. I know you are upset, I'm just not sure about what part."

We have been driving around all day. Usually between calls, we stop, chat for a while and wait for the next call to come in. Today has been slow, which I'm not saying is a bad thing, but it has made for a lot of silent time and driving, basically in circles.

Finally, Tom pulls into a parking lot and throws the rig into park, then turns to me. "Not sure about what part? How about all of it, Darryn?"

"All of it?" I ask back.

"Hell yes, all of it. You are hiding from someone and I get that it's hard to trust people, but I would have thought by now you would have trusted us instead of thinking you needed to take this all on alone. Yet you go on a date one time with a guy and he knows everything, and before me might I add."

That's what this is all about? Tom is mad because Bryce knew about all of this before he did?

"Tom, he is a cop, he was there when my place got broken into."

I'm not about to tell him I called Bryce when I first found out someone had been in my place, that he wasn't even on duty that day. Tom may throw me out of the vehicle if I tell him that part.

"Darryn, it's not just that, you are staying with a guy you barely know. Don't get me wrong, Bryce is a great guy, I've known him and his brother for a while now. I know you are safe there with him and knowing him like I do, he will take care of you and Kendall…"

"Wait, Tom, are you mad because I didn't call and ask to stay with you guys?" I interrupt him when I figure out what this is all about finally.

"Darryn, you aren't getting it. It's not just one thing, it's the whole thing. We have been partners now for a while, I thought we had a friendship where you trusted us, that's all."

"Tom, you and Heather are the first friends I have had in years. All my partners before you I barely talked to while we were working, let alone went to their house for dinner. I lost all my friends throughout the time I was with Brett. By the time I finally found enough nerve to leave him,

I had no friends left, and I had no family even before him. My situation isn't something I brag to people about. Trust me, there were a couple times I thought about talking to you, you are very easy to open up to, but I didn't want you looking at me differently."

"What do you mean by that?"

"I didn't want you to know the weak side of me. I'm not proud of that time in my life. Allowing myself to be in that kind of relationship. To be honest, if I wouldn't have gotten pregnant with Kendall I may never have left, so basically she saved my life."

Tom starts to say something, but I stop him. I don't need him to sit here and tell me that I'm not weak, I left, that makes me a strong person and all of that. Like Bryce, Tom would never understand because he has never had to live it.

"Tom, you have a home, with a beautiful family. I didn't want to bring all of this to you guys. I could never do anything that I thought might endanger your family because of my mistakes and this mistake may very well follow me home one day, literally!"

Tom just sits there staring at me for a moment. I study him as he thinks about everything I have just told him, that's when I see the look I dread, he feels sorry for me.

"Please, Tom, don't look at me that way."

"What way is that?"

"Sorry for me."

"It's not what you are thinking, Darryn. You think I'm feeling sorry for you because of what you went through and for having no one in your life to turn to. That's not it at all. I feel sorry for you because you don't see what an amazing person you are. How strong you are. It may have taken you getting pregnant to leave, but you did it, regardless of the circumstances that led up to it. You had no one to help you once you did leave. You found a safe spot for your baby and yourself, and you found a way to support the both of you starting with nothing. You have made a home for yourself and Kendall. She is happy and healthy.

That's not the actions of a weak person, Darryn. You have far more strength than a lot of people, you just refuse to see it."

I feel a tear roll down my cheek and I quickly wipe it away. These last couple of days have been an emotional roller coaster and it is exhausting, but for the first time in a very long time something feels different. My chest used to feel heavy, like a ton of bricks were just sitting there. One by one these last couple of days it feels like those bricks are being taken off, my chest feels lighter. I know this is all far from over, it won't be over until Brett can no longer hurt either one of us, but I don't have to do it alone anymore.

"You need to realize what an amazing person you are, Darryn, and if it's the last thing I do, you will start to see it."

"Thank you, Tom, for everything you and Heather have done for us. I am so sorry."

"Bryce just better not be making you sleep on the couch."

My smile fades, sleeping on the couch, no. *He should be making me sleep in my own bed though,* I think to myself, thinking back to last night. Last night was amazing. I have never experienced anything like I did last night with Bryce.

"Why are your cheeks turning red, Darryn? What is going on over there between the two of you?"

I quickly turn my face away from Tom and look out the side window. Now if that doesn't look guilty, I don't know how more obvious I could be.

"Bryce has given us his spare bedroom to use."

"Are you using the spare bedroom?" Tom asks accusingly.

"Yes, sleeping with a two-year-old is a ton of fun, so if I come to work grumpy you now know why." I look back at him, hoping that with a little eye contact it will convince him everything is only a friend's relationship status with Bryce and I and we can change the direction of this conversation.

He isn't buying it, it is written all over that smug smile he is giving me. "It's all right to like him, Darryn."

Like him, I'm married to him! I want to yell out. The ring hanging against my chest feels like it is burning me.

"Sorry, I didn't mean to tease you. However, it is all right to like the guy. You are allowed to be happy, Darryn. Our shift is almost over, so before we head back, just one last thing and I will let it drop. No more secrets, from this point on you let me know what's going on. Promise?"

I just nod my head. There already is another secret, one that when he does find out, I'm sure there will be no end to his wrath when that all comes out in the open.

"All right, well let's get back, and then I'm going to follow you to the station."

Follow me to the station, when did that happen? I never asked him to do that.

"Bryce called me this morning," he answers my question before I can ask it. "Don't even try and argue with me about it, I will be following you each day after work to the station."

I just take a deep breath and sit back in my seat. I know they all think they are doing their best to help me, but in the midst of helping me they are all putting their families in danger and I'm not feeling real good about that.

WHEN I ARRIVE at the station, Bryce is waiting for me. My face instantly heats up the second he looks at me and smiles. We haven't talked about last night. This morning when his alarm went off, I jumped out of the bed and basically ran to the spare room. I was waiting for him to come knock on the door, or catch me in the hallway coming out of the bathroom and insist that we talk, but he didn't. I got ready and sat in the room for a little while trying to dodge the whole thing, but realized I would have to eventually leave to go to work, and I really wanted some coffee before we left. Taking a deep breath, I entered the kitchen, but to my surprise he never brought it up. He was all calm and cool leaning up against the counter, drinking coffee and looking at his phone. He said good morning and then asked if I was ready to go. I was relieved and disappointed all at the same time. What had I expected? I jumped out of bed and ran out like the room was on fire.

Walking up to him, he looks over my shoulder and stretches out his hand. Crap, I forgot Tom followed me into the station. I told him I was fine, but he insisted.

"Thanks, Tom," Bryce said as he shook his hand.

"No problem. I will meet you guys here tomorrow morning and make sure she gets to work," Tom offers.

"That's not necessary…" I start but am cut off by Bryce.

"I appreciate that, but we have a car that is going to follow a little ways back, we are hoping to catch him following her at some point," Bryce explains.

I, on the other hand, am starting to get a little pissed. They are both talking like I'm not even standing in front of them.

"Hello," I say to Bryce, who hasn't said a word to me yet. Why that bothered me so much, I'm not sure.

Tom laughs behind me. "Let me know if you need anything. See you tomorrow, Darryn." Then he walks away.

Bryce looks down at me with an amused look on his face. "Were you feeling a little left out?" he asks.

"You guys were talking like I wasn't even standing here. When were you going to tell me you were going to have me followed?"

"Darryn, you haven't said more than a couple of words to me since last night. You shot out of bed so fast this morning, you seemed like you couldn't get away from me fast enough."

I look around to see who is close enough to be able to hear our conversation. No one is around, I take a deep breath. I don't think the whole station needs to know what is going on between the two of us, where Bryce, on the other hand, doesn't seem to care who may be around to hear our conversation.

"Can we please go now? I would rather not talk about this here, plus I've missed Kendall and I'm ready to go pick her up now."

Bryce points down the hall toward the back of the station. "Lead the way."

THE DRIVE over to Bryce's parents' house is quiet. Bryce asks how my day was, if I had talked more to Tom, but nothing about last night. He isn't going to bring it up, he is waiting for me to say something. Once we walk into the front door to pick up Kendall, she comes running down the hall and into Bryce's arms. My heart stops for a moment. I have always been her world, the one she ran to, now everything is about Bryce and I'm not quite sure how I feel about that. I'm happy she likes Bryce, it definitely makes our living arrangement easier, but I'm not used to sharing her attention.

Once home, Bryce goes out and throws a few hamburgers on the grill, I give Kendall a bath, and we eat dinner. Bryce and Kendall are in full conversation of her overnight stay with Grandma Karen and Grandpa Steve. It does warm my heart to hear her talking about how much fun she had. How Karen and Steve have accepted her with open arms. Bedtime story doesn't last long for her. I don't think I make it off page three before she is sound asleep. I just keep reading the story out loud.

Kendall has her bed here now, I am going to just use the bed Bryce already had in here. My bed went into storage. I should go out and talk to Bryce, I just don't know what to say. We have nothing else to talk about except the events of last night, and I'm not sure what we need to talk about. I look over at the bed I will be using and it looks empty, lonely. Last night was one of the best night's sleep I have had in a very long time. Being with Bryce last night was amazing all around. I have never experienced feelings like I had last night, but the best part wasn't the sex, which was amazing, it was the sleeping. I felt safe. I didn't feel like I had to be on alert. I hate to admit it but I don't want to sleep alone tonight, I want to be in Bryce's arms again.

I can't sit here all night. It is still pretty early. I can hear the television on in the front room. If I sit here all night Bryce will know I'm avoiding him, I just don't want him thinking it's for the reason he will believe it's for. I'm pretty sure he is thinking I regret last night. I want to slap myself, what the hell is wrong with me? How old am I? I'm an adult and I need to start acting like one. We need to talk about this, we can't live under the same roof and act like last night didn't happen.

Tucking Kendall in, I figure it's time to go out and face Bryce. Taking a deep breath, I walk out of our room and down the hall. I find Bryce sitting on the couch, a beer in hand, his socked feet propped up on the coffee table, watching television.

"I brought you a beer as well, but it may be a little warm now." He points at a beer sitting on the table.

I understand his meaning. I have been in the room for a while, but I didn't realize how long until I look at the clock hanging on the wall, it is almost ten.

"Yeah! Um, sorry about that, I fell asleep for a moment as well," I lied. When I look over at him, I can see he knows I'm lying.

I want to run back to the room, why is this so hard to talk to him about? I watch as Bryce picks up the remote control and turns off the show he is watching.

He pats the couch cushion next to him. "Darryn, we need to talk."

Nodding, I walk over and sit down, but not next to him on the couch. I take the chair.

"Darryn, I've tried to wait for you to talk to me, but that isn't working, so I'm going to bring up last night. We need to talk about it."

Again, I just nod. How does one even start a conversation of this kind of subject?

"Do you regret it?" he asks point blank.

I guess that's how you start this kind of conversation, just go straight to the point. Now how to answer the question. I can tell him yes, I regret it and then he will probably tell me that he is sorry and swear it will never happen again, and knowing Bryce, it won't happen again. And that's what I fear if I'm being honest with myself. I think my fear is that I'm already starting to have feelings for him, and repeats of last night are only going to grow those feelings, and then how do I leave him when that time comes without destroying my heart?

Bryce stands up from the couch and crouches down in front of me. "Darryn, please talk to me."

I can't lie to him. "I don't regret last night," I finally admit, my voice so low I'm not sure if he even hears me.

"Why did you run out of the room this morning?"

I shrug. It isn't something I can answer because I don't know the answer myself.

"Darryn, if we want this to work, I need you to be able to talk to me."

Have this work? What does he mean, is he talking about this so-called marriage? That brings my eyes up to his. For a moment I would have sworn I read something in his eyes, maybe this is a little more than just a protection detail for him.

"What do you want me to tell you, Bryce? I was scared and confused. Everything happened so fast yesterday, and when that alarm went off this morning I realized it wasn't all a dream and it terrified me for a moment."

"Darryn, I understand everything was a whirlwind yesterday, but if I pressured you at any point last night, I'm sorry." Bryce stands up and backs away from me.

He is misunderstanding what I am saying. How do I explain it without telling him how I feel? Before I can try and explain myself, he walks away and heads down the hall to his room. He just walked away from this. He didn't give me a chance to explain. I hear a door close and my heart sinks. I can't sit here and let him think he pressured me into anything last night, that isn't fair to him, and I can't keep running from things.

Walking down the hall, I knock on his bedroom door. "Bryce, can we talk?"

He doesn't respond, so I knock again. "Bryce, please talk to me."

Still nothing! I'm not going to let him go to bed thinking he did something wrong last night. Opening the door, I realize he isn't in here. The shower is on in the bathroom and my whole body heats instantly, thinking of him naked and wet. Flashes of last night run through my head and an ache starts in my core. Before I can talk myself out of something I hope I don't regret, I quickly undress, leaving my clothes in a pile on the floor. I take a deep breath and open the bathroom door. Steam rushes out, hitting me in the face. I can see the silhouette of him in the shower, and my fear is now completely gone and replaced by a need for him. All I can think about now is having his wet body pressed to mine, that's what gets my feet to move.

Opening the shower door, Bryce doesn't turn around. He has his hands braced against the wall and his head hanging down, water cascading over his head. Stepping inside, I shut the door and wrap my arms around his waist, pressing my front up against his back. I feel his body tense, but he doesn't move or say a word.

Ducking under one of his arms, I bring myself to stand in front of him. His arms drop away and his head comes up, but he doesn't touch me. He isn't even looking at me, he is looking up over my head. Bringing my hand up to the back of his head, I force him to look me in the eye and that's when I see it…fear.

"I'm sorry, Bryce, you misunderstood me, or maybe I was just not explaining it right." I realize I can't let him go on thinking he did something wrong last night, or pressured me into something I wasn't ready and willing for, not with him knowing my past.

The questioning look is all I get. He is only touching me because I have pressed my body against his, which he is affected by, I can feel the proof against my belly. But other than that, nothing.

"I'm not upset by what happened last night with you. I wanted it just as much as you did and it was great, that's not what scared me this morning. Being held by you all night and waking up to you this morning scared the hell out of me not because of what we did leading up to it, but coming to realize what was happening to me after everything."

"What does that even mean, Darryn?" Finally, he speaks!

I can't back down from this now, if he decides after this that we need to figure out different living arrangements for Kendall and I then so be it. "Bryce, I'm starting to have feelings for you and that is scaring the hell out of me." There, it is out and in the open now.

Nothing in his facial features change, he just stands there staring down at me while water runs over the both of us. I can't tell what he is thinking, if he is mad, relieved, confused, nothing. I can't breathe and I feel the tears start to burn the back of my eyes. Looking down at his chest, I try to catch my breath, push back the tears and when I think I have myself collected, I look back up at him and that's when I see it. His eyes are changing color, to that crystal, almost clear green they get right before he is going to kiss me, and I act before I can think twice.

My hands go up and into his wet hair and I press his head down to mine, taking his lips in a demanding kiss. His arms instantly go around my waist pressing us together, it isn't enough for me though. I need him inside of me, I ache for it.

Bryce presses me up against the shower wall, lifting me up, his lips devouring mine. I wrap my legs around his waist, now feeling his hardness against my center.

"I need you inside of me, Bryce, please," I beg, not wanting to wait any longer.

Bryce moves away just enough to get his hand between us, placing himself just inside of me. I can't wait any longer so I press myself down onto him, feeling every inch of him slide deep inside. We both moan and with his hands circling my waist on both sides, he sets the rhythm. The cool shower tiles pressed against my back and with Bryce's hot, wet body moving against my front, and his hardness filling me completely on the inside, it is more than I can take. My release comes fast and hard, causing me to scream out his name against his lips. My body tightens around him, he thrusts one last time into me hard and I feel his body release. He bites into my lower lip which just heightens my release. His lips move down to my neck and he mumbles something but I can't hear what it is.

Bryce slowly pulls himself out of me and I want to scream no. I'm not ready to have this feeling end. Sitting me down on my feet, Bryce reaches around and turns off the water.

"The water is getting cold and I'm not done with you yet." He grabs my hand and leads me out of the shower.

I hadn't even noticed the cold water, my body is on fire at the moment, and it doesn't help that he just told me he isn't finished yet. We don't even dry off, he leads me out to the bedroom and over to his bed. Turning me around, he pushes me down onto the cool sheets, taking my breath away feeling their coolness against my skin. Bryce pushes my shoulders back so that I am now laying back on the bed, my leg hanging over the side. I watch as he kneels down on the ground in front of me. His eyes never leave mine, I have myself braced by my elbows behind me. With his hands on my knees, he separates my legs. He kisses the inside of one thigh and with those clear green eyes looking straight at me, his tongue dips into my now very hot and wet core. My arms are shaking so bad, they won't hold me any longer. I fall back against the bed, my hands going into Bryce's hair, pressing him closer into me. I can feel another release coming, but I don't want to give into it just yet.

"Bryce, please," I beg, not knowing what for as I push him away from me. All I know is I don't want this to end that fast.

He crawls up, his body rubbing in all the right ways against mine, and his lips claim one nipple. My hand traces down his side and finds his hardness between us. I slowly stroke down and then up, with each stroke he sucks that much harder on my nipple. I want to scream, but hold it in. I run my finger over his tip, feeling the wetness starting to bead. He is close.

His lips suck hard one last time on my nipple and then move up to my lips. "I need to be inside you again, Darryn, I can't seem to get enough of you."

Before I can respond, or maybe I should say beg him to take me, he stands up and flips me over, my front side now on the mattress and my feet on the floor. His hand caresses my backside for a moment, I wiggle myself against him and I hear him moan. I spread my legs just a little further apart and arch my back, begging him to take me now.

He enters me with one thrust, and my breath rushes out of me. With his hands on my hips, I feel him pull almost all the way out and then thrust back in with a rush. His hand snakes around and one finger slides inside my folds and that is when I lose everything. He thrusts deep inside of me one last time, and I bury my face into the mattress to muffle my scream as we find our release together. It is so intense my legs give out and all I can do is lay face down on the bed, Bryce's body covering me up and his heavy breath in my ear.

CHAPTER
Twenty~Two

BRYCE

I'M NOT sure of what just happened. One minute I'm taking a shower feeling like an asshole and swearing to never touch Darryn again, and the next I have her pinned up against the shower wall. As if that isn't enough, I think I basically dragged her out of the bathroom, pushed her down onto my bed and enjoyed yet another amazing experience with this amazing woman. Now here we are in my bed, naked, Darryn draped half across me, her head resting on my chest and I can't think of too much that would make me get up from this spot. On the other side of it, we do need to talk.

"Are you awake?" I ask.

"Hmmm," is all the answer I get back from her.

"Darryn, I know you're tired, but I don't want the same reaction out of you tomorrow morning when the alarm clock goes off as you had this morning, we need to talk about this."

She takes a deep breath and I wait. After a moment, she re-adjusts her arms so that they are crossed over my chest and she rests her chin on her hands, looking up at me. "I'm sorry about this morning, Bryce. I'm sorry about the whole day; however, I'm not sorry about last night or tonight." She gives me a sleepy smile.

"I guess my question is, are we going to have a repeat in the morning like today?"

"Tonight when you asked me why I ran out of the room this morning, my answer came out wrong. I was scared, yes, but not for the reasons you were thinking. Last night was great and I don't regret it, as well as what just happened." She takes a deep breath and then looks away from me.

"Hey, talk to me." I push a piece of hair off her forehead.

"Bryce, I'm starting to have feelings for you." She repeats what she told me earlier in the shower.

I'm not sure how to respond to her though. I'm happy she is opening up, but now I have to be careful on what I say. I love this woman and her daughter and there is nothing that would make me happier than to have her love me back, but that isn't what she is saying right now. She is admitting to having some feelings for me, it's not a confession of love, but it's a start and it gives me a little hope that this may all work out.

"And because you are starting to have these feelings is why you ran out of bed this morning?" I decide to tread slow on this subject, basically my plan is to follow her lead.

She nods her head, looking a little shy, which I find to be cute. "Look, Darryn, if we are being honest here, I will have to admit that you and Kendall have started to burrow your ways into my heart as well, but I would hope that you know that. I just married you! Do you think I offer that to all the women I'm trying to protect from their crazy ex-boyfriends?"

"How many woman have you had to protect from their ex-boyfriends?" she asks.

"Well, I will say you aren't the first, but you are the first that I have offered to move into my house and then marry the next day." I smile down at her.

"I guess that answers my next question of if I was going to have to watch my back for any crazy exes of yours."

"Look, I want you to be able to talk to me, Darryn, to be honest with me when something isn't feeling right to you. I don't want you to run and hide from me, that's not going to work too well."

Crawling her way up my body, Darryn is now eye to eye with me. "I promise and again, I'm sorry for today."

Reaching up, I bury my fingers into her hair at the back of her head and bring her lips down to mine. "Can I be honest about one other thing?" I ask before taking her lips with mine.

She nods, our lips brushing against each other's.

"I kind of like sharing my bed with you. How do you feel about just agreeing on it now so that way there is no more confusion about it in the future? Also, I was going to offer this before but didn't want you freaking out on me, but I have a whole other closet that is empty next to mine. It's yours if you want to put your clothes in there instead of trying to find room for both yours and Kendall's clothes in the spare room closet."

"Wow, it sounds like you are asking me to move into your room." She smiles down at me.

"Well, you are my wife." I put my finger through the ring that is hanging from her neck and show it to her as a reminder.

"Then I have the rights as your wife to do this." She kisses me and rubs her body up and down against mine.

"Anytime you would like, no complaints from me."

. . .

IT'S amazing how time flies when you are having fun, right? Summer is here, and the last couple of months have been uneventful in the subject of Brett. Darryn keeps asking if she can drive herself to work and take Kendall back to daycare. She says she doesn't want to wear out my mother. I think my mom will have more issues with not being able to watch her. Tonight, we have decided to go to the carnival that is going on down at the beach just for a little fun and relaxation, we have both been very busy with work.

We are standing at one of the ball throwing games when I hear familiar voices coming up behind us. Turning around, I see my sister, Charliee, along with her best friend, Jayden, her boyfriend, Travis, and another guy who I have not met yet.

"Looks like my sister is here," I say over to Darryn as I watch the group approach us.

Darryn's hand goes to her chest, she is checking to see if her ring is tucked into her shirt. She does that all the time when we are around other people, she absolutely doesn't want people to know what is going on between the two of us. Every time she does it my heart skips a little. I know it's crazy and I know I promised her I wouldn't say anything to anyone, but it is killing me. I've never deliberately stayed away from my brother and sister as much as I have the last couple of months. Not that I'm trying to hide Darryn from them, but I know the more we are together, things may come out. It's hard enough working with Derrick and not having things slip around him. My sister is a lot more observant, she will know I am hiding something.

Charliee walks straight up to me and hugs me. "Hey, I didn't know you were coming tonight."

I don't get a chance to say anything in return, Charliee's attention goes straight to Darryn. "Hi, I'm Charliee, Bryce's sister."

They shake hands. "I'm Darryn and this is my daughter, Kendall."

Charliee glances at me quickly with a little smirk before she bends down and says hello to Kendall who is sitting in her stroller.

Well, everyone is here, I figure I better make the introductions. "That's Travis, Charliee's boyfriend. That's Jayden, her best friend." I look over at the other guy and stop, I have no clue who he is.

"I'm Cameron." He extends his hand out to me and then to Darryn.

I'm going to assume this is Jayden's boyfriend.

It's nice to meet you guys." Darryn smiles at them all.

"So how did you guys meet?" My sister goes straight into the questions.

Darryn looks over at me, giving me an uncertain look. I'm not sure if it's because she doesn't want to tell Charliee how we met, or because she isn't sure how much to tell her.

I clear my throat. "We actually met the night of the explosion. Darryn was the paramedic who took care of you, Charliee."

The light in my sister's eyes fades for a moment. She has been doing great. She was able to go back to work teaching at the deaf school for the last month or so of the school year, and now that she is dating Travis, who I believe is moving in with her, Derrick and I have been needed a lot less. Which I have mixed feelings about. Derrick and I are used to having her back, checking up on her. Even though she swears she is good and she does have Levi, her hearing dog, we always worry about her. Now she doesn't need us and that is hard to stand aside and swallow as well. However, with everything going on with Darryn right now, it is working out for me.

Charliee quickly recovers her smile. "Well then, I guess I should be thanking you." She is still knelt down in front of Kendall and her eyes redirect back to her, she is hiding.

"Not at all. I'm just happy to know you have fully recovered."

Charliee smiles up at us once more. "Everyone here had a part in that."

Charliee goes to stand back up and Levi lunges forward, knocking Charliee off balance and she falls forward, almost landing in Kendall's lap. She manages to redirect herself to fall to the side of the stroller, not into it.

Charliee pulls back tight on Levi's leash. "Levi, what's your problem? Sit!"

Travis helps Charliee up. I look over at Levi. He isn't pulling any longer, I think he has realized what he just did, but his ears are up and alert, and there is a low growl coming from him. "What's wrong with him? He never acts like this," I ask as I look in the direction Levi is looking.

My senses are on alert now. Levi is very well trained, he would never lunge at someone, or chance injuring Charliee, or try and leave her. "What's wrong with him, he never acts like this?"

Levi starts to pull again. Travis takes the leash from Charliee's hand and pulls back on Levi. "He did this earlier, but I just brushed it off thinking something spooked him," Travis explains, but he too is now looking around, more alert.

"Oh my God." Charliee's voice brings my attention back to her. She is ghost white and shaking.

Jayden is the first to ask, "Charliee, what's wrong?"

She doesn't answer, but starts to shake more violently. Travis shoves Levi's leash into my hands as his attention goes to Charliee.

"Charliee, talk to us." Travis is now standing right in front of her.

Charliee points over in the direction of one of the little kids' rides. "That's the guy from the restaurant, the one who ran into me outside. He is standing there in the blue jeans and plaid a shirt, and he's wearing a backpack."

We all follow the direction Charliee is pointing and Levi begins to bark now. I can barely hold him back. The man Charliee pointed out turns around, I'm sure Levi's barking is getting his attention. The moment he realizes it is directed at him and we are all staring at him, he takes off running.

I shove Levi's leash into Jayden's hand. "Call 911, let them know what's going on. You guys get out of here now," I yell back as I take off in the direction the guy ran.

I can see the back of the guy but there are so many people around and he keeps weaving in and out of my sight. The man has a backpack, that alone is putting me on high alert. If this is the man, he has already set off two bombs—one at the restaurant where Charliee was involved and one in a movie theater. If he sets one off here, the number of causalities would be way too great, and my family is still here.

I pass a security guard and pull out my badge. "I'm a police officer, we have a possible bomb situation. Please start getting this place cleared out and call it in, tell them Bryce Brooksman had you call and is in pursuit."

I shoot everything off at the man and hope he takes me seriously. I don't even wait to see if he is following my directions, I don't want to lose the man. I turn the corner I swear I saw him go around and swear out loud. I am met with a rush of people being evacuated from the area.

Stopping, I look around. This would be a perfect chance for him to blend in and get himself out.

"Bryce, where did he go?" Travis comes up behind me, Cameron next to him.

"Where's the girls?" I ask, now concerned no one is with them.

"Don't worry, they are on their way out to the parking lot all together," Travis explains.

"Where is the asshole?" Cameron asks, looking around at all the people rushing around us.

"I don't know, I've lost him in the crowd," I answer back, looking around.

"What do you mean you lost him? He got away? Are you kidding me?!" Cameron yells next to me, taking me by surprise a little.

I look over at him with a questioning look. I get it, I want the man caught as well, but why is he getting so mad at me? "Hey, they are evacuating everyone, I lost him in the crowd." I have no idea why I'm defending myself to this guy.

Travis puts a hand on my shoulder. "Bryce, it's all right, he doesn't mean it that way. You see, Cameron's parents were both killed in the bombing that Charliee was involved in."

"Shit." What are the odds of that? I'm in shock, this guy probably wants this crazy guy worse than I do. "I'm sorry, man."

"No, I'm sorry, I shouldn't have snapped at you. Let's just look for him." Cameron won't look at me and before I can respond with something back, he takes off into the crowd.

This is going to be like looking for "a needle in a haystack" as they say. I didn't even get a good look at the man's face, by now he could have easily taken off his shirt, ditched the backpack and is blending in with the crowd enough to get out of the area. This is pretty much a useless search, but I will look until everyone has cleared and we have checked all areas.

CHAPTER
Twenty~Three

DARRYN

I DECIDE to bring Kendall back home instead of sitting in the parking lot with Charliee and Jayden. If a bomb did go off, I didn't want her anywhere near the area. Luckily I had the car keys in my purse.

It's a little strange, I have been asking Bryce for weeks now if I can drive my own car to work, put Kendall back in daycare, get back to a little bit of a normal life, but right now I'm not sure if it's from the events of tonight or what, but I am on edge. I feel like I need to keep a solid eye on my rear-view mirror to make sure no one is following us. I think I'm just paranoid, but I hate the feeling all the same. Once we pull into the driveway, I grab Kendall out of the car quickly and basically run up to the front door. My hands are shaking so bad I drop the keys trying to unlock the door.

"Mommy, okay?" Kendall asks as I bend over to pick them up.

I take a deep breath and tell myself to calm down, Kendall is starting to pick up on my uneasiness and I don't want that. "Yes, honey, Mommy is fine." I smile at her.

Walking inside, I sit Kendall down and quickly lock the door. "Let's go put your pajamas on and Mommy will turn a movie on for you in your room."

I usually read her to sleep but tonight I am too on edge. I know if I put the movie on, it won't take long for her to fall asleep. Plus she will think it's a treat, that'll make me feel a little better about skipping out on our nightly routine.

LOOKING up at the clock for what feels like the thousandth time, it's almost midnight and I haven't heard anything from Bryce. I don't want to call him and bother him if they have the guy in custody, but I will feel so much better when he is home.

My phone buzzes next to me causing me to jump. Looking down at it, I see Bryce's name and pic on the screen. "Hello."

"Hey, can you unlock the door for me? Derrick is dropping me off now."

He sounds exhausted. I want to ask if they got the guy, but I don't. I'll wait until he gets into the house, or maybe tomorrow.

Getting up, I go and unlock the door, relief flooding through me when I open it and see Bryce getting out of Derrick's car. I want to run out and throw myself into his arms, but I keep myself at the front door. They talk for a moment, Bryce turns around and waves at me, then turns back to his brother. I know they are talking about me.

Finally, Bryce shuts the car door and starts for the front door. He looks tired and defeated. That can't be good. Even exhausted, if he would have caught the guy, I would expect to see some happiness in his eyes. His walk is even dragging.

He stops in front of me at the door but doesn't say anything. I have an urge to wrap my arms around him and just hug him. I find that I want to be in his arms just as much, pressed against his body knowing everything is all right.

Grabbing his hand, I pull him into the house and shut the door. Once it's locked, I wrap my arms around his waist and we both just stand here in the entry way of the house, just holding each other.

"I'm going to guess you guys didn't get the guy." I speak against his chest, breaking the silence between the two of us.

Bryce pulls away from me and I instantly feel empty. I follow him as he moves over to the couch and sits down. "No, we didn't get him. We are thinking he was able to use the crowd when the place was being evacuated to sneak out. To top it off, I found out tonight Cameron's parents were both killed in the same bombing that Charliee was involved in."

"Wow, really?" What are the odds of that happening?

"How is Kendall?"

"She's fine. Asleep. She went down pretty easy, I'm sure it helped that I let her go to sleep with a movie on."

Bryce looks over at me, he is searching for something. "Are you all right?"

"Of course, why are you asking?"

"You always read her to sleep. You get upset when my mom tells you she allowed her to go to bed watching a movie," he points out.

Shrugging, I look down at my hands.

"Darryn, talk to me, what's going through that beautiful mind of yours?"

I don't want to tell him about how jumpy I've been since he wasn't with us, but I find that I open up to him even if I don't want to. He usually figures it all out anyway so why try and hide it?

"I don't know, I think with everything that happened tonight I am just on edge."

"Did anything happen on the way home?" Concern etches his voice. Like he doesn't have enough to be worried about already.

"No, nothing happened. Like I said, I think it's just everything that happened tonight has my nerves on alert. I will say, you won't have to worry about me begging you to allow me to drive to work alone any longer, or to put Kendall back in daycare. My imagination tonight took care of all of that for you." I hate to admit it though.

Again, Bryce just studies me for a moment. "You aren't hiding anything, right, Darryn? You would tell me if something happened or if he tried to contact you, right?"

I am nodding as he is asking. "I have no reason to keep any of that from you, Bryce. I hope you know that. I know what you have given up to protect Kendall and myself. I may want some independence back, but not that way. Like I said, I'm not even going to fight you on that either anymore."

I look up at him and could have sworn I saw a flash of anger or maybe irritation cross his face. Why, I don't understand. I just told him I won't keep begging him to let me start doing things alone any longer. I thought that would make him happy, or at least relieved.

"I'm going to head to bed." Bryce stands up from the couch and starts for the hallway. He stops and looks over his shoulder at me. "Are you coming?"

I want to ask why he all of a sudden seems upset with me, but I see the exhaustion in his eyes and I decide to let it go for now. Maybe I am just imagining things. Getting up, I follow him to the room, nothing else is said between us.

"ALL RIGHT, it's time for you to start talking to me, Darryn. What is going on with you? I've been waiting and hoping you would start talking on your own, but nothing. Are you having problems with the ex and no one is telling me?"

Tom and I have just finished our shift, I shut the door from getting out of rig and he turns to me and goes off. It takes me by surprise. "What do you mean, Tom? Nothing has happened, why would you think it has? Plus, don't you think if it had, Bryce would have told you?"

"Then what's going on with you? The last couple of weeks you haven't been yourself."

It's been two weeks since we were at the fair and Charliee recognized the man from the night of the bombing. Since that night, Bryce hasn't been the same. He still spoils Kendall and myself, if I am being honest. We are still sharing a bed, and still having sex, but something has changed since that night, I just can't figure out what. I want to ask him, but I haven't.

"I think everything is just getting to me. It's been how long now and Brett hasn't shown up anywhere. I keep wondering if I just imagined everything to begin with. It's crazy that you still have to take time out of your day to follow me back to the station after every shift. I'm starting to think this is all for nothing and just let everyone get back to their normal lives."

My heart sinks as the words come out of my mouth. Sure, that would mean Tom wouldn't have to be my personal bodyguard after work any longer, and Kendall could get back to daycare which would give Bryce's mom a break. It would also mean I would have to let Bryce go. More than once the thought has crossed my mind that he is getting tired of this farce of a marriage and that's what has changed between us. I wonder if he thinks that I have made everything up and now he is stuck in a marriage.

"Come on, Darryn, talk to me. I see the wheels turning in your head, there is something you aren't telling me." Tom's words break through my thoughts.

I can't talk to him about all of this. No one knows we are married except Bryce's parents. I had him promise me he wouldn't tell his brother and sister. We have never talked about how that is for him but I know it rips him apart keeping this from them. Not only him but his parents are keeping it from them as well. How can I sit here and tell Tom and basically beg Bryce to not tell his family?

"Really, Tom, I think it's just me getting into my own head. If Brett is around I wish he would just show himself and we can be done with all of this. If he isn't, then maybe it's time for me to get back to my normal life. Find my own apartment, give you and Bryce back your lives."

"I think you need to talk to Bryce about all of this. I'm pretty sure he will feel the same way as I do and believe it's not worth taking the risk."

"So how long do we all go on like this?" My voice raises. Quickly I look away from Tom, I can feel the tears burning the back of my eyes.

Damn Brett, he is still controlling my life without being anywhere near me. I need to get over him and the fear. There have been times when I have spotted someone in a crowd and had to look twice thinking it was him. I'm paranoid and I need to move past it, he may have finally given up on trying to find me. The note in my apartment the day it was broken into was the only thing that kept me believing he had found me. I haven't even shown it to Bryce, I almost threw it away, but decided against it and hid it in a pair of shoes I never wear.

"Hey, sorry! I didn't mean to upset you." Tom apologizes and that tears at me even more.

This man has done so much for me through all of this and what do I do? Yell at him. "Tom, I'm sorry. You have no idea what it means to me to have you do all that you are. I'm just ready for it all to be over, but that's no excuse to yell at you. Please forgive me."

"Don't worry about me, it's going to take a lot more then you yelling a little at me to make me upset. I understand, Darryn, I just want you to know I'm here if you need someone to talk to."

I give my best effort of a smile. Without anything else to say I head to my car, knowing that Tom will go to his and follow me back to the station, like every other day.

TOM TALKS to Bryce for a little bit before he heads for home after following me to the station. I go straight to Bryce's car and get in with only a wave to Tom. I figure Tom is telling about our conversation and right now, I don't care. When we get home, I am going to talk to Bryce about all of this. If Tom is noticing something was wrong then maybe it was time for Bryce and me to talk, figure out what's next.

I watch as the two of them shake hands. Bryce pulls his phone out of his pocket but I can't tell from here if he is making a call or receiving one. He ends it before he opens the door to the car.

"Hey," he says as he sits down and closes the driver's side door.

"Hey," is all I say back and then look once again out of the passenger side window, my chest hurting.

I wonder for a moment if I should just keep things the way they are, but what would that fix? Is it really that fair for me to keep Bryce in a marriage that was only created to keep my daughter and me safe? My heart may be breaking over the thought of leaving him and moving on with our own lives, but it's what's fair to Bryce. I owe him that with everything he has done for us.

I realize we aren't headed in the direction of his parents' house, but to his house. "Do we need to do something else before we pick up Kendall?"

He shakes his head, but says nothing.

"All right, then where are we going?"

"Home! Mom has agreed to keep Kendall for the night."

What the hell?! Well, now I know who he was on the phone with. "Why do you think it's all right for you to make that kind of decision without asking me? She is my child, not yours." My words are harsh and I know it, but right now I am pissed.

I see his face drop a little, but he quickly recovers it. "We have things we need to talk about and I'm going to make sure I have your full attention, and this way you have no excuse to hide from it."

What did Tom tell him? I know trying to argue with him is a waste of time, so I just sit back, cross my arms over my chest and sit in silence for the rest of the drive back to the house.

Once we pull into the driveway, I quickly jump out of the car, my keys in hand, and go into the house. Bryce follows right behind me, shutting the door behind us.

"All right, what the hell is going on? And don't tell me nothing." The words are out of his mouth the second the door clicks shut.

We are standing in the living room and from the stance Bryce is taking, we aren't going any further until we talk. Maybe this is a good thing. I'm pissed at the moment which will make it a lot easier for me to tell him what I have been thinking and not hold anything back.

"Tom tells me you are thinking about moving out."

Out of everything Tom could have told Bryce, that is what this is about. Not that I am worried I had imagined all of this, or that I thought Brett has given up way too much, but that I was moving out. "That's not exactly what I said."

"All right, then tell me, Darryn, what exactly did you say?"

I have never really seen Bryce mad at me, not like this at least. It's strange, when Brett was mad at me I wanted to run and hide, my stomach would feel heavy with not knowing what he was going to do. I didn't trust him. With Bryce it is completely different. I don't want to run and I'm not scared. I know Bryce wouldn't do anything that would hurt, at least not intentionally. That's when it hits me, I am completely in love with this man and I need to let him go.

Taking a deep breath and fighting back the tears, my heart is feeling like it is being pulled apart into two pieces. "Bryce, we haven't heard anything, or seen anything since the night I thought I was being followed. Maybe it was all just my imagination."

I'm not about to tell him about the note left at my apartment that day. He would never let me go if he knew about it. That night Brett was in my apartment and he wanted me to know about it.

"Darryn, I'm not ready to assume that. Yours and Kendall's safety is way too important to me to chance that."

"Bryce, you have totally turned your life upside down for my daughter and me. Not only that, but Tom has to get home later at night because he has to follow me around. It's not fair to anyone."

"I asked Tom about all of this at the beginning. He is actually the one who offered. I only asked him to make sure he was with you during working hours."

That warms my heart. Tom is a great friend, but it still isn't fair. "Bryce, I'm done depending on everyone, I need to get on with my life and you guys with yours. You should be concentrating on the bomber, taking care of your family, not worrying about mine."

Bryce just stares at me. I can tell he wants to say something but what, I have no idea. "Look, I work tomorrow, I think I will go and pick up Kendall from your mom's after work, without Tom following me, and then after tomorrow Kendall will go back to daycare. I have this weekend off, so if you don't mind us hanging out here until then, I will look for an apartment."

"You're my wife, Darryn!"

He surprises me a little. It's like he is trying to convince me to stay. He even said when this was all discussed that after it was all over we would be parting paths. I have to admit, my heart jumps a little with hope that just maybe he will want me to stay, that he has started to feel for me as I have for him.

"Bryce, you married me to keep me safe, I can't keep allowing you to put your life on hold anymore."

His arms are folded across his chest and he is just staring at me. I shift back and forth on my feet, wanting to just run and hide in Kendall's room. All he would have to do is tell me he cares for me. I wouldn't even need to hear that he loves me, just knowing this is more than a protection detail would make me stay.

"Look, I think it's best if I sleep in the spare room with Kendall for the next couple of nights." I need some space and time to think. Plus, each night I'm in his arms is another night I fall that much deeper for him.

CHAPTER
Twenty~Four

BRYCE

I KNOW the last few weeks things have been a little strung tight between the two of us. I want to talk to her about it but always talk myself out of it. Now look where that has gotten us, Darryn is talking about moving out. It's the last thing I want. I was hoping, and to be honest I thought, I had seen a little side of her that may have started to care a little more for me, but obviously I was wrong. I want to tell her that I have fallen in love with her, but I don't think she will believe me on that right now. She would think I am just telling her that to get her to stay.

I don't think the threat of her ex is her imagination. I have no idea why he is waiting so long to appear again, and maybe he has been around the whole time. We have been careful not to have Darryn alone. I have done everything I can think of to make sure he couldn't follow her to my house or my parents. He may just be waiting for us to slip up, and Darryn and Kendall moving out could be that slip up.

Now she wants to sleep in the spare room. I can't even imagine not having her next to me at night anymore. I know words aren't going to keep her here, and I have a couple days to convince her to stay. One thing is for sure, she isn't sleeping in Kendall's room.

"Look, I can't stop you if this is what you want to do. I will help you with whatever you need and I hope you always know that you have me if you need me, but as for the part of sleeping with Kendall…" I close the space in between us and wrap an arm around her waist. Bringing my head down to hers I stop, our lips almost touching. I can feel her warm breath and it takes all the strength I have not to claim those lips, and then beg her to love me like I love her. "It's not happening. If all I have are a couple more nights with you, than I want you wrapped around me, and me deep inside of you every minute that we can."

Darryn takes a sharp intake of breath and her eyes go wide. I may not be able to tell her how I feel, but I plan to show her as much as possible, with a small sliver of hope that she will change her mind before this weekend. I'm not going to let her go, I just need to convince her of that.

I don't want to give her time to argue with me and decide to use her surprise to my advantage. I claim her lips before she can say another word. If there is one thing I know for sure, it is the chemistry between the two us. I feel her hands go to my chest and I wait for her to push against me. It will be difficult but I will let her go. I never want her to feel like she is being pressured with me. But instead of pushing me away, each hand grabs a fist full of my shirt and holds on. That's all the answer I need. Picking her up, I cradle her in my arms, my lips never leaving hers. Quickly I walk down the hallway and into our room, sitting her down on our bed.

She looks up at me. I know she is battling with this, and I will stop if she tells me to. "You aren't going to make this very easy for me, are you?"

Her question surprises me a little. I'm not the one who has decided she needs to move out. From the look in her eyes I would say it's the last thing she wants to do. That gives me a little hope that convincing her may not be as difficult as I thought it might be. I need to show her how much she means to me, I need to prove it. Words aren't going to be enough with her, they never have been.

I need her to make the next move. To know this is want she wants. We stare at each other for a few moments and I know she is battling with herself. Here we are, her sitting on the bed looking up at me, and all I can do is stand here looking back at her waiting.

Her hands finally come up to my stomach and she gently pushes me back so that she can stand. My heart drops, she is going to walk away from me and I'm going to have to let her. Shutting my eyes for a moment, I have to fight the urge to shake her. How does she not know my feelings? I may not have voiced them but I know I have for damn sure shown them.

"Bryce, open your eyes." Her voice is low.

Opening them, my heart stops. A single tear is rolling down her cheek. With my thumb I wipe it away and fight the urge to pull her into my arms and just hold her.

"I don't want to sleep anywhere else than in your arms." Her words shock me, but what confuses me more is the fact that more tears are rolling down her cheeks now and she looks sad.

"I know I have to let you go, it's the only fair thing for you," she continues, and my heart sinks once again. She is still planning on leaving me and now all I am is more confused than before.

"Darryn, you don't have to let me go…" She stops me before I can tell her that I love her. Screw all my thoughts before, she needs to know.

"Bryce, I've already made up my mind and nothing you say is going to change that, but I'm not ready to let go of you yet. I know this is unfair to ask, but I need to be with you until that time, that is if you want me."

I have a huge urge to shake her again. Then I realize nothing is going to change this stubborn woman's mind and right now, I just need her. I will figure out a way to make her see what she means to me, but for now I will let her think I'm giving into her.

"I'm yours, Darryn, for as long as you want me." With my hand at the back of her head, my fingers digging into her thick hair, I claim her lips once again.

Darryn's body crushes against mine and her arms go up over my shoulder, her fingers now in my hair. Neither one of us wants to let go, which gives me a spark of hope. I love this woman more than words can express and I will get her to see that.

My fingers relax in her hair and I slow the intensity of the kiss down. I don't want this fast, I want it to be something that makes her think, something she has never experienced before. I don't want to have sex with Darryn, I want to make love to her.

Moving my hands down to the bottom of her work shirt, I slide my hands up and bring the shirt up and over her head, only separating our lips to move the shirt past them. Trailing my hands back down her arms, my hands span each side of her waist, squeezing slightly, pulling her hips tighter against mine.

I hear a low moan escape her. "I want your shirt off, Bryce. I need to feel your skin against mine."

Who am I to argue with her? I stand in front of her and allow her to work my shirt up my chest and over my head, it lands on the floor next to where hers fell. I watch as she then reaches behind her back and she removes her own bra. Her hands then start at my biceps and trace a path up and around my neck, her nails now lightly scraping my scalp, our bodies pressed against each other. She pulls my head down and kisses me.

I bring one hand up, brushing my fingers against one very tight nipple. Trailing kisses down her neck, I finally reach her nipple with my lips, lightly kissing the hard bud. Just that one slight touch and Darryn's knees buckle, her arms tightening around my neck to hold herself up. Pushing her back, she sits down first on the bed, and with a slight push from me, she lays back.

Before joining her, I strip out of my remaining clothes, her eyes watching my every move. Now that I'm standing before her completely naked, all I can think about is her entire body naked against mine. Her nipples are tight and begging to be touched, so with each hand I cup a breast and squeeze slightly, then tug lightly on each nipple. Her eyes close, her head goes back and her back arches, thrusting her chest out to me, begging me for more.

My hands now travel down to the waist of her pants and I slowly pull them and any remaining clothing down her legs. Bending down, I start at her knee and start trailing small kisses up her thigh. My eyes never leave her face, I like watching her reactions to what I'm doing to her. Her eyes are closed, her hands clutching the sheets on the bed. The higher I go, the more my body pushes her legs apart. I tease her a little more as I blow on her heated core. I'm rewarded with another moan. Ever so lightly, I lick up her outer folds and then trail my tongue up over her belly, her ribs and then finally to one tight and begging nipple. Sucking it fully into my mouth, my hand covering the other, my name fills the room. Darryn's legs wrap around my waist, which almost causes me to lose all control once I feel her hot, very wet center on my hardness, but I'm not done with her yet.

Darryn, using her hands, presses my head down, which is my sign to suck a little harder, nibble a little more on the nipple, and pinch a little harder on the other. Between the little sounds Darryn is making, and her body rubbing hot and wet against mine, I am about to lose my mind.

I move my one hand from her breast and down to her heated center. Teasing between her folds, I find her just as wet as she is hot. Leaving her breast, my lips trail kisses up her neck and claim her lips once again.

"Please, Bryce, I need you," Darryn begs.

"Darryn, I need you," I say as I take myself and enter her slowly, causing us both to moan this time.

I will never get enough of being inside this amazing woman. Her body tightens around me, pulling me in even deeper as her legs tighten around my waist like she is afraid to let go. Pulling out, I can feel just my tip inside of her, and when her body shivers I almost lose myself completely. I thrust deep inside of her once again. I repeat the motion again and again, each time a little faster and a little harder. I can feel her body beginning to quake around me, each time tightening her around me more and more. I'm not sure how much longer I am going to be able to hold back.

"Darryn, please." I now find myself begging her.

That's all it takes, again my name fills the room, and I'm pretty sure hers escapes from my lips as together we find our release. Feeling her body pull me in deeper and deeper, all I can do is hold her tight and listen to both of us trying to breathe.

I'M NOT GOING to let her go! Somehow, some way, I will get her to stay with me! For now, I just need to convince her to allow things to stay the way they are so that I don't worry about her while trying to convince her and on top of that, work right now is crazy with trying to catch the bomber.

Since that night at the carnival, Derrick and I have worked nonstop trying to figure out more about this guy.

"Hey, are you awake?" I whisper in Darryn's ear.

She doesn't say anything, just nods her head. She has her head laying on my chest so I can't see her eyes.

"Can I ask you a favor?"

This question brings her eyes up to mine with her head tilted back, now resting on my shoulder.

"I know you said tomorrow you wanted to start driving yourself to work and taking Kendall back to the daycare, but I want to ask that you wait on that. You asked to give you until this weekend so I'm asking the same thing. Plus, it gives me some time to break the news to my mom, she is going to be lost without Kendall." I try to lighten the mood.

"Bryce, I don't want Tom to have to worry about me any longer. I know your mom and dad love Kendall, she loves them and I'm not trying to take her away from them, but I feel bad about turning everyone's lives upside down."

"Tom is going to worry about you regardless if he has to be there to follow you or not. You are the only one who thinks Brett isn't around, just for your information. As for my parents, trust me, you didn't turn their lives upside down, you gave my mom a grandchild to spoil and she is enjoying the hell out of it."

She looks away from me again. She does this when she doesn't want me figuring out what she is thinking. She seems to believe I can read her mind. That talent isn't needed with someone who tells you everything with their eyes.

Shifting us around, I place her under me so that she can't hide from me as I tower over her. "Darryn, please do this for me."

Her eyes soften and I see tears start to well up, I have to hide my shock. It's at this moment I realize she cares for me, I can see it. This is why she hides from me, she doesn't want me to see it. Finally, she nods her agreement to my request.

"I'm going to make you see it," I state with a smile on my face.

She gives me a puzzled look. "See what?"

"How much you mean to me."

Her eyes go wide and I hear her sharp intake of breath. I don't give her a chance to argue with me or question it. I claim her lips and for the second time tonight, we make love.

THIS MORNING, I expected Darryn to try and convince me that she could drive herself to work from the station and not have the unmarked car following, but to my surprise she didn't. We drove to the station, she even kissed me goodbye. It was almost too easy, but I didn't have time at work to really think about it.

Charliee just left the station. We received a good lead today on the bombing case and wanted her to come identify the guy from a picture we were able to pull up. She did great but I can tell all of this is finally wearing her down. Since she has been seeing Travis, she hasn't needed Derrick and me as much. We are both happy she has found someone and Travis is a great guy, but I'm a little worried about her. We need to get this guy and end all of it, for all the families' sake.

"Hey, are you all right?" Derrick asks, sitting across from me at the table.

I hadn't even heard him come into the breakroom. "Yeah, just a lot going through my mind."

"Any word on the ex?"

I just shake my head.

"Are you sure that you're all right?" he asks again.

"I'm concerned about Charliee. She is trying to be so strong about all of this, but today I can see how tired she is. We need to find this guy. Charliee is strong but she is going to break soon." If I direct this conversation toward Charliee maybe Derrick won't ask me anymore about Darryn.

It's getting harder and harder every day to keep my marriage a secret. Right now is when I need to talk to him the most and I can't.

"Maybe we should talk to Travis…" Derrick is interrupted by another officer running into the break room.

"We have had another bombing," he informs the two of us.

"Where?" Derrick beats me to the question.

"Old abandoned building, which is what concerns all of us. It's not a normal target for him."

"We are going," I say as Derrick and I push past the officer standing at the door.

My phone goes off in my pocket. I ignore it. Then it goes off again. Pulling it out, I see Darryn's picture. I want to let it go, but something is telling me to answer it.

Swiping my screen, I answer as we are running out to the car. "Darryn, is everything all right?"

"Bryce, I'm sure you have heard about the bombing."

"We are on our way now, can I call you back?" We both slam through the door leading to the back lot where all the patrol cars are parked.

"Bryce, that's why I'm calling. We are here on the scene, we were called out."

Something is wrong, I can hear it in her voice. "Darryn, what's wrong? Are you all right?" I stop dead in my tracks.

"It's not me, it's Travis, Charliee's boyfriend," she informs me.

I want to be relieved she is all right, but the feeling is overtaken by now knowing something is still very wrong. Derrick is giving me a questioning look, I put my hand up telling him to hold on.

"Darryn, what do you mean it's Travis? What's going on over there?"

"We just got here, there was another bomb inside the building. When the firefighters went into the building it went off, trapping two fire-fighters inside. Travis is one of them."

"Damn it!"

"Bryce, what's going on?" Derrick asks from above our vehicle's roof.

"Darryn, keep me posted as you hear anything. We were going to come that way, but I think we are going to have to go to Charliee's, I don't want her hearing this some other way. Please be careful, there may be more."

I want to tell her to leave, but I know she can't. She has a job to do. Now I kind of understand what our parents go through with both Derrick and I being on the force.

"Poor Charliee, I will let you know anything I find out." She quickly hangs up the phone.

"Bryce, what the hell is going on? Is Darryn all right?"

"She's fine. There was another bomb in the building that went off, this time unfortunately there were firefighters inside. Derrick, Travis is one of the trapped."

"We need to get over to Charliee's," Derrick says then gets into the driver's seat.

He is backing out of the space when I reach the passenger side and get in. One of the hardest parts of our job is having to inform someone that something has happened to one of their family members. Those people you don't know though. Having to tell Charliee that Travis is trapped and we don't know if he is alive or not is going to be one of the hardest things we will ever have to do.

When we pull up to the house, we notice Charliee's Jeep isn't in the driveway. She and Jayden must have gone somewhere after they left the station today.

"She isn't home, we need to find out where she is." Derrick pulls out his phone to text her.

"Wait, here she comes, she just came around the corner. Who is going to be the one to tell her?" I ask, dreading this whole conversation.

Charliee pulls into her driveway, I can see the puzzled look on her face. Derrick opens his door and starts toward Charliee. I get out, but stay by the car. I can see Derrick's hands moving in front of him as he walks up to her.

I watch for a moment, Charliee asks why we are here. Derrick looks back at me with a look of dread in his eyes. I didn't say he was the one who had to do this, he just jumped out of the car. I see his head tilt back, Charliee is getting irritated, you can see it all over her face. Derrick doesn't need to do this alone so I walk up to join him.

"Charliee, maybe we should go inside," Derrick suggests.

"Where was it at, guys? What are you not telling me?" Charliee asks like she didn't even hear Derrick. He must have already mentioned the bombing.

"The explosion was at an abandoned building this time." Derrick is dragging this out.

Charliee's shoulders slump with relief, but then you can tell she figures out something isn't being said and she glares at both of us. "Dammit, guys, what are you trying to tell me? Just say it already, please."

Derrick places a hand on each of her shoulders and Charliee's relieved look moves to complete panic. Derrick looks her straight in the eyes. "Charliee, when the firefighters went in, a second bomb went off. Two guys from Travis's department are missing. Travis is one of them."

"Take me there," Charliee demands. She doesn't cry, she doesn't panic, she just starts walking toward our patrol car.

Derrick stops her by grabbing her shoulder and turning her around to face him. "We don't even know if it's safe, or if there is another bomb, Charliee."

This argument isn't going anywhere. Either we are going to take her or she is going to go alone. Derrick looks over at me for some help. "At least if she is with us, we can watch her," I suggest.

"Mom and Dad are going to kill us." Derrick motions for Charliee and Jayden to get into the back of the car. He stops her before she gets in though. "You need to promise us that you will stay with us."

AS SOON AS we pull up to the building, Charliee starts barking orders to let her out. I get out of the car and open her door, but I block her from getting out. "You need to promise me you aren't going to do anything stupid, Charliee."

She just stares up at me. She is pissed but I don't care, her safety is more important to me than her being a little pissed off. "Promise me, Charliee, or I'm shutting the door and locking you in this car."

Honestly, I'm pretty sure she could shove me aside if she really wanted to right now, she looks pissed.

"Fine, I promise! Now move!" she yells at me.

I stand there for a moment and we just glare at each other. Finally, she starts to step out and I move out of her way. If Darryn was the one trapped in there, I would do anything to get to her. I have to put myself in Charliee's shoes right now.

I watch her for a moment as she just stands there, Levi standing in front of her, staring at the front of the building. My heart drops. I can't imagine what she is thinking right now. My sister has been through so much. She has always been a very strong person. She has never let being deaf stop her from anything, or ever used it as an excuse. Derrick and I have always been extremely protective of her, but as she grew up we realized she didn't need us as much as we thought she did. Since the night of the bombing that almost took her from us, I have noticed that she has tried to show she is good, that she is healing mentally and physically just fine. Physically I will give her, she was up and ready to go back to work long before the doctor released her, but mentally I have seen that the whole event has taken something from her. Travis has been her wall, the one she has turned to, not Derrick and me. It's been hard but I know Travis is a good guy and is taking care of her. If he doesn't make it through this, I'm worried for Charliee.

Jayden comes and stands beside me. "You know if anything happens to Travis, Charliee isn't going to bounce back from that very well."

I nod. "That's actually what I was just thinking myself."

"There hasn't been any chatter on the radio from inside of there?" she asks.

I just shake my head, everything has gone pretty quiet since they brought the other firefighter out. "The other firefighter is awake and talking to the paramedics, hopefully that's a good sign for Travis."

"Why haven't they pulled him out yet?" Jayden asks, but I know she isn't expecting me to answer. More just talking out loud.

I look over to see Darryn standing by her rig. "Hey, stay with Charliee, will you, Jayden? Make sure she doesn't go anywhere other than right there. I will be right back."

Jayden walks over to Charliee, I head over to Darryn.

"How is she doing?" Darryn asks as I approach her.

"Not good, I'm worried about her."

"Do you think it was the best idea to bring her here, Bryce? Who knows what to expect when they do find him." Darryn states the one thing I have thought since we agreed to bring her.

"Trust me, if we hadn't brought her then she would have come here on her own. This is the only option Derrick and I figured we had," I explain.

My phone vibrates in my pocket, pulling it out I see it's my mom. *Crap, here we go,* I think to myself. "Hi, Mom."

"What's going on, Bryce? We turned on the television and it's on every channel. Right now I can even see you and Darryn." My mom is panicking, but she hasn't said anything about Charliee yet.

Looking over my shoulder, I see all the news crews and cameras pointing in our direction. How the hell did they get this close? Sure, they have distance between them and the building but we have no idea if there are any other explosives and if so, where. I am about to tell my mom I have to go so I can talk to whoever is in charge of this whole mess when my mom yells on the phone.

"Bryce, why did that look like Charliee and Levi running into that building?"

What the hell? I turn around just in time to see my sister disappear into the opening, and hear Jayden scream after her. I don't even say anything to my mom, I shove my phone at Darryn and run to where Charliee disappeared.

Derrick reaches the entrance before I do, I follow behind him as we make our way over all the debris. It's hard to see but we can hear Levi's bark. Then we hear Charliee scream and we both stop dead in our tracks. We look at each other, listening. Levi has stopped barking, but somehow we hear Charliee's voice over all the other commotion as she tells someone she has found Travis and to hurry up. Both Derrick and I start in that direction.

Derrick reaches her first. She is sitting on the ground, Levi pawing at the debris in front of her, and she has Travis's hand in hers. I run a quick eye over her and that's when I notice her leg. It is bleeding badly and bent in a strange way.

"Derrick, look." I point for him to look at her leg. "We need to get her out of here."

Derrick grabs her shoulder to get her attention. "Charliee, let them do their job. I need to get you out of here, your leg is really bad."

"No, I'm not leaving him, Derrick, he hears me." Charliee pulls away from Derrick's grasp and turns her attention back to Travis.

Derrick looks back at me. As much as I want everyone out of this building, I can't say I blame Charliee for wanting to stay until they get him out. I nod to Derrick and we both get to work helping them uncover the rest of Travis's legs. The faster we get him out, the quicker we will get Charliee out.

What feels like an hour probably only took us no more than five minutes to finish getting Travis out. I look down at Charliee's leg, blood is starting to pool under it. Tapping Derrick on the arm, I get his attention.

"Her leg is bad, we need to get her out of here now."

Derrick nods. He turns to get her and that's when she tries to stand to follow the guys out carrying Travis, and her scream echoes through the building. Derrick quickly scoops her up in his arms and heads for the opening, I follow right behind.

Once we clear the building, they guys carrying Travis head to one ambulance while Derrick carries Charliee over toward Darryn.

"Derrick, no, you need to take me over to Travis, please," she begs him, but this time it isn't going to work. I can see her trying to look over Derrick's shoulder to see Travis.

Derrick's steps don't even hesitate, he just keeps right on toward Darryn who is waiting for us. I notice she has my phone up to her ear, probably still on the phone with my poor mom. I kind of threw it at her with her still on the line when I saw Charliee going into the building. She puts it down just as we reach her.

"I think the three of you just gave your mother a heart attack," Darryn informs us as we walk up and sit Charliee down on the gurney.

I give her an apologetic smile for leaving her to deal with my mom.

Darryn looks over Charliee's leg. "This isn't how I wanted to get to know you better, Charliee," she says, looking up at her, then gets busy cutting her pants.

I watch as Charliee's leg becomes more visible and notice it is a lot worse than I had thought inside. Now I want to kick myself for letting her stay. Who knows how much blood she has lost, and it is broken for sure.

I notice my phone laying on the bumper of the ambulance, my mom's picture popping up again. I reach to answer it but am stopped when I hear Charliee scream again. Turning around, I find her trying to get up from the gurney. Darryn is trying her best to control her but Charliee isn't having it, even though she looks like she is going to pass out at any moment. Something has her all riled up again.

Reaching across I try to help, but Charliee pushes against me. "Bryce, the bastard is here." She is now pointing over my shoulder.

Looking in the direction she is pointing, all I see are reporters. What is she thinking she is looking at?

I turn my attention back to her. "Who's here, Charliee, who are you seeing?"

Her face is pale, her eyes glassing over with tears, she looks terrified and pissed. "Bryce, he's here. He stayed and watched. Look at the guy standing next to the female reporter. He has on a dark blue sweatshirt. He's the one, Bryce."

Turning around once more, I find the guy she described right away. It is the same guy in the picture we had Charliee come down and identify earlier today. She's right, he stayed and watched. I don't want to spook the guy this time like we did at the fair. We can't let him get away this time. Turning so I don't seem to keep my attention on him, I bring my radio up and describe the guy.

"Jayden, you stay and help Darryn with Charliee, who knows what she will try to do," I say, then quickly turn and start walking in the direction of the guy. Derrick is by my side, I can see other officers moving to surround him. He isn't getting away today.

The closer we get to him, the more aware he is becoming. He is looking around, frantic like, and grasping a backpack he is wearing. What if he has another bomb? Before I can voice my fear to my brother, the guy takes off. He isn't getting away today. Both Derrick and I start after him.

Leaning my head over to my shoulder, I talk into my radio. "He is making a run. Derrick and I are right behind him. Block him in, but he is ours."

The chance isn't given to us. Before we know it, one of our K-9 units is outrunning us and I swear it happens in slow motion as we watch the dog jump up, grab the guy around the arm and drag him down to the ground. Derrick and I instantly stop, waiting for his partner to call him off.

Derrick and I watch as they roll him over and cuff the guy and just like that, it's over. We watch as someone from bomb control comes over and secures the guy's backpack. Standing him up, the officer starts walking in our direction.

"Sorry, guys, didn't mean to step on your toes, I had already released him when you came over the radio," the K-9 officer explains.

"Don't worry, probably better for it to happen this way," I state back, fighting the urge to pull my gun and just shoot the guy in the leg or something. Let him feel a little of the pain that he has put so many other people through. I know that really isn't a great thing to think, but I have to admit it went through my mind.

"They all deserved it," I hear the guy mumble under his breath.

Derrick and I lunge together. Who the hell cares if we wear the badge, now I just want to beat the shit out of the asshole! Before we can reach him, each of us has an officer holding us from behind and one in front, pushing us back.

"That guy better rot in jail for the rest of his life!" I hear Derrick yell next to me.

Jail is a little too nice for this guy, I think to myself.

CHAPTER

Twenty~Five

Darryn

CHARLIEE IS BREAKING MY HEART. She isn't talking or looking at me, but I can see the tears rolling down her cheeks. We hit a bump in the road and I watch her face scrunch up in pain.

I poke my head up into the front of the rig. "Hey, Tom, radio over and see if you can get any information on Travis, please."

"Sure, how is she doing? I'm trying to miss the bumps."

Patting his shoulder, I answer, "She is hanging in there."

Sitting back down, I look over at her dog, Levi. He hasn't moved. He just lays next to her, his head on her arm, and stares at her. I pat him on the head. "You are such a good boy."

He looks over at me from the side of his eyes and then instantly back to Charliee. I tap Charliee on the arm, she slowly turns her head to me.

"He is a great dog."

She looks down at Levi, strokes his head a couple times and gives him a small, sad smile, but at least a smile none the less.

"Hey, Darryn," Tom calls up from the front.

"Yeah."

"They said he is still unconscious, but is breathing on his own. They just arrived at the hospital."

"Thank you, Tom."

We have to drive so much slower because of the severity of Charliee's injured leg. Looking back down at Charliee, she has her eyes squeezed shut. This job is so much harder when you know the patient.

Tapping her on the arm again, she opens her eyes. "They just reached the hospital with Travis, he is breathing on his own. That's good news."

"Is he awake?" Charliee speaks for the first time.

Sadly, I shake my head no. "Charliee, that doesn't mean it's bad."

"I should be with him."

"There is nothing you can do right now but wait, they wouldn't let you go back anyway. By the time we get you to the hospital and your leg taken care of, you will probably not have to wait long, if at all, to see him."

She stares at me for a moment, her eyes searching my face. "Do you love my brother?"

Now there is a question I wasn't expecting right now. I look at her puzzled for a moment. At first I don't think this is something we really need to talk about right now, but then after thinking about it for a moment, if it helps her keep her mind off Travis for a moment then I will talk about it.

I look to the front and notice Tom's head tilted toward us now. He heard Charliee's question. Looking back down at Charliee, I realize you never know when something in your life is going to change, it's too short not to live it fully.

"Yes, I'm very much in love with your brother," I admit out loud for the first time.

"I'm glad, Bryce deserves to be loved by a great woman. Don't get me wrong, I love both of my brothers more than words can say, but Bryce deserves it. He isn't out to play and send them on their way like Derrick can do. Bryce has never been like that. He wants the happily ever after, the family. Every time I have seen him look at you, I can see it in his eyes. You have caught him."

I don't know what to say. Charliee seems to think Bryce is in love with me from what it sounds like. My heart drops a little. If only she knew the whole story. I want to tell her how wrong she is, how he is only doing this as part of his job. I feel the ring against my chest and it's a constant reminder that we are only playing at this relationship.

I want someone to talk to and Charliee seems so easy to talk to. I am about to tell her she is so very wrong but Tom speaks first. "Darryn, pulling in now."

"Good news. We have finally made it. Let's get you inside, get that leg fixed up and you up to Travis, all right!"

Part of me is happy the conversation is over, but another part of me is a little disappointed that we didn't get to talk. I miss having girl friends to talk to.

TOM and I just finished getting Charliee transferred over into the care of the nurses and my phone is going off for the third or fourth time. Pulling it out, it's Karen. "Hello."

"Darryn, Jayden told me you were the one taking care of Charliee, how is she?"

I can hear the panic in her voice and can only imagine what Steven and she are going through right now. "We just got her in, it was a slow ride over because of the injuries to her leg. I can't say for sure but I know she will need stitches and my opinion is I think she broke it, but to what extent I'm sorry, I can't say."

"Okay!" She takes deep breath.

I can hear her repeat everything I just told her to Steven.

"Have you heard anything about Travis?" she asks next.

That's when it hits me, they have Kendall, that's probably why they aren't already here at the hospital. "Karen, I'm so sorry I didn't think about this earlier, you have Kendall! To answer your question, no, I haven't heard anything except he was breathing on his own, but still unconscious when they arrived here at the hospital, but you two should be here."

"I didn't want to bring Kendall down to the hospital," she explains and I feel terrible. They shouldn't be worried about taking care of my child when they should be here with theirs.

Looking at my watch, my shift isn't over for another two hours and Bryce is still working, but after he gets off he should be here, not worrying about Kendall or me. "Karen, let me call the daycare center real fast and make sure she is all right with you dropping her off there, you two should be here right now."

"I thought Bryce didn't want Kendall there right now?" I can hear the concern in her voice.

"Karen, she will be fine, right now it's more important that you are here. Charliee needs you."

Karen is quiet for a moment, I know she is torn right now but it really shouldn't even have to be a decision. Charliee needs her here. "Let me call you right back." I hang up before she can say anything else.

Carrie over at the daycare is excited about seeing Kendall again. I text Karen and give her directions to the place.

Tom walks back in from restocking the rig. "Everything all right?"

"Yes, just trying to get everyone's information and get Kendall settled so that Charliee's parents can come down. I feel bad I didn't even think they wouldn't come here because they had Kendall. I'm sure Bryce is going to want to come here after he gets off. I'll meet him here after we get off, make sure everything with him is all right and then I will pick up Kendall from daycare. I already spoke to Carrie over there and she said she will keep her as long as I need her to.

"Are you sure that's all a good idea, Darryn?" Tom has concern written all over his face

"I really don't want Kendall hanging out here at the hospital if I can help it."

"I can go and pick her up and she can stay with us, I'm sure it would just break Heather's heart to have her around tonight," Tom says sarcastically.

Tom's wife is so sweet, but I don't want to put them out any more than I already am. "I appreciate the offer, but honestly I think Carrie may be mad if I don't let her stay. It's been a long while since she has been there, she was very excited when I called and asked about Bryce's parents dropping her off."

"All right, but if anything changes know the offer is still there." Tom starts out of the emergency room, me following close behind.

THE LAST TWO hours of work seemed to drag by, and I haven't heard anything from Bryce except a quick text letting me know they did get the guy, and that he will have to stay at work a little later. I just text him back saying I will meet him at the hospital when he is done.

I have met Travis's parents briefly and his sister. Jayden, I have spoken to very briefly, but I think some other stuff is going on with her. She is here but her head seems to be somewhere else. She looks like she needs someone to talk to, but we really haven't met officially, except at the fair that night and that was just a quick introduction, so I don't ask any questions.

"Darryn." I hear my name from behind me. Turning around, I see Bryce and Derrick coming into the waiting room.

Bryce walks up and gives me a small kiss which surprises me, we have never shown any affection other than hugging when around people. I look around but no one seems to think anything of it, or maybe they were just not paying attention. His mom and dad are sitting with me, so he hugs them both as well.

I notice he is looking around, but for what I'm not sure. "Where is Kendall?" he asks.

"I had your mom drop her off with Carrie at the daycare. Your mom didn't want to bring her here to the hospital, and I agreed, but they needed to be here for Charliee and Travis. Carrie was more than happy to take her. She told me she was good with her until we head home, she figured we would want to be here until things calmed down a little and we learned a little more information."

He stares down at me. I can tell he isn't happy with the decision, but there weren't many choices to pick from really. Maybe I should have let her go to Tom and Heather's, I don't think I would be getting the look I'm getting right now from Bryce.

"Bryce, she is fine. Would it make you feel better for me to go pick her up while you go up and see your sister and Travis?"

He stands there contemplating it. I can see him battling with which way he should go. Finally, he takes a deep breath and shakes his head no. "No, I'll go up real fast, make sure Charliee is doing all right and then we can go over together."

He looks exhausted, I have to hold back from going to him and wrapping my arms around him. "All right, I'll wait down here for you. While you are up there, I will call Carrie and make sure everything is all right and let her know we will be there to pick Kendall up in the next hour."

"Why don't you come up with me?" He is holding his hand out to me.

Shaking my head, I motion to the elevator. "I'm good, you go talk to your sister. When she is out and Travis is better, there will be plenty of time for me to get to know your sister better, right now I think she just needs her family."

Wrapping me up in his arms, he holds me tight and I feel his warm breath in my ear. "You are family."

I should be happy to hear him say that. I have never been part of a family really, but this one is only temporary. Tears burn the back of my eyes. I need to smile, Bryce doesn't need anything else to worry about right now except his family.

Pulling back, I turn him toward the elevator and give him a little push. "Go, I'll be good down here. Give Charliee a hug for me."

When the elevator doors close, I pull my phone out and call Carrie. It rings, and then rings again. That's strange, she usually answers pretty fast. After the fourth ring, I get her voicemail. I don't leave a message, she must be busy with something. I will give her a couple of minutes and try again.

Karen comes up to me, wrapping her arms around me in a hug. "You should have gone up with him."

Pulling back, I smile. "He needs time with his sister."

"You know he loves you, right?" Karen smiles at me, but there is a sadness in her eyes.

My heart slams in my chest seeing the disappointment in her eyes. "Karen, I'm sorry I have dragged your son into my problems. He deserves so much more than what I have got him involved with."

Karen is shaking her head the whole time I speak. "Darryn, I couldn't be happier that he picked you. You need to stop thinking he is doing all of this because it's part of his job. My boy is head over heels in love with you, it is written all over his face every time he looks at you."

That's exactly what Charliee said earlier today. If I am being completely honest with myself, I would admit that I know he has feelings for me. He has shown me every time we are together. I think he just deserves better than me and my problems that follow me everywhere. If I tell myself he doesn't care, then I can walk away from him.

"You know all of this, don't you?" Karen asks.

I can't even look her in the eyes. I can't admit to knowing it.

"And you love him!" It isn't a question, and when my eyes level with hers she smiles, the sadness in her eyes gone. "Darryn, you need to tell him, then you guys can stop living like this marriage is some dark secret and start enjoying a life together."

Start a life together? That won't be possible until Brett is out of my life and I know he isn't. He is around, why he is sitting so idle right now is what is puzzling me.

My phone vibrates in my hand, scaring me to the point I almost throw it across the room. Taking a deep breath to calm my racing heart, I look down and see Carrie's name on the screen.

"Hello."

Nothing. She doesn't say anything back.

"Carrie, are you there?"

Again, nothing back. I pull back my phone to see if the call dropped but no, it shows we are still connected. Putting it back up to my ear, I am about to try one more time with saying her name but I hear a faint noise in the phone. Hitting the buttons on the side, I make sure my volume is all the way up. Maybe she pocket dialed me. I am about to hang up and call her back but then I hear a voice over the line that causes my blood to turn ice cold and my heart to drop.

"Brett!"

No, this can't be happening. How did he know where Kendall would be? I try to listen to what is being said but it is hard, everything sounds muffled. How long has he been there? Are Kendall and Carrie all right? All these questions need answers and I need to get to my baby.

I reach into my pocket to get my keys and they aren't there. Where the hell did I put them? Thinking about it, realization hits me like a ton of bricks. I don't even remember grabbing them when I got out of the car. Are you kidding me? I don't have the keys to my car and Bryce is up with Charliee. I have no way to get to her. I want to scream.

"Darryn, what's wrong?" Karen asks behind me.

I spin around. "Karen, I need to use your car, please."

"Sure, honey. Steven, Darryn needs the car keys. Is everything all right?"

I want to yell hell no, everything isn't all right, but I just need to get to my daughter and now.

"Darryn, maybe you should wait for Bryce to come back down." Karen takes the keys from Steven and hands them to me.

I don't even answer her. I grab the keys, more forcefully than I probably should have, and run out to the parking lot. I want to scream when I realize I have no idea where they parked. *Calm down and think, the keys have a panic button on them*. Pressing and holding the button, I wait. The car's alarm sounds off in seconds.

I hear a voice from behind me. Turning, I see Bryce. Wait, no, that's not Bryce, that's Derrick.

"Darryn, wait!" He starts running in my direction.

This family has been through so much today, I can't allow him to get involved with all of this. Brett is my problem and once and for all I need to deal with him. I'm done running, I'm done looking over my shoulder. I'm done letting him run my life.

Getting in, I shut the door quickly, starting the car and pulling out. Derrick is next to the car as I start to drive forward.

"Darryn, stop and open the door."

"I'm sorry, Derrick, I have to go." I press down on the gas pedal and pray that I don't hit Derrick as I pull away.

Looking in the rear-view mirror, I see him running back into the hospital. He is going in to get Bryce. I know once Bryce finds out I left, he is going to be furious. I didn't tell anyone where I was going, he won't know where to find me. I feel bad because I know he is going to panic, but I need to fight this battle alone.

The drive to the daycare is only fifteen minutes from the hospital but I feel like it takes hours to get there. I pull up alongside the curb, parking behind a dark-colored car similar to the one that was following me that day. I jump out of the car, leaving the keys in the ignition. My phone is vibrating in my pocket again. It's been going off constantly for the past ten minutes or so. I know it's Bryce. Running up the walkway, I stop dead in my tracks as I reach the door.

Standing there, arms crossed over his chest, is the one man I had hoped to never see again in my life.

"Darryn."

"Where is my daughter?"

He unfolds himself and steps out of the doorway, stopping only a foot away from me. "You mean our daughter."

I want to scream in his face that she will never be his daughter, but right now I have to keep a level head. "Where is Kendall and Carrie, Brett?"

He motions with his head to the inside of the building. "Both inside and before you ask the next question yes, they are both fine."

My knees threaten to buckle with relief, at least they are both all right.

"We have all been waiting for you," he announces with a smug smile on his face.

That means he has been here awhile. This kind of surprises me, he had all the time he needed to take Kendall and run, why was he waiting for me to get here?

I'm all of a sudden very tired. I realize I'm over being afraid of him. "What do you want, Brett?"

He looks around and then motions for me to enter the building.

"If I go in then you need to let Carrie leave, she has nothing to do with any of this."

"Do you think you are in a position to be making demands?"

I take a step closer, closing the space between us. My skin crawls from being this close to him. Looking straight up at him, I repeat myself. "If you want me to go inside, then you need to let Carrie leave."

Brett laughs and it sends chills down my spine. "Wow, Darryn, you have grown a backbone. That's kind of sexy." He runs a finger down my cheek.

It takes everything in me not to flinch away from his touch.

His hand drops back down by his side. "Fine, the only reason I kept her was to keep the kid quiet. Actually, we will all be leaving now. You and the kid are coming with me. I'll be honest, I'm a little surprised you don't have that cop boyfriend of yours with you."

I can't hide the surprise that I'm sure shoots across my face when he calls Bryce my boyfriend. It causes Brett to laugh.

"Do you honestly think I don't know everything that has been going on? Come on, Darryn, give me a little more credit than that. I know you have been living with him, I even know where the house is. You drive to work with him every morning to the station and then you drive from there with an unmarked car following you and then that partner of yours follows you back to the station every night after your shift. An older couple has been watching the kid, I'm going to guess they are the cop's parents."

I want to throw up, he has been following me and he has figured out everything. Why wait this long to make a move? If he calls Kendall "the kid" one more time, I'm going to slap him across the face. Before I can voice anything, he grabs me by the arm and pulls me inside.

Kendall spots me the moment I'm inside. She starts to run toward me, but Carrie holds her back and Kendall starts to cry.

"Keep her quiet," Brett snaps at Carrie.

"It's all right, Carrie, let her come to me." I pull my arm out of Brett's grip and bend down to catch Kendall, who is now running at me.

"Grab her stuff and let's get going," Brett says from behind me.

"Where are we going?" I ask, trying to waste time as I try and figure out a way out of this, plus with Carrie still here maybe he will give some information for her to hear.

"That's not important right now." Brett's voice is starting to become agitated. I need to keep him from getting mad, no telling what he will do then.

"Brett, you promised me Carrie could go," I remind him.

"Darryn, I'm not leaving you…"

"Carrie, you don't need to be a part of this," I interrupt her. If she is able to get out of here then that is one less person I have to worry about. I am pretty sure Brett isn't going to hurt her, but I don't want to take any chances.

"Darryn, do you honestly think I am going to just let her go before we can get out of here? I don't need her calling that boyfriend of yours before we can get out of town."

I screwed up, I didn't tell anyone where I was going because I wanted to handle this myself. Now I realize I made a very big mistake. I should have thought about Kendall. The main reason I ran to begin with and now I have basically handed her back to him. What did I think I was going to be able to do alone?

"Give the lady your phone and let's get going. I don't want you getting any ideas about trying to contact anyone, or anyone being able to trace your phone." Brett has thought of everything. This is why it took so long for him to make a move, he had been waiting and he knew I would mess up at some point.

"I'm so sorry, honey, Mommy messed up," I whisper to Kendall.

CHAPTER
Twenty-Six

BRYCE

IT WAS hard to leave Charliee. I wanted to just sit there and hold her as she cried. She is tired and hurting again, this time just not physically. She is still one of the strongest people I know. If that had been Darryn laying there and me in Charliee's spot, I'm not sure I would be able to handle myself as well as she is. There is no question in my mind about how much Travis means to her.

When I step out of the elevator, Derrick basically runs into me trying to get on. "What's the hurry?"

"Man, I was on my way to get you. Darryn just left out of here in Mom and Dad's car and she was in a hurry."

What the hell is he talking about, why would she leave and with our parents' car? "Where was she going?"

Mom came up behind Derrick. "Honey, something is wrong. All I really heard was the name Carrie and Brett."

I feel like someone punched me in the stomach. Brett! Carrie is the daycare's owner, what is going on?

"Darryn and I were talking and her phone went off, when she answered she said the name Carrie. A moment later her face went white and I heard her say the name Brett. Bryce, who is Brett?" my mom asks, but I see it written all over her face, she has an idea who Brett is.

I don't need to answer her, she knows just by looking at me she has assumed right. "Bryce, you need to go find her."

"Would someone like to tell me what's going on, please?" Derrick cuts into the conversation.

I need to get to Darryn. "It's her ex!" I yell at him over my shoulder as I head for the doors.

Derrick is following me out and I'm happy to know I have the backup, plus he may have to make sure I don't do anything that's going to get me fired from my job, because so help me if that bastard has done anything to either one of my girls!

"I'm assuming when you say the ex, you are talking about the one she has been running from. What the hell is going on today? Is there a damn full moon or something and all the nuts are coming out?" Derrick runs to the passenger side of my car and gets in.

I don't say anything, I just need to get to my girls and fast. I am just hoping I'm not already too late. I throw my phone at Derrick. "Call her."

Come on, Darryn, pick up the phone, I chant over and over to myself as I watch Derrick put the phone up to his ear.

"No answer, it went to voicemail."

"Try again, and don't stop calling until she picks up," I command.

I never thought a fifteen-minute drive could feel so long, and even though we hit a number of red lights, I didn't stop for any of them.

Damn, this would be so much easier if we were in the squad car. I would do anything for a siren right now.

Finally pulling up to the daycare, I see my parents' car parked along the curb. That is one small relief knowing this is where she went. Together, Derrick and I jump out of my car.

"What's the plan? Do we even know if they are still here?" Derrick asks as we approach the front of the building.

That's when the front door opens. I draw my gun, my brother following next to me. First, out comes Darryn holding Kendall, and then who I am guessing is Brett behind her.

"Hold it right there, Brett!" I yell, my eyes instantly locking with Darryn's. I see the relief flood over her face.

The world slows when I see him pull a gun from his back and point it straight into Darryn's side. Kendall starts crying and I have never felt more helpless than I do at this moment.

"Bryce, keep a straight mind," Derrick whispers next to me.

I'm trying, but seeing a gun being held on your wife makes things a little more difficult, I think to myself.

"She has no right to keep the kid from me, she is mine." Brett pushes the gun harder into Darryn's side and when I see her face scrunch up, I almost lose it.

Taking a deep breath, I try to remember our training and talking someone out of their gun, not acting fast and getting someone killed, good or bad guy.

"Well, as far as I'm concerned that's my wife and my child you are holding at gun point and I'm not going to allow you to take them from me!" I shout back.

From my side view I see Derrick's head whip around to look at me in shock. Darryn's eyes go wide and even from as far away as I am, I can see the tears form and fall down her check.

Suddenly, everything happens at once. Brett spins Darryn around to face him, then pulls Kendall from her arms as he brings the gun up and hits Darryn across the head with it. I watch as Darryn crumbles to the ground. Then the one word is cried out that I never understood until right now the impact it could have on a man.

"Daddy!" Kendall cries, her little arms out straight in front of her reaching out to me.

That one little word puts my feet into action. I'm not going to take a shot at the guy, he has my little girl in his arms, but I'll be damned if he thinks he is getting anywhere with her.

Shoving my gun into my back holster, I charge him, I don't care that the gun he is holding is now pointed straight at me. I will die before he hurts my girls anymore. I faintly hear my brother call my name as I see a figure come up behind Brett. It's Carrie. All at once I see her silhouette bring something up over her head and come around, hitting Brett in the back of the head. A shot from his gun goes off just before he falls to the ground, Kendall being dropped from his arms.

I hear Derrick yell my name, I see Darryn come to from the blow to her head, and I feel fire burning through my bicep. Reaching where Kendall fell and is now crying on the ground, I quickly pick her up, grab Darryn by the arm and basically drag her out of Brett's reach.

When I feel we are far enough away from any danger, I look over my shoulder and see that Derrick is putting cuffs onto Brett, while Carrie stands over him still with what I think is a bat over her head, ready to take another swing if need be. I can hear sirens coming down the street, it's over and my girls are safe.

Kendall's little arms are wrapped so tight around my neck I can barely breathe, but who needs to breathe, right?

"Bryce, you're bleeding." Darryn touches the side of my arm and pulls her hand away with my blood on it.

"I'm all right, it just grazed me." I look at my torn sleeve.

"How did you know where I was?" she asks.

"Mom heard you say Carrie's name and Brett's. It didn't take much to figure it out. But Darryn, this would have been a lot easier if you would have just told me what was going on. If something would have happened to either of you, I wouldn't have forgiven myself."

"Bryce, I'm sorry. I knew he was here and I couldn't let him take Kendall. Your family has been through so much, and with everything that happened today I didn't want to be the cause of anymore pain. Look, I got you shot." She points at my arm.

"Damn it, Darryn, when are you going to get it through that thick head of yours? You two are just as much a part of this family."

"Bryce, you married me to keep me safe…"

I can't believe after everything, that's what she still believes. "Darryn," I interrupt her. "I didn't have to marry you to keep you safe. Trust me, I would have figured out another way if that was all it was. I married you because from the day I met you I knew you were someone special. It didn't take long for me to realize I was falling in love with you."

"Seriously, man, first I find out you are married and then I have to watch you run full speed toward a man holding a gun at you. I'm not sure what I should punch you for first." Derrick comes up next to me looking a little pissed off.

Right now, I don't really want to deal with him. I just want to take the girls home.

"Hold that thought, Derrick." Darryn puts up a hand to stop my brother. "Did you say you are falling in love with me?"

"No, I'm not falling in love, I have completely fallen, Darryn. How have you not seen this already? I have done everything I could except say the words to show you how much you mean to me. But if that is all I haven't done then maybe this will make it sink in." I grab her by the back of the neck and bring my lips down to hers. Just before we kiss, I say against her lips, "I love you, Darryn, and I'm not letting you go." I then seal those words with a kiss that I hope expresses them to the fullest.

"I love you, too, Bryce." Darryn finally admits the one thing I have longed to hear from her.

"I love you, too, Daddy." Kendall's little voice breaks through our trance.

Darryn's eyes go wide at her little girl's words, then she looks away, almost embarrassed.

"Darryn, next to you telling me you love me, that is the next best word I could ever hear," I assure her.

"All right, now that everyone knows of the love, my turn. I have only one question. Does Charliee know about you two being married? Because I'll admit I'm a little pissed that I didn't know, but knowing what Charliee will have to say to you about it definitely makes it so much better." Derrick smirks at me.

I ignore my brother. "Come on, let's go home." I lead the three of us toward my car, I'm ready to take my family home!

"**COME ON,** Darryn, we need to get going or we are going to be late for our own reception."

"Daddy, I'm ready." Kendall comes out of her room, twirling as she walks down the hallway in her what she calls "princess" dress. She has been so excited to wear it, we had to hide it in our closet so she couldn't get to it. If it was up to her she would be wearing it every day.

"All right, I'm almost ready, let me just go put on my shoes." Darryn comes out behind Kendall.

Derrick was right. When Charliee found out I had gotten married and hadn't told them, she didn't talk to me for a couple days, then she yelled at me! Basically she was mad because she had a sister and a niece she hadn't known about. Derrick was more disappointed I think than mad. Before this we told each other everything. I think this just proved to him that we do have lives that each of us might not know everything about. Trust me, I heard about it for about a week in the car at work and every once in a while when we see Darryn on a call, he will make some smart ass comment, but it's all right, all in all we are a family and I couldn't be happier.

Charliee and Mom insisted that since the whole family and our friends weren't at the wedding ceremony then we needed to have a reception, we didn't even argue it. I think Charliee being able to help Darryn with all the plans sort of made up for her not knowing.

"All right, I'm ready, let's go." Darryn comes flying out of our room and down the hall. My heart skips a little at the sight of her. I am one very lucky man.

When we pull up to the reception location, Charliee and Travis are waiting outside for us. Charliee is still sporting a walking boot, but her leg is healing quickly and she should be out of it in a couple weeks. Travis was lucky, he came out with a concussion and a few broken ribs. He was back at work two weeks after getting out of the hospital.

"It's about time you two got here, everyone is waiting inside. Let me go in and tell them you are here." Charliee turns and a fast as possible, walks back into the building, pulling Travis along with her.

"If it wasn't for your sister, I would never have gotten all of this put together," Darryn confesses.

Walking in, we are greeted with applause and congratulations from all of our family and friends. Kendall runs straight to Grandma Karen as soon as we walk in. Charliee grabs our hands and leads us over to the head table.

Dinner and toasts are started right away, honestly the evening is moving along in a blur. We are asked to take the floor for our first dance by the D.J.

Standing up, I hold my hand out to my beautiful wife. "May I have this dance?"

Taking my hand, Darryn smiles up at me and my knees almost buckle. Leading her out to the dance floor, I bring her into me, wrapping an arm tight around her waist.

"I'm sorry you never got a big wedding, I hope this makes up for that." I kiss her lightly on the lips.

"Bryce, this is all perfect. I wouldn't change a thing. Even the events of how we came together I'm thankful for. I know it sounds weird, but without my screwed up past, my life now would never be this amazing. I never imagined I could ever be as happy as I am with you."

This is the moment, I think to myself. Pulling back, I get down on one knee in front of her. You can hear all the gasps of surprise from the guests around us.

"Darryn, you have made this chase one of the best experiences of my life. I believe I started falling in love with you from the very first time you turned me down for a date and trust me, I asked many times and you turned me down each and every one, and each time my heart became yours a little more."

Pulling the ring box out of my pocket, I open it up and hold it up to her. "I'm not going to propose, I've already gotten the honor of making you my wife. I'm going to kneel before you and make you a promise. I promise to spend the rest of my life proving to you my love. Waking up every morning telling you I love you, and going to bed showing you my love every night. I promise to be your strength when you are in need of it, your best friend when you need someone to talk to. Darryn, there are no words that can express my love for you, but I plan to spend the rest of our lives proving it to you. I love you!"

Slipping the ring onto her finger, I stand up and wipe the tears away from her cheeks before I claim her lips in a kiss with promises filled within it.

"I have something for you as well." Taking my hand, she takes a step back from me and then places it onto her stomach.

All I can do is stare. "Are you serious?" I finally find my voice to ask.

She just nods.

"We are going to have a baby?" I ask in disbelief.

Again, she only nods.

Everyone around us is clapping and cheering but I only see my wife. This amazing woman who already gave me the gift of her love, a beautiful daughter, and now another child.

Crushing her against me, I claim her lips and she laughs against mine.

"I love you, Darryn!"

"I love you, Bryce!"

Silent Forgiveness

BOOK 4

CHAPTER
One

DERRICK

"MAY I DANCE WITH THE BRIDE?" I ask, tapping my new brother-in-law on the shoulder.

Charliee makes a beautiful bride! I stood there next to my brother, both of us being asked by Travis to stand up with him, and watched our little sister walk down the aisle on our dad's arm. Kendall, our niece, throwing flowers and Levi, Charliee's hearing dog and best friend, carrying the rings on his collar, both proudly leading Charliee and my dad down the aisle. My mom in full tears as she stood and watched her little girl walk down the aisle to her soon-to-be husband. Charliee stopped and gave her a kiss before they take those last couple of steps and my dad gave her away to the new man in her life, Travis.

The pastor's voice faded to me as I looked at my brother, who only had eyes for his wife Darryn, who was asked to stand with Charliee, and their little girl, Kendall. They are expecting their son soon. My brother and sister have now settled down. Not sure if I'm really ready for the whole wife and kid thing yet, but I have to admit standing there at the moment and seeing how happy Bryce and Charliee was did make me feel a little left out.

"Hey, are you all right?" Charliee's voice breaks through my thoughts.

"I'm dancing with my sister on her wedding day, how do you think I'm doing?" I tease her, leaning down and giving her a kiss on the forehead.

"You couldn't be my protector my whole life." She squeezes my hand and I see the tears form in her eyes.

"Hey, let me make this perfectly clear. Just because you have Travis, who I hate to admit is a great guy, but don't tell him I said that, we need him to fear us a little. We will always be your protectors. That's a job I never expect to retire from."

A tear rolls down her cheek and I brush it away. Wrapping her arms around my waist, she hugs me tightly and I blink a couple of times to keep myself from crying. Rubbing her back, I hug her for a moment and pull back slightly.

"Come on, no crying. This is your happy day, right?" I try to change the mood of the conversation.

Quickly she wipes the tears away and smiles up at me. "I just have one last thing to say. I will always need you and Bryce, no matter who comes into my life. I love you!"

"I love you, too." I kiss her once again on the forehead.

"Sooo, when are you going to find someone to settle down with?"

And there it is, the question I should have been expecting from my sister. "Right now I can say I'm good with life."

"Trust me, people don't come into your life on a schedule, my brother. I personally can't wait to see you fall to your knees over a girl."

"Waiting is what you will be doing, because I have no intention on tying myself down any time soon. You and Bryce may be ready for all of that and kids, but I'm good right now."

"Don't you want kids while you are young enough to enjoy them?" She makes it sound like my hair is graying and I should be retiring soon.

I look over at Bryce who is dancing with his wife, Kendall attached to their legs dancing with them. They look like the perfect little family, what tops off the whole picture is Darryn's round belly between them. Bryce was good with dating someone with a child, and he is a great father to Kendall, but I have to admit when he told me Darryn had a daughter, I thought he was nuts for getting involved with her.

"Do I want kids? Sure, one day. But you make me sound like some old guy, I have plenty of time for the whole wife and kid thing," I defend myself.

Looking back down at her, I notice she isn't even looking at me, which means she has no idea that I just answered her. Instead, she is looking to our right with a huge smile on her face. I follow the direction she is looking and I expect to see Travis, but I don't. I have no idea what she is smiling about.

I squeeze her hand to get her attention. "You know it's rude when you ask someone a question but don't pay attention to the answer," I tease her.

She releases my hand and brings her other one off my shoulder.

"What do you think about Sam?" she signs to me.

Laughing, I realize my suspicions were right about her having me escort Travis's sister Sam down the aisle was a plan to try and put the two of us together.

"I kind of figured you had a hidden agenda behind all of this," I sign back.

"Come on, Derrick, the chemistry is there, we all see it."

Looking to our right again, I now see Sam. That is why Charliee was signing, she wanted to talk about someone without bringing attention to it. Samantha, or as she has told me "Sam", has a fire inside of her. I'll admit that did pique my interest in her. She doesn't back down from anything. We bantered back and forth all night last night at the rehearsal dinner, she never missed a beat, and she kept me on my toes. That red hair fits her spirit. As for the chemistry, last night I did find myself, a couple of times, having to hold myself back from grabbing her and throwing her over my shoulder and not releasing her until we were in my bed. I would love to see that spirit in bed.

I'm sure today we made quite the sight walking down the aisle together. She doesn't look like she is even five feet tall and if so, not by much, and I'm 6'3". She is so tiny I find myself wanting to tuck her up against my side and hold her there. It's strange, I feel like I want to protect her, although she clearly makes it known she can take care of herself.

Sam turns as though she knows I'm looking at her and the smile she sends my way almost buckles my knees. It's a dare, maybe a promise, a need, or maybe just a tease, but I feel it through my whole body.

"Like I said, chemistry." Charliee's voice brings my attention back to her.

"Give it up, Charliee." I lead her over to Travis. "You can have her back now." I smile down at her and kiss her on the cheek, hearing her laugh as I walk away.

I need a beer! Eyes set on the bar, I head for it, not making it far before I hear that one little voice that gets me every time. "Uncle Errick, Uncle Errick."

Turning, I see Kendall in a full run in my direction. No matter what anyone tries with Kendall, my name is Errick not Derrick. I personally like it, it's kind of our thing, my little nickname from my niece. Bending down, I catch her as she launches herself into my arms.

"Dance, Uncle Errick." Her little arms go around my neck and she puts her cheek against mine. How can anyone say no to this little lady? I may have thought my brother was nuts for getting involved with someone with a kid, but I can't imagine our lives without this little girl in it.

Spinning us around, her little squeals and laughter fill the room. "Again, again."

A couple more and I have to stop before I drop her. Looking up, my eyes lock once again with Sam's. It's not a look of sarcasm, or tease, it's one of want.

Kendall wiggles in my arms, bringing my attention back to her. Sitting her down on her feet, she looks up. "Love you." Then she is off running somewhere else.

I need that beer now!

CHAPTER
Two

THE MUSIC IS GREAT, and I have definitely had my fill on drinks I think. The dance floor is full and it's getting pretty warm. After this song I think I need to go and sit down for a while.

The heat instantly goes from warm to blazing. Someone is pressed up against my back. His hands are on my waist. Normally I wouldn't allow someone I don't know to dance up on me like this, but for some reason I don't want to pull away. I'm dancing with a group of girls and not one of them seems to have noticed someone has joined our little circle.

His legs are spread and his knees are bent on either side of my legs. I reach around and grab his thighs. His muscles flex and I hear his deep intake of breath in my ear. His shoulders are curved around me, he has completely engulfed my body with his. It's weird, this is just a dance and I feel protected, wanted.

The music slows, but I can't seem to move out of the cocoon of a man wrapped around me. All the couples are coming together on the dance floor, we can't stand here like this and not bring attention to ourselves. I start to pull away and his hands tighten on my waist.

"Dance with me." His deep voice vibrates down my spine.

I know that voice, but I'm not surprised; I'm excited it's who I thought it was. Spinning in his arms, I finally come face to face with a pair of crystal eyes that are searing through me. Derrick!

We must make one heck of a sight. I'm only 5'1" and Derrick is well over six feet tall. His back is hunched over, so that he can wrap his arms around my waist. Nothing is said as we sway slowly to the music that is playing.

With the song finally ending, he stretches himself up to full height. "Would you like something to drink?"

I need to keep a clear mind right now. "Water actually would be great," I answer and have a need to punch him in the arm when he smiles down at me like he knows why I have decided to stay away from anything to drink that can alter my actions.

Grabbing my hand, he leads me off the dance floor, toward the bar. "Come on, Pint, let's get you water."

Digging my heels in, I stop walking and pull my hand out of his. He turns around with an amused smile. "What did you call me?"

"Pint! It's a fitting name for you. You're like pint-sized."

"Maybe for someone who is ten!" I point out, standing up to him and stretching to my full height, which I still only come to about the lower section of his chest.

He starts laughing but his arm snakes around my waist, pulling me up against his chest. I'm not even sure if my toes are even touching the ground. His hard chest against mine sends a rush of fire through my veins and I find myself wanting to have this man wrapped around me completely.

No one has ever affected me like Derrick does. The first time I met him I was with Charliee having dinner. It was a quick introduction, but even then I found myself wondering what it would be like to have this man's hands all over my body. Since then we have only met in passing. When my brother was involved in a bombing and in the hospital, I came home from school and stayed for a week. We would see each other in passing at the hospital but no conversations happened really.

Last night at the rehearsal was the first time we were actually around each other for more than a couple of minutes. I'm sure anyone watching us would have thought we were either old buddies, or lovers trying to hide our affair with all of the bantering we were doing back and forth. Then the nickname shot across his lips—Pint, really? I've had nicknames about my height my whole life. Depending on who was giving me the nickname would decide on how I reacted to it. When Derrick called me Pint it felt like a bucket of cold water was splashed over me. Now I'm pressed up against his chest and I feel like I'm on fire; a cold bucket of water sounds refreshing.

"Derrick, let go of me. People are starting to look," I say between clenched teeth, my hands on his chest trying to push back and put a little space between us.

His arms only become tighter around me. Between the alcoholic beverages I have consumed this evening and the delicious smell of this man, I'm finding it hard to keep up the fight.

"Do you honestly think I care who is looking at us?" His tone is husky.

I keep my eyes forward and staring at his chest. I know the moment I look up into those eyes I'll be lost and find myself not caring about anything other than crawling up this man and begging him to take me.

What the hell is wrong with me? I want to slap myself. This isn't like me at all. I have never had a guy have this kind of effect on me. Yet, I know if Derrick was to let me go right now I would be very tempted to throw myself back at him.

I need to get some space before I say or do something I regret. Wiggling myself out of his embrace, I take a step back and a deep breath. I'm afraid of what I'm going to see when I look up into those eyes, but I need to seem in control.

"I do care. Now if you will excuse me." I take the first couple of steps to get around him, my knees wobble and I want to curse myself for the reaction my body is having to this man.

Looking up at a side glance as I pass him, I notice that little smirk. That stiffens my back and my legs and drive me to get around him. Looking forward I see the sign for the restrooms and I head straight for the Women's room.

The door closing behind me, I'm relieved when I notice there is no one else inside. Slumping against the counter, I take a couple of deep breathes. This is crazy, why this guy? I have been in school now for almost four years and I have been able to keep myself from being consumed by any guy, wanting to make sure I concentrate on school and get my degree. Sure, I've gone out with friends, had a good evening, danced with guys, let them buy me drinks, but nothing past that. I knew I didn't want anything getting in the way of me getting my degree in Nursing. It's actually been pretty easy to keep to that rule. You can't miss something you have never had, right? One of my roommates asked me once if I was gay. She didn't understand how I could say no to all the invitations I had. A concept most people these days just don't understand. I'm a couple of months away from graduating and now isn't the time for anyone to come into my life, Derrick included.

Grabbing a couple of paper towels, I wet them a little and rub the cool cloth against my neck and pat my cheeks. I can feel the heat from my skin through the thin cloth. It's late, and I'm sure I could leave and Travis and Charliee would be fine with it. I'm sure they are very ready for everyone to be on their way so that they can get to their suite for the night.

Grabbing the rubber band off my wrist, I wrap my hair up into a messy bun and take a couple more deep breaths. Quickly I walk out of the door and down the hall, seeing my brother and Charliee talking to an older couple. I grab my purse off the table and start to head in their direction. Passing a large pillar, I see out of the corner of my eye an arm snake out and wrap around my arm. I'm quickly pulled around, my back now flat against the pillar and a very hard body is pressed up against mine, pinning me in place. I have only a quick second where I am staring into the crystal eyes of Derrick before his head bends down and he claims my lips.

My knees buckle, I need something to hold onto. My hands come up and grab onto the first thing I can find, which I'm assuming is a part of Derrick's shirt because of the feel of material. I have never been kissed like this. Like I'm needed and wanted more than air for another person. His lips are soft, but the kiss is strong. There is a plea, one begging me to feel the same as he does. Fire shoots through my veins and right to my core. I find myself having to fight the urge to crawl up his body and beg him, for what I'm not sure, I've never had these feelings.

"Samantha." My name vibrates against my lips. I usually hate hearing my full name, but there's something about Derrick's voice saying it. I find myself wanting to hear it again, and again.

My face is being cradled on both sides by his hands. There is something so intimate about this kiss, I feel like I'm the only woman who could fulfill this man's thirst right now. It's a very powerful feeling.

"I only wanted a kiss." Derrick's voice is low, almost sounding painful. "I'm realizing just a kiss from you isn't going to be enough."

What is he telling me? His forehead is pressed against mine, his breathing just as labored. I have this need pulsing from my core, almost like my body is begging me to say yes to anything he wants. Why Derrick? What's so different with him than any other guy I have met?

"Samantha, tell me yes, please," he begs.

Hot liquid shoots through my body at the sound of my name again. Grabbing the hair at the back of his neck, I bring his head down to mine and claim his lips, crushing them to mine. He crushes my mouth with his, his tongue darting between my lips to find mine.

I hear someone moan, and feel it vibrate through my chest. Was that me? Derrick adjusts his body, now completely pressed against mine. I can feel his hardness against my belly. A need I have never felt before shoots through me.

"Derrick," I beg against his mouth, rubbing my body against his.

He pulls away suddenly. I'm so dazed, I'm not sure what's happening. All I know is I'm not ready to stop kissing him. Taking my hand, I allow him to lead me. We are leaving the room where the reception is being held and going into the hallway of the hotel. We get to an elevator and I watch as he pushes the up arrow. Suddenly he wraps his arm around my waist and pulls me into his chest, claiming my lips again. The ding of the elevator arriving has him pulling away and as the doors slide open, he pulls me inside. I'm in such a trance I find myself following him without any questions. Derrick only waits for the doors to close. Pinning me to the wall, his lips claim mine again. My hands go to his chest where I grab a fist full of his shirt in each one. What is he doing to me?

Again, the ding of the elevator has him pulling away from me. The doors open once again and I find myself being led down the hall, almost in a run. Derrick pulls a card key out of his pocket and as if in slow motion, I watch as he slides the key into the door and as the green light goes on to signal the door is unlocked, my body goes cold. I watch as Derrick opens the door and goes to step inside, still holding my hand and expecting me to follow him inside, but my feet are frozen to the floor.

Looking back at me, he has a puzzled look in his eyes. "Are you all right?"

What the hell happened to me? How did I end up here, in a hotel room with Derrick? Looking at his questioning eyes, I find it hard to say anything. I have never had a problem telling a guy no. Problem here is I'm not sure I want to tell Derrick no. My body is begging for me to say yes.

Derrick pulls me back into his arms, but I can't look up into those eyes. I know I'll be lost as soon as I do. "Sam, look at me."

My forehead falls forward and rests on his chest. His hands rub up and down on my back.

"Tell me no, Sam, and I will walk you back downstairs." His tone is begging me not to say no.

I need to tell him no. I need to run back downstairs and away from him, but my feet won't move. Then I make the big mistake of looking up at him and it's over. All it takes is one look and all I can do is nod at him. He takes my hand once more and slowly pulls me into the room. I faintly hear the door click closed behind me.

My back is now pressed against the door. Derrick is towering over me, bracing himself by his hands on the door above my head. All I can do is stare straight at his chest. There is still a little voice in my head telling to get the hell away from this guy before I do something I'm going to regret later, but with each inhaled breath of Derrick I take, my body is winning out on the argument.

"Samantha, look at me." His voice is a husky whisper and again with my full name, fire shoots through my veins again.

My head drops back against the door, I close my eyes. I feel Derrick's body rub against mine, I jump when I feel his lips lightly kiss my neck. I have to lock my knees so that I don't end up on the floor.

He trails small kisses up my neck to my ear. "What are you doing to me?" he whispers in my ear.

What am I doing to him? What the hell is he doing to me?! I want to yell back, but before I say anything his lips claim mine. My arm instantly comes up and around his shoulder and my fingers find the very short hair at the back of his head. I feel him straighten to his full height and my feet come up off the floor. Derrick's hands cup my backside, my legs wrap themselves around his waist. There is no way I have any control of my body any longer, I would never climb up a man's body and hold on, yet here I find myself completely wrapped around Derrick.

I don't even realize he has moved us away from the door until I feel the soft bed against my back. For a second panic splashes over me, but then Derrick's tongue finds mine and all is gone. I want this man, who cares about tomorrow and what happens. Right now, I want this man and I want him now.

I hear myself whimper when Derrick pulls away from me. It's completely black in the room and I can't see anything. I hear rustling of something but I'm not sure what. I sit up on my arms, trying to get my eyes to adjust to the dark so that I can see where Derrick went. I jump when I feel his hand grab my foot.

"Sorry, didn't mean to scare you." His voice is soothing, calming.

He removes one shoe and then the other. I hear them hit the floor. My nerves start up again, I can't do this. I'm about to tell him that when I feel his hands slide slowly up my calves, past my knees. My whole body jumps when I feel his hot breath against one of my thighs; when his tongue starts trailing up my thigh, I fall back against the bed.

I have never been touched like this by a guy. I have a need I don't exactly know how to explain or how to fulfill. Every bit of my blood seems to have rushed to my very core and is now just all collected there and pulsing. That very small voice that was yelling at me to stop him is now gone and I have to bite my lip to keep from begging. For what I'm not sure, but all the same I find I have a great need to beg for something.

My hands are fisted into the comforter and I have to try and control the need to press my body against his roaming lips. When his lips leave my skin, I hear a small whimper escape from me. Before I can wonder what Derrick is about to do next, his lips claim mine. It's not a soft kiss, it's strong yet needy. My hands come up and connect with his now naked chest. That's what he was doing, his shirt is off, but I can feel the material from his pants against my legs. I allow myself a second to appreciate the feel of his muscles as I run my hands across his abs, then up over his chest. I feel his muscles under my touch every time he moves, his skin is warm. I bring my hands up and under his arms around to his back. Then down to his backside. His pants are on, but by the feel of the loose fabric I'm going to say they aren't buttoned.

In one quick move, Derrick is now laying under me. Even as dark as it is in the room, I can see the crystal color of his eyes as they seem to glow. I can't seem to look away from him. I feel the zipper to my dress as he glides it down my back. Another quick motion and I feel my feet on the ground, but Derrick is sitting on the edge of the bed in front of me. My dress instantly falls down my body and onto the floor. Charliee had picked out strapless dresses for us bridesmaids so now I find myself standing in front of Derrick in nothing but a lacy pair of underwear.

My eyes have finally adjusted some to the darkness. I watch as Derrick's eyes roam over my body.

"Samantha, there isn't an inch of you that I don't want to taste." His voice is husky and I'm not given a second to let his words sink in before his mouth finds one of my breasts and sucks it fully into his mouth.

My knees buckle and his arm goes around my waist to hold me up. My hands are on his head, pressing myself into his mouth. I can feel the heat between my legs, and a pulse that is begging to be given some attention to. He has one hand teasing my other nipple, and with each tug from his mouth I feel it all the way down into my core. I am barely aware of the lace material being slid down my legs, and how I managed to step out of them without falling over I'm not sure, nor do I spend much time thinking about it.

Derrick stands in front of me and spins me around, I feel the back of my legs hit the side of the bed. I can't stand any longer, so I sit down and watch as Derrick removes his remaining clothes. I don't get much of a chance to admire the man standing in front of me, Derrick places his hands on my thighs and gently pushes my legs apart so that he can kneel on the ground in front of me between them.

One hand travels up over my stomach, through the valley between my breasts and once he reaches my chest, he pushes me back gently. I don't resist. I lay back, resting myself once again on my arms. Our eyes lock and I watch as he leans forward and kisses the inside of one of my thighs. I feel like I should be embarrassed or maybe not so bold, but for some reason all I want to do is beg him for more.

With each kiss, he moves up my thigh and closer to the most heated part of my body. One more and I can now feel his warm breath against me. I moan and my head falls back. As he leans forward, his shoulders widen my legs, opening me up even more for him. The first touch of his tongue and I shoot up on the bed. His hand comes up, covering one breast and holds me back some. His tongue dips in a little more this time, I hear myself moan. A couple more times and I feel my whole body beginning to shake.

"Derrick, please." I'm surprised by my own voice, the plea behind it. I'm begging him.

In a quick movement he stands up, moves me more up onto the bed and is now laying over me. "As much as I would love to keep tasting you, I need to be inside of you."

I feel his hardness pressed just on the outside of my very hot and wet center and I have a strong need to thrust my hips forward to push him inside, and then realization slaps me in the face.

"Derrick, I'm not protected."

"Damn it, how did I forget?" His words surprise me as he quickly gets up and I see him searching the ground for something.

I really only see his shadow in the darkness, but I quickly realize what he is doing when I see him stand up and watch as he puts on protection. Before I can say anything, he is back hovering over me.

"I have no idea what you did to me, I never forget protection," he defends himself.

I have very mixed emotions right now. On one hand, I know this isn't a first for Derrick so I'm glad to hear he usually protects himself, but on the other side of it, I find myself feeling a little jealous thinking of the women before me. How many were there?

Derrick doesn't give me much time to really dwell on it, his lips claim mine, his tongue darting in and finding mine. Once again I feel his hardness up against me. Derrick pushes his hips forward slowly and I find myself holding my breath, waiting for what I know is to come. I may be a virgin but I'm a nursing student, I know what to expect.

"Derrick, please." I'm surprised to hear myself beg him.

I can't help the scream that escapes from my throat as I feel myself tear when he pushes past the proof.

CHAPTER
Three

DERRICK

WHAT THE HELL *is wrong with me?* I think to myself as I'm searching for my pants that have my wallet inside. I never forget protection. I have never slept with a woman and not used protection, and here I find myself not even thinking of it with Sam. It's actually a little unnerving to realize the effect she has on me to get me to forget something I am adamant about. No matter how much a woman tried to convince me that she was protected, or how great I have heard it is without that barrier between us, I refuse to not protect myself. Again, not ready for kids!

I feel like it takes forever to get myself settled and back to Sam. I devour her mouth with mine and find her still very ready for me. I thrust forward slightly and her nails instantly dig into my back. Sliding in a little more, I moan as I feel how tight she is around me.

"Derrick, please." Her voice pleads with me and I can't resist any longer. My tongue darts into her very inviting mouth and with one quick motion I enter her.

"What the…" I freeze. I feel the barrier as I thrust past it, unable to stop once I realize what I have just done, and the scream that escapes from Sam confirms it.

Sam's nails I'm sure have left marks on my back. I don't move, my face is against her neck. Her nails retract a little and I realize she is slowly relaxing, I can feel the muscles around me contracting and that is not helping me right now.

Sam was a virgin! Why didn't she say something? I have questions, a few of them, but with her body pulsing around me I'm finding it hard to think of anything other than having her completely. It's hard to hold still when all I want to do is pull out and thrust back deep inside of her again.

"Sam, you should have told me."

"Would you have not wanted this with me if I had?" she asked.

Not wanted this? "No, I just would have taken this a lot slower. I'm sorry I hurt you."

She wiggles a little under me. I take a deep breath, trying to calm myself and this need for her down. She is so tight around me.

"I'm good. Please, Derrick." There is that plea again.

I brace myself on my arms so that I can see her face. Slowly, I pull out and then I test her as I slowly thrust back into her.

We both moan. "Sam, you are so tight, I'm not sure if I can hold back much longer." I need to be honest with her.

Her arms go around my neck, her hand at the back of my head. She brings my lips down to hers and just before she kisses me, she whispers, "Don't hold back, Derrick, I need you." Then she kisses me like I am her life line, thrusting her hips up, pushing me deep inside of her.

That's it, all control is gone. I quicken the pace and start to feel her pulse around me, she is close. It's her first time and I plan to make sure she doesn't forget it.

"Come on, Samantha, give yourself to me."

The room fills with my name as her body pulls me further and further into her with each pulse of her release. I pull back and with one last deep thrust, I can't hold my release back any longer.

Neither of us move, we just lay here. The only sound in the room is our heavy breathing, both of us trying to catch our breath. I'm sure I am crushing her, but I find it hard to move away. Something inside me wants to stay like this all night. What is that all about anyway? I'm not the type of guy who takes a different woman home every night. Yes, I have had my share of women, and yes, a couple have been one-night stands but normally I have some sort of relationship with them first. None of them have ever stayed the night at my house, to me that's too personal. I haven't stayed a full night with them either. Sure, I don't run out right after, but we don't fall asleep in each other's arms either. Again, too personal.

Shocking myself even more, I'm not ready to say goodnight to Sam. I slowly start to slide myself out of her still very tight clutch, and I hear her sharp intake of breath.

"Are you all right?" I ask as I move over to the bed next to her.

Sam surprises me when she rolls over onto her side and snuggles up next to me, resting her head on my chest. She doesn't answer me but I feel her head nod against me. Again, I'm not into the cuddling, but something in my chest expands and I bring my arm up and around her back and shoulder, bringing her in a little tighter against my side.

OPENING MY EYES SLOWLY, I realize a small amount of light is coming through the slit in the curtains of the room. What time is it? Reaching over onto the night stand, I feel around for my phone but it's not there. *It must still be in my pants pocket from last night*, I think to myself. Turning my head, I expect to find Sam still asleep in the bed next to me, but all I find are empty sheets. Sitting up, I listen for the water in the shower. Nothing. She's gone! How the hell did I not know she got up and left? Sure, I had a couple of beers last night, but nothing that would cause me to knock out like that.

Sitting up, I grab my pants up off the floor, pulling my phone out of the pocket. Checking the time, it's almost nine. Sitting there for a moment, I think back to last night. I know we laid there for a little while but then I got up to clean up a little; I know she went to the restroom afterwards, but returned to bed. I know I laid there for a least an hour holding her close to my side, but neither of us said a word. I know she had fallen asleep, she has this cute little snore I found out last night. So when did she get up and leave is the question. Was she mad because I didn't say anything last night? Honestly, I didn't know what to say. What do you say when a woman gives herself to a guy for the first time?

Last night was a first for me, too. I have never spent an entire night with a woman. I feel a little disappointed to not wake up to her this morning. Like I'm missing out on something. I'm disappointed that she left. These are all new feelings for me, why am I having them now? What makes Sam so different? She has fire inside of her, she gives the fight and sarcasm back. She doesn't do things just to get a guy's attention. She actually comes across as though she would be all right without a guy in her life. She is spunky, but there is a tender side of her as well. I saw it last night a couple of times. Before I found out about her innocence on the whole sex thing, I couldn't figure out what was going on. As soon as the proof presented itself, it all made sense. I just wish she would have said something before then. I know she had a few to drink, I would have made sure she wasn't letting the alcohol lead her into something she would regret.

Maybe that's why she left this morning without saying anything. Maybe she woke up realizing what happened and was upset. I need to talk to her, but how? I don't have her number, and I really don't want to text Charliee. Not only is she on her way this morning to her honeymoon, but she will start asking all kinds of questions if I ask her for Sam's number. Calling Travis just isn't an option at all. I'm sure he would hear the guilt in my voice the moment I said hello. I held the man at gun point on his first date with my sister, I can only imagine what he will want to do to me if he finds out I took his sister's virginity and we haven't even been on a date.

Rubbing my face, I look around like the answer is going to just pop up out of the air. This is crazy, maybe I should just leave her alone. She is the one who left, I don't have to be the one who feels guilty about that. I haven't done anything wrong, I should just let this go, move on. Yes, I should, but I can't.

Jayden was Charliee's Maid of Honor, maybe she will have Sam's number since she had to set all the bridesmaid stuff up. I can just text her, make up some stupid excuse and get Sam's number from her, she probably won't ask a single question before sending it to me.

Grabbing my phone, I find Jayden's number and shoot her a quick text, then decide to go and grab a shower while I wait for her to answer me.

CHAPTER
Four

I **WOKE** up this morning before the sun even came up. I was hot and couldn't figure out why I couldn't kick off the covers to cool down. Then like cold water being splashed over me, the memories of the activities from last night and who I was with cooled me down quickly. I couldn't kick off my blankets because I didn't have any on, I was lying very naked with Derrick. I had gone into the bathroom last night to clean up and when I came back to the bed I had laid back down, this time with my back curled up to Derrick. I didn't want him to ask all the questions and he didn't, he just wrapped himself around me and held me. Strangely I had fallen asleep pretty quickly.

Waking up this morning and having everything crash over me again, I realize I don't want him to ask those questions this morning either. What do I say when he asks why I chose him? I can't even blame it on having too much to drink. Sure, I had a good share but not enough to not know what I was doing last night. There is just something about that man that I am drawn to and after last night I realize it scares the hell out of me. I feel bad leaving this morning with him still sleeping and I can only imagine what he will think, but I have to.

I make it home before five and my parents are thankfully still sound asleep. I take a shower and lay back down, figuring I can get a couple more hours of sleep. No such luck. Every time I close my eyes I feel Derrick's body against mine. It doesn't help I have a slight ache between my legs to remind me of last night. I knew my first time would be uncomfortable, painful, but I don't even remember the pain. I can still feel Derrick inside of me, and how good it felt to have him push deep inside with each thrust. How his tongue felt on my breast, his lips against mine. I'm starting to have the fuzzy sensation again in my stomach, and a need in my core. What the hell is wrong with me?

Lying here is doing me no good. Throwing the covers off me, I get up and look around. I still need to pack and now seems like as good a time as any. Maybe it will keep my mind off last night. I'm leaving to go back to school tonight. My flight leaves at six, and I won't be back until after graduation in two months. By then maybe I will be ready to see him again. It's obvious it's going to happen, I can't ignore him forever, all family functions we will be forced together.

Checking my phone, it's now seven. The sun is up and promising a beautiful day. I'm expecting to hear movement in the house at any time. The knock at my door surprises me and I knock my knee against the footboard of my bed.

"Damn."

"Sam, are you all right?" My mom's voice comes through the door.

Rubbing my knee, I make my way over to the door and open it. "Yeah, I'm fine, just knocked my knee is all. Not paying attention I guess."

"I'm surprised you are up. When your father and I left, we couldn't find you. What time did you get in?"

"Sorry, that must have been the time I walked outside to get some fresh air with one of the girls. It was getting hot in that room." I couldn't even look at my mom as I spoke to her. I busied myself with walking over to my suitcase, totally ignoring the question about the time I got in.

"All packed?" I can hear the sadness in my mom's voice.

"Come on, Mom, don't go getting all sad on me. I will only be gone for a couple months, then I graduate and I'm all yours again."

"I know, it's hard to believe you are already graduating. Don't get me wrong, I'm so excited for you and you have worked so hard. Your dad and I are so very proud of you and even though it's killed me every time you have left to go back, it's hard to believe how fast it's gone."

On those endless days of studying, I felt like I would never make it to this point. Graduating and getting into a hospital seemed forever away. My job here in Washington at the local hospital is already set and ready for me when I finish my test, which luckily is only two days after graduation, and then I'm set to work the ER department. It's exciting and terrifying all at the same time.

I will be moving back home, but saving to get my own place. I'm ready to be on my own. I'm ready for the new chapter of my life.

"I came to ask if you would like to go out and get some breakfast with your father and me this morning. I was going to cook, but decided against it."

Laughing, I don't blame her. Yesterday was a busy day, I'm sure they are exhausted. I know I am. Of course, my exhaustion has nothing to do with wedding preparations. I feel my cheeks heat up just thinking about last night again.

"Sure, breakfast sounds good."

"All right, well get ready, we will be leaving soon." Mom closes my door and I hear her walk back down the hall.

Flopping down onto my bed, I lay back and take a couple deep breaths. I need to get a grip. This is all crazy. It was one night. Sure, a considered important night for a girl, but I'm not a girl, I'm a woman who made a choice and I need to move on. I have to admit, it was a very nice choice to be made. I smile to myself, envisioning Derrick standing in front of me, naked. He was one very good looking guy, losing my virginity to him will never be regretted.

DAD PULLS the car up to the curb of the airport. "You sure you want us to just drop you off here, Sam?"

My phone vibrates in my pocket. Pulling it out, I don't recognize the number on the screen. I ignore the call, if it's important they will either leave a message or call back. "Dad, this is great. No reason for you guys to pay for parking to watch me check in."

Getting out of the back seat, I round to the back of the car to pull my bag out of the trunk. I only have a carry-on this time, so Dad couldn't use needing to help carry my bags as an excuse for them to come see me off.

Dad is already pulling my bag out; he hands it to me and gives me a kiss on the cheek. "Love you, honey. Be careful and we will see you in a couple months."

"Thanks, Dad. Love you, too." I turn to find my mom now standing on the walkway. I walk over and give her a hug. "Love you, Mom."

"Love you, too, Sam. Please be careful. Call us when you land. Someone is picking you up at the airport, right?"

"Yes, I have everything taken care of, I promise I am getting back to the dorms safe and sound." I hug her once more then head for the doors.

Turning, I watch as they pull away. I'll be honest, I would much rather stay than go. I was so excited to leave and go to college after high school. Get a little space, do what I wanted to do, and it was great, for the first month maybe. My family is extremely close and not being able to see them every day is hard. When something happens, like my brother being involved with a bombing, it takes so long to get to them. I don't get to have Friday night dinner with them, or the weekend barbecues that my parents always have. This time because of graduation coming up and finals to prepare for, I flew in Friday night, was there for the wedding yesterday and then back on the plane today to make sure I don't miss classes tomorrow morning. I am looking forward to the normal family life again.

Checked in and through all the fun security, I'm now just sitting here waiting for my flight to be called to board. I remember the earlier phone call and check my phone to find that whoever it was did indeed leave a voicemail.

Tapping on the screen, I bring the phone up to my ear. The voice on the other end shocks me. "Sam! Hey, this is Derrick. I got your number from Jayden. Honestly, I don't know what to really say here on a message, I would much rather have been able to talk to you this morning."

I flinch, he sounds not so much mad as maybe disappointed. Which I am finding to be a little surprising.

"Anyway, you have my number now, so give me a call." Then the line goes dead.

I know I'm not the first girl Derrick has slept with. I would've thought he'd have been happy to not have to worry about me being there this morning. Just "another notch on the bedpost" thing for him. Derrick is a nice guy, very good looking, but a huge flirt. If there is one major difference between Derrick and his twin, it's their demeanor. I really don't know either of them that well; all right, I know Derrick a lot more personally now than his brother Bryce. Bryce is very calm, laid back. His eyes are soft, he is more withdrawn. He allows Derrick to be the center of attention and I think he likes it that way. Derrick is all about having the attention. His eyes are playful, and he is very confident with himself, and very persuasive. He screams sex, and what amazing sex it was.

I feel my cheeks heat up and look around to see if anyone has noticed. I'm sure if you were looking at me right now, you could figure out what is on my mind. I clutch my thighs together to stop the throbbing that has once again started just by thinking of Derrick.

Looking down at my phone, I wonder if I should call him back. What do I say? Hey, sorry I ran out this morning, or that I didn't tell you last night you were about to have sex with a virgin. There is no easy conversation. Then what, where do things go from there? I'm not back home for another two months. Calling him back is not going to fix me leaving without a word this morning. Sure, I can say sorry, but not much of anything else.

My flight is announced and I decide that's my answer. I have to go, so calling him now isn't an option. It was a night, with an extremely hot guy, that I won't have any regrets from. By the time I get back he will have definitely moved on and I will have a new job to keep me busy. It's not a big deal.

CHAPTER
Five

DERRICK

THE SOUND of Bryce's phone announcing yet another text message goes off. It's been dinging with that alert for the past five minutes straight. "Who the hell is texting you? Please don't tell me Darryn has become one of those wives."

"Excuse me." Bryce looks over at me but I ignore the expression he is giving me. "What is your problem anyway? You have been in a bad mood for a week now, what's going on?"

"Nothing, I'm just sick of hearing your phone go off every three seconds. I know Darryn's bored, being on light duty and all, but does she have to text you that often? At least silence your phone so I don't have to hear it."

"All right, what the hell is wrong with you? You're either going to start explaining why you have been in a dark and gloomy kind of mood for the past week, biting off anyone's head that even talks to you, or I'm going to punch you for calling my wife 'one of those wives', you decide."

Bryce is right and I know it. I shouldn't be taking all of this out on him or Darryn, she is amazing, but I honestly can't tell him what is wrong. I'm not real sure of the problem myself to be honest.

"Sorry, I'm not sure what's wrong. I've just been on edge lately. Not sure why really." Laying my head back against the headrest of my seat, I close my eyes and then it happens again. Sam laying under me, naked, begging me with her eyes to not stop. I can still feel her nails as they scrape down my back, it's getting warm in this car.

"Derrick, you aren't telling me something and the look on your face right now just confirms it." Bryce's voice brings me back.

"Nothing you want to hear about, trust me." Sam isn't just some girl I slept with. She is our brother-in-law's sister.

"Come on, Derrick, don't keep things to yourself."

I glare over at him. Like he has any room to talk after keeping that he got married from both Charliee and me. I found out when he had a gun pointed at him by his wife's ex-crazy.

"Look, I said I was sorry, you said you understood," Bryce defends himself.

"I lied."

"Let me put it this way then. Either talk or stop sulking, either one I will take."

"I'm not sulking." A call comes over the radio. Saved by the emergency.

"This doesn't mean you are off the hook," Bryce warns as I flip on the sirens and flip a U-turn to head to our call.

"Bryce, just let it go."

Slamming on the brakes, the car throws both of us forward as a car turns out onto the street in front of us. Words escape under my breath as I make my way around the idiot driver.

"Maybe I should be driving today." Bryce pulls on his seat belt, tightening it across him.

"Shut up, that asshole pulled out in front of us. Would you have wanted me to hit him instead?" I ask sarcastically.

IT'S BEEN A LONG DAY, and thankfully it's finally over. We are pulling into the lot at the back of the station when once again, Bryce's damn phone goes off.

"Can you not put that damn phone on silent?" I am yelling at my brother over his phone, what is wrong with me?

All right, I'm officially concerned for myself now. No woman has ever had this effect on me, so why Sam?

"All right, Derrick, what the hell is wrong with you?" Bryce tucks his phone into his pocket, he is probably afraid I'm going to take it and throw it out the window.

"I slept with Sam." The words fall out of my mouth before I can stop them.

Nothing comes from the seat next to me. Looking to my right I see Bryce looking at me, eyes wide and his lips pressed together in an attempt to not laugh.

"I know, trust me, you don't have to say anything."

"You are talking about Sam, as in Travis's sister, correct?" Bryce asked.

"Yes, Sam as in Travis's sister," I confirm, like we know any other Sam.

"When did this all happen?"

Taking a deep breath, I glance out my side window. "The night of the wedding."

"So that's where you had gone. Charliee was looking for you before she left for the evening. Now that I think of it, Travis had made a comment that he couldn't find his sister either."

Looking over at my brother I now have a need to punch him, he is messing with me about the comment about not being able to find Sam.

"Sorry, I'm not laughing because you slept with Sam, I'm laughing because I can only imagine what Travis is going to say when he finds out you slept with his sister." Bryce sits there laughing at me.

"He is sleeping with our sister!" It sounds desperate even in my own ears and Bryce confirms how stupid it is when I look over and see the look he is giving me.

"I'm pretty sure they didn't sleep together before the first date." Bryce makes the point even though I read it all over his face.

I rub my face. "I know, it was desperate."

"Is this what has you all edgy this week? What happened, it's not like you haven't had a one-night stand with a woman before, what's so different this time?" Bryce makes me sound like some sort of player.

I'm debating on how much to tell him, but it's out there and I find I need to tell him all of it. "She was a virgin."

Nothing but silence fills the car. I looked over and see the shock on my brother's face, then almost disgust. "Don't give me that look, Bryce, I didn't know."

"How didn't you know? There is a very obvious sign, Derrick." He asks the question that is written all over his face.

"Shut up, man. What I mean is she didn't say anything, that's when I found out. Without too much detail, by that time things were pretty…intense." I try to find the right words without too much information.

"Is this why you have been so grouchy all week, because you feel like an ass for sleeping with her, taking her virginity and then leaving her?" Bryce knows my feelings on sleeping over.

"Actually, she is the one who left, not me. This is going to surprise you but I had stayed and when I fell asleep, she was sound asleep in my arms. When I woke up, she was gone. I called Jayden that morning and got her number, even tried calling her, but she never called back," I explain everything to him.

"Wait, you spent the entire night with a woman?" Bryce's eyes are wide with shock. "Was that out of guilt for taking her virginity?"

I've never wanted to punch my brother as much as I do right now. "Can we get off the part of her being a virgin?"

"All right, let's talk about the part of what Travis is going to say when he finds out you slept with his sister."

"That's the main reason I called Jayden for Sam's number instead of Charliee, less of a chance of Travis finding out," I explain. I can't imagine Sam is going to go up and tell her brother she slept with his brother-in-law.

"Okay, so if you aren't freaking out because she was a virgin, then it's because she left without you knowing and hasn't called you back, which brings up another question, why is that bothering you so much? Unless…" Bryce doesn't finish what he is thinking and he doesn't have to, I know what he is thinking.

Sam has somehow gotten under my skin. It bothers me that she just up and left some time in the middle of the night, or that she hasn't called me back. It bothers me that I've allowed myself to let her get to me. Why is Sam so different, why can't I stop thinking of her?

"Oh man, I couldn't wait for this day to happen, I just didn't think it would happen this soon. My brother has fallen for a woman." Bryce says it out loud, something I haven't been able to do.

Taking a deep breath, I lay my head back onto the headrest of my seat and close my eyes. I decide I hate this feeling, that's one of the reasons I stayed away from relationships, they drive you crazy. This one isn't a relationship, it was just one night of amazing sex and I'm already losing my mind.

"I'll admit, it's going to be a lot easier to handle this cranky side of you knowing that this is what is causing it. You have crossed over."

That's all I can take. Reaching across, I punch him in the arm. "Shut up."

"So are you going to try and call her again?" Bryce pushes the conversation forward, laughing at me still.

Shrugging, I have no idea what to do. "Really, I'm going to turn into one of those desperate guys who calls a girl nonstop instead of picking up on the hint that she doesn't want to talk to me?"

"Derrick, calling a girl a second time is far from that desperate guy who makes a hundred calls a day."

"I don't know, I should probably leave it alone. She obviously doesn't want to talk to me." I'm not going to call again. I'm not going to be that guy. If she wants to talk to me, she has my number now.

"Are you going to tell Charliee?" Bryce asks.

"Why, what good would that do? Then she'll say something to Travis. You do remember I pointed a gun at him on his first date with Charliee, right? What do you think he is going to do when he finds out I slept with his sister?" I point out.

"True, but on the other hand, Charliee may be able to talk to Sam and find out what's going on," Bryce suggests.

"We aren't in high school, Bryce, I'm not going through the friend to see if the girl likes me," I say sarcastically.

"Not what I meant exactly. When does she come home again?"

Shrugging, I have no idea. I know she is away for college, that she is going to be a nurse, I think I even over heard her mom telling our mom that she has a job here at the hospital when she graduates, but I have no idea when that is.

"Well this should be fun then." Bryce is being sarcastic as he opens his door and gets out of the car.

I watch as he walks to the back door of the station and disappears inside. I need to get over all of this. Sam doesn't want to talk to me.

CHAPTER

Six

Sam

THINGS ARE CRAZY RIGHT NOW. The next week is going to get far more hectic. I have my last final tomorrow morning, my parents, Travis and Charliee are flying in on Tuesday for my graduation on Wednesday and Thursday we all jump back on a plane back to Washington so that on Friday, I can take my State Board. To top everything off, I wake up this morning feeling like I am going to throw up. I don't have time to get sick.

"Hey, you don't look good, you feeling all right?" Cammie, one of my roommates, asks as I sit down on the couch by her.

I love this dorm set up, it's been my home for the last four years. Its multi-level, each level has a small kitchen area and small living room, with four separate bedrooms off from that area. Two of us are in each room, so it's like having seven roommates.

Cammie is one of my best friends here at school. She and I have been roommates for the past two years. I get along great with the others on our floor but she and I just seemed to hit it off the best.

"Don't even talk about it, I'm refusing to be sick. I don't have the time." My stomach rolls again. I close my eyes and push the feeling away.

"Well, look at it this way, at least you have the weekend to get rid of it before your parents show up," she points out.

"I have one last final tomorrow, sick isn't an option." I lie down, putting my head down on the armrest of the couch and my feet up on Cammie's lap.

"Why don't you go lay down for a little while, I'm sure it will pass. You have been running around like crazy, and if not on the move you have been studying. You are probably just exhausted. Go lay down for a couple hours, I'm sure you will feel better when you wake up," Cammie suggests.

It sounds like a pretty good idea actually. I haven't had much sleep and my head has been spinning with everything that still needs to be done.

"I was going to start packing today, then study a little more."

Cammie rolls her eyes at me. "Sam, you can pack this weekend. After tomorrow it's just a waiting game until graduation, plenty of time to pack. As for studying, I know I'm wasting my breath but I'm sure you know everything inside and out, but I also know that's not going to convince you not to study anymore. Just go lay down for a while, get some rest, I'm sure you will feel a lot better and then you can study after."

She has a point about having this weekend to pack. Sleep does sound good, and I definitely don't need to be sick for tomorrow. "All right, you have convinced me, I'm going to go lie down. If I'm not up in two hours, come drag me out of bed, please."

Cammie just nods her head in agreement. I roll myself off the couch and go to lie down. The second my head hits the pillow, I don't think it takes me long to fall asleep.

Cammie was right, when I wake up a couple of hours later, I feel a lot better. She invited me to go out tonight but I don't want to risk not feeling well for tomorrow so I decide to stay in. I study for a couple hours then order some pizza, which is strange because I'm not a big pizza eater, but tonight it sounds great. Sitting down I watch a movie, eat half the pizza, then decide to go to bed and get some rest. I don't want to risk going to bed late and waking up sick. I think Cammie was right, life has been nonstop and I have had some pretty late nights, all I need is some rest. Better get it now, because next week is going to be a marathon of activity.

SATURDAY MORNING, the smell of bacon is what wakes me up. My eyes fly open and my stomach rolls. What the hell? I woke up yesterday feeling great. Took my test, even went out with Cammie and a couple other friends for dinner last night to celebrate it all being over. I had a couple drinks but not enough to wake up with a hangover.

Another strong scent of the bacon, and it goes straight to my stomach. Lunging out of bed, I run for the door, throwing it open and slamming it against the wall. I feel bad when Cammie sits straight up in bed, but don't have much time to really think about it. I make it to the bathroom, slamming that door shut, and to the toilet just in time for everything to come up.

There is a faint knock at the door, but I'm afraid if I raise my head, I'll throw up again. "Sam, are you all right?" Cammie's voice comes through the door.

I can't answer. I hear the handle of the door, and then it opens just enough for Cammie to poke her head in. "Sam?"

My head is still in the toilet. "I must have eaten something last night that was bad."

Cammie comes and pulls my hair back for me. "We ate the same thing last night, Sam, I feel fine."

She's right, we did. Then what the hell is wrong with me?

"Sam, if I didn't know you were a virgin then I would be asking if you were pregnant." Cammie hands me a wet wash cloth. "I mean you weren't feeling good the other morning, fine in the afternoon, yesterday nothing and then sick again this morning."

She is laughing but I'm now in a complete panic. There is no way, Derrick was protected. Thinking back, my blood goes cold. It's been just about two months since I've been home, but I had my period, right? I had to have.

"Sam, what's wrong? You look like you are about to pass out." Cammie looks me over, no longer laughing but now with concern etched across her face.

I sit there thinking about my last period. I had it a couple of weeks before the wedding, I know that for sure, but now that I think about it I don't recall having it since I've been back. How did I miss that? I can't be pregnant.

"Sam, talk to me, what's wrong?" Cammie tries again.

I can't talk, I can't think. How did I allow this to happen? Cammie pulls me up to my feet and starts walking me out of the bathroom and back into our room. I'm not sure if I'm ready to leave the bathroom yet, my stomach is still rolling, but I'm in too much shock to do anything other than be led by her.

I sit down on my bed, burying my face in my hands. Cammie kneels down in front of me. "Sam, talk to me, something is wrong."

"I haven't had my period in two months." My words are muffled by my hands.

"Did you say you haven't had a period in two months?" Cammie is trying hard to understand me.

I just nod my head, this can't be happening. I have spent the last four years making sure there was nothing that could interfere with me graduating and starting my career, which meant no sex. Only way to assure birth control is to not have sex at all.

Then Derrick enters my life and my mind forgets everything and my body takes control. Tears well up in my eyes. What's going to happen now? How could I allow this to happen? The tears fall down my cheeks and I start to sob uncontrollably.

"All right, Sam, you are scaring me. What's going on? Start talking." Cammie pulls my hands away from my face.

"I'm pregnant," I blurt out.

"How are you pregnant? You know you have to have sex to get pregnant, right?" Cammie asks sarcastically.

Rolling my eyes, I take a deep breath. "Yes, I know you have to have sex, Cammie."

"Then how are you pregnant?"

"When I went home for my brother's wedding…"

"Wait, you had sex when you went home and you didn't tell me?" Cammie cuts me off.

Again, I just nod. "With who?" she asks.

"My sister-in-law's brother," I whisper.

"Did you not use any protection?" Cammie looks at me wide-eyed.

"You know I'm not on the pill, there was no reason for me to be on it. I had a rule and I was good at sticking to it. Then I meet Derrick and well, rules be damned." A small laugh escapes. If she'd seen Derrick she would completely understand.

"Okay, so what, he couldn't use any protection?" Cammie asks, sounding a little mad.

"That's just it, he did. I told him I wasn't protected, he made sure he was." I throw myself back on my bed, covering my eyes with my arm.

"All right, look, let's not jump to conclusions. This could just be a weird form of the flu. You have been really stressed out with everything going on, that could explain why you haven't had a period and you are saying he used protection, so let's not freak out just yet. Let's go out and buy a test, take it, then go from there." Cammie tries being the voice of reason.

She's right, I can't start to panic without knowing if I actually am. I know with stress my body could go through changes, meaning no period, not unheard of, and my immune system could be down which could make me sick. We used protection, so the likelihood that it's just me being worn down is pretty good.

Sitting up, I rub my hands against my legs a couple of times. "How about we go with me just being stressed and just wait and see if this goes away."

If I don't take the test and I get better then we know, right? I try to convince myself.

Cammie's laugh has sympathy behind it. "Honey, I know this is a little scary, but it's better to know for sure than to sit around waiting and thinking about it. If you don't get one then you sit here and worry about it anyway. Let's just find out. It's not going to change no matter which way it goes."

She's right, but if there is no proof, it's still possible it's not true. I'm thinking crazy and I know it, but this can't really be happening. Everything is going great right now and on track. What if I am pregnant?

"Sam, stop, you are going to drive yourself crazy thinking everything that you are right now. Get dressed, I'll go with you and we'll get this figured out. Once we know, then you can decide what's going to be the best thing to do, but let's not freak out yet." Cammie knows what's flying through my mind and she's right. I need to take a test, then decide what's going to happen.

MY PARENTS, Travis and Charliee should be landing in about an hour. They are renting a car and are going to call me when they get to the hotel. I've been packing all weekend. I will be flying back with all of them on Thursday because my State Board test is on Friday. My dad hired a moving van to come pick up all of my stuff to take back to Washington, along with my car. Driving all of my stuff back wasn't an option once I found out the date of my test.

Looking around, I can't find anything else to do at the moment, just wait. Sitting down on the couch, I start getting antsy. Getting back up, I go back into my room and look around.

"Sam, relax, you need to sit down and relax a little." Cammie is a procrastinator and is still packing.

"I just need to make sure I didn't miss anything." I open the closet for probably the tenth time and look inside.

"Just like the last six times or more that you have opened those doors, it's empty. Nothing has jumped back inside since you left the room." Cammie laughs behind me.

I wish something was in here so I could throw it at her, I think to myself. "Maybe I should just head over to the hotel and be there when they all get there."

Cammie turns me around by my shoulders to look at her. "Sam, breathe. Everything is going to be all right."

I fight the tears that I have only let go of when no one is around, but Cammie must notice them because she wraps her arms around me in a tight hug. That is all it takes and the tears fall down my cheeks.

"Sam, everything is going to be all right, you are just exhausted. Tomorrow you will graduate, then you will be back home, which I know you have missed like crazy. You are going to ace that State Board and if you think this is all crazy, wait until you get into that ER unit."

What am I going to do without this crazy woman in my life? "Are you sure you don't want to move to Washington instead of Texas?" I pull away from her so that I can get a little control on my emotions.

"I've been away from my country roots long enough. Plus, I'm looking forward to all the cowboys I'm going to get to work with." Cammie winks at me.

Cammie is going to work with one of the local professional bull riders there in Texas as his personal medic during training when she goes back. It's perfect for her. Cowboys, cowboys and more cowboys, with the opportunity to travel when he does. I'm so happy for her. It sounds exciting but not something I would have been interested in. I want the stability of the hospital and not waking up in a different city every morning.

"As long as you promise if you are ever in Washington or close by, you will call me so we can get together."

Cammie hugs me again. "You aren't going to get rid of me, my friend. Of course we will see each other."

My phone vibrates on my desk. Walking over, I see my mom's picture on the screen. I hit the green button on the screen. "Mom, are you guys here?"

"Yes, honey." Mom is laughing on the other end of the phone. "Were you worrying we wouldn't make it?"

"Not at all, I'm just excited to see all of you. Are you already at the hotel?"

"No, not yet, your dad is getting everything settled with the car. They gave us this little two-door. Have you tried to put a hundred and twenty pound dog in the back seat of a car that size? It's not happening."

Charliee brought Levi, her hearing dog with her, he is never left behind. "Do you guys need me to come pick them up? I have a four-door, he will fit in the back seat."

"No, your dad is handling it. They were told when we booked it we needed at least an SUV. Anyway, we should be heading over pretty soon, just wanted to let you know we are here."

"All right, well I will head over and meet you guys at the hotel and we can decide what's for dinner then," I suggest.

"Sounds good, see you in a little bit. Love you, honey." Mom hangs up the phone before I can respond.

"They made it?" Cammie asks as I shove my phone into my back pocket.

"Yeah, they are having a small problem with the rental, but if I know my dad, he is handling it and I won't be surprised if he gets some of the money back if not all of it."

Cammie looks at me puzzled. "What's wrong with the car?"

"Charliee, my sister-in-law, is deaf and she has a very large hearing dog named Levi, he is beautiful. They don't all fit in the two-door car they set up for them," I explain.

"That's right, I remember you mentioning that about your sister-in-law. Do they need me to take the truck over? I wouldn't mind, definitely enough room for him in the back," Cammie offers.

"No, Dad is getting it taking care of. Plus, Levi thinks he is a person, he sits inside." Laughing, I pull my phone out of my pocket and pull up a picture I have from the wedding with Travis, Charliee and Levi, with his bowtie on, and show it to Cammie.

"You're right, he is beautiful."

Shoving my phone once again in my back pocket, I grab my keys and purse. "Yes and he is very protective of Charliee, he doesn't leave her side."

"Are you heading over now?" Cammie sits on the edge of her bed.

"Yep."

She sits there staring at me, the question she wants to ask written across her face.

"Do you want to come with me? I'm sure my parents would love to see you." I ignore the question I know she wants me to answer.

"No, thank you, I already made plans for tonight, but you have a good time with your family. I'll see them tomorrow but tell them I said hi." Cammie sits with a knowing look on her face.

"All right, see you later." I hurry out of the room and away from Cammie's questioning glare.

"SO SAM, Charliee and I have something for you." Travis looks over at Charliee who hands me a gift bag.

"You guys shouldn't have gotten me a gift, you guys being here is all the gift I want." I take the bag, pushing my chair back from the table a little to set the bag in my lap.

"It's not really a graduation gift." Charliee's smile is stretched from one ear to the other.

Now I'm interested. "Why are you giving me something then?" Looking over, my dad has his arm around my mom's shoulder and they are both beaming. Travis can't keep his eyes off Charliee, the proud husband who just adores his wife.

"Just open it." Charliee is almost bouncing in her seat. Even Levi has sat up and is looking over the table watching.

Pulling out the tissue, I come to what looks like a little shirt. Pulling it out, I see that it's a white onesie for a baby, and my heart jumps in my throat. Turning it around, it reads "My Auntie says I get my good looks from her." All I can do is stare at it.

"Sam, you are going to be an aunt." Travis breaks the silence.

I'm going to be an aunt. Charliee is pregnant. I feel a tear roll down my cheek. I look up and see four bright smiles staring at me waiting for my response. My mom is crying, my dad's chest is pushed out just a little more. They have wanted nothing more than to have grand-babies.

My stomach rolls, oh no. Shoving the chair back and letting the bag fall from my lap, I sprint for the bathroom before I completely embarrass myself in front of everyone in the restaurant. I make it into a one of the stalls and close the door just in time for my dinner to reappear.

Once I'm done, I stand to open the door and realize I'm still holding the little shirt in my hand. Walking out of the stall, I go to the sink to rinse out my mouth. Leaning against the counter, I stare down at the shirt again. It's not the words that have me staring back down at it, it's what that little shirt represents. A little human, a baby. I hear someone enter the restroom but I can't seem to pull my eyes away from what I'm holding.

"Sam, are you all right?" Charliee's voice breaks through the fog in my head, she's concerned.

I now feel terrible, this should be a happy time for her and my brother. I'm excited for them, I really am, but realization just hit me and I can't seem to hide it any longer. I need to come to terms, this is happening.

Looking up at Charliee, the words fall from my lips before I can stop them. "I'm pregnant."

Charliee's eyes spring open wide. "Sam, I pride myself in reading lips well but I know I make mistakes every once in a while, so maybe this is one of those times. What did you just say?"

Charliee knows she read my lips right. No matter how fast I talk, she has never missed a beat. I have tried to remember to slow down around her but she is amazing with her ability to read lips, people who don't know her have no idea she is deaf.

"Charliee, you know what I said. I'm pregnant," I repeat myself.

I haven't said it out loud until now. I didn't even go into the bathroom to look at the little stick after I peed on it, I made Cammie go and look. When she came out I didn't need to ask, her facial expression told me everything that night. I cried for about an hour and then busied myself with packing, putting myself in denial that it was real.

Cammie hasn't said a word about it since then, she has been waiting for me to bring it up and that hasn't happened until now.

Charliee is in shock and guilt now overwhelms me. "Charliee, I'm so sorry. This is your moment, your happy news, and I have completely ruined it. I'm so excited for you two, I swear I am."

Charliee wraps her arms around me and the tears start to flow, I hold onto her tightly as my parents' happy smiles flash through my head. They are extremely excited for Travis and Charliee, as they should be. I don't think I'm going to be able to handle seeing the disappointment when they find out about me.

Charliee pulls away a little so she can see my face. "Sam, who is the guy? What are you going to do about leaving here, or have you decided to stay?"

I don't know what to do, but I don't want to lie to Charliee. "He isn't from here."

Confusion etches across her forehead. I take a deep breath. "It's Derrick's," I blurt out.

Charliee's eyes go as wide as they can and she leans back a little more. "Derrick who?"

She knows who I'm talking about. I hand her the shirt. "This applies to the both of us."

No emotion, no words, her face is a complete blank. My heart drops. "Charliee, I'm so sorry."

"When did this happen?"

I take a step back, putting a little space between us. "Your wedding. Charliee, I'm so sorry…"

I'm cut off when Charliee wraps her arms around me and hugs me tight. "I'm going to be an aunt again." I hear the tears in her voice but they aren't sad ones.

We hold each other for a moment then I realize if we don't get back to the table, my mom is going to be the next one coming through the door and I'm not ready for all of that right now.

Pulling away, I wipe the tears from my cheeks. "Charliee, besides my roommate you are the only one who knows. I can't tell Mom and Dad right now, they are so excited and proud of me graduating. I don't want that to go away yet."

"Sam, your mom and dad are always going to be proud of you, this isn't going to change that."

"I'm just not ready yet. I know I have to tell them and I will, just not now."

Charliee nods her understanding. "What about Derrick?"

I have to tell him as well, definitely not ready for that conversation, but since Charliee knows there is nothing to hide now. He will have to be told.

"I will tell him, just not sure how or when."

Charliee's eyes search mine for a minute. "Everything will be all right, Sam," she reassures me.

I wish I was that confident, but I'm not, I'm terrified. For right now I am going to get through graduation and State Board, then I'll worry about the rest.

When we get back to the table, my mom looks concerned. I walk straight to Travis and give him a hug. "I'm so excited for you, congratulations."

He pulls away, setting me back a little, concern in his eyes. "Are you all right?"

"Yes, sorry. I had the flu earlier and I thought I was good, I think it was a little too much food and my body wasn't ready for it yet. Sorry, the timing sucked."

Travis searches my eyes, trying to reassure himself that I'm all right. I feel bad about lying to him but there is plenty of time to see the disappointment in his eyes later.

Sitting back down in my chair, I find it hard to look over at my parents. My mom will know something is up, she always does.

"Honey, are sure you're all right? We can pay the check and go, you don't need to be sick for your graduation." Mom looks around for the waitress to get the check.

"Mom, I'm good, really. Like I said, just too much food too soon." I look up long enough to speak to my mom but then look away before she can study me.

CHAPTER
Seven

DERRICK

**WHAT were you thinking?

I stare down at the text that I just received from my sister. What is she talking about? That's a very loaded question.

**Would you like to be a little more specific?

I don't have to wait long for a response.

**The night of my wedding. Ring any bells?

It hits me, she is with Sam for her graduation. Charliee and Travis flew out with his parents this morning. I haven't heard from Sam since she left my hotel room sometime that night. What happened, my sister walked off the plane and she just blurted it out?

It's been two months. I've started to text her at least a dozen times, then I'd erase them instead of send them. I haven't dated anyone, I haven't slept with anyone since Sam. Bryce thinks I'm sunk, that I have found that one woman who stops you in your tracks and no one else even makes you look twice. I'll never tell him that I think he's right. It's happened a couple times. Out having a beer, the girl gives me the eyes, but I have no interest. Why am I so hung up on one girl that I slept with one time? Another text chimes through.

** Are you ignoring me now?

I would like to, yes! I know that if I don't respond she is going to keep texting. I'm actually surprised she seems upset by this, she is the one who tried to pair us up.

**If I'm not mistaken, you were the one trying to play match maker, I'd think you would be happy.

There is a part of me a little irritated, but then there is that part that is happy to hear Sam is still thinking of that night. Why tell Charliee now? I would think they have been in contact with each other since the wedding. Why did Sam just now tell Charliee about that night?

I know Sam is coming back here to Washington after she graduates. I was able to get a little information from my sister. She told me that Sam has a job waiting for her at the hospital as an ER nurse, which means we will probably run into each other at the hospital. With her brother married to my sister, if we don't see each other during work, we will definitely run into each other at family functions, especially now that Travis and Charliee are expecting a little one.

Travis and Charliee had a little get together last week with our parents, Bryce and his family, myself and Travis's parents, and shared the news with everyone. You would think with both my brother and my sister giving my parents some grandbabies they would be happy, but no, the first thing my mom asked me was when I was going to settle down and join my siblings in the family bliss.

My sister hasn't respond to my text.

**Are you ignoring me now?

I throw her own words back at her.

It takes a minute but her response comes through.

**You're right, I'm sorry, that all came across wrong. I think I am just surprised is all. She will be back in a couple days, promise me you won't ignore her call when she tries to reach out to you.

Wait, what? Why do I feel like I have missed something? Charliee makes it sound like she knows Sam is going to be calling me. I'm not sure how I feel about that. Why now after two months? Why couldn't she call me back after I called her that next day?

**Charliee, why do I feel like you know something that I don't?

I can't shake this feeling like I'm missing something.

**Just promise me Derrick, I don't know the whole story of what happened between you two, but when she does try and talk to you, please give her a chance.

I want to tell my sister to tell Sam not to bother, I'm over and past it all, but I can't because if I'm being honest with myself, I want to talk to Sam. I haven't stopped thinking about that night and it's driving me a little crazy. Maybe if I can talk to her I can get past her.

**All right, I don't know what this is all about, but I promise I will talk to her.

**Thank you, Love you.

I have a lot of questions I want to ask her, but I have a feeling she isn't going to answer any of them. I will just have to wait and see if Sam actually calls.

**Love you too.

WHEN MY ALARM goes off I realize I haven't slept at all. I wanted to text my sister a number of times throughout the night and make her tell me what was going on. The more I laid here and thought about it, the more it bothered me. I almost called Sam, even pulled her number up a couple of times, I just couldn't hit the call button.

Getting to work, I throw the car keys at Bryce. "Here, you can drive today." I normally drive, today I just think I'm too distracted.

"I'm having one of those twin moments. Last night I was very restless and now I see you this morning and I know something's up. Want to talk about it?" Bryce shuts the driver door but doesn't start the car.

"Last night Charliee texted me, Sam told her that we slept together." Looking over at Bryce I see the confusion I am feeling.

"Why would she tell her now?" he asked, puzzled.

"That's exactly what I want to know. Then she made me promise that when Sam calls, I will answer her call and not ignore it." I pass him my phone with the text messages from Charliee. "This is our conversation from last night."

Bryce glances over them and hands the phone back. "Any idea on why now? Did you ever try and get in touch with her other than that day after?"

Shaking my head, I stare down at the screen of my phone, like all of a sudden all the answers will just appear on it. "No, I almost did a couple of times but I figured why push for something she obviously doesn't want to have anything to do with. I'm not going to beg her to talk to me."

"I understand, you don't have to explain it to me. Why don't you just try and call her? From what Charliee says she is going to call, why wait? It seems to be driving you a little crazy." Bryce starts up the car and pulls out of the parking spot.

"I almost did a couple of times last night. I haven't slept at all and the more I think about it, the more questions I have, but she graduates today. I don't want to ruin all of that with this conversation. I will just have to wait." That's sounds a lot easier than I think it's going to be.

"I have to say I have never seen you so distracted by a woman, it's kind of nice to know you aren't immune to a woman's charm like I thought that you might be." Bryce is trying to hide the smile but it's not working.

"What's that supposed to mean, immune to a woman's charm?" I question my brother.

"Come on, man, you have never let a woman get to you like Sam has. All I'm saying is it's nice to know you are just like the rest of the male gender out there. There is that one woman that is going to put you to your knees."

Put me to my knees? Really? What is he babbling about? "Sam isn't under my skin if that's what you are trying to say."

Bryce laughs out loud and I find that I want to punch him. "Oh no? Then why have you not gone out once since Charliee's wedding?"

"How do you know I haven't gone out? I don't need to call you first before I go somewhere. I do have other friends I hang out with." I try to sound convincing but I can hear it myself, I'm not.

"Then there is that officer, Kelly, you know the one who flirts with you every morning, begging with her eyes that you just ask her out, but I think you just like the flirting. Anyway, you have been dodging her as well. Come on, Derrick, you are talking to me. I know you, stop denying it." Bryce gives me the look like he dares me to try and deny it, but I can't. Damn it, he is right.

Rubbing my hands over my face, I look out the passenger side window. "What the hell is wrong with me?"

"Man, I warned you. When the right one comes along there is nothing you are going to be able to do about it. Brother, I think you have found that one." Bryce has that damn smile on his face again.

"Found her? One night, that's all we have had, Bryce. One damn night, and to top it off she left in the middle of it without a word. How can I be hooked on a woman who wants nothing more to do with me?" I ask out loud, but am more speaking to myself.

"That's just it. You have finally come up against a woman who isn't following you around like a puppy dog, flirting with you nonstop, begging you with her eyes to choose her. Sam is running from you, not to you. She's not making it easy for you." Bryce puts it out there.

"So you are saying I want what I can't have." I want to clarify.

Bryce nods. This is crazy, I swore I would never be one of those guys and look, here I am, realization smacking me right in the face. I'm one of those guys.

IT'S BEEN two weeks and nothing from Sam. I have no idea what my sister thought was going to happen but she somehow misread the conversation completely wrong. The worst part is it's still driving me crazy. Bryce has even threatened to talk to her himself, he says I'm impossible to be around right now. Why can't I just move on? She obviously doesn't want to have anything to do with me, but I just can't seem to get that one night, just one damn night, out of my head.

My phone vibrates next to me. It's a text from my sister.

**Why aren't you here???

Wow, three question marks. Why she needs to ask that question is beyond me. Yes, she and Travis invited me to Travis's parents' house tonight for a little congratulations barbecue for Sam. She received notice yesterday that she passed her State Board test, which now officially makes her a nurse. There is absolutely no reason for me to be there, did Charliee really think I would show up?

**Busy!

I look around my living room. Yes, I'm extremely busy. I have leftover pizza sitting in front of me on a paper plate, not touched, and an open beer I have only taken a drink of sitting next to it. The television is on, but I'm not paying any attention to what is on, I think it's some kind of infomercial. Yes, very busy guy!

A box flashes up onto my screen with Charliee's name on it.

**I was hoping to talk to you.

About what? She can talk to me anytime, why there?

**Charliee what's going on?

My sister is keeping something from me, even in text I can tell. Plus, every day for the past two weeks she has texted me asking the same question. Has Sam called yet? To be honest, I'm done with this game. I want to know what's going on and what better way than to have both of them there together to tell me what the hell is going on?

**I'll be there in a few.

I type back quickly as I head to my room to change. Tonight, this ends. I need to move on from Sam, what better way to talk to her than in person? Then maybe my sister will back down as well.

CHAPTER
Eight

SAM

CERTAIN SMELLS, and it doesn't matter what time of the day it is, get to me now. I never know what's going to set off my stomach anymore and living with my parents, keeping this little secret hasn't been the easiest. When the smell of hamburgers from outside drift into the house when someone opens the back door, my stomach rolls instantly and I'm happy I am standing with Charliee. She is the only one here who knows about the baby. So when I take off for the bathroom without a word, I know she won't ask any questions.

When I decide that my stomach has settled enough to go back to the party, I rinse out my mouth using a little mouth wash my mom always keeps in the guest bathroom, and walk out the door to find Charliee standing in the hall waiting for me.

"Why haven't you called Derrick?" she asks, her phone in hand.

What am I supposed to say to him? Hey, sorry I left without a word that night, or never called you back, but guess what, I'm having your child. "Charliee, can we talk about this later?"

She shakes her head no. "Sam, you need to talk to him. You need to tell him." She looks down at my still flat stomach.

"Why? Do you honestly think your brother is going to care?" I shout, then look around, thankful no one is close by.

Charliee's eyes go wide. "Yes, Sam, I think my brother is going to care that he is going to be a father. Why would you think he wouldn't?"

It isn't fair that I am yelling at Charliee, but she just isn't backing down from this. Every day I get a text asking why I haven't called Derrick. I take a deep breath. "Charliee, I need you to let me do this on my own. Things have been a little crazy since I have been home. I will talk to Derrick, I promise."

Charliee looks down at her phone, she must have gotten a text or something. She puts the phone in her pocket, gives me a hug and then turns and leaves me alone in the hallway. What just happened? I yelled at her for no reason, that's what happened. I need to find her and tell her I'm sorry. I walk down the hallway to the living room but can't see Charliee anywhere.

"Sam, are you all right?" Mom's voice comes from behind me.

Turning around, I see the concern in her eyes. "I'm great, Mom, why?"

"You look a little pale. Are you sure you are feeling all right?" Why does she always seem to have a look like she knows?

The doorbell goes off and I give my mom my best smile. "I promise, Mom, I'm good. I'll get that." Turning quickly, I go to the door, thankful for the interruption of the conversation. That is until I open it.

"Derrick!" Why is he here?

He doesn't say anything, he just stands there, our eyes locked. I can't breathe; just the sight of him takes my breath away. *How corny does that sound?* I think to myself.

"Sam, who is it?" My mom's voice comes from behind me, causing me to jump. I feel her come up behind me, looking around to see who is at the door. "Derrick, we are so happy you could join us. Sam, let him in."

I can't move. Derrick looks back at me from my mom, a small smile on his face. "Thank you for inviting me, Mrs. Kendricks."

That smile about drops me to my knees. My hand grasps the door knob tighter and I lock my knees.

"Sam, let him in." I shake my head at my mom's words, I need to get a grip on myself. Slowly I move aside and as Derrick walks past me, I'm reminded of that night. His smell alone makes me want him.

He doesn't say another word to me, just follows my mom out to the back yard. I want to run, leave this house, Derrick, everyone and just hide for the rest of the night. Looking out to the front yard, I wonder if anyone would realize I was gone.

DERRICK HASN'T TRIED to speak to me once since he got here. I'm relieved, but find myself a little irritated, or maybe more disappointed as well. Looking around, everyone is outside and enjoying a beautiful June night. Dad has the fire pit going. This was the one thing I missed the most when I was away for school. These little family barbecues. Looking around at everyone, my eyes lock with Derrick's. That pulsing feeling I get in my core when I think of him is happening again. Those eyes, I remember them from that night the most. Even in a dark room you can see those eyes, crystal in color. Right now they are full of questions, ones I don't think I'm ready to answer.

Turning away, I go into the house. Once in the kitchen, I grab a glass and pour some lemonade, something I can't seem to get enough of. I take a drink and enjoy the cool feeling as it goes down my throat.

The temperature in the room changes and my nerves are on alert. I feel him against my back, his arms wrap around me from both sides, pinning me to the counter so that I can't turn around.

"Are you going to ignore me all night?" His voice is quiet and warm as his words whisper in my ear. His body is tight against my backside. I'm finding it hard to breathe.

"There is nothing to talk about." I find a little voice, but it's not much, I'm not even sure he heard me.

One of his hands goes to my arm and turns me around to face him and he takes a step even closer; I'm not sure how much closer he can get. Once facing him, his arm goes around my waist. We are so close I have no choice but to look up at him.

"Why didn't you call me back? Better yet, why did you leave without saying anything that night?" He gets right to the point.

I try to look around him, praying that no one is paying any attention to us, but I can't see around him. He is so tall and I am so close to him, but I'll admit to myself it feels good to be in his arms again. I find that I have to fight the urge to cuddle into him even more.

"Do we have to do this tonight, Derrick?"

He nods his head. "Yes, and you have no one to blame but yourself. You have been home for two weeks, Pint."

Pint! There is that name. As much as I want to yell at him to never call me that again, I can't, I kind of like the way it sounds coming from him. Between his chest being pressed in front of me, with his smell surrounding me, and his low voice which seems to vibrate through every bone I have every time he talks, and those eyes, damn, they are changing to that crystal clear color, I'm finding it hard to think straight.

"We can't stand here like this, Derrick. What if someone sees us?" I try to wiggle a little room between the two of us and find that is a big mistake, all it does is rub very strong, hard parts of him against very sensitive parts of me.

"I'm not worried about who sees us, but if you are then you better figure out a place we can go and talk or we are doing it right here." He isn't going to let this go I'm finding out.

I take a deep breath. "Fine, we can talk, but not here."

He stares down at me for a moment then takes a couple steps back, and my knees almost buckle without his support to hold me up. Turning, I lead him to the stairs, my room is the only place I can think no one will barge into.

Once we are both inside my room, I shut the door and turn around. Maybe this wasn't the smartest place to go, my eyes go directly to my bed. Quickly I move over to the window and look down at everyone in the back yard.

"What do you want to talk about?" I ask without turning around.

"Let's start with why did you leave the night of the wedding without a word?" The question is straight and to the point.

"Come on, Derrick, I may have been a virgin, but I wasn't stupid. You aren't the type of guy who wants to cuddle after a night in bed with a girl." My words are harsh I know, but he can't deny it's true. I know Derrick's type.

"How do you know what kind of guy I am?" My accusations have bothered him, I can hear it in his voice.

"Tell me I'm wrong, Derrick," I challenge him.

Silence stretches through the room. He can't tell me I'm wrong. My heart drops a little. I know I'm not wrong, what will be his reaction when I tell him about the baby? I can't look at him, I'll lose it if I do. "Derrick, there really isn't anything else to say."

"Sam, would you please turn around and talk to me? This isn't a conversation I want to have to your back," he pleads.

I can't act like it doesn't bother me that he isn't interested in anything other than a night here or there with a girl if I'm looking at him. Looking down at my hands, I shake my head. "Derrick, there really isn't anything else to say," I try again.

His hand clasps down on my shoulder and he turns me around. "I have something else to say, Sam, and I don't want to say it to your back."

He takes my hands and takes a couple steps back. He sits down on the edge of my bed, which puts him below me. "Sam, I'm not going to lie to you and say you are wrong about the type of guy I am."

My heart drops, hearing him admit to it isn't something I was prepared for, or how I would feel hearing it from him. I have to blink a couple times and look up and away from him to keep the tears from springing to my eyes.

"So let me ask you this, if you knew what kind of guy I was, why did you give yourself to me that night? Why did you decide I was going to be your first?" His question is blunt and has me bringing my eyes back down to him in shock.

"Why me, Sam?" he asks again. I try to step back and pull away from him, but he isn't releasing me. He stands up and crushes me to his chest. His knees are bent so that we are eye to eye. "That night wasn't only your first, you changed something in me that night as well. That was the first time I wanted to keep a woman in my arms through the night, but I woke up to an empty bed. So you are right, that is the type of guy I was, but something that night changed and I realized I didn't want to be that kind of guy anymore."

I don't realize I am crying until his hand comes up and with his thumb, he wipes the tears off my cheeks. I look into those eyes and I'm lost. His lips brush mine, I need to pull away, put distance between us, but I can't. Before I know it, my arms are wrapped around his neck and my fingers dig into his hair at the back of his head. He stands to his full height and my feet leave the ground, my legs wrapping themselves around his waist. He holds me like I weigh nothing. He moans and it vibrates through his chest against mine.

"What are you doing to me?" he whispers against my mouth then claims my lips in a kiss that instantly makes my core pulse with a need for him.

A loud knock at my door brings me back to reality. "Sam, are you in there?" My brother's voice comes through the door.

My legs fall from around Derrick's waist and he sets me down on my feet. His forehead is against mine, both our breathing is labored.

Again, Travis knocks on the door. "Sam?"

"You better answer him or he may come in on his own," Derrick whispers.

He's right and I definitely don't want to have to explain this to him right now. "Yes, Travis, I'm in here."

"Hey, Charliee isn't feeling the best, we are going to take off, but we wanted to say goodbye," he says through the door.

"You know, the first time I met him I held him at gun point in my sister's living room and they were only going on their first date. I can only imagine what he will want to do if he finds me in his sister's bedroom making out with her," Derrick jokes in a whisper.

"I'll be right down, Travis, just give me a minute," I yell loud enough for him to hear me through the door.

He doesn't respond, but I hear his footsteps going down the hall. "Charliee has told me that story actually." I think back to that night when I first saw Derrick.

Charliee and I were meeting for dinner and he had come in after work to pick up his dinner. Even that night I was drawn to him. We had spoken maybe a whole sentence to each other but I couldn't get him off my mind after I went back to school after that visit. When I came back when Travis was involved with the bomb, there was no time for socializing. I was more concerned about my brother, but I'll admit, the couple of times we ran into each other in passing I felt the electricity between us. Then came the wedding. Charliee had told me I would be paired up with Derrick and I was sure I saw a little mischief in her eyes when she told me. Even though I wouldn't have told her I was like a little high schooler who wanted to jump up and down over being thrown in with the cutest guy in school for a project kind of thing. Never in a million years would I have thought I would be pregnant with Derrick's child.

"Go downstairs, I'll stay up here for a few moments, then make my way down." Derrick offers a way for this to stay between the two of us.

He probably doesn't want his sister asking any more questions than I do.

I nod and pull out of his arms, something I find very hard to do. When I get to the door, I look over my shoulder, and he just smiles at me. No, "I'll call you later," or "call me later," just that smile. My chest feels heavy, but again I don't say anything either.

Walking down the stairs, Travis and Charliee are standing with my dad by the front door. "Are you all right?" my brother asks as I approach the three of them.

I look at Charliee and I see the question in her eyes, she even has a small smile on her lips. She knows I was up there with Derrick, damn her for being so observant. I see it written all over her face. I give her a slight shake of my head, hoping she will understand. She does, her smile instantly leaves her face. I know she is disappointed in me, but it's just not the right time, or maybe I'm just not ready to tell Derrick yet.

I bring my attention back to my brother who is glaring at me a little strangely, I put the best smile I can on and hug him. "I'm fine, I was just looking for something real fast."

He pulls away and searches my eyes. I keep eye contact with him, because I know the second I look away he will know I'm not telling him something. "All right, well I hope your first day at work is great, call me if you need us for anything. We love you." He leans over and gives me one more hug then turns to open the front door.

Turning back to Charliee, I want to yell at her to stop looking at me like that, she is great with the guilt look. "I'll text you later," she tells me before she wraps me in a tight hug.

I know all of this is hard on her. Derrick is her brother, she is keeping a pretty big secret from him that has to do with a huge change in his life, but she is respecting my wishes by allowing me the time I need to tell him myself.

I watch as they leave, shutting the door behind them. Turning around, I look up the stairs. I see the shadow of my bedroom door opening. "Come on, Dad, let's get back to the rest of the party outside." I lead him away from the stairs before he sees Derrick.

CHAPTER
Nine

DERRICK

SAM IS HEADING BACK to the backyard with her dad when I come out of the room. I think about going back out there but decide against it. I want to speak to Charliee a little, something about tonight still doesn't seem finished. I feel like I am still missing something, but Charliee and Travis just left and there really isn't any other reason to hang around. I should go and say goodbye, my parents are still here, but I feel like that may raise a few eyebrows on why I'm not back there now. I'm not really worried about what people think, that is if they figure out something is going on between Sam and me, but she seems to be. Leaving just seems like the right option at the moment, I'll deal with my mom telling me how rude it is to just sneak out later.

The look Sam gave me as she was leaving the room is etched in my mind as I drive home. Like she was waiting for me to say something. I'm not saying I won't call her later, but honestly I feel like now it's in her ballpark. She made it very clear on the type of guy that she thought I was. Being honest with myself, she wasn't wrong and I saw the look in her eyes when I confirmed that she was right, but I tried to tell her something changed that night, that maybe that kind of guy isn't who I want to be.

I don't disrespect women, my mom would have beaten the life out of me if she ever heard that I did. Women were always aware of what they were getting with me. Was it necessarily right, maybe not, but I haven't met anyone I wanted to take things further with. Then this pint-sized virgin comes into my life and sends my mind into a whirl-wind. Even tonight, it took everything in me not to walk right up to her and kiss the hell out of her and then make her tell me why she walked out on me that night. I didn't care who was watching or knew what was going on between us. Then while we were up in her room, I wanted to crush her in my arms and beg her to give me a chance to prove to her I'm not that guy anymore.

She isn't fooling anyone either, she was affected by me as well. You don't wrap your legs around someone like she did me and claim you aren't affected. Now my question is why is she fighting it? She looks almost scared; maybe instead of waiting on her to convince herself, I should convince her myself.

Pulling up into my driveway, I turn off the car and sit there for a moment. Damn it, my brother is going to love this.

Picking up my phone, I find Bryce's name and push call. After the second ring, he answers. "Hey, what's up?"

"Where were you guys tonight?" I ask, a little surprised when I didn't see them at the get together. I know we were all invited.

"We were going to go, but then Darryn started not feeling too well so we decided to stay in. I called Travis and let him know. I'm assuming you went and to be honest, I'm a little surprised," Bryce says on the other end.

"Yeah, that makes two of us. I wasn't going to go, but Charliee texted me and told me I needed to be there. I decided I needed to figure out what was going on so I dropped by."

"And what did you find out? I'm assuming you finally spoke to Sam."

"Well, I found out she thinks I'm a player and decided that she would walk out on me before I could walk out on her." I broke down the conversation to the short version for my brother.

Bryce laughs on the other end. "So she has you figured out is what you are telling me."

That hurts a little, why does everyone make me out to be some lady user or something? "For one, would you guys stop making it sound like the only thing I do is sleep around and leave them with a broken heart or something?" I feel the anger boiling up inside of me.

"Hey, man, sorry, that's not what I meant," Bryce starts to defend himself, but I'm getting tired of hearing it.

Taking a deep breath, I realize maybe I'm more embarrassed now about my past relationships because I now kind of know what it feels like. I didn't expect anything from Sam after that night when we began the events of the evening. Then something changed, and when I woke up and found her gone it felt a little empty. That's when I realized maybe even though there is an understanding, it doesn't necessarily make the situation easier when you wake up alone the next morning. The big difference is I haven't snuck out on someone. It's all straight up from the beginning.

"She did something to me, Bryce, even after seeing her tonight all I can think about is wanting to see her again," I finally confess.

"Well, it's official, you have crossed over, man. Little advice, don't fight it, just fall to your knees gracefully." Bryce hands out the advice.

At least he didn't say, "I told you so," I think to myself. "Thanks for the advice. You're working tomorrow, right?"

Darryn is due any day, Bryce and I are usually always on the same shift, but he has been taking off days to be home with Darryn if Mom can't get over there to help with Kendall.

"I'm planning on it, unless this little guys decides tonight is the night," he explains.

"All right, I'll see you in the morning then. Call if that nephew of mine decides he is ready."

"Will do." Bryce then hangs up the phone.

I sit there staring at my phone. As I scroll through the names on my phone, I stop on Sam's. This is crazy, how does this happen so fast? I hit the button on the side of my phone instead of the call button, shutting the phone down. I'm not calling her tonight. I want Sam, I'll admit that, but I need to know that she wants me as well. I need to know she believes I'm not going to just use her like she has voiced that she fears I'm going to do, at least that's what I'm getting from what she said earlier. I've called and I was the one who went to her tonight, it's in her ballpark now.

HAVING sirens on a vehicle comes in handy when you get the call that the newest member of the Brooksman family is deciding it's time to arrive. Bryce got the call from Mom saying that she was heading to the hospital with Darryn, whose water just broke, just before we were heading out of the station to start our patrol.

"I knew I shouldn't have come to work today." Bryce keeps looking at his watch, his leg bouncing like crazy in the passenger seat.

"Relax, we will get there, Bryce." I try to hide the little smile on my face at how nervous my brother seems right now.

It takes about ten minutes from the station to reach the hospital. I pull up to the front of labor and delivery and drop Bryce off at the door. "Go on, I'm going to call into the station, let them know what's going on and park the car."

Bryce doesn't respond, he throws open the door and starts running. I don't think I have ever seen my brother this nervous.

After calling the station and parking, I go inside and find Mom sitting in the waiting room alone. "Mom, everything all right?"

"Yes, I just came out here with Kendall once Bryce got here." She pointed over at my niece who is sitting at a little table, coloring book and crayons already spread out in front of her.

Kneeling down, I kiss my niece on the forehead. "How's my favorite girl?"

She looks up at me holding a purple large crayon in her hand. "Color, Uncle Errick?"

How do you say no to that? I'm sure I look pretty comical sitting in the little kid chair, my knees up to my chest, but I'll risk looking a little dorky for this little girl. "I would love to color with you." I take the crayon from her hand.

Charliee arrives about thirty minutes later, my dad coming in right behind her. An hour later Kendall is starting to get antsy. "I'm hungee." She gives me those puppy dog eyes that she knows how to use on me.

"Come here, Kendall, your mom packed you some snacks in here." My mom picks up the backpack and starts looking through it.

"Mom, I need to move a little. I'll take her down to the cafeteria and get her a little something to eat," I offer, needing to walk a little.

"If you are sure, that would be great. This isn't easy for an adult to sit and wait for, let alone a three-year-old." Mom looks relieved for the offer.

I hold my arms out to my niece, "Come on, little one, you are coming with me. Let's go see if we can find some cookies or something."

Down at the cafeteria we find cookies and some crackers, along with some fruit punch that Kendall asked for me to buy for her and share. Not really my choice of drink, but again can't say no to her. Checking out, I turn to head out and come face to face with Sam.

"Derrick!" Her eyes are wide with surprise.

It's been almost a week since her little party and I haven't heard from her. "Sam! How are things going here for you?"

Shrugging her shoulders, she smiles a little. "Good, I think I'm finally getting over the nerves. Hello, Kendall, how are you?"

Kendall holds up her cookies. "Cookies."

Sam laughs and it hits me right in the chest. I'm not sure if I ever remember hearing her laugh. I know her smile can send fire through my veins, but her laugh sets off every nerve in my body.

"I see you have cookies, are you sharing with Uncle Derrick?" Sam asks, looking straight at Kendall. I think she is avoiding eye contact.

Kendall wraps her arms tightly around my neck, smashing us cheek to cheek. "Uncle Errick."

Sam's smiling eyes finally come to mine and I have to lock my knees. What the hell just happened? "What time do you get off work tonight?"

Sam's eyes stay on mine, like she is trying to read my mind. Her smile has faded a little. She looks back at Kendall. "What are you guys doing here?"

She is ignoring me. That's fine, I've realized waiting on her to call me was probably not the way to go. I'm not going to be that guy that begs, but I'm going to be the one who makes it real hard to say no to, I decide.

"Brother coming," Kendall answers.

Sam's eyes shoot over to me. "Darryn is finally having the baby?"

"Yep, we were all wondering if he was ever going to join us." I lock eyes with her, daring her to look away.

There is something behind her eyes. Something she wants to say but she is fighting it. "Sam, what time are you off tonight?" I ask for the second time.

She just stares at me for a second, but she doesn't look away. I can tell she is trying to decide if I'm worth the effort and I want to tell her to just give me a chance. Finally, she takes a deep breath, "I'm off at six."

"I'll pick you up at your house at 7:30 then." I don't ask because I know she would say no right away.

Sam just stands there staring at me. She wants to say yes, I see it written all over her face, but she is fighting it.

"Come on, Pint, give me a chance."

CHAPTER

Ten

THERE IT IS AGAIN, that nickname. Every time he says it I want to crawl up into his arms and cuddle into his very inviting chest. When I turned and saw Derrick at the cashier with little Kendall in his arms, her laughing at something he was saying, I froze. If I would have kept moving then he would never have seen me, but no, I was standing there staring straight at him when he turned to leave. Now here he is, in uniform, holding his niece and looking very good. He is amazing with that little girl. She is his world. I couldn't keep my eyes off of them during the wedding rehearsal and then the day of wedding. There is something about a guy who will drop anything for a child. That thought brings me back to our little one. He has no idea that he is going to be a dad and I'm making his sister keep this very large secret from him, and it's just not fair.

"Uncle Errick a chance." Kendall's little voice breaks through my thoughts.

"Yeah, give Uncle Errick a chance," Derrick repeats after her.

I can't help but laugh, the two of them make quite a pair. "Well it's a good thing for you, Errick," I pronounce his name like Kendall, "that you have such a cute supporter." I reach across and tickle Kendall's tummy.

"Is that a yes?" Derrick asks, his eyebrow raised up with surprise.

We need to talk, I need to tell him. *If for no other reason than for Charliee,* I think to myself. So much can go wrong with keeping this a secret, the number one thing being it coming from Charliee instead of me. Not that I think she would tell him on purpose, but the possibility of it slipping is big.

Looking up into Derrick's eyes, I see hope in them, maybe I was wrong about him. "It's a yes."

Kendall starts clapping her hands. "I know how you feel little one," Derrick says to her, but his eyes never leave mine.

I can't help but laugh again, but my nerves are already making themselves known, which in turn starts turning my stomach. I'm not lucky to be one of those women who only have morning sickness, mine will hit at any time of the day, like now. I need to get away before I embarrass myself.

"I'll see you tonight, but right now I need to get back to work." I start to move around him.

"We should probably get back and see how the baby is coming. See you tonight."

I turn to see Derrick and Kendall waving at me as I walk away. My heart leaps as I envision him with our little one, but then falls when I realize he may want our little one, but what's to say he will want me?

I put on the best smile I can and throw a quick wave back, then my stomach rolls and I realize I need to get to the restroom.

LOOKING at the clock for the tenth time at least, it's almost time. I have no idea what the plans are for tonight so I pick a simple sundress that can go casual, or maybe a little fancier. I should have asked what he had in mind for tonight but it was either ask questions, or throw up all over him. I'm not feeling the best right now and I want nothing more than to call him and tell him I'm not feeling well and need to cancel, but I can't keep pushing this to the side. I want him to hear this from me, not his sister.

As I was getting ready, though, I realized I should have told him I would meet him somewhere. With him picking me up, I have no way to leave without him bringing me home. What if he wants nothing to do with either of us once I tell him about the baby?

I hear the doorbell downstairs, Derrick is here. I'm thankful my parents went out for the evening, it stops all the questions they would have with it being Derrick here. Looking at the mirror one last time, I look down at my still flat stomach.

"All right, little one, here goes nothing."

The answer back is my stomach rolling. I know what that means. Closing my eyes, I take a couple deep breaths and talk myself out of throwing up.

"I hope this isn't a sign as to how the night is going to go."

The doorbell rings again. I need to get downstairs. Slowly I open my eyes and my stomach settles. Grabbing my small sweater, I make my way down the stairs and to the front door. I reach for the knob and my nerves are making my hands shake. Slowly I open the door, and there standing in a dark pair of jeans and a long-sleeved button-up shirt, sleeves rolled up and looking sexy, is Derrick. Nerves instantly turn to desire. Damn, he looks good. Our eyes meet and his eyes have already turned a crystal green, fire shoots through all of my veins and collects at my core. I grip onto the door to keep from throwing myself at him. What is wrong with me? I read somewhere about pregnancy hormones and how some women experience an increased need for sex while they are pregnant. Well, when you have a man standing in front of you that looks as good as Derrick does I can see where there is a need, regardless of being pregnant or not.

"Sam, you look amazing." Derrick's deep, low voice breaks my trance.

I need to get control of myself. "Thank you, you look pretty good yourself."

He holds out his hand to me. "Ready to go?"

Looking down, I'm afraid of what is going to happen if I touch this man, even if it's just his hand. Instead I nod and walk through the door, shutting it behind me and turning to lock it before we leave, giving me the excuse to ignore his extended hand.

"So what sounds good for dinner? I was going to pick a place and realized I don't really know what you like, so I decided we can pick something together," Derrick says behind me.

I have to keep myself from sighing out loud with relief. One thing I feared was where we would be going because certain smells set me off instantly.

"What do you think about something simple like pizza?" I suggest, that is one thing I am already craving I realize.

"A woman after my own heart, that is one of my major food groups." His laugh vibrates through me and a need burns deep down. This is crazy, I need to get a grip on myself.

PIZZA AND LEMONADE, a perfect dinner in my books right now. I sit back in my chair and watch the man across from me as he finishes his beer. "I forgot to ask, I'm assuming the baby came since you didn't call and cancel for tonight."

Nodding his head, Derrick sets his empty glass down on the table. "Yes, I'm officially an uncle again. Mr. Brayden Zachery Brooksman decided to join us at about two this afternoon. Very healthy baby boy. Mom is doing amazing, Bryce was cracking me up. He is so proud and his chest pushes out at least a couple inches each time he shows him off to someone new. Kendall just wants to hold him and carry him around like her baby dolls and gets upset when Mom and Dad tell her no."

I watch as he plays with the empty glass in front of him. "I'm happy to hear they are doing so well. I was going to try and stop by after my shift but I wasn't sure if they were up for all the extra company."

"They wouldn't have minded you stopping by at all, you would just give Bryce someone else to brag to." He laughs a little, but his mood has seemed to change.

"Everything all right?" I find myself asking.

He looks up from the glass and gives a small smile. "Yeah, just been thinking is all."

"Do you want to share?" I probe at him to keep talking.

Shrugging his shoulders, he leans back in his chair. "It's nothing really. I thought I had my life at a good spot, happy with my niece to spoil, and laughing at my brother and sister for being tied down, but then I see Bryce married and a dad, Charliee married and pregnant. I thought I was good with not being there yet, but something has changed."

My heart skips a little, maybe I was wrong about Derrick. "So what, done with the bachelor life?"

Leaning forward, forearms now resting on the table, Derrick laughs. "I'm not sure exactly what kind of guy you think I am, Pint. Sure, I'll admit, I wasn't into the whole serious relationship, tie yourself down to one woman, get married and have kids thing, but I'm not a player either."

"Come on, Derrick, you are a flirt," I point out and dare him to tell me it's not true.

Nodding, he truly laughs this time and the sound almost turns me to liquid. "I won't deny flirting a little here and there…"

"A little? Every woman you meet wants to chase after you and beg you to take them after they spend just a couple seconds with you." I point at our waitress, she has been by this table I can't count how many times asking if he needs anything else, most of the time speaking right to him and acting like I wasn't sitting across from him. "Our waitress probably already has her number written down and is just waiting for me to get up or something so that she can slip it to you."

Shaking his head, Derrick laughs. "Jealous, Pint?"

"Please, why would I be jealous? It just proves the whole player thing. You like the attention, admit it," I challenge him.

He just sits there, eyes locked with mine.

"Fine, you want me to prove it, watch this." Pushing my chair back, I can see the question in his eyes. I give him a small smile and then turn and head for the restroom.

Walking inside the restroom, I go over to the sink and wash my hands. Drying them off, I figure I've given her enough time. I know our waitress saw me get up and walk away. Walking back out, I pass her as I walk back to the table. She won't even look me in the eyes as we walk past each other.

Sitting back down, I give Derrick a questioning look. "So was I right?"

He doesn't say anything, he just nods his head and then turns what I think is the check around and there it is, her name and number.

"This doesn't mean I'm a player, I didn't even flirt with her," he defends himself.

He doesn't understand, he doesn't need to actually say anything. His eyes, smile, body, they all flirt on their own. Even that boyish grin he is giving me is sexy. He is a walking flirt!

"I just wanted to prove a point, Derrick."

"What point is that, because some random woman gives me her number that makes me a player?" he asks. His mood has changed again, he seems almost irritated now.

"No, that's not what I was proving. Look, I'm sorry, I just wanted to prove to you that women flock to you." I feel the need to defend my actions now.

"Look, Sam, like I said at your house, sure I was in a place in my life where I was happy with maybe an evening with a woman and then we part our ways. It wasn't often, but yes, every once in a while I would go out with the guys, have a few to drink and meet someone, but it wasn't an every night kind of thing. I can't even say it was a monthly thing. I'm not like Bryce, who was ready to find a wife and jump right into having kids."

Not ready to find a wife and jump right into having kids? Out of all he said, that one sentence slams into me like a fist punching me in the chest. Not so much the wife thing, but having kids. We are having a kid.

"Can you take me home, please?" I grab my purse and stand, walking toward the front door without waiting for him to respond. I need air or I'm going to lose everything I just ate.

I basically run to his car. Leaning against the passenger side door, I take in a couple deep breaths of the cool evening air and my stomach settles. This is why I should have brought my own car. Then I could just leave. It's almost tempting to just walk home.

"Sam, what's going on?" Derrick is next to me, I didn't even hear him walk up.

"I'm just ready to go home." I can't look at him, I'll lose it for sure and I don't want to cry right now.

"No more running from me, Sam, you need to tell me what's going on." He is now blocking me with his body.

My back is against the car, his arms are braced against the frame of the car on either side of me. He isn't touching me but I can feel the heat from his body. I keep my hands to my sides, the moment I touch this man it will be over for me.

"Derrick, why are you doing all of this? Why call me after that night? Why come to my party, and why dinner tonight? You just said yourself you aren't into serious, so what are you playing at right now? Do you feel guilty because I was a virgin? Do you think I'm going to be one of those girls who gives my virginity and not leave you alone? What is it?" The questions flood out of my mouth.

"Come on, Pint, do you not listen to anything I say when we are talking? Obviously I don't think you are going to hunt me down after giving yourself to me the first time, it's kind of the opposite. If my memory is correct, I'm the one who has called you, came to your party looking for you and wanting to talk to you, I'm the one who asked you out dinner tonight, I was the one left alone in a hotel room after one of the best evenings I have memory of."

My eyes shoot up to his in shock. Best evenings for him? How is that even possible? Before I can say anything, his lips claim mine. My knees buckle and I slump against the car. Derrick's arm goes around my waist to hold me up. His tongue instantly finds mine and my arms go up around his neck, my hands burying into his hair at the back of his head. He is completely hunched over, bending down to my height, so no other parts of our bodies are touching right now. We are standing in the middle of a pizza joint parking lot, anyone walking by can see us and all I can think about right now is tearing his clothes off right here.

Derrick pulls away slightly, our lips barely touching. "Sam, give me a chance, please. I can't promise anything but I can tell you there won't be anyone else. That night something changed, I changed, and I am asking you to give me a chance to prove it to you. You did something to me, Pint, and I tried to walk away from it, but I can't." He trails little kisses over my cheek, over my neck and around my ear.

"I'm pregnant," I whisper, barely able to hear myself. I'm not sure if he heard me at all.

Then his kisses stop and so does my breathing. He doesn't move for a moment but then his head comes back up to look me straight in the eye. "What did you say?"

He is so close to me, I want to look away but I can't; he is everywhere and I can't move. My heart is thumping so loud I hear it in my ears and I wouldn't be surprised if he could hear it as well. I didn't mean for it to come out like this. I didn't want to have this conversation in a parking lot, but it's out now.

Taking a deep breath, I look him straight in the eyes. "I'm pregnant," I repeat.

His eyes squint like he is trying to figure out if he heard me right, but he doesn't move. I can't breathe and I think I may throw up. I need some air.

"Did you just say you are pregnant?" he asks.

I can only nod, I'm afraid that if I talk, it's not the only thing coming out of my mouth. He finally steps away from me and I take a deep breath, my hand going to my stomach willing it to not roll again. I can't throw up right now.

"Who's the father?"

I freeze, did he honestly just ask me that? "Excuse me?"

"Who's the father, Sam?" he repeats himself.

I have never wanted to punch someone as much as I want to punch him right now. "Really, Derrick? What, you think that since I gave myself to you, I went back to school and went on a rampage and slept with a bunch of guys or something?"

"What the hell am I supposed to think, Sam? You have ignored me since the night of the wedding, how am I supposed to know what you did, or who, when you went back to school? I personally think it's a fair question to ask."

"You are the only one I've slept with, Derrick," I whisper, embarrassed that he even needed to ask. Why would I be here with him if I was pregnant with someone else's baby?

Nothing, he just stands there, hands on hips, staring down at me. Like he is trying to figure out if I'm telling him the truth or not. That only pisses me off.

"Take me home now." I turn and try to open the door so I can get into the car but it's locked. Screw him, I don't need him to take me anywhere. I turn and start walking away from the car, pulling my phone out of my purse. I'll call and get a ride home.

I don't get far before his hand wraps around my arm and stops me. "Where the hell do you think you are going?"

"I'll call a cab," I hiss between my teeth.

Derrick wraps an arm around my waist, pulling me back to the passenger door. He opens it up then cages me in. "Get in the car, Sam. We aren't done talking and you aren't running from me this time."

"There is nothing to talk about, Derrick." I'm speaking to his chest; I know if I look up and see the anger in his eyes, I'll break down completely.

"Like hell there isn't. Either you get in the car, or we can have this talk right here in the parking lot. You decide." Every muscle in his body is flexed right now. He isn't moving.

Rolling my eyes, I turn and sit down in the seat. Derrick shuts the door for me. I watch as he rounds the front of the car to the driver side. I can't cry. I won't let him see how much it hurts to know that he had to ask if he was the father.

CHAPTER
Eleven

DERRICK

I'M NUMB. Out of all the reasons I could think of why Sam was ignoring me, never did being pregnant ever enter my mind. I have questions, but I can't seem to find my voice to ask them. This must be what shock feels like. This is why I was getting all the texts from Charliee.

"Charliee knows, doesn't she?" I'm finally able to speak.

She doesn't say anything and when I look over at her, she nods her head. "She didn't say anything because I asked her not to. Please don't be mad at her."

Her voice is low and I find that I want to reach across and at least hold her hand, but I need some questions answered first. "When did you find out?"

She takes a deep breath and looks out the side window. "Right before graduation."

I can feel the tension in the car, my mind is spinning with questions and facts that I'm just trying to separate. Before I know it, I'm pulling up to Sam's house.

Throwing the car in park, I sit back in my seat. I start to ask another question when she turns to me, her eyes shining with tears. "Look, Derrick, I'm not expecting anything from you. I didn't tell you expecting you to do the right thing or anything. I'm completely capable of taking care of this child alone."

Before I can respond, she throws open the door and quickly gets out of the car, slamming the door shut and running to her front door. I can't move, all I can do is sit here and watch her once again run from me.

I'm going to be a father! I have to keep saying it, it's just not sinking in. An hour ago if someone would have pulled me aside and said, "Hey, your world is about to be turned upside down," and then left me to think about it, I could honestly say having a child would never have entered my mind. I used protection, but I'm not an idiot, I know those methods aren't a hundred percent. What is supposed to happen next? I want to go and pound on the door and make Sam talk to me, but I'm not sure if anyone else is home and if they are, if they are even aware of all of this yet. I don't want to cause Sam more stress tonight.

Pulling my phone out of my pocket, I send her a text.

**You can't keep running from me Sam. I will call you tomorrow, we need to talk!

I don't wait for a response. Throwing the car in reverse, I back out of her driveway and pull away from the house.

I need more time to think about all of this as well. I know I'm not going to allow Sam to raise our child alone, I may not be ready for children but I'm not walking away from mine. I want to call Bryce, but he is still at the hospital and he doesn't need all of this right now. The only thing they need to think about right now is their new little one, not the one I have on the way.

Charliee, she knows what's going on and Travis is at work, so I won't need to worry about facing all of that right now, but Travis and I will have to talk. I don't want him thinking I don't care about Sam or our child and that all needs to come from me.

Pulling up to the driveway, I see the light on in the living room, which means Charliee is home. Walking up to the door, I ring the doorbell and wait. It doesn't take long for Charliee to answer it, Levi standing right next to her.

"Derrick." She looks surprised to see me and then her expression changes completely. "Sam told you."

It isn't a question, she knows I'm sure just from my facial expression. "Yes, she told me."

"Derrick, don't be mad at me, please. I didn't want to keep it from you, but I knew it wasn't right for it to come from me either," she defends herself.

"Charliee, I'm not mad at you. Can I come in, please?"

"Of course, I'm sorry." She moves aside and waits for me to enter the house, shutting the door behind me.

I go straight to the couch. Sitting down, I run my hands over my face a couple times and then leaning back, rest my head back against the couch cushions. "Travis doesn't know yet, does he?"

Charliee shakes her head. "I only know because when we told her about me being pregnant, she ran for the restroom at the restaurant we were eating at and I volunteered to go and check on her. I don't think she meant for it to come out, she had just found out herself. I think she was just needing to say it out loud and I happened to be the one there when she did."

"I'm not going to apologize for it happening, Charliee, we are both grown adults," I defend myself.

Charliee sits down on the recliner. "Derrick, I'm not mad, what did you guys decide to do now?"

"Honestly, we didn't talk about it much, I'm sure I'm to blame for that. We went out to dinner tonight. We were standing in the parking lot, kissing, and all of a sudden she just blurted it out." I give her the short version of the night's events.

"She just told you in the parking lot of the restaurant?" Charliee's eyes are big with shock.

"I think she was just as surprised as I was."

"All right, and what did you say?"

"I asked if the baby was mine." Charliee's eyes fly wide open in shock so I continue before she can throw her wrath on me as well for asking that question. "Look, I know, she was just as pissed as you look right now, but come on, Charliee, why wouldn't I ask that question? She hasn't talked to me since that night, how am I to know she didn't have someone back in college and the reason she was ignoring me was because of that?"

"Derrick, do you think she would have agreed to have dinner with you if she had someone else?" Charliee defends Sam's actions.

"Look, all right, maybe it wasn't the best first question, it just all took me by surprise, Charliee. I knew something more was going on with all your texts you have sent me, but I would have never guessed it was me becoming a father." Standing up, I walk over to the window.

"So what happens now?"

That's the question I have been asking myself for the past couple of hours. Turning, I face my sister again. "I have to get her to talk to me first. We didn't talk much, once I pulled up to her house she basically told me she wants nothing from me and that she is planning to raise our child alone."

"Derrick, you aren't walking away from this, are you?"

I'm shocked my sister thinks that is even an option in my head. "Charliee, really?"

She gets up and comes to stand in front of me. "I'm sorry, I know that isn't something you would even consider. How do you feel about Sam?"

That's a very good question, I think to myself. "I'll be honest, I don't know. I haven't thought of anyone else since that night with her. I can't seem to shake her from my mind, I'm turning into one of those guys. You know, the ones who don't know how to take the hints that the girl isn't interested."

Charliee laughs and gives me a hug. "I don't think she isn't interested, Derrick, trust me. I have seen the way she watches you, and the way her eyes brighten up when we talk about you. I'd put money on the fact that she is very interested. I think she is just scared. She is afraid the only reason you will want her is because she is having your child. You have to understand where she is coming from on that."

Pulling Charliee away from me, I admit, "I was falling hard and fast before tonight and that was before knowing she was carrying my child."

"Then convince her of that." Charliee looks like she is daring me.

"Charliee, I'm going to be a dad, that's a little terrifying." I feel the tears well up behind my eyes.

Charliee's eyes water up and she once again wraps her arms around me. "You are going to make an amazing dad, Derrick.

IT'S BEEN two weeks since Sam told me about her being pregnant. I have called, texted, driven to her house I can't count how many times. She is completely ignoring me. When I have been to the hospital a couple times, I hoped to catch her and make her talk to me, but no such luck, I haven't seen her. I thought about having her paged once over the intercom at work, but realized that was her place of work and not the best place to have a conversation about our child or relationship. I am running out of options and I'm going crazy.

"Derrick!" Bryce yells at me. I turn my attention from the ambulance to my brother. "All right, what the hell is going on? This is my first day back and I see what everyone is saying, you are completely distracted."

Looking over my brother's shoulder, I see two other officers from our department looking at me as well with questions in their eyes. I look back over at the lady sitting on the curb with her young daughter, both pretty shaken up but luckily, neither is injured. Mom is pregnant, the moment I saw that my mind went straight to Sam. I was supposed to be going over there to take the statement from the woman but realize I haven't moved.

"Hey, can one of you talk to the woman over there while I take care of this?" I hear Bryce ask behind me. Then he grabs my shoulder and directs me back to our squad car. "All right, again I ask, what's going on with you?"

I haven't said anything to anyone. I wanted to figure this all out with Sam before I said anything to anyone else. Charliee had already known what was going on. I think back to when I found out my brother had kept from all of us that he had married Darryn, I was pissed and couldn't understand how he could keep something like that from Charliee and me. Now I get it.

I'm going crazy and Bryce is right, I'm distracted, and in my line of work that's not a good thing. "Sam's pregnant," I finally admit to my brother.

Bryce just stands there staring at me like I've grown a second head or something. Resting my arms on the frame of the car right above the passenger door, I rest my head against my forearms.

"Bryce, I don't know what to do. She is ignoring me right now and I don't know what else to do to get her to give me the time of day." Looking up, I look over at my brother with pleading eyes.

"Are you sure it's yours?" Bryce finally speaks.

I throw my hands up. "See, now I asked that very question and both Sam and Charliee got pissed."

"Wait, Charliee knows? How long have you known?" Now Bryce just looks offended or mad.

"Couple of weeks…"

"Why the hell am I just hearing about this now then?" Bryce interrupts me.

"Really, man, you want to go rounds on keeping secrets?" I throw back at my brother.

Bryce nods as he looks around. "Not happy about it, but I get it," he admits and calms down a little. "Tell me what's going on."

"There isn't much more to tell. Since the night she told me she has been dodging me. I've called, texted, gone to the house a number of times. Either no one answers or her parents tell me she isn't home."

"Do you think they know?" Bryce ask.

Shaking my head, I've wondered that a few times, especially with her mom. "I'm pretty sure if her dad or Travis knew anything I would have received some kind of call by now. Her mom I don't think she has told, but something tells me she might know something."

My phone buzzes in my pocket. Pulling it out, there is a text from Charliee.

**Sam passed out at work, they admitted her, don't know much more.

"We need to go." I run to the driver's side of the car.

"Derrick, we are in the middle of an accident here, we can't just leave." Bryce stands in front of the car.

"Charliee just texted me that Sam passed out at work, they are admitting her into the hospital. I need to go, Bryce."

Bryce runs to the other officers on scene, I watch as he tells them something. They both nod and as he turns to head back to the car, I get in.

Bryce jumps into the passenger seat. "I told them we have a family emergency, they said they had everything under control. Let's go."

Sirens blaring, we make it to the hospital in record time. Running inside, I find Travis and Charliee, along with Mr. and Mrs. Kendricks all in the waiting room.

"Bryce, Derrick, what are you two doing here?" Travis, looking very puzzled, asks as we walk up to them.

I look down at Charliee and then back to Travis. "How is Sam?"

Travis gives me a bewildered look, but Charliee is the one to answer. "We haven't heard anything yet, they said a doctor should be out soon to give us some information."

"Were you two here already, is that how you know what's going on?" Travis asks, still giving me an odd look.

"No, Charliee texted me," I answer, not sure what I am going to do if the questions keep coming.

Mrs. Kendricks jump up from her chair and we all turn to see the doctor coming into the room.

"Hello, I'm Dr. Mitchelson. Sam was on duty when she passed out. She is very dehydrated so we have started her on fluids but we are running tests to find out why and just waiting on those to come back. She is resting right now, but is there anything you can help us with on why she is so dehydrated?"

Both Mr. and Mrs. Kendricks shake their heads no, Charliee looks over her shoulder at me and I understand what she is wanting from me. "She's pregnant," I inform the doctor.

Both Mr. Kendricks and Travis's heads swing in my direction, I meet both their eyes in turn. I'm not backing down on this and I want them to know that. I'm not ashamed and I don't plan to not be there.

"All right, well that definitely explains everything with the dehydration. She hasn't mentioned any of that yet, but she has been in and out so we haven't been able to ask a lot of questions. Has she been sick a lot? Do we know about how far along she is?" The doctor asks me directly this time.

I shake my head no. "I'm sorry, I can't help you with all of that," I answer, a little embarrassed.

"She has to be close to three months, and yes, she has been sick," Charliee speaks up.

Travis's eyes swing to his wife in shock now. "You knew that she was pregnant and didn't say anything to me?"

"This isn't the time, Travis," Charliee snaps back.

"Doctor, can we go in and see her?" Mrs. Kendricks asks.

He nods. "Yes, follow me."

The Kendricks follow the doctor and Travis looks between Charliee and myself. "Does someone want to tell me what's going on now?"

"Travis, don't be mad at Charliee, she just kind of got stuck in the middle of all of this." I need to be straightforward with him and now is probably just as good a time as any. "The night of your wedding, Sam and I 'spent the evening together' is the best way I can say it. Anyway, Sam found out right before graduation that she was pregnant. She told me a couple of weeks ago and hasn't spoken to me since, and not from lack of me trying, that I can promise you."

He turns his attention to Charliee. "When and how did you find out?"

"The night we told her about us being pregnant and she ran from the table, that's when she told me," Charliee explains.

Travis looks between myself and my sister and then leaves, going out the doors to go outside. Charliee starts to follow after him but I grab her arm, stopping her. "Let me go," I sign. We were already gathering attention from people around us.

Charliee looks toward the doors, then back at me. "He is mad, maybe now isn't the time," she signs back.

"This is the perfect time, trust me." I need to talk to Travis, make him understand his sister is important to me and that I wouldn't treat her any differently than I expect him to treat my sister.

Charliee takes a deep breath and nods. Walking out, I find Travis sitting on one of the benches just outside the entrance. He is bent forward, his forearms resting on his thighs, his head bent down.

Sitting down next to him, I take a deep breath. "We should probably talk, man."

Travis looks over at me, I'm surprised when I don't see the anger I expected. "Derrick, if you were any other guy I probably would have taken a swing at you already."

"Travis, I get it, I promise. I remember holding a gun in your face the first time I met you and you were only taking my sister on a date, and before you say anything, I know this is different. I can't say the way all this happened was the right way, but I want you to know I plan to be there for Sam no matter what. Even before I found out she was pregnant I had been trying to get her to call me, but now she isn't having anything to do with me. I wish everyone could have found out differently but honestly, I'm happy it's out there now. Of course your sister may never speak to me again."

"I'm going to be straightforward with you, Derrick. Do you care for my sister in any way?"

Do I care for his sister? The woman is driving me crazy, and I've never wanted to shake a person as much as I want to do it to Sam. "Travis, your sister is different. I'll be honest with you, I had no intentions of following you guys' and my brother's path of marriage and children any time soon, I didn't think I was ready. Then Sam came into my life and well, I've thought of no one else, even before I found out about the baby. I'm not saying having a child isn't scaring the hell out of me, but I'm willing to make things work with Sam if she would just give me a chance and if for some reason things don't work out, I will never leave her to raise our child alone."

Travis looks back down at the ground for a moment. "I'll be honest with you, having a child is scaring the hell out of me as well." He stands up and I follow, we are now eye to eye. "You trusted me with your sister, now I'm trusting you with mine."

Nodding my understanding, I shake his outstretched hand. "Now if only I could get your sister to trust in me as well."

"Sam likes to act tough but she will cave, just keep pushing her." Travis looks over my shoulder so I turn and see my sister walking up to us.

"Hey, your parents came back down and asked if we want to go up and see her." She is unsure of how things are going between Travis and me, I you can hear it in her voice, plus I imagine she is still worried that Travis is upset with her.

"Yeah, we will run up real fast." Travis turns back to me. "Are you going up to see her?"

We need to talk, but now isn't the time. She needs to get better. "Now probably isn't the best time, plus we are on duty. We actually left an accident scene we were working on when you texted me."

"Derrick, she may give in a little if she knows you came to check on her," Charliee suggests.

"I agree, I know my sister, Derrick. You need to go up and see her. Why don't you head up before us?" Travis is now pushing.

Mr. and Mrs. Kendricks come out of the hospital and make their way over to us. I don't get nervous easily, but I am now. I didn't plan to have all these conversations at the hospital with Sam's family, but it's kind of a relief that it's out now.

"Mr. and Mrs. Kendricks, I know there is a lot we need to talk about…"

Mr. Kendricks raises his hand to stop me. "You are both adults, Derrick, I think you need to speak to each other first. The situation isn't ideal, I'll admit that, but it happened and we will support Samantha."

"I understand, sir. For the record, though, I have no intention of having her do this alone. I'm trying to be there, I just need to convince her to allow me to help." I want to make it clear to her parents that I'm not one of those guys who is going to walk away from my responsibilities. "I care for your daughter and not just because she is carrying my child."

Mrs. Kendricks walks over to me and wraps her arms around me in a hug. I'm so shocked it takes a minute to respond. "We know you are a good guy, Derrick, even if we had never met you we would know by how much Charliee talks about you and your brother. Samantha is stubborn and very independent, well, she likes to make everyone think that at least. Just keep pushing and prove to her that you want to be there, she will come around."

"I may need your help with that." If I have her parents on my side maybe I can get them to help convince her to talk to me.

Bryce comes out of the hospital at that time. "We need to get going." He runs past me heading to our car.

"Look, tell Sam I was here, I will call her later. And if someone could keep me posted, I'd really appreciate it." I follow my brother to our patrol car, kind of relieved he had a call come through. I want to be up there with Sam but I'm sure her parents told her that I told everyone she is pregnant and I'm sure she isn't real happy with me right now. I need to put a plan together to get her to talk to me and now that I have everyone backing me up, maybe it will be a little easier.

CHAPTER

Twelve

SAM

AFTER SOME FLUIDS and a little rest, I am allowed to go home. I ride home with Mom while my Dad follows in my car since I was working when I passed out. The ride home is quiet, and I know my parents are disappointed in me. I am just starting my career and I had a one-night stand that led to being pregnant. I know this isn't every parents' ideal situation for their child. I want to be mad at Derrick for telling everyone, but it would have come out one way or another today after what happened and something tells me Mom isn't as surprised as I expected her to be.

We pull up to the house and I see Derrick's car parked along the curb. I'm not sure if I'm ready to talk to him. Pulling up into the driveway, I see him step out of his car. He leans up against it, his arms crossed across his chest.

"You need to talk to him, Samantha." Mom turns the car off and gets out without another word.

Sitting here for a moment, I decide it's time for me to give in a little. He wants to talk, I'll let him get out what he wants to say and then maybe he will move on. Taking a deep breath, I open the door and get out slowly. I'm still a little woozy, all I really want to do is go inside and up to bed.

Shutting the door, I turn and find Dad now over with Derrick talking to him. He doesn't look like he is yelling or anything, which honestly I wouldn't expect from my dad anyway. He never yelled, even when we were growing up, but there was something about his calm voice that would scare us more.

I watch from a distance but I can't tell how the conversation is going. I know they have already spoken once at the hospital, Travis told me a little when they came up to see me and I had to apologize for putting Charliee into the middle of all of this.

Squinting against the setting sun, I watch as Dad and Derrick shake hands. Dad turns and walks to me. "You need to hear him out, Sam."

"Dad, I'm not sure if I can trust him." My parents know what Charliee has told them about the boys. He doesn't know about how Derrick doesn't do relationships, about the playboy he is, the flirt.

"Honey, there are many things that can change a man, a woman and a child are two of those things. You happen to have both working for you. Hear him out. I know you think you can do this alone, but why do it alone if you don't have to? I believe he is sincere, you need to hear him out." Dad gives me a kiss on the forehead and then leaves me to face Derrick alone.

We stand just staring at each other for a moment. I can feel the electricity that shoots through me every time I'm near him. I think that's what scares me the most, the way my body reacts when we are around each other. I have no control and that scares the hell out of me.

After a moment, he pushes away from his car and starts toward me. My heart leaps up into my throat. I need to get control, this is nuts, but just watching him walk toward me is doing something to me. My head feels a little light and I don't think it has to do with passing out earlier today. Leaning back against the car, I use it for support. Derrick must notice because his pace quickens and he basically trots the last few feet that is separating us.

"Are you all right?" He wraps an arm around my waist and I have to keep my knees locked so that they don't buckle.

This is why I have stayed away, just his touch, even one that is just out of concern is making me weak. *I can't fall for him, he isn't going to stay,* I keep repeating to myself.

"I'm good, thank you." I try to step out away from his embrace but he isn't letting go. "Look, Derrick, I'm tired. I know we need to talk, but can it wait?"

"Sam, you have been ignoring me for the past two weeks. Everything is out, everyone knows and I know if I give you that time, you will go back to dodging me. I have already spoken to your dad, you are coming home with me. I know you need to relax but we need to talk and he has agreed."

What? My own dad is throwing me to the wolves. "You told my dad I'm going home with you, like right now?"

He just nods his head. If I go back into my house, especially without Derrick, my dad will start asking a lot of questions, and then Mom will join in. Now I have to decide which is going to be harder. My skin is burning where he is touching me. Definitely being alone with Derrick is going to be harder, but I really don't have the energy to deal with both Mom and Dad right now.

"All right, fine, I will go home with you and we can talk. Maybe then you will leave me alone." I pull myself out of his hold and start for his car.

"We will see about that," I hear him say under his breath.

I turn to ask him about what he just said but he grabs my hand and leads me the rest of the way to the car, opening the passenger door for me, then after I sit down he shuts it. More of a gentleman gesture, but I have a feeling he is doing it more to make sure I don't make a run for it.

The ride to his house it quiet. So quiet that when my stomach starts to grumble it's heard through the car. I cross my arms over my stomach, trying to hide the sounds but no such luck. It gives way again, only this time louder.

Without saying anything, Derrick grabs his phone when we stop at a red light and I see out the corner of my eye that he is flipping through his phone log. Over the car speaker, I hear the phone ring.

"Thank you for calling Chester's Pizza Palace, how can I help you?" A girl's voice comes through the car.

"Yes, can I place an order for delivery, please? I would like a large pepperoni, green pepper and olive please, extra thick crust and extra cheese," Derrick goes straight into ordering.

I don't even hear the girl respond or Derrick give his address, I'm in shock that he remembered the pizza I ordered from our date.

He looks over at me and smiles. "Sorry, I hope pizza is all right. I'm assuming since you recommended it for our date, you are good with eating it."

Great, he is charming as well. How am I supposed to pull away from him when he keeps proving to me that there just might be more to him than I thought?

"Pizza is good, actually that's all I crave and all I find that I want to eat, and I drink lemonade." I lean my head back against the headrest and smile at him. It's the first time I have felt relaxed around him and I'm finding it's not as hard as I thought it was going to be.

Surprising me, he makes a sharp turn into a corner gas station. Pulling up to a parking space, he throws the car in park, opening his door. "I'll be right back."

I watch as he hurries into the market and back to the refrigerator section. I can see him through the windows the whole time he is in there. He quickly makes his way back to the checkout stand and within a couple minutes, he is coming back out the doors, a bag in hand. Getting back into the car, he sets the bag down on my lap. Looking inside, I have to fight back the tears. What's wrong with me? I'm crying over lemonade.

"I had to pick between and pink and regular, but I remember you drinking regular at dinner so hopefully that will work."

All I can do is give him a nod. I'm afraid if I say anything the tears will begin to flow and I don't want him to see me cry over a drink. Looking out the passenger side window, I take a couple deep breaths. I jump a little when I feel his hand touch mine. He laces his fingers with mine and squeezes gently. That does it, the tears start to flow down my cheeks and I instantly become embarrassed when a sob escapes from my throat.

Once again he turns sharply into a driveway, only this time it's a shopping center. Throwing the car in park, he pulls on my hand. "Come here."

Shaking my head, I keep my face turned toward the door window and with my free hand I wipe the tears from my cheeks.

"Pint, come here." He lets go of my hand and before I can say anything, he reaches across, unbuckles my seatbelt and then he lifts me up and drags me across the center of his car to sit on his lap.

I want to fight him, but the moment I feel his chest against my side I melt against him, the tears once again flowing down my cheeks. This is crazy, I'm crying over nothing. I know my hormones are going to be more out of whack but this is insane. I'm crying over pizza and lemonade.

Derrick hasn't said a word, he just sits there running his hand up and down my arm letting me cry like a crazy woman. Sitting up, I wipe the tears from my face and take a couple deep breaths. I try to scoot myself off his lap and back to my seat but his arms tighten around my waist.

"Derrick, I'm good." He still doesn't release me and I can't look at him because I know my eyes are all puffy and red.

"The pizza should be at your house soon and I'm starving."

He laughs and finally loosens his hold on me. "All right, if I know anything about a pregnant woman it's not to mess with her when she's are hungry."

Wiggling myself back into my seat, I realize how cold I feel when I'm not against his warm body. It only takes another five minutes or so before we are pulling into his driveway. The pizza driver is sitting at the curb.

Derrick unfolds himself out of the car and walks over to the driver. Getting out, I round the front of the car and wait for him at the walkway that leads up to his house. His lawn is nicely kept, and he has a little porch with a porch swing hanging from it.

Derrick walks past me and up the couple steps to the front door, I follow carrying the bag with my lemonade. He unlocks his door, pushes it open and steps aside for me to enter first. Walking in, I'm surprised at how clean and put together it is. The floors are hardwood, and you walk into a large great room. The living room is the perfect size, he has a leather sofa and recliner. A throw rug in front with a coffee table. A large screen television mounted on the wall. I'm surprised when I notice the wall decorations and pictures hanging all around.

There is a large pub-style table in the dining area of the room with six chairs around it, even a centerpiece sitting on the table. The kitchen looks all updated with the top-of-the-line appliances and very clean. There is a center island with the stovetop and above it the vent with all the pans hanging from it.

"Why do you look so shocked?" Derrick grabs the bag out of my hand as he walks past me and sets everything, along with the pizza, down on the counter.

"Did your mother decorate this place?"

Laughing, he pulls plates down from a shelf above him. "No, believe it or not, I am responsible for everything you see in here. Actually Mom doesn't have a decorative eye at all, it's Dad and me that do all the decorating.

There is no hiding the shock on my face. "All right, show me the rest of the house real quick then because I'm a little curious."

Coming around the counter, he grabs my hand and leads me down the small hallway, the whole house seems to have hardwood floors. The first door we come to he opens and I look inside to find a small office. Large dark wood desk, filing cabinet, lap top sitting on top of the desk, very clean.

We move to the second door and that's the bathroom, he opens another door and it has a fully set up gym inside. We move to the door at the end and I figure it to be the master bedroom. Walking in, I'm surprised by the very large dark redwood king-sized bed, nicely made, dresser to match, and a large leather recliner sitting in the corner. To the left it opens up to a very large master bathroom, big sunk in bathtub, large shower with the rain effect kind of shower head directly above it. Double sinks and a huge walk-in closet, with an island in the middle with drawers all around it. Everything is immaculate, nothing out of place. Not the bachelor pad I was expecting to see.

"I will admit, I'm very shocked. Your home is amazing." I look over my shoulder at him.

He is leaning against the doorframe of the walk-in closet, his arms crossed at his chest. He looks so relaxed. "Do I dare ask what you were expecting?"

Shrugging, I walk past him and back into the bathroom. "I'm not sure, but it had a pool table and video games in my vision."

"The pool table is in the garage actually, I made that into my game room. Air hockey, pinball, that kind of stuff, kind of a man cave I guess you can call it."

My stomach grumbles and Derrick laughs. "Come on, Pint, let's get some food into you." Grabbing my hand, he leads me out of the room and back to the kitchen.

Sitting down at the table, I watch as he pulls a couple slices of pizza out of the box and places them on the plates. He grabs a glass and fills it with ice, then pours one of the bottles of lemonade into it, pulls open the fridge and grabs a beer for himself. Balancing everything, he motions for me to follow him into the living room where he places everything down onto the coffee table.

"Sam, we need to talk." Derrick sits down next to me on the couch.

"I know and we will, I promise, but can we eat first?" I give him a shy smile and look down at the pizza, my stomach grumbles yet again. I haven't eaten much today and what I ate earlier came up shortly after. I'm starving.

Derrick grabs a plate and hands it to me. "Would you like to watch a movie while we eat?"

Taking a large bite of my pizza, all I can do is nod my head as an answer. I have to fight the moan that threatens to escape as I'm chewing, it tastes that good.

Laughing, Derrick gets up from the couch and picks up a large case filled with movies. "Any preference?"

"A comedy or action is fine." I take another bite of my pizza and sit back, surprised at how comfortable I feel right now. We need to talk, I'm not going to be able to dodge it any longer, but for some reason I'm not nervous about it anymore.

Three slices of pizza later, I settle back against the couch, not fighting when Derrick puts his arm around my shoulders and pulls me into him. Tucking my feet up and under me, I curve myself into his side. This feels right, like this is where I belong.

My eyes start feeling heavy, I fight them but it has been a long day. The doctor told me I would be tired and needed to rest. He even took me off work for the next three days. Not sure when it is but I fall asleep pretty quick.

I wake up when Derrick picks me up. "Where are we going?"

"To bed, Pint." Opening my eyes, I see that we are heading down the hall toward his room.

"Derrick, I should really go home."

"Sam, it's two in the morning, we both fell asleep. You have had a long day and need your rest. I promise to behave myself, but we are not sleeping on the couch when I have a very comfortable bed."

Walking through his door, he walks over and sits me down on the bed. I watch as he opens a drawer and pulls out a t-shirt, handing it to me. "I'm sure it will hit you at the knees so it should work to sleep in. If you want to try a pair of my sweats you can but I'm pretty sure they will end up at your ankles as tiny as you are."

I want to argue with him to take me home, but how fair is that to him having to drive me at this time of the morning? Looking over at the bed, I remember back to the last time we were in bed together and my insides instantly warm up. None of that can happen tonight, I was instructed by the doctor to take it easy, get my strength back, so all we will be able to do is sleep.

"All right, may I use the bathroom to change?" I don't even wait for the answer, I'm so tired I just want to change and crawl into bed. It looks very inviting now that I'm looking at it.

Taking me only a moment to change, I come out to find Derrick sitting on the edge of the bed in a pair of basketball shorts and a t-shirt. The covers are pulled back and when realization hits that we will actually be sharing a bed for the night, my insides start to heat up. A low pulse starts in my core. I need to get a grip on myself.

"Do you always sleep in shorts and a shirt?" I ask, pretty sure I know the answer. I can't see him as the type that sleeps with a lot on.

He shakes his head and laughs. "Um, no. I'm usually only in under-wear, but I didn't want you to be uncomfortable so I decided a little more tonight was a good idea.

Surprisingly I'm a little disappointed, I hurry up onto the bed and lay on my side facing away from him so that he doesn't read the disappointment on my face. I'm pretty sure I didn't succeed because I hear him laugh as he gets up and turns the light off in the room. I feel the bed dip from his weight.

"I've never slept with a guy before." I can't believe I just said that out loud.

Derrick grabs my shoulder and rolls me onto my back. "Come here, Pint."

It's like a natural reaction, I scoot over and rest my head against his chest as his arm wraps around my back and pulls me into his side a little tighter. I feel his lips brush the top of my head.

"It's a first for me as well," he whispers against my hair.

How is that even possible? I want to ask him, but I find my eyes quickly falling. I feel warm, safe, wanted. This isn't how I saw this night going, and I wouldn't admit this to anyone else, but I find that I don't want to be anywhere else.

CHAPTER

Thirteen

DERRICK

WAKING up this morning with Sam tucked in tight against me felt right. I expected to wake up and freak out, but I actually found that I slept better than I have in a long time. I slept so well that it was almost nine when I finally woke up, six maybe seven is usual for me. It feels so good to have her pressed up against me that I don't want to get up, but after about an hour I decide she needs her rest so I get up, take a shower, make some coffee, then think about making breakfast but I'm not sure when she will wake up or what she could keep down. Obviously she is having a hard time with keeping food down if she was dehydrated yesterday to the point of passing out.

My phone buzzes on the coffee table. Reaching over, I see it's Bryce. "Hey, man, what's up?"

"What, it's only my second day back, I couldn't have driven you that crazy already that you had to request a day off already," my brother teases.

"Last night I decided to take today off so that I could get things settled with Sam."

"So, are you going over there today? Did she finally decide to talk to you?"

"She is actually here already. I met her at her house yesterday when her parents brought her home from the hospital, then I brought her home with me." I wait for the million questions but nothing but silence stretches over the phone. "Bryce, you still there?"

"Yeah, sorry, I'm imagining the 'I told you so' and you begging a woman for a relationship." I can hear the laughter in his voice.

"Thank you, glad you are being understanding right now." I roll my eyes and fight the urge to hang up on him.

"Look, man, you didn't believe me when I told you about the powers of a woman, especially the one that would knock you to your knees. I tried to warn you but no, not happening to you. Here not only have you found that one woman, you are now going to be a father. It's like Christmas morning for me." Bryce isn't going to go easy on this, he is going to rub this in my face at every moment he can.

Hearing feet shuffling down the hallway, I turn to see Sam finally awake. "Look, I need to go." I hang up before he can say another word.

"Good morning, how do you feel this morning?" My eyes sweep over her and my breath catches in my chest. She is still only wearing my t-shirt that hits her just above the knees. She has pulled her hair up onto the top of her head and her eyes are still looking sleepy. I have never wanted any woman as much as I want her right at this moment.

"Surprisingly, I feel really good this morning." She sits down on the sofa, her legs pulled up under her.

Sitting down next to her, I fight with the urge to lean across and kiss her. "Are you hungry?"

"Not really yet, it usually takes me a minute to wake up and figure out what sounds good and that may stay down."

We need to talk and I don't want to keep pushing it back, we should have talked last night but it felt nice to just sit there watching a movie. Something I didn't think I would enjoy doing was just hanging out with a woman at home, on the couch. I'm realizing I'm just like every other male, just needed the right person. Damn it, I'm starting to sound like my brother.

"Sam, we need to talk and I don't think we need to push it back any longer. I know the last time we spoke I didn't say everything I should have or probably reacted the way you wanted me to and I'm sorry, but you said one thing that night that we are going to clear up right now before anything else. You told me that you were going to raise our child by yourself and I want you to know that you aren't. I'm going to be there to raise my child. I can't, nor do I want to walk away from my child or you, for that matter."

She won't look at me, she sits there playing with the hem of the t-shirt, twisting it around her fingers. I sit watching her. She takes a couple deep breaths, twists the shirt, and then straightens it back out, only to repeat the actions again. I'm not going to push her, we can sit here all day, but we are going to clear everything up before I take her back home, even if that means she has to stay the night again. She isn't running from me.

"What is it that I need to do so that you give me a chance to prove to you, Sam, that I want you in my life and not just because you are pregnant? I haven't been with anyone, flirted with anyone, or gone out with another woman since that night." I lay everything out to her, I'm not going to sugarcoat anything. I want her to know how I feel and that it's not just because she is having my child.

Again nothing, I want to shake her to make sure she is listening to me. "Sam, tell me what can I do to prove to you that I want you and it's not just a phase or short-term or something I need to work out of my system or any other excuse I know that is running through that head of yours right now. I've officially fallen and hit my knees!"

Still nothing, what can I do to get her to believe me? Grabbing her hand that is once again twisting my shirt, I pull her hand over and place it against my chest right above my heart. "Feel that, how fast it's beating? That's you, Sam, that's what you have done to me."

Her hand fists into my shirt and when she looks up at me finally, my heart stops when I see the tears falling down her cheeks. With my other hand, I reach up to wipe them away but am stopped when she pulls me to her by my shirt, claiming my lips. Shock isn't even a good word to use for what I'm feeling but it takes me only a moment to accept what she is offering me.

Moving up onto her knees, she is now above me, her hand still tight in my shirt, the other tightly holding my head to her, fingers digging into my hair, almost like she is afraid to let go of me. Wrapping my arms around her waist, I pull her in tight against me, kissing her back with just as much intensity that she is giving me. Letting her know I need to hold onto her just as much as she needs to hold onto me.

She was just in the hospital yesterday, this shouldn't be something that goes any further, but I can't stop her. I'm going to take what she wants to give, but I'm going to make her decide the pace. Her tongue finds mine and we both moan. Pushing me back, I'm now resting against the armrest of the couch and we are chest to chest. Her hips start to move against mine and it takes everything in me to keep my hands from roaming her body. Wait, we need to be careful, I need to think above my needs and prove to her just that.

One of the hardest things I have ever done in my life is place my hands on Sam's shoulders and gently push her back. She opens her eyes and I see all the questions flying through them. "Sam, as much as I would love nothing more than to lay here and let you keep going, we need to one, remember you were just in the hospital yesterday and two, we need to talk."

She stares at me for a moment and I'm pretty sure she even pouts a little but finally she pushes off me and retakes her place on the couch from earlier. "Derrick, I don't know what you want me to say."

"I want you to tell me you are going to give me a chance to prove to you I'm not the guy you seem to have dreamed up in your head that I am. Sam, I'm not a player like you seem to think. I just hadn't found that one that I wanted to go further with and I'll be honest, I wasn't in any rush to find one either, but it doesn't mean I was sleeping with someone new every night either."

"What changes that all now? If you weren't looking or in any hurry, why me? Why now if not because of the baby?" She crosses her arms across her chest and gives me a challenging glare.

Man, she is stubborn. "Sam, there is nothing I can say to prove to you I'm sure, you are just going to have to give me a chance to show you."

"So what are you saying, you want us to date?" Her face screws up like she smells something bad.

"That would probably be a good place to start, since we kind of missed that part in the beginning." I try to make her laugh, but she doesn't find it very funny I'm guessing from her eye rolling.

"What if I want more from you than just a couple dates here and there?" She is giving me a challenging look.

"I'm not planning on this only being a couple dates here and there, Sam. I'm willing to give you all of me."

Her eyes roam my body and her breathing becomes uneven. "So you are saying I will have free reign to do as I please with you, when I want to?" She gives me another once over, pushing up onto her knees and once again she pushes me back and we are now back to where we left off just a little while ago.

"What do you want from me, Pint?"

Her hands move to the bottom of my shirt and pulls it up and over my head. "What if I said right now what I really want is this?" She runs her hand over my chest and down over my stomach, stopping at the edge of my jeans.

"Sam, I will never say no to you when you want me, but how are you feeling?" I will say no if it means she will end up back in the hospital if I don't.

"Last night I'll admit I slept the best I have in at least the past month, and I'm not sure if you have been told this but women who are pregnant have a tendency to have raging hormones, which means you are going to have to keep up." Unbuttoning my jeans, she slips both hands into the waistband and slides them to my backside, pushing them down.

Lifting my hips, she moves down as she pushes them over my hips and down my legs, standing only briefly to pull them over my feet. She then lets them drop to the floor, leaving me lying there in only my boxer briefs. Straddling my legs, she moves up and settles herself against my very hard member. She only has the thin layer of her underwear on against mine, I can feel the heat from her and it only makes me harder. In one quick motion she has my borrowed shirt up over her head and forgotten on the floor. Leaning forward, her breasts are now pressed against my chest and her hips are making the slightest motion against mine.

My hands span each side of her waist and I press her down harder against me, she moans and makes small circles with her hips. All the while our lips are only an inch apart but our eyes are locked, her fingers in my hair. She presses a little more against me and her eyes fly open wide.

"Derrick, I need you in me now," she begs.

"Sam, I don't have any protection right now."

She stops instantly and looks at me like I've lost my mind. "What am I going to do, get pregnant?" she says sarcastically.

Rolling my eyes, I playfully smack her on the backside. "Not exactly what I meant, Sam. Look, I've never had unprotected sex and we have to have yearly physicals. I just had mine and everything came back clear."

She surprises me when she quickly stands up and slides her remaining garments down her legs. I pull mine down my legs and before I can say anything more, she is back to straddling me, her very hot and wet center now pressed against me.

"I would say I want more of the whole foreplay but right now all I really want is you inside me." Raising just enough, she surprises me when she reaches down, grabbing me and placing the tip of my hardness just inside of her very wet entrance, then in one quick motion she sits down onto me until I am fully inside of her.

Never before have I gone bare inside a woman and nothing could have prepared me for how good it would feel. Sitting straight up, I bring Sam's legs around my waist and now I am eye level with two begging breasts. I'm so deep inside of her I don't want to move, just savor the feeling of how tight she is around me. Leaning forward, I claim one begging, very hard nipple and suck it into my mouth.

Sam moans and her heads falls back. Her back arches, begging for more, which in turns pushes me further into her. I'm ready to lose myself, this is insane. My hands on her hips, I need her to move now. I guide her back just enough and then pull her hips back, nipping at her nipple at the same time. Again, Sam moans but now she is taking control of the tempo. She is pressing my face into her chest and sliding back and forth, each time a little faster and harder than the last. I can feel her body starting to tighten around me and I know she is close. I bring one hand up to cup the other breast, her nipple between my finger squeezing just hard enough, the other I nip once again with my teeth. She slides back one more time and when she thrusts back as my name is screamed and her body constricts around me with release, each pulse pulling me deeper and deeper inside of her. I finally let go, spilling myself inside of her. She pulls my head back with my hair and her lips find mine. Her legs are tight around me and before I realize what is going on, she is once again moving against me. She's not finished and I'm more than willing to keep up with her for I'm still very hard inside of her.

She pushes me back without missing a beat. I manage to get an arm under her and flip us around so that she is laying under me this time. Her tongue finds mine and I shove myself deep inside of her, she is so tight I can barely hold yet another one of my own releases. Sam's hands have moved down to my backside and she is pressing me tight against her. I pull out just so that the tip of me is still inside and with one thrust I fill her as deep as I can get. That's all it takes, her release shakes her whole body. She bites down onto my lip to keep from screaming and once again I fill her with my release.

It takes me a moment to move but I don't want to put all my weight onto her. We are both sweating and I realize she hasn't eaten anything yet. Pulling out of her slowly, she wraps her arms around me and for a moment I think she is going to protest.

"Sam, I would like nothing more than to stay this way with you all day, but we need to think of your health and the baby's health. We need to get you something to eat." Stretching myself out next to her, I pull her body up tight against mine.

"Now that you mention it, food sounds good."

"Okay, so before we decide on what to eat I have one thing to say."

She looks over her shoulder at me and my heart I swear does a flip in my chest. "This doesn't end today, Sam. I need you to tell me that you understand that. I want to make this work between us and not just for the baby."

Her hand goes to the back of my head and she presses my head down to hers, she brushes her lips lightly against mine and then smiles. "All right, but please don't break my heart, Derrick."

That is a direct punch to my chest. For the first time, I am seeing the vulnerable side of Sam and I see the fear in her eyes. "That goes the same for you, Pint."

CHAPTER
Fourteen

SAM

I STAYED another night at Derrick's and this morning I had to threaten him with not coming over anymore if he called off work yet again. I am feeling great. I kept all food down yesterday and so far this morning there are no signs of morning sickness. I am ready to go back to work, but the doctor has taken me off for a couple of days and Derrick is agreeing with him. I'm just not good at sitting around doing nothing.

Pulling up to my house, Derrick leans over and gives me a kiss. "How about dinner tonight?"

"Aren't you sick of me yet? We just spent the last two days together." Leaning my head back against the headrest, I take him in with my eyes. He decided we needed to shower together this morning which caused him to get a late start out of the house and to the station. Plus he needed to drive me home so instead of changing into his uniform at the station, which he informed me he usually does, he had to put his uniform on at the house. I, on the other hand, had absolutely no problem with that, I love seeing him in uniform. It actually took a lot of self-control not to let him call in and take the day off and then strip him back out of that uniform.

We spent the majority of yesterday in bed, I just couldn't seem to get enough and he was more than willing to fulfill every need I had.

"Actually it was one day and an evening and I'm pretty sure I can handle a repeat of last night once again tonight." Leaning over, he kisses me right under my ear and my insides turn to mush.

It is going to be near impossible to tell this man no, especially with my hormones right now. "All right, but I want pizza and tonight, you are bringing me home after dinner. I have to work tomorrow."

"Why don't you meet me at my house and then you can go to work tomorrow from there?" He has an answer to everything, doesn't he?

My body is screaming for me to say yes, but we need to pull back a little. "Derrick, if you want me to go to dinner tonight then you need to bring me back home afterwards." I try to sound serious, but he is nibbling on my neck and it's getting harder to concentrate.

"Are you sure you want to come home tonight?"

Right now I'm not sure of anything except that I want to pull him to the back seat of this car and rip that uniform off him, then beg him to take me in many different ways. Taking a deep breath, I place my hands on his shoulders and push him back and away from my neck.

"You either agree to bring me home, or it's a no." I give him the choice and have to hold back a giggle when I see him right himself in his seat and then have to adjust his pants that right now seem a little tight. I'm glad I'm not the only one affected by his little play of the neck.

"All right, fine, I'll play this your way for now, but only if you agree to a walk on the beach after dinner as well."

I see something in those eyes, I'm just not sure what to make of it. There is still so much we don't know about each other yet. Sure, we have amazing chemistry in bed and we are having a baby together, but other than what Charliee has told me, I don't know a lot about Derrick. A walk would definitely give us some time to talk a little more without a bed so close.

"You have a deal, what time should I be ready?"

"I get off at six so I should be here no later than seven if that works for you?"

Leaning over, I brush his lips with my own and a low moan escapes from his throat. I'm glad I can affect him the same way he does me. "I'll see you tonight." I kiss him to say goodbye.

Hurrying out of the car before I can't stop myself any longer, I run up to the front door and wave one last time, watching as he pulls away from the curb.

Stepping inside, I shut the door behind me and start for the stairs. "Samantha, is that you?"

"Yeah, Mom."

Walking out of the kitchen, she is drying her hands on a towel. "How are you feeling?"

"A lot better actually, I haven't thrown up at all since the day before yesterday."

We haven't had any time to really talk since they found out I am pregnant. The ride home from the hospital was pretty quiet and then once home, I left with Derrick. I know we need to sit down but I'm not ready to hear how disappointed they are with me.

"That's good. Why don't you go up and take a shower, freshen up and then come down and we can talk. Dad is at work so this will give us a little mother, daughter time. We can even go and grab some lunch if you are feeling up to it."

There is no reason to keep putting this conversation off so I just nod and then go upstairs to my room. I hate feeling like a teenager again. I need to start looking into my own place.

I take my time. I have the longest shower I think I have ever taken. Basically I stand under the water until it turns cold and is no longer relaxing. Standing in front of my closet for an hour it seems like, I'm trying to decide on jeans or go comfy for the day and wear sweats. I would usually just wad up my hair in a wet bun, but decide to blow dry it out and even curl it. I tell myself it is so I won't have to do it later for dinner tonight with Derrick, but I know I'm just procrastinating to keep from going down and having this conversation with my mom.

I don't know why I'm so worried. I'm a grown woman with a great job, I can take care of a child. I shouldn't be so worried about having this talk, but I know it has nothing to do with my job or how old I am. I'm sure my parents' dreams for me were not to become a single mom.

I've never had any problems talking to my parents, especially my mom, but this seems so much bigger and for once, I'm nervous. I'm not sure if I can handle seeing or hearing the disappointment. I can't stay up here forever and I'm sure if I don't get downstairs my mom will eventually end up at my bedroom door.

Taking a deep breath, I head down the stairs and find Mom sitting in the living room reading one of her and Dad's gardening magazines.

Sitting down in the chair across from her, she puts the magazine down on the table and takes a deep breath.

"Mom, look, before you say anything I want to say I'm sorry. I'm sorry for not telling you and Dad and you having to hear it from Derrick while I was in the hospital. I'm sorry that I've disappointed you and Dad with being reckless and becoming pregnant at all. We were protected, but I am an adult, I have a good job and I know I can raise this baby."

There, it's all out. I thought I would be able to breathe but no, it still feels like there's a lump in my throat and I can't manage to look my mom in the eyes. They have never been disappointed in me before and I'm pretty sure I'd completely break down to see it now.

"Sam, I suspected you were pregnant."

My eyes fly up to my mom's with that statement. "What do you mean you suspected? How?"

"Honey, you have never been real good at keeping secrets. You as a little girl always thought you were being so sneaky about hiding stuff, but I hate to tell you, you weren't." My mom laughs and I take a deep breath for the first time in what feels like hours.

"Mom, I know you and Dad are disappointed in me…"

"Disappointed? Sam, why would you think that?" she interrupts me. "Sure, I'm not going to say this is what we had in mind with you starting a family. Sure, every parent wants to see their child find a partner and get married, then start a family, but Samantha, you are twenty-four years old. You have an amazing career and I know you are going to be a great mom. Your father and I are not disappointed in you at all, we couldn't be more proud of you actually. Plus, I'm pretty sure you will not be doing this alone because you have a very supportive family, and Derrick isn't going to be that kind of guy to just walk away. He is hooked."

My eyes go wide with surprise. "What do you mean hooked?"

"Come on, Sam, that man has it bad for you. I'm not very surprised you couldn't resist yourself around him, he is very good looking."

"Mom!"

"What? Honey, I may be your mother, happily married and twenty plus years older than him, but sweetie, I have eyes and those two boys inherited some very nice genes. They are hard not to notice."

I can't argue that point with her. Getting up, I walk over and give my mom a hug. Why I was so worried, I don't know. My parents have always supported Travis and me. I know this isn't ideal, but my mom isn't going to be disappointed in having another grandchild to spoil.

"So I'm guessing you and Derrick were able to talk things over. I'm getting the impression you aren't being very easy on him."

"Mom, Derrick is a flirt and he isn't the type to settle down for a relationship, let alone being a dad and in a relationship. I knew I could do this alone, but I'm not sure if I could if he would have broken my heart, so I wasn't giving him a chance to break it. But before you ask, yes, we did talk and yes, I gave in and decided that I will give this relationship thing a try. I'm just hoping the broken heart doesn't follow."

"Sam, no one can predict the future. You both have a lot to learn about each other and who knows, you may find out it's not going to work out, but I know for a fact that man is going to be a part of this child's life regardless of the outcome of a relationship. It's scary to put your heart out there, but something tells me you won't be broken-hearted at the end."

I wish I had my mom's confidence. "Only time will tell."

"Why don't we go get lunch and you tell me more about this very good-looking boyfriend of yours." Mom gets up from her chair and gives me a hug, whispering to me, "Don't ever think that your father and I are disappointed in you, Sam. Please always be open with us."

Blinking a couple times, I manage to keep the tears back, but I can't speak or I know I'll lose the battle with them so I nod my head instead.

LUNCH WAS NICE WITH MOM, she is so excited to be having two grandbabies on the way. She has waited so long, she kept repeating. I'm glad everyone knows now, I hated keeping this from everyone, especially my mom. I needed my mom, I had questions and fears I wanted to talk to her about and we did at lunch. I cried a little more, but then we decided no more tears, I was going to be all right. With or without Derrick, I have the support I need either way.

I have to admit these last couple of days with Derrick have been good and I'm looking forward to dinner tonight with him, but I'm still treading lightly with him. I know I can fall for him and fall hard and I don't want to get hurt, and Derrick can hurt me. We need to learn more about each other, he swears I'm wrong about how he is and I hope I am. I will admit, I have developed a need for him, just thinking about him I find myself shifting trying to calm the need I have for him.

DINNER WITH DERRICK WAS GOOD, we just talked about growing up with our brothers and sister. I was also able to learn more about Charliee and what it was like for the boys to grow up learning sign language and the countless times they thought they were going to have to step in because someone was teasing her and of course, they made it their mission to make sure no one harmed her physically or mentally, regardless if she knew what was going on or not. They quickly learned though that Charliee was completely capable of protecting herself, which didn't surprise me. Charliee is strong inside and out and she doesn't want to be treated differently just because she is deaf and she shouldn't be, she keeps my brother on his toes and I love it.

The night air is chilly but it feels refreshing. There isn't a moon tonight, so I hear the water more than see it. One of the things I missed the most when I was away at college was the smell of the salty air.

We don't say much, we just walk, listening to the waves and holding hands. We come up onto a bonfire that seems to have been abandoned. "Do you want to sit for a little while? It looks like they left a couple more pieces of wood."

"Sure, it's a little chilly, sitting by the fire for a little bit will be nice." I watch as Derrick lays the blanket down that he grabbed as we got out of the car.

Sitting down, he pats the ground between his legs for me to sit between. I'll be honest, I have missed him today so sitting up against him with his arms wrapped around me sounds very inviting.

"Derrick, you've been kind of quiet tonight, is everything all right?"

"Just thinking really." His arms tighten around me and his hand settles on my slightly rounding stomach.

"You want to share?" I push him, fearing he may be changing his mind about us.

"It's funny. When Bryce told me he was moving Darryn and her daughter in with him after only knowing them a very short time, I told him he was crazy. I think it was a day or two after their first date."

This is what he was thinking about? "Wasn't it more for protection though?"

Darryn had told me her and Bryce's story the night of the dinner rehearsal for Travis and Charliee's wedding. I'm sure I got the short-sided story but I could have missed something.

"Actually yes, Bryce had told me it was for protection. That's what he told Darryn as well to get her to marry him the next day, when really he had fallen head over heels for her and figured that was a sure way to keep her, trick her into marrying him."

I knew this part of the story and it wasn't as bad as Derrick was making it sound, at least not Darryn's side of it. "I heard he kept it from you and Charliee for quite some time."

"Yeah, I never thought my brother would keep something that big from me."

I had to stop from giggling, he sounded like a little boy being told he couldn't go out and play with his best friend or something. "That's what you are thinking about right now? I thought you were over all of that, forgive and forget."

"I've forgiven him for it, I understand why he did it. I understand now why he did all of it, even after I told him he was insane."

I'll admit I'm a little confused now. Sitting up, I turn so that I can look at him. "You have lost me."

"I understand now why he moved them in so fast." His eyes lock with mine and they will me to understand his meaning.

"Derrick, what are you saying?" I have a pretty good idea what he is saying, but I don't want to say anything if I am reading him completely wrong.

"Sam, I don't want to frighten you away, or have you think the only reason I make decisions is because you are pregnant."

Derrick is scared, I see it in his eyes and I'm sure this isn't something he is used to. He is uncertain of himself right now, or maybe with us, and that scares him. My heart flops in my chest and I have to fight the urge to reach up and touch his face. I want to know where he is going with all of this.

"What are you saying, Derrick?"

"I want you to move in with me, Sam."

It doesn't shock me as much as I thought it was going to, but he is right about one thing. "Derrick, we just started this relationship thing and for you, I'm kind of your first real relationship from what you have told me. Moving in seems a little fast, I promise even if this doesn't work out between the two of us, I'm not going to keep you from the baby if that's what you are worried about."

"Sam, that's not what I'm worried about at all, were you not listening to me when I said that wasn't the reason? After we are done here, I'm going to take you home and then go home to my place. Thinking about it, I realize how empty it sounds. Sitting here holding you I realize I don't want to let go, I want to hold you like this all night. I liked having you to say goodbye to this morning when I went to work."

There are no words of love, which am I ready to hear them anyway? Maybe that's what scares me. What if I move in and then things don't work out? My heart is already telling me that I'm falling for him and fast, if I moved in and he ended up not wanting me I think it would destroy me.

"Derrick, I believe you when you say this isn't all because I'm pregnant, but I think it's a little fast. I'm not going to say no with the possibility of never, but no for now and let's put a little time behind our relationship first."

He wants to put his argument out there, I see it in his eyes, but instead he nods. "All right, but we are going to visit this conversation again."

I bring my hand up to the back of his head and press his head down so that I can kiss him. I meant for it to be only a small kiss, but his arms tighten around me and his tongue finds mine. Instantly I feel the heat rush to my core and the wet warmth. Turning my body to face him, I climb up onto his lap and wrap my legs around his waist. I'm wearing a sun dress and I can feel his hardness pressed against the restriction of his jeans.

Feeling very bold all of a sudden, I sit back slightly and slip my hands between us. I unbutton the button and slowly slide the zipper down. "Sam, anyone can walk by."

He is right and before that would have stopped me. I have always wondered how anyone could have sex in public with the chance of anyone being able to see them. I never understood the need or desire of it, but right now all I have to blame it on is baby hormones, because right now I could care less who is walking by and what they see as long as I have this man inside me.

Sitting up on my knees, I adjust myself a little closer to him, push my underwear aside and wrap my hand around his now free hardness. Slowly I sit down onto him, adjusting the head of him into my very hot and wet center. I can see his face by the light the fire is putting off and I hear myself moan as I watch his eyes close and feel his hands go to my waist, pushing me further down onto him.

"Don't tell me no, Derrick, I need you. I need this," I beg as my arms wrap around his neck, for now he is fully extended inside of me and it feels so good.

"Sam, I will never tell you no, trust me." He claims my lips in a kiss that has me pressing down even harder onto him. I'm not sure how much more of him I can take in but right now, I'm willing to try more. I just can't seem to get enough of him.

Rocking against him, it doesn't take long for that feeling to take over. Everything inside of my body is starting to shake. I can feel my walls convulsing around him, pulling him deeper and deeper. I rock against him a couple more times and everything explodes. I faintly hear my name in the distance. Wait, no, it is in my ear, but everything is muffled by the ringing in my head.

Hugging him tightly to me, his arms are just as tight around my waist. After a couple deep breaths, realization slowly starts to return with each breath after. Pushing back, I realize we just had sex on a public beach for everyone to see. Panic is starting to set in. The more I push back, the tighter Derrick's arms become around my waist to hold me to him.

"Relax, Pint, if you push off me that fast and in that much of a hurry, you are going to hurt me. Give me one second," Derrick whispers in my ear.

Relaxing a little after hearing his voice, I look around to make sure no one is around. After a moment Derrick lifts me up slowly and I feel him as he slides out. I have to hold back the moan that almost escapes from my chest and push that need for him once again back. I may have lost my senses once, but I'm not going to do it again.

Derrick sits me back a little and I adjust my clothing as he settles himself back into his jeans again. "I'm going to guess that has a little to do with pregnancy hormones. Bryce talked a little about that when Darryn was first pregnant."

I start to question why he and his brother were sharing their sex lives with each other, but I'm sure it isn't as it sounds. "Yeah, it's a little intense at times."

"So it's just not because I'm sexy as hell and you can't resist me?" Standing up, he reaches down and pulls me up as well.

"You are a little sexy, so I'm sure it has a little to do with it." I like this playful side of Derrick.

CHAPTER
Fifteen

DERRICK

"CHARLIEE, I need to ask you a favor." I asked my sister out to lunch because I needed her help. I would have asked Bryce but I think what I'm missing is the female eye.

"Sure, what can I help with?" She takes a large bite of her hamburger and her eyes roll back in her head.

"I'm kind of glad you suggested this place for lunch, I thought there was no chance to ever be sick of pizza. Well, that changes when you are dealing with a pregnant lady who only eats pizza. I have been wanting a good burger for a while."

"I'm sure Travis would understand your problem right now. All I want is this place's hamburgers and chili cheese fries. He doesn't even text and ask any more on his way home, he just shows up with it. Pregnancy craving are no joke."

"Maybe I should call Travis and Bryce and the three of us go out for a good steak or something."

Charliee nods her head in agreement but doesn't stop to say anything as she shovels in a fork full of chili cheese fries.

"So back to that favor, I was wondering if you would come with me to help pick out a crib and dresser for the baby."

Charliee swallows her food and wipes her mouth with a napkin. "Isn't that something Sam and you should do together?"

"I'm sure it is, yes, but I have been trying for the last three months to convince Sam to move in with me and she keeps saying not yet. She is six months along, I'm getting a little nervous. So I decided to start on the nursery. I have already moved all my weight equipment out to the garage, that room is bigger than the other room so I decided on that one for the baby. I've painted the walls, I just went with gray for right now."

"You two are still sticking to not finding out the baby's gender? How am I supposed to spoil my niece or nephew if you can't tell me which one to buy for?" Charliee and Travis just found out they are having a girl, but we decided to wait.

Charliee and Sam are due only about two weeks apart from each other so the grandmothers have been going crazy with baby shopping and baby shower planning.

"Sorry, you are just going to have to wait. Anyway, I'm not going crazy with the decorating and trust me, I can, but I do want her to be part of that. I have a couple different sets that I like, I thought maybe you could give me your opinion."

The waitress comes and takes our empty plates, Charliee then orders a hot fudge sundae. "If you were Bryce asking I'd understand the need for an opinion, but Derrick, you decorate better than me."

"I like them both, just wanted a woman's opinion to help me decide. If I ask Mom she will have me buying so much more and her mom I'm afraid will say something to her about the room."

"Can I ask you a personal question? You can tell me to mind my own business."

"What's the question, Charliee?"

"Do you love Sam?"

"Yes, I love Sam," I confess for the first time out loud.

"Have you told her you love her?"

"No, not in words exactly. I've shown her in a million ways but the actual words have not been said yet."

"Derrick, have you ever thought maybe that's what is holding her back from saying yes? She is probably scared, probably thinks the only reason you keep asking is because it's getting closer to the baby being here."

"She has to know I care for her, Charliee, and we talked about the whole 'it's not just because of the baby' thing. She has told me she believes me when I say it's more than that."

"Derrick, she may have said it, but you haven't given her any real reason to believe it. What's keeping you from telling her?"

The fact that she may throw the words back in my face, I think to myself.

"Derrick, I think you need to tell her. I'll put money down that if you tell her you love her, she will agree to move in." The waitress sets a very large sundae in front of my sister and her eyes get very excited. "I would offer you some, but honestly I don't want to share."

Charliee has never been a greedy person, so seeing her like this is hilarious. "So will you come with me?"

She pulls a large spoon full of ice cream, chocolate and caramel up and shoves the whole thing in her mouth. "Sure, I'll come help."

After watching my sister take down a sundae in record time, we head over to the furniture store where she helps pick out what I hope will be the items that convince Sam to finally move in. I'm hoping with seeing the nursery started she will understand that I'm ready for our relationship to step up.

· · ·

SAM HAD TEXTED me from work and asked if I could barbecue her some chicken tonight for dinner. I was shocked by the request, but extremely happy to have something other than pizza. I am just bringing it in when she comes through the front door. She looks exhausted. Setting the plate on the counter, I walk over to her and wrap my arms around her waist, then claim her lips.

I place a hand on her now very round, very pronounced belly. "Busy day at work?"

"Crazy, I'm not sure how I'm going to make it through the last couple of months at the rate I'm growing. I swear I'm twice as large as Charliee and we are only a couple weeks apart from each other."

"Pint, you are quite a bit shorter than Charliee so it just seems that way. Maybe you should see about doing light duty at work."

"I'm still on probation, Derrick, at least for another two months and it's bad enough that I kind of hid a pregnancy at the beginning. I don't need to give them any other reason to let me go."

"They aren't going to let you go, Sam, you are amazing at what you do and they see that. If you are having a hard time, promise me you will talk to someone about going on light duty. You don't need to end up in the hospital again."

She wants to keep arguing but she decides against it and just nods. "Is dinner ready? I'm starving."

Kissing her forehead, I grab her hand and have her sit down at the table, then round the counter to serve up our plates. "After dinner I have something to show you."

"All right and then how about after that, you and I go and lie in the bathtub for a while."

It has become part of our nightly routine when she is here, which is pretty much every night. That is one of the things that confused me when we talked about her moving in. She has clothes here, and everything she needs to get ready for work, but she refuses to move in here permanently.

Sam tells me about her day and some of the crazy stuff that came in while we eat. I clear off the table and she tries to get up and help with dishes but I make her another glass of lemonade and sit her down at one of the bar stools at the counter while I clean everything up.

Drying my hands, I throw the towel on the counter and grab her hand. "Come on, I have something I want to show you."

She willingly follows me down the hallway but gives me a very puzzled look when I stop at the door that used to serve as my workout room.

Opening the door, I stand aside so that she can enter first. "There isn't much to see yet."

I had put up the crib and the dresser is against one wall. Charliee talked me into a rocking chair she spotted while we were there today and I found a very large dark brown teddy bear to sit in the corner of the room.

"Without knowing what we are having I went with a gray for the walls, that way we can pretty much put any color with it," I point out when she still hasn't said anything.

Walking over to the crib, Sam runs her hand over the side rail, but she won't turn to look at me so I go to her. Standing in front of her, giving her no choice but to look at me, that's when I see the tears.

"Hey, why are you crying? Do you not like them? We can take it back and you can pick something out you like better. Actually, Sam, I'm hoping that I can convince you to move in here and help me get this house ready for our family, starting with finishing up this room," I ramble on.

I wasn't planning on blurting it out just like that but it just came out and now with it all out there, the only thing I can do is wait for her to answer me. Nothing comes but more tears. Wrapping my arms around her, I pull her in against my chest. We only stand like that for a moment before she pushes me away from her and when I look down at her this time, I see anger.

"Sam, what's wrong? Talk to me. If you don't like it we can makes changes." Again, nothing comes from her.

Suddenly, she turns and storms out of the room, I figure she will go to our room but she surprises me even more when she turns the opposite way and goes back to the living room. Grabbing her keys and purse, she heads for the front door.

Grabbing her arm before she leaves the house, I pull her back inside and shut the door. "What the hell is wrong? Talk to me."

"Let go of me, Derrick, I'm going home."

"You are home, Sam!" I yell. "You are here every night, we say goodbye to each other every morning before we go to work. Most of your clothes are hanging in the closet, that's not my room any longer, it's ours. I was hoping with getting the nursery started you would realize I'm serious about this and us, but for some reason you are holding back. Why?"

She turns to the door and tries to open it again, but I keep it shut. "You aren't leaving until you talk to me, Sam."

"Damn it, Derrick, let me go! I want to go home," she says between clenched teeth.

"Again, I'm going to repeat, you are home."

"This isn't my home, Derrick, it's yours."

"Is that why you won't move in, because it was just mine first? Fine, I will sell the house and we will go find another one together if that's what you want. That's all you had to tell me, Sam."

She takes a couple deep breaths and I can tell she is fighting back the tears. "I don't want you to sell the house, Derrick, I want you to want me and not just because I'm having your baby!" she yells at me, then with strength that surprises me, pushes me away from the door and runs outside and to her car.

I am in so much shock I can't move. She thinks the only reason I want her here is because of the baby. We have talked about that a hundred times and each time she has told me she believes me when I say I'd want her even if she wasn't having my child. Well, this ends tonight, I'm going to make her understand I'm in love with her because of who she is, not only because of who she is carrying.

Grabbing my keys, I run out to my car and head to her parents' house, hoping that's where she was going. Pulling up to the house, I'm relieved to see Sam's car parked alongside the curb. Running up to the door, I ring the doorbell a couple of times and wait.

Mr. Kendricks is the one who answers. "Derrick."

"Hello, Mr. Kendricks…"

"Please, Derrick, how many times do I have to tell you? Please call me Kevin," he interrupts me. "If you are looking for Sam, she is up in her room with her mom. She is pretty upset, not sure the whole story, but maybe you should give her a little time."

"No offense, Kevin, but I don't agree. If I let her simmer on this I may lose her altogether and sir, I love your daughter too much to have her walk away from me."

"You know, I'm pretty sure she was sobbing about something regarding you not loving her." He stands his ground in front of the door, not letting me pass the threshold.

"Yes, sir, I'm sure you did and that is because I am a stubborn ass who hasn't really told her I love her in so many words."

Kevin surprises me when he laughs. "I get it, Derrick, trust me, but women need reassurance. You can't beat around the bush with matters of the heart with them, they don't understand that. They need the words."

"I completely understand that, sir, and I plan to make her understand that I love her and just to give you a heads up, I'm trying to get her to move in with me. I think with the baby coming we need to be together, under one roof."

"I agree, but there is another way to reassure that, one I would feel a lot more comfortable with when we are talking about my baby girl."

I understand his meaning completely. "I have to get her to believe I love her first, sir."

"Point made." He moves aside to let me into the house and points up the stairs. "Good luck."

"Thank you," I throw over my shoulder as I take the stairs two at a time.

Knocking on her door, her mom is the one to answer. "Mrs. Kendricks, may I please speak to Sam?"

"Only if you start calling me Anna." Then she steps past me and heads down the stairs.

Walking into the room, I find Sam looking out her bedroom window, her back to me. When I shut the door she doesn't move, she isn't going to make this easy.

"Sam, you need to stop running from me. Things would be so much easier if you would just stay and talk, but I'll chase after you and make you see that for once and for all, I'm not only with you for the baby. You turned my world upside down that night at the wedding and that was long before I knew anything about the baby. I went from enjoying the bachelor's life to becoming that guy who won't take no for an answer. I had never slept overnight with a girl and that night when we fell asleep together, I found myself wanting to hold on and not let go. I swore I'd never be one of those guys that a girl turned to mush. One who said stuff like wanting to not let go, love sleeping with you in my arms, waiting for your call, worried when I don't hear from you, or the one I thought I would never say is me being jealous when another guy looks at my girl. I thought finding a girl who I wanted to move into my home and make a life with was far from this time of my life, I would have thought the day I told a woman I was completely in love with her was far in my future, but then here you came into my life and proved me wrong in so many ways. I can't wait to start this family with you.

Just you, me and our little one. I can't wait to know that every night after work, I get to come home to you and we can tell each other about the crazy people we dealt with that day, then sleep with you every night, only to wake up and say goodbye as we go to work. Sam, I love you and I will make you see that it's not just because you are going to be the mother to my child, but because you are the woman who proved me so very wrong."

I watch her shoulders as they shake, I know that is a sign that she is crying. I want nothing more than to go to her and wrap my arms around her and tell her everything is going to be good, but I need her to come to me this time. I swore I would chase her down and make her see my feelings for her, but she needs to stop running from me and to do so she needs to make the first move toward me this time.

I just stand there and wait for what seems like hours, but never once does she make a move like she is going to turn around. I realize one of the hardest things I am going to do is walk away, but something tells me I need to do just that.

Turning, I walk out of the room and fight with every step I take down to the front door not to run back up and get on my hands and knees. The only thing that stops me is she has told me time and time again she understands it isn't all because of our baby, basically because I wouldn't allow the conversation to stop until she told me that she believed me. This time I'm not going to push, if she comes to me then I know for the first time she actually believes I love her, baby or no baby.

That doesn't stop me from looking into the rear-view mirror all the way home, hoping she'd come around and was following me home. Walking into the house, it feels empty and this is the first time I've allowed myself to wonder what would I do if she didn't come to me? I know that if by tomorrow morning I haven't heard from her, I won't just walk away, I'm going to fight, but for now I need her to think about it without me talking in her ear. I have said everything I can, it's all up to her now.

I'm not going to be able to sleep, but a shower sounds like a good idea. Stepping inside, I lean back against the shower wall, close my eyes and let the steaming water fall over and around me. It is taking everything in me not to drive back to her house. This is going to be a very long night.

CHAPTER
Sixteen

DERRICK JUST TOLD me he loves me. He didn't just blurt it out, he had all the words to go with it as well. I couldn't turn around, though; I was afraid he wouldn't be standing there and I would realize I just imagined that he told me he loved me.

Finally taking a deep breath, I turn and find myself standing alone in my room. Wait, there is no way I imagined all of that, he was here, he told me he loved me. Where did he go? Why would he come over to tell me he loves me and just leave?

"Samantha Amber Kendricks, what is wrong with you?" My mom comes barreling into my room, my dad right at her heels.

All I can do is look at her dumbfounded. I'm not even sure what just happened. I could have sworn Derrick was here, but I turn to find him not in my room and my mom giving me that glare. There it is, the disappointed look I have feared since I became pregnant, although I'm pretty sure this has nothing to do with the baby, at least not directly.

"How could you just let him leave without saying anything to him? I won't lie, I was standing outside your bedroom listening to the whole thing and he sounded so sincere. That boy loves you, and you just let him walk away." Mom is going off, but honestly I didn't hear much past the part where she confirmed that Derrick was really here.

"I'm thinking we may need to kick you out so the only other choice you have is to move in with Derrick. Please tell me that is not the direction we need to go," Mom threatens me and as I look over her shoulder, my dad is standing there nodding his head in agreement with her.

I know my parents would never kick me out, but this is their way of telling me I need to open up my eyes and once and for all trust Derrick with my heart. "Mom, do you really think he meant it? He isn't just saying it because of the baby?"

"Honey, that man loves you, little one or not, trust me." My dad comes up and gives me a hug. "Sam, the question left is, do you love him?"

I don't have to even think about it, I'm just scared that he will realize he doesn't need me to be in our baby's life. "Yes, Dad, I love him, too."

"Then you need to go and tell him, stop all this running scared and using the baby as a shield."

I don't want to stand there talking or thinking about it any longer. I want Derrick and I need to get to him now to tell him I love him, too. Grabbing my keys and purse once again, I make my way down the stairs.

"Maybe we should take you over there," my mom suggests as she watches me do a small waddle down the stairs.

"No, I'm good, plus I think I will need my car to get back and forth to work from my new home." I smile and shut the front door behind me.

The drive over seems to never end. I hit every red light between my house and his. If there is a slow driver out tonight, I am behind them. I even honk my horn a couple of times trying to get people out of my way. Finally, I pull up to the house. I take a deep breath when I see his car parked in the driveway, which means he is home, thank goodness.

The front door isn't locked. Walking inside, Derrick isn't in the front room or the kitchen. "Derrick," I call out, but no answer.

That's when I hear the water from the shower running. Walking into the bathroom, I see Derrick standing there against the wall of the shower, the water just running. Seeing him standing there, naked, water cascading down his body, is doing something wicked to my insides, but that needs to wait, at least for now.

Quickly stripping out of my own clothes, I'm surprised when he doesn't look up when I open the shower door. My hands can't seem to stay to themselves, I reach out and lightly run my fingers over his chest.

He jumps, almost falling from the slippery wet shower floor, his eyes flying open. I can see it takes him a moment to realize it's me standing in front of him, it's almost like he doesn't believe I'm really standing there. Once again my hands go to his chest and before I know it, I'm smashed against his body, his arms tightly around me, his face buried into my neck. He just holds me like he is afraid if he lets go, I may disappear.

His wet body against my wet body ignites a fire that I can't seem to ignore. We need to talk but right now I need this man inside of me more. "Derrick." His eyes come up to mine. "I need you to make love to me."

His eyes turn to that crystal green color that makes my center throb with need. It's the color that tells me he needs and wants me as much as I want him. In one motion he picks me up in his arms and carries me out of the shower. I feel like I'm as light as a feather when I'm in his arms, even though I'm six months pregnant.

He doesn't stop for a towel, he sits me down on the bed still wet from the shower. His lips are on mine, then he trails them down my neck and to one very tight, begging nipple. He sucks it deep into his mouth and my back arches, begging for more. "Derrick, please, I need you now."

His hand traces down my side, over my hips and when it comes around and into my center, my whole body arches off the bed and I push myself more into his hand. "Sam, you are so ready for me."

He moves up above me and looks me straight in the eyes. He places the tip of his hardness against me and I stop breathing. I want to thrust my hips up so that I can have him fill me completely but I wait for him. His eyes are locked with mine. "Sam, I need to know why you followed me."

The heat in his eyes cools and I see the fear, he needs the reassurance about my love as much as I needed it from him. Bringing my hands up, I cup his face. "I love you, Derrick Brooksman."

He releases a deep breath at the same time he pushes himself completely inside of me, filling me more than I could have thought possible. "I love you, Samantha."

His lips claim mine as his hips find our rhythm. It isn't rushed this time, we aren't pawing at each other begging for more, he sets a pace and he reminds me over and over of his love for me.

I can feel my release building, it takes only two more thrusts of his hips and I explode around him, holding him tight against me. He pushes a little deeper inside and his body shakes with mine and together, we find our release. This one so much more intense than any we have shared before tonight.

I'm not sure how long we lie there, I know neither of us sleep, he just holds onto me tightly.

"Sam, I need you to understand something. I love you, and you carrying my child only makes me love you that much more, but I swear to you it's not the only reason I love you. I need to know that you finally understand that and believe me when I say it. You can't keep using it to tear us apart. This baby brought us together, I'm not sure if you would have given me a chance without a baby, but I would have chased after you even if there was no little one."

Turning myself over, we are now lying face to face. I bring my hand up and cup his face. "I'm sorry I have been so difficult, I'm sorry for running from you. You scared me, Derrick. I have a hard time believing that a guy like you would be interested in a woman with no experience. You have probably had all types of women and yet none of them caught your attention enough is what you told me, I didn't understand what made me so different."

"You challenge me, Sam. You gave yourself for the first time to me. It's a gift I have never been given before."

"So you're saying I got you because I was a virgin?" I ask, laughing.

"No, well yes, actually, kind of. For some reason you knew my so called reputation, or at least what you thought my reputation was, and you still trusted me. Then you ran, and for once I wanted to chase after someone. You are stubborn, fiery, confident, smart and it's kind of cute how pint-sized you are."

"So what you are saying is I challenge you?"

"That you do, and at the same time I have seen your fear, your insecurities and your need to be held and told it's all going to be all right. I want to be the guy to keep up with all of you, Sam, and if I'm being honest, I don't mind even a little game of chase as long as I know you aren't running from me in fear of my feelings, but the excitement that will follow when I catch you."

"Why don't we skip the chase for now and just get to the excitement part, because I think I need you one more time tonight at least."

STANDING and looking into the now finished nursery, my heart speeds up a little. This is happening! In a couple months our little one will be here, we will be responsible for a new little life. Both of us take other people's lives into our hands every day, but this is so different. Walking around the room, I run my hand over the crib that Derrick picked out, the top of the dresser combo changing table. The closet is open and all the clothes are hanging neatly, boy clothes on one side, girl clothes on the other. The hardest part of not knowing the sex of the baby was the clothes shopping. Derrick did a great job decorating his home, I was very impressed the first time I came over, but he went above and beyond on this room. I basically watched and placed things where he told me to put them. Home decorating is definitely a surprised talent of Derrick's I would have never guessed he possessed.

I've been living here for a little over a month now, time is flying by. I think Derrick has made it his mission to prove to me how wrong I was about him, and I will admit I was. I thought of him as nothing but a flirt, a ladies' man, a player. I couldn't have been further from the truth, well at least about the player part. The man is a magnet to women but I can't hold that against him, he is extremely good looking. Add the uniform and well, there is no surprise women can't keep their eyes away from him, but he is mine and he does everything in his power to make sure I know it. I know now how stupid I was for running from him. Thinking he didn't love me, when I look back to before he told me in actual words he loved me I can now see all the little things he did to let me know, like starting this room for example. He wasn't telling me, he was showing me, but I was so determined to prove he was the guy I thought him to be and that the only reason he had any interest in being with me was because of the baby. I hope he forgives me for everything I have put him through. I know I was only being cautious and I know he knows that, but I doubted him and I had no reason to do that. I was judging him by what I thought him to be and not what was being shown to me. Looking back I see it all now, I'm a very lucky woman, and this little one is going to have an amazing dad.

Sitting down in the rocking chair, I lay my head back and close my eyes, rocking slightly back and forth. I cover my very large stomach with my hands and wait.

"Are you all right, Pint?" Derrick's voice fills the room and the kicking begins.

You little rascal, I think to myself. The baby only kicks when Derrick talks or touches my belly. How the baby knows it's his hand and not mine, I have no idea.

"I'm good, just sitting down for a moment."

Walking over to me, he kneels down in front of me and places his hand over mine. "Is he kicking around in there?"

"Only when you walked in and started talking, like always. I don't know why you think we are having a boy, the way kicking starts when you talk, I'm thinking a Daddy's girl."

"You sure you want to go to my parents' house for dinner tonight? If you aren't feeling well I'll call and tell them we won't be making it."

Bringing a hand up, I run it through his short hair. He is very attentive and the further along I get, the less I'm doing. He cooks, cleans, and does all the laundry. I feel guilty but at the same time thankful for not having to do it, especially after a full shift at work. Every night we soak in the bath for about an hour together, having an extra-large bathtub comes in handy when someone is as round as I am right now, and he massages my shoulders and back. Spoiled I am by this man.

"No, we are going. I'm fine. Plus, my parents and Travis and Charliee are going to be there so we can all go over last minute baby shower details. We need to be there."

Since Charliee and I are only about two weeks apart for due dates and basically friends and family are almost all the same between the two of us, we decided to have just one baby shower together. Looking around the room, I'm not sure what we even need one for, every time we go shopping Derrick goes crazy. There really isn't anything we need, but my mom couldn't be stopped, then you add in Derrick's mom and both grandmothers were impossible to say no to.

"If you are sure you're up to it then we better get moving." He stands up and holds a hand out to me to help me up from the chair.

Standing up, I wrap my arms around his waist and raise my head, waiting for him to come down to my level for a kiss. Between this stomach and our height difference, some things have become work, like kissing him. We have definitely had to become inventive on some of the activities.

"I love you, Pint," he whispers as he kisses my forehead.

"I love you, too."

CHAPTER
Seventeen

DERRICK

"SO ARE you ready for all of this?" Travis comes up behind me, slapping me on the shoulder.

Standing in the kitchen, I watch both my sister and Sam open the mountain high size pile of gifts that were brought today. "I'm not sure if anyone can be really ready for all of this, are you?"

Shaking his head, we both laugh. "No, I can honestly say I have never been as scared as I am about being a father. It's exciting and terrifying and the amount of stuff you need for someone so small is unbelievable. A child cannot possibly wear that amount of clothes before they grow out of them, but what I was meaning is what's coming up next, are you ready? My sister hasn't made any of this very easy on you since the beginning."

"You're telling me. I never thought I'd be that guy who chases after a woman, I thought all you guys had lost your mind."

"Honestly, man, and don't get this the wrong way, but I didn't have to chase after Charliee. Now Bryce, on the other hand, had to go about it the hard way."

We both laugh because my brother had to trick Darryn into marrying him for "protection" before he convinced her he was in love with her.

"Charliee was yours from the moment you pulled her out from that building, and I thank you for taking such good care of her. Bryce and I couldn't have asked for a better man for her."

"Stop, you will make me tear up." Travis pretends to wipe a tear from his under his eye.

"On a serious note, Travis, I hope you know your sister means just as much to me."

"Derrick, I know how Sam is, she is full of life, will give her last dime even if she needs it more than you do, but she is a fireball and a sass. She is very independent and swears she needs no help from anyone. You will have your hands full with her."

Laughing, I'm reminded of the other night when she came home from work, all upset because her head nurse told her she was either going to take desk duty for the rest of her pregnancy or she was putting her on leave. I had been trying to convince Sam it was time to ask for light duty, she came home exhausted after a shift at work, but she was determined to prove that she could do it. Why, I'm not sure, but the other night when she came home ranting and raving about it, I secretly wanted to send thank you letter to her head nurse because she was never going to listen to me.

Sam looks up at me holding up a pink little shirt that says "Daddy's Girl" and a blue one that says "Mommy's Little Guy."

"You know, you two didn't think it was hard enough to prepare for a baby so you decided to not find out the sex either. Charliee has been going nuts over the theme of the room and we know we are having a girl, how did you two do it?"

"As long as the baby is healthy, we are good with whatever. The room is just neutral colors, we can always add a few little details after the birth. Now clothing is a whole new topic. I think I may have to give up my side of the closet until we can take half of it back." I roll my eyes as Sam holds up yet another set of boy and girl clothing.

Looking down at Levi, Charliee's service dog and best friend, I start to laugh. He is almost completely covered with little pink clothing. He just lays there and allows Charliee to keep piling them on. "Look at poor Levi, he looks exhausted already."

That dog won't leave my sister's side, when the little one comes it should be very interesting to see how he reacts. He will probably be just as protective of the little one as he is with Charliee.

"I'm not kidding you, he will walk into the baby's room and just lay there, and any time he is lying next to Charliee on the couch his head is on her stomach. I'm sure I have nothing to worry about when I'm at work, that dog will make sure Charliee knows exactly when the baby needs her. We have been talking to Levi's old trainer and she says they usually pick up on their new job pretty fast and after watching him, I don't doubt that."

I'm about to respond when both Charliee and Sam stand up, starting to say their thank yous to everyone for the gifts. "That's my cue."

Walking out to where Sam is standing, I take a deep breath. "Excuse me, ladies, but before you say thank you to everyone, I have one last gift for Sam."

Walking up to her, I want to laugh at her questioning eyes. I'm trying not to show the uncertainty that I'm feeling right now. She has fought me every step of our relationship, so I'm not very confident on how she is going to react now.

"Derrick, what could you possibly have? Between today and all the crazy shopping sprees you have been on, there is nothing else I can think of that this little one needs."

Charliee moves to go and stand next to Travis, and I laugh along with everyone else when Levi finally stands up, all the clothes falling to the floor, and follows her. When I look back at Sam, the puzzled look on her face has my heart almost stopped completely.

Taking her hands into mine, I bring them up to my lips, kissing each one. "Sam, the first time I met you, you were having dinner with my sister. We said hello and that was the extent of our conversation. That was the first time you challenged me, even though it was just with your eyes. You know exactly what I mean, you have family here so I'm not going into details."

Everyone in the room laughs, tears well up in Sam's eyes giving me the idea that she has finally figured out where I may be going with this.

"Then you came back when Travis was in the hospital. The first time I saw you in the hospital, I saw the fear in your eyes. All I wanted to do was wrap you up in my arms and tell you I understood, I knew the fear, worry and how scared you were. I felt all of those things with Charliee in the hospital. From that moment I knew you were going to have an effect on me, I found that all I wanted to do was protect you, I just didn't realize the full impact of it at that time. Then came the wedding of your brother and my sister, again details are not needed." I rub my hand over her belly and whisper for her only, "You gave me something very special that night," and I watch as her cheeks turn red.

Everyone starts yelling "no secrets," "we can't hear you" and the two of us laugh. "Sorry everyone, some things will stay between the two of us, but from that night on you have made me chase you every step of the way. Everyone has waited for the 'Bachelor Brother' to fall to his knees and well, Pint, you are the one who knocked me down and I'm ready to be a father and a husband."

Getting down on one knee, I pull the ring out of my pocket and hold it up for her to see, still holding her other hand with mine. "Samantha, will you please do me the honor of becoming my wife?"

Her hand tightens around mine. Her other is busy wiping the tears from her cheeks. Taking her hand with mine, I set them on her belly. One big kick is felt instantly.

We both laugh. "Look, this little one agrees."

She takes a couple deep breaths. "I have one request first."

I raise my eyebrow in question. "We get married before this little one arrives."

"If you say yes, we can leave and get married right now."

"One party a day is enough so it doesn't have to be today, just as long as it's soon. I can't wait to have you as my husband, Derrick. Yes, I'll marry you."

The room erupts into yells of congratulations and clapping. Slipping the ring on her finger, I stand, claiming her lips on the way up.

Soon I'm pushed away by all the women trying to get a look at my choice of ring and the guys are pulling me away, slapping me on the back with congratulations. I take the first solid breath since I walked over to her and relief floods me. She didn't even have to think about her answer. I read no fear or worry in her eyes when I asked her, she actually seemed to encourage me by squeezing my hand when I think she realized what I was going to ask. Did I really expect her to run today when I asked the question? No! We have been doing great since she moved in. She hasn't questioned my feelings for her, and she doesn't hold back on showing her feelings for me. It hasn't been all flowers and sunshine, sure there have been arguments here and there, but I would be more worried if there weren't any. Nothing is perfect, especially in a relationship. Perfect means something is wrong, we are far from perfect and I'm fully in love with what we have.

CHAPTER
Eighteen

"I CAN'T BELIEVE how fast life can change. Here I am about five weeks away from having this little one," I rub a hand over my very round stomach, "and getting married in a week, which I never wanted a holiday wedding, I always thought that was torture on a family. Life has a way of proving to you no matter how well you plan for what you think you want in your life, it can change in a matter of moments."

Charliee and Jayden nod in unison as I talk. If you look back at our little group, none of us have had the traditional meet the guy, date and get married, there seems to always be a very entertaining story behind each relationship.

"Is everything ready for the wedding?" Charliee grabs another slice of pizza, her eyes savoring it like she hasn't eaten all day, but she is on her third slice.

"How the heck are you staying so small, Charliee? I look like a whale next to you!" Already having two slices myself, I could easily finish the rest of the tray if I wasn't sharing with two other people.

"I try to control the amount I eat, but I'm hungry all the time. I swear we are having a boy. A girl couldn't want this much, could she?" Grabbing another slice, I swear it's going to be my last.

"Sam, stop being so hard on yourself, you are a lot shorter than Charliee, you will seem rounder. I think you look so cute at your four-foot-nothing height and that little round belly." Jayden reaches across and rubs my belly.

"I'm five-foot-one thank you, don't take any inches away from me, I need all I can get," I correct Jayden.

"So the wedding, do you need any help?" Charliee asks one more time.

"No, between your mom and mine, they went from baby shower mode straight to wedding mode. They have taken care of pretty much everything. I just need to make sure Derrick and the guys go and get their tuxes and don't forget. That was the only job my mom gave me. Why she gave me something to remember when my brain is mush right now is beyond me, but I have text reminders popping up on my phone at least twice every day."

"Pregnancy brain is no joke, I can't believe the stuff I forget," Charliee agrees with me.

"A Christmas Eve wedding, I'm a little jealous." I catch Jayden looking down at her hand, the one we thought by now would be the home of an engagement ring.

"I always wanted a spring wedding honestly, but like I mentioned earlier, life always has a way of showing you things can change quickly. I know it sounds a little old-fashioned and a little late, but I would like to be a wife before this little one joins us and we are pushing time right now. I would have had it earlier but both our mom's begged me to at least give them a month to plan."

"Maybe I'll be able to plan a wedding for next Christmas." Jayden holds up her empty finger to us.

"Jayden, be patient. Trust me, Cameron isn't letting you get away."

Charliee tries to reassure Jayden but Jayden just rolls her eyes, taking a frustrated bite out of her pizza.

Charliee looks over at me and winks, keeping a little secret between the two of us. Cameron is crazy about Jayden.

"Whatever, it figures I'd find the guy who wants to take his time." Jayden takes another bite.

"I think what I love about Cameron is that he knows he is driving you crazy with all of this," Charliee adds and Jayden throws her napkin at her.

Yes, life has definitely not gone the way I had it all planned, but I wouldn't change a moment of it. I may not have planned on a husband and child this soon to starting my career, but I couldn't see it any other way now. Plus, look at what came along with it. I now have an amazing sister-in-law and great new friends, life right now is great.

"I'm going crazy watching all of you getting married and having kids," Jayden pouts.

"That's exactly why he is probably waiting, Jay, why be blended into the craziness now. He is waiting to make it all your time, not having to share all the attention," Charliee defends Cameron.

Jayden thinks about it for a moment, then her face softens up. "That's why I love that man."

Charliee and I both laugh. "Jayden, we should not have to remind you of this about your man," Charliee points out.

"I know, I know. It's just hard to watch everyone around me having their weddings and babies. I want to be part of that club, and you know I hate feeling left out." Jayden looks around shyly, like she just realized how selfish she had been sounding.

"Trust me, when you are eight months pregnant you are going to want to slap us for not telling you how miserable it is. You can't sleep, you can't stop eating, everyone is telling you to watch your weight, you have pain somewhere all the time, and that's an everyday occurrence." Charliee tries to de-glorify it for her.

"Yes, but just think of the little one you are about to have," Jayden throws back.

"Trust me, that's the only thing that makes it all right at the end of the day when all you want to do is sit there and cry," I add, understanding everything Charliee is explaining.

Charliee looks down at her watch. "Ladies, we have an appointment to pick up dresses that we are going to be late for if we don't get moving."

MY MOM FOUND the perfect little church for our ceremony today, and then we will have a small reception at the Brooksman home, which is already decorated immaculately for Christmas. They go all out for the holiday, with one of the largest and tallest Christmas trees I think I have ever seen in a home.

Cammie flew in yesterday to be here for me as my Maid of Honor and Charliee, Jayden and Darryn are my bridesmaids. Kendall is now a pro at being the cutest flower girl ever to walk down an aisle.

I'm alone in the bride's room right now and all I can do is stand in front of the mirror and stare at myself in my empire sweetheart-style wedding dress, my hands rubbing up and down my belly. This is happening! In a matter of minutes my dad will walk me down the aisle and give my hand to Derrick. I'll be Mrs. Brooksman. Wow, it's all so surreal.

"Honey, are you all right?" My dad's voice surprises me, causing me to jump a little. I didn't even hear him enter the room. "Sorry, sweetie, I didn't mean to scare you. I knocked but you didn't answer. I became a little worried, so I just came in."

He walks over to me and with the gentle hand of a father, he brings his hand up and wipes the tears from my cheeks. I hadn't even realized I was crying. I quickly push the rest of them aside with my own fingers.

"Sorry, Dad, I didn't hear you. I'm fine."

"Sam, you don't cry very often, talk to me," he insists.

Turning my eyes back to the mirror, I feel the tears starting to fall once again. "I'm so big."

My dad's laugh fills the room, he turns me away from the mirror and into his arms. "Honey, you are beautiful and very pregnant with my grandchild. You are not big, you look amazing. My little girl is all grown up, I can't believe I'm giving you away today."

"Dad, don't start crying or I'll never be able to stop and then I won't be able to walk down the aisle and Derrick will think I ran again." I push out of my dad's arms, worried that if I don't I may never. They feel safe.

"There is no running, Derrick has made me promise that I will hook your arm around mine and walk you down the aisle to him, locking all doors if need be," he jokes, lightening up the conversation.

"I hope he forgives me for everything I put him through."

"Sam, there is nothing to forgive, you were protecting your heart. There is nothing wrong with that and Derrick understands that. He is a good guy, and I know he will take care of you and your little one. I'm so proud of you, Sam." Once again his eyes shine with tears.

Hugging him tight, I then pull away and grab a tissue. I dab under my eyes, cleaning up my makeup, grab my flowers then loop my arm around my dad's. "Come on, Dad, it's time to walk me down the aisle."

We walk to the door but he stops just before he opens it. Looking up at him, he leans down and kisses me on the forehead, smiles and then opens the door. We walk the short distance to the double doors that will lead us into the chapel. Everyone is lined up and ready to go.

This is really it. I take a couple deep breaths and in the distance I hear the music begin. I watch as one by one, each set of couples walk through the doorway.

"My turn, my turn." Kendall starts hopping on her toes, a huge smile on her face as she skips through the door way.

"You ready?" my dad asks, his hand tightening around mine on his arm.

The music changes and the wedding march begins. I look up at my dad, his smile is reassuring. One last deep breath and I nod my head. I can't speak, I'm afraid if I do the tears won't be held back.

Turning the corner, my dad stops for a moment. I look down the aisle and standing there is one of the most handsome men I have ever seen. Derrick is standing proud, the pastor on one side, his brother on the other. I can't see anything or anyone else, all I want now is that man standing at the end of the aisle waiting for me. I take the first step, pulling my dad with me, now very ready to be walking toward my soon-to-be husband.

I can hear the laughter in the far distance from the guests as I basically pull my dad down the aisle. Derrick's smile beams and I have to hold myself back from running to him, as though running is even an option right now with how big I am, but I would have walked as fast as possible.

Finally, we reach to where everyone is waiting. I hear the pastor in the distance but I have no idea what is being said, I can't seem to take my eyes off Derrick. I thought he looked good in his uniform, Derrick in a tux is a whole new level of wow.

My dad places my hand into Derrick's and I know I'm where I'm supposed to be. I'm with the man I'm supposed to spend my life with, and everything is right. I hand my flowers over to Cammie, Derrick takes my hand and places it with his onto my belly. There it is, the large kick that happens every time.

He leans down, placing a kiss on my stomach and then he comes up and places one on my cheek. "You look amazing, Pint," he whispers for me only.

"I'm so sorry," I whisper back, the tears threatening again.

He gives me a puzzled look. "What do you have to be sorry about?"

My fingers caress the hand on my stomach, I bring the other up to my lips, kissing the back of his hand. "I fought you so much, if you wouldn't have been so persistent this would never have happened and I would have missed out on something amazing."

He lets go of my hand and with a gentle finger, he wipes the single tear that escapes. "It was worth every sleepless night, every phone call I made, every text I sent and every fight we had, Sam. I'm not letting you run from me again, I'm holding on tightly."

"I'm holding you to that." Pushing up as high as I can go on tippy toes, he meets me the rest of the way and our lips meet.

"Well, since you just jumped to the best part, we now need to begin the rest." The pastor speaks over us, all the guests laughing and clapping.

"WHAT DO I need to do or say to get you to take me home instead of going inside?" I ask as we sit in the driveway of Derrick's parents' house.

Derrick turns to me, concern in his eyes. "Are you not feeling well? I'll take you home, they can have the reception without us."

Laughing, I adjust myself in the seat. "Derrick, I'm feeling great actually. It's just that since the moment I caught the first glimpse of you in that tux, all I have wanted to do is take it off you."

Derrick leans across the center of the car and claims my lips in a kiss that promises what is to come later. "We will get to all of that, I promise, but we need to go inside. We still have a part to play tonight."

"I know, it was just wishful thinking. Just promise me later, I get to take every inch of your clothing off, and have you any way I can imagine."

"Tonight and every night I'm yours to do with as you please, Mrs. Brooksman." He gives me one more very deep kiss and then before I can say anything in response, he gets out of the car.

I watch as he walks around the front end of the car and over to my door. Opening it, he holds his hand out to help me out of the car. He shuts the door behind me and before he can lead me to the front door, my hand goes up and around his neck, pulling his head down to mine, and I claim his lips once again in a deep kiss.

"If you don't knock that off I'm going to find a room here and not wait until we get home. I'll break a major rule of never having sex in my parents' house." Derrick is completely breathless and I'm excited to know just my kiss can do this to him.

"I won't complain." I give him what I hope is a sexy smile.

Shaking his head, he grabs my hand and pulls me toward the front door. I follow, laughing.

CHARLIEE COMES OVER and squats between the two of us at our table. "I think it's time for the garter and bouquet toss, I guess you can say."

This is the only reason I didn't beg Derrick to just take me home, I wouldn't miss this part of the evening.

Charliee stands in the middle of the room. "If I can get everyone's attention please." She looks around, watching for everyone to bring their attention to her. "All right, we are going to need all the single ladies up to the front for the bouquet toss."

Grabbing my flowers, I wait for the few ladies to come forward. There were only a few, including a couple nurses that I invited from my shift at the hospital, Cammie and Jayden. Turning around with my back to the ladies, I stand there for a moment.

"One, two…" I turn around and walk up to Jayden. "It's your turn, my friend." I place the flowers in her hand and then turn her around, where Cameron is waiting on one knee.

Derrick walks up to stand next to me. "You ready to go home now, Pint?"

"Yes, please."

WALKING INTO THE HOUSE, we head straight back to the bedroom. Derrick is walking behind me, unzipping my dress as we walk down the hallway. My dress falls as we walk into the room. He turns me around and drops to his knees in front of me, his hands on either side of my belly. He leans forward and kisses my belly.

I'm standing in only my heels and panties, he is kneeled in front of me in full tux, and even as large as I am I feel sexy. Slowly he slides my panties down my legs. I place my hands on his shoulders as I step out of them, now only in my heels.

"We are keeping the heels on, you look very sexy for one, and a little taller for two." He stands back up in front of me.

"Well you are in way too many clothes and I am very ready to help you take care of that." His tie is loose around his neck, so I pull it off and let it fall to the floor. Unbuttoning each of the buttons on his shirt, I lean forward and trail kisses down his chest as it becomes exposed. Pushing it down and over his arms, it falls forgotten onto the floor.

I bring my hands back up his arms, over his shoulders and down to his chest, down his very flat and rigid stomach to the top of his pants. I'm not going to do this slowly. I have wanted him naked too long to go slow right now, I just want his naked body against mine.

I unbutton and push the zipper down, his hardness springs forward. Wrapping my hand around him, I slide it down to the base and then slowly back up. Derrick's eyes close and he moans deep in his throat. Once again, down to the base and slowly up to the tip.

"Sam." My name escapes as a breath from Derrick.

Pushing his pants down his legs, I step back and watch as he quickly steps out of his shoes, pulls his pants off and drops them to the floor, and quickly remove his socks, standing up straight once again, now completely naked. My eyes travel his body, this is what I have been wanting all day and it's finally mine.

Derrick crushes me to him, claiming my lips. Leaving the shoes on was a good idea. His lips kiss along my jaw, down my neck and around one begging nipple. He bites slightly and my breath catches, my head falling back, my hands in his hair pressing his head harder to me. Heat rushes to my center and I feel the wetness between my legs.

Derrick walks me back and my legs hit the bed, thankfully since I wasn't sure how much longer my legs were going to hold me up. Leaning back against the mattress, Derrick trails more kisses over my belly. I watch as he kneels once again in front of me. My breath hitches when I feel his hot breath against my heated center. The first touch of his tongue and I almost lose all control with just that one motion.

"Derrick, please," I beg.

His answer is to sink his tongue deep inside of me. My hands in his hair, I pull knowing I'm probably hurting him, but not able to stop.

"Sam, you're so hot, so wet."

"Derrick, I need you, please."

Standing up, he pulls me up as well and quickly turns me around, bending me over, my hands on the mattress, my backside to him. His hand on my thigh comes around and pushes my legs apart, I can feel his hardness between my legs. I press my backside against him, begging for him to enter me. I need him deep inside of me.

His hand comes around and he cups one breast, squeezing. "Please, Derrick, now."

With his other hand he glides himself into me. The tip enters and I press my hips back against him, pushing him further inside. Arching my back, it feels so good the deeper he slides in. He slides out and slowly pushes back in, each time a little deeper.

"Faster, Derrick."

His deep laugh rumbles through him and vibrates inside of me. My forehead falls to the mattress, and I can feel my muscles starting to tighten around him. His hand goes around and a finger slides over that very sensitive nub, and that's all it takes. My release is strong and my arms can't hold me any longer, I fall against the bed.

Derrick picks up his pace and it only takes a couple more thrusts before his hands tighten around my hips and he finds his release as well.

We don't move for a couple moments, but he finally slowly pulls out, creating friction inside of me, reigniting my need for him once again. Standing up, he wraps his arms around my waist, hugging tight against my back.

"How does a bath sound?"

Grabbing his arm, I bring him around and push him down onto the bed, climbing up to straddle him. He is ready again as well. Slowly I sit down onto him, slowly letting him sink deep inside once again.

"I'm going to need you at least one more time before we head to the bath."

Derrick's hands cup both breasts and he pinches my nipples between his fingers. I push him into me the rest of the way and we both moan. This has become my favorite position since becoming so large.

It doesn't take long before we find our release together once again.

CHAPTER
Nineteen

DERRICK

"SO IS married life everything you thought it would be?" Bryce asks as we pull out of the station yard starting our shift.

"It's only been two days." We only had our wedding day and Christmas day off, then back to the real world.

"Kind of sucks you guys don't get to go and enjoy a little bit of a honeymoon."

"Sam only has two more weeks of work and then she starts maternity leave and I'll have a couple weeks after the baby, so timing isn't the best for a honeymoon. We will plan for something later."

"Did she go back to work today as well?" Bryce looks shocked.

I just nod.

"What is she trying to prove? Darryn was off by this time of her pregnancy and I know Charliee is on Christmas break for school, so she has a couple weeks off anyway."

"I've tried, trust me. I keep telling her to put in for leave but she keeps saying she isn't ready. She is going to work up until the day, but I only convinced her to take off the two weeks before by a compromise. She wanted to work until the day she delivered, I wanted her off starting now, we settled on two more weeks and the only reason I gave in is because she is sitting behind the nurse's desk all shift. I understand where she is coming from though, she is worried about her job and trying to get through the probation period."

"I get it, but I'm sure they wouldn't have let her go."

IT'S BEEN a long day and all I want to do is be home with my wife, relaxing in a very warm bath with her. Smiling to myself, I realize how a year ago, not even that, I would have rolled my eyes and laughed at anyone who would have said this would be my life and I would be completely content with it.

We have just pulled into the back lot of the station and like clockwork my phone rings and Sam's face appears on the screen.

"Hey, Pint."

"Just want to let you know I'm on my way home." She sounds exhausted and I want to argue out the point once again that she needs to take leave.

"All right, we just pulled into the station so I'm going finish a little paperwork and change real fast and I'll be on my way as well. How about I pick up some dinner on the way, and then we can relax for the rest of the evening."

"Sounds good as long as part of that relaxing is in the tub." I can tell she is smiling without even seeing her. She has become used to our nightly relaxing soaks.

"Already planning on it, just be careful driving home. I'll see you in a little bit. Love you."

"Love you, too."

. . .

PAPERWORK TOOK LONGER than I thought, Bryce and I are finally heading to change when Bryce's phone goes off. "It's Darryn, I'll catch up. She is probably stuck at work and needs me to pick up the kids from Mom and Dad's."

"I'll see you tomorrow then."

"Hey, hon, what's up?" I hear as I start to walk away. "Darryn, slow down, what's wrong?"

Those words stop me in my tracks and something in my chest changes. I can't explain it, but it's cold and hot at the same time. Turning back around, Bryce's eyes are wide and full of worry. "We are on the way."

"What's going on, is Darryn or the kids hurt?"

"Derrick, it's Sam, she has been in a car accident. Darryn is there on scene, we need to get going. It's bad."

I'm running past him as he is finishing his sentence and I know he is following. I can't wait, jumping back into the squad car I'm in reverse and moving before Bryce is even in the car.

Pulling up to the gate, we have to wait for it to slide open. I swear it's moving an inch a minute. "Damn it, hurry up."

"Maybe I should drive," Bryce offers.

"Where are we going, Bryce?" Throwing on the sirens and lights, I slam the gas as the gate makes it wide enough for the car to fit through. I hear the cross streets but Bryce's voice sounds like it's in a tunnel.

Bad accident! That's all my head is repeating over and over, everything else is in the distance. I don't see cars around us, or the lights as I run through intersection after intersection, all I know is I have to get to Sam.

The sun is setting and I can see all the lights from the emergency vehicles at least three blocks away. Finally after what seems like hours, we pull up onto scene. I'm not sure if I even stop the car before I jump out, all I can see is a full-sized truck and two other vehicles smashed all together.

Pushing past everyone, I finally come up to the scene and stop dead in my tracks. Sam's car is smashed between the truck and another vehicle about her car size. From what I can see the truck ran into her passenger side, pushing her into the car that must have been in the lane next to her. Sam's front windshield is broken out of the car and one firefighter is half inside and it looks like a paramedic.

"Derrick." I hear my name, but it's not registering who as I run to the front of the car.

That's when I see Sam, not responsive, her body slumped over the center console of her car. "Sam." I hear the scream but don't realize it's from me until I have a firefighter standing in front of me holding me back.

"Derrick, wait." I hear the voice, but I can't take my eyes off of Sam.

"Let me go, I need to get to her." I push against whoever is stupid enough to try and hold me back.

"Damn it, Derrick, stop." The voice again, I recognize it but don't know who it is, and that's when I feel the second pair of hands on me.

"Derrick, wait." That's Bryce's voice and it brings me back. My eyes focus and that's when I realize its Travis and Bryce in front of me.

"Travis, is she...?" I can't even ask the question.

"They have a pulse, but we need to get her out. We can't do that if you are in the way." Travis pushes me back again.

"That's my wife and child in there!" I yell.

"And my sister!" he yells back.

It all flashes back, Charliee under rubble from the building, Travis being carried out by fellow firefighters, Bryce being knocked back when a bullet entered his body, now Sam, lying lifeless, her car smashed around her.

"Is she alive?" I can barely hear my own voice.

"They have a pulse, we are working to get her out, you need to let us do our job. Trust me, I'm not going to let anything happen to her, she is part of my world, too. We need to pull it together for Sam and your baby." Travis is trying to stay calm, I can see it in his eyes though he is worried, but he is right. We are trained to work around personal feelings and get the job done.

I take a couple deep breaths. "All right, what needs to be done?"

"They are working on getting the other car moved away from her car, we are hoping to get to her that way to pull her out. Darryn is inside the small space next to her working on her until we can get her out. I need to get back over and help."

Travis is right, I'm pulling away help for Sam. He needs to be doing his job, not worrying about me. "I got him," Bryce confirms to Travis.

"I'm fine, I'm under control," I reassure both of them. "Let's get her out."

"Derrick, get over here and talk to your wife, she is slipping on us!" Tom, Darryn's partner, yells over from the car.

That puts my feet into motion. I run over to the car and climb up onto the hood. Darryn has her sitting upright in the seat now, I look over at her. "Her pulse is weak," she confirms and I can see she is fighting the tears as well.

Hanging half out and half in the car, I take her hand and rest it on her stomach, my heart skips when I feel a faint kick against our hands. "The baby just kicked," I confirm to Darryn, she smiles.

"Come on, Pint, you need to fight for us. Our little one needs you to hold on," I beg her, squeezing her hand tighter. I'm trying to push past all the blood, her stillness, trying to concentrate on the small movements of her chest. As long as that movement is there, she is still with us.

There are commanding voices all around me, instructing on what to do. I feel helpless. This is my wife and child who need me and I can't do anything. Another kick, but this time it's so faint, my heart sinks.

"Travis, the baby, we need to get her out of here. They are both fading and I can't lose them, move that damn car now!" I yell over my shoulder and turn pleading eyes to Darryn.

"Derrick, I'm trying, there is only so much we can do with her in this car." Darryn reads my begging eyes.

Pulling myself further into the car, I place my forehead against her stomach. "Come on, little one, you keep kicking. As long as Mommy can feel you, she will fight."

A stronger thump hits against my forehead and I can't help but smile. "You are just as feisty as your mom. Come on, Pint, hold on there. We will get you out soon, I promise."

"Keep talking to them, Derrick, her pulse is a little stronger again. She hears you," Darryn reassures me, her fingers against Sam's throat feeling for the pulse.

"Derrick," I hear the whispered voice of Sam and my head shoots up. Her eyes are still closed, maybe I just imagined it.

That's when I feel her hand tighten just a little around mine. "Sam, can you hear me?"

I wait but hear nothing, but her hand tightens once again. "Come on, Pint, I know you hear me. I know you feel the baby, hold in there."

"I'm sorry." It's faint but I know I heard her this time, I'm not imagining it.

"Pint, you have nothing to be sorry for, just hang in there with me. We are working on getting you out, you have the best with you. Travis, Darryn, Tom, and Bryce are all here working on getting you out, all you have to do is stay with me."

Another faint kick, not the strongest sign, but as long as the little one is kicking my heart is beating. "Do you feel that, Sam? I know you can, our baby is all right."

I'm not sure at this moment who I'm trying to convince more, her or me.

Then those words happen I fear the most, "I'm losing her pulse." Darryn's voice sounds far away. Sam's head falls over to one shoulder, her hand no longer holding mine. It went limp.

"Sam, Sam! Don't you leave me! Come on, fight!" I yell.

"I have no pulse, Tom, I need to start CPR as best as I can right now." Darryn's words confirm my worst fears, I'm losing her.

Everything seems to be in slow motion. I watch as Darryn works hard to keep my wife, her sister-in-law, alive. I watch as she blows each breath into Sam's mouth, her chest rising for a moment just slightly. I know there is yelling going on around me but with each second that goes by I feel my heart sinking more and more. I press a little more on her stomach, but no thump is returned.

Finally her driver's side door is pulled away from the car, orders are being barked all around me. Sam is pulled out of my grasp and pulled from the car. Darryn follows after her. A gurney is there waiting, she is strapped on all the while Darryn proceeds with administrating CPR.

Someone grabs my shoulder and pulls me back and out of the car. It's Bryce, he is saying something but I can't hear him. I can't move. If I'm not over there I can't be told that she is gone. I watch as they wheel her over to the ambulance. Darryn and Tom jump into the back, that's when I see the paddles, the last hope to bringing her back.

Another paramedic goes to shut the back doors and that puts my feet into action. I start to run toward them but am pulled to a stop. "No, I have to go to her, she needs me."

"Come on, we will follow in the car. Let them do their work, she has the best with her." Bryce is pulling me to the squad car.

I watch as the ambulance pulls away, maneuvering through the traffic, racing to save my wife and child's life.

"Let's go, let's go." Travis's voice comes up behind us as he runs with us to the car still in full gear. It puts my feet into motion. I go around to the passenger side, Bryce takes the driver's and Travis crams himself into the back seat.

As we pull out onto the street, all I can focus on is the fading ambulance lights blocks in front of us now. My world is fading from me with those lights. The only sound in the car is of the sirens above us, signaling for cars to pull over as my brother weaves in and out of traffic, trying to catch up with the ambulance and get us to the hospital as quickly as possible. I hear a sob escape from someone in the car.

"Derrick, she is a fighter, she will make it." Bryce tries to comfort me and that's when I realize the sob was from me. I can now feel the wetness on my cheeks.

I hear Travis speaking behind me, I think he is talking on his phone, probably with his parents. He isn't giving them full details, that much I can hear, which is probably for the best.

We finally pull up to the hospital, the ambulance is already unloaded. Jumping out of the car before Derrick can stop it, I run for the double doors, hoping I can catch them before they enter into the emergency room. I need to be with her.

One of the nurses behind the desk runs around the desk to stop me before I'm able to reach the double doors to the emergency area. "That's my wife, you need to let me go back."

"Officer Brooksman, you will have to wait out here. Sam is in good hands, you know that, but you can't go back there."

I want to argue with her, but I know it's not going to do any good. Now it's just a waiting game.

"Was she breathing?" I'm not sure if I want to know the answer.

"Yes, they were able to get a pulse on their way here. I promise I'll let you know if I hear anything more."

Travis and Bryce come running in at the same time Darryn and Tom come back through the doors from being back with Sam.

"What's going on with Sam?" Travis asks.

"We were able to get her pulse back and keep it after we paddled her, so that gives us hope. Unfortunately we have to wait now," Darryn explains.

"What about the baby?" I find myself asking.

"They are working on all of that now, when we were walking out they were hooking up all of the monitors." Tom answers this time.

All we can do now is wait. The air in this place seems thick all of a sudden, my chest feels heavy, and I need some air. Turning, I head back to the double doors leading outside. Sitting down on the bench, I take a couple deep breaths of the cool air. Placing my elbows onto my thighs, I bury my face in my hands. My world is inside in someone else's hands and I'm out here where all I can do is wait.

"Uncle Errick, Uncle Errick." A little voice brings my head up just in time to catch Kendall as she throws herself into my arms.

Her little arms go around my neck tightly and all I can do is wrap mine around her little body and hold on tight. It takes everything in me to hold back the tears. Looking up I see my mom and dad walking toward us, Mom carrying Brayden.

"How is Sam?" Mom's eyes are full of worry as she switches Brayden to her other hip.

"We are waiting right now, they said they will tell us as soon as they get information to the nurse's station." Kendall wiggles out of my arms and I kiss her on the forehead.

"How are you holding up?" my dad asks.

All I can do is shake my head. Taking a deep breath once again, I'm trying to keep the tears back.

"Is Bryce inside?" Mom asks as she takes Kendall's hand.

I just nod and watch her and the kids disappear into the hospital.

"Derrick, it's all right, you don't have to be strong around us." My dad waits for my mom and the kids to disappear inside.

"Dad, I don't know what I'm going to do if I lose them. I have no idea what's going on in there and I feel helpless."

"Believe me, I understand, but she is in the best care and they are going to do everything they can to make sure you don't lose them. Have faith."

Faith, all I have done is pray since Bryce informed me she was in the car acci-dent. I prayed for each little breath I watched Sam take as we waited for them to get her out of that car. I prayed for each little kick I felt letting me know our little one was still with us as well. I prayed with each breath I watched Darryn breathe into my wife's mouth, that it would be the one to bring her back to me. I even prayed that I be taken instead of them, I think to myself.

"Derrick, Sam is strong and a mother seems to fight even harder when she needs to protect her little one. They will both pull through this." My dad is trying to be positive and I know that, but he didn't see her when there was no life in her, when her heart stopped.

"If anyone will fight, it will be Sam." She has fought with me since day one.

"Why don't you come inside with me, maybe they can give you a little news on what's happening."

Standing up, I stand there for a moment and stare at my dad. I know now what they went through as we waited to hear something on Char-liee. "Dad, what am I going to do if they don't pull through?"

My dad wraps his arms around me. Here I am a grown man, in police uniform, being held by his father. What a sight we must be, but I need this from my dad right now. You are never too old or too masculine to need your parents and right now I needed this, to know I wasn't alone.

"Son, if it's meant to be that they don't make it, know we are always here to hold you up and help you move on." His arms tighten around me and I can no longer hold back the tears, I cry on my dad's shoulder.

AS MY FATHER and I walk back into the hospital, one of the nurses comes out the big double doors. "Officer Brooksman?"

I know the nurse, we actually went to school together. I almost correct her about the formality but right now all I care about is my wife and baby. "How are they?"

"The doctor sent me out here to tell you we are sending her in for a C-section. Your wife's breathing is labored which is causing less oxygen to the baby, he feels it will be safer to deliver the baby now."

"Is it safe for Sam and my baby to do that now?" Putting Sam through surgery to deliver when she is having labored breathing didn't sound safe to me.

"Your wife is stable at the moment so the doctor feels it's the best time. The longer the baby goes with limited oxygen, the more issues the baby can have. I promise we will take good care of her and your baby."

I know they aren't waiting for my permission, she is just out here to inform us what's going to happen next. I nod and watch as she disappears back through the doors. I want to run after her and be with Sam. I always figured I'd be in with Sam when she delivered, holding her hand and bringing our child into this world together. Being able to come out to the waiting room where all of our family is waiting to hear the news of little boy or little girl. Instead I'm standing here waiting to make sure everyone makes it through alive, no care of if it's a boy or girl. That excitement is gone, replaced with fear of them just surviving.

· · ·

EVERYONE IS HERE NOW, in little groups talking to each other, waiting. Every once in a while someone comes over and gives a few words of encouragement, and all I can do is nod. Levi, Charliee's hearing dog, hasn't left my side. His head rests on my leg and he just sits and waits with me, it's strange how it seems to help a little.

The same nurse from earlier comes through the doors once again. I can't read her expression so I don't know what to expect. There is no smile, no remorse in the eyes. "Officer…"

"Please call me Derrick, enough of the officer stuff. How are they?" I interrupt her.

"Sorry, Derrick. The doctor would like for you to come with me, please." She doesn't wait for me to answer, she turns and starts back through the doors.

Why isn't she telling me anything? My feet feel heavy and I find that once she disappears into one of the rooms, I can't seem to bring myself to follow her.

Her head pokes out of the door. "Derrick, it's all right, come on in."

That's when I hear the faint sound of a little cry, our baby! I want to move, but my feet can't. We were supposed to do this together, I still don't know how Sam is.

The nurse takes my hand and leads me into the room, I have no other choice but to follow her. I expect to see Sam but she isn't in the room, just a bunch of people with scrubs on. How many people does it take to deliver a baby?

Our doctor, whom I didn't expect to see, turns around along with another doctor. "Derrick, this is Dr. Maher, he is the ER doctor who has been with Sam. I happened to be on call tonight, when I heard what had happened I rushed right down."

"How is Sam?" I'm concerned that I don't see her anywhere.

"Sam is stable right now. The C-section went well and Mommy pulled through, we have already moved her to a room and are running some tests, but I have a little surprise for you and wanted to tell you first."

A surprise, the only surprise I want is for them to tell me everyone is going to be all right. One nurse turns around and she is holding a little bundle in her arms. "Derrick, I would like you to meet your son," the doctor introduces.

Before I can move toward him, a second nurse turns around. "And I'd like you to meet your other son," Doc introduces again.

"My other…" I'm speechless. Standing before me is two nurses, both smiling at me holding my sons in their arms. Before I can say anything, they both walk over and hand me both of them, one in each arm. My legs feel a little shaky, but I lock my knees. I have no words as I go from one little face to the other.

Finally, I look up at the doctors. "How did we not know there were two?"

"Well, it's rare, but not unheard of. One was hiding behind the other and they are identical. There have been a few very rare incidents where with identical twins, one hides behind the other and during ultrasounds their hearts beat as one so we don't catch it. Congratulations, Derrick, you have two very healthy baby boys."

I'm speechless. Walking over to a chair, I need to sit down before I fall down with my sons in my arms. All I can do is stare down at their sleeping little faces.

"It's also rare for an identical twin to have a set of identical twins." The doctor comes over and pats me on the shoulder.

I SIT with my boys for as long as the nurses will allow. I don't want to let go, they are giving me hope that life is going to be all right. The only way they convince me is to let me know I can finally go in and see Sam. Reluctantly I hand each one over, kissing them on the head and telling them I love them.

My happiness quickly fades when I walk into the room they have Sam in. She is hooked up to the machines, a tube coming out of her mouth helping her breath. A sound I never thought would sound comforting, the beeping of the heart monitor, is the only sound in the room. The constant beep tells me she is alive.

"The doctor will be back in shortly to talk to you." The nurse pulls a chair closer to the bed before she leaves me alone with my wife.

Sitting down, I look Sam over. She has a bandage around her head, her face is covered in bruises, both eyes black and blue and swollen. Her right leg is casted and laying on a pillow. Her arms are covered with bruises as well. I have no idea of internal injuries.

Carefully I take her hand into mine and bring it up to my lips. "Sam, you need to keep fighting, you need to wake up. You won't believe this but we have two beautiful little boys who are waiting to meet you. Here you always wondered why Charliee was so much smaller than you. Well, she wasn't carrying two little lives in her." I laugh, remembering how every time she would see my sister she would get so frustrated, wanting to know how she was keeping the weight off. I always told her it was their height difference, it seemed to suffice her for a little while, but that stopped working the closer they came to due dates.

"Sam, I'm so proud of you." The tears once again fall and I brush them away, frustrated. I'm done crying, I need to give her strength to wake up, and crying isn't helping anything.

The door to the room opens and the doctor I met earlier comes inside. "Hello again, Mr. Brooksman."

"Please, call me Derrick."

"Well, Derrick, congratulations on the two perfect additions to your family."

"Thank you. Can you tell me about my wife now?" I don't want to sound ungrateful, but I need some information.

"Well, right now we have Samantha in an induced coma. With the injuries she has sustained from the accident and the C-section, I think it's the best way to keep her comfortable for now. She has a very severe concussion and we are watching that very carefully. We had to glue up a pretty nasty gash in her forehead and that's why you see the bandage around her head, I felt the glue would keep the scar to a minimum. She has a couple broken ribs, luckily nothing pierced a lung. Her right ankle is broken, so we casted that for now. In a couple days we will do some x-rays and see if we can remove the cast and she can get along with only a boot."

"So you are saying she will pull out of this?" Hope sparks with all of his talk about things "in a couple days."

"Derrick, right now we are paying close attention to the head injury. I'm not going to sugar coat anything, it's serious and we won't know more until we take her off the medication that is keeping her in the coma and see how she reacts. The next forty-eight hours are important, but she is a fighter, she's proven that already, so I'm thinking she is going to keep fighting."

"Thank you for everything." It's a lot to take in, I feel like I'm in some kind of dream, maybe parts of it a nightmare.

"The nurses need to come in and run some vitals, why don't you go and let everyone out in the waiting room know what's going on. From what the nurses up there are telling me they are all getting a little restless and there is some news we are sure you want to be the one to tell."

I'm sure everyone is going crazy, I've been back here for some time. Standing, I lean over and kiss Sam on the forehead over her bandages and then on her hand that I'm holding. "I'll be back," I whisper to her. I don't want to walk out, I'm afraid something will happen when I'm gone, but I need to go and talk to the family.

"Don't worry, we will let you know if anything happens. She is resting right now, go talk to your family." An older nurse places her hand on my shoulder to reassure me.

"Do you know where my sons are at?" I hate that everyone is apart right now.

"They are in the nursery," the nurse confirms.

"Is there a way I can show the boys to my family? Maybe it will give them all some hope to see how well they are doing." I think of her parents and Travis, maybe seeing the boys will help them get some reassurance that Sam is a fighter. I know it helped me.

THIRTY MINUTES LATER, the whole crew is led down the hall to a waiting area that no one is in. With a boy in each arm, I proudly walk into the room to introduce the boys to their new family. The moment I walk in, shock is apparent on each of their faces. No one was expecting the second baby.

"There are two them!" My dad's voice can be heard above everyone else.

"Derrick, did you know you were having twins and didn't tell us?" Bryce comes over and looks between the two bundles in my arms.

"No, this is just as much of a shock to me as it is for you guys." My mom grabs one baby and Sam's mom the other.

"How did they not know there were two?" Charliee asks, looking a little concerned as she and Travis look at each other and then down at her stomach.

"From what the doctor told me, it's not unheard of but rare. They are identical twins, one was hiding behind the other and their heartbeats were in unison, so every time we had an ultra sound the two different heartbeats were never picked up on."

"Derrick, how is Sam?" Travis asks, still in his turn-out pants and work t-shirt, but not the rest of his gear.

"They have her in a drug-induced coma for now. They said she has a severe concussion with a large gash across her forehead, a couple broken ribs, nothing pierced the lungs though luckily, and a broken ankle. She is pretty bruised up, especially around the eyes, I'm thinking from the airbag when it went off, bruises up and down her arms. The doctor said for now it's a waiting game with such a severe concussion. The put her in the coma because of the swelling on the brain and then having the C-section, they figured it would help with all of the pain. We will know more when they take her off the meds and then we wait for her to wake up."

"Can we go and see her?" Sam's dad asks.

"I'm sure they will let you go and visit, but I'm warning you, with all the wires and the tube coming out of her mouth for breathing, it catches you off guard for a moment."

AFTER TALKING with the doctor and nurses and because of the late hour, they allow everyone to go in real quick to see Sam. I stay back in the waiting room with the boys. Bryce decides to stay with me.

"Where are Darryn and the kids?" I hope she isn't out in the other room with the kids, I know they have a policy about the age of kids here at the hospital.

"Tom and his wife came and picked them up since we don't have a vehicle here. The kids were getting a little restless, so Darryn decided to take them home. I told her I would call her as soon as we heard anything.

"And have you called her?"

Bryce pulls out his phone. "I'm thinking now is a pretty good time to show her your little surprise."

He uses the video call on his phone and I wait with the boys, ready to show Aunt Darryn the little surprise.

"Hello." Her voice comes over the phone.

"Hi, babe, I want to introduce you to the new members of the family." Bryce turns the phone around and I see Darryn on the screen.

"Hey, I'd like to introduce you to your new nephews."

"Derrick, do you realize you are holding two babies?" I see the shock in her face.

"Yes, we had a little surprise today when they went to deliver one, they found an identical lookalike hiding behind his brother."

"Let me see, let me see." Kendall's voice comes over the phone and she pulls it out of her mom's hands. "Uncle Errick, there are two."

"Yes, there are, you are going to be a busy big cousin."

"Ahh, they are so cute." Kendall's nose is enlarged on the phone screen for that's all I can see.

"Kendall, give Mommy the phone back, please," Bryce instructs from behind the phone.

Darryn's face comes back into view. "Derrick, how is Sam doing?"

"Short version, it's the whole forty-eight hour watch deal. They have her in a medically-induced coma, it's a waiting game now. Darryn, I want to thank you for everything you did today, you saved Sam's life and these little ones, because you kept a calm head on your shoulders. There is no way to express how grateful I am."

I hear myself getting choked up and my arms tighten around the boys as I fight the tears to stay back. Bryce turns the phone off me and he says a quick goodbye to his wife. He shoves the phone into his pocket and holds his arms out.

"Can I hold one of my nephews?" I place one of them in his arms.

"Bryce, what am I going to do if she doesn't make it?" My worst fears I finally voice.

"Derrick, she is going to make it, hasn't she proven that to you? Come on, she is fighting or these two wouldn't be here right now. They are healthy because she fought, she isn't going to give up that fight now."

Looking down, I run my fingers down a little chubby cheek. "They don't even have names yet, I can't do that without Sam."

"I'm sure it's all good for now, no one expects anything different under the circumstances. Derrick, relax and don't worry about anything other than these two and Sam, names can wait, I'm sure the grandmother's will be here to help. Darryn and I will get whatever you need and I know Charliee and Travis aren't going anywhere either."

"Bryce, it's killing me to be away from Sam now, but I don't want the boys to be alone either."

"Why don't you see if they can bring the boys into the room with you guys? What can it hurt? That way you have everyone together, plus it might be good for Sam to hear the boys."

Bryce has a good idea, I am going to bring that up to the doctor in the morning. "Have you heard what happened?"

"From what witnesses said, the truck ran the red light, and from the looks of where Sam's car and the other car were he wasn't going slow either. He plowed right into Sam's passenger side, which smashed her into the car next to her."

"Was anyone else hurt?"

Bryce shook his head. "Nothing like Sam. The kid in the truck was bruised up a little from the airbags going off, and the woman in the other car had no injuries, just pretty shaken up is all. I'm sure we will get a little more information tomorrow."

Two nurses enter and explain it is time to feed the boys. I know I should have asked to be the one to do the feeding, but I want to get back to Sam as well. For now I'm going to accept the help and let the nurses take care of it. Tomorrow I'll talk to the doctor and maybe we can get the boys moved into Sam's room, that way I can look after all three of them.

IT'S BEEN three days and all I know is I thought taking care of one baby was going to be a lot of work, two is impossible. I'm thankful for our mothers and the nurses, if not for them I'm pretty sure my sanity would be gone by now. I started out insisting that I was the one to feed the boys, change them, bathe them, all the stuff a parent is supposed to do, but by the second day and only having a couple of hours asleep in a forty-eight hour period, I started accepting the help being offered.

The doctor approved my request to have the boys moved into the room with Sam. They slept together in one crib next to the cot that was brought in for me, although I have yet to use it. Sam was taken off the medication to keep her in the coma, so now it's a waiting game for her to wake up.

I must have dozed off while feeding one of the boys, because I shoot up in the chair still holding my son and his bottle. That's when it registers with me, the sound, it's the heart monitor. Flying out of the chair, I push the nurse's button and place my son in the crib with his brother. Both boys are crying right now, the monitor is going off in a high-pitched constant sound and all I can do is wait.

Everything happens at once, two nurses come in and grab the boys, a group of nurses fill in pushing the crash cart, preparing the paddles to use on Sam. One nurse is trying to get me to leave the room, but I'm not going easily.

"Sir, we need you to wait outside, let us do our job," the nurse keeps repeating, but all I can do is push back and watch as my wife lays there on the bed, lifeless.

Finally, a male nurse is able to push me out. He closes the door behind him, leaving me to watch through the little window. It is all in slow motion, the paddles are prepared and then comes the shock, nothing. I can't hear anything but I can see that they are preparing for another.

Life is constantly changing. Small or big, nothing is for sure. One minute you can be telling your wife you love her on the phone and planning the perfect relaxing evening, and the next watching her fight for her life. Our family has definitely learned to love strong and never take life for granted. Tragedy tests your strength and bond, my family has proven all of that a number of times in the last couple of years. It makes you want to fall to your knees and ask how much luck can we have before it runs out?

I have no idea when I moved away from the door, or when I got down on my knees. I'm not sure how long the doctor sat there kneeled down in front of me saying my name before it registered to me that he was there. Maybe I didn't want to hear and I was choosing to ignore the doctor. If he can't tell me then it can't happen, right?

Finally, I am able to focus in on him, and slowly, very slowly, I start to make out what he is saying. "Derrick, we got her back."

It takes a moment but it finally sinks in. "You mean she's all right?"

The doctor puts his hand on my shoulder. "We have her heartbeat, it's slow but it's steady."

"Why is this happening?"

"Not sure to be honest, we are going to run some more tests."

"Can I go back in now?" I need to see for myself that she is all right.

"Sure, but we will be taking her out for some scans shortly."

Getting back up onto my feet, I shake the doctor's hand, thanking him. "Don't thank me, I have an amazing team working here and each of them love Sam. Not saying she is getting special care or anything, but they are going to make sure everything is done to get her through this."

I understand what he is saying, we have the same camaraderie at the station. Opening the door to her room, there is still one nurse in the room checking the heart monitor but everyone else has cleared out.

Walking over, I sit down in the chair next to her. I watch as the nurse works, I can't seem to keep my eyes off the monitor. I stare at it for so long I'm sure I'm breathing at the same time she is. Her heart beats and so does mine.

The nurse gives me a small smile and then finally she leaves the room as well, leaving Sam and I alone.

Taking her hand, I squeeze it tightly between both of mine. "Sam, I'm going to be honest with you, I'm not sure how much more my heart can take. I need you to wake up. Our boys need you to wake up. Do you want to know when the first time I fell in love with you was? That night at the diner. Yes, I'm talking about the first time we met. Funny how I saw you before I even realized you were sitting with my sister. You looked up and I swear your eyes pierced right through me. I wouldn't have admitted it then, not sure if I really knew it myself then. On the night of Travis and Charliee's wedding something changed completely, I could no longer deny it. You had given me something so special that night, you had given me hope that I could find that one who I wanted to change for. Wife and children were nowhere in my spectrum of considering, but here I sit watching you slip away from me and I can't believe I ever thought I would be able to live a life without this kind of love. To top it all off, we not only have one perfect son, we have two. I never thought I could love two little humans as much as those two. You gave me all of these gifts, Pint, and I need you to be here to share in this amazing life I honestly never foresaw myself having. Our sons are being named Baby 1 and Baby 2 right now. They need names and I need you to be awake to help me give them those before it's too late and they grow up being called One and Two. I refuse to name them without you."

Her hand flinches in mine. I hold my breath, waiting to see if I really felt it or it was my imagination willing myself to have thought I felt it. Nothing happens. Maybe it was just a muscle twitch, the doctor said that might happen.

"Are you trying to tell me you don't like the names picked for the time being?" I wait and there it is, I know this time I felt her hand squeeze mine.

"That's right, Pint, keep fighting it, keep pushing. I know you can hear me now, it's all right to rest. Take as long as you need. As long as I know you can hear me, I will sit right here and wait."

TWO MORE DAYS have passed with no signs that Sam is any closer to waking up. The nurses from labor and delivery brought me up a rocking chair so that I can rock the boys during the day. Right now both boys are laying on my chest fast asleep, they are the only things keeping me together. They need me and I need them just as much.

Closing my eyes, I lay my head back for a moment. If I can close my eyes for just a second I will be able to function clearly again, but right now I'm running on steam only. I swear I just shut them for a moment and I couldn't have fallen asleep, but something wet touching my hand startles me awake.

My arms tighten around each little body in my arms and I look around, confused for a moment on what's happening.

"Sorry, we didn't mean to wake you." Charliee's voice fills the room.

I look to my left and find Levi sitting beside the rocking chair, his head resting next to my arm. "I must have fallen asleep, I only meant to close my eyes for a moment."

"Derrick, you are exhausted. Why don't you let me stay here and you run home and take a shower, get some clean clothes, take a moment for yourself."

Charliee has only a few weeks left before she delivers and by the look of her eyes, she isn't getting much sleep right now either.

"I'm fine, plus I can't leave. What if Sam wakes up and I'm not here? I'm not letting that happen."

Charliee points at the chair next to Sam's bed. "May I?"

"Of course, how are you feeling?"

"I have a whole new respect for Sam. She had to carry two of these little ones. I don't know how she did it, and I'm not even working right now."

"She is a fighter, one way or another. She started with fighting me on this relationship and once I convinced her to trust me, she started fighting me on working up to the time these two were due."

Charliee puts her hands out and wiggles her fingers at me. "Please bring me one of my nephews."

Getting up, I walk over and place one sleeping baby in her arms. I watch as she looks him over. Running a hand over his blond hair, and little chubby cheeks. She stretches out five little fingers. "Derrick, they are perfect."

"Trust me, you won't be saying that if you were here during diaper change. Wow, can these two fill them up."

Charliee laughs, causing Levi to get up and walk over to her. His nose goes straight to the baby. "So I know you two had names picked out for a boy and girl, what was the one you came up with for a boy?"

"She liked Aiden for a boy."

"And what did you like for a boy?"

"I kept trying to get her to go with Kaleb."

Our little one that Charliee is holding brought his head up at the moment I said Kaleb.

"I think he likes it." Charliee runs a hand up and down his back and I watch as he buries his face into Charliee's chest and then falls back to sleep.

"I can't name them without Sam, Charliee, it's something we are going to do together."

"I think they are perfect names."

I jump out of the rocking chair so fast I almost forget I am still holding one of the babies. Levi jumps to attention and Charliee looks at me confused.

CHAPTER
Twenty

SAM

I'M HEARING a conversation around me and from what I can make out it sounds like Derrick and Charliee. Why can't I open my eyes? They feel so heavy, but I can see light through them.

As I lay here listening, I can hear them talking about baby names. Why are they discussing a second boy's name? I try to open my eyes again. The light is becoming brighter, now my head is starting to pound. It forces me to close them tightly again, but I want to know what's going on. Derrick sounds exhausted, I can hear it in his voice.

Once again I attempt to open my eyes. Objects are starting to take shape. My head hurts but I don't care, I need to know what's wrong with Derrick. I blink a couple of times and Charliee comes into view. She is sitting in the chair next to me, but she is holding a baby it looks like, but from what I can make out she is still very pregnant. Who's baby?

I need to close my eyes for just a second, maybe some of the pressure in my head will go away. The moment the light is gone the pain subsides. I fight the urge to go back to sleep. Once again I fight to open my eyes. Things come into focus faster this time, but the throbbing is almost unbearable.

I look down by my feet and there is Derrick, sitting in a chair, with a baby in his arms. Wait, why do they both have a baby? The pain in my head has me shutting my eyes again. I listen as they talk. My body wants me to go back to sleep, but my curiosity has me fighting it.

"I can't name them without Sam, Charliee, it's something we are going to do together." I hear tension in Derrick's voice.

He said he can't name them, Derrick wouldn't be talking about naming a baby, much less babies unless...

"I think they are perfect names," I manage to say. It's a whisper, but I know Derrick heard me because when I open my eyes just enough, I see him launch out of the chair.

"Derrick, what's wrong?" Charliee's voice sounds concerned.

Derrick is quickly in my line of vision. "Sam, can you hear me?"

"Derrick, my head feels like someone is hitting me with a brick and won't stop." My eyes want to close, but I need to know what's going on.

"Hold on, let me call for a nurse." With him so close I finally get a good look at him and he looks run down. He hasn't shaved, his eyes are bloodshot and have dark circles under them.

Then I see the bundle in his arms. "Who are you holding there?"

Derrick looks down at the baby against his chest. Even as tired as he looks, pride is shining in those eyes I love so much. "I'd like you to meet our son."

Next to him, Charliee stands up and joins Derrick. "And our son."

My head hurts so bad I'm seeing doubles and I swear Derrick just introduced me to two sons. Closing my eyes for a moment, I wait for some of the pain to calm down and then once I think I can handle it again, I open them and I'm still seeing Charliee and Derrick, both holding a baby.

"We have twins?" I have so many more questions but they are going to have to wait.

"Yes, Pint, we have twins. Identical boys, who are ready for names as soon as you are up to it."

My arm feels like lead, but I manage to bring it up and touch the hand of the baby in Derrick's arms. "I like the names you two just came up with, Aiden and Kaleb."

"Then Aiden and Kaleb Brooksman it is, we will work out middle names later." Derrick's voice fades as I fight as hard as I can but can't keep my eyes open any longer. The pain in my head isn't allowing it.

"I CAN'T BELIEVE how perfect they are." It's been a week and I'm ready to be home with my babies and my husband. It took a lot of persuading but I finally talked Derrick into going home and resting. He came back shaved, freshly dressed and he even stopped for a haircut before coming back to the hospital. Now we are waiting on the doctor to find out when I can go home.

"Even after the diaper changing and no sleep, you think they are perfect." Derrick holds up Kaleb and kisses him on the cheek.

"You haven't really allowed me to do much of anything yet, I'm going to make sure the doctor lets you know it's all right for me to take care of them as well."

"Pint, you don't understand what the last couple of weeks have been like. I lost you twice, I had to sit here and wonder if I was going to be able to go on if you didn't make it. The only thing that kept me hopeful and sane are these two little guys. I'm going to be a little smothering for a while and you have nothing else to do but allow it. You are still healing and I'm going to make sure you don't end up back in here once you are home."

I know Derrick isn't telling me I can't take care of my babies, he is telling me that he is going to take care of us and that's one thing I love most about him. I can only imagine what he has gone through, not only worrying about me, but taking care of the boys at the same time. From what the nurses have told me he wouldn't allow any of them to help very often.

"I get it, trust me, I do, but all I'm saying is I can start sharing feeding and diaper duty, we can divide and conquer."

CHAPTER

Twenty~One

2 MONTHS LATER...

"I NEEDED THAT." I join Derrick on the couch.

"I'll agree, it was nice to have everyone together. A family dinner was a good idea, Pint. Are the boys asleep?"

"Out cold, they have been passed around so much it took no time at all for them to fall asleep." I take the beer out of Derrick's hand and take a drink.

"Did you notice how whoever was holding Kinsley, Levi was sitting at their feet watching? We thought he was protective of Charliee, no one is going to get near that little girl." He takes his beer back from me and finishes it off.

"I'm pretty sure the boys will sleep through the night, and I'm thinking there is one more thing that would end this day perfectly." Getting up, I hold my hand out to him.

"What do you have in mind?"

"I'm pretty sure you will like what I have in mind." I turn and start for our bedroom. I listen for his footsteps behind me. He has turned me down for the past week but tonight I'm not taking no for an answer.

At our bedroom door, I look over my shoulder and see him round the corner to the hallway. Going into the bathroom, I start the water for the bathtub. I quickly undress and put my bathrobe on. When I come out of the bathroom, he is sitting on our bed.

"There is one promise you have not kept since that night of the accident." Walking over to him, I hold out my hand to have him take and stand up.

Pain flashes through Derrick's eyes at the mention of that night when I was almost taken from him. "What promise would that have been?"

He's surprised when I take the bottom of his shirt and pull it up and over his head. Letting it fall to the floor, I run my hands down his chest to the waist of his jeans. "You promised me a relaxing bath."

Derrick grabs my hand before I'm able to unbutton his jeans. He brings it up to his lips and kisses my knuckles. "I'll promise to take a bath with you if you promise to behave yourself."

Nothing I say is going to convince him that I'm all right and I expected him to fight me on this, so I'm not going to talk him into it. I'm going to seduce him into it.

Pulling my hand from his, I take the belt of my robe and pull it apart. The robe opens and I let it fall off my shoulders. Now I'm standing in front of him completely naked and he can't deny it's having an effect on him. His eyes are the first sign, they instantly turn crystal green. I take a step toward him, closing any space between us. There is no hiding his hardness.

"Your body isn't telling me that you want to only take a bath." I cup him through his jeans.

"Sam, I won't deny I want you, it's been hard to say no, but ..."

"There is no but, Derrick. The doctor cleared me yesterday at my appointment, I even asked and he cleared me for all activities."

"You asked the doctor if we could have sex?" His eyes are wide with shock.

"I knew it would be the only way that you would stop telling me no, I even had him write it down so that way if you didn't believe me, I had proof."

He reaches out for me but I step back and turn, making my way into the bathroom.

"You know, you really need to stop running from me." I turn to find him standing in the doorway, no longer wearing his pants.

I step into the bathtub and sit down, leaving a large area behind me for him to join. The water splashes over the tub when he sits down, wraps his arms around me and pulls me up tight against him.

Turning my head to see him, I place my arm behind his head and bring his lips down to mine. He pulls back just before our lips touch. "I'm thankful every day that you made me chase after you."

"I'm thankful that you never gave up on the chase."

Shift

BOOK 1 SIGN OF LOVE CIRCLE

Cammie, Sam's best-friend, from Silent Forgiveness gets her HEA!

For Cammie Mitchell, getting her dream job was a complete surprise. As a certified, Texas country girl, she was ready to put her medic degree to good use as a personal medic to some of the best riders in Texas. Stepping into an arena, she finds herself shocked to discover that bulls are replaced with bikes. It seems her dream may have just taken a strange and dangerous new twist.

Kade Maddox is arrogant. And he knows it. This playboy and number one best motocross rider in Texas, has only on thing on his mind; winning. That is, until Cammie walks into his life as Sandy's Racing's new medic.

With one trying to keep things professional and the other trying to become the top rider of his sport, neither are prepared for the shift about to happen in their lives.

Grab your copy today!

amazon.com/dp/B08W23F6J1

About the Author

USA Today Bestselling Author, Tonya Clark, lives in Southern California with her hot firefighter hubby and two amazing daughters. She writes contemporary romance featuring second chance, sports, MC, shifters, suspense, and deaf culture-inspired by her youngest daughter.

When not hiding in the office writing, Tonya has the amazing job of photographing hot cover models, coaching multiple soccer teams, and running her day job.

Tonya believes everyone deserves their Happily Ever After!

Sign-up for Tonya's newsletter at www.tonyaclarkbooks.com for book news and you can find all of her books on Amazon.

instagram.com/authortonyaclark
amazon.com/author/tonyaclark
bookbub.com/authors/tonya-clark
goodreads.com/authortonyaclark
tiktok.com/@authortonyaclark
youtube.com/@authortonyaclark8621

Also by Tonya Clark

<u>Sign of Love Circle</u>

Shift

For the Love of Brayden

<u>Colorado Storm Soccer Series</u>

Slide Tackled

Game Plan (Releasing April 2023)

Off-Side Trap (Releasing Summer 2023)

<u>Standalone</u>

Retake

Entangled Rivals

Driven Roads

Healing Tristan

Shame on Me

Hidden Flight

<u>Anthologies</u>

Storybook Pub

Storybook Pub Christmas Wishes

Storybook Pub 2

Young Crush

Tricks, Treats & Teasers

Caught Under the Mistletoe

Imperfect Date